Emperor of Dust

Jonathan Spencer is from south-east London, the great-grandson of a clipper-ship captain who brought tea from China. He served in the Canadian army, studied ancient and modern history, and has lectured at universities and private associations on the subject of Napoleonic Egypt. He writes historical non-fiction under the name Jonathan Downs, his major work a revised account of the British acquisition of the Rosetta Stone, *Discovery at Rosetta*, (London 2008; Cairo 2020). He speaks several languages, has trained with the former Russian National fencing coach, and has lived and worked abroad all his life. He currently lives in the Western Cape in South Africa.

Also by Jonathan Spencer

The William John Hazzard series

Napoleon's Run
Lords of the Nile
Emperor of Dust

JONATHAN SPENCER

EMPEROR OF DUST

CANELO

First published in the United Kingdom in 2021 by

Canelo
Unit 9, 5th Floor
Cargo Works, 1–2 Hatfields
London, SE1 9PG
United Kingdom

A CIP catalogue record for this book is available from the British Library.

Print ISBN 978 1 80032 477 0
Ebook ISBN 978 1 80032 075 8

Look for more great books at www.canelo.co

Printed and bound in Great Britain by Clays Ltd, Elcograf S.p.A.

1

For G.C., a traveller from an antique land

Βασιλεὺς βασιλέων Ὀσυμανδύας εἰμί.
εἰ δέ τις εἰδέναι βούλεται πηλίκος εἰμι, καὶ ποῦ κεῖμαι,
νικάτω τι τῶν ἐμῶν ἔργων.

King of kings, Ozymandias am I.
If any would know how great am I, and where I lie,
Let him surpass but one work of mine.

From fallen colossus of Pharaoh Ramesses II,
and inspiration for Shelley's poem, 'Ozymandias'
Diodorus Siculus, I.47
1st century BCE

Part One

Babylon

Hunter

The reeds of the Nile Delta rustled in the wind, the afternoon heat hanging in the glimmering distance, a rippling lake of molten silver, floating above sharp sands. Stark and bright against the green of the waving grasses, a crane picked its way delicately through the shallows, raising one thin leg slowly, then placing it with care, waiting, motionless. The world seemed to have awoken unscathed from a terrible dream, of thunder and cannon, of ships and fire, and now lay quiet, a picture of peace, unaware of the works of man, knowing only the sun and the wind, whose breezes shivered the surface of the cooling floodwaters.

Far in the distance to the east, the town of Kafr-Shahabas baked silently at the edge of the mirage, its walls glowing white in the glare. Just beyond the outskirts, two local *fellahin* farmers in long, threadbare *galabeyyah* smocks sweated up a steep bank to the dusty road; between them they hefted a heavy sack of meal up the slope from a flat-bottomed punt in the reeds. After only a few paces, they staggered and stopped, the man behind losing his grip and dropping his end of the sack, cursing at the other – then both stood still, staring along the road to the west, in the direction of Rosetta. One of them pointed. The other peered more carefully, then backed away, his voice rising in panic.

Alarmed, a flock of sacred ibis took flight. Immediately the horizon was alive with spray and flashing wings of black and white, the birds' shrieking calls filling the air, the startled crane joining them, the water sheeting off its plumes as it flapped into the sky. Shouting to each other, the two men tried to snatch up the sack, its weight too great for their haste, dragging it a few yards before abandoning it, running to the town's gatehouse, waving their arms, calling out. Figures appeared in the arched gateway of the curtain wall, some with muskets, looking along the main road then ducking back inside, waving the *fellahin* in to safety.

3

Far off, among the marshes and flooded islands of reed, unseen by the people of Kafr-Shahabas, a hand rose up, two fingers pointing to the left, then sank out of sight. Lying on the muddy banks of grass and stubble, Marine Sergeant Jory Cook's narrowed gaze flicked in the direction of the signal. They all heard the noise: the dull thump of hooves, the clinking of buckles and tack. Horses. The French had come.

'*God save Bristol…*' he muttered. 'There they are.'

Half submerged next to him, William John Hazzard, Captain of Marines, stared through an eyeglass. 'Move them closer.'

Cook looked to Marine Private Warnock on his right and Corporal Pettifer on the left. Like Hazzard and Cook, they lay in the water and mud, hidden by clumps of reed, partly in Marine scarlet and partly in Bedouin garb, dark *keffiyah* headdresses for the sun and *binish* robes. Warnock clutched a feathered native tomahawk from the Americas in one hand, Huron, he had said once, Pettifer a giant wide-mouthed Royal Navy musketoon blunderbuss.

They were old hands from long before the Battle of the Nile, and what they had now called the Malta Chase – Nelson's dash across the Mediterranean to catch Napoleon Bonaparte's invasion fleet; these marines had done it without Nelson, or anyone else, and had engaged the enemy in the invasion of Malta on their own. Cook glanced at Pettifer and saw the big Cornishman's frown. 'Better'n blockade duty, ain't it,' said Cook.

'Aye Sarge…' Pettifer glanced over his shoulder at Tariq, their Huwaytat scout, who gave a brief whistle.

Behind them, ten *Bedu* of the Beni Qassim rose up silently from the knee-deep water and darted across the terrain among the tall grasses, stopping, sinking down, then rising again until in position. The area was floodplain, criss-crossed by drainage ditches, tracks and trails, the main thoroughfares forming a rough grid of hard-packed dusty roads rising above the low-lying wetlands. After the annual flood, the Delta had become a sodden well-spring of new life, bordered by parched scrub hills and sandy desert, untouched by the kind hand of the Nile. The Beni Qassim drew within twenty yards of a junction of tracks meeting the main road, sank down, and waited.

Hazzard looked where the ibis had taken flight, and zeroed his eyeglass on the distant town. It was walled, a small fortress. Despite the reflections of the water and the diffuse heat playing with his vision, he

4

could gauge it was over half a mile away. He was soaked, but pleased for it, his back baking in the sun's heat. To their left the ground rose and fell in humps and tussocks of grass and rock. He scanned the wide road running across his view, from a low palm-studded ridge at the far left to the distant town on the far right. Trotting over the ridge on his extreme left, a line of horse appeared. It was not cavalry. They were civilians, riding in a loose group, ten or twelve of them, at their head two older men in uniform.

Cook recognised one but not the other. 'God save Bristol,' he muttered. 'It's that fat little oik, Menou…'

Hazzard said nothing, peering through the scope. Cook could see his hands trembling. In other times he might have taken that for fear or nerves. They had known each other now for over six years, from Spithead to Cape Town, and Bombay to Bengal – but since the events of the last few weeks, Cook knew it was a sign of something far worse: anticipation.

Menou was the Governor of Rosetta and a general in Bonaparte's army: he would normally warrant an escort of at least two hundred horse, but Hazzard could see none. A source had told them that Menou was on a local tour, and that two troops of cavalry had ridden east from Rosetta – the only reason could be escort duty. Hazzard had positioned 9 Company to intercept.

'Psst, Sarge,' hissed Warnock. 'Where's the flamin' escort?'

Cook glanced at Hazzard. 'Good ruddy question.'

Hazzard swung the scope back to the civilians. They were relaxed, laughing, looking back over their shoulders. Then Hazzard understood – they had deliberately left their own cavalry behind, and were feeling pleased with themselves. They were all much the same, the civilian savants, Bonaparte's academics: still with the air of tourists, on the lookout for remarkable sights, antiquities and ruins.

Several of them broke from the party and rode ahead, crossing Hazzard's line of sight on the main road to Kafr-Shahabas: he could see a well-dressed, dark-skinned man in a fez and two guides in turbans. Hazzard followed their dust-cloud as the three headed towards the town at a light gallop. The rest of the group to Hazzard's left followed more slowly at some distance, enjoying the scenery. He recognised another of them from his dinner aboard the Orient that fateful night so long ago: Vivant Denon, the kindly painter, who had been to Naples and knew Sir William and Lady Hamilton, raising his glass as Hazzard had parried the other savants' derogatory comments, Oh lo lo! Touché!

The memories burned, though he had grown numb in the weeks since the battle in Aboukir Bay. But he could not stop the flashes in his mind: of Sarah, of the black, soulless eyes of Derrien, Citizen *Croquemort*: the 'Mortician' – and fury raining down all around them in the debris of Bonaparte's flagship.

He had survived.

And Sarah had not.

His failure to find Derrien had brought a smouldering hatred, for Derrien and for himself. After plotting a course from Sir William Sidney Smith's map, they had charged across the Delta to the road where Bonaparte had received the news from Derrien of the loss of the fleet in battle – but of Derrien there was no sign: only rumour persisted of the 'man in black'. That had been weeks ago now, hard weeks long gone. In his rage, Hazzard had led the Beni Qassim through French camps, killing sentries, burning tent lines, taking munitions, horses and mules, spreading havoc where they could. But none of it satisfied, and Derrien was nowhere to be found.

Sarah.

He saw the raging decks of *Orient*, the great ship sending aloft clouds of burning sailcloth and rigging. HMS *Orion* and *Alexander* closing their gun ports and backing away, *Leander* and *Theseus* pulling back for fear of catching the fire they had caused as *Orient* broke apart, her rails and masts leaping with flame; the figure of Jeanne at the rail, running back to the fire for the boy, for the captain's son – until the final ear-splitting explosion, and *Orient* was no more.

As he watched them, Hazzard felt the anger rising, his chest pounding, *Gone, all of them, gone.* He closed his eyes at the scope, knowing he was shaking, knowing Cook was watching, the old nursemaid, the grizzled oak that he was. This time, he determined, *this* time, he would find news of Derrien. Perhaps Fate had intervened after all, and brought him one who might know: the overfed former aristocrat turned revolutionary, General Jacques-François Menou, not a hundred yards away.

'Stand by,' he said.

Cook kept his eye on the group of horses and murmured, 'Clear aye.'

–

All agreed that General Menou was a pompous oaf, devoted to his regulations, yet here he seemed to be delighting in the company of his Rosetta *savants*, a far cry from the uneducated soldiery. Beside him rode the laconic General Auguste Marmont, an aide to Bonaparte, colleague and sometime companion of Menou, 'taking the air' as he called it, though their ride was uncomfortable at best.

'Surely you cannot be serious, Jacques.'

Menou gave a harrumphing cough. 'Whyever not, Auguste? These people, they show no resentment, do they, bear no ill-will to their conquerors, and accept that we come to save them.'

'Save them,' said Marmont. 'From whom...?'

'From the Mamluk, Citizen General. Who else? Look how happy they were to see us at that last place, er, that Desouq place. Lodging us in a palace, by God! Feasting, those dancing women...' He went quiet a moment as he recalled the lascivious pleasure. 'Quite extraordinary... and I feel it could be a lesson for our own humble nation, indeed I do.'

'But conversion? To Islam? You go too far, Jacques, surely.'

'*Général en chef* Bonaparte has said we must mingle with the population. Their religion is very important to them – and to him. You heard the sheikhs at the last town. Loved us. Loved us!'

Marmont suppressed a smile. 'But you are neither Egyptian nor Arabic.' He cocked a quizzical eyebrow. 'Would you take the customary four wives...?'

Menou glanced at him, alarmed. 'Four...?' He shook his head. 'Well, one must make sacrifices,' he said. 'Religion in the Republic is banned, for good reason too, damn the Church.' He thought a moment longer. 'And it will put me in good standing with Bonaparte. He is the future,' he declared. 'We two, we were there at the beginning remember, he and I,' he rumbled, puffing out his chest, 'in the battle for Paris, saving the Revolution on the 13th *Vendémiaire*, commanding the guns in the streets.'

'Mm,' said Marmont, somewhat dubious of Menou's heroism. 'Which he cleared with the cannon, if I recall.'

'Indeed, Citizen General! At my behest it was too, knowing his skill. And Barras agreed! And look at us now – conquerors!'

Marmont watched the guides reach the town of Kafr-Shahabas. He looked behind them. 'Should we not wait for the others, and the escort...?'

'Oh, nonsense. All the more lesson to them for dropping behind. Dolomieu and his damned horse, I ask you.'

'It was an awful beast, that horse,' admitted Marmont. 'How could he possibly control it. Dolomieu is as ancient as those ruins we saw last...'

'Citizen Denon!' called Menou over his shoulder at the back of the group. 'Do you not delight in the scenery, Citizen?'

Vivant Denon rode up beside Menou, in a broad-brimmed linen hat, his face shining with sweat. 'The arid sands of desert around us, yet all lies among flashing floodwaters. Truly, a *bellevue*, is it not...' He waved a hand at the horizon, the shadows, ridges and marshes. 'It is almost too much, hm? Louis Auguste, what say you?'

Louis Auguste Joly, a younger man of twenty-four, rode up eagerly to join them, pleased to have been invited. 'Yes, it is all such beauty, Citizen Denon!'

'Aha, bravo! The birds, the sky, it is all so magnificent, *mon général*,' continued Denon, 'that we two have scarcely sufficient paint to do it justice.'

'But well said, well said,' approved Menou. 'A man of the sublime, dear Vivant, excellent. And what say you, Citizen Joly? You are a draughtsman, are you not.'

The young man hesitated, 'Oh, *mon général*, it is so, but also I paint, hoping to learn from Citizen Denon...' He held a hand up to shield his eyes from the sun. 'Forgive me, *général*, but what is this up ahead, at the little town...?'

They heard distant shouts – then a musket-shot.

Menou brought his horse to a halt. 'What on earth...'

From the direction of Kafr-Shahabas they saw a growing cloud of dust as Dr Fayyad, the man in the fez, came galloping back along the road towards them, shouting and waving, '*Turn! Turn! They are come upon us! They are come upon us!*'

Far ahead, the two mounted guides argued at the gates of the town, riding in circles, shouting down at a small group of armed men, the guides' horses whinnying in fright. One of the townsfolk saw Menou and the *savants*, pointed and called out. There was a loose volley of musket-fire, the balls pinging off the dusty road and into the shallows either side.

The two guides called down at the people to stop, but in vain: a mob poured out of the gates and charged towards them, pelting the guides with stones. Another volley of musketry rapped from the town walls, kicking up the dust and sand. The guides lashed their horses and raced back to the *savants*, shouting and pointing to their right – across the marsh on a parallel road from the rear of the town came another group of armed figures at the run. They were trying to get behind the party of *savants* and cut off their retreat.

'*Mon dieu*,' gasped Menou, 'we shall be flanked…' He raised a hand. 'Turn! Turn, I say, and ride for your lives!'

Another musket volley boomed. Denon cried out with alarm and was nearly struck as the doctor charged by. 'Dr Fayyad…!' called Denon. 'Doctor! What has happened!'

'They will not parley! They threatened the sheikh's guides! They mean to kill us all! Ride!'

–

'*There*,' said Cook to Hazzard. Just as the shots rang out from Kafr-Shahabas, they saw the cavalry escort emerge from behind the low ridge on the far left – along a rough raised dirt track, a shortcut through the marsh leading to Menou on the main road. There were fifty at least in a column of two files, in dark blue coats powdered almost white with dust, their plumed cuirassiers' helms flashing in the sun. Having heard the shots they were now riding to the rescue, but were still some way from the *savants*. There was no doubt what they would do to the townsfolk once they reached Kafr-Shahabas. Cook tried to identify them. 'Dragoons…?'

Hazzard focussed the eyeglass. He could see no dragoon holster pistols or saddle-carbines. They carried only swords. 'No. Light cavalry.'

There was a cry from the marsh, *Estaeed…!* The column of French horse faltered when those Beni Qassim already dispersed among the grassy banks suddenly stood, muskets at the aim, and fired a broadside volley. The edge of the track vanished in a cloud of powder-smoke and dust, and six of the cavalry went down at once, the horses crying out as they stumbled across the narrow track surface and fell, tangling the legs of the troopers behind and in front. A second volley tore through them and nearly a dozen more at the rear of the column fell in screaming confusion, a sergeant calling out, *Chasseurs! Chasseurs! Aux armes!*

But the cavalry could not escape. Heeling round a junction in the dusty distance came a group on horseback, charging into the marsh, water spraying from their hooves, straight for the cavalry's rear. Under his flying robes the leader wore an officer's waistcoat and boots, and held aloft a Royal Navy sword. It was Lieutenant Marmaduke Wayland, six Huwaytat and Awlad 'Ali *Bedu* and the rest of Hazzard's marines.

Cook cursed. 'Jaysus. Bitten off more'n he can chew...'

'Come on...' Hazzard scrabbled to his feet, the water sheeting off his sodden *binish* robe and scarlet coat beneath. The plan to take Menou would have to wait: Wayland and the cavalry came first. He unwrapped his Lorenzoni pistol and fired a shot in the air. '*Horses to me! Yallah!*'

'*Up, ye dozy buggers, and juldee!*' roared Cook, and the remaining Beni Qassim burst from the reeds among them, drawing their swords. The horses were brought in from behind, charging along a path from the sandy banks. Sprinting through the shallows, Tariq raced to the lead horse and leapt into the saddle, pulling another to Hazzard, who jumped up and took the rein. 'Jory! Forget Menou for now,' he shouted, turning the Arabian about, 'those troopers will wipe out that town, and Wayland's on his own!'

'Sir! Volley-fire first like we planned—' But Hazzard charged off, head down, straight for the cavalry column. Cook spat with anger, '*Jesu, bugger an' blight! Petty, Knock-Knock! Get after him, steady the line and maintain volley-fire till he's in among 'em!*'

'*Aye Sarge!*' called Pettifer at the run, the heavy blunderbuss in hand.

'*Kuq!*' called Tariq, 'You need I stay? I go?' he asked hopefully.

'Go on off after him damn ye, Tariq!'

Tariq drew his Yemeni *jambiya* dagger. 'No prisoners...?'

'*Isri ya! Hurry up, ye li'l bugger!*'

Tariq smiled his murderous little smile and kicked his heels in. '*Yallah!*'

The Beni Qassim riders fell in some distance behind Hazzard as they rode through the marsh, the spray flying, leaping the small islands of grasses, heading for the dirt track and the disordered column of French cavalry fifty yards away. They were still in two files, side by side, their officers shouting, troop sergeants bawling out as troopers turned and spun in different directions, turning to deal with Wayland's approaching charge from their flank.

Splashing through the marsh, Warnock and Pettifer called out the time, *Make ready! Fire!* The Beni Qassim in the reeds fired another volley, and more horsemen fell, some tumbling down the banks into the water and mud, the track too narrow for them to manoeuvre. Hazzard urged his horse onward, *Come on, come on,* and he bounded over a drainage ditch and onto the track. He turned to face the cavalry and kicked his heels in.

The flying mane of the horse obscuring his vision, he charged headlong at the column, sighting down the middle of the two files of riders. He put the reins in his teeth, reached over with his right hand and drew the ivory-gripped scimitar bumping against his left thigh. The razor-edged steel flew from its white scabbard, and he thought of Sheikh Ali-Qarim, *Hadeyya. Gift.* With his left hand he drew a shorter curved *shamshir.* He leaned forward, heading straight for the lead pair of cavalry officers. They drew their sabres and the cry went up, *Mamluk! Un Mamluk!*

Hazzard thrust out his arms, becoming a broad Mamluk scythe at full gallop, and charged between them with swinging blows, *cutting,* the swords flashing over his head in an arcing X, lashing out, letting the power of the horse drag the blades across his targets, feeling the metallic clang of a parry, the scimitar cutting *down.* A flailing windmill, he drove straight through the centre, crashing into their knees, their stirrups, slashing at the horses, the riders' thighs, necks, backs and shoulders – anything in his path, the horses screeching and rearing. He heard himself shouting, the rage darkening his vision, his limbs weightless, the Beni Qassim cheering behind, *Al-Aafrit al-ahmar! Al-Aafrit al-ahmar!*

The two streams of the column split apart, horses diving down the steep banks into the marsh, some riders unseated, falling into hidden troughs, horses collapsing onto them, their legs trapped in sinkholes, Wayland coming up fast in the other direction, sword raised, *Marines to me!* The remainder of the cavalry broke and charged off, *En avant,* leaping through the shallows, one horse going down with a scream, another stumbling behind, the riders thrown, the water spraying in clouds of mist as they plunged on regardless, to reach the relative safety of the main road. Fallen cavalrymen rose from the mud, trying to run, then dropped, hit by *Bedu* bullets. Barely twenty of the French escaped, the Beni Qassim in pursuit.

Wayland approaching at a trot, Hazzard hauled on the rein and turned to look, the swords hanging at his sides, his chest heaving, the horse snorting, tossing its head. The marsh track was strewn with the dead and injured, riderless horses staggering off into the muddy waters. Cook and the others were running towards them. Hazzard looked for Menou on the distant main road, now halfway to the town gates: the mob from Kafr-Shahabas had overrun the tourists.

–

'Turn your mounts! Turn I say!' called Menou – but with the approach of the angry townsfolk the young man riding beside Denon, Louis Auguste Joly, fell from his horse, sliding off the saddle. Instead of climbing back up, he tried to run.

'Louis!' cried Denon, leaning down to him. 'Here! Here, give me your hand!'

'*Non, non!*' Joly was wild with fear, ignoring the hands reaching down to him, the shouts too confusing.

'*Come up, Citizen!*' ordered Marmont. '*Behind me on my horse!*'

Another burst of fire rapped and echoed across the shallows, and Joly screamed in panic, '*Help me!*', out of his mind, dodging about between his colleagues.

Menou watched the townsfolk rushing towards them. 'We have but moments! Citizen Joly! *Mount again this instant or we are lost!*'

Denon and another tried to pull him up but he would not come, and ran off to the banks, falling into the water, only to be seized by the first of the townspeople. Menou called out to the escort, still too far off, '*Au secours! Cavalerie!*' A man with a rough-hewn knife reached up to Menou, but Marmont knocked him down and Menou kicked with his boot, '*Away! We must away!*', and the group rode off to meet the remaining cavalry mounting the road in the distance, Denon looking behind at the screaming Joly, '*Louis! Louis!*'

–

Hazzard watched as the mob charged back to the town gate, dragging the terrified Joly among them. '*Jory! Out! Get over there!*'

Cook turned and looked, then called out, '*Petty! Get 'em in!*'

Hazzard rode to the first of the fallen cavalry officers and jumped down. The Frenchman looked up at him, a lined face, a bushy, curling grey moustache, his eyes wide. The man was older than most, and wore the flashes of a troop major, a *Chef de bataillon*. Bloodied from chest to brow, his helmet gone, he looked bewildered and soon to breathe his last. Hazzard seized him by the jacket-front. '*Ecoutez-moi!*' shouted Hazzard in French. 'The Citizen *Croquemort!* Where is he! *Rosette? Alexandrie? Répondez!*'

The cavalry officer blinked, uncomprehending. '*De... de l'eau...*'

'Derrien, Major! *Où est-il?* Where is he!'

'I do not know...' the officer gasped, closing his eyes. Hazzard swung a goatskin round from his shoulder and held it to the man's lips. He drank, then half-opened his watering eyes. '*You are... le diable... rouge...?*'

Al-Aafrit al-ahmar.

The Red Devil.

Hazzard looked down at himself, the scarlet of his Bombay Marine coat showing through his open *binish* robe, his muddied headdress dripping on its faded gold braid and bastion loops, its Indian orders long since tarnished by salt and sand. The major's head sank back and he said no more. Hazzard looked down at him, and let out a long breath.

Wayland looked down from the saddle and sheathed his old '96 Pattern sword with a scrape of steel. A checked *shemagh* covered his head and face, tufts of his blond curling hair visible at the sides, bleached almost white by the sun now, stark against his reddish tanned skin, his eyes betraying new experience, no longer the young and eager lieutenant he had once been.

'A long ride,' said Hazzard, moving back to his horse. 'Well done.'

Wayland nodded. 'We broke cover once we saw them. Had to distract them if you were to reach the road.'

Tariq trotted up to him, pulling his mount behind. 'Hazar Pasha,' he said with a quick bow, and pointed across the marsh at the rising dust on the main road and the disappearing shapes of Menou and the *savants* riding off with the remaining cavalry. Cook, Pettifer and Warnock jogged back to him, waving an arm. '*Sir – they got one o'the Frogs—*'

Hazzard mounted and they all rode to join the main road ahead, eventually reaching the growing mob outside the gates of Kafr-Shahabas. Far from a simple group of outraged villagers, they had been organised: a line of men with muskets stood in two trenches before the gates, and there were men on the aged battlements of the gatehouse and adjoining walls.

'They were waiting,' said Wayland.

'The cavalry will be back, no doubt.' Hazzard looked at the shouting mob in the rising dust, *Bedu* horsemen joining them, riding round several shouting figures, screaming in each other's faces, arguing. 'But this...'

He rode towards the gate but a phalanx of unknown *Bedu* stepped out, muskets ready. They were in dark blue or black *keffiyah* headdresses, some in turbans, some not, homespun patterned robes, bandoliers of powder flasks across their chests, pistols in their belts, workmanlike: *soldiers*, thought Hazzard, *but whose*.

The Beni Qassim were curious as well, and immediately suspicious, facing each one of them, neither looking less fierce than the other. The young Frenchman, the captured *savant*, had gone. Hazzard then saw him being dragged through the old wooden gate. '*You there. Stop that man!*' He nodded at Tariq. Tariq bellowed out at them, ignoring the *Bedu* with muskets, '*Waqafa!* Halt!

It had no effect. The mob began to jostle their way through the gate, farm tools in hand, herding staves and pikes, an older man brandishing a broad-bladed cleaver overhead. Cook moved between Hazzard and Wayland. 'Don't ruddy like the look o'this...'

'Shots in the air, sir...?' suggested Wayland.

The remaining marines jogged up behind them, Pettifer with his blunderbuss, Warnock with his tomahawk, followed by the others. '*Ere!*' came a shout from behind as Kite, Hesse and De Lisle came at the double, Handley, Porter, Napier and Cochrane close behind. 'What's the news then, Petty?' asked Kite, his quick eyes sizing up the scene.

'Don't bloody like it, Mick,' muttered De Lisle, cocking his four-barrelled turnover pistol.

Sgt Jeremiah Underhill checked his priming pan and cocked his musket, glancing at Cook. 'What's all this then, Jory boy?'

'Don't reckon we're invited, 'Miah,' murmured Cook.

'Come on.' Hazzard kicked his horse and they pushed their way into the group, *Isri ya. Yallah, yallah*, and the mob parted, the Beni Qassim still watching the armed *Bedu* carefully.

The assembly burst into the small square behind the gatehouse and spread out, their cries bouncing and echoing around the whitewashed mudbrick buildings. The *savant* was dragged into the centre, four men pulling him by his outstretched arms, his face streaked with tears and twisted in utter terror.

Hazzard ducked through the low gateway and rode into the square, the elderly man with the cleaver already poised over the *savant*, his companions bending the sobbing Joly over. He was going to behead him.

'*Jory!*'

'*Hold yer bloody business there!*' Cook fired a shot, and the crowd jerked like a startled animal, falling suddenly silent. The Beni Qassim spread out in front of Hazzard's horse, Underhill and the marines taking up positions.

'Crowd control, sah!' shouted Underhill in his best parade-ground voice, further frightening the locals. 'Shoot the man shoutin' loudest and damn them all – old rule never fails, sah, 'appy to oblige.'

One of the armed *Bedu* stepped forward and waved a hand at Hazzard and called in broken pidgin French. 'Hanglais! *Pah por vooz! Nonn!*' He pointed at the young *savant*, '*Aadow!* En'mee de noos! *Leh fransaya ennmi!*'

After a moment's silence, the crowd roared again and surged forward, urging the old butcher to do his work. Hazzard kicked the horse forward and drew his scimitar, shouting at them, '*Ana al-Pasha al-ahmar! Ana al-Aafrit al-ahmar!*' He threw back his *binish* to show the full scarlet of his Bombay Marine jacket, the Mughal orders still glinting, Tariq shouting more in Arabic, *Hazar Pasha!*, calling down at them to obey, to be grateful for his protection, the friend of Murad Bey, beloved of the *Bedu*, defeater of the French Sultan *al-Kebir*, with *Nelsoun amir al-bahr* at Aboukir. The *fellahin* peasants shrank back as Hazzard called down at them in English, '*You will not do this.*'

Four of the unknown *Bedu* came forward, muskets slung over their shoulders, at ease but wary. Their leader called up at him in French. '*Parlez le français?*'

'*Oui,*' shouted Hazzard, '*Je suis l'anglais.* I am the Englishman, the Devil in Red, and I say you will not permit this infamy!'

The leader undid the *shemagh* scarf from his face, revealing a scarred and weather-beaten soldier's expression, staring eyes and a grizzled beard: an older man, and experienced. 'I am Sheikh Qahir ben Sayyid Baibars *al-azim.*'

'Where are you from?' demanded Hazzard. 'You are not Awlad 'Ali, Blemi or Maaza – *what then?*'

'We are Al-Tarabin,' said a voice from behind, and Sheikh Qahir bowed and stepped aside. The speaker removed the *shemagh* from an elaborate golden *iqal* rope-circlet, to reveal a smooth, delicate face – a woman. She looked up at Hazzard, her caramel skin sharply defined by the deep blue of her *keffiyah*, flowing *kaftan* and *binish*. Beneath the *binish* Hazzard could see the glint of pearls.

'So. *Al-Aafrit al-ahmar. Le diable rouge,*' she said in rough French. 'I am Shajar al-Durr.' There were shouts and calls, *Shajar, Shajar!* 'We are the Tarabin *Bedu*, of the Sinai,' she said, and raised her voice louder in Arabic, speaking to the crowd. 'We are the guardians of Egypt.'

Hazzard looked down at her. He could not help but think of Sarah, and how very different they looked, yet how very similar they truly were. They would have been kindred spirits. 'My compliments.' He frowned. 'Shajar al-Durr…? Tree of… pearl?'

She nodded. 'Yes,' she said, as if acknowledging a shared secret. 'They have called me so for some time.'

'Since she threw out the Turk from Nuweida,' said Sheikh Qahir. 'And made him beg for his riches.'

The Tarabin behind all cheered: *Shajar al-Durr! Shajar al-Kebir! Shajar!*

Hazzard recalled, somewhere, a history, an account of a queen of the Mamluk, from very long ago. 'You have come late,' he said, 'There are no Mongols here.'

She gave a brief bow of the head. 'Now, *my* compliments.' Sheikh Qahir murmured something to her, indicating the crowd and she looked up at Hazzard. Negotiation had begun. 'You do not command here.'

Hazzard indicated the men of 9 Company behind. 'These are the Marines. Of England. Soldiers of the sea. Friends.' *Soldats de la mer, amis,* he had said, then Tariq translated for the crowd, *Junud al-bahri! Sadiqi!* The townsfolk looked at them, Hesse in his short *galabeyyah*, his pointed hussar's moustaches exotic against his white *keffiyah*; others were in *binish*, but all wore some vestige of their British scarlet. Hazzard's voice bore a note of warning. 'You would not want them for an enemy.'

The sheikh growled and reached for his musket, but Wayland whipped a hand to his holster pistol and Cook took a step towards the *Bedu*. 'Steady now, lad, or ye'll regret the day.' It needed no translation.

Qahir stood still. He waved back at the crowd. 'And these are the poor, who seek justice.'

Hazzard looked at them, at their ragged clothes, their sunken cheeks and hollow eyes. The French had not done this to them – scarcely a month had passed since the Battle of the Nile: their lords had done this instead, over years of neglect. But France had invaded, and Mamluk greed had been forgotten. 'Do the Tarabin oppress the people as the bad Mamluk lords have done?'

'No. I am Qahir ben Sayyid! Protector!'

The *Bedu* chanted again, *Qahir! Qahir! Baibars al-Kabir!*

Hazzard nodded at Tariq, then pointed at the wretched boy, Joly, and addressed the crowd. 'This boy is not a warrior!' Tariq translated. 'He is but a student! A man of books and wisdom, like the learned men of the Al-Azhar Mosque!'

Qahir raised a fist angrily. 'The men of the Al-Azhar do not invade!'

More cries went up and Hazzard called out, 'If he dies the French will kill you all! Sar'nt Underhill!'

'*Sah!*'

'If that old fool moves, shoot him!'

Underhill stepped forward with his musket and several of the townsfolk backed away from him in fright. His beard was thick and matted under his chin, but his burned and scarred upper lip was bare, the skin pocked and blasted by decades of fire – with his Marine scarlet, *binish*, sword-bayonet and pistols, he looked more terrifying than the Tarabin. Underhill raised his sawn-off musket and Pettifer stepped up beside him, his wide-mouthed blunderbuss an enormous cannon. The crowd moved away still further.

Shajar watched. 'You depend on these people for support, yet you would kill them?'

Hazzard remembered Shubra Khit, the dull-eyed Hasim Bey, before he charged to the Nile in the hopes of rescuing Sarah. 'Shajar al-Durr – Tree of Pearls you may be, but if you do this the French will destroy this town, brick for brick, man, woman and child. Then spread across the Delta looking for us all. Understand? *Comprenez?*'

The old man with the cleaver lowered his hands and stepped back and Joly recovered slightly, feeling there might be hope, and appealed to Hazzard. '*M… m'sieur? Je vous en prie…!*'

'What is it you seek here, Englishman?' asked Shajar.

Hazzard looked down at her. He hesitated, then declared, 'I seek the man called Derrien. The man in black. The Dark One.'

The Tarabin either side of Shajar murmured to Sheikh Qahir. Clearly they sought Derrien as well.

There was a shout from atop the wall, more calls from outside the gate, from the Tarabin and townsmen. Curious for the view, Cochrane had climbed up to the gatehouse battlements, and now called down, '*Sir! The potheads're back!*'

Wayland tugged his horse about and shouted up at him, 'Be clearer dammit, Cochrane!'

Cochrane put a hand to his bony face and called down more loudly, '*About two 'undred 'orse, sir,*' he said, muttering, '...doin' the devil's work, aye.'

The cry went up and the crowd burst into panic, calling out, *Fransaya, Fransaya!* and pushed in from the gate. 'Sir!' called Wayland, 'Time to be off—'

Hazzard appealed to Shajar. 'Not *this* man. Not this young man of learning. He did *nothing*. He is a student. He—'

There were several shots from the wall battlements, the sound of hooves growing louder, and the crowd screamed. Hazzard turned his mount to look through the arched gatehouse and saw a dust-cloud rising on the main road. Underhill shouted, '*Sah! Request command!*' and he turned back, but it was too late: the old man brought his cleaver down on young Joly's neck, the boy's screaming cut suddenly short. His head thudded to the ground. There was a cheer and the crowd rushed in to pull at the body, the old man spitting at it. Underhill lowered his musket.

'*Christ God,*' spat Cook.

'That ain't right,' muttered Napier, the big broken-faced boxer.

'Leave the buggers to the Frogs, sir,' swore De Lisle.

Hazzard had collapsed forward slightly in his saddle, as if losing a breath, his head hanging. 'Mr Wayland. Gather the men...'

Wayland spun round and called up to the wall, 'Cochrane! Kite! To me! We're out!'

'Sah!' called Underhill, fighting off the townsfolk still pouring in the gateway. 'Request to position firing ranks until we kill enough of the murderin' buggers—'

Hazzard looked down at Shajar and her men. 'Who *are* you? *Who*, damn you!'

'We fight the French across the land, in Sinai, in the Delta, in Cairo—'

'Alone? With the Mamluks? The Turks? Who!'

She reached up and handed him a coin. 'Here is proof. From the kingdom of England.' It was a British guinea, solid gold. On its obverse was struck the unmistakable profile of the king, GEORGIVS III DEI GRATIA.

'Who gave you this?'

'An officer—'

'An *Englishman*?'

'From a ship.'

'*Was it an Englishman!*'

She looked back at him. 'It was from an *anglais*, yes. We raise the revolt in Cairo. They swear to support us.'

Sickened by the brutality before him, Hazzard flipped the coin back at her with disgust. '*You lie*. The English cannot yet land an army to support you. You will be crushed in the same day.' He stabbed a finger at the headless body of Joly. 'If this is your form of protecting the people here, then you have failed. Stay and be *damned*, and watch as your enemy destroys this town and enslaves its people.' Outraged, he turned on Sheikh Qahir. 'So, grand Sheikh. Feast upon your glorious victory, for I have not the stomach for it.'

Kite and Cochrane came skittering down the stone steps from the wall, taking the last two in a jump. 'Sir! Frogs at an 'undred yards – looks like a general or two wiv 'em. Proper cross they are an' all.'

Hazzard turned his horse, Wayland close behind. 'Go,' said Shajar. 'We shall handle these French. If they find you here they will burn the town.'

Hazzard kept his eyes on her and shouted, 'Marines to me! Beni Qassim! *Ilal amam! Forward!*'

Muskets booming across the floodplain beyond, Sheikh Qahir began ordering his men to posts at the gate, on rooftops and along the wall – but Shajar al-Durr watched Hazzard and called out after him, 'We shall meet with you again, *M'sieur l'anglais!* When we bring revolt to Cairo!'

Hazzard looked back at her. The marines doubling up with the Beni Qassim riders, they clattered through the town and out the opposite gatehouse by the small mosque, as the Al-Tarabin muskets began to snap and bang behind them. Hazzard went through the gate, glad to leave the doomed town. He was still no closer to finding Derrien, but he had found something else: a new danger.

Cook and Wayland brought up the rear and rode up beside him. They kicked the horses into a canter and soon disappeared into the dust, heading perhaps for Damietta, perhaps for Sinai, and the endless desert beyond.

Phoenix

Cairo glowed with late summer heat, the approach of autumn bringing no respite. The domes of the mosques and towering minarets gleamed gold and bronze, melting into the ochre and limewash of the buildings. The harsh, medieval stone battlements of the citadel chopped at the hazy skyline, a brutish military monument in its midst.

His hands clenched tightly behind his back, *Général en chef* Napoléon Bonaparte, the new Alexander, the new Conqueror of Egypt, stood alone on a high balcony, looking out over the rooftops of his Babylon, brooding, silent, feeling untriumphant, unvictorious. His twenty-ninth birthday had come and gone, and the Nile had flooded, the great 'Nilometer' renovated by the *savants* the new gauge of the inundation's progress. And his battle-fleet was sunk, the remains a collection of hulks and hospital ships, so much useless, wasted oak.

'They will mock me,' he murmured. 'No matter my successes, no matter my victories. They will mock all the same. As they did Caesar...' He looked down, biting his eyes shut in the intense heat. In his featherlight embroidered silk and cotton tailcoat he had some relief, but few moved in the streets, the sun was too high – only the river stayed alive, boats of all shapes, punts, large *djerms*, tall *chebeks*, plying up and down, docking at distant Bulaq, *feluccas* and their sloping yards heading downriver with the current. 'Louis...'

Bourrienne, his oldest friend, came forward from inside. A small, vigorous man, now grown somewhat more portly, he stepped into the sunshine. 'I am here.'

'What do they say...?'

Bourrienne took a breath and moved his spectacles an inch, then back again. Louis Antoine Fauvelet de Bourrienne was more than Bonaparte's friend, he was ambassador, secretary, and confidant. He was also watchful. 'The general staff regret the loss of the ships of course,' he began, 'but... above all they do wonder,' he added quietly, 'how we intend to get home again.'

Bonaparte nodded. 'I had hoped they would *want* to stay. Tamarisk and jacaranda, orange blossom in their gardens, half-naked concubines cavorting for them every night... Is this not paradise enough?' He shook his head. 'I should never have used the Army of Italy. Never.'

Bourrienne said nothing, but waited.

'Brueys,' said Bonaparte. 'Dying at his post, his leg taken by a ball. Du Petit-Thouars blown in half and propped on a cask to direct the battle. Heroic. But futile.' He shivered his shoulders, suddenly angry. 'Trullet shooting himself in his cabin, *ma foi*. So they should have, all. A *fleet*, Louis. An entire battle-fleet, gone. That old fool.'

'Brueys?'

'Sitting snug in his private bay, believing it safe as a Rhine castle. He did not know Nelson. I warned him – repeatedly.'

Bourrienne nodded. 'I know. Indeed I have the copies of your orders, all signed. You told him to set sail three times.'

'Of course I did.' He turned. 'And *they blame me.*'

All remembered the moment, where they were, what they had been doing, when they had heard the news that the fleet was sunk, destroyed by the English. By Nelson.

In Bonaparte's case, on a desert road, a column of cavalrymen behind. He had heard a shout and ordered a halt, the dust-cloud of an approaching messenger all too clear behind them. The sound of the frothing horse's hooves was heavy as the wounded rider made his way towards them – and the sight of him: torn, bloodied, burned, wild-eyed and maddened, his shaking hands passing over the written despatch that spelled the ruin of all their hopes and dreams.

Defeat.

Thankfully for Bourrienne, Bonaparte turned from the sight of Cairo and returned to the shade of the palace. He had occupied the former residence of Muhammad Bey al-Elfi, which he had found abandoned, as with many of the palaces in Ezbekiya belonging to other high-ranking Mamluk leaders. He surveyed the large, comfortable room; decorated pillars supported the ornate carved ceiling high above. There were cool white walls, rugs, and gleaming polished marble steps to a lower level, festooned with couches and cushions, lit by arched windows. Devoted Berber guards, freed from the Knights' servitude on Malta, stood either side of each doorway. He glanced at his desk, the balcony windows behind, a flamboyant and ornate piece in the Moroccan style, geometric designs picked out in ivory and mother of pearl.

Two secretaries awaited him, with Gaspard Monge and Claude-Louis Berthollet, the two senior *savants* of the scientific Commission. They were seated in low-slung carved chairs upholstered in soft leather. The two older men were patient, waiting for the return of their protégé. If ever Bonaparte had a father-figure to whom he could turn in times of difficulty, it was the stellar conjunction of the pair before him, Monge and Berthollet. However, they were not lazing, but rather observing, with a scientific curiosity. Before the desk, also waiting for Bonaparte, stood another, one now almost universally despised.

He leaned to his left on a walking-stick of bleached sycamore with chased silver mounts, his heavy frock-coat discarded in favour of one in cooler black Egyptian cotton and linen, a black cravat at his throat. His right arm hung stiff at his side, a discreet glove to hide the burns and protect his skin from the sun; under his sleeve the glove reached near to his elbow and the site of a bitter wound; new scars rose from his neck to his forehead, the right side of his face darker than the left – all from burns received in the last dying moments of the flagship *Orient*, at the debacle of Nelson's victory in Aboukir Bay. Despite the glove his right hand was still quick enough to dip into his pocket to retrieve his small screw-barrelled pistol, though slightly too stiff to squeeze the trigger as quickly as he once could.

Master of spies, with the rank of Collector in the *Bureau d'information* from the Ministry of the Interior, Jules-Yves Derrien waited in sweating discomfort, the man who had not prevented the disaster in the bay – the man who had let Hazzard live. The man whom Bonaparte could blame.

Derrien glanced behind him at his two new Bureau deputies, the broad-necked and sturdy Citizen Blais, and the hatchet-faced Citizen Peraud, both hard, wiry men like Derrien. They stood quiet, bare-headed, in nondescript dark coats, heavy-headed canes in their hands. They had been co-opted from Alexandria after the death of Masson, and had proved the most amenable to Derrien's peculiar methods. They bowed in unison as Bonaparte approached the desk, and Derrien lay several sheets of paper on the blotter. 'Your weekly reports, Citizen General.'

Bonaparte glanced at them as he sat, as if ignoring him. 'I see.' He skimmed through them quickly.

Derrien added, 'And a final tally of materiel lost… in Aboukir Bay.'

The stiff silence in the room thickened still more deeply. Bonaparte read, whispering, '*Nom d'un nom…*'

'Citizen Conté,' began Derrien, 'is now machining the replacement tools he needs, for those lost in the *Orient*, and other vessels. Though his fire-engine has been rebuilt and there are hopes for a model for Cairo. He still promises a balloon ascent for the New Year celebrations.'

Monge adjusted his waistcoat with some satisfaction, a paternal pride in his tone. 'I told you so,' he said. 'Give him a push and he shall achieve wonders.'

Bonaparte nodded. 'News of Desaix?'

'Citizen General Desaix is moving south in pursuit of Murad Bey, who has retreated into Upper Egypt, in the region of Aswan. It would not be unimaginable that their aim is to entice General Desaix away from the capital.'

Bonaparte glanced at him. 'Are you suggesting this is a clever tactic rather than mere retreat?'

'General Desaix is one of your best, Citizen General—'

'*You need not remind me.*'

The voice was like a lash. Derrien closed his eyes. He had grown accustomed to at least one tirade per meeting. The two Bureau men shifted uneasily. 'As you say, General.'

'And?'

'As are his cavalry detachment, the best. If they were too far from the capital when they were needed…'

Monge interrupted, 'I believe Jacques Cavalier is with him,' murmuring his approbation. 'Very wise to send Cavalier, General. Excellent man, excellent.'

Bonaparte nodded to Monge, happy to be distracted. 'He is. Though he had some trouble with that depot colonel, Lacroix.'

'Yes,' said Monge, 'threatened to knock his head off in a duel.' He glanced at Derrien. 'All because of your *anglais*.'

Derrien could not let that lie. 'I assure you he is not my *anglais*, Citizen Professor.'

Bonaparte threw down the pages with annoyance. 'And what of him. Have you found him? Seen him? Heard of him?'

'No, Cit—'

'Then *kindly do so!*' Bonaparte threw his hand out in sudden anger at the deputies behind him. 'Have you not enough men, not enough informants? Is it not enough you allow *Mademoiselle* Moreau-Lazare to be murdered in so brutal a fashion and then let Mr Hazzard *escape*? *Again?*'

Derrien said nothing, his mind racing with images of those last moments in the fury of Aboukir Bay. How he himself had escaped remained a blank in his memory, flashes coming only at rare times, or when he slept: Hazzard in the lamplight, the ship exploding around them, diving into the dark and falling; crazed rubble and cries of the trapped; a pair of cannon-balls joined by a length of chain, crashing through the stern, a whirling diabolus, a device of Satan himself, roaring through the bulwarks – and falling again, until the crash of impact in the water, ice and fire filling his throat. How had he survived indeed.

He had told Bonaparte nothing of the truth of Isabelle Moreau-Lazare, nor her secret identity, but had taken pride in revealing the treachery of Bonaparte's own acquaintance, the *comtesse* de Biasi. That Isabelle Moreau-Lazare, Bonaparte's mistress, had been quite possibly the most successful British agent he had ever encountered was a special surprise he was reserving for an appropriate crisis.

Sarah – of course! How very English, Mr Hazzard.

Sarah Chapel. How he had struggled to keep her to himself. Yet still the memory thrilled him.

She was mine.

Mine.

'There was a disturbance, Citizen General,' began Derrien with some hope of distracting Bonaparte further. He turned and took a sheaf of papers from Peraud, the taller and by far more ambitious of the two, while Blais, perhaps more instinctual, watched the *savants* closely, as if trying to detect their intentions. '…At the town of Kafr-Shahabas, a suburb in the Delta, near Shahabas Ammer—'

'I know where it is,' snapped Bonaparte.

Monge chuckled. 'Of course he does…! The general studies every map by the millimetre. As should you,' he said, looking at Derrien, '…Citizen *Croquemort.*'

Blais noted the insulting jibe, 'the Mortician', and watched Berthollet for signs of assent, but Derrien ignored the old man. 'Unlike the resistance at Mansouria some weeks ago, the townsfolk here were prepared and well organised. Governor Menou led a party of *savants* on a minor expedition and was well received by the sheikhs of Desouq, feasted and accorded all ceremony.'

Bonaparte sat back, pleased. 'Excellent. He is considering converting to Islam, as I declared all officers should.'

'Would he really?' asked Berthollet, scandalised. 'The idea of Menou in robes. How appalling...'

Derrien waited a moment before continuing. 'When they approached Kafr-Shahabas, they were met by gunfire and a mob.' He glanced at Monge and Berthollet. 'The townspeople captured one Citizen Joly, a draughtsman from the *École des Ponts et Chausées*, I understand.'

They were alert now, and Berthollet sat up, the horrors of the battle on the river at Shubra Khit all too fresh in his mind. 'What? Well, what became of him...?'

Derrien kept his report as matter of fact as he could; it always had the greatest effect. 'The governor and his party had split into two groups, leaving Citizen Dolomieu and others behind at some distance, the foremost outrunning the escorting detachment of horse. The cavalry were attacked by Bedouin, and Citizen Joly suffered some form of mad fever, and would not remount his horse. He ran from his colleagues, who were forced to retire quickly. When they returned with the cavalry they found Citizen Joly's headless body.'

'*Oh mon dieu*,' gasped Berthollet. 'The poor boy. He was barely...'

Monge was furious. '*Par bleu!* How *dare* they...! A – a draughtsman, an *artist*, of all things! By *God* I would burn them down myself!'

Bonaparte regarded him as if hearing the news of Aboukir Bay all over again, his face draining of colour, a quietly shaking rage, then imperceptibly subsiding. 'Take a detachment of artillery and destroy Kafr-Shahabas. Not a wall or hovel is to be left standing. Every captured male to be conscripted to the *sapeurs* as army labourers, females to the brothels. The sick and infirm shall be shot. I will *not* be defied like this!' He threw himself back in his chair, then held up a hand. 'No. No, the Sheikh of Desouq is to organise this, as he would any unrepentant town that did not pay his taxes.'

Derrien nodded. 'It shall be done, Citizen General. However,' he added, 'what is more of concern is the organisation of the resistance. Local informants speak of the Englishman, yes, but also of a band of Bedouin come with some authority from the Sinai, Al-Tarabin Bedouin, greatly respected and deadly warriors. It is my suspicion they were sent by order from Acre – from one Ahmed al-Djezzar.' Bonaparte looked up in reaction, as if he knew the name. 'I understand it means "the Butcher", Citizen General.'

After a moment, Bonaparte rose from his chair. He glared out the window. Bourrienne reminded him, 'He offered insult to Citizen Beauvoisin in parley, this so-called Butcher. Not reasonable. Possibly why the sultan in Constantinople uses him as a disposable tool. Though he rules all of Syria.'

Bonaparte nodded. 'He swore to throw me into the flames, I believe.' He looked out at Cairo again, possibly seeking some form of escape.

Bourrienne glanced at Monge and the others, making light of it. 'Threats in the desert. No more than the wind. Or,' he turned to Monge, 'what did you call it, Professor?'

'*Mirage*, General.' Monge nodded, looking away, possibly thinking of Joly. 'All to do with perspective...'

Though some had been injured at Shubra Khit, Joly had been the first direct *savant* victim of the expedition. Derrien watched for signs of dissent, disharmony, anything he could use to claw his way back into power. 'That may be so, Citizen General, Citizen Professors,' he said with insincere deference. 'But if they have come to foment rebellion, then they might come with the permission of the sultan in Constantinople. We must assume, therefore, that Minister Talleyrand's diplomacy has not yet been a success.'

Bourrienne knew of Talleyrand's mission, and his involvement in the scheme. 'If he fails,' he lowered his voice, 'then we are at great disadvantage.'

'I have drafted a communiqué for the Ministry, Citizen General,' said Derrien, turning to Peraud once again. He handed Derrien a number of copies. Derrien placed them on the desk. 'To inform the Directory and remind them of the urgency of a diplomatic mission to the Ottoman sultan.'

'Talleyrand,' scoffed Bonaparte, looking at the despatch. 'More hot air. Nothing but *shit* in a silk purse.'

Monge said nothing, but took a deep steadying breath. 'He had been the one hope.'

'The largest enemy in the world on our doorstep,' said Bonaparte. 'As Ashurbanipal knew, if you have Palestine you must take Egypt.

As Ramesses knew, if you have Egypt you must control Palestine. Axiomatic. If they force me, I shall burn them all…'

Bonaparte looked out through the window again at Cairo, unseeing. The atmosphere took on a slight chill. Monge glanced at Berthollet. 'We have barely established the Institute, General, surely you can take some time, just for yourself…?'

'I take three hours per night to myself,' he said in response. 'Only fools need more.' He moved back to the balcony and looked out. 'To protect what we have achieved here I will march the army through the gates of Constantinople, Isfahan, Baghdad and Bombay if I have to.'

'Surely the men deserve something of a rest,' suggested Berthollet with a pained expression, glancing at Monge hopefully. 'This Murad business, retreating to the south…'

It was a poor ruse, but it came with Monge's support. 'Quite so, Claude, let them have their donkey-races and whatnot. I hear they chase about on ostriches now! Plucking the tail feathers for hats! Ha.' He laughed briefly. 'Cairo has welcomed them.'

Bonaparte was unconvinced. 'Cairo has welcomed their money…' He looked to Bourrienne. 'Louis, what is the diplomatic position?'

Bourrienne read through Derrien's draft but did not have to think too hard about it. 'Exposed. If the sultan does not align with France, we can no longer claim to be here as liberators on his behalf. If we attack Syria and Palestine we would reinforce the sultan's position within his empire, his subjects rallying not only to his cause but to God's.' He looked at them all. 'We would become open enemies to the endless armies of Islam, including Egypt.'

Bonaparte nodded, almost mocking. 'So we should do nothing. Stay here, safe in Cairo.'

There was an uncomfortable silence. 'That may not be advisable, Citizen General,' suggested Derrien.

Bonaparte looked at him. 'Well?'

As ever, Derrien did not flinch. 'A number of depots report losses of munitions and firearms.'

Bonaparte looked up at this. 'Losses?'

'Not losses, Citizen General,' said Derrien. 'Thefts would be more accurate.'

They all listened now.

'To date we have no accurate inventory of longarms owing to the cargoes lost in Aboukir Bay. Some weeks ago swimmers were sighted diving down from punts, going into the wrecks to loot them, for reward, or sale to us or other buyers.'

Bonaparte was a commander who knew the details of every depot in every district. He looked through a sheaf of reports. 'The quartermaster at Aboukir Fort claims two hundred 1777 Pattern Charleville muskets. Is this then inaccurate?'

'That report is what *should* have been allocated to Aboukir Fort – not what is currently in the armoury. He admitted to my agent—' Behind him, Peraud took a half-step and gave a brief bow, '—that he has been unable so far to account for his full allocation. Some firearms, powder and shot were simply never received. He assumed them missing, or stolen.'

Monge looked away. 'Good God...'

'And considering the confusion within the city after the Mamluk beys abandoned the capital, there are doubtless several thousand Ottoman muskets in circulation as well.' Derrien then did what he had always done, let the truth itself sow its own brand of disquiet and uncertainty: 'I am not convinced Cairo is the safe place we believe it to be.'

–

Some distance from Bonaparte's palace in Ezbekiya, through the new bazaar that led to the southern areas closer to Old Cairo, several streets had been renamed by the soldiers, *Bastille, Faubourg, St Denis*, all bright with a post-nightmare relief that life could continue, and the tenuous hope that things perhaps might improve. With its proliferation of European cafés, many serviced by expatriates of France, the area had been nicknamed Little Paris. Here, a soldier's tunic button could buy him little, though they were common currency everywhere else, for the café owners knew the value of their wares, and accepted only the *franc, piastre* and *scudo*, the *dinar, drachma* and *dirham*.

Outside one popular haunt, prudently renamed after the Revolution '*Le Citoyen*', *the Citizen*, a few tables had been put out in the shade of a broad awning, the frontage of the café open to its dark interior, revealing a curving bar with seating, stools and benches, and rugs and bolsters in the shade for smoking. Spread over two tables at the front, beside Mrs Nasim's stall of cotton *shemagh* and *kaftan*, slouched the unsoldierly sight of Fusilier Gaston Rossy, his dusty boots resting comfortably on another chair, the giant, Pigalle, occupying virtually a table to himself and young Fusilier Antonnais, scarred and aged years since the invasion only two months earlier.

Watching them protectively from the bar in the café's cool interior, among the local Arab men in fez and turban, was *Sergent-chef-major* Achille Caron, Senior NCO and *major* of the 75th *demi-brigade de bataille*, 'the Invincibles'. Rossy and the others were some of his most prized *enfants*, his children – his best platoon, the *Alpha-Oméga* skirmishers, *Le Premier et Dernier*: the first the enemy sees, and the last, and without question the deadliest *chasseur* unit in Bonaparte's expedition.

'I could become well used to this new life, *Chef*,' said Rossy to Caron behind. Rossy closed his eyes and rocked his chair backwards until it bumped against the central column which propped up the Citizen. 'So long as we are kept out of trouble. I think I was made for the good life.' He took a sip of a tall lemonade with sliced lime, and several long shots of illegal *grappa*, extending his grubby yet dainty pinkie. 'Ahh, *c'est bon, la dolce vita*.'

Caron looked out at the square, at the small central fountain, at the two- and three-storey tenement buildings all around, music twanging and wailing from somewhere, listening to the raucous voices calling, the women working on the doorsteps and in doorways, somewhere a goat bleating – and he did not disagree with Rossy. Nowhere could he see enemy cavalry, cannon bursts or lines of guns: for now, that was over. 'Trouble will find us soon enough, *garçon*,' he murmured. 'She always does.'

Pigalle looked up from his playing cards, tiny in his huge paws. 'Which is the one higher than the knight of the swords...?'

'The jack or the king, *M'sieur* le Pig. With the little K in the corner, for the German.'

'There is no K. Or a queen. I think it is lost.' Pigalle frowned, looking at the cards as if they were broken and needed fixing. 'I tell you this always.'

Rossy glanced at him, taking one from the deck. 'Ah. Those are not the German cards, Pig. These are Mamluk cards, no queens.'

'Huh. *Stupide*. How can I play Aluette if they keep changing.'

Caron watched them paternally. He indulged them with free time – they had earned it: they had fought their way from the Vendée to

Holland, up the Rhine and down to Rome, and from Malta to the shores of Egypt. They had survived the Battle of Shubra Khit and the Battle of the Pyramids. Before the night march to Alexandria, Colonel Junot had threatened the army that they must march or die: the Alphas had marched, and not died. They were too experienced, said Rossy, and Death did not want them.

Their greatest exploit, however, had been to step in and foil Lacroix's plans to destroy their *anglais*, the Red Devil. They had rescued him from slow murder in the sun – for nothing so tawdry as honour, they protested, but something greater: they had hated Lacroix. And Hazzard, they knew, was the old soldier, their *anglais*, whom they had captured in Valletta – their personal prize. At the enquiry, they had been acquitted by saving a valuable prisoner for the *général en chef*, and Lacroix had been demoted to captain and put in charge of the depot latrines.

Their reverie was disturbed by a slight figure, an Egyptian, scurrying across to them with brisk little steps, at once determined yet deferential. He had come through the heat of the square from his barbershop opposite. '*M'sieur* Rossy, *citoyen effendi*, will you come now, for the shaving?'

Rossy looked puzzled. He ran a hand over the two-week growth of patchy and grimy beard and his flowing moustaches. 'Raff, I am not certain, you know. I am liking my grand moustaches. They make me look distinguished.'

Raff stopped short. 'But, no no, *effendi*, your hair.'

'What of my hair? Is it too long?'

Raff shook his head, very insistent. 'We must shave it, oh for the heat, oh for the health, *effendi*.'

Rossy put a hand to his head. 'I will not be bald like you Egyptos, even if the heat demands it.'

Then Raff understood and smiled up at the sky. 'Ah, no no, *effendi*, I see, I see, oh no no, not the hair *there*.'

The Alphas looked up, all very interested now. 'Which hairs where then?' asked Pigalle, looking at Rossy with curiosity.

Raff spread his hands modestly. 'The hair, *effendi*, that makes for the hot heat and the discomfort in the trousers. All for the health.'

Rossy tilted his chair forward slowly till he came to rest with a thump, and looked at Raff through narrowed eyes. 'Am I right in thinking that you wish to shave my... my *saucisson*?' He wiggled his little finger. 'My *saucisson spécial de Toulouse*?'

Pigalle took it very seriously. 'I would be careful...' he murmured, returning to his cards.

'But yes, *effendi*,' continued Raff. 'All must be shaved, for the little fleas, and biting things and—'

'Raff, are you making a living of handling people's private parts?'

'Ah no no, *effendi*. Always the customer he, or she, holds things away that I might not cut...'

Even more interested now, Antonnais looked up from his mint tea. 'Ladies? You shave the ladies?'

Raff was proud of his work. 'Oh yes, *effendi*, and very grateful they are indeed yes!'

Rossy made a face. 'I am not sure of such a fashion, Pig, are you? I like to find a little furry home when I see *chérie* under her skirts. It is the French way, *non*?'

Still concentrating on his cards, Pigalle nodded ponderously. 'I agree.'

'Oh no, *effendi*,' enthused Raff, his hands up to the heavens, 'the beautiful ladies, they do enjoy it so!' He looked away, suddenly shy. 'They show me so...!'

Rossy cocked an eyebrow, making a decision. '*Chef*,' he called over his shoulder, 'I wish to become a barber. I wish to resign from the war and make ladies grateful.'

'Very wise,' said Caron.

'Still,' sighed Rossy, 'must I let my *saucisson* into the hands of a man with a razor...?'

'My sympathies are for whoever handles your *saucisson*,' grunted Caron as he took a swig of beer.

'Mine too, *Chef*,' agreed Rossy.

Another figure appeared from one side, a soldier. Exhausted, he crashed down into a chair, another Alpha, St Michel, the sniper. He propped his Austrian rifle-musket against the table and removed his spectacles with a gasp, running a hand over his head. '*Mon dieu*. This heat. It is worse than the bowels of the Château d'If.' He grabbed a glass of water by Antonnais and drained it in seconds, then saw Raff. 'Oh, *putain*, you have not come to shave my *cazzo caldo* again, Raff, *merde alors*...'

Raff stamped his foot. 'But it is important, *effendi*!'

'You will not circumcise me with your damn razor! Be off with you.'

Raff wagged a finger at them. 'And that is *another* worry of mine, *effendi*! That none of you is circumcised! The health in the desert, the sand, the heat, the little biting things...' He mimed a small nibbling animal.

Rossy was about to reply when he saw movement on the other side of the square, by the dark archway to the narrow *souk*. He tensed, sitting up slightly.

St Michel detected the change in his demeanour, as did Pigalle and Antonnais. They looked into the blinding sunshine, trying to search the shadows beyond. As they did, a dark figure emerged from the bazaar, from among the silks and jewellery stalls, a European – but a rare one, for he was not beset by voluble traders. A few tried, then fell suddenly silent, backing away from him, something fearful rising in them. He wore a broad-brimmed hat, black coat and cravat, a glove on his right hand, and had a distinct limp, using a walking-stick. The Alphas recognised him at once – one of their dearest enemies. Caron set down his beer glass. '*Mon dieu. Le diable.*'

Last seen at a makeshift brigade camp in the Delta, his hands twisted behind his back as Colonel Lacroix tried to take the *anglais* once and for all. Rossy's voice was just above a whisper. 'Citizen *Croquemort.*'

Their paths had not crossed in the months after the destruction of the fleet and Hazzard's escape – even since they had returned to Cairo on recuperative leave, they had neither seen nor heard anything more of him, and assumed him dead.

Raff the barber bowed. '*Effendi,*' he said, then scuttled back to his barbershop.

Derrien noted the Alphas at their tables, the strangely *Parisien* feel to the café, its sign, the slate board offering meals and the *prix fixe* menu. He stopped and stared at them a moment, then approached.

'*Calisse de merde...*' murmured Rossy, his hand reaching for the pistol at his hip. '*Chef...*' he said with warning.

Caron stayed on his stool at the bar. '*Ça va, garçon.* We just wait.'

Rossy cocked his pistol, just in case. 'The true soldier's motto, *Chef...*'

Derrien stopped in the shade of the café awning, a dark silhouette framed by the blaze of the square behind. He looked at each one in turn, Rossy, St Michel, Antonnais, Pigalle – and then Caron.

'*Sergent-chef-major.*'

Caron nodded. Derrien had remembered his honorary rank. 'Citizen.'

Derrien looked at them again. 'Is this all that remain?'

Rossy spoke carefully. 'We are the *chasseurs à pied*, Citizen. We do not need numbers. But yes, we are here.'

Derrien shifted his weight, his leg giving way slightly, and his arm twitched. Without exception, each man snatched up his musket. The Arabs at the bar with Caron turned, concealed muskets emerging from their robes – the Alpha-Omegas were all there, after all, in the open and incognito. Much of the noise in the square died down as onlookers saw the stand-off, the guns, the tension among the soldiers. People hurried out of the way, pigeons flapping into the sky in alarm.

'So,' said Derrien. 'There you all are.'

Caron muttered, '*Ça suffit,*' *enough*, and they relaxed their weapons, but remained alert. None trusted Derrien and all knew that the stories about him were entirely true. Caron emerged from the café, to stand beside Rossy. 'And what can we do for you, Citizen.'

Derrien almost smiled, his news bringing some small amusement. '*Sergent-chef-major,* you are now under my command, by order of the *général en chef.*' He handed over a folded sheet of stiff paper. It rattled in the hot wind as he held it out.

Caron took it and opened it. He read the signature, and recognised the seal. He looked up. 'A temporary command.'

'No,' said Derrien. 'As I see fit.'

'No,' corrected Caron. 'A temporary command.'

Derrien took back the order. Carefully he folded it away into his inside pocket. 'As you wish to believe. Time is limited. There is a schedule, but it is unknown to us. And we must find it out.' He settled his hand on his walking-stick once again. 'We have an important task.'

'And what might that be?'

Derrien looked at the Alphas at the bar, so convincing in their turbans, *keffiyah* headdresses and robes. '*Chef,*' he said, eyes glittering with some small triumph, 'we are going to prevent Cairo from exploding.'

Whirlwind

The rain spattered on the beaten cobbles of Horse Guards Parade, the bright stone buildings rendered dark by a menacing September sky. The cries of drill-sergeants echoed across the quad as a platoon of the Coldstream Guards marched in perfect line abreast, the crash of their hands on musket forestocks mingling with the clatter of hoofbeats and carriage wheels in Whitehall. It had been freakishly warm in the last few weeks, and the autumn rain came as something of a relief to London – but brought little relief to the hard-pressed Commander Charles Blake, RN, who hurried through the shortcut to the adjoining Admiralty buildings next door. The Horse Guards clock over the quad struck two. He reached the rear gate and the Marine sentry, who fumbled with his ring of keys.

'Good afternoon, Tom,' said Blake.

The guard opened the outer gate and they went through to the inner. 'Afternoon sir...'

'Is your mother all right now?'

He unlocked the inner gate and saluted. 'Doc Philips said she's doing much better sir, thank you very much.'

'Glad he could make it,' said Blake with sincerity, and passed into the rear courtyard, the marine locking the gate behind him. Blake continued on to the mews stables and carthouse, up a set of steps to the rear door. He got out of the rain and shook off his hat – then felt a drip land on his head. He looked up at the leaking skylight far above. He smiled, thinking of Hazzard going up the backstairs on that last occasion. *When had that been? Six? Seven months?* 'Yes. We must fix that...'

He ascended the stairs and reached the top landing. The top floor of the Admiralty was quieter than the lower, containing as it did the conference and chart rooms, more a rarefied atmosphere of rank and decision than administration and activity. Just a few steps away was a door marked '63', his offices, and those of Sir Rafe Lewis, head of Admiralty Intelligence. To his right he saw the chart room, the door open, a few Signals officers sorting the sheets for the coming briefing. Blake recognised one of them and called in a stage whisper, 'Mr Pryce... *Mr Pryce—*'

Lt Pryce of Signals looked up from the broad table and came to the door quickly. 'Yes, Commander?'

'Are they in the conference room or His Lordship's suite...?'

'Oh, yes sir, the suite apartment, sir. They've only just arrived.'

'War Secretary as well?'

Pryce nodded with commiseration. 'Afraid so, sir.'

'Thank you, John. Could you make sure someone brings in tea this time?'

'Got the Trojans working in the galley now sir. Might get some sandwiches too.'

Blake smiled and walked off, his heels loud on the worn planks. Years he had served at sea, and years now he had served here, in this grand palace of spies and lies. He smiled again at the thought of William John Hazzard, who would have said precisely that.

His gait slowed at the thought of what had happened, of the Battle of the Nile, as all now called it, of Hazzard's fiancée, Sarah Chapel – and Blake's own part in the tragic affair. He offered no excuse for himself, but he likewise felt no forgiveness for the brutal heart of his chief, Commodore Sir Rafe Lewis, Head of Intelligence and the infamous Room 63, so willing to discard the people once under his command. What he and Lewis had done, he felt – and always had felt – was tantamount to a pact with Lucifer, their perfidy etched in blood upon their souls, to be brought out and thrust upon them come Judgement Day. For all his conscience, Blake knew he had sold himself to the darkness of the greater good – which, in his experience, inevitably demanded the greatest evil.

He approached the twin doors and two marines in scarlet and black round-hats, spatterdashes and boots came to attention, one of them turning, knocking, then opening the door. Blake stepped inside into a panelled corridor, a hatrack and mirror over a console table to the left. A young rating in bluejacket livery, breeches and white stockings took his cloak, stick and hat and he paused at the mirror, then moved on without looking, for fear of what his reflection might impart. Hearing the murmur of voices, he took a breath and walked round the corner, the apartment revealed before him.

To the right, three tall windows rose behind a large oaken desk set upon a broad Persian carpet of rich burgundies and creams, dotted with sabre-legged chairs and small occasional tables, the light winking from glazed bookcases and the sharply cut facets of crystal decanters. To the left, the room extended to a comfortable set of French bergère chairs and soft cushions in worn damask, a low table between them, an Adam fireplace in black marble at one end – the whole set before leaded lights, with a view through the foliage of elms and oaks to the Thames beyond.

Standing by the fireplace were three men, brandies in hand: First Sea Lord the Earl Spencer, the Secretary of War Lord Melville, and Commodore Sir Rafe Lewis – who gave Blake a sharp look, as if to reprimand him for being late.

'My lords, Sir Rafe,' said Blake, putting his heels together quietly and bowing his head, 'My deepest apologies.'

Spencer waved away his concerns without rebuke. 'Not at all, Commander, good of you to come at such short notice...' The Earl Spencer had been fending off not only the French and the Irish but also the clamorous demands of his noble colleagues on the Board of Lords Commissioners for over a decade. Blake had met him long ago, and what he saw now was a weary, exhausted man. Melville was quite different: a Scots general, he was well-known as an opponent of current naval strategies. Bewigged, in frock-coat and with a brass-topped cane, he looked very much the picture of the army that had marched to victory at Blenheim decades earlier. Sir Rafe, on the other hand, was a closed-faced, harsh man in short iron-grey wig and austere coat, workmanlike, dark and hard-bitten: the picture of a long-serving Royal Navy officer.

Spencer indicated seats for everyone and settled himself down, the young naval rating bringing Blake a belated brandy on a silver tray. He noted that the earl looked particularly tired. Blake raised his glass, 'My lords, your health, most welcome on such a day,' and they joined him, draining and setting down their snifters, ready to work. Blake sipped his discreetly and set it down.

'Mr Blake,' said the earl, 'what is your assessment of the situation?'

Blake had been prepared for this. There was no doubt Lewis had supplied the earl with as many facts and figures from different sources as anyone could need, but Blake had a way of giving the true feeling of such data, without compromising their facts.

'My lord, my lord Secretary,' he said, nodding to Melville. 'As Sir Rafe is aware, I was once a fellow-officer of Mr Hazzard. I know him well.'

'Then come along, sir,' Melville burst out, 'are we seriously to concede he was as much to thank for the victory at the Nile as Nelson?' he demanded with a snort. 'Stuff and nonsense. Reports are rife, and we have them all now, safe under lock and key, that there were marines *ashore*, engaging enemy gun emplacements while Nelson led the charge at sea. Some damn fool even suggested he saw scarlet aboard the flagship *Orient* before she blew up. Absurd, surely.'

Blake thought a moment, as if to give weight to Melville's concerns, though he did not. 'Mm. Yes sir. But, knowing Mr Hazzard as I do, that is most probably what happened.'

Melville stared back at him. 'Even Berry of the *Vanguard* said this fellow had reconnoitred the French fleet from the damned masthead of the *Orient*! Climbed the thing in broad daylight for a wager with 'em… it simply can't be.'

Again, Blake nodded apologetically, a peculiar sense of pride passing through him. 'Then that is what he did, sir.' He smiled briefly. 'William Hazzard is a quick study. I understood he dined with Bonaparte as well when aboard the *Orient* as his prisoner.'

'By *Judas*,' whispered Melville. 'It's *true*?'

'I cannot account for what was said, my lord, but,' he smiled briefly, 'we have it on good account from two of our former agents, since passed to us.' He glanced at Lewis, who scowled: the fate of Sarah Chapel and the *comtesse* de Biasi was a sore point between them. 'It was that same night he leapt from *Orient*'s upper gundeck into the sea for rendezvous with Nelson.'

Melville looked away, aghast. 'God Christ above.'

'Oh Henry, really,' said Spencer wearily. They were quiet a moment and Spencer put a hand to his forehead and sighed. 'How would you sum up his position, Mr Blake?'

Blake glanced at Lewis, but Lewis gave him no counsel in return, merely a raised eyebrow and a shrug. Blake cleared his throat. 'That Mr Hazzard will never leave Egypt, my lord, nor the Egyptians, while they are in danger.'

Spencer nodded. After a moment he put his hand down and looked out at the green of the dripping leaves twitching in the falling rain. 'Will he be able to survive, in Cairo? In Egypt, for so long?'

Blake was uncertain how to respond. 'He is very hardy, my lord.'

'His lordship is concerned,' said Lewis, speaking for the first time. 'Cairo might see an uprising. Though tactically we cannot yet support it.'

Melville responded almost angrily. 'We *must*. If the French lose their grip on the capital their forces will be split. As every day passes they consolidate their position and India is *still at risk*, sir.'

'What then?' asked Lewis. 'A landing, sir? We have but a handful of ships blockading Egypt and no men to land.'

Spencer glanced at Lewis. 'How few ships are we reduced to now?'

Blake answered, '*Zealous*, *Swiftsure*, *Alexander* and a few light frigates, my lord, under Commodore Hood. Malta is also blockaded and we fear Naples may need support shortly.'

Spencer nodded sadly. 'The blockade is anathema to our captains, they do despise it so.' He waved a hand at Lewis. 'But what, in its stead? Open battle at sea with a reinvigorated enemy, and the likelihood of hundreds of lives lost?' He shook his head. 'I own that I am tired of all this, Henry, I truly am...'

Blake felt suddenly very uncomfortable, and made to withdraw. 'If you would prefer, my lord...'

Spencer shook his head. 'No, no, do please stay, Commander, I am beset is all, truly, you are needed.' He looked to Lewis. 'Sir Rafe? What of Commodore Smith?'

'Commodore Smith still has the trust of the fleet sir, and the Sublime Porte in Constantinople. He is now in command of the Levant, while Nelson recuperates in Naples from his wounds received at the Nile.'

'We have despatched orders of confirmation to that effect, Sir Rafe,' confirmed Blake. 'The commodore will rendezvous ashore with Mr Hazzard, for resupply and briefing.'

Melville grew thunderous. 'My orders were very clear. Your Mr Hazzard was to retire from the field – and he did *not*.'

Before Lewis could answer Blake spoke in Hazzard's defence. 'He is not one to do so easily, my lord. Even if under Navy discipline, which he is not.'

Melville turned wide eyes upon him. 'He is a commissioned officer. Paid up to Captain of Marines—'

'If you will pardon me, my lord, he is an *Exploring* Officer, more an unofficial agent, if you will, under the aegis of Room 63. And owing to his original letter of permit, which gave him—'

'From Pitt and the like,' muttered Melville in recollection. 'I was *forced* to sign that document, sir...'

'Indeed, sir, but owing to that commission he is not subject to military or naval command or order – and is therefore free to disagree with them.'

'And you let a man like that stay active? With India in the balance?'

'Believe me, sir,' said Lewis, 'if I could, I would recall him.'

Spencer looked to Blake. 'Would you, Commander?'

Blake did not hesitate. 'There is hardly a man with a keener sense of the tactical and strategic implications of the French occupation of Egypt, my lord, than Mr Hazzard. He does not court followers, yet attracts them. From what Sir Sidney has told us, my lord, he has not only the marines of the Special Landing Squadron but also a sizeable force of Bedouin irregulars sworn to him. They call him Hazzard-Pasha, and other Bedouin tribes call him the *afrit al-akhmar*, I understand. The Red Devil.' He looked at Lewis. 'Mr Hazzard is an old India hand, and would scarce let anything threaten the subcontinent, were he able to prevent it.'

Lewis nodded. 'Beloved of the Wazir and the Mughal Emperor, my lords. A rare and precious commodity. Though a damned nuisance.'

Melville burst out, 'Then I want him out of the desert and leading a command in India, fighting Tipu Sultan in Mysore, not digging up mummies and whatnot.' He looked at Lewis and Blake harshly. 'Will he leave off, if so commanded?'

Lewis shook his head. 'No, sir, he will not.'

'Then we can no longer trust him.' Melville was harsh, realistic. 'We are on the verge of breaking the Turks from France, of forging a new alliance – and setting the sultan against Bonaparte. By God, we cannot afford to have such a man in place without check.'

Spencer got to his feet and moved to the window, his great embroidered coat falling in folds around him. 'When I learned of his personal tragedy I was cut to the quick, Sir Rafe,' he admitted. 'I felt ashamed at our part in it... and that I had not the time to shake his hand before he set sail. We are Agamemnon and Odysseus... Pelleas and Priam…' He watched the rain thoughtfully. 'And he is young Achilles, driven and wasted by, well, by *us*, and our old men's fears. Such burden and sacrifice is unwarranted for any one man, nor the men under his command. I wish them home,' he said, turning, 'safe and sound, a king and country's gratitude for those who have suffered so terribly, while others have gloried.'

Blake looked at the earl at the window, the rain tapping at the glass, a reminder of the sea, of sail, and the open skies, and the crews who plied beneath their canopy. Few like Spencer had such empathy. He would be sorry to see such a man retire.

Lewis got to his feet. 'My lord. It has been a busy week and a busier morning,' he said, possibly doing so for Spencer's benefit. 'We shall endeavour to recall Mr Hazzard and his men, before it is too late. I will send an order to that effect.'

Spencer turned his head. 'Thank you, Sir Rafe. Commander,' he said to Blake, 'I am grateful for such kindliness of spirit as yours within these often bleak halls. Your views are always most welcome.'

Blake met his eye, then bowed. 'I am grateful to be of service, my lord.'

Blake turned to go, crossing the apartment to the entrance hall, listening as Melville followed with Lewis. 'But what do we *do*, Sir Rafe,' continued the Secretary of War. 'This isn't Jolly Jack Tar's purview any longer but mine, John Bull in his brute red coat. And I need time to gather an army to fight in Ireland, in India, and now, damned Egypt on top of it all.' He looked about, angry. ''Tis my position we leave the damn Frogs to rot there in the desert while the Turk takes his revenge – and keep Hazzard out of the damned way.'

Lewis took a moment, then said, 'If Jack Jervis steps down, my lord, Nelson wants command of the Med, but the earl shall not give it to him. Instead we have Lord Keith standing by.' He glanced at Blake, 'Isn't that right, Mr Blake?'

Blake took his cloak from the earl's servant. 'Yes, Sir Rafe. So I believe.'

'And?' said Melville, 'How would Nelson take that?'

'Nelson is not in a position to argue, my lord, sitting in Naples amid glory and adoring ladies. But Smith has orders for Hazzard, and we have arranged that Keith will enter the Med for a quick tour of the blockade fleets.'

Melville understood: Lord Keith would give Hazzard his orders direct. 'And if your man still refuses to comply, sir?'

Lewis glanced at Blake. 'I wouldn't say, my lord, that Mr Hazzard will remain an active threat in Egypt for much longer,' he said grimly. 'He is riding the whirlwind.'

Blake paused a moment at Lewis's words, then took his hat and stick from the liveried servant. He made his goodbyes and stepped into the dark panelled hall beyond, once again amused that everyone had so gravely underestimated William John Hazzard. He left Lewis talking with Melville and hurried down the corridor to the backstairs, wondering just how to get a message to a renegade horseman in the middle of a war.

–

The tents of the Beni Qassim spread out under the stars and a low crescent moon, on rising ground overlooking the cool water of a small oasis rather than under the palms on the lake's shore – both to keep a good lookout and to avoid the scorpions. The marines of 9 Company set their billets among the large and spacious dwellings of the *Bedu*, more than comfortable among the rugs and lanterns.

Weeks had passed after Kafr-Shahabas. The marines of 9 Company had moved across the Delta, from Lake Maryut south of Alexandria, to the marshes and inland seas near Damietta, and into the desert approaches to the Sinai Peninsula, ever on the watch for the French, who seemed as scattered as the herdsmen they encountered. That they had found no trace of Derrien grated on them all – the thirst for revenge had become as pressing for the men as for Hazzard.

'I could get used to this lark,' said Kite, settling down next to Warnock and Napier on a sloping bank of sand. They looked out over the marshes to the Nile, the hard compacted sand littered with stone, a few rising hulks of rock here and there, palms in clumps and rows marking the passage of floodwater, undergrowth lush and blowing in the night breeze. The sky above was a deep indigo, the stars dripping light upon their heads, the moon luminescent. 'From the Isle o'ruddy Dogs to livin' the life of a rajah,' concluded Kite, 'Not ruddy bad, eh?'

Handley, who had been with Hazzard and Cook at the Cape three years earlier, former Ship's Master and their only sailor, looked thoughtful a moment and scratched at his grizzled ginger beard. 'You been to Injia then, Mick?'

'No, 'Andy,' said Kite with a pensive sigh, 'but I know it's there. More champagne anyone?'

Someone laughed and shoved him over.

'Ain't no bloody rajahs here mate,' muttered Warnock. He scratched at his forearm. 'Flippin' robes gimme the ravin' ab-dabs. Bitten all over I am...'

Kite glanced at the rash and Handley craned his neck for a look. A bulging black blister and small abscess had formed where Warnock had been scratching. Warnock had been known as a 'Burnt Man' aboard ship, his red and blackened skin a souvenir of Nelson's failed attack on Tenerife – but in Egypt he had darkened still further, passing easily for a Maaza or Khushmaan from the south, his pocked skin telling the tale of his service. Tonight he wore a *Bedu* turban, wrapped over the dead scar-tissue where once an ear had been.

'That's a camel tick, Knock-Knock,' said Kite. 'You got to dig 'im out, with 'is eggs an' all.'

'We ain't got no ruddy camels.'

'Yeh, well we ain't got a dog but we got fleas.' He took a draught of water. 'Go see the doc.'

'Potty Porter ain't no doc,' complained Warnock. 'The Whitby Poisoner more like.'

'Give over, mate. You told him you was all bunged up so he gave you somethin' to let it all out. And we all suffered.'

The others began to chuckle, but Warnock was serious. 'It ain't no bloody larfin' matter mate—' More of them began laughing, including the Bedouin, who did not really understand, but thought it good to watch the English clowning. 'I had ten shits in a 'arf-hour Mickey! Couldn't squat fast enough for days.' The marines roared even louder. He picked at his arm. 'Bloody little nits...'

Hesse joined them, the little Austrian settling himself cross-legged into the sand. Warnock glanced at him. 'You look more like a local every day, Essy.'

'I have found my true calling perhaps,' said Hesse mysteriously, rolling the spiked ends of his moustache into sharper points. He cut into a persimmon and took a bite. 'These people. Hard lives.'

Warnock kept examining his arm. 'Huh. Bully for them. Try Whitechapel after dark.'

Napier blew into the lock of a blunderbuss pistol in his lap, unhappy. 'I put the oil on like you said, Mick,' the big man said, 'but the sand's got in it now, an' it's all manky.'

'I said keep it *dry*, Nappy. Dry as the dust and then you can just blow it out.'

'Nah,' said Warnock, 'oil, mate, *lots* of it, and keep it *clean*.'

Kite then looked at Napier's feet. 'Arthur, mate, I been meanin' to ask. Why are your boots so bloody big?' He pushed the toe of the left with his thumb. 'There's easy an extra inch in there, mate.'

Napier frowned. 'I always asks for boots too big, Mickey. Gives me coinfidence.'

Handley and Kite looked at him, and even Hesse frowned. 'Eh?'

'Coinfidence,' he repeated, looking at them. 'Y'know. Walkin'. I put me foot where'er I fancies, wivout no fear nor nothin'. Rocks, scorpiums, them big hairy spiders or slippy decks, nothin' worries at me.'

Then Kite got it. 'You mean *confidence*.'

'Eh? When?'

'Yeh, Nappy, you know there ain't no such word as coinfidence, don't you? You're mixin' up confidence and coincidence.'

'Oh.' He looked puzzled. 'You callin' me igronant?'

They started to laugh all over again.

'No, it's just… Well,' explained Kite, 'coincidence is when two incidents 'appen at the same time that are most unlikely. Like you steppin' in your big boots on the very spot where Knock-Knock dropped his missin' ear—'

Warnock shot him a sour look. 'Leave me ear out of it.'

But Napier shook his big head and the others kept laughing, Napier demanding an explanation, *Wot you lot larfin' at?* Finally Hesse leaned over with a slice of fruit. 'Have some persimmon, Arthur. And look at the stars, and be happy.'

–

Hazzard and Cook sat by the fire where Tariq was heating a coffee-pot. Its lid rattled as it boiled, hanging from its iron hoop over the flames. Much had changed in the months since the return of Nelson, the battle in Aboukir Bay – and Sarah. The darkness had settled into Hazzard's spirit forever, it seemed, and made its home as time had blurred one action into another, one attack into another – until the bitterness of each day had eaten into him to create an eternal night.

Cook recognised something was wrong, had seen it before years earlier, and kept a wary eye on him. Hazzard had stopped fearing, stopped caring, pushing his chances ever more foolishly, as if testing Fate to see what new horrors she could unleash, finding none more awful than any he had already endured. He strode through fire unconcerned, sleepwalking through destruction – and some of the Beni Qassim feared him, as all might fear an evil spirit. Hazzard's marines knew better: he was Nelson and Jervis in one, and they guarded him, their captain.

Porter regularly tended wounds Hazzard would otherwise have ignored or not noticed. When Hazzard relented, let Porter tend him, his care was as fine as that of a doting mother, the soft-spoken Yorkshireman becoming something akin to a conscience.

'One inch to the right, sir,' Porter murmured at the fireside, inspecting a cut at Hazzard's neck, 'and your carotid would be opened.' He looked round from behind Hazzard's bare shoulder, the firelight flickering on his spectacles. 'And that would be that. Seven or eight seconds, it's said.'

Hazzard nodded. 'Mm.'

Porter blinked at him, accepting that would be his only response. 'You're not a 74 sir, with three decks and oak planking...'

'I know, Porter.'

'Well, it's nowt I can fix up with a poultice of fishhead soup now is it, sir.'

Hazzard twisted to look at him. 'Would that work?'

'Only in Whitby, sir.'

Hazzard stared off again, lost in his thoughts, Cook watching him, Tariq silent. 'This world was once green,' he said in a far-off voice.

'It was, sir,' agreed Porter. 'Then we little angels came along, didn't we.' He bent forward and bit off the thread and began tying a knot, dabbing the wound with astringent on a cotton pad. 'There, sir. Do not raise your arm over your head for at least a few days or I'll have to stitch you up again.'

Hazzard stared off, thinking of weeks past and former lifetimes only months gone. 'Thank you, Porter.'

Porter leaned closer. 'If you'll pardon me sir, y'not made o'bloody stone. One day you'll chip. And I can't stitch that.'

Cook nodded. 'Listen to him, sir. Ma knows best.'

'Mm.' Hazzard murmured, 'You're an old fusspot, Porter.'

'Aye. But not a worker of miracles, sir.'

'Neither am I,' said Cook. He looked over at the fire. 'Y'anymore tea in the pot?' he asked Porter. 'For that would be a ruddy miracle.'

Wayland joined them, dropping his sword beside him in the sand, a bowl of mutton, French army rice, dates and *labneh* in his lap. He extended his bad leg stiffly and rubbed it with a mumbled curse, his new habit.

Months earlier, Thomas Marmaduke Wayland, 2nd Lieutenant of Marines, would never have dreamt of joining the old hands in such a relaxed fashion. But he had changed. His command of the road in Malta during the French invasion, his sortie along the dunes and gun-emplacements of Aboukir Bay as Nelson streaked in for the kill, all had hardened him. He no longer measured himself against others' achievements, their reputations, their glories. He now had nightmares of his own which judged him.

'Pickets set, sir,' he said. 'No movement.' He ate, using the two fingers of his right hand, like any good *Bedu*. 'Something odd in those abandoned huts to the northwest, sir. A light in one of them at one point. Can't be French. Especially as we just moved here. Mustafa and Hussein have ridden off to check.' He continued eating. 'Probably nothing... some *fella*, fiddling about.'

Hazzard agreed; French soldiers rarely deserted in this hostile environment, for fear of the local inhabitants, unless they could reach a port and stow away on a foreign trader – not where 9 Company were, in the borderlands of nowhere, and the borderlands of the Tarabin.

Hazzard thought of the Beni Qassim, their unquestioning loyalty and devotion. They were a secretive clan, discussing plans with their men and making decisions only with group consent. Five of them sat round the fire, short Turkish and French carbines in hand, their dark faces turned away, looking out, keeping watch; they heard an approach and stood, out of deference. Hazzard looked up to see the three leaders come to talk: old Sheikh Idris and his two nephews. They knelt down and sat, easing their weapons and laying them down. Tariq joined them to translate.

'Hazar Pasha,' said Idris, stroking his thick greying moustache, his curling eyebrows giving the appearance of a constant smile and beaming goodwill. He nodded to Tariq and put his hands together in thanks for the translation, *shukran*, and Tariq prepared.

'Hazar Pasha,' continued Idris, 'our herds need tending, and many of us must leave for our winter homelands.'

Hazzard nodded. He had been expecting it for some time. The sun had shifted in the sky, and autumn was upon them. 'I understand.'

'This thing the French work against Egypt,' he said, pulling thoughtfully at his lip. 'It brings you an evil *djinn*, driving you into darkness.' Idris looked across the dark rocky terrain, doubtless, thought Hazzard, seeing only beauty in its harshness, life and flower in its waters, and grace where others would see only wasteland. 'But you must not fear. The *Bedu*,' he said, 'have been in these lands longer than any other of God's children. We carry the long memory of the world. We watch while the great lords of Cairo or of Constantinople fight each other, to take or destroy lands that are not theirs. We watch, and we wait. These French, this Banaparat Sultan,' he said softly, 'will pass, as all men and things do. They will go home, as do we all. As did the Romani, as did Iskender, as did the builders of the Pyramid and *Aboul Haoul*, the Father of Terrors.' Hazzard thought of Izzam and Alahum, showing him the Sphinx, and this dark name for it. 'All of these strangers…' he sought the word, '…are but *visitors*. And all shall be blown to dust, and swept out by the winds. Even the Turk will go home, after so many centuries. They that shall remain, shall be God's people, the *Bedu*.'

The Bedouin either side bowed forward and intoned, '*Alhamdulillah*,' *Praise be to God*, as if hearing words of Holy Scripture. Hazzard relished every calm word. It gave him hope, drove out a demon or two, lent him the momentary understanding that struggle was vain, that balance would always be restored. He wished it were true for Idris and his people.

'Hazar *al-hakim*, the wise, we take our leave, but some will remain to protect you, under the watchful eye of God.'

Hazzard replied warmly, 'I am grateful to you, Sheikh *al-Kebir*.' It was reciprocal praise for the older man; he had called Hazzard 'the wise', so Hazzard had called him 'the great'. Idris smiled and bowed his head politely. Hazzard turned and reached behind him, bringing out a long object wrapped in cloth, much as Ali-Qarim had once done, in the palace quad of Murad before the battle at Shubra Khit. 'This, I present to you, Sheikh, a gift, won by your bravery and triumphs… with my gratitude.'

They waited for Tariq to finish his translation and bowed. The man to his left reached out and took the object flat in both upraised hands, and passed it to Idris, his eyes wide. 'This is most unexpected, Hazar

Pasha...' He unwrapped it to reveal a gleaming French smallsword with gold hilt, carved grip and a pommel in the shape of an eagle's head.

'Torn from the enemy on the field of battle. An unworthy token of my great esteem for you and the Beni Qassim.'

Cook looked on as the older man drew the fine, gleaming blade and examined it in the firelight. 'Magnificent... *Shukran, Hazar Pasha, shukran.*'

Tariq bowed to Hazzard. 'Idris Sheikh thanks you, Hazar Pasha.'

'Much obliged, Tariq.'

Idris lay the sword down in its cloth and leaned forward earnestly. 'Will you not stay, Hazar Pasha? To lighten your spirit? Will you not marry?' He smiled. 'I have many daughters...'

'Too many daughters,' said his nephew to the right, and they laughed.

'Yes, too many daughters! And not enough sons and families...' He nodded slowly, as if considering the business implications for Hazzard. 'We have many hundreds of sheep in our lands, far from the French. You would be...' he nodded and spread his hands, 'a wealthy man of position.'

They chuckled, and for a moment William John Hazzard considered it as seriously as any other lost man would, rootless, homeless, no ship, no land, at sea in a desert, and he smiled, the fire mesmerising. Many sheep in Egypt, or many sheep in Suffolk, what was the difference, he wondered, and all too soon the warmth of the fantasy slowly ebbed – and he was returned to a *Bedu* encampment, a fire, amid an army of French soldiers, an outlaw with little hope.

'That's not a bad offer,' murmured Cook. 'And me? Have you a daughter for me?'

They laughed and one of them said something. Tariq translated: 'It would need many big daughters for you, *Kuq!*'

They took minted tea in small cups, some of the Beni Qassim behind praying to God for the last time that day, and Hazzard knew all such moments, even here in Egypt, should be savoured, were precious, and all too fleeting.

When they parted there was little left to say, though Hazzard knew these men had saved their lives, protected them, and a new rhythm had come to carry them away on a fresh tide. There remained only to be said the final farewell, as he did to Idris, '*Rabbena ma'ak.*'

May God protect you.

—

When Mustafa and Hussein reached the ruined houses they found firelight still burning in a window. Drainage ditches crossed the fields, rejected watermelons left to rot in their furrows, the leaves now damp in the cool glow of night, the smells of fermenting fruit all-pervasive. These were not permanent homes but storage huts or temporary shelters, little more than one-room hovels of limewashed daub, the mud-plaster cracked and falling in slabs from the skeleton of hide and hair beneath, the thatched roof partially collapsed.

Mustafa nodded to Hussein and they dismounted silently, moving in opposite directions around the larger of the two huts where they saw the light burning within. They heard the cawing of a bird and a flap of wings and stopped, listening.

Gripping his short carbine loosely but with some growing unease, Mustafa moved to the entrance. There was no door, only darkness, but he could smell the charring of the fire. He waited until Hussein appeared on the other side of a knot of bladed palms at the front of the hut. He made a gesture, *wait*, and Hussein nodded. Mustafa moved to the doorway but stopped dead.

'*Mustafa…?*' whispered Hussein. But there came no answer.

Hussein moved round the hut, keeping to the shadow, but stopped, an ice-cold touch at his neck. Immediately he cried out and let off his musket into the night sky. The blast and report were deafening, the double flash illuminating the shape of a demon with two faces, front and back – followed by the unmistakable sound of a flintlock being cocked.

—

The pickets at the camp appeared on the ridge at the sound of the gunshot, and the cry went up, '*Mr Azzard…!*'

Cook set down his cup and struggled up from the fireside. '*Christ a'mighty…*'

Hazzard and Wayland rode down the low escarpment onto the floodplain, Cook and Tariq behind. They saw the flickering light still burning inside the larger of the two cottages. They dismounted, split up and approached the rear. His sword-bayonet in hand, Cook peered briefly through a dark window aperture in the first building. Hazzard then found the entrance, and the orange glow within.

Wayland held up a pistol and pointed at the front window. Hazzard nodded and waited as Wayland made his way through the sharp palms – a rat scurried out in alarm and Wayland kicked at it, then stopped. Cook crept round the corner to join them.

Hazzard glanced at Cook. '*Ready.*'

Cook muttered, '*Aye…*'

He went in, the Lorenzoni pistol held out – then stopped. In the middle of the bare earth floor was a circle of stones round a campfire, a small cauldron bubbling away, the ceiling open to the sky, the smoke rising to the Delta breeze. Arranged around the room were kegs of biscuit, dried meat, sacks, enamelled army ration tins, and straw arranged as a makeshift bed. Mustafa and Hussein stood on the far side of the room, eyes wide, tin mugs in hand.

'*By all that's ruddy holy in Bristol…*' murmured Cook. He sheathed his bayonet.

Seated in a folding chair by the fire, pouring hot water into a china teapot, was a naval officer with a shock of dark curly hair, in blue cloak and brocade coat, a silver order on the breast, a broad Genoese sword at his side and a sea-service pistol swaying under his arm. He turned to them with delight. 'Ah,' he said brightly. 'Mr Hazzard. Would you care for some tea?'

Hazzard lowered the heavy Lorenzoni. It was Commodore Sir William Sidney Smith.

–

'Ah, excellent, excellent…' said Smith, swinging his sword out of the way and sitting down in the sand at their camp. He threw off his cloak and lifted the pistol sling over his head to set it down, the tassels on his gold epaulettes shimmering as he moved. 'The low Bedouin fire, shielded by the landscape so that none may see—' He held out a tin cup for Tariq, who happily filled it, devoted to the ebullient Englishman, '—but ideal for the rather wonderful Bedouin coffee-pot.' He thanked Tariq in formal Arabic, '*Shukran, Tariq effendi. Allah yusallmak.* It is good to see you again.'

'*Rabbena ma'ak, Sur Siddani effendi,*' replied Tariq with a short bow. 'It is the true pleasure.'

Hazzard watched Sir Sidney while he sipped the bitter brew. The marines and Beni Qassim sat round in a circle, muskets at ease but in hand, looking out, disturbed by Smith's sudden appearance, as if he might have brought French patrols in tow, a bad omen that they had been so surprised.

'Apologies to the two fellows, but they got quite a fright,' said Smith. 'I think it was the old cocked hat. Thought I was French. But that's my little safety-house, in case one is indisposed...' He handed the *Bedu* further cups of coffee from Tariq and bowed his head, speaking in Arabic. They smiled, embarrassed, and all was forgotten. 'Took a bit of a stroll from the beach I can tell you, but then I'm used to it, trips through Romney and Winchelsea and such.'

Hazzard took a final swallow of the sweet coffee. 'What is it,' he asked Smith bluntly, 'that brings you here?'

'Several things,' Smith replied in a businesslike fashion. 'First, we have had further sightings of one Citizen Derrien of the *Bureau d'information* in Alex, in Ramaniyah and in Cairo, near the palace in Ezbekiya.'

'*Cheerist...*' muttered Cook, throwing something into the fire in disgust.

'Yes, quite. He gads about a bit,' said Smith, handing over a slip of paper. Wayland took it, reading by the firelight. 'A list of areas and sightings, might be of use, build up a travel-pattern. But in the interim you have had such success at blowing up French munitions, camps and storage depots that you have manifestly changed the disposition of the French demi-brigades, now spreading out to fortify their hold even as far as El-'Arish in Sinai. Though the cavalry is still up-country with General Desaix, chasing one Murad Bey Esquire.'

Hazzard thought of El-'Arish. 'Is it fortified?'

'Arish? There is a fort there, yes.'

'In Tarabin lands?'

Smith looked at him with renewed admiration. 'Ah. Quite possibly, yes.'

'They will not take that lying down.'

'The Tarabin take very little lying down. They are the accepted guardians of the Sinai and, in a way, Egypt itself.'

'We know,' said Hazzard. 'We met them.'

Smith looked at him, his voice low. 'Shajar al-Durr?'

'Mm.'

'Quite beautiful, is she not.'

'I had little time to notice.'

'Have no doubts – she is extraordinary. Not her real name, more an honorary, likewise her consort, the so-called Baibars, both revered names from the past – Shajar was the only queen ever voted to rule the Mamluk, so I believe. But they are true *Bedu*, and rightly proud of it.'

'Perhaps, but they were foolish enough to permit the execution of a French *savant*, a boy, at Kafr-Shahabas. The town will soon cease to exist.'

Smith put a hand to his head, genuinely upset by the news. 'Odd's blood.' He sighed. 'I beg your pardon. That is... unfortunate. We *need* the *savants*. That is, Britain needs them – the whole damnable *world* needs them.'

'What do you mean?'

Smith took a moment, then spoke in earnest, his voice low. 'We have no idea of this country, Mr Hazzard. None. No one in Europe has really. The brief of the *savants* is to measure, record, analyse and assess everything they encounter. When eventually this information is released to a hitherto benighted world, through capture or through peace, we shall at last have a comprehensive report of the history, geography, and commercial potential of Egypt, and open new lines of trade. *We need them.*'

Cook shifted round. 'Who exactly invaded this ruddy place then? The Frogs? Or us?'

Smith considered a moment. 'By Jove. That is a *jolly* good question, Sergeant.' He glanced at Hazzard. 'How would you like to ask the admiral?'

Hazzard frowned. 'St Vincent? He's not here?'

'No. Dear Jack Jervis or, quite rightly, Lord St Vincent, has been making overtures to step down, his nerves, his health. Nelson's hunt across the seas for our mutual friend ran Old Jarvie utterly ragged. He must head back to London, and Nelson wants his post, since he cannot have mine as commander in the Levant.' He smiled sheepishly. 'Very cross, our new Baron Nelson. But the Sea Lords favour one George Elphinstone, now Vice-Admiral Lord Keith.' He took a quick sip of his coffee.

Hazzard felt a jolt. 'Elphinstone? From the Cape?'

Cook swore softly. 'By God…'

'Indeed, yes, I thought you knew him, and Lord Keith knows you, and thus would like a quick word.'

Hazzard stared back at him. Smith was no ordinary officer – Hazzard had no idea of his true rank, though he seemed to be Acting Commodore of the blockade fleet. He behaved more like an independent adventurer. But for occasional meetings with the Viennese diplomat Joseph von Hammer, Sir Sidney was Hazzard's only contact with the outside world.

He was also a bringer of bad memories, not only of the fleet, but of that hated night in Aboukir Bay, where Hazzard's world had come to an abrupt halt, and died in his arms.

'Elphinstone?' repeated Hazzard. 'Would like a word?'

'Yes. Right now, in fact.' Smith finished his coffee. 'Got a jolly-boat round the corner, ready and waiting, oarsmen shuffling about, getting bored.'

'You want me to come out to the blockade fleet.'

'Yes.'

Hazzard stared at him. Cook leaned closer and murmured, 'We got to get the men into a new camp further west, sir, away from the Frog patrols…'

Hazzard looked at Smith and said evenly, 'All of us. The marines will join me.'

Smith frowned and smiled. 'My dear chap, it's not as if you need protection, you know.'

Hazzard watched him carefully. He trusted Smith, certainly, but not his Admiralty masters. Though in London, Sir Rafe Lewis could reach out to anywhere in the world – especially to bring a rogue Exploring Officer to heel. 'Call it a rest then.'

Many of them turned when they heard this, quite pleased at the prospect. Wayland leaned closer to Hazzard from behind. 'Sir. I could take two men, confirm Sir Sidney's information.' He looked at him levelly. 'I could start at Rosetta.'

'Jolly good idea,' said Smith.

'Might as well start close to home, sir,' said Wayland, with a pointed glance.

Hazzard met his eye. Wayland clearly had something in mind. 'Very well. Take Hesse, De Lisle and Tariq,' he said. 'And we will rendezvous with you at the usual place.'

'I'll go too, sir,' said Porter, 'In case of wounds.'

Hazzard agreed. 'Very well. But keep your head down and let Mr Wayland handle difficulties.'

'Yes sir.'

Hazzard looked at Smith, and hoped he could trust him. He glanced round at them all. 'Clear in the boat?'

They all gave their *aye*, Kite adding, 'Blimey though, sir – the grub in the blockade'll be bleedin' awful an' all.'

Some laughed and Smith got to his feet. 'Good lord. I came only for Ma and Pa. They shan't expect a family of gourmets...'

'I don't care what they expect,' said Hazzard, getting up. 'If I don't like what I hear then the new admiral loses his only hope in this place.'

Smith looked at him, very much concerned. He glanced at the marines as they began to gather their things and kept his voice low, as if not to dishearten them. 'William, you are hanging on here by the merest thread. If you come for briefing we can force Keith to agree to endless supplies, food, clothing, money, powder and shot, everything, but you *must* recognise Navy discipline,' he insisted. 'You will not be alone forever here. We *will* hit them, I promise you, and hit them hard, as soon as we can. That is what he wishes to discuss.'

Hazzard recoiled at the very idea of meeting Lord Keith, of seeing the fleet again – though he too wanted to put to sea, to feel the cold splash of water, somewhere without the constant fear of discovery. 'So be it.' He broke off and took Wayland aside. '*Rosetta?*' he murmured quietly, Smith moving away a pace with Cook, '...which we both know is tight as a snare drummer's backside...'

'Mm,' nodded Wayland. 'Didn't think Sir Sidney needed to know everything, sir, just in case.'

'Quite.' Hazzard looked at him. He had come to rely heavily on Wayland, as much as on Cook, and knew he could depend on him. The hesitant boy he had met in the Admiralty with his clattering sword and blushing smile was long gone. 'So. Cairo then.'

'Sir. I'll use Sir Sidney's list and find Masoud. If Derrien is there we can track him, sight him, line up a kill.'

Hazzard took a breath. 'Watch yourself – do not engage him direct by any means. Keep it quiet. Remember: no reconnaissance is worth a damn—'

Wayland completed his old axiom, '—if you don't get back. No, sir. Tariq will get us to Ezbekiya. And Masoud will know.'

'All right?' asked Smith, suddenly at his shoulder.

Hazzard nodded to Wayland. 'Carry on then, Mr Wayland,' he said. 'We shall not be long. A night and a day.'

'Sir.'

Hazzard looked at Smith, a strange feeling stealing over him that he was glad not only that the marines were coming with him for added numbers, but that Wayland and a few of them were not – as if at least those few were out of officialdom's grasp. This prompted a memory of his exchange with Shajar al-Durr and her belief in British support. He asked Smith carefully, 'Have you given gold to the Al-Tarabin?'

Smith frowned. 'I'm sorry?'

'Coin. Guineas, Sir Sidney.'

'I fear I have given no one gold, my dear fellow. I have no idea where they might have acquired it.'

Hazzard watched him. Smith seemed ingenuous enough, but it was as Hazzard had expected – if Shajar al-Durr had indeed been supported, that support could be whipped away in a moment and denied. Sir Rafe Lewis would have done likewise: Lewis had created 9 Company without official sanction, so he could cut them off as if they had never existed – just as he and Blake had done to Hazzard and Race at the Cape three years earlier.

But this time, Hazzard had cut himself off, in a desert.

With Napoleon Bonaparte.

Hazzard made up his mind. 'Very well.'

Blockade

The oars dipped rhythmically, the foam churning silver under the moonlight. Its standard whitewash painted over with thick black pitch, the boat vanished into the surf, invisible against the night sea. Smith sat in the stern with Hazzard and Cook, Handley at the tiller as a modest honour for the only seaman among them, Kite, Warnock and the others taking up spare oars as well. As they pulled through the black waters, they looked out at the dark waves, taking in the glow of the horizon, drinking in the cool salt tang of the breeze. Jeremiah Underhill summed it up for them all.

'*Good to be at sea again, eh lads…*' he murmured.

Riding the gentle swell, all shared his strange pleasure and chorused *aye*. With their sun-darkened faces and *Bedu* robes, turbans and *keffiyah* headdresses, they were the most unlikely passengers ever to board a ship of the line. The oarsmen could not believe their eyes, and Smith watched them, amused. 'I must say, I never expected Bedouin to row so *well*.'

Hazzard looked out at the harbour lights of Damietta. It was his first time at sea since Aboukir Bay, and all he could see was Sarah's face in the chaos, *William!*, as Bonaparte's flagship *Orient* took light, and shook the cosmos. Somewhere, he heard the distant sound of his heart breaking all over again. He closed his eyes. He could still feel the sharp edge of the small picture-frame, sewn into the lining of his coat – Sarah's silhouette miniature, a ghostly reminder forevermore.

Ahead of them, still some two hundred yards off, was the rising silhouette of two ships of the line. Smith explained, 'HMS *Zealous* to port,' he said, 'and that's ours, the *Tigre*, off her starboard quarter.'

Hazzard knew the *Zealous*, and had seen her in action from the dunes of Aboukir Bay, racing HMS *Goliath* to be first at the French line, her crew's bloodthirsty cheers echoing, as Nelson had descended on Brueys. She seemed peaceful now, her sails furled, anchored at the bows and stern.

'Currently she leads the blockade fleet,' explained Smith, 'under the stentorian Commodore Hood. We are a bit thin here, I must admit, Hallowell of the *Swiftsure*, Ball of the *Alex*, and Foley of the *Goliath*. Hood and Foley get on well enough, but there is still some bad blood.' He chuckled conspiratorially. 'Foley beat him to it, you see, to the French line. So Hood's ship is often called HMS *Jealous*.'

'And the *Tigre*?' asked Hazzard. 'Not in the blockade?'

'Oh,' said Smith with his inscrutable smile. 'No, our task is somewhat more complex. Rather a... roving brief.'

In the distance, he spotted the grim shape of the Second-Rate 74-gun HMS *Tigre*. Her 24-pounder guns on the upper decks were run out, moonlight seeping through the open ports, the 32s below buttoned up for the night; four vicious Long 18s pricked out of her bows like so many medieval spikes, swivel-mounted murderers on every rail, the quarterdeck lined with giant-mouthed 36-pounder carronades. The *Tigre* had been converted to a three-decker of 80 guns. It looked the deadliest ship Hazzard had yet seen afloat. He had no doubt: this was the mobile command HQ of Admiralty Intelligence in the Levant: Room 63 had come to Egypt.

'Something of a brute now, alas,' admitted Smith. 'French, captured in '96 and renamed *Tiger*. But we like the French spelling,' he said, 'Makes the chaps feel exotic.' Smith nodded at Handley. 'Compliments to the cox'n, but do pull for the *Tigre*, would you.'

'*Tigre* it is, sir, aye,' replied Handley, glancing at Hazzard. As Hood was commodore of the blockade, they had naturally been heading to his ship, the *Zealous* – but evidently no longer. He pulled the tiller over and passed a command to the oarsmen. 'Easy to port lads, and dig for starboard.'

Someone called out, probably Kite, *izzat left or right, guv?* and they laughed, the oars knocking on the gunwale and dipping deep, the prow swinging round.

This slight change of course had alerted the marines to something unspoken, something uneasy in Hazzard perhaps. Jeremiah Underhill glanced over his shoulder at Cook, and the old sergeants communed in silent suspicion. The prow of the jolly-boat nosed round as they headed for the dark and formidable *Tigre*, her claws run out and ready to kill.

The guidelines were thrown down the portside boarding steps and Underhill was first up, leading Warnock, Kite and Pettifer, followed by Napier and Cochrane, Cook and Hazzard climbing behind. When their Bedouin boots clumped onto the quarterdeck, a young midshipman nearly tripped over his own feet as he stepped back in alarm, and they were soon faced by a squad of marines, bayonets levelled.

A Marine Sergeant stepped up, confident, incredulous, his eyes scanning their dusty robes, their headdresses, the bandoliers of powder-flasks across their chests, the bizarre Huron tomahawk hanging at Warnock's waist, the sawn-off Charleville muskets. To a man they looked like pirates from the Horn of Africa.

'Now then, Mustafa,' said the sergeant, rising onto his toes, 'Where d'you think yer off to then, eh?'

Underhill removed the loose dark *shemagh* from his scarred face, and grinned his most hideous grin, taking a deep, glorious pull on a glowing cheroot. He blew a cloud of smoke straight into the sergeant's eyes. 'My my,' he said with his rasping London laugh as the sergeant coughed, 'if it ain't Corp'ral 'ickory Dickory. Tick, tock, goes the clock, and Corp'ral Dickory's in the dock...' He laughed again.

The sergeant's eyes fairly bulged out of his head as more of them appeared over the rail, followed by the others. 'You're English...!' He frowned, his expression clearing in recognition. 'I don't believe it. Jerry-bloody-miah Underhill. Imprisoned at His Majesty's pleasure, as was.'

'Wotcher, Docky. Give us a kiss,' laughed Underhill. Dickory's baffled marines lowered their muskets and stepped back.

'And who the bloody 'ell are you supposed to be this time then, 'Miah? Ali bloody Baba?'

Underhill puffed more smoke. 'We're the Oddfellers, matey,' he said with satisfaction. 'Nine Company. Swift as night, cheap as sixpence, so mind yer manners.'

Dickory stabbed a finger at him. 'Now look 'ere, 'Miah Underhill—' but stopped dead as Smith appeared at the rail, helping Hazzard and Cook on deck. 'Gorblimey... that's...'

Underhill grinned. 'Aye, that it is, laddie-buck.'

Two hard-bitten lieutenants appeared, the midshipman piping Smith aboard. 'Mr Wright,' said Smith.

'Sir,' said Wright, the First Lieutenant, one hand on a pistol in his belt. He nodded towards Hazzard. 'Are they...?'

'They certainly are, Mr Wright. Major Hazzard, Sar'-Major Cook and the marines of 9 Company, First Lieutenant Wright – and where's Mr Tyte... Tell Ritter to lay a meal in the fo'c'sle mess and clear the manger, as Mr Hazzard's men will bunk together – they shall need a place to rest while the grown-ups chit-chat.'

Wright nodded, not the slightest taken aback. 'Very good, sir. Sar'nt Dickory, take the men for'ard and see them settled.'

'Sir.' Dickory put his heels together and grabbed Underhill. 'Come on, Baboo. You owe me a ruddy drink.'

Cook removed his turban, surprised. 'You knew we were English then, sir...?'

Wright gave him a grim smile. 'This is the *Tigre*, Sar'nt-Major,' he said. 'We have seen it all. Even your Bedouin guide here.' He inclined his head. '*As-salamu aleikum.*'

Kite pulled off his headdress and in his broad dockside Cockney said, 'That's very good, sir. You could lead evenin' prayers an' all.'

'There you are, John,' said Smith to Wright, patting Kite on the shoulder. 'Formalities complete already.'

–

Escorted by a squad of marines, Hazzard and Cook filed across the quarterdeck and past the helm in silence, two men at the wheel watching them with fascination, another two whispering, *that's Mad Billy-Jack, that is.* Hazzard felt his chest tighten, the darkness and the eerie glow of the compasses reminding him of old friends, of De la Vega and his copper-hulled frigate the *Volpone*, tracking Bonaparte's fleet in the darkness off Malta, of the giant *Ville de Paris* and the odious Major Duncan – of the *America*, and the duel with Harry Race. He stopped and looked back at the ship. Cook and Smith slowed, waiting.

The moon had vanished behind a bank of misty cloud, leaving a glow on the rolling swell of the sea, a hint of the distant Aegean in a ghostly pearlescent blue. There were no lanterns or lamps lit: HMS *Tigre* was running dark, only the white of their breeches and robes stark in the half-light. Hazzard gazed out across the decks, at the men of the Mid Watch on the gangways, up in the rigging, some clustered in the tops, others in the tweendecks, the glow of pipes in the darkness, all looking up from their labours. None spoke, all stock still at their stations, looking, at Hazzard, at Cook, the furled canvas dark against the moving cloud then bright amidst the blue-black of the skies. One of the men in the tweendecks raised his pipe in salute, as did his shipmates. Hazzard returned the gesture, a creeping sense of dread stealing into him. He turned and they continued down the passage to the stern, following Smith.

They passed cabin doors, only the gleam of polish giving them light, the blancoed white crossbelts of the marines as bright as Delta sand, a sentry turning to get a glimpse of them, then snapping eyes front when Hazzard went by. At the end of the passage, just past the stairs, Smith opened a door and they filed into the elegant stateroom of the Great Cabin.

Here, warm lamplight gleamed from every surface, ornate Persian silks drawn across the galleried stern balcony windows for the blackout. Shining mahogany and walnut tables, racks of swords, pistols and muskets, mosquito nets hanging from the beams above, swagged behind heraldic wrought-iron mountings – all so luxurious it would not have surprised Hazzard if Smith too were some sort of pirate as De la Vega had been.

Waiting was a small group of officers taking sherry. Standing in the centre of them, somewhat impatient at having waited so long, one hand atop a brass-topped cane, was Lord Keith, Vice-Admiral of the Mediterranean Fleet: an older man in long gold-embroidered dark blue frock-coat, his curling white hair rising carefree from a high forehead, a sharp, frowning countenance aged by experience, eyes all the brighter and harder for it.

He turned from conversation with a younger naval officer, possibly in his early thirties, with the saturnine expression of the harsh task-master, and Hazzard recognised him: Hood, Captain of HMS *Zealous*. Two other officers, one a wooden-faced Major of Marines in scarlet tailcoat and epaulettes, the other also a Marine Major in red, a stiff, taut man, with pale handsome face and quick eyes. Several junior officers stood behind, three in scarlet, two in Navy bluejackets. They all stopped mid-sentence, glasses poised at lips, and looked up.

'My lords, gentlemen,' said Smith, 'may I present Mr Hazzard and Sar'-Major Cook, 9 Company, Marines – the Special Landing Squadron... otherwise known,' he said with evident ironic relish, '...as the Oddfellows.'

The gathered officers cast an incredulous eye over the newcomers, at their soiled Bedouin robes, their dark weather-beaten faces, their bizarre weapons, Hazzard's gold and ivory-hilted scimitar, the shoulder-slung holster and Lorenzoni pistol, the Indian orders on the breast of his faded Bombay Marine coat – and Cook towering over them all from the rear in dark Maghrib headdress, a pistol and jewelled *khanjar* dagger jammed in his belt. Someone at the back murmured, *Are they on our side...?*

'Mr Hazzard,' continued Smith, 'may I name Vice-Admiral the Lord Keith, and Commodore Sir Samuel Hood, Captain of the *Zealous* and commander of the blockade fleet... Major Naismith, 35 Company, Marines...'

Hazzard nodded. 'Naismith.'

Naismith hardly twitched. 'Hazzard.'

'...and Major Jack Douglas, my commander of the Marines company, HMS *Tigre.*'

Hazzard came to attention. 'Sir.'

Smith frowned, just remembering something. 'Aren't you a Light Colonel in the army as well, Jack?'

'That's nothing compared to a knight of Sweden, Sir Sidney,' he replied quietly, and they laughed in their private joke. Though held in tight, John Douglas had an edge to him, and a ready smile. He put his hand out and Hazzard shook it. 'Hazzard. Good to put a face to the name. Everywhere I go I am asked if I know you.'

'I'm sure you're not, sir.'

Douglas gave him a wry grin and stepped back. 'I have a feeling we'll be seeing a lot of you...'

Keith came forward. A noble Scot from royal Stirling, his own brogue was neither Highland nor Lowland, and scarcely noticeable, it was said, unless he grew angry – which happened often enough. 'Your appearance does not come as a surprise, Mr Hazzard, after what Berry told us of you two on the *Vanguard.*'

'Delivered in a cargo net full of fish, I believe, sir...' said Hood drily. 'Absolutely made Nelson's day. Spoke of it for weeks.' There were polite chuckles all round and Cook shifted, not remembering it too fondly.

Lord Keith glowered at Hazzard then abruptly offered his hand. 'I believe considerable waters have passed beneath the keel since last we met.'

Hazzard stiffened, unwilling to speak amicably, but relented and shook his proffered hand. 'Sir. They have.' Though it grated with his inclinations, Hazzard found himself thanking the man. 'I am grateful for the services of your surgeon in Greenwich, after the Cape, sir.'

Keith nodded, more than aware of Hazzard's fretful history with the Admiralty, the bloody affair with Harry Race at the Cape – and his demand to Nelson after the victory in Aboukir Bay. 'A terrible time. And… my condolences.'

Standing ramrod straight to attention, Cook glanced at Hazzard, as if concerned for his reaction. But Hazzard merely nodded, his mind a world away with slow and unhappy realisation: the admiral had been the only outsider, for the first time in two and a half months, to bring Sarah to mind. He wondered if he were jealous of her memory; having kept her so to himself, it came as a surprise that others had known of her – or known of him either. Even he recognised he had been too long away from normal society.

'Sir,' said Hazzard, then added to Hood, 'We watched your progress from the dunes in Aboukir Bay. Fine seamanship, sir.'

Hood bowed graciously. 'Truth be told, Foley led the way. But from a marine who can captain a Spanish brig in a storm and sink two French corvettes in the process… that is praise indeed,' he replied, then suddenly hardened. 'Though I understand you refused Nelson's hand at victory.'

Once again, saw Hazzard, he was to be reprimanded for defying their god.

'I had my reasons.'

Hood waited for further explanation. Hazzard gave none.

'Very well, gentlemen,' said Smith, not the slightest disturbed by the evident tension. His landsman servant entered from behind a folding bulkhead and put a silver tray of fresh water and glasses on the long table. He poured them out as Smith moved into his low swivel-chair behind the desk, the gallery of dark windows behind, the candlelight winking in reflection. 'Do be seated gentlemen, please. Sar'-Major Cook will sit in with us, his views being of keen interest.' Half-ready to escape through the doorway, Cook hesitated and Hazzard pulled out a chair for him before sitting himself. '*God save Bristol…*' muttered Cook and removed his headdress, brushing a weary hand through his close-cropped hair.

'I understood the marines have no rank of Sergeant-Major,' said Naismith abruptly, sitting down.

Major Douglas looked at him with distaste and Cook stiffened, but Smith held up a hand. 'I should have explained, Major,' he said smoothly. 'Owing to his length of service and having a senior sergeant serving under him, Marine Sergeant Cook has been granted the honorary rank of Sergeant-Major, equivalent to a Company Sergeant-Major in the 1st Foot.'

'Hm.' Naismith seemed unimpressed. 'Presume you've earned it…'

Cook was busy pouring a glass of water and stopped. Hazzard looked at Naismith with contempt. 'Oh, he certainly has,' he said. 'More than a coffee-house officer might in Portsmouth, Major.'

Douglas stifled a smile but Naismith stared back at him, unpricked, possibly used to it.

'*An' merry Christmas an' all*,' grumbled Cook, and drank his water. Hazzard cared nothing for Naismith or his opinion and settled himself, the heavy Lorenzoni pistol clunking against the woodwork. He pulled the sling over his head and dropped it with a hollow thud on the table and waited.

Smith leaned back in his chair, as if with a sudden pleasant memory. 'I believe the Turks call it "ear to ear" or some such, or "Russian Scandal" – the players sit all in a row, the first whispering a message into the ear of the second, "I went to market with Dolly Smith and bought ham and cheese". The second chap, or indeed lady, conveys this to the next, and so on down the line until the result is compared with the original message – in most instances bearing absolutely no resemblance whatsoever.' He looked at Hazzard. 'We do not suffer this curious affliction here, Mr Hazzard. Not this evening.'

The implication was clear; what was to follow came straight from the horse's mouth: senior rank, Admiralty, Downing Street – or above. Hood glanced at him, and Hazzard nodded. 'Understood.'

Smith continued. 'It seems the Turkish sultan in Constantinople knew more about the invasion of Egypt than the French Consul Ruffin did, or indeed, more even than did we. The sultan sent out diplomatic *firmans* that Bonaparte was a criminal who had acted without authority, and that his presence in Egypt is merely temporary.'

Keith looked down, shaking his head slightly, Hazzard uncertain whether the admiral knew this already. Smith carried on.

'He did this, first, to save French citizens from being dragged from their homes and businesses and butchered in the streets, and second, to give Foreign Minister Talleyrand and the Directory in Paris the opportunity to – how shall we say – *disown* General Bonaparte. Needless to say, they have not.' He leaned forward on the desk, moving a pen and inkstand to one side. 'Meanwhile, Djezzar Pasha in Acre has threatened Bonaparte's officer *parlementaire*, and Bonaparte himself. The Ottoman Empire is currently a powder-keg, which could blow itself apart.'

They absorbed the news. Smith continued.

'My brother, Mr Hazzard, the new First Secretary at our embassy to the Sublime Porte in Constantinople, informs me that, *not* having had any word of apology from France for Bonaparte's attack, French Consul Ruffin was presented with a declaration of war by the sultan early last month, on the 2nd of September. He was politely informed that all French consuls and ambassadors were to be detained and their property seized. They now sit, drooping somewhat, in the medieval dungeon prison of the Seven Towers. All this was done over coffee, with, I am pleased to report, the most impeccable Turkish manners.'

Keith nodded, satisfied. 'At last…'

'Indeed. In all of the empire's major cities, French citizens are lying very low for fear of mob and riot.' Smith looked to Keith. 'My lord.'

Keith took a moment of thought, as if considering his words carefully. His hand clenching the top of his mahogany cane, he raised his chin to speak. 'Have you heard any rumblings in Cairo, Mr Hazzard?'

'Cairo?' Hazzard looked at Cook again. 'No sir… The French New Year celebration went off last month, but otherwise nothing of note…'

'September 21st or 22nd, is it not?' asked Smith.

'Yes, 22nd. They celebrated at the Nilometer gauge. Why, sir?'

There was an uneasy silence. Smith nodded to one of his junior lieutenants, who stepped out through the apartment door. He returned a moment later with a well-dressed Egyptian trader with dark curling moustache and beard. He bowed. 'This extraordinary gentleman,' announced Smith, 'will explain. May I introduce Herr Joseph von Hammer-Pürgstall of the Viennese consulate in Cairo.'

It was the diplomatic envoy who had guided Hazzard and Cook from Alexandria to warn the Mamluks of the invasion – and saved their lives. Hazzard got to his feet at once and took his hand, genuinely pleased. 'Herr Hammer…'

'My dear chap,' he said with his scarcely detectable Austrian accent, 'Hammer and Hazzard. Still the fearsome London solicitors.'

'So very good to see you. What is the problem?'

'Nothing good,' he said quickly and softly – adding in a fast whisper, '*Eine Nachricht.*' *A message.* A scrap of paper was pressed into Hazzard's palm as they shook hands.

Hazzard took it and Hammer stepped back. '*Mein Herr Admiral,*' he gave a brief bow of the head to Keith then to the rest, 'Gentlemen. From what we have heard from Al-Djezzar in Akka, or Acre as I believe we call it, and from the Grand Vizier, a revolt will shortly erupt in Cairo.'

Hazzard had not expected this to be the subject. 'Revolt?'

'Weapons have been passed about between the people, and I myself have seen the work of disparate resistance groups, planning and organising the erection of barricades. It has its beginnings with the Mosque Al-Azhar, and will spread from there throughout the city, passed by the *imams* and the *muezzin*'s call to prayer as a signal.'

It was exactly as Shajar al-Durr had promised in the heat and dust of Kafr-Shahabas. Smith detected Hazzard's heightened concern. 'It would be a good thing, do you not agree, Major?'

Hazzard looked at Hammer. 'When?'

'Any day now. My apologies, I seem to bring you poor tidings, my dear fellow.'

He heard Cook look down and swear under his breath, '*Jaysus an' all...*'

Wayland. Porter, Hesse, Tariq and De Lisle.

Hazzard looked from Smith to Hammer. 'How certain are you of this? There was always the threat, but, to be organised...'

'As certain as we can be,' said Hammer. 'It will involve thousands. They have amassed sticks, clubs, muskets, powder and shot, planned road blockages to cut off the French cavalry. Many in the know will close their shops or flee the city, others will be less fortunate. There are fears of criminal riot and looting, but the Al-Azhar hopes it can keep the lower element in the dark.'

Smith could sense something was wrong. 'Your thoughts, Mr Hazzard?'

Hazzard glanced at Cook. 'My second in command has gone to the capital with three of our men and their interpreter.'

Hammer looked at him. 'Herr Wayland?'

Smith was puzzled. 'But he said he was to travel to Roset—' then stopped, looking at the surface of his desk, understanding. 'Ah. I see.' He gave a nod of appreciation. 'Very good security, sir.'

God above.

'Herr Hammer,' said Hazzard, 'what parts? I – I mean, which districts?'

'So far only the Al-Azhar and into the centre, Ezbekiya is too well guarded with the royal palaces and high command, but they will close the southern gates certainly to deny access from Old Cairo.'

'What of the Institute?'

'That is in Nasriya. I have had no word of that area. I do not believe the rebels are aware of it.'

'Christ almighty...'

Smith met Hazzard's eye. 'I shall come to Mr Wayland shortly,' he said, trying to reassure, 'but, in your opinion, Mr Hazzard, from what you know of the resistance, could a revolt succeed?'

'No, of course not,' said Hazzard bluntly. 'It would be utter madness.'

'I fear I agree with Herr Hazzard,' said Hammer.

Keith frowned and spoke up. 'How so?'

Hazzard looked at Smith and Cook. 'We saw it often enough in India. Cairo has no support. Bonaparte will encircle the city, crush the rebellion with cavalry and probably bombard the capital without regard for the inhabitants, absolutely none. And for every Frenchman dead he will kill ten, fifty or a hundred Egyptians.'

'You know him well,' remarked Hammer quietly.

Smith said, 'As a gesture, though, an act of defiance, it could ring out across the world.'

Hazzard looked at him, appalled. 'Sir Sidney, this is not an island port, or a – a small colonial outpost. Bonaparte is an Oriental *conqueror*, a – a *dictator*, in a land of massacre and revenge.' Hammer nodding his approval, Hazzard spoke very clearly, so there could be no misunderstanding. 'We must dissuade them from such a move, sir – it would give Bonaparte another victory, and his troops would rally once again under their invincible general—'

Hood frowned. 'Hardly invincible, since he's lost his entire fleet...'

Hazzard was quick to reply. 'No, not his entire fleet, sir. You sank eleven ships of the line – his entire fleet was four *hundred*. Some of his transports still sit in Alexandria. Bonaparte ignored the defeat as a slight setback. It is irrelevant to his grand scheme.'

'Which is?'

'To outdo Alexander, march overland, conquer Persia, conquer everything in his path – and eventually take India. It's his dream. Europe is *nothing* to him now. He told me so himself, in Malta.'

Hammer stood firm with Hazzard. 'This is perfectly true, gentlemen.'

They stared at him, then glanced at each other. 'That is absurd, Major,' scoffed Keith.

'It might well be,' said Hazzard, 'but there is no one to tell him otherwise. He is the supreme commander.'

'Then he is bereft of reason,' deduced Keith.

'My lord,' said Hammer with a crisp bow, 'I have sat with *qadis*, *kashieffs* and sheikhs listening to the general explain how good a Muslim he is, indeed a better one than they, and why he wishes to take the Quran on a great crusade. To restore the law of Allah throughout the East.' He chuckled. 'There were many confused faces that day, sir.'

'Mr Hazzard,' said Keith, 'you are up in the Delta on operations, what could you possibly know of this?'

'Clearly more than some.'

The Lord Admiral sat up, affronted. 'I *beg* your pardon sir...?'

'Yes, how far from Cairo are you anyway, Hazzard?' demanded Naismith. 'Must be miles.'

Hazzard did not flinch. 'Damn sight closer than you.'

'Enough sir!' snapped Keith.

There was an uncomfortable silence. Cook turned to Smith. 'Begging your pardon, sir, my lord, but Mr Hazzard rode the field at Embabeh, drawin' the fire of two divisional squares, that's ten thousand men, away from the Mamluk cavalry.' Cook looked over them all. 'Few know what could befall Cairo better'n Mr Hazzard, sir.'

Smith said in a discreet voice to the others, 'Gentlemen, such are the men before you and their knowledge of the field.'

'We have all seen horrors, Smith,' remarked Naismith.

Smith ignored the slight and quipped, 'No sir, you have not. Not like that.'

Naismith had no response. Cook gathered himself. 'Sir, judgin' by the behaviour o'the French and the Egyptians in battle,' he began, 'a revolt would bring down such a slaughter upon the innocent, that I would not wish to answer for it, come judgement at the end o'my days.'

Lord Keith cleared his throat. 'This is more difficult a matter than divisions, lines, feints and tactics, Mr Hazzard. We speak of *nations*. And matters beyond any one man. *Any.*'

'The revolt then,' summarised Smith, 'would need to be reinforced.'

'By a landing,' said Hazzard. 'British troops, Ottoman troops, to meet the French army before it masses in the field, to pull them onto two fronts.'

'Which we *cannot yet do*,' said Keith with finality. 'We have *not* the men.'

'This is the problem,' said Douglas, nodding to Smith. 'If I may, sir. From what we have discovered through Acre and Jaffa, Mr Hazzard, the Ottoman levied infantry is more of a horde than an army.'

'How many men?' asked Hazzard.

Even Douglas seemed astonished by the answer. 'Near a hundred thousand. But it creates utter chaos and the sultan does not call it up lightly. It would take months to gather them,' he said. 'They would not reach Egypt before next year, the imperial eye falling rather upon Djezzar Pasha at Acre for support.' He glanced at Smith. 'Which leads us to the other matter, sir.'

Smith took the floor. 'Mr Hazzard, the coin you said held by the Tarabin.'

'By Shajar al-Durr.'

'Yes. I believe it was from part of our support to Djezzar, to bolster our agreements. The very fact that Shajar and the Tarabin had such a coin supports only one conclusion.'

Hammer nodded to Hazzard. 'It suggests that Ibrahim Bey or Djezzar of Acre has paid them to rise up.'

Hazzard could think only of Wayland and the others.

Good God.

Hazzard nodded. 'So he need not raise his own army... and can just stroll across the border when the capital turns against the French.' He looked at Hood, at Douglas, then Smith. 'We have to stop them, for their own good.'

Lord Keith started in his seat. 'What do you mean, sir? Stop the revolt?'

'Yes sir. If the people rise up in Cairo, they will be utterly destroyed, and the capital with them, not to mention my own—' Hazzard stopped.

None of the others had reacted to the news that Djezzar had paid for the uprising. Hazzard fell silent as he realised at last: they knew all of this.

'You knew the revolt was coming. And did nothing.'

Room 63.

The Admiralty.

Lies.

'My dear fellow,' protested Smith, 'we knew nothing of it, as Herr Hammer said—'

'Of *course* we did, sir!' Keith burst out, impatient with them both. 'Supposed the idea, guessed at it, predicted it, what or however you please. We *need* the revolt, sir. Egypt needs the revolt!'

Hazzard looked from one to the other, Hammer saying nothing but trying to convey something to him. Hazzard could feel his heart pounding, perhaps from Cook's recounted memories of his bloody gallop through the field, and the savage consequences at the gates of Cairo. He had forgotten the influence of Sir Rafe Lewis and the Admiralty – all of it spoke of the tortuous rabbit-warren mentality within Room 63 and Admiralty Intelligence. He had forgotten to think like Lewis – but now he saw it.

'You might want a revolt sir,' he said to Keith. 'But you want it to *fail.*'

Hammer met his eye and gave a barely perceptible nod.

'Fail?' asked Douglas, confused. 'Why should anyone want it to fail? I don't quite follow...'

'So that the sultan is forced to commit his army, join with British troops, and invade Egypt.' He looked at Keith. 'You would let innocents rise up and be crushed underfoot, to suit a strategy?'

Smith refused to accept the supposition. 'That is simply not the truth, Mr Hazzard, *surely—*'

'And what of it, sir!' demanded Keith, sitting forward. 'Who are you to question matters of such import!'

Hazzard lashed back at him, 'And who are *you* sir, to condemn thousands to certain death from the comfort of a briefing room in Gibraltar or London!'

Keith exploded from his seat. 'By *God*, Lewis was *right*. I knew this would be your way sir! Knew it!' His outrage overwhelmed them all, the junior officers behind stepping back in surprise. 'Of course it is true, sir! Of *course* it is.' He stood, facing Hazzard. 'It is the *only* way to make the sultan see that Egypt and his crumbling empire is doomed *unless he acts and we act with him!*'

Smith and Douglas were shocked. 'But surely, my lord, this has not been ratified—'

Keith interrupted him irritably. 'Horse Guards are already plotting a campaign with the Lords Commissioners, Commodore, and it *will* fail unless French Egypt is broken from within.' Keith rampaged onward, accusing Hazzard, 'Yet you presume, sir, to hold a mirror to us and reveal our *shame*? What conceit, sir! When all we seek is to restore the Mamluk, rid their nation of the *pestilential* French Republic and destroy Bonaparte! And you condemn us!'

Hazzard was on his feet. 'Yes, by God, I condemn a scheme that sheds another nation's blood with such wanton disregard...' But then he faltered. 'You struggled for negotiation at the Cape – *why not here?*'

'I would if I could,' asserted Keith. 'But I will *never* sit at a table again without a thousand guns over my shoulder *pointed down our enemy's throats.*'

Hood watched grimly. 'Mr Hazzard, it seems these are not matters for captains or conscience. Which we are plainly not permitted...'

Keith was implacable. 'Egypt and Britain need this revolt to be a hellish, catastrophic, *bloody* failure to ignite the Ottoman Empire in *outrage* sir! *We are the sultan's only hope.*'

Hazzard looked at them, hearing Nelson's words ringing in his ears from a similar Great Cabin on a similar 74-gun ship of the line:

We are England, sir – we determine the nations.

Innocents. Again.

Hazzard turned to Hammer. 'The Tarabin? Their leader, Shajar?'

Hammer shook his head. 'There is a clan of Al-Tarabin fighters among the rebels, yes. Led by one known as Baibars.'

Shajar al-Durr holding up a coin, a golden guinea.

Here is proof. From the kingdom of England.

Destroyed, shot, butchered, beheaded.

God above.

'Mr Hazzard,' declared Keith, regaining some composure and sitting once again, 'you and your men will accompany us on HMS *Tigre* to Cyprus, for suitable reward, rest and recuperation.'

'I will do no such thing—'

'—and to ensure you do not interfere with matters beyond your station sir.'

Smith tried to keep the peace. 'Mr Hazzard, I beg of you—'

Hazzard got to his feet. 'Sar'nt Cook—'

Cook stood. 'Sir.'

'By God you will mind yourself in my presence, sir—' blustered Keith.

Hazzard ignored him. 'Sar'nt, 9 Company to the portside rail. Bo'sun to lower a boat. We're going back. *Now.*'

Keith's face reddened. 'The devil you are, sir, without my leave! Major Naismith!'

Douglas looked round to Naismith, who hardly moved a muscle. He had no need. 'Already done, my lord.'

Hazzard looked at the wooden-faced major, the officer he assumed would merely run back to Room 63 and report to Sir Rafe Lewis, an Intelligence errand-boy. But it seemed he was not there for that at all. He felt the sharp edge of Hammer's message still clutched in his hand, and finally examined it:

Keith to command. But watch for Naismith – CB

CB. Charles Blake.

Hazzard's face suffused a deep red upon reading that name, the name of a former friend turned Admiralty functionary, the man behind the duel with Harry Race and the involvement of Sarah – Hazzard realised Blake's warning had come all too late for his temper. He looked at Naismith. 'What is already done…?'

'Yes, sir,' demanded Douglas, 'what have you done? You have no authority aboard this ship—'

Uncomfortable with it, Keith cleared his throat. 'Merely a precaution, sir.'

Douglas looked at Naismith, as if fearing what he might have done, or indeed, could yet do. 'What in the blazes are you, man?'

'I am a Special Marshal, Major Douglas. And, as such, accountable only to the Admiralty under the Navy Act.' He looked at Hazzard. 'Your men are currently under armed guard by my own Marine Provost deputies, Mr Hazzard,' said Naismith, 'to be released only at my command, upon reaching safe harbour at Cyprus.' He took a satisfied breath. 'Call it an escort if you like.'

'I *beg* your pardon, sir…?' said Smith, rising from his desk. 'No man, with the exception of the flag, has authority above the captain aboard one of His Majesty's ships, least of all the *Tigre.*'

Naismith handed over a letter. 'My Provosts, Sir Sidney, or rather, my marines,' said Naismith, 'are acting in accordance with a direct command received through the Sublime Porte, signed by one Sir Rafe Lewis,' he said, trumping them all, 'of the Admiralty.'

Douglas took a step forward. 'You *dare*, sir—'

'This is not the army, Major Naismith,' said Smith icily, 'we have no Provosts here, and my title is Sir Sidney if you please.'

Major Douglas stepped in front of Naismith, his heels together. 'You will show me such authority, Naismith, or be charged with attempted mutiny and thrown in a cell.'

Hazzard had one hand on the Lorenzoni.

Lewis.

'These are the men of 9 Company,' said Hazzard, 'handpicked by Jack Jervis himself, heroes of Malta and Aboukir, their names known to the *king* and the *Prince of Wales*—'

Naismith evidently could have cared less. 'I have my orders, Hazzard—'

Hood set down his sherry glass, addressing Smith. 'Sir Sidney, I fear the quality of the company has deteriorated somewhat. Kindly call my gig at once for return to the *Zealous.*'

But Cook knew the form and feared the worst. He stormed to the door and yanked it open. Two blank-faced men in Marine uniform and navy-blue sashes stood in his path, hands behind their backs. Just over their shoulders were four red-coated *Tigre* marines watching, uncertain, looking hopefully at the door. A corporal met Cook's eye. 'Bloody 'ell, Sarge… it's – *who are they?*'

Cook's hand was already on the hilt of his Arabian *khanjar* when he stopped himself. 'You knows who I am, boy?'

The Marine Corporal nodded. 'Y-yeh, Sarge. You're Cookie, who fought at the Pyramids… an' the Nile, an' saved Nelson and the *Culloden…*' The Provost backed away a pace, suddenly uncertain. The corporal saw Smith and Hood, and nodded at Hazzard in the background. 'An-an' that's Mr 'Azzard, sir… hero of the Cape and all, sir… and pride o'the bloody service…' He looked at the Provosts angrily. 'Just gimme the word, Sarge, I swears it.'

A figure appeared behind, a petty officer, stiff, stocky, a face hard as brick, his manner rigid and unassailable. 'It's true, Sar'nt-Major,' he said to Cook. 'They've shown me an order from a Mr Naismith, whoever the devil he is.'

He pushed through them and into the cabin. He came to attention in the doorway. 'Sir,' he said to Smith. 'As Master at Arms I cannot shake them. They claim their warrant lies with Major Naismith here.'

'What goes on here, sir,' demanded Keith. 'Provosts at the Great Cabin within sight of an enemy shore? This stands contrary to the laws of arms at the very least—'

Naismith slowly got to his feet, as if in quiet command of it all. 'Since it has come to this, these are measures for your protection, my lord,' he said confidently. 'Mutineers and deserters aboard. Mr Hazzard, Marine Sergeant Cook,' he announced, 'by order of the Admiralty and Lords Commissioners, for desertion of the fleet at Alexandria after the Battle of the Nile, you and the men of 9 Company are hereby placed under arrest.'

Hood cocked an eyebrow and regarded Major Naismith with a strange calm. 'If you think this a simple matter sir, you are sore mistaken. I look forward to your court-martial.'

'Sir Samuel, if you please,' said Smith to Hood. They strode to the door, just as a call came down from the mainmast lookout.

Though few knew it at the time, HMS *Tigre* had been taken.

Mutiny

The galley fire smoke had died, but the iron pots kept their heat, that morning's curried porridge of fish and biscuit having matured to everyone's taste, the proud hands of the *Tigre* insisting, *Sir Sid don't want for nuffing, mate.* The off-watch sailing hands had spread out among the benches and tables of the fo'c'sle mess, the great foremast driving through its centre to the bowels of the ship through the decks below. The doors to the tweendecks stood open for air, rows of silent 24-pounders gleaming in the night. Deckhands moved between them, cross-hatched with shadow from the overhead gratings, some disappearing into the deeper darkness cast by the boats slung above.

The grog had been flowing freely and Kite was enjoying the lime-light. Crowding the benches and tables, some cross-legged on the planks, a number of the women from below decks, the *Tigre's* marines and off-duty seamen all clustered round: these were the men who had chased down Napoleon himself, ridden with the Bedouin, and followed 'Mad Billy-Jack' Hazzard, Giant Jory Cook and 'Dead-Leg Wayland'.

'...and, 'ello, he says, I 'ave a blockage in this 'ere musket, I wonder what it can be?' Kite played his audience well, laughs all round as they waited. 'So he turns it about, like so, the muzzle up to his puzzled eye, and looks down the spout...' Kite mimed the action, one eye shut, the other peering comically down an imaginary musket barrel, 'But lo, he says, it be too dark, and I cannot see within the packed barrel. Whatever shall I do? I know, says he, I be needin' a light at t'other end!'

The cabin rocked with laughter as Kite continued his mime show of the unfortunate marine. 'So, holdin' a candle-flame in his free hand, thus – no, honest, dead straight – he puts the flame to the touchhole of his primed, loaded and rammed musket while lookin' down the barrel, and he says, 'Ere Sarge! I can see all the better now! Aaaaaand

– *bang!* – there's a ka-boom like a Spithead salute for Nellie himself, and this oke goes flyin' into the scuppers, head over heels, musket still clutched tight in his hand, all of us thinkin' his head's been blowed off and now he might at last make a good marine. But no, he sits up, his face black, his hair standin' on end and smokin' from powder an' shot, and says with tremblin' voice, *Sarge, I do believe I found the problem.'*

The company roared, Kite clanked tankards with Handley and shouted through the din, 'An' *that's* what I calls an Oddfellow, mates.'

Some of them played curiously with their *khanjar* daggers and *keffiyah* headdresses, one of them trying to tie a turban. Pettifer and Warnock sat relaxed, their backs to a bulkhead, Napier whittling a bit of wood, his thick features deep in crazed shadows, Cochrane red in the face from drink, and Underhill leaned back against the planks, another long cheroot sending up clouds of burning fragrant smoke. One of the *Tigre's* marines, Rhys, a corporal from Cardiff, whispered for fear of being overheard, 'But what's he *really* like, man? We hear he's a holy terror…' The men of 9 Company smiled and went quiet. 'Is it true, all them tales o'the Cape? Come on, man, tell us…'

Underhill laughed his dry rasp, and looked at Handley and Pettifer. Handley spoke up, the longest serving seaman of the group. 'I was with 'im at the Cape, with Petty here. We fair tore down that mountain eh, Pet, after watchin' that bastard Cap'n Race push a blade in the guts o'some poor bloody boer… and saw his scum o'the earth men murder the 'ole bloody family…'

The group fell quiet. Handley took a sip from his ale.

'Mr 'Azzard – I never seen the like… when we hit the bottom of the slope, he dropped a man at fifty paces with a snap-shot from his bloody great double-barrelled Manton pistol, took a round in his shoulder, gutted another with a spear, and blew the head off one of them caught by Cookie in the middle of rapine and murder. Petty 'ere blew another man clean off his legs with that musketoon o'his.'

The big Cornishman nodded. 'We hared down to the beach after them's who were left…' He glanced at Handley, 'From the *Stately* weren't they… and Mr 'Azzard runs at Mr Race like a ravin' beast, just as the fleet opened up on the coast, y'remember? A flamin' barrage, couldn't hear ourselves think…' He looked off into the past. 'And them two, swords flyin', Mr 'Azzard tryin' to make him surrender-like, takin' hits and cuts all over – till he hit Mr Race with that Mughal Cross o'his…' He looked at Handley. 'Opened Mr Race up from hip to shoulder and back again. Blood in the surf, all over…'

Someone gave a low whistle, the assembly agog. Underhill laughed.

'An' that's why we calls him Bloody Billy-Jack, not mad, but *bloody*. He boarded the *Orient* at the Nile, with Knock-Knock there, and Pet, decks all burnin' up, to save his fair lady...' He fell silent a moment and stared at his cheroot, then abruptly moved on, as if these were memories only for the few. 'He does nothin' without askin' what says the boat. If the boat says aye, then we carry on. And we rarely says nay.' He took another drag on the cheroot and blew smoke into the planks above. 'He leads from the front, and knows us to think like him, so's if ever we are parted, we all of us knows what to do. And that's his trust in us, all thinkin' men, and that's a fact.'

They chorused in quiet murmurs, *amen*, and *aye*.

Rhys nodded. 'How can we join, Sarge?' he asked in a whisper, 'Come on, you must be needin' more okes by now, man.'

'We ride with the *Bedu* Arabs,' said Pettifer stolidly, his deep Cornish accent rolling against those of the dockers and Londoners. 'Can't be takin' on new littl'uns, Taffy. Ain't got room.'

'We ride light and quick,' confirmed Warnock. 'Barely enough rations for us and the *Bedu*.'

'Aye,' said Underhill. 'It's true, but it's not a life for men o'the sea such as ye, boys. Out in the hot sands, with nought but rock and scrub and camel ticks...'

'Still in me bloody arm,' said Warnock.

'An' scopriums,' muttered Napier. 'They're scarifyin'.'

'An' scorpions I warrant ye, brother, aye,' agreed Underhill.

The ship's bell rang and all stopped and listened. They waited for the usual double note, but it did not come: it rang only once. Underhill frowned, looking up, the bell just over their heads on the foredeck.

There was a clumping of boots down one of the foredeck ladders. Dickory, followed by four of Naismith's blue-sashed Marine Provosts and a squad of *Tigre* marines, came through the tweendecks doors and moved through the galley to the mess, Dickory red-faced and shaking his head, pushing his way through the crowd. 'I don't know what the *bloody 'ell* you been up to, Jeremish Underhill...'

Once they reached Rhys, one of the Provosts piped up officiously, 'All ranks, on your feet, an' two paces back. *Move—*'

Dickory spun round, a hand up to him. 'Hoi, mind yer manners, you paralysed streak o'*piss*. My manor, my men, my rules, so belt up and get *back*.' The Provost stared back at him with a sneer.

Rhys looked about. 'What's all this, Sarge…?'

Dickory flung his hands up, exasperated, '*Move* dammit! All o'yer! On yer feet and move away…'

The *Tigre* crewmen and marines obeyed and stepped away, the Provosts remaining where they were, the men examining them curiously. Dickory stood square in front of Underhill and the others at their table. 'By order of one Major *bloody* Naismith, Special Marshal of arse-whatnot, you're all under ruddy arrest for some flamin' reason.'

Kite looked up from his seat. 'Do what?' he said, a half-smile still on his face. 'You yankin' me plank, Sarge…?'

Rhys and the *Tigre*'s marines looked round astonished. 'What? Give over, Sarge—'

'No, Taff, I won't,' he said. 'You will stay back and belt up.' He turned and gestured over his shoulder. 'Two Section, in 'ere, *now*.' Eight armed marines moved forward, murmuring their excuses, *I dunno do I mate*, muskets at the port.

Handley glanced at Napier and Cochrane, who watched carefully, their hands smoothly moving to their various weapons. Underhill continued smoking his cheroot.

'Now, Docky,' said Underhill, 'I don't claim to know what tales someone's been tellin' ye, but—'

'No, 'Miah!' Dickory shouted back, 'No! Yer've done it *again*, aintcha. Bloody *hell* man! Each time, *each time* I sees you, it ends up like this, with *trouble*, mate! Bloody Sumatra or the *bloody* St Laurence, no difference is it, an' I bloody 'ad enough of it!'

Rhys checked him. 'Who's Major Naismith anyhow, Sarge?' He looked at the men in blue sashes. 'We got a right to know. He ain't got no sway on Sir Sidder's boat now man!'

'He *does*, Taff! He *bloody* does…' He wiped a hand across his slick forehead, furious, frustrated. 'An' I got to do what he says till told else-wise…'

Pettifer rose slowly. 'Now Sergeant, if'n our Major 'Azzard and Cookie be in trouble, and you be part of it—' He nodded at the brass-barrelled blunderbuss in his left hand. 'I'll blow you apart, Provost, marines or no.'

The Provost looked at Pettifer and swallowed, his hand reaching for a pistol at his belt, but Dickory paid him scant attention. 'You dozy Cornish cart'orse! Doncha get it? If your major's in trouble then my *captain's* in trouble, right? So you bloody lot sit *tight* and don't move less I says so, an' I can figure somethin' out…'

A pair of running boots came from the tweendecks and they turned to look, a deckhand, and they passed the word, Rhys pushing his way back through them. He turned to Dickory then looked at the three men in blue. 'These Marine Provo's, Sarge, they got the flippin' junior officers in the gunroom, middies, lieutenants and chief petties, Mr Wright and all, won't let the hands past 'em.' He raised a threatening finger. 'Master's gone to Sir Sid, but as Gunner's Mate, I say this is dangerous in light of an enemy shore off the larboard beam. This is bloody bollocks, and I say tis full 'gainst the KRs and the Navy Act, so stuff 'em.'

They looked at the three co-opted Provost policemen, who backed away to the mess bulkhead. 'Now, Sergeant, you keep your lads under discipline, right, we didn't know nothin' about—'

'Nothin' about what, ye beggarin' bastard!' rasped Rhys, shoving him back against the plank wall, 'This is the *Tigre*, man! Not some bloody Channel Fleet scow! We engage three enemy at once and think nowt about it, you bilge-rat *shite*!'

'*Christ*,' said Dickory. 'It's a bloody mutiny, from the wrong way round.' He snapped a hand at Rhys. 'Taff, foredeck, get Mr Skellitt, look in the tops, see if he's up there with the scouts…'

'Aye Sarge,' said the Welshman, pushing his way to the forward steps. He paused and looked back. 'And if not, Sarge?'

Dickory looked at the Provosts, then whipped off his round-hat, wiping the sweat from his forehead. 'Then you ring that bloody alarm bell quick as mustard.'

'Now look here—' began one of the Navy men, backing into Cochrane.

'Shuddup you,' said Napier, and dropped him with a lazy fist. The Marine Provost crashed against a table, fell onto a bench, crumpled on the floor and lay still. Handley, Cochrane and Kite whipped up their short muskets as Napier loomed over the other two.

'Good goin', Art'ur,' said Cochrane.

Warnock advanced on them with a vicious smile, his tomahawk in hand. '*As-salamu aleikum*,' he murmured. 'That's Ab-rab for 'ow ye doin', ye piece o'shite. You're facin' the Specials right now, me shiverin' mateys, and we kill before breakfast most days.'

'Well, Docky,' said Underhill, moving through the mess to look out the doors, 'let's 'ope yer middie's up above...' He cocked a pistol. 'Else you got yourself a mad, mad monkey o'trouble.'

The sound of more running feet on the tweendecks, on the gangways and up the steps told Dickory all he needed. The next moment a call came down from the tops, and the alarm bell rang. The marines reacted at once and lurched for the door but Dickory shouted out, 'Stand *still*! You will wait for the order!'

The marines held fast, stopping dead. Dickory pushed his way past the galley to the tweendecks. Rigging hands were shinning up the yards and a tall young midshipman appeared at the door from below. It was Mr Skellit. 'Sar'nt Dickory! We have enemy sail to the larboard quarter of *Zealous* and I've been barred from the quarterdeck! Where is Mr Wright or Lt Tyte?'

'Sir!' Dickory turned and shouted into the mess. 'Right, that's bloody *it*.' He turned and drove the butt of his musket into the midriff of one of the Marine Provosts, throwing him back over a table and into the corner. '*Tigre*, to me! Stand by to clear for action, smartish, you lumpen bloody Jonahs! Turn about, cocked and locked, any stranger stops you, give 'em a round in the bollocks! Nine Company,' he said to Underhill, 'you lot follow me, we done our bit for King's Regs!'

Underhill and the others got to their feet. 'Ah, shame Docky,' he said with a grim laugh. 'We ain't 'ad a good mutiny in ages, 'ave we.'

–

The quarterdeck exploded with shouts as the marines and the Master at Arms hurried to the rail, Hazzard, Hood and Smith marching straight through the startled Marine Provosts who backed away, pistols extended, none prepared to shoot. Wright erupted from below decks, calling out 'Sir Sidney! Enemy to larboard, beat to quarters sir?'

'Yes dash it all John, action stations.'

Wright bellowed along the tweendecks, '*Beat to quarters! Weigh anchor! Where away in the tops!*'

The call came down from the foremast, '*Enemy sail off larboard bow, range two thousand yards, closing on Zealous! Gunboats!*'

The ship came alive with hands leaping to the rigging, gunners diving below decks, the retracting anchor cables screeching in the capstans, the marines storming up to the quarterdeck to take up firing positions at the stays, loading the murderer swivel-guns. Smith took a telescope from the Signals officer. 'Captain's gig for Commodore Hood at once, Mr Fanshawe.'

Hammer joined Hazzard and Cook – they found the cause of the alarm: off the port bow of HMS *Zealous*, barely a cable length ahead, was a small French frigate emerging from the distant lights of Damietta, running fast under a glowing cloud of sail, scudding along the darkened coast, her guns flickering, the staccato salvo rapping across the black waves moments later, spouts of water rising near the great 74.

Hood gave a curt bow to Smith. 'They shan't get away with this, Sidney... we can gather at your convenience.'

'Just get to *Zealous* in time, Samuel,' called Smith, 'You've an awfully good '89 Chambertin over there and I should hate it to go to the bottom.'

'I shall save you some,' called Hood as he and two lieutenants hurried to the starboard rail as the boat was lowered, a midshipman piping Hood into the night.

Zealous opened her shutter lanterns. Within moments her rigging was illuminated from the masthead, her bows, midships, coamings and decks, the huge lanterns on her flamboyant taffrail bursting into light, her name now visible, emblazoned in gold across her stern – she was as bright as the port, so that Hood could find her in the dark. Bells clanging, drums rattling, and sails billowing, her First Lieutenant hauled her round to starboard in the growing swell. 'She's lit up like Vauxhall illuminations...' murmured Smith, then called out, 'Mr Wright! Keep us out of direct line – don't steal her wind!'

Then Hammer saw them and pointed. 'There... they are very small. Are they boats...?'

Hazzard looked. In the water, suddenly visible in the reflections cast by the lights on *Zealous*, a flotilla of single-masted tartanes and cutters – each with a short naval gun mounted in the bows: deadly snub-nosed carronades – with enough power to shock a 74 if they got close enough. The call came a moment later from the foremast lookout far up ahead.

'*Gunboats in the water! Dead ahead, bearing west-nor'west five hundred yards! Making for the Zealous!*'

'What is the fear of such small craft?' asked Hammer. 'The ship, it is so big...'

Cook answered, gripping the rail, 'Them small boats can get in under her guns and blaze away at the waterline. They got to get that big-arse 74 out of it, quick... But Hood's still out there in his gig somewhere.'

Smith zeroed his scope and looked, then called, 'Twenty degrees to port Mr Wright, to shield the *Zealous*! Full sail – let her fly! Prepare a ripple and all hands to brace for collision!'

'Very good sir!' Wright shouted through a loudhailer, '*Gunnery load for langrage and rippling broadside! All hands ready for collision!*'

Cook leaned close to Hazzard. 'What in hell's a ripplin' broadside...?'

Hazzard watched the gunners ran out the double-shotted Long 18s and carronades around them. 'I think we are about to find out...'

The 80-gun *Tigre* surged ahead, *Zealous* pulling further out to sea, trying to escape the faster gunboats. Far to starboard they could see Hood in his white-painted captain's gig, the oarsmen pulling for their lives to the ship, a squad of marines loaded and rammed, their muskets pointing outboard, *Zealous* altering course to pick them up.

'That's it,' said Smith. '*Zealous* is turning to intercept him. Good chaps, Hood's lot. These dashed little gunboats are merely a diversion to keep us away from that wretched *aviso* frigate up ahead.' He looked at him, a hand on his arm. 'Do get your fellows ready to mount a jolly and nip over the side. Once we are done I'll drop you at Rosetta so you can head upriver to Cairo.'

Hazzard was surprised. 'That was expressly against his lordship's wishes, sir.'

Smith smiled inscrutably as ever. 'Perhaps you can save this captain's conscience, my dear fellow.'

'Thank you, sir.'

The *Tigre* leapt, her yards straining, the canvas bright in the dark skies, the decks now alive with running crewmen, gunners calling their stations, *aye for one*, *aye for two*, all along the portside. The gunboats struggled in the swell, their ship-killing armament weighing them down in the prow. One took a shot at the *Zealous*, a deep booming echo across the sea, a spout of water rising fifty yards off her port quarter. 'Damned cheek... Mr Wright!' called Smith. 'Shred the water!'

'Aye sir!' The lieutenant turned, Lord Keith standing at his side, looking back at Smith. Wright put up his loudhailer and roared down the main deck, '*Main gundeck, rippling broadside to port! Open fire!*'

The *Tigre*'s portside tweendeck guns roared in rapid succession from the cockpit in the bows to the officers' gunroom at the stern, each a fraction of a second behind the next, the effect a repetitive thudding drumroll of flaming muzzle-blasts, the flashes blinding, raising a terrifying curtain of explosive water geysers advancing towards the gunboats, the langrage shrapnel hissing in the air as it passed, fizzing across the boiling water's surface in a tidal wave of bursts.

One of the boats sheared off and capsized, its crew flying into the dark waves. Another bore away sharply to port, its bows dipping into a wave, inundated by the spray and towering waterspouts – the carronade lost its mount and pulled it under, her stern shooting upward into the sky, the mast and sail folding back, the crewmen vanishing from sight. Wright was not yet done. '*Lower-deck! Rippling broadside to port! Open fire!*'

The second deck of *Tigre*'s guns roared, the gunboats veering away from *Zealous*, the shrapnel chopping the water into a boiling mist, the French crewmen screaming out, knocked overboard, masts collapsing.

'*Hard a' port! Collison course! Stand by to ram!*' The drums quickened and HMS *Tigre* lurched to port, her paws swiping angrily at the sea, grinding three of the gunboats beneath her bows, the bump and crash of the shattering wood lost in the wake. Hazzard looked down as one splintered against the hull, three crewmen leaping as she overturned. One fell into the spray, two getting a purchase on the *Tigre*'s broadside, some of the lower deckhands calling out, *get 'em up get 'em up*, trying to reach down for them, only for one to miss his footing and fall, his hands up in the foaming water, the other taking one hand, a seaman holding onto him. '*Get him aboard dammit!*' shouted one of the midshipmen, but the seamen could not maintain their hold, the Frenchman tumbling with a cry.

The mainmast tops called down, '*Gunboats larboard beam!*'

They rushed to the portside and looked down: a small cutter and a Levantine tartane with sloping lateen sail and jury-rigged topyard, had penetrated the curtain of the broadside and came speeding in, heeling in the wind. The *Tigre*'s gunners opened fire, the 24s and 32s booming, the thud knocking the wind out of Hazzard with every percussion, the water leaping astern of the tartane, a cry going up, *she's too close in! Stand by the murderers!* Smith stood like stone at the rail and watched as the cutter's carronade blasted from its prow; there was a bright flash and cloud of streaming grey smoke, and *Tigre* reverberated with the impact. 'Damage, Mr Wright!'

Wright looked over the side, '*Larboard gunport sir, lower deck! Mr Tyte, fire as she comes to bear!*'

Smith watched, unperturbed, raising his scope. 'Who *are* these fellows…?'

'If she gets too close, sir…' asked Hazzard, watching the gunboat bearing in on them.

'Then we ram and overturn her,' he said.

Hazzard was already moving along the gangway. 'Jory, with me!' He shouted down the tweendecks, '*Nine Company to the portside rail!*'

Underhill appeared at the run, Warnock and Kite, Handley, Cochrane and Napier behind, running from the fo'c'sle where they had been sniping at the French far below. '*Sah!*'

'Firing positions! Mark your man and put him down!'

The *Tigre* marines on the quarterdeck murderer fired their load of grape-shot, battering the bows of the closest gunboat, but to little effect. Hazzard leaned out over the rail. The tartane was a thirty-foot craft, embellished with decorative rising rails at the prow and stern, a midships hatch, central mainmast, a *felucca* sail flapping madly. The second smaller cutter charged alongside, the men leaning over the gunwales shouting commands at the other crew.

Marines began shooting from the taffrail and gunports into the tartane but could not get low enough. The *Tigre* swung hard to port to crush the boat but the French cox'n kept her on course. It made no sense: Hazzard counted only six men, not enough to board an 80-gun ship of the line, yet she came in fast for the hull. Then he smelt the fumes – but Underhill got it first. He turned at the rail, his mouth open, his call reaching everyone:

'*Greek fire…!*'

Naphtha.

Hazzard turned and called to Wright, 'She's a fireship! Veer off, veer off! She's too close! Hold your fire!'

Wright rushed along the gangway rail and looked down. He spun and shouted to the helmsmen, '*Hard a'starboard! Hard over! Hold your fire! Gundecks fend off! Fend off!*'

Tigre heeled away, the tartane staggering in the crash of her wake, the French crew falling about her heaving decks. Harangued by what looked like the captain or a petty officer in a slouch hat, they began splashing kegs of liquid over the deck and starboard rails. With the increased range, two of *Tigre*'s lower-deck guns boomed and bracketed the smaller cutter, a third shot blowing her to matchwood. Wright screamed down, '*Hold your damned fire! Cease fire!*'

The French crew below looked up, their officer shouting at them and knocking one of them to the deck, two of them readying grappling hooks. Hazzard guessed they had been going to set her alight and dive overboard, to be picked up by the second boat – but even with the loss of their means of escape, their captain was bellowing at them to do it anyway.

A triple-headed grappling hook came sailing over the port rail, another further amidships snatching at the *Tigre* with a scream of metal and wood: the gunboat was caught fast. At once the deckhands began hacking at the lines of the hooks but one called out, '*It's chain! We can't cut 'em!*'

Cook bellowed down the line, '*Napier! Get the armourer and a ruddy axe, boy!*'

The big marine fetched a fire-axe and hefted it over his head, bringing it down with all his strength on one of the cables. He smashed the rail to splinters, but the hook clung on, digging into the deckboards. He swung again and again until there was a cheer and they called out '*One down!*'

The single mast of the tartane swaying before him, not fifteen feet from the rail, Hazzard judged the distance: it was feasible. He looked at Wright. 'We've got to get down there, take her helm—'

Wright stared at him. 'Are you mad? It's a floating fire-bomb—'

Hazzard called down the gangway, '*Underhill! Handley! Take lines and be ready to drop to take that ship! No guns!*'

'*Aye sir!*' He turned and bawled at the others, '*Blades in yer 'ands! Boarding party make ready, Frenchies for the askin'!*'

Dickory shrugged off his belts and equipment, '*Hold hard, Jeremiah, if you think yer doin' that without me!*'

Dickory and Handley slung their muskets on the portside rail belaying pins and caught lines thrown to them by deckhands, pulling them round their waists and over their shoulders, ready, Underhill poised, looking down. The hooked tartane swerved away from *Tigre*, then crashed into the hull, rising and falling, her crew falling about her deck, one of them crying out as he nearly fell overboard.

The spread of stays and standing rigging flashing just before him, Hazzard judged he could catch at them if he timed it properly. He threw off his *binish* and Bombay jacket, calling to Lord Keith, '*Mind yourself, sir!*'

Cook was already on him. '*No you ruddy don't, sir!*'

In his shirtsleeves, Hazzard clambered over the rail onto the main-mast stays and footboards, a line in hand, Smith calling, '*Mr Hazzard! No sir you shall not! Stop him, Mr Wright—!*'

Hazzard felt the roll of the ship, watched the tartane's mast, and jumped, his hands outstretched.

He flew out into space, the mast and sloping yard rushing towards him as he dropped, his hands out to catch the lines, something, anything, *clewline*, the rope burning, tugging as he swung round, pain lancing under his arm, his boot knocking into the swaying yard, the rigging catching him, flinging him round, *starboard stays*, a falling spider, swinging underneath, clutching at the ropes, his feet finding them as he bounced on the web.

He shinned downwards, the canvas of the sail thrashing at him as the yard tilted and collapsed with his weight on the botched stays with a crash. He rolled off into the tangle of rigging on the foredeck, the low rails around him a series of peeling carved pilasters. As he tried to right himself a pick-axe descended from nowhere, *Salaud de merde!* The pick-head crashed into the deck planks, and Hazzard drew the scimitar, thrusting upwards and out, water spraying across his face, *blood, ignore.*

He saw the others drop by their lines from above, bouncing against the broadside and then making a final leap into the boat: Dickory, Underhill and Handley. *Good.* '*Cut the grappling lines! Handley! Haul the rudder hard a-port!*'

The boat rocked and leapt, caught fast to the *Tigre* now by a single grapple. Handley fell amidships, a French crewman swinging at him with a belaying pin, missing. Handley struck out with his cutlass, slashing at the man's exposed midriff, and he cried out and fell, sliding down the deck and smashing through the cracked and ageing starboard rail, falling between the tartane and the *Tigre*, to be crushed against the hull with a scream.

Tigre loomed over them, her great lower-deck 32s and 24s just above, unable to depress far enough, so close their flaming wadding would set light to the deadly tartane gunboat. The sharp tang of the naphtha in their nostrils, Underhill yanked the line from his waist to be grabbed from behind. He spun on one knee and swung his short

Turkish *kilij*, taking one of the French crew across the face, another close behind, *Putain Bédoux!* a knife coming down, Dickory slamming a billy-club into the man's head and dropping him. Underhill jumped to his feet and laughed, '*Ah but ain't it good to be back at sea, lads!*'

''*Miah!*' shouted Dickory. '*Cut that grapple, you bloody lunatic!*'

Handley staggered to the stern, two frightened boys swinging swords fearfully at him, one with a pistol, the other snatching at his hand, '*Non! Tirez pas!*' *Don't shoot!* Handley aimed a kick but fell, the boat leaping, the boy with the pistol falling, clutching his leg, the pistol rattling across the deck and slipping overboard.

Hazzard looked up at the *Tigre* and followed the line from the foremost grapple – he saw it, bouncing and straining above their heads, leading to the mast. The boat pitched and he slipped to the open midships hatch with Dickory and Underhill. The store below decks was packed with barrels of gunpowder. The boat was not just a fireship: it was a bomb.

'*Judas'n'Mary…*' said Dickory.

Hazzard tried to reach for the line flexing over their heads. '*Get that cable! On the mast! It's the grappling line!*'

Underhill and Dickory staggered forward to the mast, Underhill taking up the pick-axe jammed in the foredeck. Dickory then turned and shouted, '*Sir!*' A boathook whistled past Hazzard's ear and dug into the hatch coaming. He spun away to find the French captain standing above him, dragging a pistol from his belt. '*Venez mourrir avec nous!*' *Come die with us!* He aimed the pistol into the hold. Hazzard kicked out at his knee, bringing him down with a grunt, the pistol clattering down the hatch among the barrels. He dived on Hazzard, clawing his way to the hatch, trying to reach it – if he pulled the trigger the boat would go up. Hazzard seized his arm, a bunched fist lashing out and knocking him away.

As Dickory made his way back to him with his billy-club, a small iron shovel swung down and struck the side of the captain's head with a metallic clang, and he fell limp, slumping over the edge of the hatch into the hold, motionless. White-faced with fear, one of the boys from the stern stood above him. '*M'sieur… je vous en prie…!*'

The boy dropped the shovel and Hazzard shouted up at him in French, '*Get to the stern and stay with Mr Handley! We shall get you to safety!*' The boy nodded and staggered to the rear.

Dickory and Underhill swung their pick-axes against the mast and cable, but without success. '*We got to bring the ruddy mast down!*' shouted Dickory and began to chop at the polished wood while Underhill tried to push it over, '*Go on Docky! Give it some spite!*'

The French boys at the stern clinging to the tilting rails in terror, Handley dragged the tiller round. With a lurch the stern of the cutter swerved violently from *Tigre*, the cable of the remaining grappling hook pulling her back by the mast, the craft heeling over. Hazzard slashed the stays and lines with the scimitar and got beside Underhill to push as Dickory chopped. The mast began to tilt. '*Nearly there!*'

'*Come on ye blighted beggar...!*' With an ear-splitting crack the forces pulled at the trunk of wood where Dickory had been chopping, and it snapped and moaned, sloping to starboard – but still the grappling line held. The starboard gunwale of the heeling tartane hit the *Tigre*'s wake, the spray flying, and they all stumbled, Hazzard clutching to the leaning mast, Dickory sliding down the tilting deck. Underhill grabbed him, *Gotcher Docky!*, one of the French boys crying out '*Sauvez-nous! Sauvez-nous!*' Save us!

Handley hauled the tiller over, 'Stand by sir!' and the deck eased to port.

'*We're nearly there, Underhill!*' shouted Hazzard and they fought their way back to heave at the mast.

Just behind him, the captain struggled upright, hauling himself out of the hatch to the hold, and saw what was happening. He snatched at Hazzard's boot, pulling him down, Hazzard rolling, kicking out, striking him in the cheek. The captain threw a fist and Hazzard locked his arm, rolling over once, twice, unable to draw the scimitar, and they crashed into the port rail – when there was a rending shudder throughout the ship and the mast tore from its housing, Underhill and Dickory roaring, '*Come on damn ye...!*'

The loosed grappling cable sprang back to *Tigre*'s broadside and the tartane rocked violently a-beam, Hazzard catching a handhold, the captain tumbling over the low port rail into the sea. The *Tigre* sheared away quickly, the crew calling down. The rigging tangled in the gunwales and rails, the mast dragging in the waves and sending aloft a fountain of spray, the gunboat ploughed nose-down into the water. Handley called from the rear, '*Abandon ship! Everyone off!*'

The young French cox'n and his mate jumped off the stern, Dickory grabbing Underhill, both knee-deep in the water, '*Come on, you barmy old sod!*'

'*But she's such a fine craft, eh Docky!*'

'*Go on with yer, dammit!*'

They leapt into the foaming water from the starboard rail, and Hazzard threw himself to the stern, calling, '*Handley! Get off!*' They stumbled among the flotsam of kegs and spars, as the stern lifted sharply.

Handley reached for him. '*Ready sir!*'

Hazzard took his hand, '*Go!*' and they jumped into the foam of the dying wake.

Swamped by the sudden cool water Hazzard wished he could drink it down, the dust of the desert still burning in his throat, now floating free, the scimitar bumping against his leg. He struck out for the surface, his face breaking water next to Handley, and they both gasped for air, sucking it in.

They watched as the second hook was thrown out to sea from the *Tigre*'s rail amidst a distant cheer. The would-be fireship tipped up vertically, her shredded rigging floating then vanishing, dragged under, gouts of air bursting from her hold. The *Tigre* roared past, slowing, her sails furling, her great stern galleries now bright, and the large taffrail lanterns shining far above. Just as the *Zealous* had done, Smith had lit her lights.

'Oddly enough, sir,' spluttered Handley, 'I shan't be sorry to see dry land after this.'

They heard distant cannon. *Zealous* turned back to port, doubtless now with Hood back aboard, firing an outraged salvo from her port quarter at the remaining gunboats. The battle, for what it had been, was over.

'Cab's here, sir,' called Handley, a jolly-boat on its way, the others climbing aboard.

The oars dipped, Cook in the prow, holding up a lantern, its dazzle lighting the swell, Wright leaning over, his hand out. 'Whatever do you do for an encore, Mr Hazzard?'

—

On the starboard gangway, the young French crewmen shivered with fright, and someone put blankets around them, Smith addressing one of them in French. The boy gave a stammering report and Smith turned to Lt Tyte. 'A mere child. Picked up in Corsica, never been to sea in his life, I'll warrant, dashed ridiculous. Get him some grog and a berth with the marines, away from the crew or they'll, what is it, *scrag* him, if I have the vernacular a-right.'

'You have indeed, sir.' The lieutenant looked at the boy. 'Come, *venez avec moi.*'

Hazzard watched as Douglas and four marines marched Major Naismith below under armed escort, his erstwhile Marine Provosts with him. Underhill and the others were already reunited in the fo'c'sle mess, their clothes drying at the galley fire. Hazzard shook off his soaked shirt and Hammer brought him a towel with a reflective chuckle. 'Quite an episode my time at sea…' He moved away discreetly as Cook approached, furious. Hazzard towelled his dripping hair, glancing at him.

'I am lighter and faster than you,' said Hazzard. 'There was no time and no one else.'

'Only a hundred marines is all.' He moved closer. 'Ye'll do it once too ruddy often. Sir.'

Lord Keith was busily looking to port, scanning the coast through a scope. Damietta seemed peaceful once more. Smith joined Hazzard and Cook, Hammer at his side, and spoke in a confidential tone. 'I gave your compliments to Major Naismith when I put him under arrest – for sabotage, mutiny, treason and all sorts of fascinating legalities, I'm sure they can decide something or other.' He glanced at Wright, busy with a repair party at the chopped and hacked portside rail. 'And if he falls overboard before Cyprus I explained I shan't mind a bit. Mr Wright—'

The lieutenant turned. 'Sir.'

'Jolly glad you're not wet as well, Mr Wright. Kindly inform Sar'nt Dickory that next time he truly wishes a bath he need only ask – and tell him well done. A half-tot for all with my compliments. Continue on present heading westward,' he said, glancing at Hazzard, 'Mr Hazzard and his men have an appointment. With luck he shall be in the nick of time.'

Wright nodded. 'I've no doubt he will be, sir.'

'We shall make it so,' confirmed Hammer. 'Upriver then off at Bulaq. Then, how would you say, we see a man about a horse, hm?'

Smith watched Wright head off to Lord Keith and said smoothly, 'Best not ask, but Lord Keith has made it plain that Naismith overstepped his authority, which was only to escort your chaps to Cyprus and no more. It was Lewis at the Admiralty who demanded your arrest.' He raised an eyebrow to Hazzard. 'An old quarrel, I believe…?'

Hazzard towelled his hair. 'Something like that.'

'Mm. Lord Keith will become our new commander in the Mediterranean, no doubt. But until then, I am the local despot.' He smiled. 'And you and I seem to be of one intent,' he said. 'Namely, to stop a certain Mr N. Bonaparte, Esquire.'

Hazzard wondered, and thought of Derrien again, the water, the fall into the sea triggering dark memories. 'Yes, sir.'

'In which case, my dear chap,' he said, 'ignore Lord Keith, and Lewis, and do *what*soever, and *how*soever, you damned well please. And that, as they say, is an order.'

Cook handed him his Bombay jacket and *Bedu* robes, and Hazzard nodded. 'Sir.'

Storm

Just before six, Cairo still modestly cool from the night breeze from the Nile, Wayland left the horses at a stable, taking a mule in part trade, Tariq striking a bargain with the owner for two gold French coins and several brass tunic buttons – and an unspoken threat by Hesse if the horses were not there when they returned. Porter piled the mule with their bedrolls and two of their muskets wrapped in old sacks – the mule was more to give them cover in the streets than transport: to be a group of men moving with no obvious purpose could arouse suspicion. De Lisle leading it by a rope halter, they joined the stream of early-morning tradesmen heading south into the city a mile distant.

After two months with the *Bedu*, Wayland had a few Arabic phrases, not enough to construct full sentences, but enough for appearances if need be – and though his French was fluent, he would rather not have to use it: his nerves were strung tight enough as they moved through the streets, part of the crowds, heads down, dusty *shemagh* to hide their faces, itinerant Bedouin come to market.

As they drew closer, Cairo rose around them, the *muezzin* calling to prayer, the city alive with the song of the minarets, the long notes sailing across the rooftops. They passed neoclassical European buildings in white stucco, set back behind walls guarded by thick-trunked palms; further on, endless terraces of brick or daub jostled shoulder to shoulder, fighting for light, rising to three and four storeys, some with ornate *mashrabiya* lattice oriel windows overhanging the streets. Where there were busy shops and traders below, there were tenement apartments above, the stark shadows of neighbouring structures slowly receding from their façades like an ebb tide, yielding to the molten bronze of the morning sun, which rose steadily into a cloudless sky.

Both the prosperous and the indigent emerged, sights of the lame awful for Wayland to behold, many half-blind, feeling their way with sticks to collapse into roughly upright postures in doorways – some then driven off by shop owners or custodians, and some given food and *zakat* charity by the beneficent, most bystanders looking on, too inured to their own suffering to attend the needs of another.

They heard the sounds of hoofbeats, and De Lisle murmured, '*Jaysus shite sir, cavalry on the trot...*'

'Eyes down, Lil...'

A column of French cavalry clopped down the road beside them, plumed *chasseur* helmets nodding, sabres bright against their dark blue. A troop sergeant at the front scanned the area, but paid them not the slightest attention.

A small group of young men, some in the white turban and *galabeyyah* of the Al-Azhar Mosque, gathered on the side of the road opposite. There was a shout at the cavalry and the sergeant stopped, looking. One of the young men threw a stone, and was joined by the others, pelting the French, calling out, '*Tahiyah Misr! Tahiyah al-Qahira!*' One ran round to the front of the group, raised a musket and fired.

The round missed, howling above their heads, chipping stone from the façade of a building opposite, the hurled missiles bouncing off the troopers' backs and shoulders, the horses whinnying, rearing up, one man nearly falling, a hand clutching at his head, crying out, *Putain alors!* The sergeant roared out, '*Troupe! En avant!*' and pulled a short carbine from his saddle bucket. He spurred his horse and charged after the group as they dived down a side-street, four cavalrymen following, the boom of the carbines echoing, the rest of the troop charging after others to scatter them across the road, people's screams rising.

'*Jaysus shite an' shite...*' muttered De Lisle, his hand closing on the sawn-off musket slung under his robes.

Wayland put a hand out to them. 'Like everyone else, we watch, in surprise. Tariq, how much further to Ezbekiya?'

Wayland had been to Cairo only once before in their two and a half months of operations, and was only vaguely familiar with the various districts. But he knew they should reach the wealthy Ezbekiya area, where the general staff had their HQs and homes in the abandoned palaces of the Mamluk beys who had since fled, either with Ibrahim to Syria, or with Murad, to continue the fight in Upper Egypt. In Ezbekiya they could contact Masoud.

They had come through the northeast of the city along a trade route used by overland merchants from the Delta who had no access to the Nile. They had passed through Zehar and headed to the river, moving south along the Nile, by the river island of Gezira. Minarets of mosques rose above the skyline as useful landmarks, though Wayland could not be certain which was which and relied upon Tariq.

'Ezbekiya, Ezbekiya,' nodded Tariq, pointing again, and Wayland could see the greatest of the magnificent domed mosques in the distance. 'Al-Azhar,' confirmed Tariq. 'Close by, Ouwayalande, close by... but careful hm, sh sh, we must be careful.'

The city was simmering; they could sense it in the shifting glances of the people as they hurried about their business with a watchful, fearful eye. Tariq was unnerved, something alerting him to a figure on the other side of the road, a man loitering in a doorway, watching them, noting them. He then ran off. Hesse saw him too. He asked Tariq, 'Informer?'

'Didn't like the look of him, Lil,' admitted Porter, his hand protectively over his shoulder-bag of medicines.

'Those men,' asked Wayland. 'What were they shouting?'

Tariq said in French, '*Vive l'Égypte*. Long live.' He spat. Wayland wondered if, for the Huwaytat, 'Egypt' existed in quite the same way as it did for a resident of the city.

Through a gap in the buildings they could see the Nile, feel its air, another sprawling river island stretching out in the blue waters. Tariq threaded their way through the lanes, turning down alleys, beneath hanging canopies, the dark fretwork window boxes overhead, crowds pausing to eat at stalls and cafés, smoke rising from broad steel pans over flaming coals, the heat worsening, the smells intoxicating – Tariq used one of their coins and bought them hot food from a streetside stall, and they shared out a ration of flatbread and soft, sticky mutton and dates, all the while fending off insistent offers to buy the mule.

Within another half-hour the streets branched out, the city buildings falling away to greater open spaces, the palaces rising before them, once grand homes of the Mamluk beys and wealthy merchants. Tariq slowed and stopped and Wayland looked back. 'What is it?'

Tariq held up a finger, listening. 'The *muezzin*...'

The call to prayer had changed. It was no longer a lilting song, but more a stream of commentary, partly sung as if to conceal its content. 'They call on the godly to rise up, *effendi*,' he said, looking about. The people in the streets had stopped and were listening to it as well. 'There is danger here, *effendi*.'

Wayland slowed as they came to a corner. Hesse and De Lisle moved ahead to find a wide thoroughfare blocked by an army checkpoint stiff with guards and sentries. A unit of army sappers dragged a barrier into place. Somewhere in the distance shots were fired, popping sounds, the cry of a crowd.

Wayland joined them and peered round. 'It's begun,' he said.

'What has, sir?' asked Porter.

De Lisle put a hand to the musket under his robe, one hand on the lock. 'Bloody trouble...'

Tariq nodded. 'We hurry. The *muezzin*,' he said, still hearing the calls over the city, 'he has not stopped.'

From behind the largest of the checkpoints emerged a stream of French officers, running to their waiting horses, some riding through and galloping off, shouting orders back at the checkpoint. With them came noble Egyptians in *kaftan* and *binish*, white *keffiyah* headdress and turbans, men of power, guessed Wayland, one of them bowing to the others and then hurrying away. He ran across the road and out of sight. De Lisle fell back. 'Sir. Got company. One oke, littl'un, dark turban, unarmed I reckon...'

Wayland looked round just as the man came skittering round the corner and stopped short in alarm, looking from one to the other. He was a small man with neatly trimmed beard, well dressed – and very nervous. He took a good look at them, Tariq with his walnut-brown face riven into hardened creases from endless days in the sun and wind; Porter clutching at his bag and reaching for the wrapped muskets on the mule; De Lisle and Hesse standing poised, ready – and their taller leader with the blue eyes. With a nervous little smile he said. 'Wayland *effendi?*'

Wayland sensed that he could trust him. He removed the *shemagh* from his face to reveal the stubble of some days, and said in French, '*Oui, c'est moi.*'

The small man breathed a sigh of relief and raised up his hands. '*Al-hamdulillah...*' He gave a quick bow of his head and said, '*As-salamu aleikum,*' then drew closer, speaking in French. 'I am Firaj, assistant and friend of Masoud ibn Yussuf *al-hakim*. He has seen you and says for you to follow me.'

Wayland looked about, feeling suddenly exposed. 'How did you know who we were?' Then he realised. 'That man, watching us.'

'The informer,' said Hesse to Tariq.

'One of his people, *effendi*, yes. You have been guarded, all of the morning. How do you say, it was the good guess. Come.'

They followed Firaj across the road to a lane in the shade. French soldiers went past, a sergeant shouting orders. The soldiers began banging on the doors of houses in the lane, shouting up to the upper storeys. One smashed in a door, a scream echoing from upstairs. The city was now a hostile place, and the conquerors were angry. A musket boomed, and another. They heard the sound of running boots, a shout and more gunshots.

Firaj hurried. 'This way, quickly—' He ducked down an alley and they followed.

The dark passage was deserted, heaped with rubbish, tall buildings either side, small windows open above, the clamour of sound clattering in the narrow confines. De Lisle hung back, suddenly awkward. 'Sir – pardon, but... I got a right flamin' leg on...'

Wayland stopped and looked at him. 'What on earth does that mean—' Then he understood. 'Here? Oh for God's sake man, of all the times—'

'Well I can't keep me banger under me trousers for much longer or I'll piss me trews...'

Just as Wayland spoke a French soldier appeared further on by the corner, undid his buttons and urinated against the building, ignoring them. '*He's doin' it, sir*,' whispered De Lisle. The soldier ran off in a rush, calling to someone, *J'arrive!*

'Hurry up then, dammit...'

Delighted, De Lisle ran to the corner once the Frenchman had passed, the stench of countless others foul and acrid in the hot air – but he cared little, his robes pulled aside and his white breeches opened, the musket slung from his shoulder. He sagged with relief against the stonework. 'Bloody 'ell sir, thank Gawd.'

Then a second French soldier appeared, and saw him. He looked at De Lisle's breeches, then saw the musket.

'*Eh, tiens! Vous—*'

De Lisle reacted out of instinct, his right hand fast as a snake, a Mamluk *shasqua* blade slipping straight into the man's throat. His trousers still round his knees he reached over quickly and took the top of the man's head in his left hand and spun him away as he withdrew the blade, a fountain of blood spraying from his neck. The Frenchman's eyes were wide as he gagged, unable to speak or breathe, and drunkenly sank to his knees in gasping silence, his musket falling to the ground. De Lisle hauled his breeches up and wiped his blade. 'Sorry, sir, won't 'appen again...'

'*Christ above*,' hissed Wayland as Firaj shrank in horror, his back to the wall.

'*Awahu lahh... ohh non non!*'

Tariq and Hesse helped drag the body further into the alley. They peered round to check the adjoining street just as an Egyptian in white turban and dark blue *binish* burst round the corner. Wayland snatched at his neck, pulled him round the corner and slammed him against the wall, a blade ready – but stopped, the man holding his hands up, whispering in English, '*It is I, it is I!*'

It took Wayland a moment: after two months he had nearly failed to recognise him. 'Masoud...?'

'Wayland *effendi!*'

Wayland nearly collapsed in relief and they embraced. 'Masoud, thank God...'

'*Al-hamdulilah*,' said Masoud. 'We say *al-hamdulillah*... Indeed, praise be to God...'

The young Alexandrian saw Firaj and the others. 'Doctor Porter, Private Leel...'

'Wotcher, Masoud,' said De Lisle.

'And a new face...' He gave a quick bow of his head, '*As-salamu aleikum.*'

Tariq put his hands together, '*Wa aleikum as-salam effendi.* Tariq. From Sir Siddani Smits.'

Masoud looked at the dead soldier without comment. He went back to the corner and looked into the road. There were more distant shots and the sound of soldiers running. Wayland ducked round the corner to look. 'Masoud, what is going on?'

'The city, *effendi*,' said Masoud. 'It is ready for, how do you say, *l'émeute...*?'

Wayland looked at him. 'Riot. Yes, we've seen...' He fished Smith's list out of his pocket. 'I want to confirm these sightings, Masoud, to see if we can find Derrien.'

Masoud's eyes hardened. 'The Citizen Derrien. Yes, the most feared man in Cairo.'

Masoud looked at the list and looked bleakly back at Wayland. 'Hassan in Rosetta has also this place, and this... but—' He shrugged helplessly. 'How we have tried, but cannot predict where he will be, he has no reliable pattern of movement.' Masoud thought quickly. Much like Wayland, the Alexandrian interpreter who had so desperately gripped Hazzard's hand that first day that Nelson had arrived, begging him to return, had grown in daring and confidence into an embedded spy and resistance operative. 'There are checkpoints everywhere, *effendi*, but I have the pass, I can get us through. I work with the general's aide, Devernois, at their *Quartier général*, the army command offices.'

'Which general?' asked Wayland.

'Bonaparte.'

'Good God.'

Masoud was less impressed with himself. 'I handle command despatches and general contract law, *effendi*. I do what I can. The source of much of this rebellion is at the Al-Azhar Mosque, some distance to the northeast of here. There are two safe places: Ezbekiya, and the area of the Institute, at the Bayt al-Sinnari.'

'The *Institut d'Égypte*?' asked Wayland. 'Surely that will be one of the first targets of any mob—'

'No, no, it is very discreet, quiet, I showed the house to the older man, the Citizen Monge, and he took it over, with the nearby houses. It is where they live.' He met Wayland's worried gaze. 'Fear not, Wayland *effendi*. Devernois thinks me a fool, but together Firaj and I confound them all. Come.'

They covered the dead infantryman with some discarded sacking they found and left him in the shadows, following Masoud to the next side-street. 'Come,' he said, 'we go to Nasriya... by the Al-Zahir.'

They moved out of the alley and down a short market street to a corner, no one paying any notice, and soon found themselves on a main road running north–south. A company of French troops marched past, a platoon of *chasseurs* running beside them, overtaking them, scattering around the streets. Wayland heard more gunfire in the distance.

They joined the crowd hurrying south, possibly to the citadel or the Zaheb mosque a few streets away, its Moorish castellations stark against the blue, its minaret rising sharp, piercing the sky. The roads splintered into local lanes and markets, groups of people gathering, many of them young men, some in the white robes of the Al-Azhar Mosque, some not, others shouting, pushing and shoving, arguing with each other.

Masoud skirted them quickly. Hidden by market stalls at the head of a lane was another group of men passing out muskets from a cart. Carts had come along the main thoroughfares and were stopping at certain points to distribute weapons. Once armed, the men dispersed in the nearby lanes, calling, shouting to each other.

'Come along, hurry,' said Masoud, only now aware of what they had walked into.

They rounded the corner to an open junction where they saw a gathering crowd on the far side. Standing on an upturned crate was an older bearded man haranguing his listeners. More began to gather, arguments breaking out.

'*Jaysus shite an' all...*' muttered De Lisle, slipping one hand under his *binish* to the sawn-off Charleville slung from his left shoulder.

Hesse and Porter were both loaded and rammed, Porter squinting into the distance, his spectacles tucked away. 'It's like market-day on every corner.'

Wayland leaned close to Masoud and Tariq. 'What's he saying?'

'He says,' began Tariq, 'the French are godless, without religion... More will come, with fighting vessel... ships, yes, ships of battle... as high as mountains...'

'Reckon we should scarper, sir,' suggested De Lisle.

Wayland glanced at the mule, calculating the weight and speed of the beast in the streets if they had to run for it. 'Chaps. Be ready to bolt if it comes to it. If separated, Nasriya, the Institute. Clear?'

They murmured *aye*, and began to back away. Tariq rapped a phrase at Masoud, who muttered a quick reply. More people gathered, of all colours, affiliations and tribes, some like criminal gangs firing their muskets in the air – others began to shout, raising their fists, *Allahu akbar!* With them was a man on a horse, in dark turban and robes, a musket slung openly over his shoulder. Wayland recognised him from Kafr-Shahabas. It was one of the Tarabin *Bedu*. The Tarabin horseman pointed down the street and the crowd looked.

'He say,' said Tariq, 'all French...' he looked at Wayland, 'must die.'

Masoud backed away, pulling Tariq. 'Wayland *effendi*,' said Masoud. 'We must go I think.'

Wayland needed no telling. 'Yes. Go...' he said.

The mob burst and spread like an eager flame. An enraged flock of birds, the crowd streamed out of the junction and down the streets, the sound of glass shattering, the popping of musketry and stones pelting wooden shutters, doors, screams as people fled, a man in an apron, another, both Egyptian, knocked to the ground and then blotted from Wayland's sight by the press of bodies as they kicked and beat him. They stormed into his shop, smashing it to pieces, carrying off its contents, others moving on to the next.

More French cavalry clattered down the main road, a huntsman's horn blowing, and the Tarabin on the horse rode off, the crowd at his heels, calling out, the cavalry scattering the protesting mob, swords swinging. Some turned and were run down, others turned and raised their hands, clawing at the French, a trooper dragged from the saddle and pounded repeatedly with clubs and staves, another trooper slashing at them, taking a hand, a head, his mount rearing, trampling others. Fire broke out, flames lashing at a shop, smoke belching across the main road, the streets alive with people running, yet littered with the remains of the dead and injured. A man rushed past them, seizing Wayland by the arm, as if he could be some form of shelter or protection, his face showing only fear as he ran from the scene. Wayland thought of Malta, and the flight of the civilians of Sliema from the invasion landings in the harbour, their panic, their frenzy, and he knew nothing could stop them.

Masoud led the way down a narrow lane, De Lisle and Porter running hard behind, muskets in hand. Wayland snatched their packs from the mule, Hesse pulling the braying animal at a fast trot. Gunshots and hoofbeats echoing, they ran past shops and stalls, owners slamming their doors, staff bringing in tables and chairs from coffeeshops and *ahwa* tea-rooms.

'*At some point,*' gasped Wayland, jogging along beside Masoud, '*It will be better to be French than Bedu.*'

'*Indeed, effendi. Soon!*'

The buildings rose around them from a tight grid of streets, a market trader hauling his cart in desperation, unable to pull fast enough, looking over his shoulder, running, leaving it behind. It teetered momentarily on its two cartwheels, then tipped forward onto its long, cracked harness shafts. At a junction ahead, a small mob rushed down an adjoining street across their bows, some stopping, seeing Wayland and the others. One waved a club overhead and called out.

Hoofbeats echoed and the men turned, looked, and continued running, a squad of pursuing French cavalry riding through them, the man with the club struck by the chest of a horse and thrown bodily into the corner of a building, only to be trampled by the horses behind.

'We must go south...' cried Masoud, and led them to the right, past a torn awning, potted plants knocked over, a window broken, furniture smashed to pieces, a shutter hanging from its hinges. Lying half in the road, half over the threshold of an open doorway, the stricken door shattered, an Egyptian girl in a black *hijab* leaned over the unmoving form of a woman in European dress, a man nearby on his front, the pale linen tailcoat torn up his back, a sleeve ripped away, blood down the arm. The girl saw them and waved her hands, crying out, tears streaked down her face.

Tariq keeping watch in the road, Porter dashed towards them and knelt beside the woman, reaching into his bag. She was olive-skinned, her morning dress torn, a short-waisted linen jacket gashed at the shoulder – a smear of blood ran from her forehead, and she lay unconscious.

The girl clutched at Firaj, looking at the other marines fearfully. Firaj spoke quietly to her and she replied in sobs, pointing up and down the narrow lane. 'She says it is her mistress and master, from the consul, she her servant, that they were set upon...'

Porter put a hand to the woman's neck and listened to her chest. 'Breathing, sir,' he said to Wayland, and felt round the back of her skull. 'Knock on the head most like...' He waved a small phial of salts under her nose and the woman coughed and groaned, her hands rising weakly. 'There's a good lass...' murmured Porter and moved next to the man, turning him over.

He rolled onto his back, a well-groomed, dark-haired gentleman with black moustache and beard, collar and cravat, his cheekbone black with bruising and a bloodied forehead. His eyes flickered. '*Rana*...' he gasped.

'He's with us, sir,' declared Porter, Wayland crouching down beside him, 'groggy but with us.'

'Let's get him up,' said Wayland. 'De Lisle, get the lady onto the mule.' The man sat up onto one elbow, blinking, trying to focus, saw Hesse and De Lisle lifting the lady to the mule. 'Rana—'

Porter held him fast and said in his heavy Belgic French, 'She will be well, *ne vous inquiètez pas*, do not worry.'

The man looked at them, confused at their dress. 'Fr-*Français*? I am Theokritos, *M'sieur* Theokritos, *apo tin Ellada*... from Peiraias... th-the delegation...' Stricken at the sight of his wife, he began to weep,

'She is Turkish, I am Greek, th-they said we should never have come – *what have I done*—'

They hefted him up slowly, wary of syncope, but Theokritos scrambled to his feet as they lifted Rana onto the mule, the Egyptian girl climbing on behind, holding her steady, speaking in Greek to Theokritos, who took her hand and patted it gratefully. Masoud took him by the hand, '*Éla, viásou,*' he said, *Come, hurry.*

Tariq came at a run, '*Isri ya,* fast now please…' Firaj ran onwards to another broad road, then looked back waving at them. 'This way!'

The girl holding Rana tight round the waist on the mule, they hurried to the end of the road and looked. The gathering crowds had run north, to their left, pursued by squads of infantry shooting volleys into the air, then firing into the crowds. Barricades had been dragged across the main thoroughfare, the mob rushing round them, defending them or attacking them, Wayland could not tell, some of them falling, spinning away as the muskets cracked.

'*Run!*' he shouted, and Hesse smacked the mule, honking in complaint, the girl kicking it with her heels, the tearful Theokritos alongside, one hand up to them both, Tariq and the marines covering their flanks, muskets out, trying to shield them.

The road was strewn with the dead, French and Egyptian. Fast-moving *chasseurs à pied* came dodging up the verges, from one broken shopfront to the next. One took a shot, and his fellows ran forward while he reloaded, maintaining a steady rate of accurate fire. Looters rushed from body to body, one rising up and swinging a club at Firaj, Masoud crashing into him, his hand quick into his robe and out, and the looter spun, a spurt of blood rising from his neck. Wayland watched Masoud but the Alexandrian seemed to think nothing of it. '*Wayland effendi! Come!*'

Hesse called up to the girl on the mule, '*Hold tight*—' and she nodded, her dark intense eyes wide but determined. 'Faster!' she cried in French. 'I shall not let my lady go!'

They reached the safety of the street opposite and dived into the protection of the buildings. At the end of the lane was a sharp left turn, and a mews passage between a short parade of grand houses – Masoud cried out, '*Here!*' and they dashed round the corner. At the far end was a fine two-storey house, gardens behind, spreading trees offering shade.

'Bayt al-Sinnari,' gasped Masoud, running alongside Wayland. 'The Institute.'

The houses were more like small mansions behind high walls, grand *bourgeois* residences not unlike those in London or Paris. The mule then refused to go any further, leaning back against Hesse's grip, the rope harness taut but the animal unyielding. The sound of the mob nearby was enough to spur them on, and Wayland called, 'Theokritos! Take her, now!'

The Greek plucked Rana from the mule's back, her arms going round his neck, the girl climbing down and running with them, Hesse taking her hand, her dark robes flying behind, the mule trotting off to one of the gardens, Wayland shouting out in French, 'All of you! Run! Masoud – be ready to pass us through!'

Several grenadiers in their white and grey uniforms and tall dark mitre caps turned at the gate of the house at the sound of the shouting and Masoud began to call out, '*Français! Français! Au secours au secours! Please help!*'

Seeing Hesse, Porter and De Lisle with their muskets, the grenadiers were immediately alert, levelling their own weapons. '*Arrêtez! Qui vive!*'

'*Caporal!*' cried Masoud in relief. 'I am so pleased to see you. The crowds, they are coming,' he said, fumbling with his papers, stamped, *Quartier général de l'armée, Assistant Première Classe, interprète. ADC Devernvois 23ème db.* 'I am Masoud ibn Yussuf and this is my assistant—'

The grenadier took his papers but shook his head, one hand out. 'Pass on, I cannot take you in – the Institute is closed up for—'

Wayland reached them, the servant girl in black behind, Theokritos gasping, Rana in his arms, and he spoke in his rapid Strasbourg-accented French. '*Caporal* – I am *Capitaine* d'Hauteville, on special assignment with the 25th *Infanterie de marine*, attached Division Dugua,' he said, blowing out a breath. 'This is *M'sieur* Theokritos and his wife of the Greek delegation, and they need medical attention at once—' He reached for the gate, but the corporal stepped forward and put a hand out to stop him.

'Sir, I cannot let you in—'

At that moment a company of infantry matched into the mews lane from round the corner of the building in a column of threes and crashed to a halt. Sergeants ran forward and began separating them into platoon details, two officers heading towards the grenadiers at the gate curiously.

'Sir...' murmured De Lisle from behind, cocking his musket.

Wayland turned on the grenadier, red-faced, furious. 'Yes you *will*, *damn it*, or I shall tell the QG in Ezbekiya that three men at the Institute took it upon themselves to break our trade treaty with the port of Peiraias and not give succour to a friend of the state!' he shouted, his face inches from the grenadier's. 'Or should I tell Citizen *Croquemort* that you should guard the bloody *Sphinx* in the desert for the rest of your days?'

At the sound of Derrien's dread nickname the grenadier corporal looked them over in turn, at their *Bedu* robes, their sawn-off Charlevilles, and the evident quality of the clothes on Theokritos and Rana. 'All right, all right...' He began to unlock the gate. 'What happened to her...?'

'The mob is out for blood,' said Wayland. 'Be ready.'

'I beg of you,' said Theokritos, 'please hurry...'

The grenadier corporal swung the gate open as one of the infantry officers drew closer, looking Wayland up and down, amused.

'My, my, Captain Sinbad, I presume. Been in the wars have we...?' he asked languidly. 'Or are we just overdressed...?'

Wayland shot him a filthy glance. 'Not quite. Some of us happen to work for a bloody living.'

'*Ooh dear...*' the officers chuckled between themselves, but the grenadier corporal opened the ornate iron gate for Wayland, and looked at the infantry officers with instant dislike. He snapped at his colleague, 'Check their warrants, no one inside.' He nodded to Wayland. 'Sorry for the delay sir, down there...'

Theokritos was exhausted but carried the lady down the dark passage into a spreading courtyard, the house rising all around. A fountain sprinkled in the centre in the shade of a spreading tree, and beyond they could glimpse the front gardens. Stone steps in the corner led up to an upper-floor doorway, a balcony with dark *mashrabiya* screens overlooking them, stretching over another passage.

Wayland looked up to see a soldier coming down the steps, heavy-set, older than most, coming slowly down towards them, a frown on his face. Wayland had never seen him before: it was *Sergent-chef-major* Achille Caron of the 75th Invincibles.

Revolt

Instead of heading west to Rosetta, Smith set Hazzard and the marines ashore later that same morning on the dead stretch of shore near the camp where he had found them; they had left their horses with several Beni Qassim awaiting their return. Driven by the same determination that had taken him from England so many months earlier, Hazzard and the marines set off for the capital – they were some eight hours behind Wayland, and he pushed them hard.

They thundered down the hardened dusty roads, their formation so tight they looked like dragoons to distant French infantry and Mamluks to the *fellahin*. Napier was no natural rider, but he had learned to hang on like Handley and Kite, who whooped with joy at the speed of the Arabian horses. But Cook fought him at every step.

'*There's no point cackin' us all out for nuppence in the middle o'nowhere,*' he shouted at Hazzard.

'*Their lordships are happy to sit back and watch while these poor bloody people get blown to bits,*' called Hazzard in reply. '*We might find Shajar and the Tarabin, get their men out in time – it could be happening right now!*'

'*But we can't stop it!*'

'*I've got to try, dammit Jory!*' snapped Hazzard. He thought of Ali-Qarim, of Nazir, those wasted souls, so ready to sacrifice themselves for something better – and everything had failed. Bonaparte was still here, and had walked into Cairo. '*I've just got to try...*'

The night was colder with the advent of autumn, and they made good headway along the less frequented roads, having to avoid French forces only twice – the Delta seemed deserted of its new conquerors, who doubtless felt safer in their camps and depots. They met a unit of *chasseurs* outside Mansouria, but their robes and speed put the Frenchmen off, as if it were too much trouble to challenge them. Nevertheless, the Mamluk scimitar of Ali-Qarim hung ready at Hazzard's side, and the Lorenzoni had a full seven rounds in its chamber.

They would reconnoitre first. Hazzard knew the *Bedu* did not like to enter Cairo, preferring to keep to themselves, unless travelling in force. Having come in with such fighters as the Tarabin, Shajar would have the power to get Hazzard to the sheikhs of the Al-Azhar, to Al-Jabarti at least, to dissuade the ringleaders, make them see *sense* – tell them that no one was coming to their aid, not a ship, not a single gun.

Wayland would be with Masoud and Masoud always said there were two safe places: the Viennese consulate and the Institute. It was his only starting point. Hazzard thought of Lord Keith and William Sidney Smith. '*Damn them...*' he muttered, then found himself shouting, '*Damn them!*' and charged off ahead of the others, forcing them to catch up.

Within two days they had reached Bulaq, Cairo's chief port. There were French sentries everywhere, but they were more interested in inspecting carts and baggage trains, the arch of the gate staffed by Cairo customs men busied with the offloading of cargo from the river. Hazzard looked out at the Nile, at its vast breadth. He looked at the far side, and thought of Embabeh, of rolling down the mud embankment and floating downriver with the dead, so much carrion for the vultures.

For nothing.

He resolved otherwise. *This*, he thought, *would be something.*

Their robes, *keffiyah* headdresses and turbans were sufficient to pass them through. '*Shukran,*' said Hazzard, making a sign of gratitude to the gatekeepers as they rode through at an unhurried walk, Underhill removing his *shemagh*, revealing his beard and scarred dark face. To the Egyptian guards of Cairo, here was a troop of *Bedu* from the Sinai – allies against the French. An artillery sergeant watched them go with a wary eye: but even the *Bedu* came to the grand mosques to pray.

'Strangers in a 'eathen land again,' muttered Cook next to him.

Hazzard kicked his heels in. 'Come on.'

They took the centre of the boulevard at a light gallop, forcing a path through traders with mule-teams and carts. After a mile they passed through squares and junctions, deserted but for large groups of men gathered at the corners. They slowed, watching as they went by, older men shouting at the crowd, the younger men calling back, then raising their fists and calling on Murad, calling on Ibrahim, on God himself: *Allahu akbar!*

'*Christ a'mighty…*' muttered Cook.

They moved deeper into the city. By noon the heat had set in – but trouble had already begun, their skin crawling with apprehension. The few people in the streets had begun to hurry away, some disappearing indoors, others simply rushing, pointing, fearful.

'Don't like this, Sarge,' muttered Warnock.

'Close watch, lads,' whispered Underhill, 'nice an' easy…'

They came to a long road, low tenements, cafés and markets on the right, larger civic buildings and private residences on the left, behind high plastered walls. In the distance they could see a platoon of infantry, some standing picket duty, some going into gateways, coming out, stopping, looking, waiting for some distant threat to materialise.

Hazzard brought them to a halt. They clustered together, looking out over the city. Cook nodded at the skyline. 'Bloody hell…'

Palls of smoke rose from distant fires, drifting across the rising domes, ashen shadows passing over the city. The *muezzin*'s call to prayer from the nearby minaret grew harsh and angry.

'They were right,' whispered Hazzard.

'What's that din…?' said Kite, walking his horse forward to Hazzard's left, and they listened. It was the sound of a waterfall, the same surge they all knew from below decks when the pumps were working, tons of water crashing and churning, and for a moment Hazzard feared the Nile had burst its banks. The French infantrymen in the distance began to run. Cook was first to guess.

'*By all that's holy in Bristol,*' he cursed, '*Off the ruddy road!*'

A hundred yards further up, a roaring tide of people came rushing round the corner straight towards them, smashing shops, breaking in doors, throwing stones, tearing apart market stalls, strewing goods across the street, their cries mingling with the screams of residents slamming their doors, barricading themselves in.

The French infantry fell back from their guard-posts, turning, forming lines and retiring, *Préparez! En joue! Feu!*, their volleys booming out, trying to maintain a withering fire, killing a dozen in the front of the mob but with little effect, the crowd a headless, mindless beast, unstoppable – the infantry were trampled, beaten, clubbed and stabbed to death in the road. Hazzard looked ahead: further up on their left was a set of gateposts in a high wall, a large white manse set well back from the road. He saw French soldiers struggling to close the heavy gates – they had mere moments to act.

Hazzard lashed his horse with the reins, '*Marines to me!*' They galloped up the road, straight at the oncoming crowd.

But before they could reach the elegant house the crowd found it, a tributary of the main flow pouring into the gateway. The iron hinges howled as they were torn from their mounts, the guardsmen trying to close them – but they were thrown back by the press of people, the gates crashing against their white posts with a resounding clang, one gate falling, the crowd roaring.

Charging up from behind them at full speed came a troop of Arab horse, a sheikh in fine blue and white robes driving into the mob, beating them down with a crop, his *sanjaqs* on horses beside him, trying to stem the tide. Hazzard turned and headed straight for him just as the flow of people poured around them. '*Yallah!*' he shouted down and rode through them, men diving aside, the marines following close, their muskets out, ready.

'*Salam, ya sheikh!*' cried Hazzard. '*Ana Hazar Pasha, injiliz!*' he called, then added in English, '*I ride in the name of Ali-Qarim Sheikh and Nazir ibn Salah ar-Rahman!*'

The sheikh whipped round to look at him, tugging his mount about, the dark ostrich plumes on its magnificent tack dancing, bobbing, his *sanjaqs* kicking out at the protestors roaring down the road past them.

'Ali-Qarim Sheikh,' cried one of the sheikh's men. '*Al-ma'rakati al-Imbaba!*'

The battle at Embabeh.

The Battle of the Pyramids.

'*Hazar Pasha…?*' The sheikh looked at him more closely, at the robes, the red tunic just visible beneath. In thickly accented French the sheikh called to him, 'I fear for the French citizens – as does the sultan! We must hurry—' he called, pointing up ahead at the shattered gates. '*Al-musteshfa askari!* They go into the military hospital – there are women and children!'

The sheikh charged his horse, two men falling beneath the hooves, the *sanjaqs* behind him beating down at others with whips, one firing his carbine in the air. Hazzard tugged his horse about. '*To me!*' They charged through the crowd, the people parting, streaming past them. '*Keep up, Jory, for Christ's sake!*'

'Well slow down then, dammit!' shouted the sergeant. 'Marines to me!'

'They's gone barmy, Sarge! Look at 'em...!' called Pettifer beside him.

'Then get after him, Petty!'

They charged through the smashed iron gates. Dead sentries lay splayed over low walls, in the gardens, in the stone drive, looters pulling their uniforms to pieces, the rioters madly beating clubs into the dead bodies. Others streamed through the open courtyard gardens, two men in red fez and European clothes knocked down, clubs smashed into their upturned faces. Hazzard cocked the Lorenzoni and shot one of the attackers – the man flew backwards into the fountain, and his companions bolted, heading for the main entrance.

Hazzard saw them charge through a pair of tall double doors and jumped down. '*Keep hold of the horses! Aim low at anyone who comes close!*'

He saw stables round the back, outbuildings connected to form courtyards to the main building. Inside was a main entrance hall converted into a barracks ward, dark and suddenly cool, low cots laid out in rows, fevered and injured French troops and Egyptians lying helpless. There was a small gang of some fifteen men running between the beds, stabbing in a frenzy at the screaming patients with daggers and bayonets. Pettifer ran in after him and they looked about, at the bloodied sheets, the dead arms hanging from bedsides. '*Jaysus an' all...*'

Hazzard drew his scimitar, anything to distract them. '*Yallah, majnooniyah!*' he cried, *Come, you fools!* and they looked back at him, stopping dead.

Pettifer readied his blunderbuss. 'Sir...'

They charged straight at the pair of them. Hazzard ran to meet them, the scimitar flying fast in two loops, three men falling as he spun into their centre, full circle, cutting at waist level, slicing through the crush in a tight arc, the space between the beds became a crowded fighting deck until they ran, crying out, tripping over each other, maimed and wounded, and Pettifer shouted, '*Sir! Go left!*'

Hazzard dropped low and the blunderbuss roared – five men screamed, flung back onto the beds of their victims, two of them dead, the others clutching their abdomens and groins. The sheikh appeared at the end of the hall, '*Hazar!*' His *sanjaqs* fired two shots at the ceiling and the mob fled in panic. Hazzard ran back to the doors.

'Ain't good out there, sir...' warned Pettifer, running after.

Outside, the marines cleared the main yard, firing, chasing the mob back to the road with volley-fire, the sheikh's men firing beside them. Handley called, '*Petty! Sir! They got some o'the nurses! Women! Out in the street!*'

Cook charged out first. '*Marines to me! Take 'em down, 'Andy, and no messin'!*'

Hazzard heard the screams and leapt into the saddle, *God above*, his face dripping with sweat, his heart pounding, *this is no revolt: it's a savage bloody riot* – thinking of Sarah, trying to save her as if she were out there. He hauled his mount round, the sheikh beside him shouting to his men, '*Isri ya!*' Hurry.

In the road they found a growing circle of the rioting crowd, in their midst four women being pulled and pushed in all directions – an Egyptian girl had her robes torn away and she screamed, half-naked, a stone battering her, a fist into her mouth, until she was driven to the ground, the men diving on her, kicking and hitting her with their clubs and sticks, *Fransaya! Fransaya!*

Underhill was first in, trampling a knot of men, the horse's hooves smashing into their backs, kicking them away, his Charleville barking, its buckshot dropping two. One handed, he swung the butt up and over to smash another, and another, the crack of wood sharp in the air. Handley tore in after him with Kite, Napier dropping another. The big boxer jumped down from his horse and hurled a fist, smashing the jaw of one, a straight left crashing into another. He took the man's club and waded into them, knocking them aside, roaring, taking up one of the Egyptian nurses, shielding her under one arm, '*Cocky...!*'

Cochrane charged for him and fired into the group as Napier put the girl on his saddle. Kite leaned down for one of the other Egyptian girls who managed to break free, pulled her up and rode out, hacking with a cutlass at the hands that reached for her – *Fransaya! Fransaya!* They were too late for one nurse, kicked and beaten to death, stripped and stamped upon, a smear in the dust on the road, some of them holding up her torn bloody robes in their hands triumphantly. The sheikh fired a shot from a pistol and dropped one of the perpetrators, his comrades running, stumbling over his falling body.

In the thickest group, the mob had split into factions, tugging on the wrists of two European women, yanking them back and forth, and Hazzard crashed straight through them, the horse knocking them down, rearing up, its hooves clawing at the air in fright. '*Ana al-Aafrit al-ahmar!*' *I am the Red Devil*, he shouted. '*You betray God's law!*'

The Lorenzoni boomed, a .50 calibre pistol ball crashing into one of the men holding the woman's wrists, removing most of his arm and shoulder, his companions falling away. Hazzard cranked the loading arm of the pistol and fired at the other, the round hitting the base of the man's throat, the head dropping to one side, partially severed, his body crumpling, and they scattered, screaming, *Yallah! Yallah!*

He spun the horse about, the nurse reaching for him – and in that moment recognised her: from a scene of chaos on the gunboats on the Nile at Shubra Khit, amid twenty-five thousand French and six thousand Mamluk horse – when he had tried to rescue Sarah. He leaned down for her, his hand out, '*Madame—*' She grabbed madly for his arm, '*M'sieur!*' one foot on a stirrup, climbing fast, she pulled herself up behind him, her arms strong, tight round his waist.

The sheikh rode into view beside him. '*Hazar! You must go!*' called the sheikh, '*We shall hold them! Rabbena ma'ak!*'

Hazzard thanked him, '*Shukran, ya sheikh!*' and shouted over his shoulder, '*Jory! Out, dammit!*'

'*Comin' fast's I ruddy can!*' cried Cook as he took the hand of the second Frenchwoman, who used his leg as a ladder and shinned up behind him onto the rump of the horse. '*'Miah! Get 'em out! Anyone in the way,*' he called, '*bloody kill 'im!*'

'*Out of it, ye scarlet heroes!*' shouted Underhill, Warnock riding down another, stopping, looking at the dead Egyptian girl in the road then turning, enraged, to smash his tomahawk down onto another skull, then two more, left and right, and another, the stone axehead embedding itself in bone, '*How's that eh! How's bloody that!*' Dismounting to finish one off, the axe striking again and again, *bastard bastard*, he swung his gun-arm up and fired his musket at them as they ran, the buck-and-ball load blasting two of them off their feet as they pushed each other to get away from the scene. '*Piss-waters! Bloody shitin' piss-waters!*'

Handley grabbed the bridle of his lone horse and rode up to him. '*Knocky, for Chrissake!*'

Underhill joined them, his voice roaring, '*Marine Private Knock-bloody-knock! On thy ruddy equine transport, fast as Davey's arse!*'

Spattered with blood, Warnock mounted, spitting after the crowd. '*Fackin' piss-waters, Sarge! Piss-waters!*'

'*Come on, bye, come!*'

The sheikh's men rode into the mob and drove them off as Hazzard led them at a gallop down the road. '*M'sieur,*' called the nurse into Hazzard's ear from behind, '*You are the one, from the Nile...*'

'*Where are the doctors?*' shouted Hazzard, outraged. 'The damned surgeons? *Les chirurgiens?*'

'Some at the army camps, or the Institute—'

'*The what?*'

'*Bayt al-Sinnari*—'

French infantry came at the run, horses drawing artillery-pieces bouncing on their limbers, sniping shots cracking from high windows, some of the French falling, shooting back. They came to a junction of streets, devastation everywhere, market stalls torn apart, carts upturned. A shop was on fire, groups of frantic tradesmen and stall-holders struggling with buckets of water from a distant fountain, the flames out of control. '*Down there,*' she called and pointed.

The marines behind him, they charged across the junction, French troops shouting, shots snapping behind at protesters but no one pursuing. Hoofbeats clattering with a sudden deafening echo in the confines of the narrow streets, they slowed to a walk and came to a gradual halt, exhausted. Hazzard looked round at them all.

The marines looked back at him, dusty faces and robes now black with smoke, some smeared with blood. Some of them coughed, Pettifer reloading his blunderbuss, Kite staring, Napier spitting on his knuckles and wiping them.

'All clear in the boat?' asked Hazzard.

One after the other came the *aye* he had been hoping for: they had all kept up, and had saved four. *Madame* Lascelles began to shake behind him, and clung more tightly to his back, suddenly sobbing.

'Madam...' he said, '...you are safe...'

She nodded her head and one of the Egyptian girls, sitting behind Handley, began to weep as well.

'What is your name?' asked Hazzard.

Madame Lascelles tried to take a breath, but her shoulders shook violently and she could not answer. The Egyptian nurse behind Kite reached out for her, and he brought his horse nearer so they could touch. Each held the other's hand tight.

'Bloody 'ell, sir...' said Kite.

Underhill nodded, one side of his face dark with blood and powder, the whites of his eyes bright in the dim street. 'They all done good sir, aye. Took down a good few o'them bloody mad buggers.'

'Frogs'll slaughter 'em to a man…' said Cook. '*Chrissakes…*'

Warnock stared at the ground, his free hand still clutching his tomahawk, red with blood from the street. He shook his head and spat, '*Piss-waters…*'

Hazzard nodded at him. 'Well done, everyone.' He glanced at Kite. 'Never took you for a steeple-chaser, Kite.'

'Must be all that runnin' from the law, sir.'

The marines chuckled. Hazzard could feel Delphine's sobs subsiding. 'I am… Delphine-Marie Lascelles…' she said, her voice barely above a whisper.

Hazzard squeezed the hand round his waist. 'Do not worry now, Delphine.' He glanced at Cook. 'The white robes – they're from the Al-Azhar. If they started this, Bonaparte will break them. The only safe place now is the Institute. If anything we might find Masoud or word of him, and make contact.'

'If Mr Wayland found him at all…' said Cook, looking up at the high windows above, then back up the street. 'Less he walked right into the ruddy Frog army.'

'Don't say it.'

'If they close the roads we've had it—'

'We'll have had it when the damned artillery starts up, Jory. He'll blow the place to pieces. I know him.'

'Why would he risk that? Hit his own men, hit ruddy everythin', it's barkin' mad—'

'Because it's what Caesar would do, and it's what he did before in Paris, a riot of royalists, and he laid his bloody great guns and blasted them all to kingdom come. Made him hero of the damned Revolution…'

'Aye well, let's ruddy leave 'em to it.'

'If we can get to Shajar and her men, or the Azhar, we could stop it before it goes too far, and *get them out*—'

'Get bloody who out?'

Hazzard looked back up the street. He had no answer.

'She's not here!' shouted Cook, 'She's *gone* dammit! An ye won't be bringin' her back by saving this lot!'

Hazzard stared at him.

Sarah.

Breathing heavily, Cook looked away, red-faced, staring at the road, his horse tossing its head, sidestepping, nervous at their shouting. Hazzard watched him and hated him for being right.

'I know.'

He looked at him, both of them replaying memories, of heat, and fire, of jungle or sea, of Hazzard's recklessness: from the mud and reeds of the banks of the Nile as five French divisions wheeled ponderously south in formation to take Cairo, Cook had said the same words, and he repeated them under his breath. 'You can't save 'em, sir.'

Hazzard's eyes burned, the heat, the dust, his robes suddenly choking, and he threw off one sleeve. He stank. He could feel the sweat streaming down his sides, the leather of belts, slings and straps biting into him. Was it Delphine, he wondered, feeling her behind him, her arms holding him, that had made him think immediately of Sarah, that all of Cairo was, somehow, Sarah needing to be saved.

'I can't leave them.' He thought of Shajar holding up Smith's coin. 'A gold sovereign's not worth it.'

Cook watched him. Both knew the odds were heavily against it but they both still prayed for luck. 'Aye.'

'Delphine,' said Hazzard, 'which way...'

She gathered herself, drawing her torn dress and shawl over her shoulders. It was hot but she was still shivering. 'Near the mosque – Al-Sayeda Zainab...' She pointed. 'Down there...'

Barricade

Caron descended the steps and saw Theokritos and the injured woman in his arms. He called a couple of men who ran down to help carry her up the stairs, Masoud speaking very quickly, '...*from the consulate, and this lady insists to stay at her side...*'

Wayland approached, guessed Caron was some sort of senior warrant-officer and made his report. '*Chef*,' he said, '*Capitaine* d'Hauteville, 25th *Infanterie de marine*. Found her in a doorway badly knocked about. The crowds are murderous – and coming this way.'

Caron did not recognise Wayland, but all the while he peered at De Lisle, Porter and Hesse, as if something pricked a memory, but he could not be sure what it was. 'Then come, *mon capitaine*,' said Caron, bidding the others to follow. '*M'sieur* Masoud,' he said, 'to safety, with us.' Masoud and Firaj pulled Tariq along, the small Bedouin looking around in wonder as they followed Caron up the steps.

'*Elle a la fièvre, Chef*,' said Porter in as thick an Ostend twang as he could muster – the only place he had ever spoken French on voyages across the North Sea. 'She is too hot, the concussion, it causes the humours to react. The doctor, *le grand chir'gien*, Desgenettes, is he here...?'

They followed Caron into the darkness of the house, the old sergeant calling back, 'Yes, but others as well...'

'Bloody impressive, doc,' muttered Wayland to Porter. 'Brass balls, De Lisle. Like our Yorkshireman here.'

Very uncomfortable, De Lisle hurried behind, looking about him, as if waiting to be pounced upon. 'Sounds 'bout right, sir...'

Caron moved quickly behind the men with the diplomats. Wayland marched along, very much the captain of the 25th Marines, his men behind him, their robes attracting some attention, but not much in the circumstances. They entered a side door on the first floor, and found a scarcely controlled panic. The interior was dark and cool, rising high to ornate carved ceilings. Soldiers and civilians rushed everywhere, turning tables and chairs upside-down to block doorways, carrying boxes of homemade grenades and ammunition. Soldiers handed out muskets to young men in frock coats and shirtsleeves, some still in laboratory aprons, baffled by the pandemonium and firearms instructions, *First tear the paper, then prime the pan, then – tiens, putain alors! Listen to me when I speak eh!* – a young man shaking his head. '*I study the botany, not bullets! I know not what you say!*'

Caron moved through to the wide staircase and up, his pace not slackening, shouting, '*Doctor!* Where is the *triage* room now! It should be down here! *Putain alors!*' As they passed, Wayland glanced in at plush conference rooms with rich carpets, curtains and furnishings, in another, a vast library, civilians in frock-coats, older men, younger men, a man shouting and slamming a book on a table, others standing about uncertainly, soldiers elbowing them out of the way, dragging gilt chairs and consoles to block the windows. These, he realised, were the *savants*, the men of learning. Wayland thought of his brief days at Oxford, and for a moment envied them their adventure – until he recalled its unforgiving demands, and the fate of Joly at Kafr-Shahabas. He hurried after the group up the stairs.

An ornamental floor-to-ceiling window on the first landing cast delicate shadows on their upturned faces as they climbed – dead-faced grenadiers in pale grey coats and tall white spatterdash gaiters leaned on their muskets in the corners, looking out, nervous young *savants* moving past, curious, alarmed, some trying to laugh it all off with *braveur*, others more grim.

They came to a broad corridor, the dark beamed ceilings some fifteen feet above them, great lanterns hanging at intervals, exotic potted palms, broad, spade-like ferns between day-beds along one side, some occupied by the injured, the exhausted. '*Capitaine,*' called Caron. 'This way, I may need you and your men.'

Wayland and the others hurried along, hearing shouts at the end of the corridor, the clink and clank of metal instruments, Tariq behind, looking about with wide-eyed awe. 'It is the home of a great lord, *effendi*…' He gazed at the lanterns hanging above, glancing into a room as they passed, glass cases, animal skeletons on benches, the house a combined laboratory and museum. 'I did not know men could make such things…'

Wayland murmured under his breath, 'Chaps, my French is from Strasbourg where I studied and I'm fluent – how's yours, Dr Porter…?'

'Belgium sir, first sailings and a Dutch auntie in Ostend. I read some French medical texts when I were learning the trade.'

'Good. Lil?'

'*Jeriais*, lingo from Jersey, sir, half-Anglo but I got a bit o'Norman an' Breton an' all.'

'Marvellous,' sighed Wayland. 'With an x in everything so no one can understand a word. We know Tariq's all right, and you too, Hesse.'

'*Jawohl*,' said the little Austrian, 'French and Italian from the Alps, *mein Herr*.'

'Where'd you learn English then?' said De Lisle.

'From ring-a-ring-ze rosies, by Jove.'

Caron ducked into one large chamber, then moved on, Wayland spotting high counters and a profusion of tubes, glassware, a microscope and chemistry equipment, the smells of powders and ethers, arguments raging inside, *No no no! You cannot move this, not now, ah, mon dieu—*

At the end of the corridor they saw patients on fold-out cots and orderlies moving to a backstair. They followed down to a half-landing with a raised loading-stage in a carriage entrance, a cart reversed up to it, canvas stretchers with the injured being lifted by *savants* and staff, the daylight suddenly blinding, the heat suffocating, some being carried in from slung harnesses on horses, a voice shouting, *Another ambulance! I need another ambulance!*

In their midst was a vigorous man, older than the others, in waistcoat and shirtsleeves and spattered apron, his long, dark hair tied back, a quick look about him, examining each victim as they passed by. Porter took Wayland's sleeve. 'Sir... that's Larrey.'

Surgeon Dominique Larrey moved from one stretcher to the next, cots lying in rows, *This one, no not him yet, and then this one, yes, yes, go go go, vite, vite, come!* He clapped his hands together and Egyptian orderlies lifted the pole-stretchers and moved the wounded into order of precedence, Larrey holding back a tall hanging curtain as they carried the first into his operating theatre, looking back, calling out, 'Maher – loosen the tourniquet every two minutes, wash with the salve, and I shall be out, *vite vite vite, alors!*'

Caron found the men laying the lady Rana on a chair in a corner, her head lolling, one hand up to her head, Theokritos kneeling before her, calming her, their maidservant standing close by, holding her free hand in devotion. A junior *savant* medic joined them, wrapped a blanket round her shoulders and called, 'Ashaf! Bring dilute glucose cordial and water—' He looked up at them, his eye resting on Theokritos and Wayland a moment before looking away discreetly. 'She is important then...'

'Diplomats,' said Wayland, glancing at Caron, then tried his luck: 'I will have to report it to Citizen Derrien.'

Caron snapped a look at him. 'Huh. Best of luck finding him.'

Wayland's heart fell − not that he was sure what they might do if they had indeed found him: he had no briefing from Hazzard for that − only reconnaissance.

Porter spoke in French to the doctor. 'Signs of fever? Bleeding under the skull?'

The man looked up, unused to being challenged by a Bedouin, but uncertain of his rank or influence. 'Inflammation yes, from the head wound, but local. Cranial pulse still normal though elevated. Treat with ginger, cinnamon and Jesuit's bark if need be...' He looked at Porter in a new light. 'But, yes, your compress wrap held the swelling. Well done.'

He moved off and they heard Larrey shouting in the back, *Armand! Someone to hold this man down!*

Somewhere behind them was the sound of breaking glass and someone swore, shouting out − a stone had been thrown. De Lisle gripped his Charleville and nudged Wayland. 'Gettin' hot in here, sir...'

Wayland looked round to see a group of senior *savants* striding down the corridor towards them. The foremost of them bore a ferocious expression, Citizen Gaspard Monge, Professor of the *École Polytechnique*, Inspector of Foundries and veteran of the river battle of Shubra Khit.

'*Sergent chef!*' boomed Monge. 'Having made such an impressive display upon arrival, your soldiers have moved off. And now we have a mob! They pelt us with stones eh eh! Is this to be our protection?'

'*Capitaine,*' Caron said to Wayland, 'with me if you please...'

Wayland decided sergeant-majors the world over were the same: subordinate to officers but still effectively in command. '*Oui, Chef.* What is the situation?'

'It is this...' Caron said as he marched past Monge and his outraged followers. 'The ten grenadiers we have are in position and will obey you without question. The troops, they go to destroy the barricades on foot or by horse, and I go with them, so: will you stay and guide these stout Men of Letters to defend themselves?'

Wayland caught De Lisle's eye. 'Of course, *Chef*. Where are their weapons—'

'They have them, but are afraid they will go bang.'

'I'm not,' said one behind them, young, laconic, his hands gripping a Swiss hunting flintlock – a pair of sunglasses on the end of his nose. 'Better than blasting birds in the Delta for St Hilaire. Just give me a target.'

'Citizen Jollois,' declared Caron, reaching the stairs and the high window overlooking the front. 'So you are the born killer, hm?'

'They revolt, as did we,' said one, 'when we threw off the shackles of *ancien* power. We cannot just *shoot* them—'

'I shall remind you of that when they come to batter your skull with a shovel,' said Caron. He turned. 'Listen – *écoutez bien*, hm? These are not the students of the Al-Azhar. These are not men striving for freedom. They murder, and loot. Any French citizen, men, women, their own people who work with us, beating anything that moves. All mobs are the same, do you see? Storming the Bastille or storming the Institute. The mask of the crowd brings out the beast in the man. They are no longer thinking, reasoning men but animals – and that is what battle is, *mes braves*, believing your enemy is nothing but an animal and should be killed. That is how you survive, not by reasoning with him.' He looked at their terrified faces. 'They have massacred everyone who has contact with us, Christians, Muslims, traders, merchants, anyone. If they get in,' he finished, 'they will kill you all.'

Denon the painter came forward. 'What of the boys, the young ones? Surely they cannot be asked to shoot guns—'

'And not the literaries, *je vous en prie*, I forfend!' declared a voice behind grandly.

Monge looked at him: in frilled cravat, silk waistcoat and shirtsleeves, his cuffbands romantically frayed to give the desired effect of penniless, tortured genius. It was Parseval-Grandmaison, the expedition poet. Monge was not impressed. 'All men will take up arms, Citizen, artists, poets and all. With the zoologists, physicists and chemists and engineers—' He looked to Caron. 'Shall we make bombs, *Sergent-chef*?'

'We have some few grenades...' Caron peered out the window. 'But we have no further powder to spare...' Where once there had been a column of nearly two hundred infantry, there was now barely a checkpoint and a growing mob of milling protestors at the end of the mews, some armed, most with clubs and lengths of jagged wood torn from rubble heaps. 'Citizen, I think the occasional shot will keep them back. If any one man comes forward,' said Caron, 'drop him.'

'We did more in Italy, *Chef*,' reminded Monge.

Caron looked at him. 'Yes, you did, Citizen.'

His meaning ambiguous, Monge took umbrage. '*Sergent-chef*, this is different.'

Caron agreed. 'It is. Here they put up resistance.'

Denon pleaded, 'But we must go – back to Ezbekiya... For the young boys, *Professeur*, they do not understand the danger—'

Monge looked at them all. 'No. *Never*, Citizens. This is our moment to defend our precious science, our belief in the Rational Mind, our *work*, and the very future of mankind, and protect it from—' He waved an arm at the window and the howling riot below, '—from the depredation of the *unthinking*. Even if I stand alone I shall not let them pass! Guns!'

Wayland watched them, remembering Hazzard's reports from his time aboard *Orient*, dining with them, fending off their arguments, winning some, losing others. He wondered if this was indeed the entire purpose behind the French occupation after all.

'...will you, *Capitaine*?' asked Caron.

Wayland looked back at him, not having heard. '*D'accord, Chef...*' he said in agreement, partly to maintain their cover story but also because he agreed with Monge's sentiment. He sympathised with the people, but not with a raging mob. 'Not one of them will set foot in this building.'

Monge threw an arm round Wayland's shoulder and turned to his colleagues. 'You see? Spoken like a true-born son of the Republic. What better example could we have, *messieurs*?'

Hesse nodded to Tariq. '*Absolument.*'

Caron glanced at them with a weary expression. 'Then *adieu*. I shall be at the barricades...' he grumbled, a look passing over his face in memory, 'again...' he muttered, turning away. 'I am always at the barricades...'

They watched Caron move down the steps and Monge began snapping orders to the others, each taking up a musket, none noticing the shortened Charlevilles carried by Tariq and the marines. Wayland turned to his men. 'Fusilier Hesse, Tariq, De Lisle,' he ordered, pointing to the upper landing to ensure De Lisle could understand. 'Firing points, upstairs landing with the grenadiers. If we can muster a volley I will give a command, otherwise fire at will when I give the word. Snapshots to keep them back, as in the fighting-tops – any one of them steps past that wall down there, take him dead.'

'*Oui, mon capitaine!*' said Hesse with a crisp salute. The three hurried up the stairs branching to the right, Hesse and Tariq chattering in French. Wayland turned to Porter. 'Porta,' he said to Porter, latinising his name somewhat, 'Citizen Jollois, with me!'

Another stone smashed through a window downstairs, a grenadier cursing, *putain*, the distant shouts louder. Wayland marched off to the next branching corridor, looking through the chambers to the windows to find vantage points, Jollois following eagerly. 'I've not hit one yet, Captain,' he said. 'But if it comes to it...'

'Rest assured, *m'sieur*, it will.'

Jollois grinned. 'Old *Mange* prefers us to be called Citizens...' He looked at the pair of them as they ascended the dark wooden steps. 'Why are your muskets so short?'

'An old trick I learned from an Englishman,' said Wayland, his bad leg stiffening as he mounted the last stair to the landing. 'Does he know you call him old Mange?'

Jollois shrugged. 'He should lose some weight.'

'He might today...'

They stopped at an oriel window and opened the *mashrabiya* panels to look out. The crowd had grown, but were still filling the end of the mews lane. Wayland checked the priming pan of his Shorter Charleville and gave Porter a nod. He nodded to Jollois. 'Ready?'

The crowd became a single mass, murmuring in the distance, a low thrumming that drew closer, several fingers of the mob stretching forward behind the bolder leaders, who ran forward and lobbed their missiles. Glass broke again and a protestor raised a musket and fired, the round thudding into the wall of the building and whining off in ricochet. 'Porta, if you please,' said Wayland.

Porter stepped up past Jollois. '*Mind tha' now, lad,*' he mumbled in English, took rough aim through the open *mashrabiya* panel and fired. The flash and report were both deafening and blinding, filling the chamber window with clouds of choking grey smoke. The buck-and-ball load was not wholly accurate to the range of the mob but spread its stinging load effectively, three men falling, crying out, grasping their legs, the lead stone-thrower knocked off his feet. Jollois leaned half out the window. '*Sacre…!* How did you hit so many at once!'

Wayland levelled his own musket through the panel and said, 'Sheer bloody luck…' He squeezed the trigger and the blast resounded through the hall and high chamber. Another pair dropped writhing to the ground, their friends turning to run, stopping, then going back to retrieve them, pulling them to safety. 'You see,' murmured Wayland, '…sheer bloody luck…'

When Caron reached the main courtyard he hurried down the corner steps, calling to the grenadiers out front, now crouching behind the gateposts, '*Caporal!* All men to me, form line!'

The half-dozen grenadier sentries followed him as he strode through the arch to the gate, facing the mob at the other end of the mews passage. The windows of the other houses lining the mews were now dark with broken panes, muskets cracking from the upper-floors, other *savants* taking pot-shots, rioters beating at the doors with sticks, enraged, some shooting up at the snipers, neither with much success.

They turned and howled at Caron as he appeared through the gate, and threw a salvo of stones, bricks and broken bottles, all bouncing harmlessly ten or fifteen yards away from the old sergeant. Just before him the paved mews bulged in a European-style turning circle for carriages, the mob held back from this by some invisible barrier, trying to keep just out of range.

The volume of their outrage increased as another figure charged in on horseback from the side of the Institute building, the horse whirling about, the rider's dark coat flapping: a smoke-blackened and embattled Jules-Yves Derrien.

'*Chef!* Where are your chasseur Alphas! The barricade did not go off – the fuse failed!'

Caron looked up at the enraged Citizen *Croquemort* in the saddle. 'They were with *you,* Citizen!' he accused, drawing his sword-bayonet and a pistol. 'How have you lost them! If just *one* of them has been—'

From the front of the mob a lone man came running, a long club in hand, his right arm pulling back to launch the weapon, and Caron fired his pistol just as Derrien did likewise. The man spun and buckled, hit by two rounds simultaneously, and fell just as Derrien readied a second pistol. '*Chef!* Get to that barricade!' shouted Derrien. 'If the cavalry cannot break through, we cannot storm the Azhar Mosque! *Immédiatement!*'

Seeing their compatriot fall, the crowd surged forward, a tide of anger, and Derrien fired a second pistol, shouting to the grenadiers, 'Form line! Two ranks!'

Barely a platoon, the grenadiers looked to Caron, who ordered them into formation, and they raised their muskets, bayonets fixed – but Derrien did not give the order to fire: instead, both he and Caron stared at the end of the mews, over the heads of the mob.

From the rear of the crowd, a troop of Bedouin horse burst around the corner at full gallop: some in dark Maghrib or *keffiyah* headdresses, some in turbans, *kaftan* and *binish*, robes flying as they heeled round the corner, hooves clattering on the cobbles, horses whinnying, the crowd leaping back, *Yallah…!*, some of the riders firing pistols in the air, muskets swinging low, knocking men to the ground, the mob rushing to the sides of the passage to get away, those in front running, turning to look.

Derrien's face went white. Beneath the *binish* of the leader, he saw a flash of scarlet.

'*Non…*'

The grenadiers wavering beside him, Caron stared in disbelief. 'The *anglais…*' After a moment, his mouth betrayed the faintest trace of a smile.

–

Hazzard knew the horses would charge straight into the crowd if need be, though frightened to put their hooves on uncertain ground, but he knew they would jump if led. A gap opened before him, the looters and rioters arguing, fighting each other, now all diving away, eyes wide, mouths open – he squeezed with his legs and leaned forward, calling to Delphine hanging on behind, *Hold on*, and the Arabian lifted its forelegs, sailing over the ducking heads of the front knot of protestors, crashing to the cobbles, the horse's hind legs hitting someone, a cry, Delphine gasping, her chin striking his back until she tucked her head in, squeezing tight, '*Mon dieu…*'

Hazzard saw Caron, saw the other mounted figure, but thought only of the mob behind, the marines coming in fast behind him – he spun the horse about as grenadier guards fired a volley into the air, Caron shouting '*Get her! Get the lady down!*'

Hazzard's horse wheeled about, the grenadiers' hands reaching up to take her, Delphine being pulled down, *No, wait wait...!* while twenty yards off the mob charged towards them. Hazzard shouted down in French, '*Do you have her! Do you have her!*'

Caron shouted back, '*Yes! We have her!*'

The Lorenzoni was out and in his hand and firing before Caron had finished, a spark rising from the cobbles as the heavy round skipped off the stones and a man fell, others nearby leaping away to run, only to be struck down by the musket-butts of the marines riding in behind. Hazzard's horse turned, looking for escape, its flailing legs enough to drive back the closing mob. He cranked the loading arm of the Lorenzoni and fired another shot, and more of the protesters skidded to their hands and knees to escape, sliding on the paving stones, turning, crying out, pulling at their comrades to get up and run.

Caron and the grenadiers helped Delphine to the gate, the grenadiers firing a second volley, clouds of smoke bursting, the mob trampling the wounded to escape. Cook, Underhill and the others pulled up, their terrified passengers jumping down, running for Caron and the grenadiers, *We have them!*, and the grenadiers ran forward in a crouching phalanx of bayonets.

–

Wayland looked down. '*God above...*' he whispered in English.

'*It's him...*' whispered Jollois. 'It's him! The *anglais* – from the *Orient!* It's *M'sieur d'Azzard*—'

'Maintain fire at the front of those bloody people,' said Wayland to Jollois and anyone who could hear. 'Porter,' he said, '*allons-y*,' then, to Jollois's bafflement, shouted up the stairs in English, '*Marines to me! Hesse! Tariq! De Lisle! Boat approaches!*'

Jollois ran out to the hall after him, an incredulous smile spreading across his face. '*Anglais?* Are you... *all* English...?'

Wayland looked at him and nodded out at the mob. '*Bonne chance.*'

Outside, Hazzard watched the nurses jump down, saw Caron and the grenadiers getting them in. He felt nothing odd about their collaboration against the riot, against the mob, nothing, men of duty and conscience against a common enemy. Hazzard's horse stamped its hooves, its ears pricked, its tail proud, turning about – then it stopped. He stared as the grenadiers ran across the front of the Institute, forming a defensive line, everyone rushing: all but one. In a moment of sudden stillness, he registered the other mounted figure, the dark coat, the hat, the blank eyes staring, the horse pale as death.

Derrien.

Derrien let out an inarticulate shout, Hazzard could not be sure if it were his name, or a curse, but both their pistols rose at the same moment, arms extended, the shots lost in the muffled roar of the tumult. The figure in black screamed, eyes maddened, the teeth bared, and he turned, his arm rising with a stick, beating at his mount, and fled. As if it understood, the horse beneath Hazzard leapt forward to give chase.

'*Derrien!*'

Cook watched as Hazzard charged down the narrow lane at the side of the Institute. Wayland and Porter came at the run, the others hard behind. '*Sar'nt Cook! Well met!*'

'*Sir! Hop aboard!*'

Wayland jumped up behind Cook, the others finding partners and scrambling up, Kite putting a hand down to De Lisle as he leapt onto the rear of the shying Arabian. 'Wotcher Lil—'

'Wotcher Mick. Been busy?'

'Nah. Quiet mornin'. Comfy?'

Masoud and Firaj hurried round from the side passage, Masoud holding Firaj back, calling out in French, '*They ride towards the Al-Azhar Mosque!*'

Caron saw Cook – and the two old sergeants exchanged a moment of recognition. 'The road,' said Caron in English. 'I show you. *Suivez*—' *Follow.*

Caron ran, leading them round the corner to the carriage entrance. He saw a despatch rider. '*Get off, off, putain alors! Go! Go!*'

'But *Chef*—'

The rider jumped down and Caron climbed up and pulled the reins about to ride with Cook, and charged into the empty street, the others following.

Hazzard burst into the road beyond the Institute gardens, the roar of the rioting streets louder, echoing, columns of smoke rising, more grenadiers on the lawns looking on in surprise, Derrien headlong in full gallop, thrashing at his mount, '*Faster Faster!*'

Hazzard leaned in to the gallop with no care for his direction, no sense of his surroundings, and felt that same morphia-induced unreality of that chase to the dunes of Aboukir Bay, Nelson's ships descending on the French fleet, the bells clanging, leaping work-parties, dodging the sappers and the wells... Sarah was bright in his mind, too bright, burning into him and he found himself screaming for Derrien, *screaming*, the horse not tiring, *go on go on*, tearing through the streets, left, then right, after the fleeing glossy black tail in front, its fugitive rider glancing over his shoulder, eyes wide. Strewn market stalls whipped past, women raising their arms, rubble in the street, bodies, looters fighting over tables and chairs, then diving away as Derrien shot past, his stick swinging in his free hand, smashing at men in the street to get them away, *Damn you, damn you all!*

Hazzard began to gain, but Derrien skidded into the curve of the main arterial road and Hazzard realised: *Al-Azhar – he's heading for the mosque.* The great domes loomed over the rooftops in the distance, shaking and flashing in the flying mane of the horse, armed men in the minarets sniping down at the French in the streets. He heard the faint bark of a cannon, and the whistling rush of a hurtling round-shot. There was a percussive blast far ahead, the round crashing into a four-storey house, bringing down the upper floors onto the street amid a cloud of broken stone and splintering wood, people screaming.

Hazzard saw the first barricade, the white robes of the Al-Azhar among groups of men and women throwing stones, firing muskets at French soldiers trying to advance in ranks, firing return volleys.

The next round-shot struck the barricade itself, blowing its cluttered heap of upturned carts and furniture into flying matchwood, debris sailing high into the air, protestors flung in all directions. Some began to fall, some French marksmen taking good aim. Hazzard saw one of the men defending the barricade, raising his musket, dark robes, *Tarabin*, he thought, then knew him: *Baibars – Sheikh Qahir.*

Derrien feinted right then ducked left, away to the verges of the road to a high stone wall, the horse riding alongside it, clods of earth flying from its hooves, edging closer and closer, until Hazzard grasped what he was doing: slowing, reaching out for the wall – he was going to jump. Hazzard drew the scimitar, closing on him.

'*Derrien!*'

Derrien nearly leapt but misjudged and almost lost his seat, crying out, the horse pulling away at the last moment, a tree suddenly in its path, and they careened back into the street, another heavy round-shot coming down, a shuddering crump, a shower of rubble raining down on them. When he burst through the cloud of smoke and dust he saw they were riding straight into the mob behind the barricade.

Derrien dodged again, the horse crying out, but the crowd was too thick, hands of Tarabin fighters and rioters tearing at him as he beat them away. Hazzard heard shots, well timed, well paced, all accurate, key men at the front hit, falling, spinning away.

Derrien was almost overwhelmed and Hazzard kicked out as hands reached up for him as well and he shouted back at them in Arabic, '*I am the Red Devil! Ana al-Aafrit al-ahmar! Ana Hazar Pasha!*' Another round hurtled overhead and the crowd screamed and scattered, an explosion nearby, a swathe suddenly cleared, a man with a club swinging, roaring at them, a giant, sending the mob diving for their lives. Hazzard recognised Pigalle at once.

Behind him, Rossy took a shot and a man fell, St Michel running behind, pulling Derrien away, the horse taken, the mob clawing at Derrien as he clambered onto the barricade itself, the mob closing in on all of them.

Hazzard spurred the horse and it spun in a rough circle, clearing the crowd, Pigalle almost swinging at him until he saw the scimitar, the flash of red beneath the *binish* – Rossy looked up at him and Hazzard put his hand out. '*Take it! Only one chance!*'

Hesitating only a moment, Rossy leapt across the rubble of the barricade and took his hand, jumping up behind him, swinging a carbine round and firing at another man too close to St Michel. '*Anglais!* Have you the buckshot?'

'*No!*' Hazzard fired the Lorenzoni and reloaded it, firing again.

Rossy whistled and St Michel ran to them, taking a running jump from the barricade, catching Rossy's leg and landing up beside them. '*Down there!*' Rossy pointed down the side-street and turned. '*Pig! Come on! We have a coach!*'

The horse snorted and staggered and Hazzard fired again, just to keep their heads down, to keep them away, the Lorenzoni now empty. He shoved it back into its holster and pulled the rein round as the crowd surged forward yet again. He heard a shout and looked round to see Caron and Cook charging into them, swinging down with muskets, clearing them away, Underhill and Warnock driving them off, Cook shouting, Pigalle looking up. Napier leaned down, offering a hand, the two big men gauging each other's size, their plight, and Pigalle climbed up. Hazzard kicked in his heels; the horse protested but lurched ahead down the side-street, the rioters in flight. At an empty alleyway and sudden quiet, St Michel jumped down. '*Merci, m'sieur!*'

Rossy climbed off and looked up at him, saying nothing.

Hazzard nodded. 'A debt.'

'And now?'

'Derrien.'

Rossy almost smiled and said, '*Al-hamdulillah!*', and ran off.

Hazzard turned about, Cook and Wayland coming their way, Cook shouting to him, '*No ye don't, sir!*'

'He's in there, Jory! And I'm going to kill him!'

'*Don't you dare go back in there, boy!*'

But Hazzard charged back to the crowd at the barricade, the cannon-rounds now exploding howitzer shells, the dead everywhere. 'Baibars!' he called. '*Baibars!*'

The Tarabin *Bedu* looked round and saw him. '*Hazar—*'

'Shajar! Where is she! *Get out of here!*' He kicked the horse in and took a club to the thigh, spun round and kicked out at the men closest. '*The Turks are not coming! You are alone!*'

'*She knows! I know!*'

'*Then get down, damn you!*'

Baibars cried out and spun, a musket-ball crashing into his chest, a hand out, eyes wide, blood bursting from his lips, and he tumbled down the barricade. Hazzard tried to drive the horse through the mob to reach him, then stopped, hanging his head. '*Damn them all…*'

The nearest houses had been reduced to bare skeletons, their entrails poured into leaning heaps from their top storeys, people falling, scattering, running, others looting what they could. Then Hazzard saw him, clambering down the far side of the barricade: stooping, Derrien then clawed at the rubble madly, digging with his bare hands, throwing stones and chunks of wood aside, a pistol ready.

'*Derrien!*'

Hazzard climbed from the saddle and jumped onto the rubble of the barricade, the horse skittering away into the crowd. He hauled himself up the piled carts and rubble, stumbling over loose stone and brick, determined to reach Derrien on the other side. Derrien saw him: not taking his eyes off Hazzard, he thrust his pistol into the hole he had made – and smiled. He pulled the trigger.

There was a flash and muffled bang, powder-smoke belching into the air – and Derrien scrambled down the other side, towards the French infantry, who began to run for their lives. Then Hazzard understood.

Explosives.

Hazzard tried to make his way to the side of the heap, but fell over a cartwheel, a table-leg cracking him in the knee, a musket-ball howling off a stone beside him. He got to his feet and heard someone far off, *Sir! Mr Azzard*, and threw himself off, leaping for the road, his last thought as he launched himself into space: *bomb*.

There was a whump of powder from within the barricade and the road heaved in a cloud of splintering wood and stone. Hazzard felt weightless, turning upside-down, a dull impact on his back as he struck something, *wall*, fell, and hit the ground – thinking of Sarah, *you didn't cut the quickmatch this time*, and how he wished he had been aboard when *Orient* had split the night with flame and his world had ended forever.

Memnon

The great dome of the Al-Azhar Mosque glowed in the sun, smudges of smoke still rising up to the minarets, the smells of the smouldering aftermath everywhere. The great courtyard lay open, its smashed gates and rubble testament to the accuracy of French gunners: heaps of broken stone, once ornamented arches now shattered, the expanse covered in debris – and kneeling men.

Cavalry horses snorted, stamping their feet, impatient for their reward, the troopers proud of the destruction, of having charged the breach and defeated their enemy now awaiting their fate. The great, broad-chested General Dumas sat atop his charger, looking down upon them, still enraged, spinning his horse in a tight circle, to show them all who was master of the field, who had trampled upon them despite their resistance.

A call went up, À… vous! The soldiers lining the huge quad cracked to attention, and Dumas straightened in the saddle. The conqueror had arrived.

Bourrienne, Generals Berthier and Murat behind, his aides keeping close, and a squad of dragoons marching in close escort, Général en chef Napoléon Bonaparte moved slowly through the ruins of the Al-Azhar gate and surveyed the bloody field. He looked up at the impacts caused by his bombardment and nodded with detached satisfaction. He looked about, his mathematician's gaze traversing the area mechanically, assessing, analysing, then stopped, and looked down, as if taking a moment of reflection. The kneeling prisoners knelt lower, their imams clustered together virtually prostrate on the unforgiving stone.

'Why, Louis?' he whispered. 'Why did they do it… do they not understand?'

Bourrienne leaned closer. 'Perhaps they do now.'

Bonaparte looked around at the devastation. 'They were as my children…' He looked round at them, his pale face whiter now, his voice rasping with anger. '*Was I not a good father to you…?*' he shouted. '*Did I not prove how we love God and His Prophet…?*'

Derrien stood close by in the entourage, his face still blackened from powder-smoke, the proud scars of battle. Bonaparte glanced at him. 'So. The barricades blew.'

'Yes, Citizen General. And the artillery was perfectly accurate.'

Bonaparte watched him, his last remark more for Bonaparte's benefit and the reaction of the others nearby – once again they were afraid of Citizen *Croquemort* and his influence. 'So I understand,' acknowledged Bonaparte. He nodded, deciding. 'You are now Chief of Counter-Intelligence, not only for Egypt, but for the whole of the *Armée de l'Orient.*'

Derrien considered this new title, its grandeur, its scope. He bowed his head. 'Citizen General. I offer my unceasing efforts.'

Derrien still felt the burn of his neck as it bent, as he might now forevermore, so unused to the posture was he from his exalted position in Paris of Chief Collector; but here, on the frontier, life was different: it was thrown into the sharp relief of extremes – survival or destruction, friend or enemy. If he could, he would remain friend of the conqueror. How much better, he knew, to be the Grand Vizier rather than the sultan.

'These, Citizen General,' said Derrien formally, stepping back, one hand indicating an aged *imam* in bright turban, 'are the ringleaders, and the sworn enemies of peace in Egypt.' Among them was the leader of the Al-Azhar Mosque, the aged Al-Charkawi, his pale, paper-thin skin falling in crepe-like folds about his face, his confused eyes flicking from left to right, seeing the soldiers brandishing their muskets either side. Behind him came several others, old and young. One stopped to spit at the foot of a soldier and was rewarded with a musket-butt to the stomach, tugged back to his feet by another.

'An unrepentant, as you see, General,' commented Derrien.

Bonaparte watched. 'All to the citadel,' he said, 'for execution.'

Al-Charkawi looked at them, wide-eyed, and was led off, his fellow prisoners following behind to their scaffold.

'And these, Citizen General,' said Derrien more brightly, 'are the sheikhs who wish to convey their condolence and displeasure at the uprising…'

The *imam* turned and made a swift gesture to another, standing beneath the multi-coloured colonnade of arches in the shade. A brief procession of lordly men approached, in fine robes and varied head-dress, and gathered before Bonaparte and the generals. They stopped, as indicated by the *imam*. The *imam* then spoke in Arabic, an Al-Azhar student in white *galabeyyah* at his side translating. 'These sheikhs wish to greet Sultan *al-Kebir*, and offer their loyalty.'

Bonaparte waited. The first came forward and bowed. 'Sultan *al-Kebir*,' he said, and Bonaparte offered his hand. The sheikh clasped it and touched his lips to the knuckles.

'So,' declaimed Bonaparte loudly, for all to hear, 'you were not party to this terror of the mob, these horrors in the streets that killed so many innocents of my people.'

The sheikh listened to the translation and bowed again, saying 'No, Sultan *al-Kebir*... This was not of our doing, nor of our wishing.'

Bonaparte nodded and bestowed his mercy. 'Then I forgive you, Sheikhs of Cairo, and call you friends.' He looked about at the assembly. 'I grant amnesty, for this is my wish, that we all live as one, with one mind and one heart.' This was put into Arabic by the Al-Azhar student and many bowed, the kneeling prisoners touching their heads to the ground in relief.

The procession continued, each sheikh approaching, bowing, and taking his proffered hand. As they bowed reverently and filed off to the side behind Derrien, Bonaparte leaned towards him, 'I understand we have prisoners,' he said softly. 'How many?'

'Yes, Citizen General,' Derrien replied. 'Over a thousand.'

'Did they all take up arms against us?'

Derrien knew that quite likely not all had, but it mattered little. 'They did.'

Bonaparte took the hand of the last sheikh. 'Then even as I welcome these men, you will take the heads of the ringleaders and every prisoner who took up arms.' He looked about the courtyard at the kneeling captives, their muskets stacked, evidence of their treason. 'Wait until nightfall. And throw the bodies into the Nile.'

Derrien felt a *frisson* of excitement at the command, and admired the statecraft: to shake the hands of the influential upon whom he must rely, and to take his vengeance cold, so all may shiver at dark tales of his cruelty. 'It shall be done, Citizen General.'

'And the Institute?' asked Bonaparte, strolling now, a task complete, picking his way through the debris.

'All well, General,' said Derrien, moving closer, now a confidant, already advancing himself above the generals in tow. 'A company of foot relieved them of their vigorous and brave defence of Science, led by Citizen Monge himself.'

Bonaparte gave a thin smile. 'I did not doubt it.'

Of the questionable actions of certain men at arms, notably one officer of the 25th Marine infantry and his men of uncertain identity, who brought a wounded diplomat and his wife to Larrey himself, Derrien made no mention, nor of a troop of Bedouin cavalry led by one William John Hazzard. That Hazzard had been caught by the explosion was something he kept also to himself – for he would never believe the man dead and gone until he held his severed head. He began to tremble at the thought, the memory of the chase through the streets, Hazzard's madness, his focussed rage – he had *felt* it, burning through his back, each moment waiting for a bullet that never came.

Derrien looked at the sheikhs, in a row, their chins up, each as guilty as the prisoners on their knees, but each too important to be denied. He looked at the men he must now execute, and considered that it had, indeed, been a good day.

–

Sergent-chef-major Caron did not agree. He and the Alpha-Omega squad picked their way cautiously through the rubble of their particularly favourite corner of Little Paris, hoping to find *Le Citoyen*, and a beer. They made their way cautiously to the square where they had sat at the café and been conscripted by Derrien. There was little familiar left standing.

A fire had burned out an entire tenement, all four storeys of it, and an artillery round had crashed through the top floors of another, the stench of smoke and charred flesh hanging in the air, debris all over the square from shops and stalls torn apart by looters. The wails of bereft families had faded, most bodies taken away for funeral rites and burial but some remained unclaimed.

St Michel went on ahead, his Austrian rifle at the ready. Pigalle was silent, his big face set in a deep frown as he moved slowly, looking up at broken windows overhead, then down at the shattered wood, stone and glass strewn at his feet. But Rossy was the most disturbed.

They stopped in the centre of the square, the small fountain filled with rubble, a body lying beside it and, worse, the barbershop in the corner in ruin, its door hanging, the interior blackened by fire. A foot protruded from the broken planks of an upturned cart, a broken wheel dangling. Rossy slung his musket over his shoulder and squatted down to move the wood aside, and see who it was. When he saw enough, he dropped the planks back and sat there, his head low. It was Raff, the little barber.

'*Chef*,' he said.

'Yes, *mon garçon*.'

Rossy shook his head back and forth, arguing with himself, then again, '*Non. Non, non… non*. It is *not*…' He sighed again, blowing out a heavy breath. 'It is not right, *Chef*. Why would he – *why?*' He looked at Caron, his reddened eyes sunken and black with fatigue and despair. 'Why would he save us like that? This *anglais*? *Who is he?*' He pointed at Caron, angry. 'A *saint? What then?*'

Caron stood still, looking down at Raff. '*Non, mon enfant*. He is no saint…' He sighed as well. 'He is as we are. Old soldier.'

'Then why does he not *fight* us? Why save us…'

Caron looked around, the entry to the covered *souk* bazaar blocked by rubble, a few people pulling at it, stepping back as floorboards from above swung down and fell, raising dust. 'Because we saved him?' He shrugged. 'I know not. In saving him… we saved ourselves, hm.'

'But save us for what?' Rossy gestured at the destruction all around them. 'For *this*? For *this* world?' He spat. 'For I tell you, *Chef*, I have had sufficient of it, I have truly. When my bullet comes I will welcome it and step *into* it, may God stand witness. And this general, this *M'sieur* Bonaparte, he can whistle now if he needs the musket-gun of Gaston Rossy.' He smacked his hand on a piece of rubble beside Raff. 'For he deserves *nothing*. Look what we have done. *Look*.'

The square was quiet; even the labourers trying to clear the rubble had been seized by such a sadness many simply stood and stared at the ruin all about. 'If it were not this general, *mon garçon*,' said Caron, 'it would be another, for there are always more generals.' He looked down again at Raff. 'Ah, *le Rif-Raff, mon ami*. I am so sorry we were not here. You were a kind and harmless soul.'

St Michel joined him and they pulled the cart away, tipping it over, and it crashed onto its broken wheel, sinking on a broken axle. Pigalle lifted a wooden beam from Raff's small broken body. 'They say the brothel, it is immoral,' said the giant. 'To curse, it is immoral. What then is this.' The big man threw the beam aside, revealing Raff's burnt trousers, *galabeyyah* and *binish*, lying prone, one knee bent, his arms splayed out, as if asleep. 'The *anglais*,' he said, with some thought, glancing at Rossy, 'he is moral.' He looked at them both. 'And then so are we.'

He bent down and turned Raff onto his back, the eyes staring, mouth agape, and picked him up lightly, carrying him to a clear part of the square, and laid him down gently, legs straight, his arms at his sides. St Michel watched, then crossed himself. '*In nomine patris et filii et spiritus sancti. Amen.*'

Antonnais appeared from the collapsed shopfront of *Le Citoyen*, a bottle of wine in each hand. 'We have this at least,' he said. 'To bid him farewell.'

Rossy joined him and took one of the bottles, reading a small, smudged label. 'Chianti *Nobile*. How very fine.' He smashed the neck against the wall sending a splash of red against the stone. He raised the bottle to the square. 'To Raff, and all the *misérables*, for there are too many.' He drank from the broken glass.

—

All was white, a blinding blaze, from mind to horizon. A flowing *binish*, a white *shemagh* and golden *iqal* looked in at him, into his eyes, the *shemagh* removed to show a fine moustache and delicate beard, peaceful, serene, a friend.

'*Ali…?*' he heard someone say, possibly himself.

My voice.

'*Q… arim…?*'

The face did nothing, a hand doing up the *shemagh*, covering the mouth, and it moved away, the world becoming white once again. He swayed. It was the feeling of a boat, swaying one way then another, bumping on peaks in the swell, then sinking into troughs. He drifted on a tide of his own making, hands beckoning, *come*, hands holding him back, *stay*.

Sarah.

No. Not Sarah.

Who?

And instead of Sarah or Emma Hamilton or Delphine or the dead nurse in the middle of the road, *Too late too late! I was too late!* Shouting somewhere, and struggling, *bound, hands tied, tied up, Good Christ above,* hands holding him still, a blast of pain and he gasped, a thought of a lady again, nothing but eyes in the darkness, almond eyes, a pure beauty, Mamluks with swords, a balcony and the smell of jasmine, *Can you save my husband?*

Nafisa?

The lady Nafisa al-Khatun.

Wife of Murad Bey. He had met her on that darkened landing before the battle for Cairo, a scent of blossom and gardens wafting in from below, and he had said, *How can I promise so...?*

Smith's voice, laughing, his kindly smirk, *Mr Murad Bey Esquire...*

Just as Ali-Qarim had appeared, so did she now, looking in, a black veil over her forehead, a Maghrib headdress, and only a vision of her eyes, watching him.

Her voice was soft. *'Al-Aafrit al-ahmar...'* She held up a hand clad in black, in her fingers a shining disc, gold against the silk.

Coin.

Georgius Dei Gratia.

Shajar al-Durr.

Shouting her name, but all that emerged was a whisper. 'N-n'fee... sa...'

The face of Ali-Qarim appeared again.

'Iyaqulu Nafisa,' said a voice.

Ali-Qarim peered in at him. *'Nafisa?'*

Arabic but Hazzard thought he understood some of it, his lexicon of conjugated verbs too small to identify it entirely, *he says Nafisa*, but recognised the tone, well bred, familiar, *kings and queens*, blending, dripping, draining away. Heat and ruins, rock rising red and burning, temple gates reaching to the sky, the sound of the Nile and ibis calling for Thoth, goats bleating and the strained guttural roar of a camel.

Caravan.

The swaying took him again, and he slept. Sand poured in an endless stream, the days blurring into weeks, the jackal-headed god seeing him, turning the glass, *beware: I come*, hours melting in the sun, days, shouting again, and Cook's face looked in at his, dark skin, *the auld oak*, deep-set eyes large then bulging, out of focus, one of Monge's mirages. *'Quiet now, lad, or ye'll wake the hens.'*

Underhill's laugh, the old pirate, with his smuggled rum and his fiddlers three, fooled no one, not Hazzard either, but a good man in a scrap, *'Clucky little hens Jory, just clucky little hens, ha-har...'*

A hand dropped into sight, a bloodied sleeve, limp, bouncing, *dead?*, then moving, the elbow bending to prove it was alive and he felt relief, thinking perhaps it was his own.

Who is there? Another?

When he awoke he was lying prone in the shade, but the distant blaze had returned, blinding white, his eye travelling across a desolate sweep of sloping sand and scrub, around tall, twisted bush-headed palms, their slender trunks entwined – leading to a sight which at first he could not comprehend.

A stone giant, towering over the earth, upon a megalithic throne, a god made stone, its twin just beyond, the pair sitting in balanced judgement upon him, both of them, one and the same terror.

Memnon.

Pharaoh. God. Stone reaching to the sky, the wind whistling, sand stinging their ravaged, insensate features. A place where no minute passed, no grain of sand flowed through the hourglass of Anubis.

The twin giants sat still, their broken, chipped and crumbling faces gazing blindly at the Nile and the eternal east from sixty feet in the piercing blue sky.

I am Memnon.

Behold.

The blank-faced desert stretched behind, rugged mountains of terraced rock rising in the distance, their heat glowing from flat-iron peaks, pulsing into the void of the cerulean dome above.

Behold, I am heat. I am rock. I am earth and sun and sky.

Lord of Æthiopius, son of Eos goddess of the dawn.

I am Memnon.

Grinding, crumbling, the neck of the stone pharaoh burst with fragments, a cloud of granite dust, showering sand and rubble upon its great shoulders as the terrible head in gloried rays of the sun turned with the steadiness of a breathing mountain, rumbling in discontent to turn implacably and look down upon him.

Behold.

Hazzard blinked, the stone cold to the touch, not hot, the day usurped by night, the moon shining, and he looked up at the seated Titan. His leg felt dead behind him, a lost thing. He had dragged himself up, limping across the cold sand, the scimitar in hand, the tip scraping the earth, and leaned for support against the king of kings: *Basileus Basileon, I am Memnon.*

He opened his mouth to roar with the pain, the god ignoring him, watching for the dawn. He heard shouts of running men coming for him and fell, wanting to escape, *dropping*, the leg still dead, *run*, the pain become the raging fire the stone pharaoh witnessed every morning as the sun rose, burning, burning.

His eyes registered first a soft blue and red cotton, the comfort of a cushion under his face. He had not moved, lying under shade, somewhere, and the day lived on, hot, merciless. He had a thought of young Elena, from the *Volpone* again, her softness and care, and somewhere in his psyche detected the presence of a woman. He looked, but there was none. He sucked in the air, grains of sand susurrating beneath his hands as he moved first one, then the other, *have to check*, and one leg, then another, *yes all there*.

I am whole.

Behold.

But am I alive.

–

Night fell, cool and welcome. The giants had gone and he lay in the temple. The moon hung low, its light casting ghostly luminescence on the fallen guardians all around them. Many still partly stood, though broken, studded like pillars to support the great stone roof. Lamplight glowed yellow from heads and torsos lying in the scrub, gazing at the earth or sky with placid serenity, their indignation passed to acceptance, sceptres in crossed hands, glowing as they had every night for three thousand years. Hazzard stirred and tried to roll from his front onto his back, a restraining hand immediately in place, Cook looking down.

'Easy sir. Back had some burns. Leg not good.'

With this confirmation, Hazzard felt bruising down the length of his body, from his neck across his back, the backs of his legs, even his heels – *barricade, flying, upside-down, the heap rising in a sudden spout of earth* – until a jarring crump and his jaw had clacked shut, and he had dropped onto one shoulder, falling, his knees, everything clattering together. He had not felt such complete pain since his flogging on the Indian frigate: Cook letting him down from the rig, holding him still, the deckhands gathered round in outrage, ripe for mutiny, Cook's face a mask of suffering, *I'se sorry sir, sorry sir I am*, and the blood dripping from his exposed ribs, the Mughals sewing him together, a burst sack of scars and tissue.

But oh, that had been long ago.

He looked down at himself. His leg had been tied to a splint, the ache overwhelming, and he felt the pain wash over him unimpeded by insensibility and lay his head down, '*God...*'

He could scarcely form the words as he thought them, his jaw moving, his lips parting, 'De... errien...'

Cook's expression was hard. 'Gone. Knocked down, but got up and run for it.'

All for nothing.

He looked at the broken faces around him.

As is everything. For nothing.

The man he had taken for Ali–Qarim appeared beside them in the light of an oil lamp, white robes, a dark *binish* overtop, a fine golden *iqal* circlet on his *keffiyah* headdress, a man of wealth, a man who had saved him, saved them all. A breeze blew in through the open colonnade, and he saw a faded, flaking blue celling above, powdered with stars, the man's face at last in focus. It was the sheikh, from the action at the hospital, from the dead girl in the road.

'I am Saleh al-Mansur,' he said, in good French. 'Sheikh of the lands of Ali–Qarim Sheikh and Nazir Sharif.' He waited for the words to sink in. 'I know of you, Hazar Pasha, and praise your good men.'

Hazzard struggled to understand. 'Ali–Qarim's... lands...?'

Al-Mansur nodded. 'When both brothers fell at Embabeh, I was bestowed their lands. I am, how says one, a cousin. And in your debt.'

'No. No more debts—' Hazzard sighed and tried to sit up. Cook handed him a cup of water and he drank. He closed his eyes and began to breathe slowly and regularly. 'The men...'

'All here,' said Cook. 'Petty were swingin' a club to an' fro, knockin' 'em all down, to...' He stopped then said, 'well, to get them Frogs out o'the mob.'

Hazzard closed his eyes and took a breath. 'Was not his duty...'

'No. But he knew it was right.'

'Mr Wayland...?'

'Took some bad wounds in that blast. Tried to get to you before it went off.'

Hazzard sat up as best he could. 'All right...?'

Cook nodded. 'Like flash-burns from powder, plenty o'bruises and splinters. Porter kept him alive with his potions and snake-oil. But aye, he's well.'

Hazzard lay back.

Cook knew his thoughts very well. 'He volunteered, sir.'

'Don't give me that old one, Jory—'

'He *did* though, di'nt he. An' he said so, he said, don't tell him, Cookie, don't ye dare till he be well, so here you are and you're well enough in my book so there it is: he near broke his neck climbin' that barricade after you, but his bad leg felled him in nick o'time and he dropped just as it blew the street sky-high.'

The sheikh looked on with surprise at the harshness of the words, '*Kuq* Sergeant, perhaps...'

Hazzard lay still, eyes closed. In French he said to the sheikh, 'Forgive me, Sheikh. They are all here because of me...'

Al-Mansur nodded. 'But of course. For they love you, in their way. As they should, for their pain is clearly yours.'

'Not enough of it.' Hazzard wanted to sink into the earth and never emerge.

Cook watched him. 'We're all in slings and bandage and blood, aye, but there's not a man out there who would trade it for a month o'peace in the blockade fleet, not a one – and you know it.'

Hazzard closed his eyes, memories of that first morning on the *Esperanza*, addressing them, their faces blurring, not wanting to know them – but now he did, and they were his to protect. 'Should have been just you and me, Jory...'

There was a lasting silence until Cook said it: 'We all want that bastard Derrien, for what he done. To you, to me, to Miss Sarah, and that poor little lass Jeannie on the *Orient*...' He looked away. 'And to all of us. No mistake, the lads want him too. As to bloody Bonaparte...' He shook his head. 'He's just another bastard we're fightin', but they'll 'ave 'im, some day, teach him a lesson. Ask Arthur Napier. For a-frightin' his poor auntie, and his ma and da, he'll have 'im for that alone.'

He became aware of the pendant, still round his neck: St Jude, from poor silly little sweet Ellie at home, last given him by Sarah on a battlefield – the patron saint of lost causes.

As good a lost cause as any.

'Where are we...? Thebes?'

Cook looked at the sheikh, who nodded. 'Mm. Down from Qena. Been on the move, all over, lookin' like a *Bedu* caravan, goats, few geese, and we traded some of the horses for camels.'

'Good ones,' said Saleh al-Mansur. 'They do not bite.' He smiled. 'Very much.'

'How... *long*,' Hazzard began, then coughed. 'How long have we been gone?'

Cook was evasive. 'Long enough. Out of danger. No one following.'

Hazzard watched him, but Cook did not look away. 'Well done,' said Hazzard. It was an apology of sorts, and he knew Cook knew it was.

Cook pushed himself up and stood. 'This was the easy bit. I know how to run when stuck.'

Hazzard gave a wan smile and Sheikh Saleh put his hands together and bowed, '*Rabbena ma'ak, Hazar Pasha.* I bid you sleep well tonight, *bien dormis.*'

'*Shukran, ya Saleh Sheikh...*'

Cook watched him go, and looked out at the landscape, the ruins, the desecration. 'Heathens in a 'eathen land...' He squinted up at the sky, at the lengthening shadows. 'Sun'll be down soon. I'd say we should march in the cool, but we need the rest...' He broke off and said, 'I'll send Porter over later to check on you, sir.'

Hazzard took his wrist tight. 'Sorry, Jory.' He swallowed. 'Should have been just you and me.'

Cook nodded. 'Still is, sir.'

Just down the slope from the ruined temple, at the camp of the Tarabin and Mamluk *sanjaqs* of Sheikh Saleh, fires crackled, lighting shattered gods strewn in the sand, revealed as flickering ghosts. Some played music, the women of the caravan singing, the tones swooping and diving through the group. The marines sat among them at the open tent of Sheikh Saleh, Tariq translating when they spoke – but mostly the little Huwaytat *Bedu* sat cross-legged on the edge of the carpets, his eyes half-closed, the incense of a pipe curling lazy clouds before his nose.

Beside him was Hesse; despite being from worlds apart, the pair were almost like twins: Tariq rolled the ends of his moustaches up like Hesse and the pair leaned towards each other and sang, and everyone laughed. Two of the Tarabin women who had once been chosen to train as *almeh* danced before them all, luminescent in the firelight: one pale and green-eyed, the other dark as walnut with eyes of shining jet, their hips and legs swaying then shimmering, their hands out, their torsos locked, unmoving but to the demands of the music, the *Bedu* men playing, the marines gazing entranced.

Kite stared at the dark-eyed creature before him, her smile white in the darkness. 'This is what it's all for, innit Sarge... what all o'this is about...'

Underhill lay stretched out next to Kite, sharing a pipe with the Tarabin beside him, the cloying aroma of *hashish* on the air. 'How d'ye reckon on that, young Michael,' he asked.

Kite hardly blinked, watching the dancer, her rotating hips drawing her closer to him, her eyes looking down, then rising up in time to the rhythm. 'Findin' a rare beauty...' he replied in a faraway voice, 'An' keepin' it well.'

Underhill looked at the dancers as they dipped low on spread knees, and swirled together, a pair of entwined serpents. 'It may be so, laddie.'

The dancing continued and the music echoed round the plain, swallowed up by the sand, by the rock, by the Nile, unheeded by the stone gods. Hazzard watched from his bedroll, the distant fires flaring. He thought of laudanum and what Porter might have given him, until, in a cloud of dark linen, she appeared, kneeling at his side, her face filling his vision, *almond eyes*, honey skin and a black *hijab* and veil over nose and mouth, her long dark lashes like wings as she blinked slowly down at him. Her hand removed the veil and Hazzard saw none of the ferocity he had felt at Kafr-Shahabas, but a look of concern.

'*Hazar Pasha...*' she said, sounding so different to the others.

It was the Nafisa of his dreams made real, made into Shajar al-Durr, a warrior from a deadly day in the heat of the Delta.

'Shajar...' he said.

'*Oui, c'est moi.*' Always in French, yes, it was her.

A gold coin.

Her cool hand touched his forehead and his face with a strange reverence he had not expected and he closed his eyes to this soft heaven, and began to wonder if this too were a dream as the colossi of Memnon had been, the grinding head turning to glare down upon him for his sins. '*I was too late,*' he said.

'No, no,' she replied in her French. 'You were there. It was enough. The people see you, and know they are not alone.'

'But now they are alone, forgotten...' he said. 'That is why I came to Cairo... to help them...'

She looked at him with a kindness he could not understand. She had been deadly that day at Kafr-Shahabas, yes, angry, displeased with his interference, but now she was not. 'Baibars,' she said, 'Sheikh Qahir ben Sayyid, is dead. He fell for his people, at the barricade.'

'I tried to...' As he moved, his leg grated at the knee, *the bad knee again*, he thought, running and walking through the Suffolk woods to Hedingham, to Sible Rise, *should have stayed in bed, become a reverend pastor, you bloody fool—*

'...those he pardoned.'

Hazzard gazed as the stars shifted behind her head. 'What...?'

'The General Bonaparte,' she said, 'executed the prisoners, the people...'

Hazzard watched her face swimming, the backdrop of the heavens floating on the temple ceiling above, 'Prisoners...? But—'

'Two thousand. The sheikhs, the great *imam* of the Al-Azhar...'

Two thousand.

'Wh – how did he—'

'At night. Cut their heads,' she said, *coupait les têtes*. 'Like in Paris they say. The bodies, thrown away, in the Nile...' She looked down.

Two thousand.

Hazzard looked at her but saw only kneeling misery, at the citadel battlements perhaps, got someone local to do it no doubt, not sully their own hands: old men, young men, learned men, and anyone who resisted the Republic, butchered.

Liberté, fraternité, égalité.

You were too late. We all were.

He began to shake, his back arching, and he saw through watering vision a square filled with people, the guillotine blade dropping, and the resultant cheer, and he wanted to vomit, his teeth clenching as he tried to breathe, the people paying their own terrible price with endless fear.

May God above damn the liars all—

Lewis.

Blake.

Bonaparte.

Lies.

'...are coming soon.'

'What…?' He sank back, exhausted.

'French cavalry. The General Desaix rides now from beyond the oasis at Faiyum, Murad is too far away perhaps to stop him.'

Hazzard tried to sit up, his anger driving him. 'How many are you?'

'Twenty men and ten women, and the Sheikh al-Mansur, he has twenty Mamluk and wives in caravan.'

It is enough.

'We must… prepare them to move,' he gasped. But his head swam as he sat up, *what has that bloody old nursemaid Porter given me for God's sake…*

She held him down. 'You cannot walk.'

'To hell with that,' he said, *au diable*, but she understood and held him down.

'No no, the *Fransaya* will not come for days—'

'Then we must surprise them…'

He sank back onto the bedroll, exhausted, hearing the tinkling of water in a bowl as she wiped a damp cloth over his face, her hands cool on his skin, on his chest, his shoulders. The blue night sky on the ceiling looked down, painted by the sacred artists of Memnon or Thothmes, or Seti, the stars lit for eternity: the huntsman Orion and the Pleiades, *am I here*, and the day sighed away like the sand under her cool hand. The cloth wiped him again and he sighed, *of course, I'm ill*, he thought, *of course*, hence the daydreams, hence the nightmares.

When he opened his eyes he found the night had deepened, the moon low, her form revealed in the light of the oil lamp, *she is still here*, and the flicker of a fire in the distance at the foot of the Memnons, the Titans on their thrones, men moving before them, their shadows, some dancing, others playing their music.

'Did you… take that coin,' he said, looking into her honeyed eyes, through her, 'to start the revolt…?'

She looked at him, her long eyelashes swooping, graceful birds taking flight from a goddess.

'The *imams*,' he insisted. 'Who told them to rise up… Was it Smith… was it—' He choked, '*Was it us…?*'

We need it to be a bloody, catastrophic failure, to outrage the sultan.

Lord Keith, declaring the mission.

Mission accomplished, my lord, it was bloody, and a failure.

'You are here, for us,' she whispered, as she bent over him, 'and for them.'

Several of her women moved behind her in the temple, armed, and turned facing outward, silent, on guard. She freed her hair and it fell across his vision, a luxurious black curtain, smelling of sandalwood oil and jasmine. '*Do you see me...?*' He felt the heat of her softness through the fabric of her robes, the linen warming under his hands, the fire of her curves as she bent over him, *her heat, her power*. '*I see you*,' he said, this woman become the goddess, coaxing him to wakefulness within a dream, her head thrown back as she settled astride him, life amid so much death, hope amid so much despair, and his became the breathing agony of an Osiris, holding her tight as she shuddered atop of him – and he fell, far, far into the abyss, to sleep in the cool shade of a woman called Shajar, queen of the Mamluk.

Cook awoke just before dawn. Old sea-hand that he was, he was still unable to sleep for more than a four-hour watch at a stretch. He found some of the others already awake, taking *Bedu* coffee at a fire, the cool air misting grey and dark around them. Tariq handed him a steaming tin mug, and he took it, burning his hands, blowing on it. 'Where's the Professor?' he asked – at times they still used Wayland's old nickname.

Kite turned round. 'Lookin' at the artworks, Sarge.' He put his mug down. 'Is it true, Sarge, that we 'ave to shave our heads and all?'

Cook frowned into his steaming coffee. 'What you talkin' 'bout, boy...' He took a careful sip.

Warnock blew on the top of his own scalding liquid, thick with sugar and goat's milk. 'The *Bedu* women told 'im,' he yawned, then chuckled, 'as they don't want to go foragin' about in the bushes.' For a change the group laughed with Warnock at Kite's expense.

'She was a perfect lady,' said Kite, '...for a bit.' They laughed again.

'You've broke me 'eart, Mickey,' said Handley.

'Naughty naughty,' called Napier, 'Winkey-winkey, monkey-monkey, eh, eh?' He shoved an elbow into a young Tarabin Bedouin at his side who rocked with him and laughed, despite not understanding a word. 'Eh, Ali? Eh?' Napier rarely had the chance to be comical. He nodded to them all and put an arm round the Bedouin's shoulder. 'This is Ali, my mate.'

Tariq said something and Ali nodded, smiling, and Napier thought this was grand indeed. But Cook was almost cross with Kite. 'No fiddlin' with the locals, lad, I done said so, clear as a bell, di'nt I?'

'I weren't, Sarge,' protested Kite, 'I'm just devilish 'andsome is my problem.' They fell about again and Handley threw his *shemagh* at his head. 'Well, *she* said so,' complained Kite. 'I think.'

'Aren't ye now,' said Cook. 'Wounds. Report.'

Kite lifted his left arm, assessing its movement. 'Bit stiff but good.'

Warnock nodded. 'Same, aye. Potty took stitches out yest'y but got a rub on it. Been near a fortnight now.'

'Clear aye, Sar'nt,' said Cochrane in his doleful Belfast twang. 'All's well, praise be.' He glanced at Napier and gave him a nudge. 'Art'ur. Yer man's askin' ye.'

Ali pointed at his hand as if to remind him. 'Oh yeh...' Napier blew out a breath and held up his finger. 'Got a sprinter, Sarge. Big one. Hurts.'

There was more stifled laughter and Cook sighed. 'God, boy, I do wonder 'bout you, sometimes I do.'

'Don't like sprinters.' Ali patted him and he got back to his brew, forgetting it at once.

'He's a-right, Sarge,' said Pettifer. 'Lil's wound is weepin' no end. Needs rest.'

'Doc with him?'

'Aye. One of the Beds'll be givin' him a salve, might help.'

'Good.' Cook looked at Tariq. 'Your leg better?'

Tariq was busy making flatbread. He shook his head. 'Yes, *Kuq effendi*. I am *Bedu*.' They chuckled and he grinned. They were all practical enough to know to be honest: modest heroics helped no one, an unhealed wound in the midst of action bringing danger to all.

'Right,' said Cook, taking another sip of his coffee, then looking at Kite. 'Shave whatever y'want, boy, so long as it's King's Regs.'

'There y'are, see?' said Kite to Warnock, 'No 'elp at all, you lot.'

Warnock perked up. 'Polly on the *Ville* says it makes it look bigger, Mick,' he said, 'An' you need all the 'elp you can get there, mate—'

Kite threw his mug at him and they fell about cackling all over again as Cook headed off.

Cook walked out beyond the ruined temple, looking round the columns of broken-headed gods. His *binish* and *galabeyyah* underneath were damp – ordinarily he would have sorted it out but he knew that with every passing hour the cloth would dry with the rising of the sun. He stopped a moment and looked up at the guardians of the afterworld, their expressions blank, identical, so many tin soldiers on parade, with the blessing of benign indifference to their toil. He shook his head. '*God save ruddy Bristol...*'

He then bumped into Porter, who looked all the world like one of Al-Mansur's men, until he pushed his grubby and bent spectacles onto his nose. 'It's the major, Sarge,' he said in his dead-flat Yorkshire voice.

'What is it.'

Cook pushed past him and hurried to the temple. He saw the sword and pistol lying by a rolled pack, candles guttered and the lamps cold, Hazzard's bedroll empty. Hazzard had gone.

Temple

The stars looked down on ancient Thebes, as impassive as the stone kings who had sought so dearly to join them in the afterlife. The air was cold, a northerly breeze rolling through the fingers of mountain ridges reaching for the Nile, blowing in brief gusts from all quarters, bringing the scents of sand and water in omniscient confusion.

Hazzard let the horse take him at a slow walk, the oil and leather smells of its mane filling his senses, the rhythm of its bobbing head waking him. It came to a gradual halt. He was on the plain. To his left, the rocky foothills stretched to rising cliffs, every riven bluff and crag etched in sharp relief in the half-light of the heavens above.

Far to his right, the Nile flowed by, the river the only movement in the world, its dark infinity reflecting the bowl of the sky. The raw strata of mountains rose in the eastern distance – but before them, in the foreground on the riverbank, he saw a city in ruins, vast and empty: colonnades bridged by stone joists, palms growing between, jostling for position. A towering slab-fronted gate stretched to colossal heights, built for the Titans of Memnon he had seen enthroned, through which they strode nightly, revisiting their starlit cathedral under the heavens, the obelisks to guide them as they waded across the river to bring forth the dawn.

'*Khurnak*,' said a voice in his ear, and in the darkness he heard Izzam – Izzam killed at Embabeh, trying to save him from French bayonets, Izzam who had taken three men with his scimitar before falling.

Then he saw it was Tariq, *not Izzam, no*, and relief swept over him, for Izzam had suffered enough. Tariq rode beside and just a few paces behind, his arm raised, pointing across the river to the endless temples of forgotten gods. '*Khurnak*,' he repeated.

Karnak.

He had read of it, yes, but what might it say to him if he should listen? He tried to harken to its message, but heard only the wind. The wind blew the sand in endless whispers before him. The distant columns soared, hieroglyphs upon every surface, figures holding objects, beckoning the devoted to enter the unearthly realm. If the pharaohs had sought immortality, they had achieved it, he thought, even if only in destruction.

Necropolis.

To the Greeks, it was a City of the Dead. To the pharaohs, rebirth.

Dr Muhammad, in London, his smile, his medieval manuscripts, *Here, the soul rises, do you see, like a bird...*

He looked out across the plain to his left, to the hills in the northwest, the darkness revealing what the blazing light concealed in the heat of day: a low, wide platform, the remains of old pillars like so many broken teeth marking another ruin, another tomb, another mausoleum. Shining onto it all, the light of the night sky, shadows deep and endless, the pale glow of broken stone, everything casting him small, weak.

I am Memnon.

Sand whispered in the wind, the voices of entombed demigods hissing, drawing him on, or warding him off – he could not tell. The earth throbbed with time, with the past, in the temples of Ptah. All temples belonged to Ptah, the Ancient One, about whom naught may be said, he remembered, his mind sifting the histories for when they called it *Ai-ku-ptah*, the Kappa become Gamma, the Alpha become Eta: *Eguptah.*

The House of Ptah.

Egypt.

He felt a sudden pain, that it was all *too, too old*, for such a small thing as he to perceive, a growing sadness inundating him, the burden of these thousands of creeping years weighing down on them all, *what then have you done, what then, what then can you do?*

For I am Memnon.

There was a crash ahead in the scrub and he jerked in fright – a vulture lumbered into view, its gristly head turning, red eyes flashing bright, and hopped, ungainly, flapping its coarse wings, lifting off. *Here be dragons*, he thought, set at the brow of pharaoh: *beware.*

In pale gown, a figure, walking, bare arms, a woman, her head turning to look back at him. He felt his heart palpate within his ribs, the throb of his own pulse in his ears and he stopped breathing. *No.*

Sarah.

The horse was too slow, *move, move!* The impossibility not penetrating, *move, move!* The horse began to crop quietly at scrub grasses, unperturbed.

He was clenching his eyes shut, fighting off the dread. Where seeing the Pyramids at Giza had once released him, unburdened him, these ruins, these distant reliquaries, altars and naves were crushing him with their scope, their vast, unceasing demand to worship something greater even than the earth or the heavens themselves – rendering him a helpless child among its maddening geometric shadows.

He wanted to throw his head back and cry out her name, but stared, simply stared, lost.

—

'*I said where the hell is he, boy!*'

The Tarabin lookout was uncertain whether he should fear Cook, and spoke only to Sheikh al-Mansur, who said in French, 'He saw him ride out of the camp, yes?' Cook nodded, following him roughly. 'Down to the statues. He did not wish to stop the Pasha.'

'*Christ a'mighty...*' Cook charged past them and the large tent, having roused nearly everyone in his fury that the sentries had let Hazzard leave camp unescorted.

'*Sarge! Got 'im!*'

Cook spun round. It was Handley, at the front of the temple, looking through a scope towards the Nile. The big sergeant stalked over to him. 'Well! Where away?'

Handley gave him the telescope and pointed. 'Black 'orse, on 'is own, nosin' round them two big ones.'

Sheikh Saleh joined him and Cook peered through the eyepiece. The missing Arabian was cropping at the grasses around the massive plinth of one of the twin stone giants on their thrones, but of Hazzard there was no sign. 'No flamin' saddle even – he went out with no tack, prob'ly no ruddy 'quipment or kit, firelock or ammo—' He turned and shouted. 'Someone gemme a damned horse! *Now!*'

Sheikh Saleh called to the camp, '*Hisana! Ajlibou hisana!*'

Zeinab, one of the older Tarabin women, had mounted and brought one in tow. Cook jumped into the saddle and Handley gave him the scope. 'Find the Perfessor and gimme a shout when y'do.' He looked at Zeinab. 'Speak English? *Injaleezi?*'

She shook her head, her dark eyes narrowed in a perpetual frown. '*Leh.*' No.

'Good,' said Cook 'Y'won't 'ear me cursin' me *fackin'* head off then—'

They leapt into a canter, Cook charging down the low slope to the plain, Zeinab keeping close. It was less than a thousand yards, and they covered it in a few minutes. Cook gave the stray horse a quick examination. He gestured to the woman. 'Right, Zeinab: *you*,' he said, and took a handful of the grazing beast's mane to demonstrate. 'Hold here. Right?'

She understood and nodded an emphatic yes, '*Nahm, nahm nahm*—' and looped a line round the horse's head, clucking to it all the while as Cook rode quickly round the first of the high plinths, wondering if Hazzard had fallen and crawled into the lee of one of them, lying unconscious. 'Sir...? Sir...?'

He found nothing. He rode on to the next colossus and looked round that as well, but still came up with nothing. He rode back and looked at the ground around the horse. Zeinab pointed at the scrub, shaking her head. She held up her hands, '*Jaef*—' Dry. It was too dry and hard, with few tracks not already trodden by the horse's hooves, but at least there was no blood.

Other riders approached to help, and Cook looked at other broken statues behind – they were smaller, the area strewn with rubble. He rode around them all, looking in the bushes, in the scrub, Saleh and his men doing likewise, calling out to them to watch for signs of French scouts. He rode up next to Cook.

'Hope he not in *le wadi, là-bas*,' Al-Mansur said in French and broken English, pointing for emphasis. 'In the wadi, *non*?'

Cook understood most of it, and looked to the mountains to the north and west, and saw the valley carved through the rocks, and swore again. They heard a sharp whistle and turned. He raised Handley's scope up to his eye and saw Kite and Cochrane waving a white cloth at him.

Saleh slapped him on the shoulder, hopeful. 'Come, *hayya*—!'

The stray horse in tow, Zeinab followed with the other *Bedu* as Al-Mansur and Cook charged back across the plain. They rode up through the camp and back to the temple ruins, the tethered mules braying in alarm, the goats bleating.

Cook hauled on the rein as Kite waved him down. 'With the Professor, Sarge – he's round the other side—'

'What d'ye mean, damn ye!'

He jumped down and followed Kite and the marines at a run through the temple ruins, his chest puffing. He saw Shajar al-Durr and nearly seized her by her robes. 'What'd you do? Cast yer spell on him, *did ye*, damn witch!'

But Shajar remained calm, her face uncovered, her right hand on the hilt of the dagger in her belt. Cook looked down and saw it. 'He is well,' she said, in French, and he seemed to understand. 'He has slept. With the spirits.'

His French sufficient to the task, Cook took her at her word. '*What...? Spirits?*'

She led him round the corner of the ruin, picking her way up a short slope through the rubble. There stood Porter, Warnock, Underhill and the others – and Wayland, in his breeches, boots, and tattered Jermyn Street shirt, looking over at more ruins.

'Sir—' began Cook.

Wayland turned, then held a finger up to his lips. He pointed. Further on, round the corner of the temple, before what appeared to be a giant hill of broken masonry, was Hazzard, his Bombay jacket bright against the dun brown of the stone and sand all around, out of place, the colour itself alien in such alien surroundings.

Hazzard was leaning against the stone, both hands out, his head hanging. Cook glanced at Underhill and gave a jerk of his head. Underhill understood. 'Come on lads, back to yer breakfast.' Watching over his shoulder, Underhill led them off, and Cook met his eye: he knew the drill – he was to ensure Hazzard was well, lest the men lose heart. 'Doc.'

Porter stayed. 'It's a good thing,' he said, in a low voice. 'Purgative.'

Cook nodded, not taking his eyes off Hazzard.

Hazzard moved at last and looked up at the hill of rock. It was the wreck of a statue, as large as the enthroned giants on the plain – a broken trunk lying tipped backwards, staring up at the slowly brightening sky. The smooth, massive shoulders were the height of a man from the ground, the head the length of two men. The face was gone, blasted away by wind and sand, or defaced by the angry victors of a forgotten battle. Hazzard continued to lean against it as if for support, small by comparison.

Perhaps emboldened by the reinforcement of Cook's presence, Wayland broke the silence. 'Good morning, sir,' he said in a low voice. 'You seem better disposed.'

Hazzard did not turn. '*Yes...*' His voice was a husk, a whisper like the drifting sand all around. He gazed at the enormous statue tumbled in ruins. Large hieroglyphs in a cartouche border stared back, mute, incomprehensible, of such a size as to be legible from the ground.

Wayland and Cook moved closer, each looking up at the ancient wonder, a fallen king. The beginning of dawn began to pick out the relief of the hieroglyphs, Hazzard watching its transformation in the light.

'It must be him...' murmured Hazzard.

Wayland glanced at Cook. 'Who, sir?'

'Pococke... described this place, in his book. Fifty years ago.' His breath wheezed from him, 'Diodorus Siculus... the giants, on the thrones...' He put a hand out to touch the cold stone again. Sand fell from under his fingertips.

'Sir?' Cook took another step. 'The Bedous say you took a horse last night – to the plain.'

Hazzard did not react, lost in his own world.

Ramesses.

'This is the king,' he said, 'who sacked Jerusalem... The king who defeated the Hittites, and the Nubians, and the Libyans...' He ran his hands against the stone and murmured in Greek, '*Basileus Basileon, Osoumandouas eimi...*'

Wayland glanced at Cook, who watched Hazzard carefully. Hazzard looked at the stone, his hands roaming across its smooth surface reverently. 'He wrote that there is a monument to Ozymandias... at its entrance a *pulon* of variegated stone forty-five cubits high...'

'Ozymandias...?' Wayland looked back at the temple. 'I – I don't see now—'

'Sir, you're not well,' warned Cook.

'—the figures at square pillars sixteen cubits high...' Without turning he pointed at the gods standing at the pillars beside them, the broken guardians. 'The ceiling of the temple... depicting stars on a blue field.' They all knew the ceiling of the temple, where some had passed, where Hazzard had slept, where Shajar had visited, where the oil lamps had glowed, and night was eternal.

The giants on their thrones seemed smaller now, less imposing.

I am Memnon.

See how I lie.

Broken, fallen, brought low. Mortal.

'*Nikáto ti tón émon érgon…*'

Cook made to move forward but Wayland put out a hand, bidding him wait, letting Hazzard commune alone.

Let him surpass but one work of mine.

Hazzard stared. His primeval fear of the twin Titans, sitting in judgement, left him.

'Is it,' he said, 'All for *nothing…*? Is everything… a lost cause of St Jude?' His head hung low, his shoulders shaking with his breathing, that admonishing pendant of the saint swinging before him from round his neck, *St Jude, St Jude.*

'*Jory…*'

Cook took a step forward. 'Here.'

Breathing in tune with the statue, with the rock of the mountain, Hazzard stood still, leaning on the king of kings. '*Is she really gone…*'

Sarah.

Cook watched him. He nodded to Hazzard's back.

'Aye.'

Hazzard's head sank lower. He struck the side of the rock with the flat of his hand. 'I cannot… *see her face.*'

They were quiet, the four of them, Wayland, Cook, Hazzard, and the king of kings.

'She's safe now, sir.'

Hazzard's back shook and he gasped, nodding – anything, to break the bonds and return from those green depths of the dead, floating in the warm waters of Nelson's rage, at Aboukir.

Gone.

But safe.

He saw only the sand before his eyes, and one of his boots, white with dust.

'Sergeant,' said Wayland. 'Could you retrieve that old walking-stick of mine for the major…? Perhaps Dr Porter could…'

'Yes sir…'

But Cook did not move, staring at the fallen giant with them. Above them the indigo of night yielded to the orange and red of sunrise, the blaze of Ra and the mountains beyond beginning to glow. The Memnons had brought forth the dawn, yet again.

Hazzard breathed, following his own line of thought, as if Sarah were guiding his anger into logic: *if they all lie... what then?*

Ramesses. Bonaparte.

One and the same.

Hazzard pushed himself away from the massive stone shoulders, taking a deep, shuddering breath, mumbling before the fallen god-king, angry with himself, '*I have been so blind.*' He shook his head and looked back at them, his eyes ringed with black circles, his unshaven face pale. 'It was not for India...'

Wayland glanced at Cook. 'Sir...?'

Hazzard looked up at the pharaoh. 'It was just for *this*. To surpass but one work of mine: *Nikáto ti tón émon érgon.* The inscription, written by Didorus...' He shook his head. 'King of Kings, Ozymandias am I, and any who wish to know how great I am, then let him surpass but one work of mine. Do you see? All of this, invasion, colonising, rebellion, this *destruction*. Bonaparte came for *himself*.' It was a revelation, and he gazed into its light. 'He wants to surpass Ozymandias, to surpass *Ramesses*. He wants to be sixty foot high, in stone, that all might marvel, or run in terror. He wants *this*.'

Encouraged, they came closer, the cool air clinging to the stone reaching out to engulf them. 'I don't understand, sir...'

'There's nothing... *strategic*. There is no great plan. He simply wanted to conquer Egypt.' Hazzard straightened, his heart spent. A loose chunk of stone tumbled from a crevice and landed at his feet. He looked at it. A set of rough hieroglyphs had been carved on part of it, broken off, a circle, like the sun, a serpent, an alchemical glyph of a key. *Find this*, he thought, *his broken dreams*, and pushed it under the great neck with his boot for another to discover, under the carved relief of the pharaoh's headdress evoking the rays of the sun, now dulled by the displeasure of other, more powerful gods.

He stopped, looked down. 'We *did* break his dreams,' he said, 'made them fall around his ears, but...' He shook his head. 'But he's still here. There is *something* coming, something worse, and I don't know what it *is*.' He thought of his vision, of the temple, of the vulture – *or had it been real?* 'He can get troops from Sudan. From across the Red Sea. From Eritrea, from all over, *buy* them, enslave them... He needs men.'

'How can you tell, sir...?' asked Wayland.

'*Because we sank his fleet,*' he replied, thinking of the heavy bird trying to take flight, Egypt speaking to him. 'He has no reinforcements from France... *nothing.*'

Shattered his dreams.

They turned at the sound of a footfall. It was Shajar and her Tarabin women, in their multi-coloured banded *shemagh* and turban headdresses. Hazzard looked at her, a dark shape against the dawn, in her dark robes, only the glint of the whites of her eyes showing. She bowed and Hazzard could see, even beyond the veil. *Is this all I am now*, he wondered, *a longing in a world of shadows?*

He pointed across the plain, across the river. 'What do they call that place,' he said, 'the temples, the ruins.'

The Nile glowed under the dawn, a grey reflection of the sky, the palms on the opposite bank dark, the temple columns and colonnades, gates and obelisks in silhouette as the mountains bowed to the rising of the sun.

'*Khurnak,*' said one of them.

He had no memory of getting back to the temple of blue stars, of finding Ozymandias. *Where had he been? And with whom?* 'Tariq... is he all right...?'

Cook glanced at Wayland. 'Been here all night sir. He's well, aye.'

Hazzard stared across the Necropolis, the City of the Dead, at the temples, palms and mountains. He no longer felt the crushing burden he had borne from the ancient ruins – because now he knew, he understood.

Basileus Basileon.

King of kings.

No, not you, Bonaparte, no you are not.

He blinked, and looked around as if seeing them all for the first time. He looked himself over, the *galabeyyah* hanging down to his knees, his breeches and boots, all scuffed, filthy, his open jacket – no sword, no pistol. He took a step. There was a twinge, but the leg took his weight, Cook coming forward. 'Easy now, sir.'

'He killed everyone he pardoned...' Hazzard said it as if just remembering. He looked down at the ground and wanted to spit with disgust, the bloody savagery of it all.

Their heads thrown into the Nile.

His breathing improved, and he took great lungfuls, feeling some vestige of power returning. He saw Bonaparte's face, the voice whispering to him and he could not stop it:

I am Memnon.

'*No you damn well are not,*' he hissed viciously.

'Sir?' Wayland.

'Bloody murderer,' he said, '*Bloody*, bloody *murderer.*'

Bonaparte.

Many of the camp knelt for morning prayers, facing the rising sun, their quiet chanting more life-affirming than the ravaged stone gods who listened. But disturbing the low murmur of prayer came the sound of thumping hoofbeats. Sheikh Saleh al-Mansur came at the head of a small group of riders, straight off the road past the twisting trees and across the scrub towards them, the shadows deepening in the first light of morning, streaking across the landscape. They clattered to a halt, the sand spraying, the horses puffing at their brief gallop.

'Hazar Pasha,' said Al-Mansur, raising a hand, 'You are found. *Al-hamdulillah.* These men—' He pointed over his shoulder: behind were three men in unfamiliar robes, their dark faces hidden by white and blue *shemagh*. 'They bring news from beyond Tur, from beyond the Khushmaan, from beyond even the Negev...' He spoke to one, who spurred his horse and rode forward to Hazzard, drawing to a halt.

'*A-s'lemu aalikum ya basha,*' he said in salute, his accent different, not Egyptian, then turned to Saleh al-Mansur. '*Hal ant sadiq?*'

Hazzard recognised the word *sadiq*: friend.

Al-Mansur nodded his head in assent, '*Hazar Pasha, Al-Injilizi.*' *Hazar Pasha, the Englishman.*

The messenger pulled back his veil, revealing a fine-boned black Somali face with short goatee beard and thin moustache. He looked at Hazzard then at Al-Mansur. '*El... el Aafrit el-ahmar?*'

The Red Devil.

Of all the things Hazzard felt he was, he certainly felt that much returning to him.

Hazzard nodded. '*Nahm.*'

Yes.

The rider reached for his saddle-bag, speaking while undoing its buckle, Tariq translating, 'Banaparteh-Sultan has been at Suez, he say, with his men of science... and gone, stealing cattle... and womenfolk from the *Bedu*. He is now thief. Men from Al-Sudan Bey and other rulers for his army come...'

The rider handed down a leather tube. Saleh al-Mansur took it and pulled off the cap, finding an unsealed scroll inside. He opened it out and read. He glanced at Hazzard and spoke in French. 'It is a *firman*. The Osmanli,' he said, 'the Sultan of Turks, has declared war upon Al-Banaparteh, with the Rus and the English.' He handed the scroll to Shajar to read. The rider spoke to him again, grim, proud. 'The war, he says, it is come, and so comes the Turk, in a great host of vengeance.'

The revolt must be a bloody, catastrophic failure.

And so it was, thought Hazzard. Lord Keith and the plotters had won.

Hazzard took steady breaths, his mind rushing with probabilities: it was not what Bonaparte wanted, no – but it was what he needed, as surely as he had needed action at Shubra Khit. He had come to conquer, not just preside. Now the new Ramesses, the reborn Ozymandias, could march on the Hittites once again, and sack Jerusalem.

They turned at the sound of distant hoofbeats, and saw a Tarabin scout dismount and come running. '*Silah al-fursani… fransaya.*' Cavalry. French.

Sheikh al-Mansur looked out at the Nile, at the Somali messenger. 'They must have been followed. French cavalry he says.' He asked the scout, '*Kem?*' How many?

The scout replied and the sheikh took a breath. 'Many.'

The sun emerged, casting its light over the plain and the ruins, the trees brightening, cracking as they leaned towards its warmth, the temple humming with its rebirth, the stones breathing anew. They heard a shot. The advance scouts of Al-Mansur and Shajar's Tarabin came at the gallop from the high ground behind, a cloud of dust in their wake rising like mist in the beams of sunlight.

Cook was already running down to the camp, *Mount yer arses up! One Section with Tariq, Two Section with Al-Mansur!* Still in shirtsleeves, Wayland ran to the horses, calling, *Handley!* and Handley beckoned, his arm up, his eye on the glass looking to the south, *Reckon on fifty – correction, 'undred – correction, could be two 'undred!* and Wayland called back, '*Firing positions! Load with buck and ball! Horses close and ready!*'

The marines sprinted in among the Tarabin and Mamluks, the goats bleating in fear, the *Bedu* herding them away to the shelter of the temple, Shajar's sharpshooters taking up posts behind the stone guardians of Memnon's spirit, their long Turkish miquelet muskets pointing towards the Nile. Hazzard joined them, watching from the pillars of the temple ruins with her, the painted blue sky and stars above them, and his hand squeezed her shoulder, her own hand touching his.

'I will have to leave you,' he said.

'And I you,' she replied.

'*Rabbena ma'ak.*'

God protect you.

She nodded, her eyes wide, blinking. '*Rabbena ma'ak,*' she said, her arm stretched out, unwilling to let go as he moved away. '*Hazar Pasha.*'

He looked back at her, then saw her, completely, in her dark blue linen, bandolier, pistol and dagger – her beauty, her compassion, her determination. When she sensed that he truly saw her, she let go.

A Tarabin ran to meet him, carrying the scimitar of Ali-Qarim. The stocky *Bedu* bowed and handed it over. '*Al-Aafrit al-ahmar.*' Hazzard nodded, '*Shukran,*' *thank you, yes, today I shall be the Red Devil once again.* He threw the leather buckles round his waist, and drew the sword, feeling the smooth grip which fitted so neatly into his hand, then slammed it home.

'Sir!'

Handley.

'Mr Handley.'

Handley slapped the Lorenzoni and its sling holster into his hand. 'Cleaned, loaded an' locked, sir, Frenchies, for the use of.'

Hazzard took it. 'Thank you, Handley. Mind yourself.'

'Will do, sir. Mr Wayland taught me to ride, last time.'

'So he did.'

Two thousand.

Bonaparte, I know you.

And by God you shall pay.

Hazzard glanced back at Ozymandias for the last time, as the stricken king welcomed the dawn, the heat already upon them – then out at the plain of the Theban Necropolis. The City of the Dead would soon have new souls to harvest. He saw Cook at his position with the marines.

'Jory – be ready for a run through the mountains,' called Hazzard. 'Like Peshawar all over again.'

Cook nodded with a glance at the folded rockhills behind. 'Ye're damn right there, sir...'

A cloud of dust rose from the south. The French had arrived.

Scipio

There was little they could do until the French revealed their full number or formation: Hazzard had to wait. As a skirmish force they would either have to snipe at the enemy or ambush them – or run. But Hazzard was not in the mood to run.

He left Shajar in command of the elevated firing post in the temple: it overlooked the plain and if the French came within range, her Tarabin could pick and choose their targets. Al-Mansur was already mounted, gathering his own men and riding off behind the temple ruins into the grassy foothills along a path they had chosen for just such an occasion. Each knew what they had to do. Karnak grew lighter and brighter by the moment on the other side of the Nile, the dark eastern mountains shifting into revealed focus, the rounded ancient peaks and strata coming into relief. Hazzard hurried to his horse, Tariq waiting stoically, looking southward.

'How many?' asked Hazzard, tensing, feeling the knee grate again, *Kam?*

Tariq checked the girth strap and buckles of the ornate tack. 'Company troop, *escadron*,' he said, showing his nerves, mingling French and English. 'Two hundred, or one-and-fifty, Hazar Pasha, can be more…' He stooped, cupping his hands for Hazzard to climb into the saddle, his bad left leg barely able to take the strain as Tariq pushed up, and he mounted, swinging his right leg over the high-backed Arabian saddle.

They had some sixty men in total, foot and horse – no match for two hundred French cavalry, a standard squadron column. Numbers dictated they should harass and fight a rearguard action as they disappeared into the western mountains behind them, behind Memnon, the only barrier to the desert beyond, and the beginning of the endless Sahara. But they had a plan, and it was simple, the oldest tactic on earth, scoffed Hazzard to himself, turning his mount, looking over the plain, the colossal statues below, the Nile their natural barrier. *Childish*, he thought, despising his idea's simplicity: known among Arabic commanders as *karr wa-farr*, employed by Scipio against Hannibal two thousand years earlier. And it might still work – because it was based on human emotion, not discipline.

Sixty against two hundred.

Madness.

He kicked his heels in and rode through the camp, the Bedouin rushing with their caravan belongings, hauling the camels along, the beasts roaring, laden like mules. He cantered past the humped tussocks of grass and scrub where the marines were preparing their positions with Cook. '*Jory! Three volleys then out! You damn well run! Clear!*'

Cook raised a hand. '*Clear aye!*'

He turned and saw a small group of horse led by Wayland, only a dozen of them, in the brightest robes in the camp, whites, reds and checks, Tarabin and a few of Al-Mansur's Mamluks, two of them already in heated argument, and Wayland had to shout to break them up, his pistol drawn. A call echoed across the plain and a shot was fired: the signal. Hazzard looked down the slope, past the scrub and gnarled thorn trees towards the Nile – and saw the rising dust.

'*Stand by!*' called Hazzard and spurred his horse down the slope to Wayland and his men. The sun dazzled and the twin Memnons on their thrones grew larger in his vision, one blotting out the sun. 'Mr Wayland!' he called.

Wayland shoved the pistol into his belt and drew his Mamluk *kilij*. '*Ya saif!*' Sword!

They cheered as Hazzard cantered through them. '*Hayya! Yallah!*'

They rode towards the Nile, the dust-cloud approaching from behind the promontory by the river, the ground shuddering hard beneath him. Hazzard realised he wore no *binish* or *kaftan*, only his Bombay scarlet and dark *keffiyah* headdress, and he thought, *Today they shall see a red coat.*

The indigo *shemagh* had come free from his face, flapping over his shoulder, and he tucked it in again, leaving only his eyes visible. Ahead, the sun glanced off a white lapel, then a scabbard and belt as the French cavalry rounded the corner by the river. Tariq and the scouts had not been wrong.

The French vanguard appeared at full strength, their mounts prancing, helmets flashing, dazzling, the plumes flying – they were *cuirassiers*, armed with pistol and sword, and had dispensed with their heavy breastplates in the heat. The squadron was in twin column formation, a senior NCO and their commanding officer, a major or colonel, at the head to one side in white gauntlets, golden fringed epaulettes and hanging braids, their dark blue dusted with the white of the desert, the officer pointing ahead with his drawn sabre. '*Bédoux! Préparez…!*'

Hazzard felt that same twist of nausea and power he knew from the sea, as an enemy ship turned to engage. He kicked his heels in and the horse leapt forward. He glanced over his shoulder. The Mamluk were with him in perfect formation, the Bedouin riding on the outside, their swords high, robes flying, the sun glowing through their white linens, trails of dust flaming behind the horses' hooves into columns of smoke, and he felt a pride he had not known before. *I ride with lions. I ride with fearless lions.*

And another strange thought seeped in:

Allahu akbar.

The first horsemen of the French column leapt forward into a gallop, sabres drawn, charging up to meet them head-on. The plan was for Hazzard to break when they reached the range of a pistol-shot, but the combined speed of the opposing charges was faster than he had anticipated and he did not want to break: he wanted to tear into them.

He drew the scimitar of Ali-Qarim from his left, and it flew upwards in his grip, a sheet of pain flowing up his back: *ignore.* He put the reins in his teeth, his breath sawing sibilantly past the salty leather, his jaw clenching tight enough to crack his own skull. He reached over his horse's plunging neck with his left hand and drew the second sword. The slim curved *shamshir* slipped from its sheath and he held both swords out, as Ali-Qarim had done, as the Mamluk had done. From the corner of his eye he saw the Mamluk behind had done likewise and they cried, *Ya saif Ali!*

The French vanguard jerked away suddenly then came back in line as the charge came within thirty yards, then twenty, one of them pointing, the call going up as he knew it would: *Anglais! Anglais!* The lines crashed through each other, Hazzard's twin swords scything through the first French sabres, their disciplined hanging-guard parried and struck aside by the tip of his scimitar, cutting them on the pull as he passed through them – *two*, and spinning, cutting across from behind, a man throwing his head back, his arms out, the horse rearing, screaming, a downward cut, a thigh, and a man fell, and he knew it was enough.

'*Turn! Karr wa-farr!*'

The Mamluks exploded from the back of the French cavalry troop and raced round in a tight arc, charging back up to the plain in a flying retreat, the swords sheathed, the Arabians lunging at full extension, a race to see who could escape first, *Run run!* Wayland rode beside him, both hands reaching forward to give his horse the rein it needed, a Newmarket jockey on the flat, Hazzard charging beside him, tiring, his heart hammering, *faster boy, faster.*

He risked a look over his shoulder and caught sight of two columns of enraged French charging after them, one section riding out to their left in a bid to cut them off, but the Mamluk were well ahead of Hazzard and dodged to the right, heading for the twin seated colossi of Memnon first, *yes*, he thought, *good*. The Titans stared from their thrones to the east, the sun washing them bright, the dust obscuring the world from their vision.

The Mamluks led the trailing Tarabin around the first colossus, snaking round behind the back of the other – and Hazzard watched as the French followed precisely, as if trusting only the path created by their quarry – until the shooting started.

Hazzard distinctly heard Underhill's parade-ground roar: *Fire!*

Hails of miquelet and buck and ball blasted the first French riders from their saddles, one dragging in the dust, his foot in the stirrup, trampled by the man behind, one horse trying to leap, the rider misjudging, crashing atop of them, a rolling collision of five at least. Another volley rang out, each shot finding its mark and the Mamluks cried out in retribution for Shubra Khit and Embabeh, for every man lost, some turning, cutting down the stragglers who lost their formation. One Mamluk jumped from his seat, both feet on the saddle, then sprang for a fleeing Frenchman, bringing him down, a massed cry going out, *Hunekha!*

Hazzard rode past Wayland. '*Temple!*'

'*Aye sir!*'

They led the Tarabin and Mamluks back up the long, low slope, clouds of dust billowing in the rising wind, stirred into swirling eddies, the terrain giving way to dry grasses and scrub as they continued the race uphill, the horses determined, hardly slowing. The bulk of the French cavalry now burst upon them, dodging the colossi, following

Hazzard and the Mamluks, but Underhill's section had already moved round the giant plinths and fired a second series of volleys, *Fire!* – cavalrymen flew from their mounts, just as the Mamluks had done before the French infantry squares, at the spiked castles of men.

The grasses rose and Hazzard misjudged one of the hillocks, the horse taking it in an easy leap, and he felt the rise of his stomach, floating within him, until the Arabian's forelegs thudded onto the sand and he banged back onto the saddle, his vision swimming, *mountains, reach the mountains.*

They roared past the mortuary temple, last refuge of Ozymandias, and he saw the flicker of muzzles firing, hearing nothing, as Shajar's crack-shots took more of the pursuing French – then down, away from the foothills, and he saw Cook, and heard another volley whipped away by the wind, as he and Wayland led the French past the different firing positions, each one an ambush, each one a fusillade, the French falling, another half-dozen, horses flailing in clouds of sand, crashing into the stone guardians of Anubis, to be mobbed by Shajar's daggers and knives, cut to pieces, the wind snatching away their screams, the rest following, always following.

He rode downhill back to the colossi, *open ground, yes, but not for long*, and he felt a hand clutch at his throat as he saw what he had feared, nearly half the French squadron forming line abreast at the colossi to meet them – so they had not merely been following mindlessly, but herding them as well, and now Hazzard had led the Mamluks and Tarabin back into their waiting arms.

But he had no choice. It was the plan. He looked to his left as he made the corner and began the turn. '*Mr Wayland! Behind me!*'

Wayland ignored him and spurred his mount, leading the Mamluks down to the waiting French cavalry. The French had the time to follow sabre drill: swords drawn, they held the blades upright before their faces, trotting, then their elbows swinging outward, their speed increasing, and he heard the command, *Chargez…!* The two ranks of horse leaned into the gallop, swords at full reach – and Wayland led the Mamluks straight into them.

Fifty yards, counted Hazzard, *forty, thirty*, his head snapping left and right to judge the distance and he shouted, '*Left left left!*'

Wayland broke left and the French tried to wheel, but Underhill, Pettifer and Napier stepped out from behind the second colossus and launched three heavy objects into the air – the last of their bag o'tricks.

The bundles soared over the field, and just above the front rank of horse, they exploded. The horses whinnied and shrieked, rearing up, and the charge fell apart, the natron and lime flashing bright, the black powder driving the nails and splinters into the horses, into the riders' shoulders, necks and faces, and ten fell in a broad circle, the thrashing legs knocking down those behind, the dense clouds of smoke from the burning oil-soaked wool impenetrable. The cavalry major tried to gather them, pull them back, blinded, unseated, the horses dying or galloping off – just as Al-Mansur's Mamluks came howling from the foothills behind the temple of Ozymandias.

Charging down the slope gave the Mamluks the advantage, heading into the glare of the rising sun without hesitation. Their *kilij* swords and scimitars reaching out, they burst through the French squadron and out the other side, turning in perfect unison. Hazzard watched the moment in awe, the same flock of birds he had seen so many months earlier as Murad had charged his enemy, charged the castles of men conjured from the sands.

The French tried to regroup, the fallen trying to remount, in no doubt as to what awaited them if captured; four fell at the stroke of the Mamluk scimitars, the razor-edges slicing cleanly through steel, leather, wool and bone. Al-Mansur led his troop around them in a tight circle, the dust rising in choking clouds, the French trapped, wheeling, horses rearing and whinnying, the confusion too great.

Hazzard looked back over his shoulder to the rise of the mortuary temple and his innards lurched: the French vanguard had broken off their pursuit of him and their decoy group – and now charged back down at the Mamluks, encircling their comrades by the seated colossi of Memnon. The French commander, his bright bullion-fringed epaulettes and golden braids flying behind, leapt a fallen horse, striking down with his sabre at a Mamluk in mid-charge and driving him down, breaking Al-Mansur's circle, and a cheer went up, *Ha Rou! Ha Rou!*

He tore through the centre to the first of the colossi, his sabre rolling in great circles from right to left, taking one man, unseating another, the Mamluks breaking up and pulling back to attack him alone. The officer wheeled about and charged Al-Mansur, a joust from five centuries ago, and Al-Mansur pulled his rein over, the Arabian leaping into the gallop, the white tassels on its bridle and saddle streaming behind, his gold-mounted *kilij* catching the officer's sabre and fending it off, the hilts clashing at full speed, and the Mamluks roared, *Hunekha!* Al-Mansur dropped his arm and drew first across the Frenchman's waist as he flew past, the officer toppling forward, cut, Al-Mansur holding the sword aloft and the men cheering, *Ali...!*

Hazzard spurred his horse as he heard Cook, *Out! Out and juldee with it, ye buggers!* And he saw the running figures of the marines making for the back of the temple and the path into the foothills, Shajar standing, watching, calling orders to her own people, the Tarabin running to cover, falling flat, firing, the musket balls snapping.

Hazzard spun the horse about and headed for Al-Mansur, hearing Wayland again, *Sir, sir!* but wanted to get the Tarabin out, to get Shajar out, to get the marines to cover. A section of French at full charge raced in a graceful arc and headed towards him, pointing at his Marine scarlet, *Anglais! Milord Mamluk!*

Hazzard spurred his horse to draw them away from Cook and Shajar, and they followed, *Anglais...!* Every hoofbeat on the hard ground battering his senses, he charged down to the battlefield at the colossi, other Tarabin behind him, one snapping a shot from his carbine, Wayland at his side.

'*Get after the men!*' shouted Hazzard, but Wayland pointed down to the colossi, his answer lost in the thunder of the charge. Ahead, the French had broken off and formed up again, fewer, vastly fewer, a hundred left at most – they galloped away, then split into three blocks, turning about and charging again from different points. There were simply too many of them.

'*Sheikh Saleh!*' called Hazzard, but Al-Mansur could not hear. '*God's sake...*'

Al-Mansur charged his men at the centre of the three blocks before the two wings could perform their pincer, and cut through the French, Mamluks falling, French knocked from their saddles, a Mamluk javelin slicing through the melee, taking one rider and throwing him down, the French survivors to be hit by more flying buck and musket-ball. Underhill roared out, '*Two frogs each man or I'll scrag yer proper, me beauties!*' They had not fallen back as ordered.

Hazzard looked over his shoulder to see Cook, Underhill and the marines, standing, lying, kneeling, with Shajar's Tarabin, all firing, the French falling, and he wanted to scream back at them to *go* – until he saw why: coming from behind, out of the mountain pass from far beyond the mortuary temple, with a sound like the rumble of distant guns, came a thunderhead of dust. He had seen it only once before, at Shubra Khit.

A pillar of fire.

Cavalry, at full gallop, burst across the plain in three squadrons, each in arrowhead formation, their shout echoing across the folded crags and bluffs of the blazing western mountains. *Murad Murad Murad! Allahu akbar!*

It was Murad Bey.

Al-Mansur heard the sound and turned his men about to cut back through the French, but the French cavalry paused, all heads turned to see the newcomers. Five times their number, the Mamluks swept onto the field, swords out in both hands, one with a tall bow, an arrow whistling past, the thwack of the quarrel as it struck home, a man falling. A bugle sounded among the French and the cry went up: *Retirez!*

The Tarabin joined Murad's charge, straggling French desperate, trying to get out before they were cut off. One of the French drew a pair of holster pistols and fired into the Mamluks, taking one, then another, a Tarabin *Bedu* falling from his saddle. Hazzard saw a large shape rise up from the scrub – it was Napier.

'*Ali…! It's me mate Ali!*'

Cook bellowed, '*Marine Private Napier! Get yer ruddy arse back 'ere now!*'

But the big man did not hear. He lumbered down the slope to Ali and picked him up, flinging him like a sack onto his left shoulder. Some of the French cavalry saw him and opened fire, pistol-shots pecking at the ground by his feet – and he ran, then stopped, bent again, and pulled at another Mamluk with his free hand, dragging him away from a fallen horse. Hazzard could not believe his eyes.

Napier…

Hazzard cranked the Lorenzoni and dropped the nearest French rider, but another had turned to charge. Napier hefted the second man under his free arm, the marines rushing out to him, *Covering fire!* Napier ran, his big feet stamping at the ground, his broken, beaten face twisted with exertion – until a shot rang out, and he stumbled and fell.

'*Arthur!*' Warnock and Cochrane were on him at once, trying to pull him in behind the rocks, Warnock seeking out the man who had fired. The French horseman threw away his spent pistol and Warnock charged, dodging his sabre, his Huron tomahawk hacking at the man's leg. He put a hand to the rider's boot and shoved him up from the saddle, *Come on ye shite!* – propelling him through the air to land heavily on the hard ground, his sword clattering. Warnock leapt on him, smashing his skull to powder with the sharpened stone axe, *bastard bastard*, the Frenchman's screams shrill and piercing, suddenly stopping short. Pettifer blasted a salvo of the blunderbuss, clearing the field as they pulled Ali, Napier and the other Mamluk to cover.

The French turned to ride from the field, some stooping to help their comrades, others kicking their heels in to escape, all falling back in disorder. But several by the Memnon colossi were still engaged in sword duels with Al-Mansur's Mamluks – and Wayland.

Hazzard saw Wayland charge into the tangle of horses, men and sabres, then dip down low to one side, and tear upwards at a French rider, slashing the man's girth strap, the saddle swinging off, unseating him – and a running figure, *Hesse?* waving to him from the shadow of the giant statue's massive stone plinth, being chased by a French horseman.

Wayland charged the rider, his sword held out in good hanging-guard as Hazzard had taught him, but the cavalryman drove his blade away, knocking Wayland back in his saddle. Hazzard tore down the slope, through the duels, leaping a fallen horse, *Mr Wayland!*, a Frenchman tumbling away with a cry, and he saw Wayland falling to one side, his sword battered away again. '*Mr Wayland…!*'

Wayland yanked his rein to one side and the horse jerked away from the French cavalryman – he raised his sword again but the French rider hacked at Wayland again and again, Wayland turning the horse to present a different target, a different angle. He drew a short cutlass with his left hand, whipping upwards to parry the French sabre so he could strike with the *kilij* in his right, but too late. Hazzard fired the Lorenzoni, the bullet striking the stone base of the colossus beside them, and called out again as he saw what was to come: the French sabre came down from on high, caught by the short cutlass, but sliding past it, cutting down, into Wayland's forearm.

No—

Wayland's cutlass and his severed left hand flew outward and the boy screamed, startling the Frenchman sufficiently that he pulled back, Hesse running round, firing upwards with his musket and dropping the rider to the ground. Clutching at the bloody stump of his wrist,

Wayland fell from the saddle, Hesse bringing him down, holding him tight and dragging him to cover at the base of the great pedestal of Memnon.

Hazzard dodged left, then right, a stricken horse before him, the Lorenzoni firing into a face, a man clutching at his head and falling. He burst out of the dust-storm just behind the stone colossus towering above, and slid from the saddle, pulling the horse with him. '*Hesse! Get him up on the horse! Schnell, Mann!*'

Speaking German had its effect on the Austrian, and they hauled Wayland to his feet, Hazzard taking his other arm and they pushed him across the saddle. The boy was not out cold yet, but pulled his leg over the haunch of the horse and Hazzard jumped up behind. '*Hesse! Stay in cover! Murad comes!*'

'*Jawohl, Herr Major!*'

As he spoke, a storm of Mamluk horse crashed through them, Memnon giving them shelter. Al-Mansur's men leading the way, Murad and his cohort of cavalry thundered past, the Theban plain thrumming to galloping hooves, whistles and cries. The remaining French fled, leaving the field littered with their dead, stragglers speared where they stood, one caught on foot, an Ottoman lance running him through, embedding itself in the ground, the body propped standing, a new guard to the afterworld for the colossus of Memnon, glowering above in his displeasure.

Holding the sagging Wayland, Hazzard kicked the horse towards the mortuary temple and rode, thinking only of the blood, *the blood*, his eye flicking from the field to Wayland's left wrist, and the boy's grip on it: he had known enough instinctively to seize it tight and it had worked so far, but the shock of it would be too great to keep him going and already Hazzard could feel he was cold.

'*Nearly there, Mr Wayland… hold on! Hold on—*' He could not think of his proper name, *Thomas? Marmaduke? Which? Christ…* He called out, '*Porter! Jory!*'

He reached the scrub and the marines came running, crowding round, Warnock the most fearful, *Is he gone, no he can't be gone*, Cook's hands lifting Wayland down, *Take his legs, take his legs, dammit boy*, laying him on the ground. Cook and Underhill immediately dragged off their *shemagh* headdress for a good length of fabric, and tore at the tough linen, Kite managing with his own, *Here sir*, Underhill taking it as Cook held the boy's wrist as high as he could, *Keep it up, aye* – they tied the length of cloth tight and the pulsing bleeding stopped but Wayland had gone white. Porter rushed in among them and skidded through the sand and stone beside Wayland, his bag clinking beside him. He looked at the wound.

'*Mary and all the saints…*' He held the wrist gingerly. It was cut at an angle, not clean but not badly either. A flap of white skin hung down from the top of the wrist, the ends of the radius and ulna bones glowing white, the tendons, ligaments protruding jaggedly as the tightly sprung muscle tissue recoiled, the blood vessels compressed, their darkness pooling on the remaining tissue. '*I need hot tar, lord above,*' gasped Porter, 'I need…'

He took Warnock's hands and placed them round the severed wrist. 'Hold, keep upright.' Pettifer gave Wayland a sip of water and he swallowed hard, coughing while Porter rummaged in his bag, his forehead dripping with sweat. He brought out a blue bottle and unstopped the cork – Hazzard knew it at once: laudanum. Porter put it to Wayland's lips and tapped out two fat drops. '*Time,*' he said. No one answered. Porter lashed out at them, '*What is the time!*' De Lisle rifled through the layers of Wayland's shirt and breeches and found it on a lanyard round his neck, the only pocket-watch they knew. 'A quarter past eight o'the clock,' he said.

'Right. Two drops every two hours,' said Porter. 'Next at the quarter past ten.' He looked at the wound and shook his head. '*Lord oh lord… wrap or stitch, wrap or stitch…*'

He took out a curved needle and black thread, and bit off a length, then tried to thread the needle with shaking hands. '*For blessed virgin's sake, please…*' Threading it, he pulled the thread through and made a knot. 'Hold,' he said again to Warnock, and De Lisle helped hold the wrist steady as Porter pulled the flap of skin over the stump as best he could – and was ready to stitch.

The thunder of hooves gave way to distant cheering on the plain: *Murad Murad Murad! Allahu akbar!* There was a call from behind as one of Shajar's Tarabin women pushed her way through, '*Leh! Leh leh…*' It was Zeinab – older than the others of her clan, her face lined by decades of sand and wind, her black eyes narrowed into mere slits beneath her Maghrib headdress. In her hand was a *khanjar* dagger, the curving blade glowing red-hot. She looked at Porter, and leaned over him, then nodded. '*Nahm?*' Porter understood and nodded back, '*Nahm.*' Yes.

She applied the flat of the blade to the torn flesh of the wrist. Wayland gave a brief cry, and his head rolled to one side, unconscious. 'E's passed out, doc!' said Warnock with alarm. There was a sizzling and the pop of the burning tissue, a wisp of smoke from the wound and Wayland jerked, his legs, his whole frame jarring with the pain, his head whipping to one side though he was still blacked out. She looked at Porter and nodded. '*Hassaneh.*' *All right*.

Warnock and De Lisle held the wrist tight, Warnock murmuring, 'Come on doc, you can do it a-right.' His fingers trembling, his face sweating, Porter began to stitch the flap of whitened skin over the charred stump. Zeinab held the thread away, stopping it from tangling, watching him, nodding. '*Oh lord, oh lord...*' He began to pray, '*Our Father who art in Heaven...*'

The marines joined in, led by Cochrane, 'Oh Lord guide this our brother's hand in his work, and look down upon thy servant, fallen on this field of Man's iniquity... as he did cast his life as naught in the service of others...' Cochrane looked down, his eyes closed. 'Amen.'

The others chorused, *amen, aye*, as they looked down and watched, and Porter finished.

'Done—' Porter tried to tie a knot but his bloodied fingers were no good and Zeinab took over, biting the thread off and tying it swiftly. Porter looked over his shoulder and took the length of fabric from Underhill and poured the contents of another bottle onto it, then wrapped it round the stump of the wrist, tucking it into the tourniquet. The white linen immediately bloomed with bloodstains, but no renewed bleeding. He took a breath, the woman's hand on his, nodding, a tight smile, '*Hassaneh, hassaneh.*'

'Sir...' Porter looked up for Hazzard, his own face drained and chalky-white. 'He needs to go to t'hospital. There could be gangrene, or sepsis, draining, or we might needs remove his arm at the elbow. He'll need debridement, maggots... *bloody maggots...*' His voice cracked, his shaking hand in his hair. 'I'm no surgeon, sir—' He looked down, tears on his face, '*I'm not nothin' for the lad or nobody, just a bloody quack...*'

Handley took hold of him as Porter wept out of frustration, fear, relief, who knew, but it mattered to none of them, just that he was there. Hazzard watched them, his eyes staring, the enormity of it all barely sinking in, his face flushing hot, his heart hammering, remembering their first meeting, the blushing boy with the clattering sword, their fencing lessons on *Esperanza*, letting him ride, letting him stay, *letting* him: *his fault*.

They heard a call from behind. It was Pettifer, kneeling over Napier – Porter looked over at them. 'Right, right… *done. Up.*' He pushed himself up and ran to Pettifer, Cochrane close behind. Napier lay on his back, eyes closed. Porter bent forward, an ear to Napier's lips, 'Air, I hear air… by the lord, Arthur—' He put a finger to the side of his neck, then lay his head on his chest. 'Pulse… too weak but it's ruddy there…' He jumped up and straddled the big boxer, beating his fist on Napier's chest three times, pausing, then pounding again. 'Cocky, you listen!'

Cochrane bent over him, ear to his chest, 'Nottin', doc! His heart's stopped—'

Cook slapped at Napier's face, 'Come on, Arthur, damn ye boy!'

Cochrane watched the big man's face. '*Doc, bae God,*' he cried, 'He's goin' *blue… Jaysus, Mary an' Joseph…*' Cochrane lifted Porter aside and tried to climb on himself. 'Doc – *mind, quick now, get back—*'

Porter moved out of the way as the former hangman raised his fist and brought it down like a sledgehammer. There was a loud crack to Napier's ribs, the crowd of gathered Mamluks and *Bedu* gasping. Arthur Napier blew out a lungful of air, wheezed, then breathed like a man saved from drowning, his chest expanding, his eyes widening, and he blinked. 'Cocky…?' he said 'Di–did Ali get back…?'

'*Art'ur,*' choked Cochrane with a laugh of relief, 'I t'ought ye'was gone… we all t'ought ye'was gone…'

Cook sagged visibly from the ordeal, patting the big man on his shoulder. 'Ye done it boy, ye got him back…' He glanced at Pettifer, on one knee behind, the lifeless body of Ali nearby. The big Cornishman shook his head sadly.

Porter nodded. 'Got to get that bullet out,' he said, and they rolled him onto his front. He used a long pair of tweezers to find the wound, and Zeinab handed him scissors to cut open the robes. '*God and glory…*' murmured Porter as he delved inside, more confident after Wayland. He pulled back the folds of striped wool and linen to find the .42 calibre pistol-ball staring back at him, buried in blackened tissue. The robe had taken much of the impact but the muscle had slowed its path and stopped it. '*By God in heaven…* He's got a back like sheet-iron…' He reached for a pair of long-nosed pliers, took a two-handed grip on the handles, and pulled. With a sucking pop, the ball snapped out, but he looked in, then back up at Hazzard. 'Needs a surgeon, sir. The cloth is shredded, some could be buried deep... it will suppurate.'

Shadows fell across them and they looked up to see the Mamluk sheikhs, Al-Mansur, and the towering bulk of Murad Bey himself. Murad squatted down among them, the piercing blue eyes above the hook nose burning into them all, his great shaggy beard grown greater still since last they had met, when Hazzard had warned him of the French. It might have been a happier reunion, but Murad gave him a grim smile. 'Hingleesh,' he said and bowed. '*As-salamu aleikum*—' he said, '...*Hazar Pasha.*'

Murad looked down at the childlike Napier, blinking upwards through tears, '*I tried to save him sir... honest...*' – and at the blond boy, the torn white shirt, the bloody stump of his left wrist, and knelt, patting Wayland's arm, murmuring to himself, shaking his head.

'Murad says,' explained Al-Mansur, 'Thus are the English.'

Murad sat up and lifted a charm from round his neck, an old coin, a hole cut through its centre, a fine loop of gold suspending it from its leather thong. He laid it on Wayland's chest and spoke to Al-Mansur.

'Murad says, tell any man, by my command, and receive my blessing, food, water, horse, and it shall be given, as I am the true *Amir al-Hajj* of Egypt.'

Al-Mansur bowed, as did the others, and Hazzard nodded, '*Shukran.*' It was barely a whisper but he knew what they should do. He looked at Al-Mansur. 'The river. *Al-nahara.* We're going to the river, Sheikh.'

Al-Mansur put this into Arabic for them and Murad rose and raised a hand, shouting out above their heads. There were cries at the back of the group, and Hazzard galvanised the marines into action. 'Pack up, *now*. Kite, you and Hesse get us a boat, somehow, *felucca*, punt, raft, I don't care. We've got to save Napier and Mr Wayland, so we're taking them out to the fleet. What says the boat?'

They had no hesitation, and without a glance to each other replied, *aye*.

A Mamluk rider was passed through to the sheikhs and *sanjaqs* at the front and Al-Mansur said, 'There is a craft, a small vessel – they wish to help, carry your *M'sieur* Wayland, and your great warrior, who saves *Bedu* and Mamluk alike.'

Murad took Hazzard's hand and smiled. '*Good*, Hingleesh. I *t'ank* you.'

Hazzard bowed. 'And I, thank you, sir.'

The Mamluks knotted the ends of a torn robe and set it on the ground beside Napier and bent down, Warnock, Underhill, Cook and Porter helping lift him, swinging him into the stretcher, then carried him. Two other Mamluks knelt beside Wayland with another robe stretcher, and did likewise, the boy half the weight of the heavy marine, Hazzard grateful he was barely conscious.

The regiment of Mamluk cavalry parted and the stretcher-bearers hurried, Hazzard leading them, the marines alongside. Shajar was waiting for them down at the river with the broad ferry-punt Kite and the Mamluks had found – an old man, bowing, pleased to serve, come across the Nile from his usual route on the far bank.

They were quickly aboard, Hesse dumping a number of bloodied dark blue tunics and helmets in a heap as they fell back, exhausted, the two wounded lain beside each other, Porter ministering to them, Cochrane not leaving Napier's side.

Hazzard knew only that they had to get both of them to a doctor. Shajar stood on the riverbank with Murad and Sheikh Saleh al-Mansur, the Mamluks riding the field between the colossi of Memnon, firing their carbines in the air, *Murad Murad Murad! Allahu akbar!*

The boat dipped and rocked with the waves, and was pulled into the strong current, the old man at the tiller with eyes only for their destination, the distant sea. They all stared, dark-eyed, drained.

The twin giant Memnons receded slowly, and Hazzard gripped the loose old rope stays of the boat's single mast and looked back, at Karnak, at a City of the Dead, watching Shajar al-Durr standing apart, a slowly diminishing figure in black, his veiled goddess from ancient Thebes – doubting he would ever see her again.

Tuileries

Winter had come to Paris, the grey morning revealing rooftops frosted with snow, the trees bare and shivering in the cold wind whistling down the Seine, the coal and woodsmoke of early fires choking thick on the air. The clashing chimes of Nôtre-Dame, Montmartre and others echoed distantly, striking eight. It was *primidi*, the first day of the Republican working week, and the lavish halls of the Tuileries Palace gleamed bright. A celebrity had come to call.

An escort squad of four stone-faced troopers of the 1st Cavalry marched through the broad panelled halls, past gleaming columns, their sabres drawn, their ironshod heels clicking in unison on the marble floors. In their care were three young sun-browned officers in braided coats and fur-trimmed cloaks, their swords rattling as they processed, murmuring to each other, one laughing quietly, keeping their spirits up. Many of the onlookers recognised one face in particular passing before them: barely twenty, he was the most trusted emissary of the greatest general in France – his younger brother, Louis Bonaparte, fresh from Egypt.

In gold-embroidered topcoat, sash and sword, hat tucked under one arm, he looked the very image of the Conqueror of the Orient and scourge of the Ottomans. His gaze flicked to either side at the Tuileries guardsmen of the *Armée de Paris*, and he nodded at their recognition. One after another the sentries presented arms as if to the general himself, *À… vous!*, their hands cracking on the forestocks of their muskets like rifle-shots, a voice calling out from one, *Vive le Général Bonaparte!* And others, *Vive le général! Hwa, hwa, hwa!*

Less saturnine than Napoléon, Louis looked about him with some justifiable wonder, at the beating heart of the Revolution, his dark curling hair and wide eyes giving him an approachable air, perhaps one pliable enough to coercion, but perhaps not. At twenty, he was a captain, though he had been offered colonel – something he had refused, owing to his own assessment of his experience, vanity the least of his vices.

The cavalrymen ascended the central staircase in perfect step, the pillars of the galleried upper floor of the great domed atrium casting stark shadows from lights soaring far overhead, and young Louis looked down at the guardsmen, their faces turned to watch him – he raised a hand to them and they cheered once more. He hefted the slung sabre-tache higher onto his shoulder, the messenger of his supreme commander – who was still the embodiment of all fears for the Directors of France.

In the private offices of the Directory government, they could hear the cheers. At a decorative gilt console desk in front of the tall Tuileries windows sat the cold and brittle Director Louis de la Révellière-Lépeaux, in white wig and grey frock-coat, a pair of gold wire-framed spectacles perched on his nose. He listened to the popular adulation below. An ormolu clock chimed on the marble mantel, the fire in the grate crackling. It brought him no warmth.

Possibly aware of the ghost of Maximilien Robespierre hovering at his elbow, Lépeaux kept his voice low and turned to his colleague behind, who stood looking out at the snow-powdered gates and gardens, and the smoking rooftops of Paris. 'We performed a complete *volte-face*. And this is the result. I warned you, Paul. *Warned you*. Disaster.'

'Which is why we need you, Louis, to see that it is not perceived as such,' replied his less agitated colleague, Director Paul Nicolas Barras. His hair pulled back in the modern fashion, in heavy, dark velvet frock-coat and high-throated waistcoat and cravat, the taller and bulkier Barras was possibly the most imposing statesman in France. Of the two, the ruthless and astute Barras had stayed atop the teetering and greasy pole more steadily than his rivals, and now reigned supreme in all but name. However, though leader of the five remaining Directors, Barras still needed the consensus of his two senior colleagues. And though Lépeaux, cold, slight and quick, was more amenable to Barras's corrupt manipulation, the others were not – hence their absence that morning.

'The Council of Five Hundred *still* demand we address the invasion of Ireland and England. This,' said Lépeaux, with a slap of the documents in his hand, 'this Egypt nonsense is mere schoolboy fantasy, and our heads *will roll*.'

'Not while we have Bonaparte.'

Lépeaux turned on him at last. 'I know he was your protégé, Paul, but the sainted Napoléon Bonaparte disposes of the Government of France as if we were his own personal exchequer and counting-house. He has grown tired of victory in the desert, I tell you, and will turn his sights on us very soon. If he ever returns.'

Usually the very soul of political *bonhomie*, Barras looked down at him severely. 'Be in no doubt, Louis,' he replied. 'With a single command Napoléon could call to these palace gates over twenty thousand devoted men. They would follow him through the inferno itself. Ha. And emerge with Lucifer's balls in their teeth.'

That they occupied their exalted position from a coup, supported by Bonaparte's troops, was a constant source of fear to them both: what indeed could prevent Bonaparte doing it again? They stood still, hearing the distant cheers in the main gallery welcoming their guest.

'So we see the brother quietly do we,' he muttered irritably, 'with the entire palace hallooing below.'

'Cannot be helped, Louis,' said Barras. 'Must give them something of their hero. And ours, remember that.' He moved to the fire to warm his hands. 'It is bitter. I can only imagine how he feels after damnable sand dunes and things…'

'This is an impossible position!' snapped Lépeaux, angered by this irresistible *fait accompli*. 'First we must *send* your so-called Caesar and his legions to darkest Africa, and now we must *rescue* him!'

Barras spotted a small plate of biscuit *délices* and popped one into his mouth. 'He must hear the truth first,' he said while chewing. 'And you do that best.'

'The truth?' Lépeaux was almost revolted at the sight of Barras eating. 'Hoche up in arms, Massenat calling for men in Italy…'

'As we discussed,' said Barras, his fingers daintily sorting through the bon-bons before him. 'Then I shall take him elsewhere and learn more of Caesar's ambitions.'

Lépeaux looked at him. 'And that he should stay there.'

'Perhaps…' Barras looked up at the clock on the mantel and adjusted his cravat in the mirror behind. He dropped his hands and looked at himself, a grim realisation overtaking him. 'Or pray he never returns to cross the Rubicon.' The words hung in mid-air a moment, but he turned to Lépeaux. 'For all our sakes.'

The tall double-doors opened. An official put his head round the door. '*Capitaine* Bonaparte, Citizen Directors, and escort.' He opened the double doors wide.

'Very well,' said Lépeaux. He straightened his coat, set his spectacles upon his nose, pulled his chair in more tightly to the desk, and waited.

The cavalrymen marched through the outer office and entered, crashing to a halt. Louis Bonaparte and his fellow officers stepped forward two paces and stopped. They bowed their heads. Smiling, Bonaparte went forward to meet Barras, already moving to greet him, hand extended.

'*Captain* Bonaparte,' said Barras warmly. 'Ha! It has been a while since last I said that! Ah, but he was so soon a *colonel...!*'

Louis Bonaparte nodded, an embarrassed smile. 'Citizen Director, great fondness. Yes, once captain, and now he is general. In Egypt they call him Sultan *al-Kebir*. The Great Sultan.'

Barras roared. 'Haha! Wonderful! So they should! For so he is indeed,' he said indulgently, indicating the desk where Lépeaux remained seated. 'Citizen De la Révellière-Lépeaux, of the Executive Directory. I believe you have not met.'

'No,' said Louis, and bowed his head once again. 'An honour, Citizen Director.'

'Indeed it is,' said Lépeaux.

'Captains Le Gros and St Pierre,' said Bonaparte, indicating his companions. 'My good friends.'

'Excellent,' said Barras, nodding to an official. 'Citizens, there is coffee, brandy and a fire in the inner sanctum. We shall not be long,' he said. 'Just a preliminary discussion today, eh, my good Louis?'

Bonaparte nodded, discomfited, as the pair were led out by a nondescript secretary in high collar and tailcoat. They filed out, looking back at Louis, who examined the bare desk, the few papers, the hard-backed gilt chair awaiting him opposite Lépeaux. The doors shut with an echoing click and Barras turned, taking his seat. 'And you are feeling better, Captain? Your *maladie nerveuse...*? Now that you are out of that infernal heat?'

'It was perhaps only the fever,' said Bonaparte self-consciously. 'They call it many things I am sure...'

'Mm, mm,' nodded Barras solicitously, moving his seat to the corner of the desk, giving an air of informality – and neatly distancing himself from Lépeaux. Lépeaux noticed, straightened his cravat, and turned back to Bonaparte, waiting.

'Well…' said Bonaparte uncertainly, and pulled the sabre-tache from his shoulder and opened it. 'It is my honour to present the despatches from the *général en chef* in the new Republican colony in Egypt.'

He handed over a leather-bound folder and Lépeaux took it as Bonaparte sat, his chair scraping on the cold stone floor. Possibly keen to look undaunted, Louis Bonaparte settled himself, his cloak, his sword, but his eyes flicked from the high windows to the chandeliers, the mantel, the fire, the desk, the large chamber more or less empty, Spartan, much like Lépeaux himself – and all the colder because of it. He pulled his fur cloak round his shoulders more tightly.

Lépeaux read each sheet with only a cursory glance, unimpressed. 'Before we read through these later with the Foreign Minister *in camera*, perhaps you would like to present us with a précis,' he suggested.

Young Louis Bonaparte hesitated. 'They are chiefly requests for reinforcements, Director, that I am asked to—'

'From where? France is committed to several campaigns. Funds are depleted for excursion.'

Louis continued uncertainly, 'He calls for more ships, for more men—'

'Again, this is not possible given the current economic crisis.'

Louis looked to Barras, who stared back with a blank smile. 'But we need materiel, powder, shot, coin—'

Lépeaux was unequivocal. 'The Comptroller will never allow it. The people starve and the army goes unshod, many without proper clothing, even in winter. The general will have to think again. The loss of the fleet has cost us all dear.'

The young captain looked away at mention of this. Though cast off by his brother as a minor setback, it was the only blot on the battle-honours of the campaign to date. 'The defeat was not his fault, but… circumstance.'

Lépeaux nodded. 'And that circumstance died at his post to pay the price. Though to France the loss is incalculable.'

They sat quietly for a while. Ships aside, the price of that defeat in the loss of Admiral Brueys, Captain Du Petit-Thouars and others had been dear indeed, nearly eclipsing Bonaparte's victories.

Barras glanced at Lépeaux and intervened. 'Captain… my good Louis, if I may,' he began. 'We are hard-pressed, on all sides. The Austrians have regrouped in Italy, there is movement on the Rhine, and the Turks have allied with the Russians and the English. We are facing a new coalition of enemies.' He spread his hands. 'France is under siege once again.'

'In Egypt we are strong,' asserted Louis, 'but cut off. We could come back home, and help—'

'What then of the colony? It must yield dividends to the public coffers.' Lépeaux was almost angry with the boy. 'It is as I said,' he declared coldly. 'This was *always* the danger.'

'The danger…?' said Louis. 'My brother, the general, can overcome anything. The revolt in Cairo was as nothing to him. He defeated and pardoned the rebels, and they have flocked to him. He says they are his children – children of our Revolution.'

Lépeaux leaned back in his chair. 'No reprisal?'

'He beheaded the ringleaders, yes, as would any prince of Egypt. Peace in Cairo, he says, has a simple formula: take six heads a day and keep smiling.' Barras began a jovial laugh but stopped when he saw Louis Bonaparte was not joking. 'Yet he also pardons them. They fear him. But his soldiers love him.' He gestured at the doors, as if to the guards in the halls below. 'As they do here, with good reason.'

None could tell if the boy meant to do it, but the mute threat was clear. It was just as Barras had told Lépeaux earlier: Napoléon Bonaparte was adored. Louis looked away. 'The general asks that if the invasion of Ireland or England is now no longer feasible, could we move the Atlantic Fleet to Toulon… and reinforce Egypt that way? It would break the blockade—'

Lépeaux shook his head again. 'We must defend the Channel ports from the English.'

Louis Bonaparte swallowed. 'Then I – I do not…'

Lépeaux moved a document from his side of the table and spun it round to face Bonaparte. 'Certain events have taken place recently of which the general is unaware. Primarily, the declaration of war from the Turkish sultan.'

Louis leaned forward to read the document. 'What is this…?'

'It is the despatch we were to send to the general in Egypt, but have delayed for your arrival.'

Louis scanned the page, his face flushing, the legalities too long-winded and circuitous for him to grasp at once. 'But I do not understand... if they have declared war, then—'

'Allow me,' said Lépeaux, turning it back. 'In our draft communiqué to the general we shall state he has three options. Namely, to access the Red Sea with a new fleet to liaise with Citizen Tipu Sultan, who fights the English in India. Two, to march across the Sinai Peninsula, Arabia and Persia to India, overland, gathering recruits to the army on the way...' He coughed to clear his throat, as if the words were difficult to voice, '...and three, to march into the Holy Land,' he said, 'take Constantinople... and destroy the Ottoman Empire to protect the colony of Egypt.'

Lépeaux removed his spectacles, breathing on them and polishing them with a linen handkerchief. He sat back, waiting.

Louis Bonaparte blinked, overwhelmed. 'If we must garrison Egypt... that would leave but fifteen thousand active men for battle.'

Lépeaux nodded. 'I see.'

'March to India...? I – I could not yet *name* the countries we would have to conquer, or – or treat with en route...' He sat back, astonished. 'The Ottoman Turks must have tens of thousands... or—'

'Over a hundred thousand,' said Lépeaux, 'according to our sources. A rabble, they say, untrained, levies.'

'The Turks are the deadliest troops I have ever seen on a field of battle,' retorted Louis. 'But that – that is *impossible*. How could we... *mon dieu*... I did not know...'

Lépeaux seemed to care little. 'Will you take replies back with you, Captain? Or...?'

Louis stared unseeing at the table before him. 'I – I was to take a command... in Italy.' He looked up. 'But yes, I will go back, go back to *be* with him—'

Barras held up a hand. 'My boy, that would be unwise.'

'But why? You were the great general, Director, you were there, on the 13th *Vendémiaire*—' Louis looked at him aghast. 'You gave him his first command – you would not... *abandon* him?'

Lépeaux had no hesitation in saying it. 'To spend millions in evacuating Egypt makes little commercial sense if we are in danger of attack from all sides at home. I am sure your brother the Citizen General would agree.'

'Evacuate? He would never assent to evacuation. And neither would his soldiers! They are the bravest men I have ever seen, marching eight, ten hours a day in fifty-degree heat! Who else can do this? And for whom would they? None but the general.'

Louis fell silent. Still recoiling from the shock he pushed himself out of his chair, looking about, unwilling to meet their eye. 'I am… I must report to… *mon dieu*,' he gasped, turning at last. 'If I had but a *company* of those men I could recapture the whole of Italy. And you would leave them in the *desert*…?'

'We would not,' said Lépeaux crisply, gathering his papers, 'but I am sure the general will find a solution.' He stood, his chair scraping against the cold stone floor. The interview was at an end. 'We will continue this in the week. Good day to you, Captain.'

Barras rose and led him to the door. 'Come, we shall have a cognac hm, and we shall see the better side of things, eh?'

Louis nodded. 'Yes, Citizen Director.' He looked back at Lépeaux. 'Director. I bid you good day.'

Lépeaux looked up from his papers, then looked down again, as if Louis Bonaparte's presence were already forgotten.

Barras closed the door, guiding Bonaparte into the corridor. An official approached. 'Citizen Director, the President of the Council… I apologise…'

Along the corridor came a figure striding towards them vigorously, calling out, 'So, Citizen Barras, what perfidy is this? You bring the brother of France's greatest general and exclude the President of the Council of Five Hundred for conference?'

Barras nodded kindly to the official. 'Thank you, Jean-Pierre. I called for him.'

The president drew closer, his arms out wide and Louis smiled at last. 'Lucien…'

They embraced, and Lucien Bonaparte, his elder brother, banged him on the back heartily. '*Mon dieu*, the conquering hero comes! *Voilà! Ecco l'uomo!*' He looked him over. 'Ah, the saints, you look well, thin hm, and dark as a nut, eh!' Lucien Bonaparte had the same taut physique as his brothers, but was smoother, his thick dark hair combed back from a handsome face, the vigorous guardian of their name in government.

Barras smiled and said quietly, 'He has just had the news.'

Lucien glanced at him. 'Citizen Lépeaux and his balance sheet?'

Barras nodded. 'But I am sure we can find ways,' he said. 'For there are some of us within these walls who still revere the general's name,' he said pointedly. Lucien nodded. 'And it should resound for eternity, Citizen President. Not be left to wither among dusty tombs at the ends of the earth. I will not rest till he returns the hero that he is.'

Ever the politician, Lucien smiled the same quick and closed way his elder brother did. 'Then we shall prevail.'

'Lépeaux said he must capture Constantinople,' said Louis. 'Destroy the Ottoman Empire! And what then? March all the way home through Vienna? It is madness – *monstrous*.'

'Remember, young captain,' admonished Barras, 'I was the general, as you said. And I tell you that if he *must*,' he declared with confidence, 'then he *shall*.'

They went off to breakfast together with Louis's two captains, Barras all the while content he had not pledged the support of one Citizen Lépeaux. It was a matter of insurance, he decided: for, when Caesar returned, as Barras knew he surely would, somehow, with or without Barras's trumpeted help, he would look for vengeance – and for any ambitious senators holding a dagger. And Barras saw little future in playing Brutus – for he was certainly not an honourable man.

Plague

With the onset of winter, something far deadlier than revolt or Murad and the Mamluk cavalry had crept into the military hospital in Cairo. Surgeon's Assistant *Madame* Delphine Lascelles hurried down a make-shift corridor, past the hanging screens of blankets and curtains they had erected in the entrance hall to control the movement of the air and the intrusion of the outside world, especially after the riots of October. Now the first ward was a *triage* area where Larrey and others sorted the sick and injured. But Delphine had noticed that too many of the soldiers coming in were not merely sick or injured, with malaise or the all-too common gastric complaints: it was much worse.

'Omar! Omar!' she called, running down towards the orderlies heading out the door. 'Where are the last two cases you brought in?'

Omar turned and pointed to one of the first stalls as he hurried out. 'In there, *madame* – he lies with the straw, but we need places for others come just now!'

Delphine swished back the hanging curtain – this one no more than a large *kaftan* on a pole ten feet above – and found the first of them, a soldier, dazed, moaning, his uniform open, his stained shirt showing. 'Ah, *mon dieu*, must I do everything...' She tugged off his boots; his filthy footrags fell apart and she recoiled from the smell. '*Ah alors*... Fahima! Can you help me? Fahima...!'

After a moment the curtain was pulled aside again and Fahima rushed in, a small slight Egyptian girl. 'Shears—?'

'Yes—'

She handed Delphine a set of scissors and they began cutting through the linen and cotton tunic, first one sleeve then the other, opening both sides at the shoulder. Delphine jumped back when she saw the fleas leap and cursed again. '*Mon dieu*, do they not let them bathe now, for fear of attack...'

Fahima pulled the lower part of her *hijab* over her nose and mouth. 'No wonder they become so ill.' She frowned. 'What is that...'

Delphine saw the stain by the left underarm – it was dark, possibly bloody. She cut away the shirt across the chest. There, clearly visible in the cleft of the man's pectoral and triceps muscles, was a bright purple and black boil, the size of a fist, the area around it suffused with blood.

Fahima looked at her. 'It is here now.'

Delphine nodded. 'Keep back a moment…' She strode back to the curtain and held it back. 'Hussein! Can you bring hot water!'

Fahima did not obey Delphine but soaked a cloth in saltwater and bathed the affected area. 'If it bursts, what then – is it an abscess?'

Delphine shook her head. 'No, it is what they said in Alexandria. A bubo.'

Fahima did not shrink back but froze for a moment, then continued bathing it. 'If kept clean of external pus it might—'

'No, my dear, it will not—' Delphine seized her hand. 'Come away – the fleas. There—' She flicked one from Fahima's sleeve. 'Let's get him stripped, burn his clothes and—'

A call came from beyond the foyer. '*Madame Lascelles! Madame! Where is the doctor?*'

'*Surgery Two, amputation,*' she called, then moved out of the stall and looked. Omar and Hussein were carrying another man in on a canvas cot. 'How many more?' she asked.

'Eleven in this brigade.'

'Very well. Down there, the patient in surgery, we shall take him to the recovery area and put him in the waiting stall…'

Omar and his companion carried the soldier past her. He put his arm out. 'Ah *chérie*, will you be looking after me now? *Mon dieu* I am lucky, *hein*?'

She smacked away his hand and put a palm to his forehead, walking alongside. 'You should know better than to get ill, you silly boy. You have fever.' She looked at Omar. 'Cold water wrap and two grains of powder.'

As they carried him away he called back, 'Ah, but only to see you again, *mon ange*!'

She turned back to the patient in the stall. Fahima had cut away the rest of the shirt and breeches of the soldier to reveal two other buboes, one in the other underarm, another in his groin. She was bathing the areas with more of the saltwater. It was a combination of Nile riverwater and magnesium salts, and seemed to be drying the worst of the oily excesses of the buboes. Fahima looked at her. 'Should we not cut one open…? He will not live like this. His blood is affected at three points, poisoned. If we let it out…'

'No, we cannot, surely,' said Delphine, looking down at him. 'The effluent will release too much of his blood and then become infected again with more pus—'

'I have heard it work in the Delta, *madame*…'

The soldier was lying still, his breathing shallow, a film of sweat covering his waxy face. She shook her head. 'I should be in the operating theatre… this is…'

But Fahima was insistent. 'If it is I who shall do it, then you are safe—'

'Oh, Fahima, I cannot let you do this…'

But the decision was taken for them: the soldier began to retch and seize in a tetanic convulsion. They tried to hold him still, his heart beating too fast, too strong, until with a gasp, it stopped. He fell back, and lay still. Delphine lowered her head. She crossed herself. '*Mon dieu*. The poor thing.'

Omar put his head round the curtain. '*Madame*, they call for you. *Le chirurgien*. He is finished.'

Delphine nodded, indicating the dead soldier. 'We… we have another place free now, Omar. Take him to the crem.'

Omar's eyes widened. 'Oh *madame*… Sharia law say…'

She shook her head. '*Non*. Omar, this, it is *plague*. We have no choice, *Sharia* or not.'

She went out, down the corridor. As she passed the stall with the open curtain the new soldier called to her. '*Madame*…' He did not sound so full of life.

She looked in. 'Rest. You must drink the boiled water with the medicine, it will help your temperature.'

The soldier shook his head. 'Not that…' he pointed at the inside of his left thigh, at his groin. 'Something…'

Delphine sighed. 'Oh, *mon dieu*, will you boys not leave your foolishness—'

He pulled back the long shirt and she saw it, a bubo, larger than the ones she had just seen on the dead man. She stared a moment, then turned and closed the curtain.

'What is it…?' he asked with a gasp. He was shaking. 'It feels so heavy…'

She helped him settle back but he was not ready to stop and forced his way onto one elbow. 'When… we have the boil, we lance them. We all do. We bite on a belt and a friend bursts it for you, and you shout, and he puts in a piece of wool and we go on. You must do the same.'

She looked at it, a domed swelling, so purple it was black. She closed her eyes, a sense of terror creeping through her at the thought of it. *La peste. La peste d'Egypte…*

The plague of Egypt.

There was a distant cry, shouts in Arabic, French, *Plague, plague! It is plague!* The sound of running feet. She looked at him. 'What is your name?'

'Millet… Private Millet…'

'Wait.' She called out, 'Fahima—!'

There came the sound of running feet as the orderlies rushed from the main entrance, out to the quad, anywhere but to stay in the hospital, the casual local staff, some of the French administrative staff running with them. 'Fahima! Bring a kidney bowl and a scalpel—'

Millet looked at her with a mixture of hope and horror. 'Will you… do it?'

Delphine looped an apron over her head and tied it round her waist. 'I am a surgeon's assistant. I have done worse even than this.'

A moment later Fahima appeared, a scalpel rattling in a small shining metal bowl in her hands. 'Here,' she said, and then held up a thick leather strap. 'And this. Like a boil, yes?'

'Yes…' Delphine wrung out a cloth in a basin of saltwater, then took the strap and gave it to him. 'Here.' He opened his mouth and she set it between his teeth. 'Bite.'

He bit down, closed his eyes and lay back, his breath whistling heavily through his nostrils in anticipation. Delphine took the scalpel. She had draped Millet in cloths, leaving only the bubo on his groin exposed. It focussed their attention and they stared at it. 'Fahima, the bowl, next to the wound, as close as possible…'

Fahima moved in, cupped his genitals under the cloth to one side and opened his legs, pushing the thin edge of steel against his skin just beneath the abscess. Millet found none of it as amusing as he might have earlier, his eyes darting back and forth between the women.

'Ready,' warned Delphine, and Millet threw his head back, his eyes tight shut, his breathing coarse and irregular as if he had run a mile, the belt between his teeth. Delphine raised the scalpel – but the curtain was pulled aside abruptly.

'Delphine?' said a sharp voice. 'What on earth—'

She looked up. It was the surgeon, Dr Vernond. He wiped his hands on his apron and adjusted his wire-framed spectacles, the sweat gleaming off his bald pate. '*Mon dieu*, what do you do...?'

'I am going to lance a boil...' she took a breath. 'A bubo.'

'*No*. You cannot – it would poison him!'

Millet could take no more of it and sat up, his face straining at the belt clamped between his teeth, and snatched the scalpel from Delphine – and cut.

He screamed, muffled by the leather belt, the blade shearing the top of the bubo – it belched a blackened and bloody discharge over Fahima's hand, and she kept the bowl in place, '*C'est ça! That's it!*' she cried, the bulbous dome deflating before their eyes. Millet dropped the scalpel to the floor and fell back, the belt loose from his open mouth as he screamed in time with his breath.

'Continue!' shouted Delphine and squeezed the area, the angry ooze flowing clear then bloody. 'Bandage!'

Vernond reached for the medical kit behind her and fetched a swab of linen and wool, and stuffed the pad onto the gaping tear in Millet's thigh. 'Wrap—'

Fahima took the bowl away, set it down, and passed Delphine a fold of linen crepe and she and Vernond wrapped the padded wound as Millet sank back, his face pale and slick with sweat, his eyes rolling up as he fell into a dead faint.

'This is not a treatment...' gasped Vernond, dabbing at his forehead. 'This *cannot* be a treatment... most irregular...'

Delphine stepped back, a hand to Millet's forehead. She looked at Fahima. 'Well done...'

Vernond stood back, his chest puffing, but back under control. '*Madame* Lascelles. You are not a surgeon, but an *assistant*. In future,' he said, 'you will restrict yourself – and your staff,' looking at Fahima, 'to my orders alone. Is that clear?' He softened and moved closer, lowering his voice. 'You are here at my sole dispensation, Delphine, and are my responsibility. If a soldier dies under your treatment...'

'He would have died like the other in Stall Three did ten minutes ago.'

Vernond looked at Fahima, who nodded. He swept his forehead with a handkerchief. 'I was not aware. Very well. Perhaps this can be our new protocol but, in future, I beg of you—'

After the display by Fahima and Private Millet, Delphine was disposed to lash out at Vernond, but knew better. 'I understand.'

Vernond glanced at Fahima. 'Wash, salts and the new spirit-rub. And your hand.'

Fahima bowed her head. 'Yes, Doctor.'

He would not bring himself to say 'well done' to Fahima, but went out, and Delphine looked down at Millet. His breathing was shallow, his body soaked with sweat. She stooped to pick up the fallen scalpel and discarded belt, his teeth-marks indented in the thick leather. Fahima put a hand to his forehead tenderly. 'He is brave. And cooler, much cooler. Something has worked...'

They heard the shouting first, and both looked round. There came a clatter of wheels and hooves outside, an enraged voice bawling out and the sound of running feet. *Take them! Take them now!* – and the subsequent cries, of people being dragged off. They heard a sergeant calling out a command unfamiliar to Delphine: *Form line! Make ready!* She moved to the curtain, just as Omar burst in, white-faced. '*M-madame!* Th-they are *shooting* them!'

Fire!

The fusillade echoed with a dissonant boom throughout the hospital. Delphine's first fear was another riot, and she envisaged a mob at the gate once again, her brow springing with sweat, her hands shaking, the memory of her nurses screaming: now they were screaming again. '*Non, non,* God in heaven...'

She and Fahima ran after Omar down the corridor to the wide carriage entrance and saw it all: a cartload of wounded, a platoon of infantry, and a line of six men – and three bodies crumpled at the foot of a wall in the hospital quad. They had been hospital orderlies. Delphine stared, dumbstruck. A scarred battalion commander stormed over to her, smeared in blood, dust and sand from the road, his grey moustache caked in it, his pale eyes staring at her with outrage.

'*Well! Are you another? Eh eh? Another who refuses!*'

'What are you doing!'

He grabbed her shoulder violently and spun her round to point back at the cart, his soldiers standing either side. 'They would not come near! They cry out, *la peste, la peste!* And run! Will *you* run! *Eh eh! Well!*'

'You shot my hospital orderlies?' She put a hand to her mouth, staring at him, unable to breathe. '*M-murderer!*'

He yanked her by the neck and thrust her towards the cart. '*There! Damn you! Do you see! Is* it then? Is it *plague* to which I lose my best men! *Is it! Answer me, damn you!*'

Fahima came running behind Delphine and they looked at the first man. She lifted a canvas cover from his body and bloated flies flew out into the dazzling sun, the heat already baking and drying the body, shot, bloodied, the skin yellow, his eyes fixed.

'He is… dead, *madame*,' Fahima said with finality and moved to the other. Fahima lifted a cloak from the man's head, the smell of excrement and horse manure thick and pungent; a camel-tick burst out at her and flew heavily away, and she opened the man's uniform coat. A scorpion larger than her hand crawled out of the folds of cloth and she recoiled with a scream. Behind her Omar bolted, the battalion commander seizing him. '*You!*'

Fahima shook her head, a hand to her mouth, pointing, and Delphine saw it, and another, crawling out from the man's body as the officer snatched at Fahima's hair. '*And you!*' He looked round, 'Any others! *Any, eh eh!*'

A lieutenant had another struggling in his arms, the boy who had helped Omar with the stretchers. 'Here, *mon colonel!*'

'So you refuse to treat our men with plague, *putain de merde!*' He threw Fahima into the arms of the sergeant by the line of men, who shoved her towards the wall and she fell over the dead bodies, Omar stumbling beside her, Hussein thrust in next to them.

Delphine screamed. '*Non!* She just saved the life of one of your men inside! With plague! I assisted!'

The colonel shook her off. 'Orders, woman! You will not shrink from plague at this hospital, damn you all! *Sergeant!*'

'*No!*'

Two other men appeared from behind – with Dr Vernond. Delphine nearly fell to her knees before Vernond, clutching him. 'Please, Pascal! Save them! You must!'

He looked away, shaking his head, hissing at her, '*I – I cannot…*'

'They do not refuse to treat the plague!'

'Of course,' said one of the men at Vernond's side. 'For we have no plague in Cairo. Have we.'

Had Delphine but known the calm voice she would have collapsed in fear at the sight of the blank stare, the expressionless face, the glove upon the walking-stick of bleached sycamore. It was the new Chief of Counter-Intelligence, Jules-Yves Derrien. He nodded at the sergeant. 'An example must be made. Carry on, if you please.'

Delphine turned and ran at the colonel, tugging at his arm, his rattling sword banging into her hip, his pack, the smell of him assaulting her senses. '*No no! I beg of you – please! It was a scorpion! She saw a scorpion!*'

He turned about, his arm battering her to the ground. '*Get off, damned woman!*'

As she fell she heard Fahima's cries, Omar holding her, both shaking, rooted to the spot in fear as the sergeant shouted, *En joue!* and all she could do was howl like an animal, sobbing, her breath not coming – and saw Derrien, looking straight at her as the command came, *Fire!* The muskets boomed. Fahima, Omar and Hussein were thrown back, and fell in a heap.

Delphine screamed again, flat on the ground, her hands clenched tight in the dust, a clod of horse dung under her arm, seeing only the stones and grit under her face, the boots of the men standing over her, looking down upon her – until the colonel's rough hand snatched at her thick hair and hauled her round as he loomed over her. '*You see! You see, you damn putain! You bloody whore!*'

She felt the thin piece of metal still clutched tightly in her hand, collected from the floor at Private Millet's bedside, and she swiped it across the colonel's face in a frenzy, *get away get away*, the scalpel blade slicing deep across his cheekbone and nose, his pale angry eyes wide with surprise, then slashing back and forth, opening his forehead to the white of the bone, the blood sheeting down his face as he wailed, his other cheek opening, thick flaps of skin and muscle falling forward, and she stabbed the instrument again and again into his left eye, his shaking hands scrabbling at her, others pulling her back, *Get her off! Mon dieu!* Vernond running to the man, leaning over him, the scalpel protruding from his eye, *I am blind! I am blind!*, blood spraying and Vernond plucking it out, *I need a bandage here!*

Covered in dust, manure and blood, Delphine was pulled away kicking by two soldiers, her heels dragging in the dirt as she watched the colonel clawing around in the filth, screaming, his face now a red mass of thick sheets of raw hanging flesh, all now poisoned with traces of Private Millet's suppurating bubonic abscess.

'Hold her still!' shouted someone, and Citizen Blais seized her, clutching Delphine's left arm. 'What shall we do with her, Citizen?' he asked Derrien.

Motionless, Derrien watched her and she met his staring eyes, not looking away for fear, nor for shame, feeling only hatred. 'She needs rest,' he replied, 'for the patients.' Then, with a quizzical tilt of his head, 'For we have no plague in Cairo, *madame*. Have we.'

Delphine said no more, her last furious memory of the horror of the day the dead expression of Jules-Yves Derrien, following her as she was dragged through the dirt by the hair, back into the hospital.

–

The room was dark and stifling, the heat dripping down the walls, seeping through her skin like an infection, and she screamed, *Fahima*. Her mind did not revisit the horror of that wall and the bodies, nor the insensible animal rage of that colonel, his grey bloody moustache, and malevolent, predatory eyes – none of it: instead she saw the mob of the revolt all around her, pulling at her arms, tearing poor dead Ayisha from one side to the next, her screams, her fear, and she unable to reach her – until the street burst with bullets and they began to fall and run, trampled by those men on horses.

Then she remembered the hand that came down for her, the voice saying clear and loud, *Here*, and the face of the man in red, his Bedouin headdress wrapped about his face, his eyes a burning blue as she had never seen before. *Why had he not come this time?*

Slowly she sat up on the cot, stiff, soaked with sweat, her dirty cotton blouse and shift clinging to her, her bloody apron draped on a plain wooden chair beside her, under the high window. Her eye took in the darkness and the shelves all around. It was the stock room, the cot moved in to make space in the wards for new patients.

Fahima.

The tears sprang to her eyes and she began to sob, with an anguish she had not known for years: *What are you doing here*, she asked herself, *what!* They were all mad, all of them – she had thought the hospital was the only antidote to the madness, the cure. Yet all they did was rescue boys from their insanity, patch them up and send them back again, to murder and maim.

But no, Réné had said otherwise. Réné had said they would help the people, not the army, the *people* were their main concern, with their endemic disease, their tumours and skin lesions, their blindness, their daily misery. *This is what we do, Delphine, and shall continue for as long as I am in charge, fear not.*

Desgenettes. Réné Desgenettes.

Killing them. *They were killing them!*

Fahima.

Slowly she swung her legs over the side of the cot, and nearly fainted dead away. Vernond must have given her a sedative, she thought, to keep her quiet. She sat on the edge of the bed, rocking quietly, reflecting. She had been cold-bloodedly detached when she slashed the face of that *murderer* to pieces, in the hope she could erase his face from the world forever. She closed her eyes.

Do no harm.

She saw it again, the salon at the university, where she had said, *But I am not a doctor, Réné*, and he had laughed with her.

Ah, but you do harm to me in so many ways, Delphine, for I am slain! And he mimed a dagger to his heart, and kissed her.

She blinked, her lank, matted hair hanging over her eyes, the floor swirling slowly. She rose carefully, her feet swollen. They had not removed her boots. They never remembered. She lowered her feet and gently applied pressure. She breathed.

Réné.

Quietly, the door clicked open. She watched it swing inwards slowly, and a face appeared, Sharina, her *hijab* pulled loose, her tired, smudged and frightened eyes looking in. She gasped when she saw Delphine sitting up. '*Non non non...* you must lie yourself, *madame*, for the rest, here... *please.*'

She bustled in, a heavy girl, so kind, her face streaked with her own miseries at the death of Fahima, at the death of Omar and others, Delphine knew, for they had been the closest friends. 'Sharina,' murmured Delphine. Her throat stuck, the words cloying. Sharina handed her a glass of water and Delphine drank greedily. She closed her eyes in relief. 'Are they... still here?'

Sharina froze, afraid even of the mention of the evil that had come to them earlier that day. 'The men are departed... only officers are here, the wounded.' Her French was broken and simple, but adequate, and far better than Delphine's Arabic.

'Where? *Ayna?*'

Shahina hesitated, and looked out to the door. Delphine could hear the voices of staff moving among the wards, the clink of bottles and receptacles. 'I... I—'

'Where are they, Sharina...'

Making up her mind, Sharina swallowed and nodded. 'They are in Ward Four. The stable.'

Delphine looked at her for a moment. If she went through the back door she would not pass the stable. '*Shukran.* Thank you... *bien.* That is good.'

She stood again, slowly, carefully, Sharina helping her to her feet. '*Madame,* be careful... they... the men,' she said. 'They fight themselves.'

Delphine interpreted this as 'arguing', which suited her fine. If she could get out she could get a message to Desgenettes. She took a step and felt weak in her left side, *ribs*, she thought, *they have kicked me*, and Sharina took her arm and guided her to the door. She looked out. There were no guards anywhere, so she was not under arrest. It was an ironic blessing that at last she could benefit from their constant condescension and disrespect – a mere assistant, a woman, was clearly considered no kind of threat to them, the whole nasty affair concluded.

'Sharina,' she said. 'Go home, and stay there. Tell everyone. All go home. Wait until you hear from me or Chief Surgeon Desgenettes before coming back. No one else can order you, not Vernond, no one. Understood?'

'Yes, *madame*,' she said, weeping. 'You are so hurt, *madame*... can I not—'

'No, you take care of yourself and the others. I am going to see Dr Vernond now and tell him.'

Sharina nodded, then embraced her tightly. '*Madame*...' she gasped through her tears. She hurried down the corridor in the opposite direction. Soon the orderly nurses emerged from the stalls and Sharina bundled them out to the back entrance, whispering urgently, *Leh leh leh, Madama Delfina, yallah, isri ya, hayyah*, and Delphine felt some relief. It was no longer safe to tend the sick.

Delphine moved painfully down the corridor, every breath burning, every step sending shooting pains into her hip and lower back. She paused a moment, savouring the cool darkness. It was a high-ceilinged old building, some sort of factory once, she had heard, with tall looms for weaving the voluminous one-piece linen and cotton *kaftan*, the gigantic frames leaning against walls in the disused area now known to staff as the stables. She passed a window to a rear quad and saw a boy watering several horses and mules, some grazing among the rough gardens under a tree.

She made her way slowly, stopping to rest against the wall, breathing, *they kicked me, would have kicked me to death*, and found Vernond's office, a glazed partition looking in on file cabinets, a plain table heaped with forms, papers, declarations and army adjutants' Orders of the Day pinned on a board by the window opposite. He was at his desk, writing, then stopped. He looked round, the light flashing on his spectacles.

'Delphine—?'

She leaned on the doorframe, exhausted. 'I have sent them home, Pascal.'

Vernond frowned. 'I do not understand… who have you—'

'My nurses and orderlies,' she said with some effort. 'They have gone home. They will not be back.'

'Not be back…?' Vernond rose from his chair. 'B-but you cannot—'

'It is done. If the army want to *murder* my staff then they may do all of the dirty work themselves. Move their own wounded, pull the swollen tongues from their throats, scrub the pox from their testicles and the faeces from their legs, and cart their dead bodies to the pyres, *I care not.*'

Vernond tried to calm her. 'Now, now, Delphine, I understand that you may be… well, disquieted, but—'

She looked at him, incredulous. 'Disquieted?'

'—yes, it, it was a horrible thing to happen, horrible, truly—'

'*Which you permitted.*'

He was shocked. 'That is not so! I—'

She could hear her voice break and she wanted to weep again but would not. 'They *kicked* and *beat* me… while poor Fahima lay dead in the sun! That – that *monster* called me *whore*. A *whore*, Pascal, because I am a *woman* and I am *here.*'

He crossed his arms. 'Mm. Well, I think he has paid his price, would you not say?'

She stared at him. He refused to understand. He adjusted his spectacles, her silence uncomfortable. He looked down. 'Perhaps I could have...' he murmured, then shook his head. 'But no, I did not prevent it... *could not.* I—'

Without another word she left him standing there arguing, and made her way slowly through the hospital. Vernond leaned out into the corridor, one hand hanging onto the latch, calling after her, 'Delphine, where will you go? There is nowhere...! *Delphine*—' then a curse and he slammed his door shut.

She passed the main ward filled with local patients, not the army, but the poor, the crushed, and her heart ached for them. She passed the operating theatres where she had seen Larrey apply a Bedouin cure to a new amputee and quell his pain, a schoolroom where she had seen Desgenettes himself meet with Egyptian healers, making lists of their medicines, making notes of their common ailments, and she wanted to weep anew for the *waste* of it all, as beasts came kicking in the doors to destroy. She stopped at the entrance to the old stable. She looked in the first stall.

A man lay in a fitful sleep, his head swathed with bandages, only his chin and one eye uncovered. He was barefoot, his breeches on, a bloodied white shirt open to his chest, his boots fallen near a nightstand, his uniform tunic, sword-belt and pistol hanging on the back of a chair by a wheeled trolley of jars, boxes and bowls. It was the colonel she had wounded. Her stomach lurched.

His remaining eye blinked as he woke, red and black with bruising from her blows with the scalpel and nail-strikes as he had towered over her on the ground. He turned his head slowly, recognising her.

'*You...*'

She watched him, and felt pity for him, for that remaining eye, which looked so helpless, so very confused. Perhaps anger had taken hold of him, his only concern his soldiers, for them to be treated, refused at other stations perhaps, and she felt sickened by her anger, her selfishness. He spoke again, his voice a dry gasp, and she leaned in to listen.

'*Vous...*' he sighed raggedly, '*Pu... tain...*'

You whore.

She stared down at him, feeling but half-awake. Traces of blood on the bandages marked the path of her scalpel. Without pausing to peel back the layers to check the wounds, she moved to the trolley and stooped to the bottom shelf, uncorked the stopper from a jar and spooned a measure of its white powder into an empty cup, and mixed it with some water. It hissed and frothed and she felt it would suffice, walking slowly back to the bed with painful steps, careful not to spill any, his hand rising to take it, and she guided it carefully to the gap they had left around his mouth – he swallowed, and she took the rest and poured it all over the bandaged face, from top to bottom, making sure to catch the last concentrated dregs.

His inarticulate screams began almost at once, as she knew they would, for it was not a healing tonic she had given him but a solution of corrosive caustic soda, used to clean the instruments, and she was burning him alive from the inside out with a fire that no water would ever extinguish, the deadly alkali eating into his lips, his tongue, larynx, all, burning steadily through the flesh of his face to the bone – to leave him a blackened, misshapen screaming cadaver.

With a dull-eyed expression, still not quite present, she dropped the empty cup and it bounced across the flagstones. She then shoved the chair closer to him, the sword and pistol within reach of his flailing hand, now tearing at his bandages and throat. They could end his suffering by applying one of their many breaking-irons to the back of his neck, or simply by opening his carotid artery instead. She had done similar for poor mutilated boys, her clouding eyes full of tears, their agony beyond cure. But she knew Vernond had not the stomach for that.

As she continued painfully down the corridor, his echoing screams mingled with the sound of running feet and the shouts of doctors and army officers, but were stopped abruptly by a single shot. She reached the front entrance and went out into the endless heat, wanting to go home, as she had told the others, *just go home*. Instead she took a mule, the quiet one called Henri, undoing its rein from a post and giving him a little treat from the hanging nosebag, and climbed on. His hooves thudding slowly on the road, she headed for Nasriya and the Institute, to find Réné Desgenettes.

Sultan

The former palace of Muhammad Bey al-Elfi was aglow with torch and candlelight, the cool breeze of the Nile wafting in, carrying the scent of winter jasmine and roses from the ornamental gardens, the serpentine strains of Arabian strings and flute filling the air as the new colony engaged in the levity of an *ancien* ball. Swan-necked girls from Abyssinia, their dark, lustrous skin glowing in their high-waisted French gowns, moved at the side of their young officers, the shy smiles of knowing concubines meeting, then looking away, to others from Sudan and Somalia, all former servants and slaves of Mamluk lords, now the companions of French cavalry captains and lieutenants. The powdered and perfumed French ladies of colonels and generals rubbed shoulders with their dusky beauty, all competing with the young Egyptian women in floating linen and silken *niqabs*, draped in jewels of bronze and lapis lazuli, their shadowed eyes swept in blackest *kohl*, and glowing with blues, purples and gold dust, the ancient come to life, eclipsing the rustling taffeta of their French counterparts.

Napoléon Bonaparte stood with his hands behind his back in his dark gilt-embroidered cutaway coat, watching the proceedings. He was dissatisfied, but always was with such occasions. Thoughts of Joséphine boiled in his mind, tumbling end over end in a melee of hatred and bewitched devotion. Colonel Junot beside him had presided over the final disillusionment just weeks earlier, presenting him with the evidence of letters and testimony – and his own: that Joséphine had indulged in affairs since their wedding.

'*I know, damn you*,' Bonaparte had snapped. '*Ma foi*, but what presumption it is to *tell* me.'

Junot had nodded his cadaverous head, his hollow, sunken eyes glowering. 'Since Malta I was to tell you, but you would not hear of it.'

Bonaparte simmered. '*Yes*... yes, I know, Jean-Androche.'

Junot had waited the prescribed number of moments before speaking after an outburst, and added, 'But the other lady will attend.'

Bonaparte had looked up. 'She will…?'

Junot nodded.

'And the husband…?' Bonaparte lifted a page from the papers on his desk, evasion, deflection, as if it were a matter of no concern. 'Lieutenant Fourès…?'

Junot was quick with the answer. 'The lady's husband the lieutenant is well on his way to France with the despatches, *mon général*.'

So it was that evening that Napoléon Bonaparte looked across the room, past the colourful turbans of sheikhs and amirs and their sultry mistresses, to address the delicate beauty of *Madame* Pauline Fourès, now the abandoned wife of an officer sent away with despatches, on his orders. She caught his eye once and looked off – then back again, and smiled.

An ensemble of musicians played in a corner to their far left, a dark fretwork screen erected, an *almeh* singer behind, her quavering tones light and exotic, the officers mesmerised by her absence, and their fertile imaginations. An *oud* lute and *qanun* wailed in discreet harmony, the light cotton voiles at the arched windows floating in a blessed breeze. It was, as planned, a *Nuit Arabesque*. Junot watched all of this from behind the partial cover of a swagged silken curtain, not taking his eyes from Bonaparte, Jules-Yves Derrien doing likewise beside him, odd bedfellows by circumstance.

'She will do well,' said Junot grudgingly. 'The husband?'

Derrien looked on. 'Embarked two days ago.'

'How did she hide for so long before anyone spotted her?' It was something of a rebuke, suggesting Derrien had missed something so very obvious.

But it was true: Derrien himself had been unaware that a nameless and rather pretty junior officer of Lt Fourès' brigade had in fact been Fourès' young and rather pretty wife in disguise. Several had pulled the same trick. 'She revealed herself only after reaching Cairo,' said Derrien, looking into his glass, remembering. 'I was rather engaged with an Admiralty plot at the time.' He looked at Junot. 'Not counting the cutlery.'

Junot scoffed. 'A plot which did not go well for Admiral Brueys.' He looked at him in return. 'Did it.'

Derrien replied quietly but with some satisfaction, 'It went as well as the river battle at Shubra Khit.'

Junot stared back at him. He had suffered enough condemnation from Monge for that debacle, which had nearly wiped out the *savants* and the entire scientific Commission in one day. 'An incident. Yesterday,' said Junot, to change the subject, 'at the military hospital, by the Old Gate.'

Derrien kept his eye on Bonaparte. 'A *Chef de bataillon*. Of the 86th *demi*. A surgeon's assistant.'

'Laval,' said Junot. 'He was a pig. But.' He looked at Derrien. 'Must I explain the position?'

Derrien sipped his Verdicchio. 'It is I who explains the position, *Chef de brigade*. Not you.'

Junot bit off a curse. 'Are you *still* shooting hospital orderlies and attendants?' he hissed. '*Doctors' assistants?*'

Derrien watched Bonaparte. 'Of course.'

'Have you an order in writing...?'

Derrien took another sip from his glass. 'I have more than I need in writing, *Chef de brigade*.'

Someone laughed and they watched the two, Bonaparte and *Madame* Fourès, engaging happily, Junot's expression as wooden as Derrien's. 'Perhaps there will be a divorce. It would suit all, I should think.'

Derrien regarded them carefully, watching their mannerisms, gauging the response of Bourrienne, Monge and Berthollet. Eugène de Bauharnais, Joséphine's son, passed by, glass in hand, wanting to speak to Bonaparte, but stopped when he saw *Madame* Fourès. Bonaparte said something sharp to him, and the boy flushed red before striding away, looking down, mortified, his mother evidently supplanted. He would have to be watched, thought Derrien.

The group was then joined by the melancholy General Berthier, with his sad eyes and drooping moustache. They all bowed and smiled likewise to Bonaparte, Berthier perking up as he spoke to Pauline. *Madame* Fourès was proving popular.

Several European ladies in silk and linen approached Bonaparte and his companions. The foremost of the delegation was the untouchable *Madame* Tempié, the lean and supple dark-eyed wife of a naval captain, and one of Bonaparte's favourites. Bonaparte bowed. She flapped out her fan in the old Italian court style, which he had not seen in some time, but recognised its code very well. She was angry.

'*Mon général,*' she said, 'I hear you attempted to... what was it, oh yes: to *humiliate* a doctor, in Alexandria, who refused to treat victims of the plague, *la peste,* hm? By forcing him into women's clothes and putting him on a mule...?'

The generals around chuckled, perhaps thinking it a joke, the *madame* always game for fancies at a good party. Bonaparte's smile faded. It was no joke. 'Indeed. To teach him a lesson in courage.'

'Ah,' she said, 'so you believe that since he was weak, he should be dressed as a woman.' She leaned closer to him, the men's eyes feasting on her swelling décolletage, her scent heavy on the air, captivating them all. 'I assure you, *mon général,* women are not *weak,* unlike our little men.' She flicked a glance down at his crutch. 'Or perhaps I should prove it, and meet you in the duel, hm? To fight for... how should I say,' she finished, 'my *sex?*'

The men put fingers to their collars, the voluptuous sensuality of *Madame* Tempié almost too much to bear. Bonaparte bowed gallantly. 'You would undo me, I am certain, *madame.* Though powder and shot are no friends of the true lady.'

'They would not be your friends either, *mon général,*' she laughed, a tinkling chuckle, and they joined in, none worthy of crossing her. As she wandered away, Monge leaned towards them. 'I thought we were all done for.'

But Bonaparte was not amused. 'She is the litmus test of senior opinion. *Dieu en ciel,* it is ridiculous, for she is right. Was the order published?'

Bourrienne nodded sadly. 'I fear so. But not carried out.'

Bonaparte grew angrier by the moment. 'I will have no more of – of this *plague* talk.'

Pauline Fourès linked her arm in his. 'Show me these Egyptian delicacies you have ordered for us all, *mon général.*'

He nodded, still preoccupied, but was gracious enough to let her soothe his temper with distraction. He took her arm in his and escorted her to the low tables where some ate, sitting with the sheikhs as Bonaparte had wanted, some on the dark carved sofas, a private soldier bringing a chilled bottle of Pouilly to refresh their glasses.

Derrien and Junot watched the scene, ignoring *Madame* Tempié's intervention. 'It is a success.'

Junot nodded at him grudgingly. 'She will suffice,' he said, turning to go. 'For apparently she has no odour.'

A dark-haired senior officer in pale tailcoat and shoulder-sash approached Berthollet, asked him a question, then saw Junot and Derrien – he was possibly in his late thirties or early forties, wearing a dress smallsword: it was the Chief Physician of the expedition, Réné-Nicolas Desgenettes. He touched Berthollet's shoulder and pointed at the pair, a furrowed brow deepening into anger, and he bore down on them.

'*Chef de brigade* Junot,' he grated with a curt bow, 'and *Citizen* Derrien, I understand.'

Derrien bowed, '*Médecin en chef.* An honour.'

'Not for me, *m'sieur.* Am I right in thinking it was you who allowed that *revolting* cretin of a colonel to assault my nursing staff and surgery assistants – before throwing them *against a wall*—' he gasped, still incredulous, '—to be *shot*? Like *criminals*?'

Derrien pursed his lips and tried to reply, 'Citizen General, it was not as simple a mat—'

'*How dare you, m'sieur,*' he spat, keeping his voice low. 'How *dare* you! The most *disgusting* act of brutality I have yet witnessed – *murder*, enacted upon our own *people*.'

Junot answered, 'It is the order of the *général en chef.*'

Desgenettes rasped at him, 'He denies it, damn you, Junot—'

Junot said nothing. Derrien remained unmoved. 'Citizen General, if hospital staff fear the ailments they are to treat, they must pay the—'

'*Fear?* One of those harmless souls murdered by that – that *obscene, blighted dog* of a colonel, was an Egyptian nurse rescued from the damnable riots, a volunteer of great experience, brave enough to save the life of a common soldier not minutes before by draining a diseased abscess that would surely have poisoned him to death! Is *that* your idea of fear? For I should like to see *you* do the same.'

'As I recall she refused to treat a wounded soldier.'

'*It was a scorpion, you utter fool.* She recoiled from a *scorpion* in a dead man's cloak!'

Junot laid out the official line. 'We have plague in Alexandria and Damietta. If this—'

'I forbade anyone to call it so for this very reason,' interrupted Desgenettes. 'It causes the ignorant to panic and leads to incidents *just like this.*'

Junot closed his eyes patiently and continued regardless, '—and if this behaviour continues they will only spread further rumour, which could lead to the breakdown of order yet again.'

Desgenettes looked at them both. 'I don't care a *damn* for your order, Junot, since you believe the streets will be all the quieter for the corpses you leave strewn about them.' He looked at them aghast. '*Mon dieu*, what idiots rule the asylum, who would *kill* the very people who can help us—' then, looking Derrien up and down with disgust, '—faceless, unaccountable wretches that you are, *M'sieur le Croquemort.*'

Derrien could suffer it no longer and grated under his breath, 'You will call me *Citizen*, not *m'sieur*—'

Desgenettes matched him threat for threat, leaning forward and hissing into his ear, the hatred seething from between his lips, 'Were I feeling *generous* I would call you the *shit upon my shoe, m'sieur.*' He stepped back from the pair. 'He is dead, you know? This, this Laval? This swine of a colonel? That is my only satisfaction. Drank caustic soda, thinking it some sort of treatment, then shot himself in the pain of it.' He shook his head, looking at them. '*Damn* you for this. May God protect you both in this place – for by my order *none* of my doctors will. Keep *away* from my staff and my hospitals or I shall have you dragged home in chains. By God above I shall.'

The music was at its height, but heads had turned, Bonaparte looking as Desgenettes stormed out, red-faced, slamming his glass onto a side table. Derrien and Junot watched him go.

'It seems we must look to our own resources,' said Junot ominously.

Derrien put his glass to his lips but stopped when he detected movement at the arched entrance: it was his deputy, Blais, red-faced from exertion, worried. He saw Derrien and hurried over. 'Citizen.'

Derrien bowed to Junot. 'I believe more is at stake than the good doctor believes.' He took Blais to one side. 'Well?'

–

Some guests were still arriving, on foot and in carriages, many taking their time in the cool evening air, a mere twenty degrees rather than the stultifying forty and fifty of months earlier. The garden paths of Ezbekiya Square were dotted with torches and lanterns, grenadiers standing guard with new, more exotic sentries, from the west, from the south, Morocco, Tunis, Libya, Sudan, as sheikhs and senior officers processed along the lamplit avenues towards the sound of music and song.

Just beyond, a carriage bearing the banner of the 2nd *Légère* slowed to a trot for the turn into the square and the guard checkpoints. In the plush leather-upholstered interior were renowned *Général de brigade* Luc-Philippe Verdier, and his devoted and equally renowned lady wife, the dark-eyed and kindly Italian beauty, *la contessa* Maria, known to all his staff as the Angel of the Expedition. Accustomed to the heat of Campania and Puglia, she sat comfortably in elegant silks, an Egyptian shawl drawn over her shoulders.

'If the rumours are true...' warned the general, but she happily disagreed.

'Soldiers' rumours are never true...'

'Perhaps,' he said, 'But if they are, my dear – this shall be terrible.' He looked at her, a tight expression on his handsome features, the worry evident. 'I do fear for you so, *carissima*.'

'I have ridden on every campaign with you and intend to do so again,' she smiled, her warmth lighting the cabin of the carriage. 'How else can I ensure your safe return?'

He shook his head, not smiling for her, not reassuring her – rather to frighten her, to keep her away, keep her safe. 'This will be different. There is talk of Syria. Of all the places on God's earth this will be one where I would never wish to find you at my side.'

She lowered her head and nodded, knowing his ways. 'We shall see what Puss-in-Boots says.'

He broke into a smile at last. '*Mon dieu*, Maria, you mustn't call him that, for God's sake.' Verdier squeezed her hand but she glanced out the window, frowning as the carriage slowed.

'Who is that...?' she asked, looking out the window.

Making her way along the dark pavement, as if sleepwalking, stopping periodically to lean against the high white wall, lost in the shadows of palms and overhanging vines, clad still in her stained day-dress and surgeon's apron, was Delphine Lascelles – exhausted, distraught, her hair dishevelled, her face smudged and darkened with tears and dust, one hand clutching at an obviously injured arm. She slowed and fell to one knee.

'Oh, *lo dio mio*...!' exclaimed *Madame* Verdier. 'Stop, we must stop—'

'She is one of the medical staff...' murmured Verdier. 'What on earth...'

'It is *Madame* Lascelles—' *Madame* Verdier banged on the ceiling and called out to the coachman, '*Arrêtez! Attendez ici!*' then in exasperation, '*Oh, Georges! Stop the carriage!*'

The carriage came to a halt, the horses stamping and spluttering, the driver hauling on the reins. Without waiting, she flung open the door and descended the carriage steps quickly, hiking her skirts up as she hurried to Delphine's side. 'Delphine? *Madame* Lascelles? What is it? What has happened?'

'Henri... they took Henri... the mule—' Delphine fell into her arms, eyes wide, shaking, 'I must tell him... *le docteur*, Réné...'

'Desgenettes...?' asked General Verdier, crouching beside them.

'Yes, yes – the plague... it is come to Cairo—'

Verdier looked at his wife. 'Good God. I'll get a runner. You keep her here.'

'No, Luc, we must get her inside, quickly, she is in a terrible state. Louis Bourrienne will know what to do—'

Grenadier guards came at the run, a sergeant at the front. 'You need assistance, *mon général*?'

Verdier called back. 'Is the *Médecin en chef* here tonight? Dr Desgenettes?'

The sergeant hesitated. 'The Citizen Doctor has come, yes, General – I passed him through some time ago—'

Delphine blinked, remembering. 'The colonel... is dead... I – I killed him...'

'She makes no sense,' said Verdier. 'Sergeant, help us with her into the carriage, we shall take her inside.'

'No, no,' mumbled Delphine, pulling away, 'I will find him...'

Madame Verdier close behind, the sergeant carried Delphine to the carriage and called over his shoulder, *Open the gate! Let the général and Madame Verdier through!*

Heeling and bouncing on its springs, the carriage turned, the horses trotting for the checkpoint, Georges the driver dusting their tails with his whip to speed them through to the palace entrance.

–

Sergent-chef-major Caron stood at the shadowed rear entrance of the palace of Muhammad Bey al-Elfi, the Alphas sitting on upturned crates and a low stone wall near the refuse, where the kitchen scraps were tossed daily. Fusilier Rossy looked about, disappointed. 'There is a big party inside, *Chef*,' he said reasonably, 'And I feel that I must put myself forward as a taster, to safeguard the life of my unbeloved *général en chef*.'

'That is a good idea, *Chef*,' murmured Pigalle from nearby. 'I am losing weight.'

'Precisely, *M'sieur* le Pig,' said Rossy. 'I see it as my soldier's duty.'

'I am not having you eat half the dishes before they leave the kitchens, *mon garçon*,' replied Caron, 'despite your devotion.'

'What then do we do here, *Chef*,' asked St Michel irritably. 'It is... why, it is almost *cold*.'

Young Antonnais glanced at him. 'Can that be possible, in Egypt?'

'It rained on the 25th *demi*, they say,' said St Michel.

'It should rain on the 25th,' agreed Antonnais.

'Rain or shine, this is where the anarchists come, *mes enfants*,' said Caron. 'The poisoners, the bomb-throwers. They do not come to the main gate with an invitation.'

'That is underhand,' said Pigalle.

'It is, Pig,' said Rossy. 'Shame on them—'

He broke off when he heard a call from the western entrance to the square, *Open the gate! Open the gate!* A troop of horse clattered round the bend into the quad, at their front Citizen Peraud, the second of Derrien's Bureau men. Behind, among a brace of cavalry and very uncertain in the saddle, came an unknown naval officer.

Caron moved out into the darkness to the vine-covered archway looking into the stable quad. Peraud led the way, striding over the dark cobbles towards him, past the ornamental trees. Caron held up a hand and Peraud heard the click of musket locks cocking in the darkness. The shapes of eight men of the Alpha-Omega platoon emerged. Unseen from beneath the palms, Rossy touched the muzzle of his Charleville to his neck and Peraud froze.

'Nature of entry,' demanded Caron.

Peraud looked back at their guest, virtually a prisoner. 'Special envoy for Citizen Derrien and the *général en chef*.'

Caron looked at him. 'Advance and be recognised.'

The cavalrymen stepped aside and the naval officer came forward. 'I am Captain Pichard.'

'Very well,' said Caron. 'We had been warned. Rossy.'

Rossy got to work at once, his hands swift and practised, moving through Pichard's pockets, his collar, his underarms, his breeches, his boots. 'Nothing, *Chef*. Not even a sardine.'

The back door to the kitchen scullery opened with a sudden increase of noise, of shouting voices, the banging of pots, and Caron heard the footfall behind him, knowing full well who it was. Blais appeared first, Derrien following, sweating in the cool evening air. Peraud and the cavalrymen stiffened when they saw him, the Alphas still as stone. The somewhat startled Pichard looked about, his eyes resting at last on Derrien.

'I was told to come at once—' he began.

Blais looked at Derrien. 'It is as we feared, Citizen.'

'Suspected,' corrected Peraud.

'Quite right,' said Derrien, acknowledging the difference. He looked at the man. 'Your name.'

'I am Pichard, Captain of the *Hélène*, docked in Alexandria.'

'Carrying?'

Pichard seemed surprised but answered, 'Olive oil, wines, charcoal dust, powders of potassium niter, ingots of lead—'

'Very well.' It was the easiest way to validate the man's credentials: any blockade-running captain would know precisely what he carried in his holds and Pichard had not hesitated. 'Come with me.' He beckoned to Caron to accompany him. '*Sergent-chef-major*. Leave a man at the door.'

Caron nodded. 'Rossy.'

Derrien in the lead, they passed back through the kitchens and the bustling local staff busy arranging the platters for the next course, the heat and smells of spice and scented woodsmoke almost suffocating. They went through the winding, whitewashed corridors back up to the palace's public rooms, the rough flagstone steps yielding to polished marble as they approached the main interior.

Peraud and Blais behind him, Derrien moved through the throng heading directly for Bonaparte, ignoring the looks of the staff and dignitaries. Generals 'Papa' Dugua and Berthier, Belliard and the Herculean Dumas watched, Reynier nudging Murat with a frown, knowing the signs: *despatch*.

The new first couple of the colony were sat on cushions on the floor, listening to the music, being offered food from the large round platters of beaten bronze, each held by as many as three servants, two sheikhs sitting opposite, laughing politely at an interpreter's comment. Derrien stopped just behind them, and Bonaparte looked up. Derrien bowed.

'Citizen General. A matter for your attention.'

Bonaparte was up in an instant, the festivities forgotten, and marched past his generals, bidding them follow with a look. Derrien leading, they moved through the outer corridor to a rear drawing-room, once part of the old *harim*, so Derrien had discovered, its remnants visible in its fine furnishings, hanging lanterns glowing above, delicate linens at the windows.

Waiting were other members of the general staff, the watchful General Vial, General Bon, and the stern Kléber; in their midst among the escorting cavalrymen was Caron, a young Levantine in clerical *galabeyyah* and white cap, and Pichard, his hat restless in understandably nervous hands. Bonaparte stopped in the doorway and looked at him.

'So.'

Pichard recognised him at once and bowed. '*Mon général*. An honour.'

'Captain Jean-Louis Pichard of the armed merchantman *Hélène*, Citizen General,' announced Derrien. 'Just broken into Alexandria, through the British blockade.'

Bonaparte was impressed. 'Well done. You bring news.'

Pichard nodded. 'When I explained to the port authorities that I have just now come from Cyprus with intelligence, they rushed me down here to explain personally – and to give you this.'

He handed over a scroll wrapped in a dark stained ribbon. Derrien opened it and nodded, with some glad confirmation. 'It is in a Turkic script,' he said.

'Yes,' said Pichard, 'It is one of the *firman* sent out by the sultan.'

Bonaparte took it and saw the heavy seal, the official frankings and signatures – it was no forgery. Satisfied, he held it out to the Levantine scholar. 'What does it say?'

Pichard answered, 'It declares, *mon général*, that which I learned on Cyprus.' He looked about at them. 'That the sultan hereby declares war on the Republic.'

For some time, the room remained dead silent. Bonaparte looked at the Levantine. 'Well?'

The boy nodded, reading. 'It is proclaimed,' he said, 'the sultan in his terrible power declares a state of war has arisen with France, in accordance with his allies of Britain and Russia.' The boy continued, his calm expression as undisturbed as if he were reading from a philosophical tract. 'That all persons of the French government within the empire are to be seized with their personal property, now declared forfeit. And further remonstrations of French actions in the imperial province of Egypt...'

'That will do,' murmured Derrien.

Obediently, the boy rolled the scroll, the crackle of the dry paper strangely loud in the silence, as if it were the sole arbiter of their fates. He handed it to Derrien, bowing his head and stepping back out of sight.

'Further to this,' said Pichard, 'I have learned that Ahmed Pasha, the one called Al-Djezzar, who commands Akka—' he looked round, 'that is to say, St Jean d'Acre, capital of the province, has built an army with Ibrahim Bey, and that Mustafa Pasha of the Osmanli will move south from Rhodes – their intention to recapture Egypt.'

The gathered generals looked to Bonaparte for his reaction. Bonaparte had not moved, eyes bright, decisions rising up, sorted, made. He looked at Pichard. 'How many men?'

'They say a host – the levy and the janissaries, it is difficult to—'

'*How many,*' repeated Bonaparte.

Pichard stiffened. 'Some say a hundred thousand, *mon général.*'

There was a stunned silence. The generals looked to each other: a hundred thousand swords, a hundred thousand spears – a hundred thousand demons clamouring for revenge.

Bonaparte nodded, his face unchanging. He turned on his heel and headed for the door, his power drawing them all behind. 'General Berthier,' he said, striding into the main reception hall, guests of the soirée parting like a wave, 'call a meeting of the general staff. At once. Generals of division to attend, Kléber, Bon, Lannes and Andréossy, artillery, cavalry and infantry to be mustered—'

Someone behind called out, *Vive le général*, and another *Vive la République!* The gossip had already begun, the honoured guests watching with rising apprehension, the evening festivities over, the junior officers putting down their glasses and hurrying to the doors to spread the word: *We march on Syria.*

At the front of the palace Verdier's carriage of the 2nd *Légère* charged through the gate, sentries bringing their muskets to the salute. The horses slewed to a halt across the cobbles by the pillared entrance, the equerry jumping down from the driver's bench and calling *Assistance! Quickly!*

General Verdier was out first and several of the grenadier sentries came at the run as *Madame* Verdier climbed down. 'Please – be careful with her, she is injured—'

'Call for Desgenettes,' ordered General Verdier to one of the grenadiers. 'He should be here.'

'The *Médecin en chef*?'

'Yes, quickly now,' said Verdier, Delphine in his wife's arms, murmuring.

'*Burned him to death... I – I...*'

Two *savant* physicians emerged from the palace, saw the carriage and hurried over. 'General? What has happened?' They took hold of Delphine from *Madame* Verdier and sat her in the carriage doorway, examining her, opening her eyes, checking her pulse.

'She keeps asking for Desgenettes. She is covered in bruising, I cannot imagine what has—'

A grenadier guard pointing, Desgenettes appeared at the broad portico and came at a run. 'What has—' Desgenettes's eyes widened when he recognised her and rushed forward. 'Delphine? *Mon dieu*, what happened?'

'Réné... the colonel,' she gasped, '*I killed him...*'

Desgenettes glanced at Verdier. 'Colonel Laval? *Non*, impossible. He shot himself, Delphine, a callous, murderous swine, and he is dead, good riddance.' He looked back at Verdier, as if daring him to deny it and the general seemed unwilling to disagree.

'Réné,' she said in a whisper, 'we have plague,' she gasped. 'In Cairo. Cases increasing on the hour... from the Old City, not just the people—'

'Army?'

'Like Damietta. Five yesterday, ten this morning, then more in the afternoon...' She blinked dazedly. 'I am... so tired...'

Desgenettes held her close and she winced in pain. He looked at her filthy clothes. 'My God, what did they do...'

'They... Laval... kicked and beat me... *called me whore...*' she began to sob, '*...our own army, killed Fahima...*'

A grenadier sergeant looked over his shoulder, outraged. 'Who has done this thing to you? Tell us, *mon ange*, and we shall make them suffer for it, *par dieu*, I swear it so.'

'And what did Vernond do?' asked Desgenettes.

She clenched her eyes shut, the tears streaking. '*Nothing.*'

'Then you are his assistant no longer,' asserted Desgenettes. 'You are mine, the finest in a theatre anyone could hope for. Larrey will curse me for stealing you so.'

There were shouts and cheers from inside. *Madame* Verdier clutched at her husband and asked the grenadiers, 'Is it true, *m'sieur le docteur*? Is it Syria? Is it what they have all been saying?'

Desgenettes looked grimly at her. 'Perhaps.' He glanced at the *savant* doctors. 'Let's get her to my carriage, and you accompany me, Armand. We will need splints, bandage, tissue salts of phosphor, and a winding-corset in case of fracture—'

Delphine reached up to Desgenettes, touching his cheek. 'I told you I was no doctor...'

'You are more than that, always...' He looked back at the palace of Muhammad Bey al-Elfi. 'But I think we are too late to help anyone here, Delphine...'

Inside the palace, Bonaparte heard them cheer as he headed to his upper-storey office with its terrace overlooking his new conquest, his capital, his new Babylon, the ghost of Alexander's Diadochs and generals following – and determined: no, not *just* Syria.

He would take them all.

'In my army shall be sheikhs, Turks, Greeks, Berbers, Tuareg and Maghrib, from Sudan to Abyssinia, the *Qadi* himself and the sultan's own pasha,' he declared. 'An *imperial* army of a new world. *And we shall shock them.*'

Hwa hwa hwa! Vive le général!

His Berber guards throwing open the double doors for him, he strode in, the power trembling within his limbs as he marched up the gleaming marble steps to look over the lights of ancient Cairo, to look across the history of the world – a world he would remake: he was going to show them, from the Directors in Paris to the Admiralty in London – he was going to unleash the deadliest army in the Orient, and bring down the mightiest temple on earth.

He turned and watched them file in, their faces showing strength, determination and that devotion he knew would soon move the mountains themselves: this was why he was here, why he had come.

He was going to destroy the Ottoman Empire – and bury his enemies in its rubble.

Part Two

Holy Land

Haven

Hazzard awoke to the shriek of seabirds crying on the wind, their wings extended stiffly as they floated on a freshening northerly, hovering over the busy harbour just outside his window. Fleet masts rose up to meet them, a number of gulls perching on the neatly squared yards and rigging of the Royal Navy, stark against a grey Mediterranean winter sky.

He blinked at his still unfamiliar surroundings, a bedchamber on the top floor of a house on the seafront. He was reminded of the last proper bed he had slept in, at the Palazzo Sessa in Naples, tended by the kind beauty of Lady Emma Hamilton. It had felt just as strange. There was a washstand and mirror, with large jug and bowl, a painted wardrobe and a cheval glass in the corner. The tall casement window had been opened for air, a pair of linen curtains blowing across a small desk underneath. He saw the blotter, pen and inkstand, the papers he had been writing, his reports of the last months – the last months in Egypt.

He sat up, encumbered by clouds of sheets and a quilt, and regretted it at once. His shoulder pulled as if tied by a line to his wrist and thigh, and he gasped. *Wounds.* They slowly eased, and he knew they were getting better, and he shivered stiffly. It was cold. After Egypt, he was now unsuited to anything below the hottest summer Europe could provide.

He swung his legs out carefully and sat still. He felt clean for the first time in ages, still marvelling at it, and his head hung as he sat, breathing, just breathing. Eventually he looked up at the window, and slowly stood, moving to look out.

The small Sicilian port of Syracuse looked back, a squadron of British men o'war, Neapolitan sloops, fishing boats and merchantmen dotted about the basin before him. Local labourers, sailors and officers in bluejackets, and red-coated marines moved along the quaysides and gangways. The Neapolitan guard drilled outside the distant Castello Maniace, the great turreted fort at the far end of the spit, guarding the harbour of the ancient isle of Ortygia, the heart of old Syracuse.

He looked over the ships, trying to identify them, but could not – only a few of the frigates, many from the blockade of Malta. The 64-gun HMS *Lion* was in, as was the elegant sloop the *Mutine*, and he thought of her captain, Lt Hardy, and how they had landed at Alexandria together, in the hopes of saving a nation, only to be turned away. Hazzard wanted to try to find him, if for little else than to see a familiar face, and shake his hand.

Then, in the distance, he saw her, moored by the round corner towers of the castle: HMS *Tigre*. Sir William Sidney Smith had arrived. The waiting was over. His hand gripped the windowsill more tightly as he recalled their journey.

God above. They had all come so far.

As they left Karnak behind, Hazzard had dispensed with his Bombay coat before they had rounded the great bend at Qena on the east bank. The ruined temples of Dendera off to their left on the western side, their course was steady and swift, the Nile bearing them outward, ever outward. The marines watched, caravans passing on the rocky banks, large *djerm* traders putting up sail, *feluccas* being hauled upstream by teams of men and mules. They hardly spoke, Cochrane tending to Napier, Wayland in fevered states of sleep and wakefulness under a haze of Porter's laudanum.

As they neared the confluence of traffic around the river islands heading for Cairo, they concealed the French tunics Hesse had liberated, but kept them close in case they were needed, maintaining their Arab cover legend. None but Tariq and the boatman spoke when hailed – having shared their last tobacco with him, he was their greatest friend. When they passed the port authorities and checkpoints, they found only exhausted French soldiers and dragooned Mamluk customs men unwillingly looking out at them in desultory fashion, ignoring them for a band of poor, up-country Bedouin headed back to the Delta. Hazzard wished he could breach the shore and call on a skilled French surgeon – Napier's breathing had become worse, and both men's colour had drained, the pallor of their skin appalling.

They drifted past the pyramids, the men staring in silence, Hazzard and Cook exchanging a glance, but no memories: they were too painful. Within a day they had reached Rosetta, an ancient fortress tower crumbling at the river mouth, the horizon widening until they burst into Aboukir Bay and the endless blue of the Mediterranean.

The marines helped the boatman brace his sail against the inshore breeze as they entered Aboukir Bay. As they did, all stared at the arc of the shoreline, the broken hulks of French ships hauled into the shallows, each man lost in his own thoughts, and Hazzard wondered what they had achieved, if anything, since that awful night. Cook stood at his elbow, looking out.

'The sea covers all things, sir...' he murmured.

Hazzard nodded. It was the inevitable truth: the sea, like the desert sand, could sweep away all of Man's efforts with the next tide. 'Making the world clean again.'

'Amen...'

Cochrane was leading a prayer for the battle-site, and Hazzard heard them, '...*and no man to be left o'erboard, be he jack or jolly, amen...*'

They drifted on the power of the Nile until the wind pushed them gently back towards shore, and they began to tack, hauling the sloping sail round to starboard, then back to port. Soon, they passed the shoals where Sir Thomas Troubridge had run aground in the *Culloden*, just off the fort on the Aboukir headland, where Wayland had charged a French artillery company, and saved Sir Thomas, the current drawing them on to Alexandria.

Soon after, they sighted the distant silhouettes of the blockade fleet: British frigates, ships of the line, and exotic Turkish men o'war standing on the horizon. Hazzard wondered about De la Vega and the *Volpone*, and where they were now. He removed his Bedouin *kaftan* and pulled on his Bombay scarlet, the easiest form of identification.

A fast, low frigate spotted them, her yards turning, her sleek prow coming round, her sails filling with that same north wind that had driven Nelson into the French line with power enough to change the world. She fired an unshotted bowchaser as a warning and a plume of smoke rose up. Cook waved his turban *shemagh* at them as Tariq guided the boatman round, braced to starboard, nosing over within easy reach, then reefed the big lateen sail. The frigate doused sail and drew slowly alongside. A voice called down from the rail.

'*This is His Britannic Majesty's Ship Seahorse,*' cried a midshipman. '*Who are you?*'

Hazzard gazed up at the curious faces looking down. He felt an ambivalent mix of failure, pride, shame, distrust and relief, tears gathering in his eyes. '*We ar—*' he began, then stopped, looking round at the marines – at their hollow cheeks, dark sunken eyes, filthy, dusty, scarred faces, their bloodied, torn and ragged robes, their broken, skinned hands gripping their sawn-off muskets, scimitars and cutlasses – and wondered how to answer. He thought of Aboukir Bay, the Battle of the Nile, the revolt of Cairo, and the howl of Murad's Mamluk cavalry riding to the rescue from the western hills under the shadows of Memnon himself.

Who are you?

He shouted back. '*We are 9 Company, the Marines,*' he called, '*with two wounded – and I am Captain William John Hazzard.*'

There was silence from the *Seahorse* as the midshipman took it in, then turned to his lieutenant. He ducked away and returned a moment later with the captain. More of them appeared at the rail, and soon the rigging hands in the ratlines and tops cheered and waved, whistles going up across the ship, the bell clanging on the fo'c'sle as all hands rushed to the portside rail to look.

Underhill and the others listened to the greeting and looked up, then looked to each other, no man saying a word, none jubilant, as if in recognition they were safe, yet in mourning for something lost. The captain raised his cocked hat in salute and signal flags rippled up to the masthead, snapping in the wind. Guide-lines were thrown down and sailors climbed down the steps to hook them in, a cradle swinging outboard on a boom.

With care the marines loaded Napier onto the mattress in the net harness of the first cradle, and guided it safe aloft into the sky, watching it swing gently inboard. It was not until the cradle returned and lifted Wayland up and out of the Nile barge that the marines gathered their equipment and filed up the boarding steps, the deckhands giving yet more cheers. Hazzard was the last, and turned to their ferryman, their erstwhile Charon who might well have conveyed Hazzard over the River Styx, given different circumstances. He offered two gold coins.

'For when I see you. Next time.'

The old man took them, his face creasing into a smile, and he showed off the new clay pipe in his hands, smouldering happily, courtesy of Underhill. '*Rabbena ma'ak, Hazar Pasha.*'

May God be with you.

Hazzard climbed the steps stiffly, hands reaching down to help him up. When finally he reached the portside rail, he found the officers gathered behind the captain, staring openly at them in shock. The duty watch of the *Seahorse* marines had formed up behind their lieutenant, a sergeant shouting, '*P'rade...!*' and banged to attention. Hazzard stood still a moment, looking about, at the rails and rigging, the guns, all so clean, all so foreign to him again.

'Mr Hazzard,' said the captain, stepping forward. 'Sir Edward Foote. Welcome aboard the *Seahorse*.' He smiled warmly, taking Hazzard's hand. 'Welcome home.'

The *Seahorse* surgeon had taken care of Napier's back, which he declared tougher than a First-Rate's broadside. He had reopened and widened the torn flesh to drain the area before closing, and complimented Porter on his attendance to Wayland's wound.

'I had help, sir...' said the modest Yorkshireman, and they thought of Zeinab and the Tarabin, and horses' hooves all over again, and all fell silent, Kite raising his mug of grog, the rest following suit.

They had reached Syracuse in a week. With the promise of safe harbour, the marines' injuries came blazing into full revelation, and they were taken a-bed to rest in the barracks infirmary behind the imposing towers of Castello Maniace.

Hesse kept Tariq close by, ensuring the Bedouin never felt alone, the Italian staff doctor convinced they were both Austrian Hussars. De Lisle's weeping wound was treated and healed, the physicians curious about the poultices left on it by the Bedouins of the caravan to Thebes, while Kite and Warnock moved about like crippled men. They all suffered likewise, stiffened legs having borne too much, bruised and cracked ribs wrapped, torn shoulders and arms now supported in slings. Wayland saw a specialist surgeon from Naples, and Hazzard remembered De la Vega in the Palazzo Sessa, after their first clash with Derrien, the doctor called in the middle of the night by Hamilton – and Hazzard's heated threat to the doctor echoing in his memory: *if he dies, you die.*

Hazzard and Wayland had lain alongside the men in the ward until they were billeted together in a house along the seafront. Hazzard spent the days with them – he had no intention of letting a frustrated drum-major get anywhere near them: they would not be doing drill or sentry duty on sick-parade. None dared suggest it. There was not a sergeant or flag-captain left unaware that these were 9 Company, the Special Landing Squadron – the men of William John Hazzard.

There had been a few squabbles in the old town, a few involving drink. The worst occasion was in a small tavern on their first night of freedom, when they had entered in their various degrees of uniform scarlet jerkins, sashes and shirtsleeves, Kite still wearing a sling, Underhill on a stick. The room had gone quiet, several seamen rising from a table to offer it to them, ales already coming – but a marine from the frigate *Emerald*, far beyond his measure, had recognised Underhill and staggered drunkenly to attention, blocking their path and bowing in mockery. 'Oh 'allo 'allo. It's the *Nine*, innit, eh lads? All *bow* before the Nine, eh? Blow me down an' up me arse, eh, eh?'

Underhill had shoved past him in the small establishment, the Sicilian potman and his sons well used to drunken seamen, Genoese, Neapolitan, Ragusan or British as they may have been. The man to crack first had not been Underhill, Napier, or even Cook, who was still in the doorway – but Pettifer. The *Emerald* marine repeated his curse and spat after them with, 'Boffin' about with the 'Gyppos eh, whiles we in the fleet does all the work eh, eh? Nice bit o'work if y'can get it, eh?'

Pettifer had turned and crashed his fist onto the crown of the man's head, twice, then three times, driving him down into a cowering heap on the floor in a split second. He slammed him in the back of the head again and again until the blood began to swell, the small table knocked away, Underhill and the *Emerald* shipmates calling out, trying to pull Pettifer off until Cook weighed in. When Hazzard had heard, it reminded him of himself after the Cape. No more was said of it, but the *Emerald* marine was charged with drunk and disorderly conduct, his shore leave withdrawn.

Hazzard and Cook had kept them busy, with hikes beyond old Ortygia, as if headed for Mt Etna in the north, the smouldering plume of the volcano visible through the eyeglass on the blue horizon. They grew stronger and eased into a new rhythm, the sun no longer an enemy to resist, but something to revel in, and Cook and Hazzard watched them at play – Kite with his own particular repertoire of bawdy melody, Cochrane plucking a fiddle, with local girls from the town round a fire in the hills, all hoping the endless fear would ebb forever.

On some days, Hazzard and Wayland explored the churches, the ruins of the amphitheatre, both with a silent appreciation for the finesse of the ancient Greek city. It became their own private Grand Tour, and Hazzard no longer regretted the passing of academe, as he had in Naples while viewing Hamilton's collections. Here, he could taste the salt on the wind, and could feel the life in the sunlit stones before them, without the weight of Karnak and Memnon bearing down upon his soul.

As they recovered, Cook renewed their training, Warnock and De Lisle would perhaps lead them in the knife, or compete at throwing his tomahawk at an upturned barrel, Tariq showing off with the *khanjar* – or they would practise the sword, Wayland slowly regaining his balance, compensating for the lost hand. When he stumbled on his bad leg or became tired Hazzard did not begrudge him, the men proud of every step he took.

They were a strange family to Hazzard, who had known little family in his youth, an orphan raised by his uncle. As he watched them sit, eat, and laugh among themselves in the long waving grasses, the Mediterranean beyond, it had become almost happiness – no gloom passed over him, no fearful wondering how long it could all last. Sarah had gone – not entirely, but she was no longer the admonishing reminder of failed obligation, her memory now more of warm companionship.

Delphine Lascelles appeared from time to time to him in his mind, and he wondered how she had fared in Cairo after the revolt. He hoped she was safe, her beauty coming to him in the drowsing wakefulness of early morning, out in town in the trace of a scent, or in a woman's voice – he would turn, finding it not her but another.

But he did not mourn her absence, or pine for seeing another. He now viewed the world rather with the simple fatalism of the *Bedu* and Mamluk: *as God wills it.* One day, he thought, he might be free – but never so free as he felt in those warm winter Sicilian hills, with Cook, Wayland and the men of 9 Company.

Yet still he felt the tug of an unfinished task. As he looked out over the harbour at HMS *Tigre* in the distance, he touched the ivory hilt of the scimitar of Ali-Qarim, hanging on the back of the bentwood chair beside him. He heard his calm voice, *hadeyya, gift*, and remembered the way he had revered the Mortimer pistol Hazzard had given him that first day: '*Martimar. Londan.*' He would have been a kind man, Hazzard suspected, had he known him.

Hazzard lifted his hand from the corner of the desk and found grit beneath his fingers. It was sand. He was still finding Egyptian sand in his clothes, in his boots. It had infiltrated the miniature of Sarah, which stood propped up against the inkstand before him. The remnants of Anubis's hourglass, it was embedded in his body, in his spirit – and part of him wanted to get back. Despite the constant risk all about them in Egypt, he had grown used to the quietude of the Delta, of the desert – and just as he had found in Suffolk with that first disturbing return home, he regarded the clatter of this world all around them untrue, unreal, after the struggles in his ancient world. Memnon stared down at him from his dreams still.

A signal flag went up the masthead of *Tigre*, others coming down. It seemed a reminder, a beckoning. *Very well, Sir Sidney*, he thought, *I am coming.*

He dressed, in his Bombay scarlet, in his Bedouin boots and loose soft linen breeches, the Lorenzoni, the ivory-hilted scimitar and dark *shemagh* tied round his waist, a vestigial sash: each of them kept theirs close for fear of losing it – it had become their mark, the mark of 'the Nine', as others had come to call them, and they all wore it so. He went downstairs and found Cook in the small sitting-room, browsing at a bookshelf. He was bare-headed, and wore his old cut-off scarlet jacket, white ducks, boots and cross-belt – and his sash. At his side hung a short Turkish *kilij*, his curved *khanjar* dagger jammed in his belt at the front. He turned and stiffened to attention.

'Sir.' They both knew this might be the end of their waiting.

'Ready.'

Cook nodded. 'Clear aye.'

He followed Hazzard outside. On the step the marines of 9 Company waited, Underhill snapping them to attention as Hazzard appeared. '*P'rade.*'

They strode behind him along the waterfront road, on their left the painted townhouses of officers and officials, on their right the rail and rocks of the breakwater and harbour. The horse-drawn traffic slowed before and behind, their drivers not shouting down, a donkey and cart moving past, seamen and marines standing aside. The marines marched behind Hazzard in arrowhead formation, their *shamshirs*, *kilij* and scimitars swinging, their sawn-off Charlevilles held loose and ready. Their eyes never rested – out of habit, too used to the unexpected, their eyes on each ship, *Terpsichore*, *Emerald*, *Seahorse*, the marine sentries coming to the end of the jetties, watching as they passed, deckhands moving to the rails. *That's Cookie, an' that's Petty, with 'is blunderbuss*, necks craning for a look. *That's them, bloody 'ell.* For a time they owned the road, the harbour, the fleet, behind the man who had reconnoitred the French fleet from the masthead of *Orient*, the men first on Malta, who charged the artillery at Aboukir, the men who rode with the Mamluk, just as the whispers said. The doors of the seafront opened, officers and servants alike coming out just to get a glimpse.

They passed to the end of the southern reaches of Ortygia, and the royal Neapolitan guardsmen at the iron-studded doors of the Castello Maniace cracked to attention, '*Signore.*'

Hazzard nodded, '*Per Commendatore* Smith.'

'*Prego, signore,*' said the Officer of the Guard, his left hand slapping the gleaming hilt of a sword, his right hand snapping up in salute. '*Signore* to follow me please.'

They marched through the gatehouse into the main quad, a troop of naval artillery doing drill, hefting a cannon from one gun-carriage to another, another squad practising their reloading, *Get your bloody backs into it you bone-idle blockade buggahs!* They were led through a doorway to a large room occupying the first bay of the fort, peering in at the round southeastern turret as they passed, giant 36-pounder cannons looking out over the harbour.

Hazzard looked about. The room was dark, heavy beams above rough stone walls, ornate wood panelling and tall narrow windows at the far end giving a view of the sea and a headland beyond. Out in the strait, British men o'war prowled the approaches for any unwanted ship fool enough to come too close. He had detected the scent of anticipation in Ortygia: the Mediterranean Fleet was back, and hunting for blood in the water.

Before them, a Neapolitan officer and his retinue waited at a large chart table among a group of braided bluejacket officers, lieutenants and artillerymen. Hazzard stopped dead. The Neapolitan was no mere officer – it was Admiral Sir John Acton, former Prime Minister of the court of Naples, and no supporter of Hazzard, their last words echoing in Hazzard's memory. *You forget yourself sir! For you stand in the embassy of King George of England and you play him false!*

But something had changed in him, Acton giving him a slow nod of recognition, his eyes betraying some act of unspoken contrition. But another figure nearby arrested Hazzard's attention. Between Acton and Sir William Sidney Smith stood Rear Admiral Horatio Nelson.

The marines fanned out behind Hazzard, Underhill giving low, curt commands. When Hazzard caught a glimpse of them they stood in close order behind in two ranks, arms ordered, at attention. Nelson approached. He stopped in front of Hazzard.

'Mr Hazzard.'

Hazzard noted the scar on Nelson's forehead, the new wound from the Nile, and his general demeanour. If his nerves had recovered from the pursuit of Bonaparte's fleet and the battle in Aboukir Bay, it was not obvious: he still looked grave, exhausted and troubled.

'Sir.'

'I am glad you yet survive,' said Nelson, putting out his left hand.

Hazzard shook it. 'And you sir.'

Nelson drew closer. He looked down, thoughtful, shaking his head. 'I have no idea how you did it,' he said, looking him in the eye, 'but there was, indeed, a tethered goat for my tigers.'

Hazzard remembered his words to Hardy and Troubridge before he had departed to ride to Cairo: *Tell him to come back, Sir Thomas. Tell him I'll have a tethered goat – for his tigers.*

'I am grateful sir,' added Hazzard quietly, 'For everything thereafter.'

Nelson nodded, another sad memory. 'When Tomlinson heard it was your request, he looked to his task with all the gravity I knew he would. Perhaps,' he said, 'there are times, when we can save souls after all.'

Masoud, his funeral barge on the night waters, the Nile lily, the prayers of the Beni Qassim.

Sarah. *Safe now.*

All for naught – but all in the trying. St Jude always wins.

'And Mr Wayland,' said Nelson, moving to Hazzard's right, 'there are few who can fully comprehend. But you know I can,' he said, indicating his own empty sleeve. 'It may ache but if tended at the correct intervals, it dulls with time. I have a man in London to recommend.'

Wayland grasped his left hand with his right, standing stiff to attention. Hardened though he was, the young man within still flushed with pride. 'Thank you, sir.'

'Sir Thomas sends his best regards to his good friends of Aboukir, who stopped the guns, and saved the *Culloden*.'

'Yes sir,' Wayland said, looking back at the marines. 'The greatest hearts I've ever known.'

Nelson smiled for the first time. 'They certainly are…' He moved past him, to Cook, to Underhill, to Warnock, offering his hand to

each. 'The great oaks of England. Far from home, far from the fleet.'
He moved on to Cochrane, to Napier, to Porter, shaking each hand in
turn. 'They move from sail, to horse, to guns, to musket and sword.'
Then on to Handley, De Lisle, Pettifer, Hesse. 'Our good men, our
very good men...' he said, casting a glance back at Hazzard, '...who
never stop.'

He came to the end of the row. 'And Private Kite.'

Kite stiffened to attention further, his chin rising. 'Sir.'

Nelson looked uncomfortable but spoke clearly. 'It never reached
your ears, more is the pity... but I never felt safer, boarding the *San
Nicolas* at Cape St Vincent, than when I had you and the red coats of
the marines at my side. My profound gratitude.'

Kite blinked, taken by surprise. 'S-sir...Thank you sir. I mean...'
He swallowed and looked forward again. 'Sir. My honour, sir.'

'And mine.'

He turned at last to Tariq. 'And the brave Egyptian, who lives
through turmoil untold.'

'Our interpreter, sir,' said Hesse beside him, 'Tariq ibn Hasim, of
the Huwaytat.'

Nelson bowed his head. '*Al-salam alleykum*,' he attempted, 'And
shokran.'

Tariq bowed deeply, his lined and weathered face creasing with
delight. '*Wa aleikum as-salam, Nelsoun Amir al-Bahr.* My honour,
Kapudan Pasha.'

Nelson made his way back to the table and the assembly. He looked
briefly at Smith. 'Commodore, I have court business with Sir John
here in Palermo, and must set sail, while you have business with these
gentlemen I understand.'

Smith bowed his head and smiled diplomatically. 'We certainly
have, my lord.' The two scarcely exchanged glances, not the best of
acquaintances, Smith's 'my lord' given with a barely detectable ironic
twist. Nelson gravitated to Acton and his officers, and headed out, the
junior officers coming to attention, heels cracking. Underhill gave a
low, '*P'rade... shun.*'

The marines stiffened, Nelson giving them a nod as he passed. 'I
bid you all fair winds, gentlemen,' he said, and within moments he
and his entourage were gone.

Once the heavy doors boomed shut in the outer yard, Smith
gestured to a connecting door. 'Mr Hazzard, there is a breakfast laid on

in the gunroom through there for the men. A proper feast, gentlemen, and Mr Hazzard and Sar'-Major Cook will join you presently.'

'*Sah.*' Underhill stepped one pace forward and drilled the marines through to the gunroom. As junior officers prepared the charts, Smith beckoned Hazzard and Cook to another door by the windows, and they went through.

It was the cramped office of the Sergeant of the Guard, serving as the administrative hub of the castle, a carved desk, leather-backed chair and filing cabinets, and a second door to the corridor and quad. Smith shut both doors.

'I am uncertain if you know all this,' he began, 'but Nelson evacuated the entire court of Naples and the royal family to Palermo barely a month ago, just before the city flew into revolt and the French came marching in. It's quite a mess. The French have declared it a new republic, as they are wont to do, doubtless with its own newspaper already.' He fetched out a decanter and three glasses from a cabinet and gave Hazzard a slight bow of the head. 'Your words to Sir John Acton, he admitted to me, were quite prophetic, well done.' He poured out three pale green drinks, the sharp bite of citrus on the air. 'The Neapolitans control Syracuse, of course, and the whole of Sicily, but now feel indebted to us, hence our welcome. Sir John is somewhat more grateful now for the blessings of King George.' He handed them each a glass. Cook took it circumspectly. 'Lime and lemon-juice, Sar'-Major,' said Smith. 'Keeps the scurvy away. With a dash of gin for the next bit.'

'Thank y'sir,' he said, and they drank.

Smith remembered something else. 'And Sir William Hamilton sends his most heartfelt regards, for telling Acton what's what. Apparently you rather put him in his place.'

Hazzard thought of the inflated bully he had encountered in Hamilton's study in Naples – the man outside had seemed more humble. 'I think we all had forgotten our place...'

'Very noble, but from what I know of Acton I doubt you had at all. Now then,' Smith perched on the edge of the desk. 'First, it's rather good to see you alive and well again, both of you. You've taken jolly good care of him, Sar'-Major, well done.'

Cook acknowledged a rare compliment. 'Sir.'

'Second, what news of the uprising in Cairo? I've got your report, but quickly.'

Hazzard was blunt. 'The city was torn to pieces – barricades, muskets, mostly Al-Azhar students and then of course the criminal mob itself. Ran amok, the minarets calling the people to rise up. It ended when Bonaparte bombarded the area around the Al-Azhar Mosque with cannon and broke through its gates.'

Smith watched him, assessing Hazzard's feelings. 'Just as you said.'

'Yes.'

'Resentment noted. Repercussions?'

'Anything between a thousand and two thousand prisoners executed by Bonaparte, their bodies and heads cast into the Nile.'

Smith blew out a breath. 'Good God... Al-Charkawi? Leader of the mosque?'

'Executed,' said Hazzard, 'with the other *imams* who took a hand.' After a moment he added, 'It was Lord Keith's catastrophic bloody failure, just as he wished.'

There was a brief silence, Cook looking at the pair of them, but neither was more nor less sensitive than the other to the circumstances. Smith pinched the bridge of his nose, closing his eyes, then looked out through the lead mullioned window at the sea. A frigate cruised past in the outer roads of the harbour approaches, the sun flashing on its sails, momentarily dazzling. He sat up more brightly and slapped his hands together, as if to keep his mind working. 'Very well,' he said, 'Very well. Troop movements?'

'In my report, but I'd like to see a chart.'

'Done.' Smith stood abruptly and reached for the door.

Hazzard stopped him. 'He is most probably going to attack Syria and march clear through to bloody India if he can. You do know that.'

'Then we had best stop him.' Smith looked at them both. 'I was most sorry to hear about Mr Wayland,' he said sadly, frowning to himself, as if trying to see how he could have prevented it. 'You have seen some days, haven't you?'

Cook nodded. 'I'd bloody say, sir.'

When they returned to the conference chamber, only Smith's aides remained, with Wayland, Lt Wright, Smith's first officer on the *Tigre*, an unknown naval officer and an Ottoman army officer. They had gathered round the chart table, examining the maps of Egypt, the Levant and Turkey. Smith made the introductions. 'You know Lt Wright of course,' he began.

Wright nodded with his usual inscrutable expression. 'Good to see you again sir.'

Smith indicated the Turkish officer. 'And may I present Captain, or rather, *Yuzbashi* Shafik Reiz of the Ottoman army.'

Reiz was a handsome man of about Hazzard's age, perhaps younger, somewhat taller, with short black hair, flowing moustaches and a broad smile. He wore baggy dark blue Turkish *shalvar* breeches tucked into gleaming black boots, but most remarkably a jacket of deep red, not unlike Marine scarlet, braided in gold foliate scrolling in broad bands down its centre, along the hem and cuffs – possibly emblems of rank, Hazzard assumed, but unrecognisable to his eye. At his side hung a graceful curved *kilij* sword suspended from a broad white belt round his waist. Smiling, and with a bow of his head, Reiz put out his hand and Hazzard took it, meeting his eye in the Turkish manner, and Reiz beamed in reply. He spoke in English. 'The greatest honour to meet the English officers, Wayland *effendi*, and Hazar Pasha.' He bowed his head again, taking Cook's hand. 'And the mighty *Kuq guchlu*.'

Smith explained, 'Captain Reiz is of the *Nizam-i Djedid*, the New Order army, trained by European advisers – mostly French, ironically enough.'

'We are an antique people,' admitted Reiz, 'Too ancient for our good selves, may it be. Now we have been taught to volley the musket, site great guns, and speak the French, but I,' he said proudly, 'I learn the English as well, of the good Sir Siddani.'

'*Bir onndur*,' said Hazzard, *an honour*, 'Sar'nt Cook and I served with the Ottomans at Embabeh.'

Reiz was delighted. 'So! Some here do know some of the Turkish,' he said, looking about with a laugh, the others obliging him. He bowed his head. '*Teshekir ederim, Yuzbashi*.' *Thank you, Captain*.

'Excellent,' said Smith, clearly pleased, and turned to introduce the silent man behind. 'And this, gentlemen, is Colonel Antoine le Picard de Phélippeaux, an officer of His Majesty's armed forces.'

Phélippeaux was in his early thirties, in a nondescript dark blue coat, collar and cravat, dark haired, clean-shaven. Hazzard recognised him at once as unmistakably French. Smith glanced at Hazzard. 'Like you, Mr Hazzard, Col. Phélippeaux knows Bonaparte personally.'

'You have met with him?' asked the colonel in heavily accented English.

'Yes,' said Hazzard. 'And dined aboard his flagship, the *Orient*...' he glanced at Cook, '...just before we had to get off.'

A smile played at the corners of Smith's mouth and he said to Phélippeaux, 'What did I tell you?'

Phélippeaux bowed his head. 'I am honoured. I should explain,' he said, looking to Smith, '*En français?* I am a loyal soldier of France,' he continued in French, 'but I am also a loyal subject of my king. Though I knew Bonaparte at the *École militaire*, I shall not rest until the republic falls.' He took a moment. 'He is...' he sought the word, '...*driven* to conquer, like an engine of war, for he fears being so conquered himself, as he so nearly was before his command in Italy.' He nodded, remembering. 'He will thus destroy everything in his path to seize power. Wherever it lies. It is my belief he must be stopped.'

Hazzard caught Cook's eye. The big man was not happy with a Frenchman at the table. Smith flicked a glance round the group, noticing the reluctance.

'Gentlemen. I should explain. Years ago,' he said, his voice dropping, 'in a more confused time, I was on operations in France – a simple matter really, but arrested on charges of espionage.'

Hazzard was not at all surprised. 'Espionage?'

'Mm. Nonsense really. Went to the Temple Prison actually. John here as well.' They looked at Wright. 'I even wrote to Bonaparte in protest.' He smiled. 'Blighter never replied.'

Upon their first meeting Hazzard had assumed Smith was from Admiralty Intelligence – but had not sensed the cold hand of Sir Rafe Lewis or Room 63 controlling him. He could feel his spine crawl at the thought of it. 'So, you're not merely naval officers.'

Smith gave his laconic look. 'Are any of us really, Mr Hazzard?' He considered a moment, then indicated Phélippeaux. 'But we were saved by this extraordinary gentleman.' Wright looked down at the chart table with a slight smile as Smith continued. 'He dressed himself as an officer of the constable's staff, produced a false warrant to the guardroom that we were to be moved to another prison. Next thing we knew we were marched out, put in a carriage, and spirited into the night to safety. Colonel Phélippeaux is utterly trustworthy.'

Hazzard looked at Phélippeaux, and the unassuming Frenchman smiled back at him blankly. 'It is so, I think,' he said in English, 'with many who remember the old France.'

Cook shook his head. '*By all that's holy in Bristol...*'

'Indeed,' said Smith, clapping his hands together again. 'Now. Bona fides complete, to the present if you please. We have some revelations: Mr Hazzard, the Memnonium. Your thoughts.'

Hazzard glanced at them all and took a breath. 'Sir. A Somali messenger seeking out Murad Bey in Upper Egypt found us at the Memnonium, near Karnak. He insisted Bonaparte knew of the sultan's declaration of war and was buying soldiers from sheikhs in the Sudan and beyond. Murad is being reinforced by small numbers of troops from Mecca and Yemen. He came to our aid at the Memnonium,' he said, his memory replaying the events, 'where we engaged a squadron of French cavalry, and suffered our losses...' His eye found Wayland who leaned on his cane, gazing down at the map with a fixed look.

Hazzard stared down at the shoreline of Sinai, the coast curving up into Palestine. 'There is something,' he said, 'something monstrous coming... The signs are all there, of a vast plan.' He looked at Smith and Wright. 'I believe they are going to mobilise to attack Constantinople.'

There was a short silence, Smith looked uncomfortable and took a breath. 'Mr Hazzard, in the last few weeks we have received reports of precisely what you fear. Prompted by the build-up of forces by Al-Djezzar Pasha at Acre, which now surely threaten Egypt. Bonaparte has marched east.'

Hazzard went cold. 'When?'

Wright glanced at Smith and took over. 'Two weeks ago, General Reynier's advance division set out for Katia in the Sinai Peninsula. We understand it was reconnoitred by one General Lagrange for just such a purpose. We assume they have reached El-'Arish by now and, as you said, will shortly advance into Syria – to attack Al-Djezzar at Acre.'

Hazzard stared at them, incredulous. 'While we have been here? Sitting about?'

'My dear fellow,' said Smith, 'we are watching them, never fear – and your men were riddled with wounds and injuries.'

'For God's sake... where is Bonaparte?' demanded Hazzard. 'Now?'

Wright moved to the map. 'He will be at Qaitya, here; perhaps even already at El-'Arish.' He glanced at Reiz for confirmation. 'I am told there is a Mamluk force at Arish, at the border.'

Reiz nodded. 'Yes sir, one thousand and two hundred men at the least. That is all.'

Hazzard considered the numbers. 'Bonaparte landed in Egypt with possibly forty thousand men – eight divisions, twenty-five thousand under arms, and ten or twelve in reserve, some say more...' He looked to Wayland for confirmation.

Wayland shifted on his walking-stick. 'If you include auxiliaries, engineers and sappers...' Wayland looked to Smith and Wright. 'How many are reported in Reynier's division, sir?'

Wright answered at once. 'Small. Two and a half thousand.'

Wayland got it. 'He's cut his divisions in half.'

Hazzard agreed. 'The rest left to garrison Egypt. Then Bonaparte marches with only his best thirteen or fourteen thousand men.'

'Attack the sultan's empire with so few soldiers alone?' asked Reiz, incredulous. 'Is this so?'

Wayland did not waver. 'Bonaparte would, sir.'

'Could he do it?' asked Smith.

'Not capture and hold sir, no,' said Hazzard, 'But destroy Al-Djezzar, before Djezzar attacks Egypt, yes.'

'Al-Djezzar is a deadly foe...' warned Reiz.

'Not up against a ruddy infantry square he ain't,' rumbled Cook. 'No one is.'

'Quite so, *Sergent-chef*,' said Phélippeaux with a nod.

'These are disciplined soldiers, Captain Reiz,' said Hazzard. 'The desert is no barrier to them. They march in temperatures of 120 degrees without water, their losses ignored. And what is more, they will do it,' he said, 'because they adore Bonaparte.'

'Can you show us, Mr Hazzard?' asked Smith.

Hazzard looked at the chart: *Gaza, Jaffa, Acre... my God*. They were all situated on a simple route northwards. 'He will keep close to the coast where it's cooler during the day...'

Reiz looked down with him at the chart. 'Then he knows not his terrain.'

'How so?'

'It is not hot, as in Cairo. This is rain, wind and cold. They will fight the desert – and they will fight the mud and rain as well.'

'So,' said Smith, 'horse and foot, say thirteen to fifteen thousand. Field artillery?'

'Yes,' said Hazzard. 'Twelve-pounders, eights and fours, and eight-inch or six-inch howitzers. We saw them in the battle for Cairo, at Embabeh.' Hazzard remembered them well. 'All on carriage wheels.'

'The *canon de douze*, the 12-pounder, it is not the siege weapon,' offered Phélippeaux, 'and the troops, they move fast, *d'accord*? Never stop long in the one place.'

'His mobile field-guns are perfect for that,' said Wayland.

'But not to take Acre.' Reiz looked up to Smith. 'He has nothing heavy.'

'You are quite right, Captain Reiz...' Smith looked through a number of scattered sheets on the table then gestured to an aide on the far side. 'Jardine, where is that note, with the Austrian stamp...?' As Jardine looked, he continued, 'If he wants Djezzar at Acre, he will need heavy artillery, no question—'

'I say he cannot take Akka,' said Reiz. 'It is a fortress, in the rock.'

'Perhaps, *mon vieux*,' said Phélippeaux, 'but it is old.'

Hazzard glanced at them. 'Malta too, was a fortress.'

Wayland put a finger on the chart, on the Levantine Sea. 'He'll ship the guns on transports, sir, hugging the coastline along with his troops, perhaps, weather permitting.' He looked up, a brighter idea dawning. 'Or simply send them on their way to await his arrival...'

'We wholly agree,' said Smith, stretching out to take Jardine's paper. 'Here we are...' He began to read, trying to find the relevant place, 'So on, so forth... *and heavy artillery to be put aboard a small flotilla of ships. Destination presumed first Jaffa for reinforcement or Haifa, to command the heights of Acre, for disembarkation by army.*' He handed the note to Hazzard. 'From your Mr Hammer of the Viennese Consulate. He never sleeps, dear chap.'

Hazzard took it, Cook looking over his shoulder. Coming from Hammer, it was indisputable. Hazzard read down the page more carefully: *canons de 24, Gomer mortier de 8 pouces, Gomer mortier de 12 pouces*. These were 24-pounder ship-killers and 8- and 12-inch mortars, throwing round-shot a foot in diameter. It would be more than enough to smash holes in a stone fortress – particularly ancient Acre.

'And we have intercepted a French communiqué, clearly indicating Mr Bonaparte is rather on his own.' Smith flapped it out, scanning it quickly. 'It was deciphered by our man in Palermo,' he said, and summarised, 'The Directory government cannot risk any further involvement, et cetera et cetera, and insist that he has but three choices, either to stay where he is and fend off a Turkish attack...' He nodded at Reiz who bowed his head, 'Or march into the Holy Land and take

Constantinople. Whence he can either return to Egypt or proceed overland to India and join forces with Citizen Tipu Sahib... and relieve him in his fight against the vainglorious English, so on, so forth...' Smith shook his head, handing the letter to Hazzard. 'Quite surprised they do not suggest he conquer the moon while he's about it.'

Hazzard read down the page of French, the phrases redolent of diplomatic and governmental whitewash, *that it must be considered by the General in Chief that we regret we cannot...* Smith was right: Bonaparte and his elite army had effectively been abandoned in Egypt. Hazzard cast his mind back to the Barrakka Gardens in Valletta, and a quiet conversation with Napoleon Bonaparte, on a garden seat in the sun, discussing Caesar and Britannia. Clearly Caesar was not meant to return. He found himself once again identifying with the man, sensing his thoughts: *Bonaparte had no choice.* Whoever he dreamt he was, be it Ramesses, Caesar or Alexander, he could not wait for the Turks to come to him. He was going to them.

God help them all.

Smith continued, 'Our task now, Mr Hazzard, will be to support our new Ottoman allies against this assault. The sultan believes he has the upper hand. Djezzar Pasha in Acre has created two armies, in total some sixty to eighty thousand, spread across Damascus, Sidon, and out to Rhodes, all ready to attack.'

Hazzard looked down at the chart, his eye falling on the names of cities he had only read of in antique histories: *Damascus, Tyre, Antioch, Jerusalem.* Despite depleted forces Bonaparte was invading the most ancient territory on earth, guarded by the largest empire since Rome.

'He will catch them off-guard,' said Hazzard, feeling the chill of a bloody history, the emanations from the names themselves, knowing how Bonaparte had gazed at them himself. *He will turn every battlefield into a Thermopylae, a Gaugamela, a Pharsalus.* 'Wherever you least expect him, he will attack, find the weakness in the imperial line, an unhappy joint where two nations meet – Albanians and Turks, or Moroccans, Mamluks and conscripts – and he will split your army, overwhelm you with artillery fire, throw his entire force into the breach, then wheel and surround the weaker half – and destroy everything in his path.' They looked at him, the brutality of it all not lost on Hazzard. 'But the heavy artillery is the key,' he added. 'It would tip the scales.'

'Yes,' agreed Reiz. 'He needs the guns for Akka.'

Phélippeaux said quietly in halting English, 'The walls of Acre, or Akka, *je m'excuse*, are old, from the Middle Ages, the crusades. Good siege weapons would bring them down.'

There was another brief silence, Hazzard thinking of Hammer's words: *a small flotilla.*

'So,' said Smith, glancing at Hazzard, 'when do you go?'

Hazzard looked at him, at Cook, at Wayland. 'Go?'

Reiz spoke. 'Sir Siddani agrees,' he said with a nod to Smith, 'I have the order to defend the coast towns – and thus to find the flotilla of heavy artillery, Hazar Pasha.'

'Why not take the *Tigre* to find and sink it?' asked Hazzard.

Smith cocked an eyebrow. 'Quite right, yes. However, there is a greater threat to the Mediterranean of a second French fleet, commanded by Bruix, which could relieve Egypt or Malta, attack Constantinople, or even take our ports in Sicily – including this one. And we are duty bound to protect Sicily and Turkey. I must maintain the Egypt blockade, Hood having departed and Troubridge trying to fill the gaps with the others. *Tigre* cannot be spared for long.' He leaned closer, pointing at the chart. 'I want a raid, Mr Hazzard. By the only fellows this side of Gib who can do it.'

Hazzard looked at the chart.

From Damietta… to Jaffa or Acre.

'Something else for you to consider…' Smith gave a nod to Wright, who handed across a buff-coloured sheet of paper. It was emblazoned with a coat of arms and stamped with a wax seal. Smith read aloud, 'Et cetera et cetera… *relations with our Ottoman allies notwithstanding, it has been so demanded that the physical person of one Citizen Derrien of the Ministry of the Interior be seized, and he be made prisoner, arrested either in vita or per mortem.*'

Hazzard stared, a chill lancing through him.

Derrien.

The name would not leave him in peace.

Smith continued, '*To which end, this office with the sanction of the Crown hereby promotes Marine Captain William John Hazzard, Exploring Officer Extraordinary, to the rank of Major of Marines, effective immediately,* signed, sealed, so forth.' He held out the sheet to him. 'Congratulations, Major.'

Hazzard began to tremble – he could feel the vibration of the threshing machinery, the cogs and wheels of this terrible engine that had gathered so much pace and speed, and now become an unstoppable force. This was the stratagem he had sensed at the statue of Ozymandias, a descending doom. And, to convince him, they had thrown in something for good measure.

Derrien. In vita or per mortem.

Dead or alive.

Hazzard took the note. It was not Admiralty. It was from the War Office, from Downing Street.

'I had the honour to bring this to you, *Capitaine*,' said Phélippeaux with a bow, 'Ah, *pardon*: Major. From my work with the Alien Office.'

'Alien Office?' asked Hazzard, clearing his throat. 'What have they got to do with this?'

'Nothing,' said Smith, gathering the orders and despatches for Hazzard, 'not officially. Though Wickham and the Aliens liked the idea of side-stepping Sir Rafe Lewis. But we owe this to an Admiralty officer, looking out for your interests it seems. He's liaising with the French Committee and the War House, hence his trust in Colonel Phélippeaux. A Commander Charles Blake.'

Blake.

'And I have it on good authority,' said Smith, looking at the chart on the table, his finger drawing a line from Syracuse to Crete and to Palestine, 'that Derrien is with the general staff of the expedition.'

'How do we know this?'

Smith gave a slight smile. 'It was Masoud ibn Yussuf, in Cairo. He sent word, giving the names of those from their headquarters who would attend.' He shook his head. 'They cleared their offices in preparation for their return and have been replaced by acting temporaries.' He kept his voice low, almost nonchalant. 'So, What do you say, Major?'

Hazzard looked at them, Smith, Wright, Phélippeaux. War Office or not, it was a typical Admiralty lie, he knew, Blake's involvement proving it. The promotion was meaningless, but Derrien was the bait to tempt Hazzard's appetite.

Smith straightened. 'Derrien, and the artillery. If we deprive Bonaparte of his guns we might save the Holy Land – and Egypt. The ancient world, Mr Hazzard, or what is left of it.'

Hazzard looked at him steadily. He could feel the tremors begin in his limbs, his voice flat, unfamiliar.

Derrien.

'With what support?'

'HMS *Tigre* will wave you off,' said Smith, 'But otherwise, you're on your own. The way you like it.'

'But with me,' said Reiz, stepping forward.

Smith inclined his head. 'And of course, *Yuzbashi* Reiz here will accompany you.'

'I know Yafa well,' said Reiz, sorting through the charts – he pulled out a small map of the port town of Jaffa. 'I know the quiet way in, Major *effendi*, if needed.' He moved his finger along the north wall. 'Here, the north wall finishes, by the rocks and harbour.' He looked at Hazzard and smiled. 'When I was a boy, we go inside, to markets, all times.' He nodded and looked at Smith, smiling suddenly. 'And, how do you say, I speak the *lingua franca*?' He looked about and the assembly chuckled. It was difficult to dislike him.

Hazzard turned to Wayland, then Cook.

'Jory.'

Cook nodded. 'The lads're itchin' to do somethin' sir. An' they'd do it just to get that bastard Derrien, they would.'

Hazzard knew he was right. The idleness of port had thrown them, their nerves still at high pitch. But now that they were safe, he was unwilling to let them come under fire again – he had protected only a handful of those blurred faces he had seen that first day aboard the *Esperanza*, and they were his responsibility, *his*. He looked at the sheet shaking in his hands – he could take no further nightmares.

But he wanted Derrien.

Smith looked down at the chart table. 'I have also reason to believe,' he said quietly, 'that Shajar al-Durr will be in support, somewhere, with the Tarabin and an irregular force of Mamluks, but we have no way of knowing where.' He looked at Hazzard. 'It was she who asked Masoud for your help.'

Shajar.

Lying with her in the temple of blue stars, in the house of Memnon, oil lamps guttering, the cool of the Theban plain washing over her bare back, her skin warm under his hands.

No, not again.

'She is not in this,' Hazzard said. 'Please tell me so.'

Smith shook his head sadly. 'I fear I cannot. She is their leader.'

Hazzard was silent. He looked at Wayland. 'I cannot risk you for this, Mr Wayland. For your own sake—'

Wayland leaned on his cane. 'It's all right sir,' he said. 'We have discussed it.'

Smith explained, 'Mr Wayland has graciously consented to become my personal adjutant while ashore and coordinate with the Sublime Porte in Constantinople, with Colonel Phélippeaux, as I am now an Envoy Plenipotentiary.' He gave his short, quick smile. 'He has an ear, it seems, for Turkish.'

There was a noise behind, and he turned to see the marines in the doorway to the gunroom. They stood easy, Warnock with his tomahawk hanging at his side, Underhill with a curved *khanjar* dagger jammed in the sash tied round his waist, Kite with his sawn-off musket, his arms folded, waiting. Wayland turned to Hazzard, leaning on his cane.

'Sir.'

Hazzard nodded. 'Mr Wayland.' He shook his head. 'I am sorry—'

Wayland stopped him. 'But I am not, sir.' He glanced at his bandaged wrist in the sling. 'These shall be my memories, sir,' he said, looking at them behind, 'For St Crispin's Day. And we happy few. It is what they trained for. How did you put it sir, boats dark, clothes dark? Just as you said.'

Hazzard could think of only one question for them all, the least he could do. He turned to look at them. 'What says the boat?'

Underhill looked them over, one by one, and nodded back.

'Boat says bloody aye, sir.'

Hazzard glanced at the chart once more, the names burning into him.

Derrien.

Bonaparte.

Smith gazed down at the charts. 'I am doubly pleased, gentlemen.' He took in a deep breath, shaking his head. 'I must confess to a… a certain feeling of dread, far away, out there. I cannot explain it… and wish that you might stem that despairing tide.' He nodded to himself, some hopeful decision taken. 'Very well,' he considered, 'one higher, finer purpose then…' He looked straight at Hazzard, as if with the knowledge that he communed with a kindred spirit: 'To be our conscience again, William – and save as many as you can.'

He knew Hazzard too well.

'Sir.'

Shame

The ancient Nile port of Damietta seemed smaller by far than Rosetta or Alexandria, but was the ideal location on the eastern side of the Delta, and the closest to the Sinai. Consisting of a confusion of salt lakes, sea channels and long breakwaters, the main harbour basin heaved with a profusion of Nile barges, *feluccas*, *djerms*, exotic seagoing tartanes and tall-masted chebeks. Overlooked by a medieval stone tower and the ramshackle remnants of lost crusades, the lading quayside used by the French was crowded with dockworkers pulling camels and mules to offload crates and sacks from their long-suffering backs, all into the ships destined to support the expedition into Syria.

The first of the heavy guns arrived from the western breakwater of the basin, the winter swell crashing against the rock, the spray bursting near a squad of artillerymen and a pair of mules hauling a six-thousand-pound Turkish bombard cannon on a cart. They crept slowly past the flotilla's first transports to the largest, at the end, an armed sloop, the major in charge of the cannon, *Chef d'escadron* Baudillon of the 4th Horse Artillery, bringing them to a halt.

He looked up at the ship and the boom being swung outboard, a luff tackle ready, several hands aloft lowering the lines and grapples to them. Putting two fingers in his mouth, Baudillon blew a long, loud whistle and called up, '*Capitaine Standelet! Non, non! We are too large for this tackle!*'

A figure appeared at the rail of the merchantman and looked over. '*Comment?*'

'I say again, the *frame* of the *boom*,' he pointed, 'it may break! I say you need a stronger yard, and reave your blocks to disadvantage!'

'*This is a five-ton lift, Major. We know what we are doing. What is your load?*'

The artillery major looked at his lieutenant who shrugged and muttered, gesticulating up at the man at the rail. It was some three metres in length, but wider than usual, its muzzle big enough to take a 36-pound round. He called up again, '*I cannot be certain! This is a Turkish bombard, and not a Gribeauval. It is greater than a naval gun! Three, perhaps four tons! You must rig for over five tons in case!*'

'*We do not wish for your Turkish bombard. Where are the Grib canons de 24? We expect at least six of them and the 12-inch mortars!*'

Baudillon threw up his hands. '*I am told to bring this monster to you, so I bring it, la merde! Mortars coming this morning!*'

The figure hesitated, disappeared and reappeared. '*Is it not one-hundred-fifty per pound of shot?*'

The major cursed, losing patience. '*Ah mon dieu... No, you cannot apply a Gribeauval formula to a foreign tube! It is your risk! Your boat, your boom!*' Then as an afterthought, '*Have you set your carriage or trucks ready to receive!*'

'*Very well! Un moment!*'

The major threw up his hands. 'Ah! *Putain alors*, the navy, *ma foi*.'

As the artillerymen scrambled around the heavy and ornate Ottoman gun barrel, readying its rope harness for lifting, the flotilla commander *Contre-amiral* Perrée approached with his staff. 'How goes it, *Chef d'escadron*? What is the problem?'

The major turned. 'Admiral, I said this is a madness, truly, I did. I am to haul this old relic from that falling-down tower, and to find what? This Dalmatian tub here, is not a warship and it cannot mount this gun. It is for siege, for the army, and your boat, it has not yet even considered how to stow the cannons. Him up there, he does things backwards, forwards, *à bric et brac, alors*.'

Perrée looked over the ship. They had graded the sloop as a frigate, and Captain Standelet's flagship, but it was more of a large *aviso*, a sleek polacca with a long bowsprit, square-rigged at the mainmast and foremast and a sloping lateen yard on the mizzen. It looked more like a racing yacht, with a web of rigging but very little hull – she was already low in the water. 'Yes, but where are the naval men, *Chef d'escadron*?' Perrée looked about. 'Where are the gunners? They should deal with this.'

'I have none, Admiral, only a bombardier and his section. If I had I would have left your matelots to manhandle this, this fat *putain de merde*, I tell you.' Baudillon shook his head. 'The others come by sea, thank God, in some hours – the *canon de 24*, Admiral, easier for him, naval guns.' He spat a bit of tobacco on the ground. 'Some say they are dredged from Aboukir, the wreck of *Sérieuse* and the others, in the shallows. Who knows...'

Perrée nodded – it was a sore point with them all. He cupped his hands round his mouth and called up. '*Standelet! Are you there? Captain?*'

A trio of figures appeared at the rail above, one calling down and disappearing, bringing the captain. Standelet appeared and raised his cocked hat. '*Admiral! A good day to you!*'

'Will you be ready for the tide?'

As he spoke the boom swung over, reinforced with extra blocks, the tackle rigged for the potentially heavier load, a set of grab hooks descending from overhead. One of the artillerymen jumped onto the back of the cannon to gather the harness rope-sling already dressed round the massive gun, and reached up to guide the hooks into position. They all heard the command. '*Heave!*'

They stepped back, Greek and Arab dockers fending off the cannon with poles as it rose slowly, tipping slightly, gently swinging, then stabilising. Baudillon kept his eye on the boom as Standelet called down, '*Oui, mon amiral! We are near fully laden – I have divided the Gomer mortars and their cartridges, one-fifty each, among the other ships. At least then if only one or two of us get through, we have brought some guns, and sufficient powder, and not lost it all. We await only the canons de 24 now!*'

'Very good, Standelet.' Perrée turned and his lieutenants wheeled with him, back down the quayside to the frigate *Junon*. He mounted the steps and hurried up the quarterdeck, taking an eyeglass from an ensign. He extended the telescope and looked to the south.

The Delta looked back at him, flat with saltmarsh and scrub, then rock and rising desert in the distance. The army column had long marched on the Sinai road, but he had hoped to keep track of it somehow; following the schedule blind was something akin to a hopeful prayer, or arrogant presumption by the *général en chef* that all would go as planned. After the horrors on the Nile at Shubra Khit, Perrée was loath to try that again. He pulled his collar together tightly against the wind. He wondered if any of it would work, given the weather – but the guns would arrive with Standelet, they had vowed that much. 'Cast off and take us out, Riel,' he said to his lieutenant.

'Wind is fair for Alexandria, Admiral.'

'Mm...' Perrée looked out for signs even of Bedouin. But they too had gone, along with everyone else.

Some forty miles southeast of Perrée, and far from the blessings of the sea, the army caravan marched into the Sinai desert. *Sergent-chef-major* Caron watched as a column of some seven thousand filed past in divisional echelon in the bright sun. Other columns, he knew, were marching further south. Rossy, Pigalle and the others were behind him, also watching. 'Half strength,' said Caron. '*Putain.* Two and a half thousand per division. Not just demi-brigades – hm, demi-divisions now.'

On the fringes of the mobile circus there were not just regular camp followers but rather the accoutrements of a hundred homes dragged along by enthusiastic officers: slaves, servants, mistresses and wives, on camels, in carts, with folded tents, beds, carpets and comforts. Caron shook his head. '*Putain.* They go for a pleasure outing.'

The Alphas maintained their positions as *chasseur* scouts, keeping well away from the column, looking out for any unwelcome surprises. 'They say the Turks are many.' Antonnais looked out at the reduced manpower. 'They will devour us.'

Caron nodded. 'They might, Anton. But *voilà*, see,' he said, gesturing with frustration at the column. 'They might let us stay, as tourists.'

'The scholars enjoy themselves,' said Pigalle curiously, as donkeys raced past, young *savants* bouncing on their backs, laughing, parasols in their hands.

Caron knew they would not be laughing soon. 'Come, *mes enfants*, we must catch Reynier before we rest. We must be as the *Bedu*.'

'Which *Bedu*?' asked Pigalle.

'Any *Bedu, mon garçon.*'

'But they are all different they say, and get very angry.'

Rossy spat, then threw back some water from his flask, gargling. 'That is because we are ignorant, *M'sieur* le Pig, and know nothing of such matters.'

'Huh. But I would like to know.'

St Michel sighted down his rifle, stopping when he saw distant dots. 'Turks…?'

Caron joined him and looked, then pulled out his eyeglass. The shapes moved in the distance, heading south. '*Non*. Just the *Arabes*, moving away.'

St Michel mumbled hopefully, 'Cannot be many Turks out there yet… eh, *Chef*?'

Caron looked at him. 'We will find plenty Turks soon, Micheline.' He looked at them. 'Come, let us find the others… and the *général en chef*.'

The four of them mounted their horses and rode at a light canter, overtaking the beds, tents and concubines, Caron wondering how many of those unfortunates would see Cairo again.

–

Bonaparte rode close to the head of the column, off to one side, with Berthier, the Chief of Staff, and General Louis-André Bon, one of his better commanders, a victor of Italy and the Battle of the Pyramids, a quiet, round-faced man, who sat relaxed and confident in the saddle, one hand on his hip, though with a watchful eye, ever scanning the landscape. Slightly behind came the senior *savants*, Citizens Monge and Berthollet.

Monge looked across the harsh, merciless terrain of Sinai, the morning winter sun giving them the heat of a European summer, cloud gathering high above, the wind picking up. Rock was strewn everywhere, the scrub-covered landscape rising to low hills, then disappearing into the distance towards the jagged mountains further south.

Berthollet beside him was less content, a forced excitement about him, when in reality he was nervous, weary, and ageing before Monge's eyes. He was happier in his chemistry laboratory at the Institute – the memories of their first encounters with the Mamluks and Ottoman mercenaries were doubtless still too strong. 'I am glad you came along Claude,' said Monge, to brighten his spirits. 'It would not have been the same without you.'

'Oh Gaspard,' said Berthollet, 'I could hardly let you go alone.' He gave him a wry look. 'People would talk.'

They laughed and Conté rode up just behind Bonaparte and Bon. 'I do insist, *mon général*, I could have built the sledges and carriages for the guns. I could still do so even at this late stage – they require only broad wheels, to spread the pressure. Are you certain this is truly what you wish? To send them by sea?'

'Citizen Conté,' said Bon, 'we must be quick about this. We have not the horses to draw such guns.' He grinned at Bonaparte. 'Murat's cavalry demands them all.'

Bonaparte looked at Conté, the intense stare, the angry mouth. 'I am sure you could, Professor,' said Bonaparte, 'but General Bon is right. The soldiers are already much encumbered. I need their souls to be quick and light.'

There was little comment of this aspiration of Bonaparte's, each among them having their own assessment of the troops' souls, but quick and light did not feature in their conclusions. Conté accepted it gravely. 'At your service, *mon général*.' He looked at Monge with a scowl. 'We will need those guns, Professor Monge, mark my words.' He fell behind again.

'Any reports of Reynier?' asked Bonaparte as a matter of routine.

General Berthier rode closer. 'None to report, *mon général*. He should be at El-'Arish by now.'

Bonaparte cocked an eyebrow. 'I expect it to be occupied upon our arrival.'

On the other side of Bonaparte rode the sombre figure of Jules-Yves Derrien and one of his deputies, Citizen Blais, looking very hot yet stoic in the saddle, not a master of his seat, discomfited by the finer horsemen around. Derrien cleared his throat. 'General, we had advance warning of Turkish troops at El-'Arish. Most probably General Reynier is positioning himself accordingly to seize the fort and town.'

'El-'Arish should not need taking, though, should it.' Bonaparte looked out across the desert, his long hair blowing. He narrowed his eyes. 'They should welcome us, should they not, *effendi*?' he asked of no one directly, though the sheikhs riding behind knew well enough he was asking them specifically. The *Qadi*, the chief magistrate of Cairo, bowed his head, looking to Mustafa Pasha, a Turkish second to the former Pasha of Cairo. Bonaparte had since appointed Mustafa the *Amir al-Hajj*, in place of Murad Bey, and thereby made him one of the leaders of the Mamluk government *diwan*.

Mustafa replied for them, 'Yes, oh yes, *ya Sultan al-Kebir*.'

Bonaparte nodded, apparently pleased his appointments had been so successful. 'Quite so...'

Derrien touched the brim of his hat and dropped back from the group with Blais. For a moment he looked at the group from behind with contempt – they had no idea yet of their true role. He had issued Bonaparte's wishes to the sheikhs and Turkish diplomats, framed as bluntly as an imperial summons, and they had acquiesced. Derrien had a greater faith in the complexity of the scheme than did the generals, who had come merely to trample and conquer. If Bonaparte played his hand correctly, he could smash the Turkish alliance and break England in the Levant, winning Egypt as a French protectorate, once again as friends of the sultan. And Derrien would be the architect of such power, the Turkish and Levantine diplomats, interpreters and representatives of Egypt becoming his puppets, speaking in the heart of the Sublime Porte, to the sultan himself. This was not mere soldiery to Derrien, and he would not be denied.

Blais puffing hard behind, Derrien rode further from the column, and cast about for Caron and his men. 'There, Citizen,' said Blais, pointing.

Between two rising scrub hills Derrien saw movement, the large shape of the man called Pigalle. He would never forget witnessing his giant hands shatter a musket as he bent it double before their eyes that night on Malta. He would tread warily.

'Well done, Citizen,' said Derrien. He squeezed his heels in and the horse trotted onwards, some fifty yards off the column track. Pigalle emerged, with his *Bedu* headdress and ragtag uniform of local cloth and French grey, so clouded with dust he was virtually invisible. Derrien drew to a halt.

'Where is your *sergent-chef*?'

Pigalle looked up at them and tilted his head, as if confused.

'Answer the Citizen,' ordered Blais. He had not seen the breaking of the musket.

Pigalle frowned. 'I am to say: *Moses.*'

Derrien nodded. 'Quite correct. Then I shall say: *burning bush.*'

'Then,' said Pigalle, 'he is behind you.'

Derrien turned, but there was no one, Blais turning his horse as well, looking full circle. Exasperated, Derrien turned back to Pigalle but found the big man had gone, replaced by Caron.

'A neat trick, *Sergent-chef-major.*'

'Yes,' said Caron, 'it works well.'

'I think it is time now. I want to know what happens at El-'Arish before we arrive.'

Caron looked at him, the sun in Derrien's eyes. 'I am not yours, Citizen. You know this.'

'You are under my command, remember,' said Derrien. '*My* command.'

'Temporarily,' reminded Caron. 'But I will do this thing, and scout. It is our task.' He turned to go, then stopped. 'Did you see the *Bedu*?'

Derrien said nothing then looked to the horizon. 'Where? How many?'

'Yes,' said Caron, 'that is my point.'

As one, the Alphas rose from their positions all around them. Derrien saw that he and Blais had been completely surrounded – from the slope of the low hill to the open ground, twenty men had been leaning, lying, squatting, each as covered in sand and brush as Pigalle.

Rossy slung his Charleville over his shoulder. 'It has become too easy, this thing we do, *Chef*.'

'Perhaps,' said Caron, waving them on to follow. '*En avant*. Trouble, she is calling on us, and we must answer.'

Derrien and Blais watched them go in single file and disappear behind the low hills. In a few moments, they had mounted and their horses thudded away into the distance. Within three minutes they had gone, swallowed up by the Sinai.

–

Caron and his platoon caught up with other *chasseurs*, strung out ahead of Bon's column. Command had adapted the *chasseurs à pied* to horses, to keep them fast and mobile. All of them were experienced riders and Caron had no fears for them, part of him hoping they might get camels one fine day.

They had a more direct route to the rendezvous point of Katia and onward to El-'Arish than did General Lannes or Reynier. Kléber, he knew, following Reynier hard, would be the fastest, and he wished he were with them and the old brigade, with the 75th Invincibles. He watched Rossy, St Michel and Pigalle as they rode beside him. They had survived so much for so long, but since their attachment to the *Croquemort* their risk had increased – luck would not last for such men, nor for himself. This course they had undertaken against the Turks was a dark and dreadful thing, and would result only in their ruin – of this he was certain.

Within a day they bypassed Katia, seeing only *Bedu* on camels – traders, no threats as the French rode past, Caron giving the greeting and handing out precious rations, the gift of food in the desert more valued than gold.

'*I shall miss these little charms,*' called Rossy over the wind as they headed off, '*when I am gone.*'

Caron shouted back at him. '*We shall miss it all, mon garçon, when we are gone.*'

The next morning, they reached the rearguard of Kléber's 'demi-division', two and a half thousand men strung out in column. The men of the 4ᵗʰ ran to meet them, spread out across a rough dirt track, which some had confidently called a road, since widened by the tramp of soldiers' boots. When Caron called out, a hand waved and they welcomed the riding *chasseurs* with a shout, *Vive les Alphas! Vive le Premier et Dernier!*

Whistles and catcalls coming from the marching men, Pigalle threw his arms out sideways to them giving a loud *Hwaha!* And they replied, *Vive le Pig! Hwa hwa hwa!*

When they made it to the head of the column, Caron found Kléber and his staff, and their old company commander, Captain Moiret, whom he had not seen for months.

Kléber sat tall in the saddle, his collar turned up to the wind, his wild hair blowing. 'Ah, old *Tartuf*, you are with us at last.' It was an old nickname for Caron, the 'truffle', one he had not heard in years – given after he had once sheltered his wounded officer from a barrage in an Italian forest by digging him into the ground, as if searching for truffles they had said. To many of them Caron was indestructible.

'General,' he said. 'Life in the rear, it is too comfortable. Too many cushions.'

'Of course, of course.' He shouted over his shoulder, '*Moiret! You must not let him carry news again to HQ! See how they keep him fed!*'

There was laughter, and Moiret called back that he would not. Caron nodded to the others, *généraux de brigade*, commanders of the demi-brigades: the 25ᵗʰ, 4ᵗʰ and 75ᵗʰ, sundry colonels. 'Do you stay?' asked Kléber.

'Have you word from General Reynier?'

'Only that we are catching him up.'

'There is news of Turks outside the town,' said Caron. 'Mamluks.'

Kléber swore. They had all hoped the fortress would be an easy start to it all. 'Then go, Achille, and give support. We'll see you as soon as we can.'

Caron nodded. '*Oui, mon général.*' It was good to be with the old ranks again, to be normal once more. But it would be short-lived. 'Until El-'Arish.'

Kléber touched his hat brim. '*Mon brave.*'

Caron saluted and dropped back, then led the Alphas off to the side. 'Come,' he said, 'let us find some Turks.'

They dug their heels in and rode hard, past the column; a hand up from Kléber, Caron looking over his shoulder until they were mere shadows in the distance. They reduced their speed to a canter, the rhythm too much eventually – Antonnais, the slowest, needed rest. But by nightfall they saw campfires through the eyeglass.

Caron shrugged into his cloak. Many of the men had only linen and cotton tunics and light *kaftans* or *binish*, and he wondered how they would manage in the cold. The sky was grey and heavy, and he watched it, knowing rain would come. Just after ten o'clock they reached the fires – but they were not Reynier's.

They tied the horses and fanned out behind a low rise in the scrub, the smeared night sky promising cloudy and rainswept days to come, the sand cold to the touch. Caron looked. He knew at once it was no French encampment. There were no pickets, no guards. There was a large central glow to the camp, and Caron guessed at once who they were.

'Why are there no guards, no sentries?' asked Antonnais. 'It is… odd, hm?'

'It is the way,' said Caron, 'if you do no fighting after sunset. Micheline,' said Caron, turning to St Michel beside him, 'we have found your Turks.'

–

It took an hour to ride round the camp safely without alerting the occupants. They headed to the western approaches of the town's main road. El-'Arish was a small fishing-village of leaning hovels and whitewashed buildings, some in the Mediterranean style roofed in Roman pantile, others in wood and plaster, the few roads dominated by a square stone fortress with hexagonal towers and jagged Saracen castellations. When they reached the outskirts, all they could hear was screaming.

They found remnants of Reynier's division, their path into the town inefficiently blocked by hastily contrived barricades and piles of stone, the deserted roads littered with the dead. Caron moved slowly through the town. It was the aftermath of a massacre. He counted them, men, women, and then he stopped. '*Children…?*'

They heard noises up ahead, some of Reynier's soldiers charging into a house, the muffled blast of musket-flashes bright in the darkness, the moon high. Caron dashed forward to a corner and looked round. A pair of soldiers chased a man and woman through the streets, catching them, bayoneting them as they ran and fell, their guttural cries horrible to Caron's ear. '*Mon dieu… a butcher's yard… where is the general?*'

The soldiers moved off at the double. Caron turned and waved for Rossy and the others to follow. Covering each other as they went, they moved quickly down the main road two by two, Charlevilles ready, Rossy aiming up and down the street as they went. St Michel followed, Pigalle trotting to a door, open, finding bodies in the doorway. He nudged at them then looked back, shaking his head. Caron joined him, putting a hand to each neck. They were still, no pulse. '*Par dieu…*'

A musket flashed and a ball smacked the plaster of the house next to Pigalle. He ducked, seeing a soldier in pale uniform, French, who then charged, bayonet reaching out for him. Without hesitation Rossy dropped the man with a clean shot, and he fell face-down, dead, his musket tumbling, its bayonet digging into the dirt before him.

They moved forward, Rossy stepping over the dead man – far easier to kill than explain. They reached the small central crossroads, a grassy lane leading up to the fortress at the seafront now looming tall over the town, the surf loud in their ears, the stink of the harbour at low tide. Caron saw only the dead – townspeople, no soldiers, no Turks in the dust. They lay crumpled in their doors, caught as they had tried to escape, some of them still writhing in the slow agony of bayonet wounds.

'Is this why we hurried ourselves,' asked Pigalle as he knelt at the side of a boy, no more than ten years of age, a bloody gash in his neck. '*Chef*, I like this not.'

'Nor do I, *enfant*,' said Caron.

'*You there!*'

A platoon moved slowly down the road towards them, some going to one knee, others standing, Charlevilles aimed. '*Qui vive!*'

'*Sergent-chef-major* Caron, of the 75th. And the *Alpha-Oméga.*' He held out his hands, the pistol ready.

Pigalle rose slowly to full height. He did not hold out his hands.

'*You!* Move slowly!'

Pigalle spat. '*Va te foutre.*'

The officer cursed and strode forward. 'You *dare*, you dog!' He then stopped dead. Rossy stepped out of a shadowed doorway and St Michel likewise on the opposite side of the road, each with their Charleville aimed at his head.

'I have a wager with my friend here,' said Rossy, 'that I could blow your head off so clean that it lands at his feet, so that he could kick it. Like a ball.' He smiled nastily. 'He said the same. I should like to see who wins.'

'Lower your arms, at… *at once!* I… I am *Capitaine* Andret of the 22nd *Légère!*'

'And you command this slaughter of innocents?' asked Caron, pointing at the dead boy at Pigalle's feet.

Andret looked about, then stuck out his chin. 'It was orders of the general! Subdue the town, put it to the sword!'

Caron looked at Andret's men. They were in good formation, disciplined. They were not savages – yet they had done this. 'Where is he?'

Andret looked from Rossy to St Michel. 'At the camp by the castle. We have isolated them, maybe a thousand Berbers and Mamluks, I tell you. It is now a siege.'

'Take us.'

But Andret did not move. '*You,*' he ordered, pointing at Pigalle, 'put up your arms.'

Pigalle looked at the Charleville in his hands. 'This?'

'*Yes, damn you!*'

Caron said nothing, but watched. One of Andret's soldiers, still some thirty feet off, unwisely moved forward, threatening with his bayonet. Pigalle frowned, thinking, then turned his Charleville round, holding it like a club, and with an explosive grunt flung it spinning into the man with all his strength. The whirling musket dropped him with a retch and a loud thud, his head at an impossible angle, his bloody eyes staring.

Caron stepped forward, his pistol out. 'Now take us, or stand accused, by command of the *général en chef*. We are the *Alpha-Oméga*, and you,' he said, 'are nothing.'

Rossy leaned over to Andret's ear. 'Well,' he whispered, glancing at Pigalle, 'you did ask.'

When they reached the tent lines they could smell cooking fires, and Caron detected the familiar aroma of grilling horseflesh. They moved through the camp, the men gathered round the cooking pots, one man frying steaks of horsemeat in fat on a skillet. *Putain*, thought Caron, *they are eating the horses already*.

They were passed through to the 1st Battalion of the 22nd and Andret stormed off, his men following. Caron watched him go, knowing he had started a blood feud, but cared little. They found Reynier conferring with his officers, stick in hand, squatting over a map he had sketched in the dirt. Caron liked Reynier – he had *grandeur* and *sangfroid*, and, so Caron had thought, was a true *chevalier*. He could not surely have ordered the massacre of the town. They came to a halt just outside the circle of officers and listened.

'...if they hear a sound, we are lost. Encircle, and move quietly once the centre has gone in and you see movement up the side of the camp. Understood? We move in thirty minutes with the 9th and 85th. Go, eat, be quick.' He looked up at the arrival of Caron and the Alphas.

'*Mon général*,' said Caron.

Reynier put out his hand. 'Achille before the walls of Troy. My honour. I feel like Odysseus himself.'

Caron took his hand, but with hesitation. 'We entered the town, *mon général*. That dog Andret tried to take us under guard. We killed two of his men, for bayonetting children.'

Still holding Caron's hand, Reynier's smile froze and he let go, his head sinking, and he nodded. 'Yes... yes, *Chef*. There was no other way. I... we cannot *keep* them, you see...' He kept nodding, as if to convince himself. 'Yes, yes, the men... they went too far...' His head came up. 'But we are safe now, hm? And ready to continue.'

Wary, Caron watched him, flicking a glance at the diagram in the sand. 'What is this now, *mon général*?'

'The encampment. We go now,' he said, turning. 'Will you come? I need your luck, Achille.'

Caron followed. 'A Turkish camp? We saw it.' They reached his tent, a soldier bringing out Reynier's sword and clipping it on the hanger at his waist. 'It is quiet there.'

Reynier went still for a moment, his face like stone as he stared at the ground. When he looked up, he smiled brightly once again, his old self. 'Yes, that is right.' He pointed at the fires. 'Take some meat, a hot mouth, eh, then off we go.'

'Horse,' said Caron.

Reynier maintained his fixed smile, perhaps used to it by now, his hands shaking as he tightened his belt to accept the weight of the sword. 'Mm, yes. And... some camel. It is... it is good, so they tell me.'

Caron gestured to the Alphas to follow. They reached a point outside the town, the surf the only sound at the small port, and the now-muffled noise from the camp. Before them were ranged four reduced battalions of troops – barely a thousand men, crouching, sitting on the ground, waiting in silence.

Reynier led them down a slope, the scuff of their boots in the sand and rock their only accompaniment, the glow of the Turkish camp ahead. All was quiet. Rossy whispered, '*Chef, is it a trap?*'

Caron looked down sadly. '*Non, mon garçon*, no trap. The Muslim, he rarely gives battle between sunset and sunrise...' He let out a slow breath. 'They have never met the ungodly before – for such we are.'

The small brigade split into groups and spread out around the sleeping camp, one moving to the left into the darkness, another to the right. They could hear the distant bleating and braying complaints of goats, mules and horses on the far side of the camp – they had not thought to leave even the animals on guard.

Reynier halted the main force at a rough gate of beaten posts, before a well-tramped lane of hard dirt and scrub, the firelight flickering across the elaborate Ottoman tents. The dwellings in the centre were broad and square-topped, others mere bell-tents arranged in circles around their lords, still others in lines or different styles, Albanian, Turkish and Mamluk. They could hear the crackle of the flames in the dying fires. As one the French crouched, waiting. Caron moved up beside Reynier.

'How many in the camp, *mon général*?'

'Two thousand,' said Reynier, glancing at a chased gold watch in his hand. He looked at him. 'They would do the same,' he said to Caron, 'to us. They would.'

Caron did not understand this strange ambivalence of Reynier's, hopeful yet equally so full of despair. '*Général*, what do—'

But before Caron could enquire further the group rose again, and Reynier headed off, drawing his sword. Caron looked at the storming battalion soldiers as they passed – none had loaded. Instead, they had fixed their bayonets.

Reynier entered the main gate, a block of troops behind him. Caron hung back as the first company split and moved into the first tents, and he heard strange sounds, a scuffling movement – then the men emerged, moving on to the next.

Rossy stopped beside Caron. '*Chef*... are they...'

Caron watched the storm troops, a hand out to stop the Alphas. 'Wait here for me. We will not do this thing.'

'No,' said Pigalle, his big hands shifting along the stock of his Charleville. 'I like this not...'

Reynier ducked into the entrance of the large central tent and Caron hurried after him. He found rows of bedrolls and sleeping men, the mingling smells of food, of incense and oils. The French soldiers moved in. The first raised his musket and bayonet, aiming it carefully, then thrust it downwards, pushing his bayonet through the chest of the first sleeping man. There was a rush of air as the man gasped, his eyes flashing open, the French trooper clapping a hand over his mouth to stop him struggling, the eyes rolling inward. Satisfied, the soldier yanked out the bayonet, and moved on.

The others moved along the beds, each standing above their chosen victim, thrusting down and through the breastbone, throat or ribs, through the side, through a man's eye, killing them silently. Within minutes, the tent was filled with the dead or dying.

'*Général*,' hissed Caron to Reynier, '*Mon dieu*...'

Reynier ignored him and pushed on, out the other side of the long tent and to the next, Caron hearing the muffled cries of some from other tents on the edge of the camp, the sound of boots in the dust, sounds he had feared in fitful nights for decades as a soldier in action, *to be murdered in your sleep*, the scenes before him a nightmare come true. Caron caught Reynier up by the guy-ropes of the next tent, '*Général, there is no honour in this*—'

Reynier swung round, his sword red in his hand, his whispers harsh in the eerie silence, his voice trembling. 'We are but *thirteen thousand*, Achille. They have a *hundred thousand* waiting for us.' He looked about, torn, his eyes staring, almost mad, hearing the strangled cries about him. 'Shall I not... *delay* our inevitable slaughter...?'

Captain Andret, who had already helped butcher the inhabitants of the town, had no such qualms, and burst round the corner of the tent, dark smears on his throat and face, Turkish blood black in the murderous night, his eyes flaring, his teeth bared in a rictus of pleasure and excitement. '*Général!* We are nearing the centre of the camp! It is a success! It... it is *glorious!*' He saw Caron and stopped. 'You shall have *none* of the glory.'

Caron had a pistol ready. Andret was in no fit mind and could turn on him easily, as if he were a Turk himself. 'These sleeping men deserve better, *Capitaine.*'

Andret seized him by the tunic, his bloodied spittle flying. 'Then let them *deserve* the honour of standing in battle, for they *sleep* when they should be *standing-to.*' He turned to tug at Reynier's sleeve, a demon beckoning him to further evils. '*Général, please, je vous en prie...*'

'You are a mad dog, Andret,' spat Caron. 'In my village we would despatch you with a bullet.'

'*You dare...*'

'I could no more bayonet a sleeping man than I could a child,' Caron said, 'for both are innocent in the eyes of God.'

Reynier pulled away. 'I must save us, *Chef*, somehow—'

'*Like this?*' Caron watched the soldiers moving through the tent-lines, a scene from the darkest days of Herod or Tiberius. '*Non, mon général.* You have lost me. And my men.'

Andret ran off, and Reynier blinked, breathing hard, his eyes flicking round, searching for penitence, but not finding it. A final quick look to Caron, a whisper, a plea, '*Then pray for my soul, good Achille.*'

Caron watched him hurry off among the stifled screams. The camp was alive with running French troops, yet no Turks yet stirred. He looked at his pistol. He could fire a shot in the air. He could give warning. But something stopped him, the equivalent horror of betraying his countrymen, no matter how bereft of humanity. If Reynier's men were to be damned, he decided, let them be damned by their own hand.

He turned and strode through the tent of dying men, one rolling to the floor, clutching his abdomen, a trooper of the 85th stabbing downward again with the bayonet, then again, *putain alors, will you not die!* Caron smashed his fist into the trooper's face and knocked him down flat. 'Enough! *Salaud de merde...*'

He found the Alphas still at the entrance to the camp in a defensive semi-circle, waiting, looking out, muskets ready. '*Chef,*' said Rossy.

Caron marched towards him, only another twenty paces, but St Michel pointed over Caron's shoulder, and brought his rifle to the aim.

Caron stopped. A dog barked, and St Michel fired.

A bare-chested Mamluk with sword in hand fell, not two strides from Caron's back, the first to die bearing arms in the damned camp of the sultan.

The camp exploded into pandemonium. Men roused from their beds burst out of the tents in their underclothes, robes, some naked but for a musket or sword. '*Fransisja! Fransizlar burada!*'

The French are here.

Rossy gave a whistle. '*Time to go!*'

As the camp flew into uproar the French troops charged into the awakening Ottomans, as they poured into the lanes to escape and arm themselves – dark-skinned Turks, pale Albanians, Georgian Mamluks, all running into deadly bayonet ranks, French Charleville muskets booming in volley-fire, flashing bright in the darkness.

Caron and the Alphas moved to the track leading to El-'Arish. They turned and looked back, the fires and muzzle-flashes lighting their faces, each lost to their own thoughts, the crazed shadows and silhouettes flickering as the victims fled in confusion, crying out. A dozen half-dressed bearded men, trapped by a platoon of French grenadiers, their 17-inch bayonets shoved brutally into bare midriffs, the Turks doubling over in agony, falling to the ground. Rossy broke the silence.

'Are these then men of honour, *Chef*...?'

A fire broke out and Reynier appeared before the campfires, calling a charge to the stores, his sword high, and the French cheered, following him, trampling over the bodies of the dead and dying.

Caron watched. 'I wish they were, *mon garçon.*'

Canaan

Hazzard watched the dark swell of the Levantine Sea under the glimmering indigo of the midnight sky. Swathed in a *shemagh* of warm soft black cotton, a black *iqal* circlet round his head, and a long sleeveless black *binish* over his Bombay scarlet, he sat at the prow of the pitch-painted launch, invisible but for the spray flying from her dark bows. He glanced at the marines behind, likewise with black over their red coats; not a glint of metal shone anywhere among them, their shadowed faces looking out to sea, their eyes traversing the waves, intent, thinking only of finding a flotilla of ships among the quiet of the stars.

It had taken them several days to gather what they needed: clothing, boats, ammunition – and keep it quiet. Captain Reiz requisitioned all he could from the stores aboard the *Medina*, a sleek Ottoman battleship of 78 guns that had brought him from Constantinople. Reiz had been trained in artillery, and found Hazzard a stock of powder, scrap and quickmatch, making snap-fuses and all he needed to construct the old 9 Company calling-card: the bag o'tricks, the fused woollen roll of wadding around a grenade of loose scrap-iron langrage and fine black powder, lime and magnesium – but now with deadly naphtha added, courtesy of the Ottomans. There were enough for three for each man. They had then painted the brightwork of their blades and sawn-off muskets black with pitch. It was just as Wayland had hoped for: *boats dark, clothes dark, weapons black.*

It had taken a further twelve days aboard the *Tigre* to return to Egyptian waters, Hazzard fuming, impatient – once prepared, he wanted to execute the plan. But when they scouted Damietta they found no artillery flotilla. From the quarterdeck he and Smith had scanned the broad port for signs, but saw nothing, the marines leaning through the shrouds, staring out into the dark.

'So,' said Smith, taking the eyeglass away. 'Gone.'

'Not quite, sir,' said Wayland beside him, 'we know where they're going.'

'Yes,' said Reiz, 'but which course do they take?'

Hazzard had continued to watch the coast. There were few options: the flotilla would either head for Jaffa or Acre. But, Hazzard knew, they could not arrive either too early or too late. The only solution for the captain would be to head for the first port on the chart, Jaffa. If the port were taken successfully, they could then put in and wait for orders.

'If they headed direct to Acre,' said Smith, 'they could be anywhere. Nelson missed a fleet of four hundred by a thousand yards…'

'If we do not find them at Jaffa,' said Hazzard, 'we'll continue with the shore operation, and hope you or others can intercept them at Acre.'

Smith closed his scope with a click. 'Then let us be about it.' He looked out for Wright. 'Take us back out, Mr Wright, to the drop point.'

'Aye, sir.' Wright turned away to Clark, the bo'sun. 'Make your helm east-nor'east, Bo'sun, as plotted.'

'East-nor'east it is sir then, aye.'

Wright was about to move off, but hesitated. 'And, Clarkie… keep a weather eye, so we're ready to fly, if need be.'

Smith had made ready their single-masted 24-foot launch, rigged with a dark blue gaff sail hung from a topyard which could be dropped for quick dousing. The boat swung from its tackle at the portside steps, waiting to be lowered, virtually invisible, no lamps lit, the *Tigre* running dark. Stowed centrally in the boat were their packs, each loaded with ammunition, Reiz's grenades, food and water ration. The hands lowered away, and the black launch sank out of sight.

The marines began to climb down. Hazzard had reluctantly accepted Sgt Dickory and a section of his own marines from the *Tigre*, the men who had foiled Naismith in what had become known as the Secret Mutiny. He watched them embark, *Rhys, Jacobs, Willis*, just as quiet and careful as his own men had been, *Grant, Church, Gowey, Lawler, Kehoe*. He watched and noted their faces – he would remember them.

'Can you keep up?' Hazzard asked bluntly.

Dickory smiled. 'I bet Jeremiah Underhill a month's wages on it, sir.'

Underhill moved in behind and confirmed it. 'Docky's a steady hand, sir. Just you wait an' see.'

Hazzard nodded. 'I know he is, we owe him a debt.'

Cook climbed down and Reiz went next. He stopped at the rail, and turned to shake Sir Sidney's hand. Smith said in Turkish, '*Allah'a emanet olun.*' *May God be with you.*

Reiz bowed his head to the valediction. 'Today, I stand with English gentlemen. I shall never make a boast more proud.'

Wayland had stood at the rail as they all followed Reiz, climbing aboard, nodding as they went, each with their own thoughts, seeing him left behind: regret, sympathy, comradeship, guilt – for the relief that they were not as he. Hazzard stopped before him. 'Mr Wayland.'

'Sir.' His hardened features betrayed no sign of envy or loss, but determination. 'I will get you out. That much I can promise, if I can promise anything, or the heavens come down upon me.'

'I know it.' Hazzard looked him over, strangely proud, still protective. He gave the Egyptian farewell, so familiar to them now, '*Rabbena ma'ak.*' *God protect you.*

'*Rabbena ma'ak*, sir.'

As he moved down the steps to the rolling black water Hazzard watched Wayland, realising how much he had come to rely on the fellowship of the young man slowly rising into the night before him as he descended into the darkness – a young man now no more than a silhouette at the portside rail. Cook looked up with him.

'We'll make it count sir.'

They shoved off, erected the mast and the dark canvas billowed above them. When Hazzard watched HMS *Tigre* disappear into the night, he could feel the men's intent, their silence, their concentration. They were now focussed, seeking a target. That had been some hours ago.

They headed eastward, the horizon nothing but a black swell, the faint reflection of the moon behind the winter clouds above, the only mark of their passage the glowing froth at their bows and the silver of their wake. No man said a word.

Tariq took a deep breath. Even as a *Bedu*, Tariq had made a surprisingly good sailor, his attention to the weather greater than many seamen Hazzard had known.

Hazzard whispered, 'What is it?'

The little *Bedu* nodded. 'The *Khamsin* and *Sharav*,' he whispered, 'they fight the Invader.'

Hazzard felt it too, the weak warm air of the desert blowing first from the southwest, then into their faces from the southeast, and a cooler wind from behind, blowing from Cyprus and Greece in the north: the Invader.

Hazzard and Handley sighted along the line of Cygnus and Lyra, heading for Jaffa, using the small candlelit compass binnacle in the launch, noting their speed every half-hour. HMS *Tigre* had dropped them deep in the Levantine Sea, and by two o'clock in the morning Handley calculated they were less than one hour from the western coast of Palestine. But they saw nothing.

If all else failed they would head due east and hit land, then make contact with local Mamluk forces – but the French could well have occupied the coast, and they did not know how far. Jaffa remained their only hope.

Hazzard stared out, his eyes catching tricks of refraction, the sea an undulating mirror of the sky – until Reiz heard it: he moved closer to Hazzard and whispered, '*Singing...?*'

Hazzard listened.

Tariq leaned forward. '*Music...*'

Hazzard extended his telescope. It had been hooded with an extra leather tube of some six inches – no reflection could bounce from its lens. It gave a reduced field of vision, but enough for their purposes. He swung slowly left, then slowly right. Only the black swell and glowing wave-tops moved before his eyes. He stopped.

'*Contact*,' he whispered. '*Dead quiet in the boat.*'

The marines tensed behind him, none knowing whether he had sighted friend or foe. He stared through the lens. '*Ship ahead*,' he said. '*Reiz.*'

Four barges, no masts, cabled together and towed by a sailing chebek. They were about a thousand yards away, the lights bobbing, dancing like spray on the swell. He handed the eyeglass to Reiz. The young captain looked, focussed, and looked again. The music drifted towards them, then drifted away.

'They feast,' explained Reiz, looking at Tariq. 'Hm?'

The little man nodded to Hazzard. '*Ramadan, effendi.*'

Hazzard suddenly understood. It was not the flotilla – they were Egyptian. No food from sunrise to sunset, many eating and dining into the small hours. Hazzard watched the barges and felt a strange return to their old world.

'Traders, El-'Arish?' asked Reiz. 'Or...'

Hazzard stared through the eyepiece. 'We're too far offshore... Helm, come to larboard... slip in behind them, Handley.'

'*Larboard aye...*'

The launch heeled slightly to port, and they fixed on their new target, the unwitting shepherds in the dark. Hazzard prayed for them all, and that their shepherds would lead them to haven – in Jaffa.

–

Deserted of its small Ottoman garrison, the Christian community of Gaza had opened its gates to Bonaparte – over the following four days the town was summarily looted. But after the foul weather of the march from El-'Arish, Citizen Derrien left it to the army to sort out their own problems – he had his own: his special Turkish envoys, including the newly appointed *Amir al-Hajj* and *Qadi* of Cairo had slipped away once they had crossed the Syrian border, and were nowhere to be found. That they could question who was true lord of Egypt made Derrien burn for vengeance, and he vowed one day they would feel it.

After the siege of El-'Arish, which had taken another week after Reynier's night attack on the Turkish camp, the army had lost nearly four hundred men taking the fort – partly from their own artillery. *Fools*, Derrien had thought: he had watched them site the guns in a circle around the fortress, a circle so complete that the first rounds had sailed over the castle battlements and crashed onto their own positions on the opposite side. As an ex-artillery officer, Derrien had been ordered by General Dommartin to reissue the range and elevation orders, and had done so: '*Tell that bloated idiot of a colonel to cease fire at once!*'

When Bonaparte heard of his interference, he kept Derrien even closer. 'The army does not understand,' Bonaparte had confided that night to him, Bourrienne and Monge looking on. 'Artillery is *science*, and they can barely tie their bootlaces...' He sat slumped in a folding chair at a collapsible campaign table, the wet winter wind shivering the canvas around him, the flame in the hanging lantern flickering in its glass. He was tired, shaking his head. 'They eat their own horses, then complain of no transport.'

'But surely, they had no food,' protested Bourrienne in their defence.

'*Then they should have achieved victory sooner!*' snapped Bonaparte, his hollow eyes flaring wide.

The desert had punished them further, with rain, mud and plummeting temperatures. Derrien heard them mutter and complain – they had forgotten the Revolution, the charge at Toulon, the *Vendée*, and the 13th *Vendémiaire*, all of it. The generals themselves, he thought, had forgotten the trials and suffering that had won them freedom: Bon, Dommartin, Lannes, the now subdued Reynier and the arrogant Kléber. He hated them for it. And their men straggled behind, sick and lame, stripping the dead horses and camels of their packs, and hauling the carcasses off the trail for the commissary to butcher.

Their objective after Gaza lay inland, a convenient resting-place called Er Ramieh, according to an ageing French map, though Derrien heard the locals refer to it as Ramla, a small town known for a monastic hospice. As he rode to the head of the column, he looked off to the east, at the rising mountain heights, knowing that beyond lay Bethlehem and Jerusalem, and a nightmare of twisting passes ideal for ambush. *God's house indeed*, he thought, and spurred his horse, angry with the sham of it all.

As the sun emerged briefly, to warm them with sullen reluctance, he pulled to a halt beside the vanguard commander at the entry to Ramla – a slovenly, brandy-fuelled oaf in Derrien's opinion, his spreading posterior resplendent on the thick carpet of his Arabic saddle. He slumped forward, leaning on the high pommel before him, his battered cocked hat drunkenly crooked, his bushy tobacco-stained grey moustaches drooping as badly as he. Spoiling for a fight after the rainswept and mud-caked march through flooded scrub and cloying riverbeds, he seemed disappointed with their luck – the local Muslim population had fled, leaving the Christian inhabitants to welcome the new arrivals.

'I still do not trust this,' the major had muttered, then leaned out away from his horse's neck and spat, wiping the brown spittle from his chin.

'Trust it or not,' said Derrien, 'you will secure the monastery, Citizen *Chef de bataillon*.' Derrien looked at him with revulsion – he was a fat man, he had decided, with fat appetites. 'Any monastic wines to come to Staff *Quartier général* at once. There will be no looting.'

This caught his attention, the major glancing at him then away with resignation, his plans for finding a good drink nipped in the bud. He gave a snort. 'Huh, monks. Armenian, Shia, Druzes... *Christians?* In *this* place?' He shook his head, perhaps thinking Christ had been born on the altar of Nôtre Dame de Paris, and shrugged. 'The women, they run to the monastery... they are white-skinned, you know, not veiled – *oui, pas mal,*' he said, waggling his hand back and forth as he weighed their beauty. 'Not bad, but only some are worth bedding... *Putain!* Some of the monks are prettier, ha!'

Derrien rode forward, slightly upwind of his fetid odour, and turned his mount. 'We are not here to loot or violate pretty monks, Citizen,' warned Derrien, his lip curled with disgust. 'And with evidence of either, be it from the rank and file or officers, I shall gladly assemble a firing squad.'

The major scowled. 'You are very sure of yourself, Citizen.'

Derrien looked back at him until the major blanched and nodded.

'Very well,' the major harrumphed, gathering his rein. 'Then tell the *général en chef* that, like Gaza,' he declared, 'this too shall become a place of peace.'

—

For Delphine Lascelles it did become a place of peace. Once the town was occupied, she and the last nursing staff followed a group of Franciscan friars through the narrow lanes to the monastery in the heart of the town, a broad stone building with fine masonry arches and buttresses, a Christian bell tower rising above, not unlike a Muslim minaret. The sun shone at last, not as sharp as in Egypt, and Delphine hung back from the other assistants, closing her eyes to feel its warmth.

The Franciscan Monastery of St Nicodemus and Joseph of Arimathea had the same quietude as the small Cluniac convent outside Paris where Delphine had been educated, before the Revolution. When she entered the cool, polished stone interior, she allowed herself to breathe, slowly and deeply, for the first time in a long while, her senses resting in its familiarity. But, within moments, she heard Desgenettes' voice up ahead, and the serenity was gone – she had work to do.

She moved through a tall archway, the light pouring in all around, rough stone block walls, gleaming polished stone floors, a bright niche with a statue of the Virgin and, above, vast whitewashed vaulted ceilings casting curved shadows across the scenes below. The central hall opened out before her, and there in the middle of it all stood the Chief Surgeon.

'Delphine—' He corrected his delight with a self-conscious smile, and a slight bow, and moved towards her, an arm out to bring her in. '*Madame* Lascelles, how fortunate. The good Father Abbot here was just explaining to me where we may lay cots, palliasses, and stretchers for the patients.'

Delphine looked about. Still there were crowds of nervous women clustered together with the friars who were trying to calm them. The hall seemed to be their refectory, monks and doctors' orderlies moving large tables, and she knew at once Desgenettes would want these for surgery. The monks' cells would be ideal for cots, and possibly two or three patients each, as isolation units, she thought, just as the monks had lived. 'But where will the brothers, excuse me, the friars go? Where will you go, *mon Père?*'

The Father was Greek, an older man of more than sixty in a rough grey and brown habit, bald but with a short silver beard. He bowed to her, his lined face crinkling further, and replied in good French, 'You are very kind to think of us, *madame*. I am *Père* Michel. But have no fear, we gladly relinquish our place for the sick and infirm.' He smiled. 'It is why we are here.'

She took in his kindness like a balm. After the Cairo revolt, the affair of Laval and the plague – not to mention the deaths and wounds at El-'Arish and the march – she needed *somewhere*, she thought, somewhere to rest herself. Desgenettes watched her. 'The abbot, *pardon*, *Père* Michel, has been magnificent, and dealt with the army with considerable courage.'

Father Michel watched Delphine as well, his smile warming her. 'Please, *madame*, allow me to show you where your patients or nurses may reside…'

In his touch she felt his care, care from a world that had laid siege to the core of her beliefs: in God, in Man, in herself – and she followed in silence, Desgenettes watching with concern. When they had passed into the first of the corridors, she stopped and found herself weeping, Father Michel before her, her shoulders shaking and her breath coming in short, shuddering gasps.

'You have suffered much,' said the abbot quietly. 'Your care for others is tested, yet still you do care, for all.' Without the slightest movement, he wreathed her in the rays of the sun. 'And you are very strong.'

She caught her breath. Was it fear, fatigue, *what was it?* She could not tell.

'Come,' he said, leading her down the corridor to the cells. They passed narrow windows set in deep stone sills, revealing glimpses of the blue of the sky, and the bright stone of the town about them, and she calmed. 'Thank you,' she said.

He looked at her, spreading his hands, and said kindly, 'But I have done nothing, my child.'

She found Desgenettes later, in the refectory, his staff moving briskly about, folding screens erected, crates of stores open, the friars helping. The cots were already filled with the sick and wounded, the last of the invalid column still not yet arrived. Delphine took a breath and pulled back her sleeves and joined them. The new hospital, within the hour, was full.

The soldiers seemed cowed by their surroundings as they ate, sitting in groups by the sunlit walls, looking about as if they sensed the spirits about them, holy or otherwise, according to conscience. Without many exceptions, the battalions could be found on their knees, humble, receiving the healing benedictions of the Franciscan friars, most hoping their repentance could be stored up in heaven for the horrors they might soon enact. And the truly fearful among them could detect the tremors of a vengeful God, an Old Testament God in this land of Moses, rumbling in the desert beneath them.

–

Two days later, Caron and Rossy dashed across a babbling irrigation stream in a dense fruit plantation. Everywhere there were olive groves and the scent of orange and lemon blossom drifting all about them: spring had come, and March had dawned brighter than the weeks before.

They had gone far ahead of the column to scout for Kléber and the 75th. Their specialist Egyptian guide unit had spread out far to the southeast, scouting for General Lannes, but Pigalle, St Michel and the others were not far off in the undergrowth with Captain Moiret and the rest of the Alphas. Caron had felt the touch of the friars at Ramla, and he had fears for what was to come – unlike anything he had yet endured in the field, he felt a primeval fear.

He whispered through the trees to Pigalle, '*Quick, mon garçon, then back.*' He called to Moiret, '*Capi, we are clear.*'

Captain Moiret gave Pigalle the nod, and the big man pushed his way through a tangle of branches – but he soon stopped at the edge of the trees. After barely five minutes he came back, and leaned out of the wood, Moiret behind.

'*Chef,*' said Pigalle, 'it is big.'

Caron and Rossy moved through the trees, hands on the low gnarled boughs overhead, then went down in the grass, finally pushing through a screen of old olive and milkwood grown into a rambling hedge. The scene suddenly revealed itself. Caron stared.

'*Mon dieu.*'

Before them, just across a number of beachside gullies slick with water draining into the harbour basin, rose fortified Jaffa. Crenellated stone walls flanked by square towers encircled the town, mounting a crowded hill nearly a hundred and fifty feet above the sea. Stark shadows slanted across the multi-coloured reefs of Andromeda's rocks, where legend claimed she had been chained to await the Kraken, the morning tide washing in, the spray crashing. Markets spread from the quaysides up the twisting lanes to the city walls, the people thronging the narrow streets, a host of small craft bringing fish, fabrics, salts and spices. Seabirds swooped over the rooftops, crying at every jetty and landing-stage, floating past the brightening stone walls warming to the sun. This was the city of the Canaanites, conquered by David and Solomon, Thutmose and Alexander, ancient of place, ancient of name – the sons of Abraham and soldiers of Joshua hearing Caron's every breath and his every thought: it was, to Caron, as indomitable as God Himself.

He sank back and lowered his head. Rossy looked over at him. '*Chef?*' He crawled to Caron through the brush, twigs snapping, dead leaves rustling. '*Chef? Ça va?* What has happened? You hit?'

Caron simply sagged forward, his head down. Rossy shook him, an incredulous half-smile on his grimy unshaven face. 'Eh, *tiens, Chef,* you are making me afraid, you know? We never pray unless… well, you know…'

Slowly, Caron rolled onto his back, blinking, gasping, 'It is too much… too much, *mes enfants.*'

'Too much, too much? *Putain alors,* eh, nothing is too much for us, *hein*…?' Rossy tugged open Caron's collar, pulling the grey tunic wide, the white cotton of his shirt open, his hand reaching for his water-bottle. 'Ah, you need the wine, I know, *Chef*, but we have none here,' he said, putting the bottle to his lips. '*Chef*, some water...'

Caron drank, then pulled his face away, closing his eyes, his breath coming with a wheeze. '*Mon enfant...*' he began, but said nothing more for a while. 'I am... too tired, now, of all this... too old, to bring down this fortress of God's place... for *nothing...*'

Pigalle joined them, the others coming over. 'What is wrong?' asked the big man.

'He is tired, that is all,' said Rossy hopefully, 'Eh, *Chef*? Eh, *papi*?' He laughed. 'Remember how you said never to call you that?'

Moiret appeared behind and crouched beside them. 'Achille, *Achille*. Is it thirst? Salt?' He delved into his own pack looking for something, anything. 'We did not come all this damn way,' he said, 'from pissing in Toulon harbour, to storming the gates of Cairo...' He pulled out a packet of salt tablets, made by the *apothécairers*, 'for you to fall down half-dead in a stinking Rif harbour town...' His hands were shaking as he opened the packet.

Caron waved him away, looking up at the sky. '*Capitaine...* this land... this is His place. See how we besmirch it... as we have done to everything... everywhere.' He closed his eyes and took a deep breath.

Rossy sat back, baffled. 'We are the soldiers, *Chef*, it is what we do – you tell me so. Now, *come*.' Rossy hauled him upright, Moiret taking the other side.

Half-upright, Caron looked about himself, as if only just realising he was there. For the first time, he felt his years. He stared. 'It will be a siege, *Capitaine*. Am I the devil's son, that all I see is how to destroy...'

'We are all, *Chef*,' said Moiret. 'For that is what we do, says Rossy, hm, and we let others build after.'

'Tell the general... the *sapeurs* can force a breach,' Caron said quietly, in a haze. 'The wall, it was here before ever man had cannon. The mortar... it is old, worn by the southern sun...'

'Good. Yes, you will tell him,' said Rossy, trying to pull his uniform coat together. 'We like the siege, hm? We sit, we talk, we play cards, and eat and laugh while they quietly starve, hm? All good for us, the brave soldiers staying alive, eh, for that is what we do.'

Caron tried a brave smile. 'I know, *mon garçon*, I know.' He looked to Moiret. 'We shall not leave this place, *Capi*. Part of our soul will lie here, buried, forever.'

Moiret watched his face, his lined, haggard face. 'Then let us haunt it all together, my old friend.'

They were silent a moment. St Michel joined them. '*Capi*, a runner from the *Quartier*. He says the *général en chef* is in the tent in the lemon trees, between the two divisions.'

Caron took a breath and exhaled slowly. '*Très bien.*' He was ready. 'Get this old soldier to General Lannes. He must be told...'

Moiret looked up. 'If you please, *M'sieur* le Pig,' he said, and the giant leaned over, offering his massive arm to his old sergeant and Caron grasped it. Pigalle lifted him in one breath.

'So,' said Caron, doing up his tunic, 'this is Jericho.' He adjusted his belt and looked at Moiret. 'And once more we are the trumpet... Let us find the music-master.' They strode off into the orange trees in search of General Lannes.

—

Not far off, Derrien rode through the citrus groves with Berthier and Lannes, Bonaparte a short distance ahead, personally reconnoitring the southeastern curtain wall. 'Old Caron was right,' said Bonaparte, looking up at the stonework. 'This was built long before the days of artillery. These walls have never tasted modern iron and powder.'

Derrien looked up. By one of the square towers he could see men running along the battlements, pointing, shouting down, the city rooves rising behind in sandy pink, the citadel towering over them all.

'Night attack,' said Berthier, looking at the ground before them. It was rocky yet more or less level to the walls – there was no moat or ditch to protect the town. 'Storming ladders onto the rooftops, and we go in.' He looked back at the fruit trees behind. It was open ground for a short distance, but the groves had grown so thick and close, the defenders would not be able to see beyond them.

'No. We need a *breach*,' insisted Lannes, and Bonaparte listened – he always did, to Lannes. 'Made by the guns, Berthi. Or my men exhaust themselves climbing and have nothing left for the Turk inside.'

'Huh. So speaks the Roland of the Holy Land,' Berthier shook his head. 'We have not the guns nor the time, *mon seigneur* Rolo. And a breach murders men by the score...'

Lannes sighed. He was a vigorous man in his thirties, used to getting things done properly. 'The 12-pounders could breach if they are sited at the right point – combined fire should tear these down in an hour or so.'

Derrien could just see the 12-pounder field-guns behind, through the trees, the artillerymen waiting for their dispersal instructions. Bonaparte went on ahead, and Berthier chirruped to his horse. 'Come, he rides on...'

When Derrien looked round, the others had moved off, and he saw Bonaparte far ahead of the group of generals. A movement on the top of the wall caught Derrien's eye and he saw Turkish soldiers on the rooftops, crouching, some rushing to lie down, muskets in hand. He could do nothing but shout. '*Non! Protect the general! Get him back!*'

He spurred his horse through the group, past Berthier, past Lannes, and the coterie of aides including Eugène, Bonaparte's stepson, who also took up the cry, '*Protect the general!*' But they were too late.

The shots began almost at once, a musket-ball thudding into the ground beside Derrien's horse as he dodged right, then left, the whip of the whizzing balls familiar to his ear from old battles of lost years – Bonaparte still not aware of the threat from above or choosing deliberately to ignore it. More shots cracked and Bonaparte's horse jerked away, starting, and he threw up an arm, almost toppling, his hat flying to the ground, his heels kicking immediately, the horse digging in to gallop just as Derrien and the young aides raced round his exposed left flank to shield him, clustering about him as they rode him back to the trees, their hands pulling him down, '*Général! Général! Le général en chef!*'

Derrien looked on as Bonaparte was dragged from the saddle, Berthier and Major Detroye getting him down and into cover, half-carrying him to lie under the trees, Lannes beside him, '*Napoléon? Are you hit?*'

But Bonaparte shook them off, getting to his feet, '*Enough! Enough...!*' He looked himself over, the aides dusting him off till he swatted them away.

'You are not hit...?' asked Eugène.

Bonaparte patted himself all over. 'Nothing,' he said, touching his shoulders, chest, legs, 'Nothing...'

Lannes looked down his back. 'Nothing here.'

Then Lt Croisier rode to them, jumping down, in his hand Bonaparte's hat. '*Mon général...*' He held it up, with a note of warning in his eyes. The gaping hole was visible for all to see. A bullet had passed through the cocked brim and gold braid at the rim, and through the opposite side, just missing the crown. Two inches to the right, and Napoléon Bonaparte would have been struck dead.

Bonaparte took it, examined it, and smiled. He put his finger through the hole and held it up, showing them all. 'So. For the second time, I owe my life to my height of five foot two inches.'

After the shock of the sudden crisis and near calamity, the assembled generals laughed with relief and did their best to guffaw and clap each other on the shoulder, old soldiers all, a *bon mot*, even here under the guns of the enemy, what *sangfroid* – but their glances betrayed the same fears as Derrien who felt the creeping chill: had he fallen, *what then*. Bonaparte moved away from them. 'Eugène...'

For that moment, Eugène became Joséphine's son once again, and approached. '*Beau-père...?*' Stepfather?

Bonaparte had turned away, shaken, one hand on a low treelimb, the other moving from his sword to his stomach, his face a deathly bone-white – not with fright, but with a quaking rage. His voice a low rasp, he gave his orders: 'Send word to Dommartin and his artillery. I want five batteries here to the south, one to the east with Bon, storming troops in the orange groves...' He stared off into the distance, his hands shaking. 'Volney was right. They are mere *garden walls...*'

Eugène watched him carefully. 'Five batteries...?'

'*Yes*. Range, one hundred and fifty metres, field guns, mortars – *all*. To open fire *at once*—' He turned his furious gaze upon his stepson. '*And do not stop until this petty little town lies in ruins.*'

Eugène de Beauharnais nodded fearfully, glancing at the fruit trees, at the field guns concealed among them. '*Oui, papa,*' he said, and ran for his mount. He and Croisier galloped along the line of citrus trees for a dirt track, overhung by blossoming boughs and screened by thick hedgerows of mimosa. Soon they disappeared, shouting for the commander, *Prepare the artillery! Prepare the batteries!* Within moments they all heard the snorting and stamping of horses and the squeaking wheels of the field-guns and howitzers as they were rolled into position, ready for dispersal.

Bonaparte recovered, smacked his dusty hat against his thigh, then again, in rage. He strode back to his horse. The laughter had stopped, his staff aware that some dread corner had been turned, and that Jaffa would not escape his wrath.

Siege

Hazzard kept his eye hard on the barges, their rise and fall on the swell of the sea, ensuring they did not overhaul, keeping well back. '*Handley*,' he hissed. '*Heading?*'

Handley checked the compass. It was sunk in its small housing, bobbing and floating, in a polished cup of mirror-bright metal, its gathered light enough to read its fixed direction-needle, north floating by his midriff as he leaned forward to read it. 'Oh-four-oh degrees sir, that's near east-nor'east a quarter east. Though it's bloody dark sir...'

'Stop yer moanin', 'Andy,' said Cook, 'it's a lovely night.'

Handley looked at him. 'I shaved for this voyage I'll have you know.'

'And yer ma an' all,' murmured Cook and they chuckled.

They pulled in far behind the barges and Hazzard looked out, ducking below a forward stay, extending the eyeglass to its full focal length. The coastline leapt into view, a series of low black humps and inclines against a glowing backdrop. He traversed left, the lights of the barges bright and dappling in the eyepiece, scattering reflections over the dark. Then something beyond.

Port lights. A rising set of complex structures, pale in distant lamplight, marking the rise and fall of rooves, walls, a hill – a town.

'*Land ho*,' he said.

There was only one possibility. Tariq looked over his shoulder.

'*Yafa*,' he whispered with a nod of certainty.

Jaffa.

They had made it. Reiz patted Hazzard's shoulder, pleased. It was as if he were the host, and he wanted his country to welcome them. 'You *see*? You *see*, Hazar Pasha?'

Hazzard spied out the coastline to the south of the port, slowly traversing left, then back again, then higher, his eye catching the smoking flashes of musket-fire. He lowered the glass.

'The French are here,' he said. 'Skirmish of some kind...' He handed the glass to Reiz.

Reiz took it and scanned the darkness. 'To the south and east of the town,' he began, '...were plantations. Of orange and citrus, of olive. When we were children, we—' he stopped. 'There...' He leaned forward slightly. 'Artillery,' he mumbled. 'They have the guns in the trees.' He lowered the scope and looked at Hazzard, worried. 'They dig for the artillery. *Entrenchement?*'

Hazzard nodded. 'Same in English. Must be digging batteries.' He looked forward. 'The town has not been taken...'

'The French are masters of this,' said Reiz. 'A few hours, they will finish.'

If such were the case, the heavy artillery flotilla would not dare approach the shore until the town was taken, if they came to Jaffa at all. The tactical plan had seemed straightforward: take the flotilla if encountered. If not, reconnoitre the waters around Jaffa and depart at once to Acre and intercept. Jaffa was far less important than Acre – but the thought of it being overrun had chilled Smith: *I have a feeling of dread out there, somewhere. I cannot express how or why.*

This, thought Hazzard, was at the root of why he had been sent. It was certainly not to arrest Derrien. To make an ad hoc landing, infiltrate French lines and capture Derrien, with no knowledge of troop disposition or the merest intelligence of *whether he were even there*, would put the entire company at too great a risk. Hazzard might have attempted it with Cook alone, but not with twenty men. Somehow, Smith had known Jaffa would fall – and that something terrible might happen. They were on a rescue mission.

Of the heavy-gun flotilla, they had seen nothing. They had no idea what sort of ships to look for: coastal luggers, huge *djerms* from the Nile or French frigates. So far there had been nothing at sea but these barges sailed by Egyptians, clearly not French. Hazzard glanced at Reiz. 'What of the harbour?'

Reiz turned the telescope to the lights of the harbour mouth. Spray burst against two arms of breakwater rocks that reached out crablike into the sea, creating a natural shelter for the port. But the port was alive with small ships, tartanes, Levantine sloops, cutters, all blocking the narrow entrance in their haste to escape. High tide had swelled round the fishing-fleet which had lain beached, but now bobbed at anchor and rough rock-moorings, other boats drawn ashore, lying cocked to one beam or the other on the mud far to their left, on the northern side. A few larger vessels rode at the outer reaches of two rock jetties, but not many.

The port began to move in the optics of the scope – they were drifting north on the current, and would soon pass the harbour mouth. '*Jory...*'

Cook leaned over Tariq. 'Sir?'

'We're either early or late. The French might have surrounded the walls, but are concentrating on the southern and landward side, in the east. They might not have reached the north yet. We can't get into the harbour – it's blocked solid. We can beach on the north shore, reconnoitre, and still get in behind the walls.'

'Use the port as a base? Wait for the heavy guns?'

'If the French don't get in first.'

Cook nodded slowly, weighing it up. 'Aye, and we can see what the Frogs're up to, better'n out here.'

Reiz nodded, not taking his eye from the glass. 'We go left of the... how you say, the rocks and wooden landing, there, the quay? On north side.'

'Good...' Hazzard passed the word back, 'Handley, bear to larboard, find a place with those fishing-boats and get us ashore.'

'*Larboard aye.*'

The launch swung to port, the yard swinging, moving with them, catching the wind, the sail cracking slightly above them – in the silence it had sounded like a rifle-shot, but none but they would have heard it.

The marines prepared. Kite and Warnock were busy eating handfuls of dates and nuts from their rations, as were many others, and taking small sips of water, Underhill and Dickory passing the order, *wrap your locks, plug your barrels*, and they set to it, the oilcloth wound tightly about the black muskets, a thick cork jammed in the muzzle. Reiz made his way to the stern to guide Handley, pointing to the shoreline. '*To the left side... there, past the big rock, yes...*'

They drifted past the port, the clamour reaching their ears, distant musketry crackling louder, a boat laden with troops making its way to the south, armed men running along the southern jetty, another boat further ahead in the surf, only now just visible. Hazzard watched through the eyeglass: the town was mounting a raid on the French artillery positions. The chebek and the Egyptian barges they were following had hove-to, the music cut short, the singing stopped, as the alarm in the port became evident. 'Handley, be quick about it.'

The walls on the north side of the town glowed in the lights of the harbour mouth, the spray bursting against the rocks nearby, the fishing-boats Hazzard had spotted evident on the shore along the beach. Reiz pointed. '*There – yes, yes!*'

Handley pulled the tiller and hissed at Kite and Porter, who hauled on a line, bracing the gaff tighter, bringing the launch into the northern current and cutting across, the pull on the tiller strong. They nosed in towards the bobbing fishing-boats. A large tartane, with long, sloping lateen sail scooted past, leaving port just in time. The northern arm of the town wall lay just as Reiz had described, stopping short of the beach, finishing in a jagged rocky outcrop, an effective barrier against a landward assault but enough of a gap to make it along the shoreline.

The beach and fishing-boats drew closer with sudden speed, the surf crashing onto the rocks. Handley called to Hazzard, '*Sir – dousing sail!*'

'*Very well – stand by your oar!*'

Handley unwound the stern brace by his side. '*Yard in line, let go your sheets and braces and lower your topyard!*' Porter, Hesse and two of the *Tigre* marines let go the braces and the topyard dropped fast to the mainyard, quick hands reefing it tight, *clear!* But the launch swung towards the nearby rocks, spray bursting over the side, the ebb of the surf tugging and throwing her back out, the flow lifting her with sudden force, the marines fending off with their musket-butts, short paddles now in the water, digging hard.

'*What's the draught?*' Handley called to Reiz, but Reiz did not understand. '*How deep is it?*' he tried, looking down into the roaring spray.

'*Two fathom,*' said Reiz. He pointed to the shoals and sand, and a pair of boats with rising pointed sterns, tarpaulins stretched over their gunwales. '*We go there.*'

It was not in much cover, fairly exposed, but the ground rose towards the walls not twenty yards to their right. Hazzard decided it was close enough. '*Now, Handley! Get a move on!*'

Even above the burst of spray and the slap of water on the rocks Hazzard heard shouts, a cry or alarm, and they all looked – in the darkness beyond the shore lanterns were swinging more violently, and getting brighter. The French had spotted them. Hazzard dispensed with subtlety.

'*Cover positions! Kite, Pettifer, on the bows. Dickory, cover the portside, the rest ready to land. Get to ground, touch, keep low, run, and make for the end of the walls by the rocks. Clear?*'

'*Clear aye!*'

The shouts grew more insistent. They had barely five minutes to abandon the craft and reach the walls before they were caught, the launch a floating death-trap. The launch heaving, Kite and Pettifer moved forward quickly, Pettifer's brass-barrelled musketoon blunderbuss packed with shot, a murderer as deadly as a poopdeck swivel gun; Kite resting his musket on the port bow gunwale, covering it as the spray blew in bursts over them.

'*Reiz! How deep?*' called Hazzard.

'*One fathom!*' cried Reiz, looking over. '*We come to land!*'

'*Get us in, Handley! We cannot be caught in this boat!*'

Handley called the orders, '*Dig down to larboard lads! Bring her round!*'

Reiz looked over, heard the shouting, and looked to Hazzard. '*Less than one fathom! It is safe!*'

The shore was barely five yards away, but far enough to slow them down. '*Jory! Get 'em out and over and onto that beach! Go!*'

'*Aye sir! On yer landlegs ye lubbers, like Davy's after ye!*'

They piled overboard into the water, muskets high over their heads, their feet scrabbling to the rocks on the bottom, Dickory's head going under, splashing up, coughing; Rhys the Welshman grabbing him and pulling him along, the Arab robes dragging, all of them running as if through molten lead. They hit the shore and clawed their way up the incline, the beckoning walls to their right. The *Tigre* men were ready first, five setting up on one knee, whipping off their oilcloth wrappings from their musket locks, tugging out the cork plugs from the barrels as the first French came running – then stopped short.

'*Turques! Les Turques! Reculez! Repliez!*'

They were too late. Dickory gave the order.

'*Volley fire One Section! Fire!*'

The first volley of four roared, the flash blinding. '*Reload! Two Section! Fire!*'

A second blast of shot from another four muskets roared out as Handley tossed the anchor outboard and jumped with Reiz and Hazzard, Kite and Pettifer covering them from the prow of the boat as a squad of French made a second sally. Hazzard shouted to Dickory and the rank of marines busily reloading, '*Tigre, hit the decks!*' and the

Tigre men flattened themselves at once. Pettifer's blunderbuss roared, the flash bright, loud and frightening enough to send the French scouts back, two flying into the night, others running. Hazzard charged up the beach.

'*Walls! Now! Nine Company, cover the Tigre!*'

Cook formed them into a rough firing line, Kite on one knee beside Hesse, Porter and De Lisle. '*Make ready! Fire!*' As the volley blasted, Dickory led his men running down the beach to the crumbling corner of the wall. The ancient stones sloped down to the sea, many tumbled into ruins at the shoreline, its masonry grown into the jagged salt-encrusted rocks now bursting with spray. In the muzzle-flash Hazzard saw a French company suddenly illuminated. '*Jory! Out!*'

Reiz and Hazzard ran to them, the loose stone beneath their boots rolling, skidding, the rest running, Cook hanging back – '*Bag o'tricks!*' He hurled the dark bundle, its sparking fuse marking its course, and they all dropped flat. There was a dazzling flash and double report of the grenade exploding and the naphtha bursting in the front ranks of the French. Men were thrown back, phosphorescent flames leaping over them, their screams shrill as they ran back into their own ranks, their comrades diving away from them.

'*Up! Go!*' Hazzard led them along the beach, Pettifer firing a second shot from the blunderbuss, more crying out, lanterns opening, beams of light bouncing, playing across the shore, the white facings of the French uniforms suddenly bright then fading. Musket-fire popped from the top of the wall, Reiz calling out to them in Turkish, waving his arms. The covering fire grew with intensity and the French fell back, some firing, the balls whining off the stonework all around them as they reached the rocks and the edge of the wall.

After most had jumped up and begun to clamber through the rocky outcrops, Hazzard heaved Reiz up the first boulder to Cook's waiting hands, a musket-ball chipping off the mortar to his left, his elbow on the old stones, *watch out, jagged rock*, seeing a sandy path used by the locals, *well done Reiz, yes*, and threw himself over, the stones of the wall rising above him, *watch out watch out*, Rhys on one knee just above him on the sloping wall, firing, Underhill taking a fistful of Hazzard's robes and hauling him up, *Gotcha sir*, Ottoman soldiers on the other side looking up wide-eyed, Pettifer behind him, *Come on Petty!* the pair of them getting half over the rocks, *Go sir!* De Lisle was suddenly beside him, firing another blast of buck and ball, their hands pushing Hazzard over.

Hazzard tumbled down the far side to the rock path, skidding down the loose stone, Cook and Dickory catching him, *steady aye*, the Turks around them, calling, their hands out to help Pettifer and De Lisle, the wall alive with musket-fire, Turkish soldiers assembling on the top of the curtain wall, shouting firing orders, '*Atesh!*' *Fire!*

Volleys boomed into the darkness, lanterns swinging in the night as the exposed French ran back to their lines. Hazzard bent over, breathless, hands on his knees, chest heaving. Cook leaned on the rock and ancient stone wall beside him. 'Well,' he gasped, 'that were too easy weren't it.'

Hazzard nodded, panting, '*God save Bristol.*'

'*God save Bristol, aye...*'

A Turkish officer moved among them, a skin of water in his hands, the men taking a grateful drink, Reiz talking to him until he came to Hazzard. The Turk stared, seeing the braid, the orders on the Bombay coat beneath, cracked his heels together, stiff to attention, his hand snapping to the brim of his soft red fez. '*Binbashi.*' Then, with some reverence, '*Hazar Pasha... Kuq guchlu...*'

Cook nodded. 'That's right, lad. *Kuq* it is, aye.'

Reiz removed his own soaking red kepi, his black hair plastered wetly over his forehead, a broad smile. 'He knows your names, he says, as do all. He calls you Major.' He pointed to himself, 'I am captain, *Yuzbashi* – you, major, *Binbashi*. Yes?'

Hazzard caught his breath and returned the salute. 'Right, thank you. *Teshekir ederim.*'

Reiz beamed, his white teeth bright in the lamplight, then looked over the high rocks, to the edge of the wall. 'Is it always so?'

Hazzard looked out at the sea crashing, the boats bobbing: the port of Jaffa, in the Promised Land. 'Welcome to the marines.'

Reiz nodded, an arm round his shoulder. 'I like this thing we do, you know? Why, you could almost be a Turk.'

–

Turkish soldiers ran through the streets, lanterns held high, waving terrified people along, trying to keep the roads clear – but to no avail, the approaching dawn bringing new fears rather than new hopes: families ran through the hilly streets, shutting up their homes, mothers pulling wailing children – all to get away before the French closed in. Some went to the north gate in the hope of flight up the coast, others down to the harbour hoping to get boats, the quayside crowds growing, soldiers turning people back.

Reiz had spoken to the young Turkish officer who had welcomed them at the wall, a Lieutenant Hamit, and translated his comments for Hazzard and Cook. 'He takes us to north side and south side, as you ask.'

'Good, I want to see the French line.'

'We know the buggers're already round the north...' muttered Cook.

'That might have been a scouting patrol, or advance light company,' said Hazzard. He looked out at the shoreline, dimly revealing itself in the first streaks of grey in the sky. 'If we can find a hole there could be a way to break people out.'

Cook jabbed a finger to the south. 'Whiles that lot want to break in?'

'Precisely.'

'*Christ a'mighty...*'

They were already up high in the town, passing through the twisting lamplit lanes between ranks of tall narrow stone buildings. Hamit led them to a gate at the side of a vacant blockhouse, and onto the roof of a similar structure which opened onto a street some two storeys below. They looked out over the walls and battlements, two of the square towers rising like Roman milehouses, the dark sea glowing with a last reflection of the moon.

On the landward side he could see the lamps and fires of Bonaparte's camp. He pulled out the eyeglass. A column was busy moving into position in the distance, possibly a mile away. To the east he saw a camp in the process of waking, pickets changing, in its centre a single battery of guns. He focussed the lens as best he could. 'Twelve-pounder. Large howitzer... six- or eight-inch perhaps. Nothing heavier.' They had beaten the heavy guns to Jaffa. Otherwise, he realised, the guns were making hopefully for Acre, guided by Bonaparte's confident timetable.

He handed the glass to Cook, who peered through it and nodded. 'Aye. An eight. Why aren't they firing yet?'

Reiz replied, 'That is not breach battery. Breach battery is south, says Hamit. With many guns, so they say.' He looked at them both. 'The French teach us many things – big guns, small guns. This,' he said, indicating the north east battery, 'is not full siege.'

276

'What's the garrison here?'

'I believe four thousand,' said Reiz, looking out. 'But some are not present in the town.'

Hazzard sized up the French troops – before them lay only one division. The column he had seen far off on the north road would be another, the rest lying to the south. Some busied themselves, clearly visible, moving back and forth with scaling ladders, as if preparing for the assault. A handful of French soldiers, blankets round their shoulders, stood drinking steaming coffee from tin mugs, staring up at the town walls. A Turk fired a musket from a battlement. There was a shout of reprimand. The French soldiers had not even flinched, well out of range. 'Let's see the south.'

They moved off the rooftop and back down to the road, going round to the east and down a sloping street, Turkish soldiers looking on, watching the marines in their unfamiliar garb, but impressed by the sight of Reiz in red, an officer of the elite *Nizam-i Djedid* – the new army, a professional. Hazzard looked up to the ornate gates of a tall blockhouse, two, or maybe three storeys high, commanding the town heights, and Hamit said a word to Reiz, who translated, 'The citadel.'

They continued down into the town, to the buildings overlooking the gatehouse and walls on the southern slope of the town hill. There was an open band of waste ground outside the walls, but beyond that stretched hundreds of acres of plantations, evidently the fruit trees and olive groves described by Reiz. Concealed within the trees, their camps visible in clearings and access lanes, lay the bulk of Bonaparte's army. Hazzard counted the battalion groupings and realised there were easily close to ten thousand among the mass of flickering lights.

Despite the sallies by Mamluks and Turks that previous night, the French had managed to dig in four batteries of assorted guns behind ramparts of rock and felled tree-trunks. Horses trotted through the orchards, towing limbers to the guns, grenadier storming troops forming up, ready. 'That,' said Reiz, pointing, 'is the breach battery.'

There were two central batteries with a number of 12-pounders and 8-inch howitzers. They could certainly force a breach, thought Hazzard.

He looked back at the road to the marines. 'Underhill, Dickory, bring them over.'

The two files broke up as the men moved forward to look over the French army, the first light appearing dim over the mountains on the horizon. Underhill moved up next to Cook. 'Now,' he said in his low rasping whisper, 'what we goin' to do with that lot, Jory...'

'Buggered if I knows, 'Miah...'

Hazzard looked at them. 'Listen, everyone, we're too late. The big guns never arrived and the French have dug in. If they were still a mile off we could have raided at night, gone in, snatched our man – or killed him.' There were murmurs of approval all round. 'As it is, we're going to see how things move here today, and try to help the townspeople as best we might. There are innocents here, women and children, and we saw what happened in Cairo.' There were further murmurs of *aye*, and Hazzard concluded, 'I want to take the fight to them, as planned, where he least expects it, but if it comes to it, we help the people first – get as many out as we can, and then find those damned guns before Bonaparte does, tip 'em into the sea and watch his bloody scheme fall apart.' He glanced at Cook. 'No man is to engage the enemy independent of his crew. Sar'nt Cook, what do we never do?'

Cook came to attention before them. 'We never give up the ruddy boat, sir.'

Dickory had been well primed, and the *Tigre* men called it as loud as 9 Company did. '*Never give up the boat!*'

'Now let's be about it,' said Hazzard, 'and look over every part of these walls.'

'Aye, sir.' Cook turned to them. 'You 'eard the major, divisions into four sections, corporals and sergeants, rations as ye go.'

Hamit strode towards them from the street and snapped to attention. '*Yuzbashi! Kahve!*'

Reiz saw him and waved it in. 'Coffee,' he said to them, 'for our guests, who are given by God.'

A large man with a bushy moustache and white coat joined them on the rooftop, two men pushing a wheeled brazier, the smoke sharp on the cold breeze. Soon he stood among them, a large copper *ibrik* pot on a long handle at work, pouring into army ration cups for the wide-eyed and smiling Turkish soldiers, handing them round, *Teshekir, teshekir, thank you*.

Hopeful of a hot drink to rival the French, the marines headed back into the road, Underhill lighting a pipe, sharing his tobacco with a Turkish soldier. Reiz hung back, watching Hazzard, incredulous, and said to him quietly, 'You speak to them as you would any man, as if equal.'

Cook nodded. 'Aye. He does.'

Reiz was still perplexed. 'But what is this *boat* of which you speak? We are on land...? Where is the boat?'

Hazzard watched the marines and Turks, moving into the sloping cobbled lane, porting their arms, Dickory and Underhill dividing the town into areas, the Turks showing them the way. Hazzard sipped at the sweet coffee. 'The boat is all of us,' he said. 'Welcome aboard.'

–

Doctor Pascal Vernond looked in on the last of the wards in the new Franciscan hospital in Ramla. They had used the austere beds of the monks, some merely large wooden shelves in places, and as many folding cots as the army could spare – though the quartermaster resisted, as some of the patients were locals and not French troops. As he passed back down the corridor to the hall and the largest ward, the main doors flew open. A despatch-rider staggered in, looked about, frantic, and saw Vernond. '*M'sieur le docteur* Desgenettes?' he cast about, 'I need Desgenettes!'

'I am Dr Vernond, but the Chief Surgeon has gone to Jaffa with the army.'

The rider looked at him with hope. 'I have wounded on the Jaffa road, my troops, too *too many*, n-nearly all of them – *please, je vous en prie*—'

Delphine appeared from behind one of the nursing screens and hurried over. 'What has happened?'

Vernond indicated the rider. 'An attack – which road?' he asked. '*Which road?*'

The man was stinking and dusty from the road, exhausted, tipping back his water-bottle to drink, gasping. 'On the north branch road to Jaffa, an ambush, we were foraging...'

Vernond turned to Delphine. 'Fetch Dr Savary and two assistants.'

'I shall come.'

'No,' he said brusquely, 'I mean, no, Delphine please—'

'*Mon dieu*, I must, Pascal. I am the only surgery assistant, you know this—'

Vernond threw up his hands. 'Oh very well Delphine, as you say, then we will need the usual,' he said. 'We have no ambulance now, so take the stores cart – is Pierre still here?'

'Yes I hope so...' Delphine rushed through the back doors to the whitewashed rear passages and kitchens, where the monks were preparing lunch for the patients, and out to the quad. They had a small stable and manger for the hospital carthorses: worth their weight in gold to the army, Desgenettes had fought off the grooms of Murat's cavalry and the Horse Artillery to keep them in Ramla with the hospital. '*Pierre...!*'

A young man in shirtsleeves and old waistcoat appeared from a low doorway to a storehouse. '*Madame?*'

'The horse and cart! Quickly! There are wounded to collect!'

Pierre touched the brim of his straw hat in salute, '*Oui madame!*'

She rushed back into the kitchen area, several of the friars looking up from their work, their young harmless eyes startled, worried, '*Madame* Delphine *effendi*? Is *bien*?'

'I need lint and wadding, Fra'Giancarlo, where is the key? It is not on its hook...'

'Ah *sì, sì,*' said the young Italian, bustling round the table to a small cupboard. 'The Father found it on the floor, he did not know...'

'*Merci*—' She rushed off into the adjoining store-rooms, the light bouncing bright from the pale stone walls and polished floors, found the tall glazed cabinet in the corner and fitted the key. She gathered several packets of lint and cotton wadding, paused, took a flexible band for a tourniquet, used in amputations, *just in case*, and shuddered at the thought, *how do we do this, how*, slammed the door shut and locked it, opened a cupboard beside her and pulled out a large leather bag, checking its contents. It had the basics, but not enough for more than a few wounded. Hurriedly she threw in the extra materials, took the bag and rushed back out to the quad.

Pierre was just harnessing the second horse as Vernond and Savary appeared with two Maltese nurses, Adella and Maria, two hard-faced girls who had travelled with the army all the way from Valletta, and through the battle of Shubra Khit. The despatch-rider clattered into the yard on his horse, turning about, the horse stamping, its hooves clacking on the cobbles. 'We go!'

Hat in hand, Vernond hurried up onto the driving seat beside Pierre, Savary and the nurses climbing into the back of the flat-bottomed cart. 'Delphine! Come, *vite alors!*'

She threw her bags in the back, and Dr Savary helped her clamber up the iron mounting-rail to the flat boards with the others. 'Do we know how many yet?'

'He says too many, *m'sieur le docteur*,' she replied, 'left by the road.'

Savary shook his head. '*Mon dieu*, the army...'

They lurched forward, Pierre lashing the team of horses into a fast trot. Within thirty minutes the rider led them to the spot on the northwest road to Jaffa and the coast, empty fields of gnarled olive and scrub for miles, dotted with lines of top-heavy pines and low trees. Delphine stood in the back, her hair blowing in the dusty wind, her hands on the backrest board of the driving seat in front. She saw shapes ahead on either side of the road, lying partly on the grassy verges. Vernond pointed for Pierre, having to shout over the rattle of the cart. '*There – we can stop in the middle so we do not carry them too far.*'

The rider had come to a halt and jumped from his saddle. Then Delphine saw them, five shapes half in the grass, three to the left, two on the other bank by a line of gnarled wild olive trees, one sitting up, dragging himself to his fellow, the rider calming one of the three on the left. They stopped and Vernond jumped down with Pierre. 'Delphine!'

Savary helped Adella down, and Delphine pushed herself along the boards of the cart, her skirts tangling on her boots, helping Maria with the bags. 'I have the neck-breakers,' said the Maltese nurse grimly, in case they had to despatch any who were too far gone.

The cavalryman waved at them. '*Hurry, here.*'

Vernond and Savary ran to him on the left side of the road. The worst was unconscious, with a violent vertical sword-cut that had chopped down across the left shoulder, the arm held in place only by the chest and back muscles. His face was waxen, but he was breathing. Vernond pushed his spectacles in place and Delphine watched him: a brilliant yet arrogant man, she thought, once kind, but hardened by all this, his balding pate now brown from the sun, his remaining tufts of hair now bright silver by comparison. He put out a hand to Adella. 'Strap.'

The nurse reached into her bag and took out a canvas belt. Vernond wrapped it round the man's shoulders, nodding to her. 'Lift,' he said, looping it under the good right arm, the soldier groaning. 'A good sign,' he murmured, tightening it to close the wound and bring the limb back into position before they could amputate it properly back at the hospital. Savary joined him.

'We have lost one, Pascal, and the other has a head-wound with likely fracture.'

'I will see the others,' said Delphine and crossed over the dirt road. The sun was hot on her back and she got a water-bottle ready to hand, kneeling by the first of the pair. His friend was half-lying atop the other. '*Please…*' he said, 'He is hit…'

Delphine gave him water. 'You lie back now, just there, so I may roll him…'

The soldier fell to his side in pain, the grass bending, rustling, its green now marked with red. Delphine looked to his companion. He was lying face-down, a wound in the centre of the back – a gunshot, she saw. She lifted him carefully, two fingers to the side of his throat. There was no pulse. She rolled him over and his eyes stared back at her, dark, glassy. Gently, she let him roll back and moved to the other man, busily taking a drink from the bottle. 'Is he… all right?'

'You rest. Where are you wounded?'

He grimaced and rolled away from her, showing his back. The grey-green cloth of his coat had parted cleanly, sliced open from one shoulder-blade to the opposite hip, the slashed lining and shirt showing a razor-sharp cut the length of his arm.

Her heart thudding, she knew very well what had caused the cut, having seen it for weeks now.

A Mamluk scimitar.

'Lie still now, just a moment…' She looked over her shoulder, but Adella and Maria were assisting Vernond and Savary with the head-wound, Pierre and the cavalryman already carrying the first man to the cart on a stretcher. She looked down at the boy before her, a bottle of pure spirit in her hands, and a pad of lint. 'What is your name?' she asked him.

'*Andre, madame…*'

'Andre. I have a brother called Andre,' she murmured. 'Now, a little sting…'

She applied the pad, dabbing along the cut, removing torn clumps of material now stuck to the wound, and he gasped with the pain. 'This is a very good cut, Andre, it should heal very well.' She lay a crepe linen bandage along its length, and envisaged the stitching process – too long for out here in the field, and she knew Vernond would want to leave it open for a drain, but would have an opinion on anything she did.

Her thoughts were interrupted when the cavalry despatch-rider called out and Pierre shouted, the sound of galloping hooves from nowhere, and her last stray thought, *at last, we do need some help.* But the road disappeared beside her, obscured in a cloud of dust, horses charging past, and she heard shouts from the other side of the road. One horse stamped to a halt nearby, turning, screeching, the smell of it overpowering in the choking dust. Andre struggled from her in the grass, scrabbling for his weapon, but a lance struck down and buried itself into his back. Delphine screamed, a face looking down at her with confusion, a beard, chainmail hanging from beneath a turban of white, a cloak, great boots filling her vision. *'Isri ya bent! Isri!'*

A hand seized her by the back of the neck, clutching her shawl and hair, and she flew to her feet, a scream caught in her throat, Vernond crying out, *Delphine,* and she saw Adella fall back, a horseman riding her down, their cavalryman aiming a carbine as he spun about in the saddle, vanishing in a blooming cloud of smoke. One of the Mamluks fell, the horse charging off, dragging the rider from the stirrup.

'Pascal!' she cried, but the Mamluk above shook her, pulling her along, almost lifting her off her feet, and she felt the cloth at her throat choking her, gagging, her toes struggling for a purchase on the road as she was flung against the back of the cart. *'Deh-danss!'* ordered the voice, *'Dedanss! Yallah!'* She took it to mean 'inside', and climbed stiffly up, wondering where Pierre had gone, the cavalryman, the wounded men.

Vernond was thrown against the rear of the wagon, his spectacles cracked, hanging from one ear, two Mamluks in red turbans shoving him forward, and he climbed up, Maria virtually thrown in beside him – she turned and spat at them. The men laughed. One reached in for her and pulled her up, and cracked her across the face with the back of his hand.

The Mamluk in white shouted, leading the two riderless horses on a line behind him, another leaping to the driving seat of the cart, lashing the harness team forward and the horses whinnied with fright. Delphine fell back as the cart bounded forward, the planks rattling against their bolts, the cart shuddering along the road, her eye catching the bodies left behind, the wounded soldiers very still now, their cavalry despatch-rider dead – Pierre, Savary and Adella, dead. The dust rose in a dense cloud around them, the sun beating down as she looked out upon the distant mountains that led, the friars had said, to Jerusalem.

–

The first light of morning revealed the landscape around Jaffa further, and Hazzard watched the distant plantations turn green, the browns of the distant scrub deepen. The first flash of isolated shots in the trees came moments later and they turned to look, hearing the delayed bark of the percussive report, watching a trail of smoke and the thump of the round-shot striking the open ground just short of the massive southern gatehouse, sending a dark column of earth high in the air.

Reiz had not moved, peering at the French positions with his eyeglass. 'It begins now.'

A second shot followed, the report echoing around them, but this time there was a crash of stone, and they knew they had hit the walls. '*Jaysus*…' murmured Cook. 'Here it comes.'

The walls of Jaffa began to reverberate to a thunderous barrage: the 12-pounders blasted furiously at the same spot on the south wall, the howitzers booming, explosive shells sailing up and crashing down. A house was obliterated in smoke and part of its streetside façade collapsed, revealing the upper storeys within. Dickory and a handful of the *Tigre* marines came at the run. '*Jaysus*,' gasped Dickory. 'Rhys, get back to One Section and gather at the rdv, and I'll get Two Section—'

'Aye, Sarge…'

The marines ran off, Dickory touching his brim to Hazzard. 'Sir, I'll get 'em together and wait for you down below.' Another salvo howled over from the French lines, and they staggered at the irregular thump of geysers of earth and loose stone. Dickory straightened again. 'Can't really trim sail and dodge this lot, can we sir?'

Hazzard looked out at the groves. 'Get them down there, Sar'nt, then we can do some dodging.'

Dickory nodded, pleased, and gave Cook a grin. 'Mind yer 'ead, Cookie.'

'And you, Tick-Tock.'

Dickory ran off down the lane to the town, another round coming over, a howitzer, and Hazzard called out '*Down!*' They dropped, and the shell crashed into a road far behind. Reiz led them off at a crouching run, calling over the din of the barrage, 'You still think the north, and not the south?'

More shots rained down, blasting at the south wall, the town shaking, people's cries below, the town shuddering to each impact. 'Yes, I do,' said Hazzard, 'Bonaparte needs to overwhelm quickly! He will storm the northeast or east while you defend a breach in the south.'

'Then we must go and speak it so in the citadel!'

They ran, the lanes shaking with each blast, and soon the French guns found their rhythm, a constant barracking from the smaller guns as the 12-pounders struck the walls on a flatter trajectory, maintaining a constant maddening bombardment. The Turkish guns returned fire, their reports muffled, deeper, each round propelled by a howl of air like a rocket – but to little effect, the bursts visible in the confusion of citrus groves but too few, too widely dispersed.

The French ignored the fire, constantly pounding, and buildings crashed in the southern sloping lanes, Turkish soldiers falling back from their rooftop positions. A howling wind rushed over them, and they threw themselves flat as the cobbles erupted, a terrace of houses collapsing with a rush of sound like the sea – Hazzard thought, *it's like the sea, the waves breaking*.

When they reached the lower lanes, the streets were thronged with townspeople. All those who had not prepared were now running for their lives – Christian, Muslim, Armenian, Turk, Arab, Levantine and Hebrew alike, making for the port in the hopes of a ship. Near the harbour, Underhill and his section were guiding people away from blocked lanes, *No this way, ma, this way*. The Turks sent units to the twin quays, waving their hands, trying to stop the boats from leaving prematurely, as artillery shells came crashing into the water, sending spouts reaching into the morning sky. Families crowded the long south jetty, calling out to fishing-boats to take them off, mothers handing their children down to strangers to get them to safety as more blasts hit the walls, the crumbled southern edge by the port breaking away in a blast of brick and mortar-dust, sending clouds of sharpened stone into the defenders, toppling soldiers and civilians into the port, their arms thrashing in the water for rescue.

Cook grabbed Hazzard by the arm. 'Sir, there. At the water's edge.'

Hazzard and Reiz pushed their way through the crowds to find Napier holding people back, as Pettifer formed a firing rank from his section of six. A small boat loaded with French was making an attempt to enter the port from the south side of the town. The marines knelt, waiting as Pettifer called the tune. '*Mark your man, let 'em come! Ready...!*'

The French boat swayed and nearly tipped, the infantrymen inside overcrowded, some trying to stand, raising their muskets, an officer getting to his feet in the stern, shouting. It heeled to one side of a rock, listing to starboard, one man nearly falling overboard, losing his musket into the water, others trying to drag him back, the boat pitching violently as Pettifer brought down his hand.

'*Fire!*'

The bows of the boat burst with splinters, sprayed by buck and ball, the officer catching some of the flying shrapnel, falling backwards into the water, Pettifer stepping to the fore. '*Reload!*' levelling the musketoon to his hip and pulling the trigger. The water erupted, boiling with stone and shot as the prow of the boat flew to pieces, an old white-haired NCO throwing his hands to his face, sagging over the gunwale, their calls audible even over the barrage, '*Demi-tour! Demi-tour! Repliez!*'

Pettifer called it again. '*Fire!*'

The boat's paintwork and planking burst into a cloud of musket-shot, another man falling over the side, the boat capsizing, but Pettifer did not relent. '*Any bugger gets out o'that, let 'im ruddy 'ave it!*'

Hazzard saw a second boat behind turn, the men paddling backwards with their musket-butts, the lesson a good one – they now knew the port was defended. '*Pettifer!*' he called, '*Back to the rdv!*'

'*Aye sir!*'

They rushed back to the docks, a Turkish *Mulazim* lieutenant coming to blows with a man trying to pull away in an empty boat, a family trying to get aboard. The officer dragged him round by the neck to the quay and beat him over the head with the butt of his pistol, Reiz shouting at him to stop, pointing to the family, '*Place them in the boat!*'

'*Yes Yuzbashi!*'

The artillery came in fast and constant, the blasts shaking the south wall, some of the Turks standing ready, charging their bayonets as if suspecting a breach by the harbour at any moment. But the shelling stopped.

Hazzard looked around, the sudden end of the barrage deafening in the woollen silence. Everyone had stopped in their flight, their panic subsiding for just that moment. 'Jory – let's get them together, quick.'

'Aye...' Cook moved off and called in Pettifer and the others, pushing through the crowd to see the *Tigre* men, 'Dickory! *Tigre* to me!' Underhill, Napier, Cochrane, Hesse and Tariq hurried back into the town towards the citadel. A trumpet sounded.

'Is that yours?' asked Hazzard of Reiz.

Reiz shook his head. 'I know it not, this signal.'

They ran uphill, the marines following, dodging through the lanes, loose debris tumbling from demolished houses, now heaps of rubble – then heard the trumpet again. The Turkish troops began to run with them as well, all heading to the tall buildings in the centre, and Hazzard realised what it was: *It's a French trumpeter – it's a parley.*

When they reached the upper town, Hazzard saw only a mass of soldiers at a guarded gate, a furore of shouting, a group in the centre – and lofted above in its midst, a tall staff, a white flag tied to its tip.

'A truce? What in hell...' muttered Cook.

'We've got to get in there,' said Hazzard, turning. 'Marines, to me, two files.'

Reiz snapped a command to the men in the crowd before them, and they parted with a sudden jerk. 'Come,' said Reiz to Hazzard.

Hazzard and Cook tucked in behind him and made their way through the Turkish troops, many bowing, some clasping their muskets with wide frightened eyes – they pointed when they saw Reiz in his distinctive red uniform, flanked by what looked like a company of Ismail'i *assassin* in their black *shemagh* headdresses, red coats and *binish* robes. The marines moved without word and the Turks watched them go, chattering volubly once they had passed through the iron gates.

Reiz led them into a dark interior. A sergeant turned and bowed, every movement sharp, crisp, unmoved by the shouts and raging voices within. He led them into a large hall, easily two storeys high, a viewing gallery above, tapestries hanging on the stone walls, ornate lanterns, chairs, a large table – and roughly a hundred imperial Ottoman officers and soldiers in a variety of uniforms: Arabic, Persian, the pale faces of Circassian Mamluks and Albanians, the dark faces of Nubian Egyptians, Yemenis, Syrians – and in their midst, a portly older man with greying beard and moustache, in robes, turban, high collar and chain of office.

Reiz whispered to Hazzard, '*Abdullah Aga. Governor.*'

The source of the argument lay with an officer, his arm upraised, pointing at a ragged group behind him in a dark corner, their hands behind their backs, some forced onto their knees – prisoners, most of them French, some Arab, some women among them. But the focus of their intent was a pair of French officers standing stiffly to attention before Abdullah – a young trumpeter, a boy, the other an ensign, possibly eighteen years of age at the most, thought Hazzard. He listened to the ensign speak.

'...*une reddition honorable, offerte par mon général, général en chef de l'armée d'Orient, conquérant de l'Égypte, des Mamlukes, de Murad et d'Ibrahim Bey – et ami de Sultan Selim lui-même.*'

It was honourable yes, but an arrogant declaration, thought Hazzard, the Turkish and Syrian nobles and officers staring at the pair blankly. The Turkish officer by the prisoners shouted again, pointing at his captives. Reiz interpreted. 'The French officer declares this an honourable surrender, offered by his general, the conqueror of Egypt and the Mamluks, but friend to the Sultan. This man here,' he nodded to the man by the prisoners, 'demands the heads of these prisoners in payment for the murder of his men at El-'Arish, and the breaking of oaths by the French, for Gaza and Ramla.'

Hazzard looked at the French ensign in his white breeches and smart blue coat, the white flag hanging above, just touching his dark curling hair. A Turk seized him, pinning his arms back, the white flag clattering to the floor, shouting, and Hazzard's memory flashed with images of young Citizen Joly at Kafr-Shahabas. The officer by the prisoners considered a moment then sent back an angry reply, '*Evet.*' *Yes.*

'*Good Christ...*' murmured Cook.

Reiz closed his eyes, nodding, 'This officer, he says, yes. He will suffice.'

'*Suffice?*'

They threw both boys to the stone floor, holding them down on their hands and knees, and Hazzard whispered to Reiz, 'No... don't let them.'

Reiz looked about, given the circumstances, they had been largely ignored. 'I... do not know how...'

A sword was drawn and raised, its blade suddenly bright and Hazzard could not stop himself.

'*No! Do not!*'

Heads turned at the shout and the unfamiliar tongue.

Hazzard stood still, his chest heaving, his eye casting about for anyone of rank within the group before him. 'You *must not!*'

Reiz swallowed hard, then took control. He cracked his heels to attention and marched forward to within ten paces of Abdullah Aga, the two French boys in clear sight before him. Hazzard and Cook followed, the marines catching on, keeping close in a tight formation behind, muskets ready. Hazzard could hear Dickory – *Christ Jaysus 'Miah*, and Underhill's low rasp in reply, *Easy lads, easy...*

Abdullah Aga looked at the marines, the Arab robes and scarlet coats beneath, then at Reiz, at the gold-braided red jacket, at the red fez kepi, the belt and sword.

Reiz saluted, his chest out, his chin high. '*Kaymakam!*' he shouted to Abdullah, and announced himself, '*Yuzbashi Shafik Reiz, Nizam-i Djedid!*'

Abdullah shuffled closer, the links of his chain of office clinking as he moved, looking him up and down. '*Nizam-i Djedid?*' He raised a vague hand at Hazzard and the marines, in mute question to Reiz. Hazzard took it to mean 'who are they'.

'English!' Reiz shouted back. 'Sir Wiyyam Siddanni Smits!'

An outraged Turkish colonel stepped forward and shouted something at Abdullah, gesturing again at the French prisoners, then pointing at Hazzard. But Reiz continued, '*Hazar Pasha! Kuq Chavus guchlu!*' he declaimed to the hall, looking up to the gallery, 'Malta! Shubra Khit! Embabeh! Abuqir! *Nelsoun Amir al-Bahr Kapudan Pasha!*' He was calling out their battle honours. 'Kahire! Karnak! *Murad Bey'in arkadashi!*'

Abdullah listened to Reiz's declaration, reacting to the mention of Nelson, the 'High Admiral', but the last, *friend of Murad Bey*, seemed to hold the greatest sway. A Mamluk sheikh came forward and spoke in eloquent Arabic, his hand out to Hazzard, his words swift and graceful. Reiz bowed to him and whispered to Hazzard. 'He says you are well respected in Egypt, battle-lord of Murad, saving the innocent of Cairo, known to the *Bedu* and Muhammad Bey al-Elfi.'

The officers and men began to exchange glances, the officer by the prisoners shouting back at Reiz, Reiz replying curtly with the evident self-confidence of the *Nizam-i Djedid*. But another took up the cry and soon the room rang with a single word, *Intikam!*

Revenge.

The officers raised their arms, shouting, the troops chanting the call, for El-'Arish, for Cairo, for all of their betrayed truces and talk of peace, Hazzard called out, unheard, '*If you do this, Abdullah Aga*,' he cried, '*Yafa will be destroyed!*'

The crowd seized the two boys and pulled them through the hall back to the door, Abdullah Aga calling after them, his hand out in commandment, Reiz shouting out his protest, but heaved aside by the force of the crowd.

Intikam! Intikam!

The marines jostled the Turks away from Hazzard, '*Sir, this way—*'

Hazzard turned, looking into the dark corner where the prisoners knelt, flashes of faces, hands held out, men, women, voices crying, *effendi, effendi!* The tide of people carried him out of the hall to the gate, the enraged troops surging from the building to the southern gatehouse, this their chance to show Bonaparte what awaited him. Within five minutes they reached the southern wall, the sun bright above, Hazzard and Cook shoved along by the men at the back.

The group stilled suddenly in a dread silence – followed by a loud cheer. A moment later, the two bloody heads were raised on the tips of two lances, bobbing over the southern gatehouse parapet, the soldiers shouting, cheering, one group dragging the bodies to the gatehouse rooftop, holding each headless corpse by the hands and feet, swinging it, and tossing it over the wall, first the ensign, then the trumpet-boy. The soldiers danced and waved, their delight moving to anger, shouting down from the walls, some firing their muskets at the French a hundred and fifty metres away.

Hazzard pushed his way out and burst from the edge of the crowd, Cook and Reiz close behind. '*Christ God above...*' he cursed. 'He has his excuse now...' He looked up, watching them, jubilant, victorious over the two dead boys. 'At last,' he said, 'Bonaparte can now cry havoc.'

Sack

Caron, Rossy and fifty sappers of the forward engineers unit had watched the two dead bodies fall to the ground with a dull thud, lifeless limbs bent askew, folding and collapsing either side of the bloody trunks. Fallen puppets, dumped like so much carrion meat. It was not that they had been beheaded, thought Caron, but that their corpses had been tossed over a city wall like rubbish.

'*Mon dieu...*' whispered Caron, '*Les idiots.*'

There had been a moment's silence across the army – shock perhaps, he thought, and then Caron heard it, a rising earthquake of sound. Every soldier in the southern ranks roared.

'This was too much,' said Rossy, shaking his head, 'too much for the mad ones of the *demis*. They keep to their ranks, to their formations, and now they will go wild. After El-'Arish, after the raids at Ramla, the revolt...'

'Now,' Caron agreed, 'it will be a true madness.'

The guns expressed the troops' rage, pounding at the same point of the wall, some of the Turkish soldiers flying from the battlements as they burst in sudden storms of stone, a constant blast in the Alphas' ears as they lay beneath the trajectory, looking at the open waste ground before the old walls, watching the rounds strike, time after time, the stone exploding, some cheering in the hopes of a breach, and Caron knew – they *wanted* to get inside. The word went round: *grenadiers to storm, grenadiers to storm, with Lejeune!*

Général de brigade Rambeau charged across the front ranks as they assembled in the orange trees, sword in hand, furious, the massed group shouting back, *hwa hwa hwa!* After half an hour of continuous firing, the guns adjusted and the impacts crept up the wall, detonations crashing through the mortar, the Turks' cries no longer cheers, the wall shattering high at the top, then in the middle, the base remaining stoutly intact, banked by the Roman earth and stone behind. The 12-pounders and howitzers delivered the final punch and drove a crashing hole through the wall, and the army cheered. As all realised what had happened, there came a sudden eerie stillness.

Caron looked out at the broken wall, the heap of rubble, and he closed his eyes, his heart sinking. '*Mon dieu...*'

In almost total silence, a captain of engineers and a company of the 22nd *Légère* charged forward, followed by Colonel Lejeune and the grenadiers. Caron watched them run across the open ground from the orange trees to the breach, the Turks staring, as if stunned. The silence was broken by General Rambeau, screaming an ear-splitting command, '*Covering fire!*'

The orange groves erupted with musketry and the battery guns opened fire, howitzers hurling their shells into the town, smashing the stonework of the buildings behind, throwing the Turks back as the first unit stormed the breach. Turkish soldiers reappeared time and again, musket-fire pouring down from the walls and overlooking houses as the French launched themselves onto the heap of rubble and up into the breach.

Lejeune raced through them, his sword held high, a company streaming out behind him as he clambered up the slope of broken stone, his men falling all around him. One soldier collapsed into his arms – he caught him, then set him down before charging onwards, the dead giving him purchase to climb further as he called to them, the men cheering, until the musket-fire burst around his feet, the rounds exploding on his chest. His sword flew up from his stiffened arm, his head thrown back, his back arching, and Lejeune fell.

His body tumbling back down the hill, the Turks renewed their fire, the engineers not retreating, but falling, flying off their feet – within moments, they were dead to a man. Further enraged, another company charged over the killing zone and Caron looked to Rossy, at his staring eyes, his unshaven face, nervously chewing. 'When will be our turn, I wonder...'

Rossy looked at him. 'Long after *m'sieur le Turc* has run out of his little bullets – that is when we go, eh *Chef. Oui?*'

'Yes, *mon garçon*. When they are friendly again.'

Another salvo roared overhead, shaking the ground, the troops securing the base of the breach, Rambeau himself now charging onwards leading the grenadiers, thrown back, and charging again, kicking through the bodies and rubble to the right side of the breach, the Turks firing ceaselessly into his men. When Caron saw General

Lannes himself rush to the base of the breach, he knew their time would come soon. 'Rossy,' he said, 'Rolo, he goes. Pass the word, be ready.'

Rossy moved to go but a captain dodged through the trees to meet him. '*Sergent-chef* Caron?' he shouted over the barrage, '*Capitaine Aymé, Sapeurs, 22nd light company.*'

Caron looked at them – he knew sapper engineers were hard men, axes and picks in hand, pioneers, miners and skirmish troops all in one. Aymé was scarred, older than a breathless ensign with glory in his eyes: he had done this before. 'Yes, *Capitaine*?'

Aymé looked at the breach, flying with shrapnel and musket-balls, Rambeau raging with the grenadiers, hauling a small 3-pounder cannon himself, aiming it to fire up at the wall at the left of the breach, Turks falling, French falling. 'We shall have cover fire in five minutes,' he said, 'the signal is the guns stopping, then a single shot, then the barrage of cover begins for fifteen minutes. We go inside the breach to the left, you see? We take the house there, which is pinning Rambeau down as he tries to go *right*.'

Caron looked at the breach, steadily filling with bodies.

'When your barrage comes, I will consider it.'

'The *général en chef* commands it.'

'I will be happy to follow the *général en chef* as I followed him up the heights of Toulon to capture the English guns, and dragged him from fire on the bridge at Arcole.'

Aymé looked away and cursed. 'I need you and the Alphas, *Chef*.'

Caron nodded. 'I know, which is why I do not throw them away. Rossy, you, Antonnais and St Michel are the fastest. We go, scout, then the rest follow with the perfect, accurate barrage over our heads.'

'Yes, that sounds very safe, *Chef*,' said Rossy, staring hard at him.

'We will end the siege, take the town,' said Aymé hopefully.

Rossy chewed on his tobacco, looking at him, the orange trees casting shadows on his whiskered face. 'If my *papi*, the *Chef*, is hit, *Capitaine*, I kill you, hm? *Bien*.' He moved off into the trees, Aymé watching him.

The barrage stopped.

Aymé looked at a watch. 'Soon.'

Caron checked his pistols. A single round hurtled overhead and burst on the wall beside the breach. Caron sighed – he had hoped the army would prove its usual self, but today it had not.

Aymé nodded over his shoulder to his men. '*Now.*'

The afternoon was split apart by a new salvo of thunder, the upper stonework of the battlements exploding. Turkish soldiers were thrown back into the town, a house collapsing, its rooftop folding in on itself, the trapped men crying out as they disappeared in belching plumes of dust and smoke. Aymé was up and running before Caron knew it, the sappers running after, one kicking Caron as he passed, *old putain eh*, and Caron looked for Rossy.

'Quick – we go left. Use the dead sappers to protect you as they fall. See where we are, then back if we fail, yes? This is bad, *mon enfant.*'

Rossy nodded. 'I know – bad, yes.' He called the others. '*Micheline! Anton! We go be foolish heroes!*'

Caron got up and followed the last of the *sapeurs*, the fury of the barrage above, the crackle of musketry and thump of Turkish guns answering, hearing himself shouting, roaring against the endless noise, a nightmare through which he had put himself for too many years, the ground alive around him with fountains of earth marking the smack and whip of each bullet, each one reaching for him alone, trying to consume him, his arm leaping with a hammer-blow and he cried out, stumbling, *up, old Tartuf.*

He ran, throwing himself onto the first of the dead, Rossy ahead, *Come Chef! I smell cooking!* The loose stone tumbled all around them with each frantic scrabbling step, sappers ahead, one throwing his axe, a Turk falling back with a scream, *dead men, dead men everywhere*, a tangle of boots and hands hooking at his feet, elbows snaring him, *stop, do not*, snagging him, and he cried out again, '*Begone, begone! Putain!*' He lost his balance, then leaned forward and rushed up the mountain of tunics and belts and dead backs, dodging left behind a wall, *wall*, the shells crashing, deafening, '*Rossy!*'

A shattered ruin appeared ahead of him and he threw himself inside, the sudden dark engulfing, Rossy shouting from in front, *Here Chef, this way!* They were in a house, *the* house, the *left* house, running then falling down a set of steps, following Aymé and the sappers, a Turk shouting out, Rossy squeezing off a quick shot, the man falling, '*Micheline!*' St Michel ran past him to take the front while Rossy reloaded, five of the sappers ahead, waving them on, *This way this way!* They ducked through a collapsed wall draped with dead men in robes, in uniforms – Caron grabbed up a pistol, checked the pan, *loaded*, burst into a chamber with a broken window, shutters blown out, Caron finding himself surprised, *what a charming home*, as they fell onto the cobbles, the afternoon daylight suddenly blinding.

Jaffa. They were in.

Before him, a road, opposite a tall building, everywhere people running, a woman and young boy stopped and stared at him, then screamed, whisked away in a cloud of smoke as she was shot from the side, her body flung to the ground. One of the sappers ran past, pausing to slam his heavy pick-axe into her head, the wailing child reaching up to him as he swept it away with a violent kick and it bounced against the stone of the doorway opposite, fell and rolled away, dead.

Caron saw this world in a dull roar within his mind, his eyes blurring, *a child, now a child*, the sappers looking like Turks themselves with their soft kepis and wrapped turbans, or sepoys from India, he thought, the sapper turning with a smile, '*Eh, old putain hein?*' And Caron shot him, his abdomen bursting with the heavy dragoon bullet, his eyes bulging, Caron not caring, feeling nothing, *scum from the inferno, I shall not die with you*.

More shots, a sapper knocking him away, swinging a fist at him, and Caron ducked – a quick reflex, easy for old *Tartuf*, ramming his sword-bayonet into the man's floating ribs, and putting a boot in his chest and shoving him off his blade, already turning, already forgetting him. Turks gathered in the street, stopping, turning. *Conscripts*, he thought, throwing their muskets down and their hands in the air. After the two dead boys, their headless corpses at the wall, there would be no quarter – they had become vengeful Titus at Jerusalem, Trajan at the gate, killing all before them. The storming troops thrust their bayonets straight through them as they screamed, trying to surrender, boots in their throats to yank the spikes free again, more grenadiers bursting from the house on the right, Rambeau leading them, shouting, '*En avant!*'

He ran to Rossy, saw Antonnais fix his bayonet and charge into the Turkish group, taking one, knocking a musket away, thrusting, another and another, '*Chef!*' Caron called to him, '*Anton! Venez!*' and ran to the corner, his two pistols up, ready, a squad charging them up a road, an officer at the front, the blinding sunlight throwing stark shadows on their faces, their slouch hats dark. Caron raised a pistol and fired and the officer fell. The soldiers stopped, hesitant, more of the grenadiers coming up behind them, cutting into them with bayonets, axes and picks, and they spun about, caught, dropping to the road, a few managing to run.

Pigalle burst into view, swinging his musket, a new Samson, the Canaanites falling all about him, '*Chef! I am here!*' Rossy and St Michel either side, Rossy shouting, '*Chef! Come! We keep them back, Chef!*'

Turks came leaping from the rooftops, tumbling into the streets, short-swords out, swinging, taking down Rambeau's men, the French pushing them back. Pigalle picked up one by the arm, hefting him overhead, musket-balls peppering the ground around him – '*I am Pigalle! And where I plant my boot, there shall I not be moved!*' – and threw the man into the nearest mass of defenders. Rambeau and the grenadiers roared and charged, the 22nd *Légère* following.

Antonnais took Caron's arm and pulled him along to the others and they sheltered for a moment, *I must look, I must see*, he thought, *for mes enfants, just for mes enfants.* He watched the Turks run uphill, deeper into the upper town to their citadel, a flood of pale French coats pouring through the shattered houses on the breached wall.

'We go!' said Rossy.

A Turkish soldier was caught on a French bayonet, his hands reaching for safety as he cried out and fell, five grenadiers swarming round him, stabbing downwards again and again, one drawing a broad cutlass and slamming it down several times, tearing, wrenching at loose skin, chopping again and finally yanking the head from the hacked neck with his bare hands and throwing it high into the street, '*Voilà, putain!*' the men cheering.

'*Sacre...*' said Rossy, crossing himself. Caron knew it was the end – the end of Jaffa, the end of the Turks, and the end of them all, as the last vestige of humanity drained away with the God that had long since departed that dread and damned place.

–

Hazzard was down, rolling among the Ottoman dead in the street as General Bon sent his storming brigade through the eastern breach, almost unopposed. He heard Cook calling, '*Sir! We're out!*' and he sprang to his feet, the scimitar hot in his hands, the blade swinging left in an arc, a scream, a face with bulging eyes falling past him – *two*, he thought, and ran, '*Marines! Up and out!*'

Reiz shielded him from another lunge with a bayonet, parrying the forestock of a musket and swinging his broad-bladed *kilij* with a firm backhanded loop, a body dropping to the flagstones. '*We go!*' he called, stumbling, Underhill behind him, taking his collar. *'C'mon wi'ye, yer Eminence!'*

They ran into a broad vaulted passageway, then burst out the other side and down a set of wide steps, tall, shadowed buildings either side. At the bottom was a broad square lined with houses, lanes going off. Bodies lay in doorways, looters looking up, caught, darting off, other townsfolk running past, a cleric gathering a family, emerging from a house, the halloos of the hunting French echoing in the surrounding streets. The marines ran to them, Underhill pushing them along, *'Come on boy! The devils're after ye!'*

Hazzard looked back up and saw them, at the top of the steps, French troops stopping, pointing, then charging down after them. He looked round, saw too many civilians still in danger. *'Firing ranks to give cover!'*

The marines formed up, Cook bawling out, *'Front rank make ready!'*

Hazzard watched the French draw closer, pouring down the steps, bayonets levelled. *'Front rank!'*

The front raised their sawn-off Charlevilles, Warnock grinning at Kite. 'Difference 'tween you an' me, Mickey, me ol'mate…' he laughed in the back of his throat, aiming, '…is I really do want to kill 'em…'

The first of the French saw them too late, the sun too bright, the shadow too deep. *'Fusiliers! Arrêtez! Arrêtez!'*

Hazzard called the order.

'Fire!'

Warnock smiled. *'Knock-knock, twats…'*

The volley burst in a choking cloud of grey smoke. Cramped by the confines of the lane, the front of the French charge flew backwards, bodies tripping the men behind, tumbling head-first down the steps, their comrades stumbling over them as Cook shouted, *'Second rank!'*

Hazzard called out, *'Fire!'*

The second volley made the remainder turn and run back up the steps into the men following, the buck and ball fizzing off the stone walls, Pettifer's musketoon roaring.

'Up and out of it!'

They broke and ran to a lower lane and saw the Turks running across their bows, all in the same direction, and Reiz stopped Hazzard. 'They go to the citadel!'

The marines ran on, Cook getting them over the road, and Hazzard looked up at the tall stone buildings, unable to move.

The prisoners.

'Reiz...'

The women prisoners.

The Turkish captain stopped. '*Yes, Binbashi!*'

Cook saw them and turned. '*What in hell you doin'?*'

Breathing hard after their run, Hazzard appealed to him, 'Reiz, we've got to get them *out*. I saw women among the prisoners – *Abdullah will execute them all.*'

Reiz looked back up the street. They could hear the fighting but knew the Turkish troops would be unable to staunch the flow of the French for long. '*Yes! Come!*'

Hazzard shouted to Cook, '*Jory! Get them down to the water! Rdv at the harbour road or north jetty!*', then ran for the citadel gates, Reiz hard behind.

Cook was furious. '*Sir! Dammit, boy!*'

They dashed across the road to a winding side street. Pounding on the uneven flagstones beneath their feet, he followed Reiz precisely, dodging left, *stall*, and right, *steps*, as the nimble Reiz leapt obstacles. They burst onto the next road, old men, old women, faces become masks of terror, children crying, running past them as they fought their way up, up to the citadel where all would be safe. Reiz looked up and down, trying to get his bearings. '*Yes! This way!*'

Hazzard followed, recognising the street, *lamp on corner, yes*, and found two crushed houses falling, the gates of the citadel flung wide, a tide of Turkish and Ottoman uniform flowing through the gateway, civilians, men, women, in turban, in Hebrew *kippah*, in Arab *keffiyah*, one gate torn from its mount, and he knew that was what he had seen – her face. *He had seen her face again, among the prisoners.*

Delphine.

The Turkish guards had abandoned the gates and stood by the massive wooden doors, a castle keep, the army pouring in, Hazzard and Reiz forcing a path to the right with the few civilians seeking shelter, *great hall*, a startled face, a dark kepi, *their sergeant at arms*, Reiz demanding, '*Chavus! Tutsaklar nerede?*' *Sergeant, where are the prisoners?*

'*Yolumdan chekil!*' he shouted back and shoved him aside. Reiz swung him round by his jacket and smacked him across the face, firing a rapid stream of outraged Turkish at him. The sergeant pointed after the civilians, '*Evet, evet!*' Reiz nodded, '*This way! We go! Order is lost!*'

He pulled Hazzard along, under the gallery beams above, past dark doorways, seeing sudden bright light from narrow window embrasures. They found a set of ancient stone steps down, a press of people below, crying out, wrangling, soldiers shouting, people hurrying. '*The south door!*' called Reiz, leading him down the stairs.

They burst from the staircase to find a crowd of people rushing to a low arched door to a rear quad – and a flood of soldiers pushing their way in, some going up the stairs, some going down, orders echoing in the yard outside. Hazzard ran along the corridor, *cell doors, Christ above*, some open, some closed, hands reaching through the bars, cries in Turkish, Arabic, French. He looked in them all, frantic, and was knocked from behind – he turned to find two men, an Arab, a Turk in a white cap and a woman, a blanket drawn over her hair. *No, not her.* Desperate, he called out into the crowd, '*Delphine!*'

Among the group rushing for the door a face looked round – a woman beside another, in *hijab* and a dark robe. She put a hand to her companion's shoulder and the woman turned.

Yes.

'*Delphine!*'

Her hazel eyes, filthy bruised cheeks, a gently pointed chin, the dark curls hanging down, a French face, he remembered, somehow different to that in his memory but now recognised. *Yes, it is she.* Her arms around his waist on the horse in Cairo, her hair on his neck as she pressed herself tight to him in the gallop, and he remembered it all. *What is your name?*

Delphine Lascelles. Surgeon's assistant.

She saw the black *binish* first, then the red coat, the red sleeves – and Hazzard. '*William…!*'

She turned against the flow of the crowd, her hand reaching out for him, her nurse Maria beside her – and behind, Dr Pascal Vernond, battered, a bloodied face, in ragged *galabeyyah* smock.

'*This way,*' Reiz led them to the open door, the light dazzling, a yard, walls, a sloping road. '*Down the steps, vite, vite!*'

There were barricades beyond, troops running to their positions, sergeants shouting at them, swatting the air with switches above the civilians, driving them out, herding the townsfolk out of the citadel precinct, arguments raging as to who had let them in, pushing them out into the street, their arms outstretched for help, '*Evlerinize gidin!*

Evlerinize gidin!' Go to your homes. Reiz called to him, *'They want us out!'* he laughed. *'They guide us out!'*

Hazzard looked at the disparate group in the street and shouted, *'Reiz! Bring them all – we'll get them to the waterfront.'*

Reiz called out to them, calling over their heads, beckoning them. They saw the red uniform of the *Nizam-i Djedid*, turned, obeying, hoping. Hazzard could think only of a single objective, and hoped it was still there: the chebek they had seen when they had landed with the launch – it was the only chance to get anyone out.

'How did you find us?' gasped Delphine close behind, holding Maria's hand, Vernond close behind.

They ran, Hazzard pulling her along, Reiz behind, hurrying the small crowd of townspeople, calling out to them, *'Chabuk, achele et!' Come along! Hurry!*

Turkish guns barked again from the heights, the air thudding with the report. Hazzard tried to make sense of the streets but could not recognise their route. The thoroughfare was clogged with Turkish troops, some running in the opposite direction, all for the citadel, some forming line – the French were close. *'Reiz, get us down to the marines at the waterfront!'* he shouted.

'This way—' cried Reiz, leading them down into the shadowed lanes, deep and dark after the sunlight. Hazzard saw the garrison building down below, smoke belching from its lower windows, muskets crackling, the noise confusing the ear, barracking round the echoing roads.

The lane ended and they came to a broad set of steps, tall palms waving high above, throwing crablike shadows across his vision. At the bottom was a road running left and right, littered with dead mules, upturned carts and bodies, Turks running at the double. Hazzard looked up and down. *'Clear!'* They clattered down the stairway, some stumbling, a robe tangled, one falling, others picking them up, a shoe catching, falling off. They ran across the road at the bottom after Reiz, Hazzard pausing at the side to count them off, *sixteen, seventeen... twenty... thirty.* He had no idea so many had followed.

Hazzard pulled Delphine along, hearing her gasps, in his mind Sarah behind him, *No, not Sarah; no, not here,* a blast of musketry behind, and he looked back up to see French troops running on the road above, seeing them, stopping, firing, a woman crying out, falling, the rest running down the steps.

'*Hazar!*'

Reiz.

He turned to find Reiz with a Turkish sergeant and a line of soldiers. They ran to the right, following the group of townsfolk, and he heard the commands '*Hazirla! Atesh!*'

The volley boomed, and some of the French were caught on the road, some on the steps, falling, rolling. The Turks stepped forward and thrust their bayonets into any that came within reach, Hazzard hearing the war-cry he had heard on the field outside Cairo, *Vur un, vur un!*

The garrison lay just ahead, the water of the harbour just beyond. Reiz guided the families down another street, the water of the port visible at the end, and they found themselves at the edge of a market square. Hazzard stopped and stared, Delphine clutching his hand tight. '*Mon dieu...*'

The French had run wild – Turkish soldiers, arms raised in surrender, were run through by bayonet charge, no quarter given, the enraged French clubbing and kicking the wounded to death, the sounds of breaking glass, the screams of women as they were dragged from the market shops and dwellings, people thrown from balconies above, crashing to the ground to be bayonetted or bludgeoned by musket-butts and axes. Anything that moved was attacked: a bloodied old man falling to his knees, his head cracked; a daughter's hair jerked back, a bayonet pushed through her neck; children running, then vanishing in a cloud of musket-shot, small bodies dropping to be trampled by French boots. A French officer of the 22nd *Légère* shouted out, '*You will stop this,*' trying to restore order, '*Stop this at once!*' A soldier beating a head to spatters on the stones with his bare hands, the officer shooting him dead with his pistol, two other men turning and running the officer through with their bayonets. Vernond stared, his twisted spectacles held by trembling hands. '*Mon dieu*, Delphine... they have become as animals.'

'We must go back,' she gasped, taking hold of an old woman and her grandchild, 'we must get the people back, William!'

'We can't! We—' Hazzard looked back up the lane, but their path was now blocked by approaching French, the waterfront but a street distant. '*Reiz! Get them through,*' he shouted, '*get them through!*'

Reiz looked at the maelstrom of murder before him. Hazzard took him by the shoulder, the young man's dark eyes wide. '*No faces!*' shouted Hazzard. '*Yes? The French have no faces! Understand!*'

Reiz stared at him, the pair of them shaking, and nodded together, '*Yes, Binbashi! No faces, none!*'

Hazzard looked to Delphine. 'Here,' he said, handing her the Lorenzoni. 'Four shots left. After you fire, crank the arm all the way round.' He loaded it for her. 'Then aim and fire again – yes?'

'Y-yes…' she stuttered.

Hazzard drew the scimitar of Ali-Qarim and turned to Reiz, '*We go together! Evet?*'

'*Yes, Binbashi!*'

Reiz called to their charges and raised his *kilij*, '*Chabuk!*' and waved them through the square, running beside them, Hazzard at his left facing the centre of the square and the French, their red coats too hard to resist. Someone shouted, '*Anglais!*' – and some turned and charged, hands reaching out with knives, bayonets, some holding their empty muskets like clubs.

The first came, maddened, a pack on his back with fur in the bedroll, his Charleville and long bayonet levelled, three others behind him. The first fell with a scream as Reiz opened his neck with the *kilij*, another vanished in a cloud of smoke as the Lorenzoni boomed, his head jerking back, a terrible cavity where the right eye had been. Hazzard looked at Delphine reloading it – her face determined, no fear, her chin down, her eyes wide – and she fired again.

Hazzard dodged a bayonet, slipping the scimitar up to the man's neck and opening his throat; another, and Hazzard threw himself against Reiz's back, the scimitar looping, *take the hand*, a scream and staring eyes, *now the arm*, cutting down, the musket falling harmlessly with the limb, blood dark on the ground, and he thought of Wayland. Reiz broke into a knot of French blocking their way to the harbour road, knocking two muskets aside left and right with the *kilij*, the angled blade rising and scything across the tops to the shoulders of the first, then the second, throats bright with a spray of blood, their eyes wide, falling.

But others got through, one of them roaring as he charged, bayonetting a man carrying his wife, his back arching as he cried out, falling to one knee, the Frenchman withdrawing, trying to bayonet another – and the Lorenzoni boomed from behind, the French trooper dropping, his head loose, tilting forward, the jaw open, hanging, as he sank to the ground, Delphine obscured in a cloud of smoke as she cranked the loading arm. Hazzard waved at her, '*Delphine! Come!*'

Vernond behind her, Delphine aimed the Lorenzoni again, the gun blasting, a soldier thrown off his feet, and she ran after them, Vernond shouting, '*Go, Delphine! Please!*' He cried, shaking her. '*Suivez-le,*' shouted Vernond, '*Follow him!*'

'*Maria!*'

The nurse behind her was yanked back by a hand grasping her hair, but she wheeled about, a dagger in hand, and rammed it in the man's face again and again and he cried out as he fell back, staggering away. '*Madame!*'

The last of the townsfolk rushed past with Reiz, but still the pale coats and mitre caps of grenadiers poured into the square. Delphine and Maria ran to Hazzard, Reiz already gone ahead, and Hazzard called to Vernond, '*Doctor! Come! Venez vite!*'

Vernond looked back at the mass of French tearing through the square, some seeing them, pointing and charging. He looked at Delphine. 'Go. Please,' he said, doubtless knowing the soldiers would not stop to question who they were, French or Turkish, Muslim or Christian – their bayonets cared for nothing. He thrust Delphine forward, '*Je vous en prie.*' *I beg of you.*

'*Non! Pascal…!*' she cried, but Hazzard pulled her away. '*Non…!*'

The light flashed off Vernond's broken spectacles and he turned to face the grenadiers, his arms out wide as if to embrace the soldiers of the Republic, their bayonets become battering rams, striking his chest, his abdomen, his throat, *Salaud de merde!* crushing the air out of him as he collapsed, choking, retching, falling forward onto them, grasping their muskets as he fell, slowing them as they tried to withdraw. Three of them staggered back, trying to prise their bayonets loose, cursing him, kicking him as he sank, their musket-butts battering his shoulders, head and neck, their incoherent screams of rage unbearable.

Choking with tears, Delphine stumbled behind Maria, '*Pascal…*'

Hazzard pulled her onwards. '*Come! He's bought us a moment!*' They broke through onto the harbour road, and Hazzard stopped. Before them were ranged two ranks of muskets, a firing-squad, Reiz nowhere in sight. Hazzard took the Lorenzoni from her, but knew it was empty, and all too late – then understood.

'*Down,*' he said.

She looked at him, eyes wide and terrified. 'What?'

Hazzard threw Delphine and Maria to the ground and fell on top of them, his hands over their heads, the sound of shouts and boots coming from behind – and Cook's voice roared out, '*Hit the bloody decks! Front rank! Fire!*'

The blast sent clouds of smoke over them, and Delphine cried out, the choking stench of sulphur and cordite overwhelming, a musket crashing onto Hazzard's back, dropped by a dead man, a body across his legs, flaming wadding from the volley landing on his hand, on Delphine's hair. He threw it off, Cook roaring, '*Reload! Second rank!*' and he heard her say, '*Now?*'

He whispered, '*Not yet.*'

'*Fire!*'

The air overhead burst again with smoke and powder, more men falling behind them. '*Up,*' he said, dragging her with him, '*Come on!*'

Hazzard ran for the end of the line, *Porter, good man,* a hand taking his arm, pulling him in, one of them nodding to Delphine, to Maria, *Afternoon ma'mselle,* Reiz up ahead further along the harbour road, their flock still with him, '*Binbashi!*'

Hazzard raised a hand. '*Evet!*'

Yes.

He looked for Cook. '*Jory! Get to the damned boats!*'

'*I'm ruddy busy over 'ere!*' he shouted. '*Front rank! Pick yer target! Fire!*'

The buck and ball blasted along the road in another hail of fire and a squad of grenadiers flew backwards, *au couvre, au couvre,* survivors dodging back into the square for cover. Cook gave the order, '*Retire! Second rank, withering fire!*'

The front rank stepped backwards two paces through the *Tigre* men behind, who lowered their muskets to shoot from the hip, just as more French emerged from the square, hesitating when they saw the line of black robes and scarlet tunics.

'*Second rank! Fire!*'

The soldiers dived too late, an arm rising, a musket falling, Pettifer stepped forward with the musketoon, roaring, '*Get 'em out, Cookie.*' He cocked the heavy-sprung lock, '*Have that,*' and pulled the trigger, the brass muzzle belching smoke. Two men fell, the trunk of one twisting and dropping, the legs standing for a moment longer, then folding and collapsing.

'*Right!*' roared Cook, '*On yer landlegs, and run like Davy wants ye for supper!*'

The road ran parallel to the shoreline, a stone breakwater on the water's edge, the waves smashing against the rocks, washing across the road as they ran. It was fifty yards to the north quay, past harbour cranes, booms and hanging nets, a boat raised on a slipway, rocks of turquoise and green and the spray of the water crashing below. The jetty was crowded with boats at the quayside, mostly oared cutters and Levantine *djerms* with exotic high prows and sterns. But they seemed useless considering the evacuation before them – there were no large boats in the harbour.

Turkish troops gathered from the garrison, the French still occupied with the town. A squad of Turks led Reiz and Hazzard's group of civilians, *twenty-one*, counted Hazzard, *only twenty-one now*, and he charged to the quay, the marines pounding hard behind, *Dickory...? Napier...? Underhill?* He saw most of them, 9 Company and the *Tigre* – but some were missing.

'*Where are they?*' he breathed, Delphine running along beside him. 'The ships, where are all the bloody—'

Delphine pointed and called out, '*There!*'

Just beyond the reef he saw what he had hoped for:

Chebek.

He found Cook. '*Where in hell's Napier and Dickory? Where's Kite?*' He looked about but could not see them anywhere, searching the faces – *Pettifer, Hesse, Tariq...*

Cook turned. 'I can't find 'Miah or ruddy 'Andy nowheres either!'

Hazzard looked for Reiz, and called, '*Reiz! Where are all the ships?*'

'*Not good for big ships, Hazar!*' he cried. '*Small boats always take people out!*'

'*We must get these people to that chebek!*'

Hazzard pushed his way through the crowd, another group and another, uncertain, fear on every face, *too many, too many.* '*Nine Company to me! Tigre to me!*' He looked at them, and saw Cook was right. Napier was gone, as was Handley and Kite. 'Where is Underhill? And Dickory?'

But Dickory was nowhere to be seen either. Hazzard tried to see past the Turks, *Handley dammit where are you*, seeing Pettifer, De Lisle, Porter, Hesse and Cochrane, Warnock – the *Tigre* men called out, and he saw them as they came running, *Rhys, Lawler, Church*, but not Dickory – or Kite and Underhill. '*Where's the Sarge?*' asked Rhys, '*Where's your Ship's Master?*'

Cook roared out, ''*Miah! Sergeant Underhill!*'

But Hazzard knew they had no time. '*Jory – we're getting them to that chebek, got me?*'

Cook turned. '*We're not leaving 'Miah behind in this bloody place!*'

'They have time to reach us, but we must get these people into these boats and off—'

Cook spun round, angry. '*We can't take 'em all.* We don't have the launch no more cos o'that bloody square.' He hissed at him, 'We can't get the men off if we take all the civvies sir.'

'We're taking them.'

'How! We'd need the damned launch to get the boys out!'

'*I am not going to let bloody Bonaparte win again!*'

'*And who says you can stop him, boy?*' Cook was shaking, his teeth set. '*Who? Look about yer!*'

A round-shot howled overhead and crashed into the harbour waters, spray bursting by the reef, people screaming with fright – but Cook hardly noticed, the marines watching, stock-still. 'God *damn* it to *hell*! *If you think this is all for you and he, then what's that make you? Eh?*'

He stared down at Hazzard, his red sunburned skin scarred and torn, his face stiff with anger. They could hear artillery ranging on the port, rounds whistling, the explosions creeping closer. Hazzard looked across the quays, at them all – the families, their fear, the French troops in the lanes above, the screams.

'Jory, *look* at them! We can't just—'

Cook shook his head, his voice low. 'You can't save 'em all, sir. You never could.'

Delphine put a hand to his shoulder, imploring. 'William,' she said, 'you must get away from here. I will be safe…'

Hazzard looked at her, incredulous. '*Safe? Here?* These men have run *amok*. You have *no* idea what awaits…' He squared up to Cook. 'Then we lead every damn boat in this bloody little harbour out to that chebek – and if anyone tries to scuttle away empty, we bring him bloody back or shoot him dead.'

Cook thought a moment. He nodded. 'Done. One man each boat, five boats, leaves enough for rowin' our own if we can find one.'

'Right. *Reiz! Volunteers!*' shouted Hazzard. 'We'll put one man each in five boats to get them out.'

Reiz nodded. 'Yes, there are abandoned boats! Not all boatmen have come.'

Pettifer stepped forward. 'Sir, behind's at least three empties an' lots o'families with littl'uns.'

'Very well – *go*.' He saw the young lieutenant nearby and shouted, '*Mulazimi!*'

The officer turned. '*Binbashi!*'

'With him, yes? *Evet?*'

The Turk looked at Pettifer who took him by the arm. '*Come on sir, let's get to the doin's of it*—' The big Cornishman pushed through the crowd to the other side of the jetty, and the lieutenant seemed to understand, giving orders to the soldiers, pulling boats in, hauling them over to the dock, loading the families in. Pettifer climbed in one, taking up the oars, Rhys joining him in another, his sing-song Welsh accent cutting over the din, '*Arright now, bach, no need t'be pushin' mind...*'

Warnock and De Lisle came forward, De Lisle shouldering his musket and pack. '*Sarge! We'll take two! C'mon Knocky.*' Warnock stopped in front of Cook.

'If Mick's with 'im, Sarge, he'll get 'im out. Mickey always does.'

Cook nodded. 'Aye...'

More artillery came whistling down, Cook shouting again, despairing, looking round, '*Jeremiah Underhill!*' He looked about, and Hazzard heard him quietly, 'God *damn* ye, 'Miah... God *damn* ye...'

Delphine and Maria began to organise the people into lines for the different boats, Hazzard pulling her back. 'You're coming with us, whatever happens. Stay close.'

'Leave me to this, William. This is what I do.' She called to one man, '*Non non non!* Wait behind there, you, tell him! *Dites-le!*' She looked back at him. 'William, *you cannot* take all these people. *C'est pas possible* – you must get away yourself!'

A howitzer shell tumbled through the air with a howl and burst in the water, sending a dark mountain of spray into the sky, people screaming. Hazzard searched the crowd for any sign of the men, anything. 'Jory! Take over! I'm going to look in the road!'

'Oh no ye damn well don't, *sir*,' shouted Cook. 'Then we lose you too!'

Hazzard ignored him and was about to push his way out when Reiz seized his arm and cried, '*Binbashi! Look!*'

Hazzard turned. Another salvo of howitzer rounds burst on the water, sending towering spouts aloft all around – and through them the launch of HMS *Tigre* came swinging into view, Handley at the tiller, Underhill, Dickory, Napier and Kite heaving on the oars. '*Pull! Dig deep, ye damn' heroes!*'

Handley waved at them. '*Who called fer a cab then?*'

'*Wotcher, 'Andy!*'

'*Get in fer Chrissakes!*'

The boat careened into the quay, the port gunwale banging into the dockside, hands seizing it, taking the lines, Cook cursing under his breath, '*Jere-bloody-miah Underhill, I'll scrag ye for this I will, I ruddy swears it...*'

Underhill laughed, 'Ah Cookie my son, did ye miss me now?'

The launch shuddered, rocking from side to side in the swell. Hazzard called to Cook and Reiz, '*Warnock, De Lisle, Pettifer and Rhys to follow in their boats, and we get as many in the launch with us as we can, and make for that chebek!*'

There were near ten in Warnock's creaking and peeling bright blue and yellow jolly-boat, another nine in Pettifer's, Rhys taking in an elderly man in Hebrew robes, scrolls clutched in his arms, Hazzard calling to them, '*Wait for our lead then follow!*'

Another shell roared overhead and smashed into the rocks fifty yards off. Reiz, Maria and Delphine handed the people down to Cook, who settled them in the launch. Musket-fire crackled within the town, stray shots skimming the waves. Another heavy round rushed overhead, a spout of water bursting from beyond the Andromeda reef – Hazzard guessed they were trying to hit the chebek, but it was just out of range: they wanted to stop the exodus. '*Hurry! Isri ya! Chabuk!*'

Another round rushed past, the townsfolk screaming, all ducking low, Underhill taking a young girl, lifting her down, *come now, me daisy, that's it*, getting her mother in, wreathed in robes and *hijab*, Dickory calling out, '*Twenty's our lot sir!*'

Other small boats were making their way towards the chebek, the captain setting sail, not taking on passengers. '*Jory! We've got to make that ship or by God I'll put holes in her myself!*'

'*Aye aye!*' He bawled down the launch, '*That's twenty-three! We're done!*'

Hazzard took Delphine's hand to help her aboard. 'Come.'

A mother and father looked in the boat, the woman clutching a young child and Delphine said, 'They go first William...'

Hazzard looked in the launch, heavy, overladen, listing to port. 'We can take no more—'

But she put the woman and child into her seat, the father shouting back, waving his arms, '*Hayari, hayari!*' *No*, and disappeared back into the crowd.

Hazzard took her arm, 'Delphine, *please*. Your Doctor Vernond died that you might *live*.'

She stared at him, a hand to her mouth, and choked. '*Oh God...*'

He brought her down into the launch, Maria holding her hand, and Delphine leaned against her, burying her face, Maria staring dead-eyed, exhausted.

Reiz looked down at them. He did not move, his arms tucked behind his back. Hazzard offered his hand to help him into the launch, but the Turk hesitated. '*Binbashi*... Others must go. I am *Nizam-i Djedid*. I shall stay.'

Hazzard looked at him and understood, but would not let him. 'No. I need you now more than ever, *Yuzbashi*. For these people, and to find the heavy guns and save Acre from a similar fate.' A round howled overhead, another geyser of water bursting, spray sheeting over them, people wailing.

Handley called out, '*Sir! Got to get underway...!*'

'But, *Binbashi*—'

'If Acre falls, so falls Constantinople. We must find the guns, *and I cannot do it without you*.' His thrust his hand out to him, waiting.

Reiz met his eye. He took his hand. '*Yes, Binbashi*.' He climbed into the launch and he sat, staring back at the town glowing in the sinking sun, hearing the screams of his people, now abandoned in favour of others. Without the slightest change to his calm and resolute expression, his hand gripped the *kilij* at his waist with such ferocity that it shook.

Hazzard wasted no time. '*Handley, after that bloody ship! Set your braces and haul the topyard sheets!*'

'*Casting off astern!*' Handley shouted, then called, '*Hessy, cast off for'ard!*'

Underhill and Napier pushed the mast into its socket in the midst of the terrified passengers, the children howling as more artillery plunged into the sea around them, one crashing near the jetty, throwing people into the water. They set the swinging boom of the gaff mainyard, the boat rocking low in the water. With no room for oarsmen the marines dived for their short paddles in the scuppers, and began to paddle hard, Cochrane and Napier hauling the topyard high, '*Sail aloft!*'

The paddles dug into the swell hard and fast, the current pulling them forever to starboard and the north. Handley kept the tiller hard over, the chebek unmoving beyond the reef. '*Harder!*' called Hazzard, paddling from the portside. '*Dig, lads! Dig!*'

Behind them Hazzard saw the trailing boats pull away from the jetty, *Warnock, one, Pettifer, two*, then the others emerged, *De Lisle, Rhys*, all of them. In the launch they set up a rhythm, *One… one… one*, the boat rocking, the swell sloshing over each side, their passengers shrinking from it in fear. A blast went up in the town by the waterfront, stone and rooftiles rising into the sky and raining down into the harbour.

The sail drew them southward to the reef and the chebek beyond. '*Easy to larboard, dig and hold to starboard!*' called Handley, hauling the tiller over. The gaff swung against its braces, billowing in the wind, and the launch skidded through the gap in the reef and out of the harbour.

The chebek had still not made full sail, but she had weighed anchor and was pulling into the northerly current. '*Hesse! Tariq! When we draw close enough, chop your way aboard and make the captain heave-to! If he refuses, seize the ship!*'

The Austrian flung up a salute, drawing his fighting knife. '*Jawohl, Herr Major!*'

They passed an overloaded punt, people in the water hanging onto the sides, reaching out in appeal to the marines and the launch, and Handley shouted, '*We'll do it in four lengths, sir! Ready on yer bows!*'

Cook shouted out, '*Load and lock, buck an' ball! An' keep them muzzles out the damn water!*'

The launch heaved up with the deep swell, rising past the reef, and the passengers cried out, Handley steering as if to ram the chebek. Hazzard watched as the ageing broadside of the old trader drew closer and closer, the bows of the launch rising on the swell once again.

'Handley…'

'*Nearly there sir…*'

'*Handley dammit, don't hit the bloody thing!*'

Handley hauled the tiller round hard and shouted, '*Let go your sheets an' braces, douse yer sail!*' Cochrane let go the topyard sheet and the short yard slid down the mast to the mainyard boom with a crash of flying rope. The launch skidded through the water within arm's reach of the chebek's peeling broadside. Reiz cocked his pistol and fired a round in the air, shouting out to the men at the rail in Turkish to heave-to. Knives in both hands, Hesse and Tariq leapt for the chebek's bulging planks.

Using the knives as climbing picks, they clambered up the side like monkeys and jumped over the rail, the figures on deck raising their hands. Kite grabbed a trailing line and began to climb the side. *'Boarding party, follow yer nose!'*

Four of the *Tigre* men jumped after, the launch rocking, the people crying out, lurching for the gunwales. Hesse threw lines over for all, Hazzard reaching for one and pulling himself in. *'Reiz! With me!'* He looked to Delphine, his voice suddenly quiet amid the clamour. 'Keep down, just in case.'

Hazzard pulled himself up, his knees and hips banging into the wooden planks of the hull as he swung, bounced, then climbed, walking the wooden wall to the rail above. He clambered over, nearly falling to the deck.

The marines ranged before them, muskets ready, the crew in a cowed circle on the open deck by the mainmast, wide-eyed, their hands up. A fat grizzled man stepped out, his chin rising arrogantly. *'Kapudan, ha.'*

Reiz crashed to the deck behind Hazzard and staggered forward, his sword out to the captain, in rapid Turkish explaining that he hereby commandeered the vessel in the name of the sultan, and that if the people below were not lifted from the boats, the captain would surely go over the other side, without a boat.

The chebek crew jumped to their tasks, throwing down rope ladders, one of them leading Handley and the launch to their well-worn and meagre boarding steps. They helped the refugees to the deck as the marines passed them up, the four boats behind coming in fast, Pettifer and the others rowing them in and waving to smaller boats to come – and some did, another forty souls at least.

Hazzard moved to the rail as Delphine and Maria climbed the boarding steps, his hand out to her. She met his eye, a memory of Cairo flitting between them. 'Come,' he said, and once again she took his hand.

When all were aboard, Hazzard leaned on the rail, exhausted. He looked out and watched Jaffa being sacked – a small walled port, its children fleeing the wrath of a new pharaoh, but with no pillar of fire to hold him back. This time, he thought, Exodus was a much smaller affair.

He looked across the decks – Reiz gave him a nod, and Hazzard thanked God for him. He saw Delphine in her ragged wet gown, a blanket thrown round her – captured by Mamluks, she had said, the very idea making him ill; she had already begun tending to the refugees. He was proud to know her, but occasionally had to stop himself, stop feeling too much: *she is not Sarah.*

No, he thought, but he felt at least one of his deep wounds beginning to close.

Cook joined him at the rail, and Reiz too, the sting of seawater in their throats. They looked back at the town being torn asunder, by horrors neither had seen anywhere else on earth.

And Acre was next.

Savage

The command tent among the orange groves was silent. The generals stood, listening – sporadic gunfire, screams, *still the endless screams*, thought Bonaparte as he looked out at the walls of Jaffa the following day, columns of smoke rising, drifting down the shore. The sack had lasted all through the night and all through the morning, the dawn lit by flashes of powder and shot, lanterns swinging in the dark on the shattered rooftops and the collapsed tower ruins. There were still sounds of laughing men and screaming women, bottles breaking, and the occasional flight of locals from the broad, corpse-filled breach: a Turkish soldier and his family, running, stumbling through the rubble, a child in his arms, wife holding his hand – and then the shots, arms flung up in shock, and the three fell, soldier, woman and child, amid the laughter of the crack-shots responsible.

'We must… *do* something, general…' murmured Lannes, looking on, furious, impotent.

'It is too dangerous,' murmured Berthier. 'We have lost three officers already, gunned down by their own men. It is a madness, *madness*. It will burn out.'

Bonaparte looked, his eyes wide, staring at his creation. 'Which brigades,' he said. 'I will have them *decimated.*'

Lannes looked at him with an incredulous frown. '*Decimated?*'

Bonaparte turned. '*Yes,*' he shot back at him. 'Every tenth man, *dead*. I will not have this. I will *not.*'

Lannes appealed to him. 'Then let me go. It was I who held open the breach…!'

They watched as a drunken French soldier appeared at the top of the rubble slope, a bottle in hand, swigging from it, then tugged open his buttons and urinated down the hill of debris, the spray spattering on the bodies before him. After waving the bottle about, cheering, he then adjusted his posture to redirect the stream onto one of the figures they had just shot in the back – the dead mother – his comrades laughing and pointing.

'That man,' said Lannes to Berthier, his teeth clenched. 'I want him dead. Today.'

Berthier shrugged. 'Then kill him, Rolo…'

Lannes strode out of the tent area, past the dragoon guards to a squad. '*Ten gold piastres to the man who drops that salaud de merde! Right now!*'

Berthier turned away in a sulk, shrugging his shoulders, his hands up questioning the world, but he had no answer. Moments later came a succession of three shots, the first two sending up clouds of stone and dust in the breach, the third knocking the man backwards, his arms out. He did not move. Bonaparte showed no reaction. Berthier looked at the others, seething, wanting to say something, inarticulate, sniffing angrily.

Jules-Yves Derrien broke the ensuing silence. '*Mon général.*' He held up a watch to show him. 'It has been twenty hours. I believe it subsides.'

Bonaparte raised his eyeglass and looked at the burning town. 'We do not have the time for this…' The town jumped into focus, the high stone buildings in the centre rising like a *donjon*, a Norman keep atop its conical *motte*. He lowered the scope. 'Fetch my adjutants. They will restore order,' he said, the menace clear to all present. 'In my name.'

–

An hour later, the breach seemed quiet. Sappers and labourers of the 22nd and 75th were pulling bodies from the slope of stone rubble, spilled from the broken walls and shell-damaged buildings, many of the dead piled atop each other where they fell. The sentries came to attention when they saw Eugène de Beauharnais and Lt Croisier, their special *aide-de-camp* sashes tied round the left arm, a white flag hanging from the tip of a Mamluk lance. They passed men at the base, and Rambeau's 3-pounder gun, now silent, and climbed a rough path at the side of the hill, a hand reaching down to help the stepson of the *général en chef*. Without a word they made their way into Jaffa.

Everywhere they looked they saw devastation: timber, rock and broken masonry in heaps, buildings collapsed, drunken men staggering about, locals trying to retrieve their dead, one begging a group of soldiers, pointing at a hand under the debris, a protruding leg, the soldiers kicking them away, one soldier striking an old man. Eugène called out, 'Y-you will stop that at once…!'

The soldier looked up and spat, nearly falling over – '*Va t'f – vaa… 't foutre…!*' – and raised his musket at them, but one of the sentries of the 75th stepped up and fired a shot. It smacked into the building behind the man, who waved his bottle at them and ran, his comrades following. The sentry, a corporal in a dark green tunic, looked at Eugène. 'It is bad, *Cap'taine*. I will accompany you.'

Eugène swallowed. 'Y-yes, thank you…'

They made their way uphill to the greatest concentration of troops, crowds of them, some pushing to get a better view of something, but Croisier and Eugène could not tell what – NCOs were raging at each other, shouting up at windows high above. A sergeant saw them. '*Capitaine*,' he said, nodding at the buildings brusquely. 'Some *quartier* of theirs. We call it the citadel. They are barricaded in.' Many turned, saw them, and fell quiet, moving aside. Eugène surveyed the scene, appalled.

The tall gates torn away, the heavy iron-studded doors had been bolted shut, the quad approaching the building littered with dead, mostly Turkish and civilian, a few French among them. With no field-gun to hand, a squad of frustrated French were thumping a heavy beam repetitively against the door, reminiscent of some medieval siege. Eugène moved forward but Croisier stopped him. 'What now…?'

Eugène Bonaparte looked about. 'I – I could not say…'

There was a cry from above in rough French, '*We shall shoot!*'

The battering of the door stopped. All eyes looked, a sergeant giving firing orders, '*Make ready! Second storey third window! Protect the captain!*' But Eugène put out a hand. 'No, no, wait!'

He watched the rifleman at the window. He moved away, the long miquelet musket withdrawn, and an older man appeared at the open shutters instead, a dark face, a deep, curving white moustache – a senior officer. He looked down.

Eugène stepped forward and held aloft the spear and its white flag. '*Luc*,' he said to Croisier. '*Come to attention.*'

They put their heels together and saluted. The old Turkish colonel bowed his head and saluted in response. After a moment he called down. He gestured to his arm, indicating the sashes Eugène and Croisier wore. 'You are senior officers *parlementaires, aides de camp*,' he called down in French, his deeply accented voice rolling across the quad. 'If you can assure us that we shall not suffer the massacre inflicted upon the town, we shall lay down our arms. If not, we shall fire upon you – and defend ourselves to the last extremity.'

Eugène swallowed, and glanced at the troops around, ready to respond.

The colonel called down, 'Have you then terms of surrender?'

Eugène Bonaparte's face flushed red, and he replied, 'Yes…!' He glanced uncertainly at Croisier. 'They are as before…!' he said. 'That is, I – yes, we do wish, *mon colonel*, to accept your honourable surrender.'

The old face looked down at them sadly. He closed his eyes and nodded.

—

In his tent, Bonaparte looked at his cot, his chair, his unlit lantern, the canvas glowing with the haze of the grey sky without. The folding table in the centre of the room lay covered in maps of Syria, Iraq, the Arabian Peninsula. Berthier and Murat stood with him, looking down at the charts, Bourrienne on the other side, Derrien in the shadows, watching. Bonaparte murmured, 'Plague… now rape and pillage…' he closed his eyes. 'Because of *Djezzar* and his army.'

'Yes, General,' said Berthier.

He waved a hand at the table, his empire. 'We came to Egypt, friends of the sultan, *friends*, and now look. *See* what he has done. *Torn us asunder.*'

'Yes General.'

'You *cannot* threaten Egypt without consequence,' insisted Bonaparte.

'No General.'

'*And we are Egypt.*' He stared down, his anger cold and bitter. 'We would become the new East, the new empire, our men wearing the turban, my *Sacred Battalions*, an army of Immortals, leading Arabs, Armenians, Albanians, Kurds, Jews.' He looked round quickly, his eyes bright, his rage and indignation burning. 'Have I not made laws in Egypt to protect the Jews? The Copts? To protect the *women*?'

They nodded. 'You have, General.'

'*Then they do this!* They *resist* and oblige me to become the destroyer! Why should I be enemy to any of them?'

They heard a distant cheer. They looked round, Berthier moving to the tent entrance. Soon the army all around took it up, cheering, some shouting, *hwa hwa hwa!* Major Detroye threw back the flap and looked in.

'General. We… we have now secured Jaffa.' He looked about at them, uncertain, then ducked out of the tent again, his eyes not settling, distracted. 'You shall see…'

They emerged to find the men in the tent lines raising their arms, cheering, the troops in the breach cheering, muskets held high, as the very young Captain Eugène de Beauharnais Bonaparte and Lt Croisier marched out of the south gate, their white flag of truce over their heads. Behind them came a ragged column of over four thousand exhausted Ottoman soldiers.

Bourrienne beside him, Bonaparte stared, his eyes widening, a shaking hand rising to his face, aghast. '*Mon dieu…*' he gasped, '*what have they done…*'

Berthier was excited, proud. 'He has done it! He has taken the citadel! With nothing but a white flag!'

Derrien listened to the others as the generals shook hands, congratulating themselves – he sidled up to Bonaparte, who had gone pale. Derrien murmured, 'They do not yet understand, *mon général.*'

Bonaparte watched them march across the wasteground towards the citrus groves, for the first time visibly shaken. 'What do they expect me to do…?' After a moment he turned to Derrien. 'Would this be the whole complement remaining in Jaffa?'

'Yes, Citizen General. Mostly Albanian, they say.'

Bonaparte continued to watch. They all stood in uncomfortable silence. Eventually he returned slowly to his table and his charts, alone, looking again at the names: *Baghdad, Babylon, Damascus, Jerusalem, the Dead Sea.* 'Everywhere, in this ancient place…' he murmured, 'is someone's homeland. Yet *everyone* is the invader.'

They watched him, the troops cheering beyond.

'An encampment,' suggested Derrien quietly. 'On the beaches, for now, *mon général.*'

Bonaparte continued to stare into nothing, his voice barely audible. 'When the battering-ram touches the gates…'

Derrien waited, patient.

Bonaparte cleared his throat. 'Stores?'

'None but for us, General, and the march to Acre, and return to Cairo.'

Bourrienne interrupted. 'The town will have stores. The commissary is presently trying to—'

'None but for us, Citizen Bourrienne,' corrected Derrien.

Bonaparte looked at Bourrienne. 'Water.'

Derrien answered. 'None but for us.'

Bonaparte cursed quietly. '*Ma foi...*'

Derrien waited. Bonaparte still looked at the maps.

'Mamluk units in the area.'

Derrien nodded. 'There are some, deeper inland, General, raiding the baggage train on occasion, Bedouin as well. And they would welcome the prisoners, take them to Djezzar at Acre, or down to Damascus to curry favour with the vizier. Or continue to harry us from all sides...' He let it fall. 'We would not reach Acre without further fighting.'

Bourrienne looked on. 'What are you saying then,' he asked, 'for it seems—'

'God, *God!*' swore Bonaparte, his whitening knuckles at his lip. '*Damn the boy.* Why, in the devil's name, have they served me thus...'

Lannes burst in. 'What is this? It is incredible! How did he do it?' His excitement ebbed upon seeing Bonaparte's face. 'But...?'

Berthier slapped him on the back. 'Now we lock 'em up and throw away the key! Ha! Lock 'em up in their own damned town...!'

Lannes looked at him as if he were a fool. 'Who, Berthi? Who locks them up?'

General Miot entered behind Lannes. 'What is this? Now we need to send them back to the damned citadel, and put a damned guard on it—'

Berthier looked to Bonaparte. 'Well... we could...'

There was silence.

Derrien looked at Bonaparte and leaned closer. 'It would be a bold stroke, *mon général.*'

Bonaparte kept staring past them, out at the column of men, in his own world.

'What would be a bold stroke?' demanded Miot. 'What is bolder than taking the wretched little port with a limp handkerchief on a pole?'

Derrien corrected him. 'We still have a campaign in hand, General Miot.'

'Have we now? My my, thank you for reminding me.' Miot stared back at him, the blood on his uniform evident to all.

Derrien's eyes glittered. 'Indeed. To take Acre, and threaten Constantinople.'

Miot looked at the both of them, then at Bourrienne. 'What are you asking, then?'

None spoke. Derrien bowed his head again at Bonaparte. 'An encampment, on the seashore, General. Where they may be... assessed.'

Bonaparte was still as stone. Then he nodded, a decision taken. 'Separate them. Artillerymen to be kept back. Egyptians to be... to be sent to the rearguard and back to the border.' Eugène Bonaparte and Croisier hurried past the tent, organising a contingent of infantry to escort the prisoners. 'Separate all those who were captured and released from El-'Arish *en parole*...' he said. 'They must be punished. And any Moroccans and North Africans... to be kept from our own Berber mercenaries.' Bonaparte looked down at his map table. 'And gather all other Ottomans.' He leaned on the table, staring down.

Derrien bowed his head. 'It would be a bold stroke.'

Miot saw Bonaparte's bone-white expression. After a moment, only he seemed to understand. 'No, no you cannot.' He looked to Bourrienne. 'Louis, for the sake of God would you—'

'*Enough*,' snapped Bonaparte. '*Enough*...' He stared down at his maps of glory, his triumphal march across Alexander's empire now become brutal, savage conquest, not liberation, not bringing hope, bringing only destruction.

Sic transit gloria.

'*Then let them fear me...*'

Bourrienne watched him. Miot could hardly keep his tongue, but Lannes held up a hand to him: *wait*.

Bonaparte's voice was hoarse. 'Let Djezzar in Acre see what will happen if he resists us.'

Derrien's urges grew in intensity. 'Let them *fear*, General.'

The generals watched him. Napoléon Bonaparte straightened from the table, hands behind his back, and turned to Derrien. 'See to the... segregation. Efficiently.'

Derrien bowed. 'It shall be done.'

He pushed past the generals at the tent entrance, Miot shouting behind him as he went, '*I will not, I will not*,' Lannes and others vaguely aware of what was to come.

—

Caron and the Alphas sat on the grassy tussocks overlooking the sandhills to the harbour walls and the wintry sea, its grey depths crashing in bright bursts against the reef where dwelt unspeakable demons, enough to swallow the souls of kingdoms, and conjure Perseus on winged Pegasus from the skies. Cloud had gathered on the horizon, distant yet threatening, the sun flashing down at intervals, but giving little warmth. A company of a line-demi filed onto the beach. And another.

There followed a ragged group of dark-skinned men, shoved along by French infantry. Puzzled, Caron looked far to their right and saw another company, with another large group of men.

'It's a whole battalion,' he mumbled. 'The 25th?'

Rossy looked out, frowning. 'No, it's the 14th.'

St Michel looked through his telescopic rifle sight. 'Are they Berbers?'

Caron shook his head. 'Berbers, yes... Moroccans...'

They were in ragged baggy trousers, dark shirts, no obvious uniform that Caron could discern, some wearing a long-tailed fez, others in tight, dark turbans. They were pushed towards the water's edge, some moving into the surf to wash their feet, splashing, then stopping, watching their infantry escort move off at the double. The two companies before them formed four ranks either side in a splayed L, a sergeant getting them neatly in line.

Caron watched as the front rank knelt, the second standing in open order, the third and fourth adjusting their position, the sergeants calling out, *hurry it up!* And soon the two companies stood still – facing the Moroccans at the shoreline. Some of them turned, realising, and began to run. Caron stopped chewing, his mouthful of bread turning to paste, his throat closing, his voice a rough whisper. '*Putain alors...*'

They were company-strength firing-squads in four rows, each twenty-five men across.

Armes...! En joue!

The front rank presented.

Feu!

The front rank of the two companies fired, great plumes of grey smoke bursting out, the first forty or fifty men at the shoreline flung back into the sea, into their comrades.

En joue!

The second rank presented. Rossy stared. '*Chef*...'

Caron was on his feet. '*Non non non*...'

Feu!

Another fifty of the Moroccan prisoners were thrown to the ground, the heavy .65 calibre musket-balls crashing through their thin clothes, bone splintering, blood spraying as they flew off their feet.

En joue!

Feu!

Some ran up the beach, cut down by more shots, others diving into the sea, swimming out to the rocks, each one picked off by a good shot, all the while the ranks firing with mechanic regularity.

En joue!

Feu!

Dissonant commands echoed along the beach against the walls of Jaffa as the other company further to their right did the same, their victims running into the water, the French firing in disciplined volleys, the Alphas watching as some five hundred men were shot to pieces, the muskets roaring again and again, *En joue! Feu!*

Pigalle stared, his breathing growing heavier by the moment. 'What *is* this, *Chef*... I like it *not*—'

'They surrendered,' said St Michel. 'They laid down their arms...'

Caron climbed unsteadily to his feet and staggered down the slope to the beach, the others following. '*Who is in command!*'

An officer standing behind the four-tiered firing-squad whirled about, his hand reaching for a sword. Caron did not recognise him. 'Keep out of this *Sergent-chef!* Back to your post! Who are you to demand anything of me!'

The Alphas raised their muskets and the major froze to the spot, Caron raging back at him, 'You will answer to the *Chef-major* of the 75th Invincibles, you *dog.*'

'*How dare you!*' He drew his sword, but the Alphas cocked their locks as one, the muskets levelled. Still the executioners fired.

En joue!

Feu!

Another officer came running. '*Chef de bataillon!* We have two hundred left and there are concerns for powder supp—' He stopped short when he saw Caron and the Alphas.

The major did not take his eyes off Caron. '*Bayonets.*'

The captain looked from him to Caron. He saluted. 'By your command...'

'*Mon capitaine!*' called Caron. 'If you refuse this order, it shall be noted in your favour!'

The captain stopped, looking back, fearful. 'I... I *cannot*...' He ran off.

Caron watched the captain go, the Moroccans swimming now, some reaching the rocks, trying to get away. The firing squads broke up, men taking independent aim, trying to hit each one off the rocks, their falling targets obliterated by the bursting spray. Some men took a small boat out, shooting the swimmers down as they met them, or bayoneting them in the back as they passed. A brief silence fell on the beach, and a call went up, '*All!*'

The major still faced Caron. 'Captain! The next group!'

Caron watched as another herd of men was pushed and jostled to the surf, now red with blood and stiff with corpses. Seeing the bodies, they tried to flee. The company ranks broke up, some still firing, others charging them with bayonets, plunging into them, kicking their dying bodies aside for the next victim, bare hands trying to stop the bayonets, snatching at them, but yielding to another rammed into their bellies. The major stared at Caron as his men moved on, butchering.

'*Who are you...?*' shouted Caron above the blasts of musketry and screams of the dying.

'*This is an order from the Quartier! I am obeying the général en chef!*'

Caron gazed at him for some while, then without a flicker of expression drew his pistol and shot him. The major fell onto his knees, a bright red patch on the white facings of his uniform, his eyes wide, and collapsed. Rossy stepped in front of Caron, angry, '*Chef. What* do we do now, *hm*?'

But Caron went around him and moved down the beach, passing the executioners, a dull look in his eye, until he found the captain. When the captain saw him, he cried out in fear and raised a protective arm, then ran from the scene. Some of the soldiers saw this and turned to look at Caron. When they saw him, they backed away and returned to the matter at hand. Many of the victims were swimming again, some dragging the wounded along the shore, the French walking slowly behind them, pausing, stabbing down into their exposed backs.

Rossy chased after Caron, taking his arm, Pigalle with him, and they hurried the old sergeant off the beach. 'He has *gone home*, Pig. I tell you, he is not here anymore, but *gone!*'

A soldier ran at them, mistaking them for the condemned, hesitated, recognising their motley uniforms, and stopped – but Pigalle smashed a fist into his sternum, lifting the man off his feet and throwing him five yards into the air, where he landed among the dead Moroccans. On the next stretch of sand the soldiers were finishing off their second group, bodies heaped on all sides, picking their way through, bayonetting the writhing wounded, kicking the bodies over to check, moving on. Others being herded to the beach saw what awaited them and began to run, only to be trampled by cavalry. Horses stampeded up and down the shoreline three abreast, crushing them, the cavalrymen slashing downward with their sabres in broad sweeping strokes.

Caron stared, Rossy and the others standing with him, watching, open-mouthed. 'What... has *happened*?'

On the crest of the rise just above them to their right, stood a group of staff officers, hands behind their backs, one pointing into the distance, commenting, an army captain running up to them. Caron heard their words, '...*orders that no further powder be expended. Bayonets alone.*'

The captain saluted, a frenzied smiling expression on his face, and ran to the shore to the edge of the slaughter. Caron recognised him. It was Andret, from the massacre at El-'Arish. Caron strode forward. '*You! Butcher! Murderer!*'

Andret jerked to a halt, saw Caron, and shouted to several nearby infantrymen. Four turned and ran at Caron, bayonets held out, the staff officers calling out, '*Halt, halt I say! Stop this!*'

Rossy and St Michel dropped the first two with shots from the hip, and as the following pair stumbled over their bodies the enraged Pigalle waded into them, knocked one bayonet aside with a swat of his left hand and seized the other by the back of the neck, forcing his face upward as he dug in his large fingers and snatched hold of the man's windpipe, and pulled it from his throat. There was a loud crack of snapping cartilage and the soldier screamed, the tongue jutting upwards with a fountain of blood. Andret stared in wide-eyed horror.

Pigalle dropped the hideous corpse and advanced on him. Andret waved his pistol and fired, the round smacking into Pigalle's shoulder harness, but the big man kept coming. Andret laughed and ran. '*Caron! I know this is you!*' his voice now a hysterical cackle. '*I know it is! I know!*' He ran for his life, down to the slaughter on the beach.

Pigalle moved away, Caron mounting the rise to the tent and the officers. 'Who ordered this!' he demanded. He recognised one of them. '*Chef de bataillon* Detroye! What is the meaning of this!'

Detroye would not meet his eyes, staring away into personal horrors of his own. '*Chef* Caron... it is fr-from the *Quartier*, from the *général en chef*. He...' Detroye paused, swallowing. 'He tries to safeguard us...' He looked down at a sheet of paper rattling in his hands, his notes. He read the date, 'Year 7, today, the 18th of *Ventôse*...' he said, reading, his words forming with difficulty. 'There were shot... more than...' his pencil scribbled with a tremulous hand, his voice a mere whisper, '...*eight hundred* Turks...'

'Today?' demanded Caron, 'What then of tomorrow? *Still more?*'

Detroye nodded, his whole body trembling, and he put a hand up to the brim of his cocked hat, which fell as he wiped his forehead. 'Th-the same... yes... The 19th *Ventôse*... there will be shot...' He met Caron's eye. 'We have lost our honour, *Chef*...'

'*Mon dieu*,' said Caron, thinking of Reynier, of El-'Arish. 'No. We have lost our souls.'

Caron looked down at himself as if seeing for the first time – his tunic, the spent pistol in his hand, the sword-bayonet on his belt. He drew his second pistol and moved off, the others following. Rossy said nothing, their task now to protect Caron from himself.

They saw further bodies, some children, boys, clutching at their dead fathers – each run through, a man with bloody eye sockets, his death writ on his face, his son of ten lying across him, his back gouged open. Rossy crossed himself. '*Sacre putains de la merde...*'

Caron pushed through the French soldiers, their eyes downcast, murmuring, the Alphas shoving them away, someone jostled losing his temper, '*Eh, putains!*' and Pigalle turned, his neck and chin still slick with a man's blood, a sergeant striding over, swearing, then seeing Pigalle, and backing away. They walked straight through more waiting Turks – none looked up, none with the fight left to break out. They passed through dead men like dead men themselves, Caron with purpose.

At a tent among the orange groves was a small group of protesting Turkish grandees and French junior officers, some standing, staring, appalled by the distant scenes – and the swelling figure of Abdullah Aga, collapsed at the feet of Napoléon Bonaparte. Bonaparte spoke to one of the generals, another civilian officer moving away, Bonaparte turning smartly, disappearing inside the tent.

Caron recognised Berthier, Bon, Miot, Monge, and Berthollet – and Peyrusse, a clerk assistant to the paymaster, shocked, staggering away around the side of the tent, leaning over to retch, vomiting; and finally the face he had expected to see at such a place – Citizen *Croquemort* himself.

'Of course,' he murmured. '*Le diable.*'

Derrien looked down upon Abdullah Aga as the prostrate governor held his clasped hands up to them all in gratitude. Caron trudged onward.

'*Chef*,' demanded Rossy, 'what do you do now, hm? *Hm?* You go shoot the *général en chef*, eh? *Eh?* If so, I will help yes, he could do with a bullet as much as any, but our boys, what do we do afterwards, when—'

Caron's voice had a dead tone to it, suitable to the occasion. 'This is not for you, *mon garçon*, not for you… keep away from them all, these men of honour.'

Rossy tried to stop him. '*Chef*… *non non non, Chef! C'est moi, hein?* Me, Gaston Rossy, your boy, you take me from the Vendée to the Rhine to the Adige, to the *pyramids*, eh? You show me the *world* and keep me *alive!*'

But Caron moved on, an automaton. Rossy stopped, distraught, his voice breaking. '*Chef! Do not go…!*' He sank to the ground, his hands over his head, shuddering with sobs, weeping, '*Papi… Grand-père…!*'

But Caron walked on, checking the priming pan of his pistol as if he had not heard, leaving Rossy crouched, his head bowed, covering himself with his arms, shaking.

Pigalle stood over him. '*Come,*' said the big man.

Rossy looked up at him, imploring, '*Tell him Pig!* He is our *papi*, and he throws his life for *this*? They are just dead Turks! Dead Egyptians! Dead Italians and dead Austrians all *dead dead dead!* What difference does it make?' His face collapsed again, and Pigalle lifted him, an arm round his shoulder, and held him.

'I am Pigalle. And where I plant my boot,' he said, his deep voice a rumble from within a mountain, 'there shall I not be moved.'

Caron headed mindlessly into the orange groves, pistol in hand, through the tent-lines, citrus and orange trees everywhere, branches brushing at him, blossom falling. As he progressed, he heard the firing-squads resume, their massed reports and subsequent cries fading the further he went, the closer he drew to Bonaparte's tent.

The green leaves of the trees parted, and he saw it – the *Quartier*, the command tent, his destination for what he did not yet know, and he heard Bonaparte talking, his clipped tones sharp on the air, angered, with someone, with everyone. Caron ignored the guard who recognised him and tried to stop him, '*Chef? Défense d'entrer, eh, no entry Chef, a conference, oui,*' but still Caron continued round the corner, round the back, through the trees, and stopped on the other side. Before him, in the ambient glow of the bleached canvas in the shade of the trees, he found the *Croquemort*, Citizen Derrien, confronted by a shocked Citizen Peyrusse.

'I have *checked*,' hissed Peyrusse, on the verge of tears, his thin curling hair wild, his clerk's coat torn, dusty, his shirt collar bent and soiled. 'The commissary has taken *four hundred thousand* rations of food from Jaffa! Four hundred *thousand*. There is more than enough for all of these men! We can, we can… *guard* them, or send them away, or—'

'You will lower your voice, Citizen.'

Derrien's deputy, Citizen Blais, looked on, ready, watching Peyrusse. The paymaster clerk raised a shaking hand to his spectacles and removed them from his reddened peeling face. '*Please, I beg of you*. We can feed them all! What was the Revolution *for*, Citizen, if not to feed *all* men – the downtrodden, the forgotten?'

'That is not your concern, Citizen…'

'It is! It is all our concern!' He looked about, stumbling away from Derrien and moving past him, Blais stepping in front of him. 'I… I… the general must be told. I shall tell him, and he shall *stop* this!'

Caron watched Derrien, and the *Croquemort's* reptilian gaze flicked up over Peyrusse's shoulder and saw him, fixing him with his basilisk stare. 'The general,' said Derrien carefully and quietly, not taking his eye off Caron, '*already knows*.'

Peyrusse froze. '*Non*… I cannot believe it…' He backed away, dropping his loose notes and papers into the grass, in the cool shade of the orange groves and citrus, the scent of blossom all about. '*Mon dieu*… we are being led by monsters… *monsters*…'

He staggered away, Caron watching him. The volley-fire of the firing-squads was now a muffled crack, followed by dissonant pops. But Caron could hear them.

'*Sergent-chef-major,*' said Derrien. 'You appear regularly at inconvenient moments.'

'It is you,' said Caron, realising. 'All of this... this... this dishonour, this treachery... it bears your mark. You whisper into his ear,' he said with wonder, 'like the serpent, a demon...'

Another set of volleys erupted, the popping sound nearly taken by the wind, carried safely out to sea. Only now did Caron remember his reaction to seeing the walls of Jaffa that first day, his fears for a terrible doom to fall upon them all – and lo, he thought, it had.

Derrien stared back. 'You flatter me.'

'You whisper, and he damns his soldiers to commit murder... on unarmed men. On *children.*'

'The aides did not have the authority or seniority to accept the surrender of the garrison, and as such the enemy was seen advancing upon our lines.'

'The aides would not have gone without his command,' said Caron, his voice hollow, echoing into an empty chasm, unheard, unheeded. 'His own son.'

Derrien took a slow breath. 'How many men, *Chef-major*, to guard three thousand?' He waited, raised an eyebrow. 'One man per ten? One per five? Two? Do we lose fifteen hundred or two thousand men to guard prisoners we cannot feed? What if they escape, an uprising, what then? Our men massacred, an enemy at our rear?' Leaning on his stick, he moved closer, as if to tempt him into his logic. 'And what of Acre? When Al-Djezzar Pasha sees what is done here, might he not yield? Whom should he fear most, the Ottomans? Or the dread Sultan *al-Kebir*, conqueror of Egypt, sacker of cities, who yet spares the life of Governor Abdullah Aga through his bountiful mercy? How many lives might then we save? *Tens* of thousands?'

'You proposed murder. He did not,' said Caron, hearing even this declaration fading, unheard, pointless.

Derrien shifted on the walking-stick, his face falling into deeper shadow from the orange trees, Blais one pace behind. 'I did no such thing, *Sergent-chef.*' He tilted his head quizzically. 'I merely agreed. As did the generals. It was, they shall say, a regrettable group decision.' He reflected a moment. 'True governance,' he explained, 'is the application of undetectable responsibility.' He frowned, the devil's advocate. 'Whose decision was it? Bonaparte's? No. Mine? No. The generals? No.' He nodded. 'It is my *duty*, you see. To protect the Republic.'

Caron watched him. 'Liar.'

Derrien's eyes twinkled bright in the shadows of the orange leaves, dappled patterns on his broad hat, his dark coat. 'Never a liar, *Chef*. Always the truth. For that is all that is ever recorded by posterity. Someone's truth.'

Caron felt the life-blood drain from him, drawn from his soul by the spectre before him. With his left hand he reached for the small, tarnished epaulette on his right shoulder, and tugged at it, then tore it free, its stitches ripping. 'I am Achille Mérové Caron—' He reached for the other and tore it off as well, a brass button clinking to the ground, the cloth ripping, 'of the 75th Invincibles, veteran of thirty years—' he yanked his *sergent-chef* sash from his chest, throwing it to the earth, 'and endless battle.' He stopped, looking down at himself. 'And I have never seen truth.'

Derrien made a sweeping gesture with his walking-stick of fine bleached sycamore. 'And so here you have, at last, today.'

With a sudden numb indifference, Caron raised his pistol and nearly reached the point of aim, before Blais raised his own much faster, and shot him.

As Caron fell, by the hands of evil men, among the orange groves of ancient Jaffa in the land of Canaan, memories played through his dimming mind from vast fields of war, when he had gathered up the colours, and gathered up the men, and walked them through the shellfire, Prussians or Austrians or Spaniards trying to kill them, but failing, *Yes, that had been a good day.* And he wanted to say goodbye to his boys, and thought, *adieu, mes enfants, adieu.*

Lightning

Hazzard picked his way slowly through the large forward hold of the chebek, the glow of his shuttered lantern lighting the posts, beams and bulwarks before him, the creaking of the hull an eerie hypnotic lullaby. He moved past the sleeping refugees, some humped in bedrolls on bunks either side, others laid out in rows on the decks, and ducked past the occasional hammock swinging to the gentle rhythm of the sea. The people of Jaffa slept, though fitfully in their dreaming fears – a child crying, now comforted by strangers, the family gone, a new one in its stead, be they Muslim or Jew, Turk, Armenian, Christian or Druze.

Cook, Underhill and Dickory had taken turns throughout the nights, two of them asleep, the other moving about on deck above. The marines had dotted themselves amongst the group at intervals. Tariq lay half-awake, a small family gathered around him. Hazzard saw Napier asleep, two small shapes tucked into the crook of each of the boxer's enormous arms. One of them sniffed and shifted, disturbed, and he woke at once, his thick fingers smoothing the hair from the face, his voice soft, *Here, mate, s'awright, eh? All goin' to be bully, in a lovely little boat on the big briny, eh…?* and Hazzard thanked God for kind hearts.

The smells of the chebek proved the captain to be a trader and sometime smuggler, the aromas of tobacco, wine and spices soaked into the wood of the ship. He had been trying to escape detection at Jaffa, but had been unable to weigh anchor owing to a broken cog in the capstan, his men having to haul it up manually, just as Hazzard and the boats had reached him. His valuable black-market stores had been thrown overboard to make room for the refugees – a chit for gold from Reiz and the promise of praise from the Sublime Porte proved more than sufficient compensation. He was now their most steadfast ally, and a proud soldier of the sultan, sailing to Cyprus with their precious cargo of frightened and bewildered humanity.

Hazzard heard movement up ahead and made his way through to the aft cabins, small storerooms and two chambers for the captain and his First Mate, each filled now with the most injured, two of them pregnant mothers to be. Delphine emerged from one of the cabins, wiping her hands on a cloth hanging from her stained apron, and saw him. He lowered his lamp.

'*Ça va?*' he asked in a low murmur. 'All well?'

She nodded. 'Maria and I, we have made them comfortable. Your men,' she said, looking out at the decks, 'have done the rest.'

'I doubt that.'

She shook her head. 'No, it is true. They make them feel safe. It is important with the injured...'

He watched her. 'You have a special touch for this.'

She looked at him, then down and away, as if ashamed of something 'Some of the times, yes.'

'When do you sleep?'

She looked at him. 'When you do.'

He nodded, *touché indeed*. 'I sleep when I know all is well. Or someone tells me it is...'

'And how often is that?'

He smiled. She did not look away. 'How do you...?' She was confused. 'How is it that you find me, at... at that awful battle on the Nile, and... and then Cairo... and now *here*? I cannot understand.'

He shook his head. 'It is only good fortune, no more.'

'No, it is... it *must* be more...' She almost wept, her voice plaintive. 'But why good fortune for me, when others *suffer* so... how—' But she could not form the words. She wiped her eyes.

'You are exhausted,' he said. 'You must sleep, Delphine, *je vous en prie.*'

'*Oh, mon dieu, Guillaume...*' She threw up her hands, her eyes closing, a hand to her forehead, ignoring the advice, finding solace in activity. 'Did you know we had two other ships behind us? With more of the people?'

He nodded. 'Yes... they followed us, thank heaven.'

'They followed *you*.' She came close to him, reaching forward, pulling his tunic together, that he might not be cold, and he thought of Emma Hamilton again, her hand on his waistcoat, in Naples, in another world. The chebek rocked gently from side to side, the bare feet of the Mid Watch above thumping lightly overhead, unhurried, trimming sail as the wind shifted, then back again. 'You are a shepherd,' she said distantly, 'is this what you do...'

Hazzard looked at her, the circles under her eyes, a beauty, but worn out, tending to every person before herself. And without warning she began to weep and leaned against him, and all he could do was hold her, her shoulders shuddering beneath his embrace. *God, what she must have endured, all of them...*

She reached up for him and he knew she was not Sarah, not at all, but Delphine, the nursing angel with dark hair and pale skin – tired, driven, who would give her food to the sick, who now gave her mouth to his. Her tears were hot on her cheeks, and he held her, her softness, not thinking anything, only feeling, regretting, hoping.

—

Heavy boots clumped on the forward ladder, voices hissing in the gloom of pre-dawn. There was a light, rapid knock on the small cabin door. Cook stuck his head in and saw Hazzard, awake, one hand on his swaying hammock, the other pulling on a boot. 'Best come see this sir.' He glanced at the sleeping shape in the cot beside him on the floor, the blanket, the tousled hair and bare shoulder of Delphine Lascelles. He said nothing and waited outside.

Feeling the chill, Hazzard threw his *binish* over his Bombay scarlet and the buckled scimitar and followed him out. 'She slept on the floor,' he said.

Cook gave him a look as they ascended the steps to the main deck. 'Did I say owt?'

As he emerged into the cold grey air he found the ship wreathed in fog. The taut stays and ratlines above vanished into a thick grey cloud, the foremast tops invisible, then clearing, then vanishing again, a strange cloying heat that yet left a chill on the skin.

He saw Cook climbing the steps to the port bows, one of the marines, Rhys the Welshman, coming to attention and giving a nod as he passed, the old sergeant bidding him hurry. The handrail, shrouds and stays dripped with the clammy touch of the mist. The portly Turkish captain, Kourosh, stood waiting for them, a hand clutching at his unshaven jowls as he looked out fearfully, the source of his concern standing quietly off the port bow. Without a word they joined him, and Cook pointed.

Not thirty yards away was a ship. It was a tartane, a Levantine trader, or rigged as one, and what appeared to be only two small-bore guns, possibly 8- or even 6-pounders, mounted on the starboard side of the main deck. She had two masts leaning astern, with long, sloping lateen yards, the limp sails hanging dead in the heavy, thick air, the loose canvas flapping in the hopes of a breeze. They could hear its lines creaking, the murmur of the deckhands talking – Hazzard could even smell their coffee.

Cook put a finger to his lips, then pointed off the starboard bow. Hazzard looked. Another shadow loomed: a second ship, rigged as a ketch, the fog so thick it enveloped them in a muffled silence broken only by the occasional whisper of air, carrying the sounds of their new travelling companions.

Silently, Cook stepped back to the chebek's foremast and pointed up, mimed a lookout with an eyeglass, then pointed dead ahead. Hazzard peered ahead but could see nothing but a grey miasma. He stared hard into the fog, his eyes uncertain of what to seek, until it became all too clear – leaping into view between the two smaller ships, came the stern of what looked like a brig or sloop of war, a towering gaff sail vanishing into the mist. A bell clanged and they heard voices – speaking French.

The fog parted momentarily. On the stern of the sloop a French tricolour hung limp in the dead air, and beneath the taffrail was a name painted with a golden flourish: *Foudre.*

Lightning.

It was Bonaparte's flotilla of heavy guns.

Captain Kourosh had simply let the northerly current pull the chebek into the usual sea-lanes to Cyprus and Acre, the most direct route. The flotilla had clearly done likewise. Hazzard glanced at Cook, the mist playing at the rail behind him, the stays blurring in the fine rain fluttering about them. The sergeant came closer. '*Reckon we found 'em.*'

Hazzard looked up at their own spread of sail. In the swirling mist he could see that they had doused the mainsails of the three masts, only staysails and small headsails aloft, Captain Kourosh hoping to catch a breath of wind when it came.

Reiz emerged from the mist on the main deck as they descended the steps with the captain. 'You have seen?' he asked, a curious tension about him. It was anger. 'We attack now?'

Hazzard sensed his thirst for vengeance – for Jaffa. 'Ask the captain to douse all sail and drop back,' whispered Hazzard. 'If any of those ships see us and open fire, we will have led these people to slaughter.'

Reiz agreed. 'Quite so.' He took the captain aside and the fat man nodded, a nervous hand scratching at his stubble, nodding, *Evet, evet, yes, yes*, anything to keep away from the French. He whispered his commands to his First Mate, and his nimble hands leapt to the rigging silently, releasing the stays, reefing the sails with the deft efficiency of the practised smuggler. Reiz returned to them, waiting. 'Yes, he does it now.'

'Boats?' asked Cook.

Hazzard calculated. 'We have the launch and the four jolly-boats.' They had strung them out on a line astern, finding no room on deck for them.

'Just the jollies then,' said Cook. 'Three. Easier.'

'Yes, the launch is too big,' agreed Hazzard. 'Five men per boat. Remainder to stay behind and guard the chebek.'

'Awright...' Cook thought it out. 'One boat to portside, to charge the decks and rigging... two boats to starboard – one to the stern, to take the helm an' go below to the officers' cabins, and t'other to the bows to get any's in the fo'c'sle. Aye.'

They looked out at the ships, and Reiz put the question. 'Which first?'

'Aye...' said Cook, considering. 'That big bugger?'

Hazzard looked out at the *Foudre*. 'Then threaten the others with her guns.'

'Where shall I go?' asked Reiz.

Hazzard looked at him, the intensity of the young man's gaze speaking volumes. 'We have done this before, Reiz, and I would prefer to know a good man is here to protect the passengers, and give orders to the captain. Will you do that?'

Reiz's face fell, and he took a heavy breath. 'Very well, Hazar Pasha.'

They looked round. The fog was thinning, but with their reefed sail the French ships had drawn further away, now dark smudges in the mist. The wind might soon pick up. He looked at Cook. 'To the boats. Quickly.'

Aboard HMS *Tigre*, Commodore Sir William Sidney Smith looked down at the chart before him, Lt Wright at his side. Beside them, Wayland and Phélippeaux examined the sea-roads into Acre. With them was Ralph Miller, Captain of HMS *Theseus*, a quiet, steady man, one of Nelson's own, a veteran of Cape St Vincent, Tenerife, and the Nile. Smith cursed under his breath. 'So, have we lost *Torride*. She is far overdue…'

Lt Wright seemed resigned to it. 'She was reconnoitring the roads to Acre, here…' he indicated on the chart, 'and here sir.' He looked up. 'What if she found the flotilla sir. The heavy guns.'

Smith sighed. 'Then she should have darted back here like a minnow and told us.' He looked down at the chart. 'Mount Carmel…' murmured Smith. 'The heights on the headland overlook the entire bay and port of Acre. With *Torride* missing, and now the fall of Jaffa, we must get word to Acre, yet also intercept the gun flotilla.' He looked at Miller. 'What say you, Rafe?'

'I can take *Theseus* at once, Sir Sidney. If Djezzar wants to evacuate Acre we can assist him, but surely such a fortress could withstand the French – especially if we find that artillery.'

'This is so,' confirmed Phélippeaux, 'and the sultan wishes him to hold fast. If Djezzar Pasha sees the *Theseus* and the *Tigre*, he will hope once again.' He looked at Smith. 'I can convince him. I shall go with the *Capitaine* Miller.'

'We must prevent Djezzar from evacuating,' said Smith unequivocally. 'If Acre falls it would spell disaster.'

Wayland stared down at the contours, the shoals, the islands and jetties of ancient Acre. All he could think of was Hazzard: there was no means of knowing whether he had failed or succeeded. 'If I may sir, the guns… If they were destined first for Jaffa, then Mr Hazzard will have found them. If he did not, the flotilla might be on a direct route.'

Smith looked and nodded. 'Straight up to Acre, quite, quite… on one of a number of courses from Damietta. Whereupon we now have a broad sea and nine or ten ships to find, where Nelson failed to spot four *hundred* of the blessed things.'

Wright glanced at Wayland. 'I for one hold with Mr Wayland, sir, that Bonaparte believes himself unstoppable and that he can stroll up to Acre on schedule. I believe the guns are coming straight to Acre.'

Phélippeaux nodded. '*D'accord*, that is, I would agree,' he said in halting English. He looked to Wright. 'What of the current? The winds?'

'The winds, my dear Antoine,' said Smith, reverting to French himself for the sake of the colonel, 'are as contrary as the god Aeolus so decrees. The current, however, is far more predictable, and flows south through the depths but eddies and turns north along the coast.'

'Then I suggest we work with it sir,' said Wright. 'If *Theseus* enters the bay of Acre and heads for the port to the north, then we can make for the south end of the bay and Mt Carmel to intercept the convoy. That leaves us a quadrant cruising zone of approximately...' He used a brass divider to measure the distance. 'Fifty miles square.'

'Fifty miles... and without *Torride* we cannot cover the alternatives,' said Miller, 'Unless fortune herself is with us.'

Smith looked down at the chart. 'Was that report wholly accurate, that Jaffa truly has fallen, I do wonder...'

Wayland shifted his weight on his walking-stick. 'From a passing trader sir, no side to him at all, nothing to gain, wouldn't you say?' he asked Wright.

'Jaffa's walls would certainly fall to French field-guns,' agreed Wright.

'Yes,' said Phélippeaux, 'they are antique, and would succumb to pressure.' He nodded. 'He and I, we studied artillery, and he is not the novice.'

'And how much dashed *time* have we?' asked Smith. 'Barely days... if Jaffa fell over a week ago, how much longer will it take that army to reach Acre, a mere three days' march.'

There was a call outside, followed by running footsteps on the boards above on the poop deck. They looked up at a knock at the door and the Second Lieutenant put his head round. 'Sir. Sail sighted off to larboard.'

Smith cocked an eyebrow. 'Larboard, is it? Good lord Mr Tyte, you sound a veritable old sea-dog...'

'I do beg your pardon sir, off to port I mean sir.' The young lieutenant touched the brim of his cocked hat in salute with a sheepish smile as they bustled out. 'Sail as yet unidentified sir, looks foreign, possibly a Turkish frigate says the Bo'sun.'

Wayland was first out, in the hope it might be Hazzard, his leg stiff, his good arm like a ramrod leaning on his stick as he stumped his way out to the quarterdeck. The wind had picked up and *Tigre* was riding the swell, spray bursting at her bows, the men of the watch, marines and rigging hands looking out to sea off the port beam. HMS *Theseus* was barely half a cable astern, her own watch looking, pointing, the tops staring out to sea, signal flags rippling up the mainmast, a voice calling through a loudhailer to *Tigre*.

Wayland took an eyeglass from a midshipman, braced himself against the portside shrouds and rested the barrel of the scope on his raised left forearm, a new skill he had mastered. He focussed as Smith and the others came to the rail and looked out, raising their own telescopes.

Wright called up to the mainmast tops. '*Range? Any other contact?*'

'*Sighted just one ship of sail, frigate, no colours, two thousand yards sir!*'

'*Very well,*' replied Wright and looked again.

Wayland scanned the horizon. At two thousand yards she would be little more than a dark shape, but the lookout called again. '*Change of heading! Turning hard a' starboard to intercept! Coming straight for us sir!*'

'*Very well,*' called Wright again. '*Open portside gun-ports and stand by your guns!*' He looked at Smith. 'Turkish?'

Smith peered through his glass. 'Italian I should say... Genoese?'

Wayland lost the shape, then swung the barrel of the scope again and caught it – a three-masted frigate, riding low and fast, its sharp prow heeling round in the tightest circle he had ever seen, the mizzen gaff sail hard over, spinning the ship about as Hazzard would have done, full sail billowing as it sped towards them. Wayland's hard-set mouth curled into the beginnings of a smile, though he could scarcely believe it. '*Good God...*'

Wright watched Wayland. 'Do you have her? You know her?'

Wayland stared through the eyepiece. 'I believe I do...'

'Is she friend or foe sir?' asked Miller, looking out.

'Surely it cannot be Mr Hazzard...' murmured Smith.

Wayland watched the ship charge against the swell, cutting through the waves, a bright flash of copper against the grey-blue of the sea as her bows reared up, then plunged again, and Wayland nearly laughed. 'No sir. Not Mr Hazzard. But the next best thing...'

He lowered the telescope, for the first time in a long while feeling a sense of hope. From the depths of a fever in a small Maltese cutter lost at sea with the marines, he would have recognised those flashing copper bows and the bravado of that racing turn anywhere:

It was the *Volpone* – and Captain Cesár Domingo de la Vega.

–

Half an hour later, De la Vega looked down at the charts with them in the Great Cabin of the *Tigre*, the curling trace of smoke rising from his cheroot, darkening before the lattice windows and decorative mouldings, a grey sea rising beyond, white-caps foaming on the waves. His son Alfonso stood silhouetted against the light beside him, Smith looking on. 'Do you see the situation, sir?'

De la Vega nodded, moving round the table, as elegant a figure as ever, in gleaming Cordovan leather boots, his collar drawn up with a white cravat, a suede waistcoat, a pistol belt, his Toledo rapier at his hip under a grey cutaway winter coat. Wayland stepped back to let him examine the coastal shoals and harbour roads.

The Spaniard had not changed in all those long months – it was as if Wayland had seen him only the week before. He had embraced Wayland tightly, a lost son, his sorrow at the severed hand palpable, his eyes tight shut in shared pain, touching Wayland's clenched right hand to his brow, then patting him on the arm, a silent promise for what, wondered Wayland, revenge or repayment in some way – Alfonso the same. Miller, Phélippeaux, Smith and Wright had looked on with some awe, Wayland clearly even more than they had surmised. Formal introductions were made with a sweeping bow not seen outside the royal court of Spain, and Sir William Sidney Smith had proved more than equal to the task. '*Señor*, it is a pleasure to see you again, even in this dread circumstance.'

'And you, *señor*,' allowed De la Vega with a bow of the head. 'Now let us see how things lie for my *hermanito del mar* – my *loco inglés*, my little brother of the sea...'

Smith had known of his licences and letters of marque from Nelson and further bona fides from Lord Keith, and had met him only the once, that terrible night after the battle in Aboukir Bay – and was clearly captivated. They could have been brothers themselves, adventurers both. Wright explained the charts and the dilemma facing them regarding the French flotilla. De la Vega pointed at the headland shoals near Mt Carmel, and looked to Alfonso. '*Muy peligroso aquí...*'

Alfonso nodded. '*Sí, las rocas.*'

Smith understood. 'Rocks, sir?'

'*Sí*, if my brother Hazzard, he sails here to Acca – ehh, *perdóneme*, *Acre*, as you say – he will find the rocks and sands. Your *flotilla pequeña*, this little fleet, it can go – ehh, *como se dice* – shallow, *sí*?'

'Quite probably.'

Miller nodded. 'Quite likely tartanes or bombs, and any other shallow-draught *avisos* they could find in Alexandria. I shall take *Theseus* to Acre, with Col. Phélippeaux – to warn the garrison and advise.'

De la Vega nodded and drew on the cheroot, Wayland sensing his thought-processes click into gear. 'Then, I say, you sail for your *canones* from Alexandria and Damietta, but I go with *Señor Teniente* Wayalande, for Yaffa. I know this,' he said, looking at them, a challenge. 'I feel it so in my bones, *sí*?'

Smith smiled. 'A man after my own heart sir.'

De la Vega nodded, businesslike, his devotion not a matter of opinion but a standing fact. '*Bueno*. With *Volpone*, we meet *mi hermanito* Hazzard – so you are free to seek for *los canones*.' He examined the cheroot. 'Me, I care not for *canones* – one gun, two gun, Jaffa, Acca,' he shrugged. 'No, I care only for *Señor* Hazzard.'

Smith glanced at Miller, and the captain nodded. 'Excellent. So be it.' He bowed his head, offering his thanks. '*Señores. Muchísimas gracias.*'

De la Vega shook his hand. '*De nada, señor. Buscamos a nuestro hermano perdido* – we seek for our lost brother. We shall find him.' He looked to Alfonso and Wayland with a brisk nod, 'Alfonso, *Teniente – vamanos*,' and strode out of the cabin and down the passage to the quarterdeck.

–

Jules-Yves Derrien rode on ahead with the vanguard battalion up the slopes of Mt Carmel, General Verdier of the cavalry alongside, the coastal wind blowing inland from their beating hooves. After a time, Derrien pulled his mount aside, letting the cavalry ride on, and looked out to sea to his left.

For hours, a division of the column had climbed the ancient tracks up the long mountain chain of Mt Carmel, through the undergrowth and pines, the stony slopes alive with flowers. Bonaparte was determined to command the heights and the valley of Jezreel as quickly as possible: it was where a pharaoh had once slain the Canaanites he had said. Derrien had felt the power of Bonaparte once again, that he was, once more, in the presence of greatness. This was the commander, he remembered, who had tended his common plague-stricken soldiers in Jaffa, who had laid his hand upon theirs to alleviate their fears and had said, '*See, it is nothing.*' Derrien had bowed – *this, truly, becomes majesty.*

Derrien had become seized by a new devotion to Bonaparte, their pact sealed at Jaffa, signed in the blood of thousands, a new-found will coursing through him to bring similar wrath to Acre and to all the corners of the earth – and none to stop them. *We are Pharaoh. We are Egypt.*

He looked up at the cavalry disappearing on the trail into the trees, the mountain promontory rising in the misty distance, a rugged stony ridge overlooking the great Bay of Acre and the Mediterranean Sea. They had very nearly made it – the advance guard was already moving to occupy the small port of Haifa just below, leaving only the bayshore and marshes to negotiate before they reached Acre itself, five miles further on – and the much-vaunted army of Al-Djezzar, the self-styled hero who would invade Egypt – *fool.*

The long rising slope beckoned Derrien on – every inch of ground soaked in the blood of millennia, vengeful tyrants, demi-gods, and thwarted liberators. He had heard the friars in Jaffa say this was where the Prophet Elijah had brought down the heavenly fire of God Himself upon the priests of Baal, and scorched the earth for all time.

Derrien looked into the plunging valleys and caves and felt a chill – a hint of the cold wind of Canaan, for a new pharaoh come to Galilee. He flapped up his collar against the breeze and spurred his horse, thinking only of the present, of a new empire, and a new god.

Hours later, temporary headquarters established on the summit and northward slopes, Bonaparte rode with his staff, cantering through his soldiers to the promontory, some of the men raising a hand to shout, *Vive le général!* Bourrienne rode behind him, Generals Berthier, Lannes, Bon and Dommartin at his side, a colour guard riding in tight disciplined precision. They passed the Stella Maris church and Carmelite monastery, its dome reflecting a slate-grey sky, cypress trees reaching heavenward, admonishing fingers waving in the wind. Soon the party slowed, Derrien up ahead, waiting at a broad stony clearing.

The generals fell back, Berthier laughing, incredulous at their progress, the view, their success, Lannes more phlegmatic and cautious. Ahead of them the sky and sea merged to a fading misty infinity, the world dropping away to nothing. Stones under Bonaparte's hooves yielded to his arrival, the winds calmed, and he walked his horse the final yards to where Derrien waited, his eyes bright. '*Mon général*,' Derrien called, 'the mountain is *yours*.'

A cheer rose up from around and behind him, and Bonaparte raised a hand to them as they shouted, *Vive le général! Hwa hwa hwa!*

Bonaparte stopped his horse and looked out. Before him lay the Mediterranean, vast and empty, the hint of distant islands mere darkenings on the horizon. To his right, the Bay of Acre swept round to the north and the medieval port itself: Acre, keystone of the Levant – a lighthouse, a spit of land, docks and jetties picked out bright, the tops of its castellated walls glowing in a weakened sun burning through the cloud, then obscured once more. He looked at Derrien. 'News of resistance?'

'Haifa, just below us, is evacuated, the port being secured by our forces, Citizen General.'

Bonaparte took a breath and looked out over the town, the arc of the bay, the tops of trees. He turned to look back at the monastery. 'They say it is built over Elijah's cave...' he mused. 'It shall be a hospital for our troops. Inform Desgenettes.'

'Yes, Citizen General.'

They looked out to sea, the staff drawing closer, now talking more animatedly. Bonaparte reached round for his saddlebag, but Detroye and young Croisier rode up beside him and handed him an eyeglass, guessing his intent. Stepson Eugène stayed further back, silent, watching – after the debacle of the surrendered garrison and executions, now evidently uncertain of his place in the pantheon of heroes. Without word Bonaparte took the telescope from Detroye, extended it, and scanned the horizon.

Derrien knew what he was looking for. 'No sign of the convoy yet, General.'

'Mm...'

In the eyepiece Bonaparte saw the fog lying heavy on the waves. Once focussed he traversed slowly left, then right, assessing Acre for assault. Much like Jaffa, a central castle rose near the eastern bastions, great square towers dominating the area. He swung the scope slowly, and elevated several degrees, his grip rock-steady. He stopped, returned, raised again, then stopped.

'What is that...'

Every officer who could do so raised their own eyeglass and looked.

Bonaparte seemed to freeze solid, his voice a choking gasp. He looked to Berthier. 'Has Perrée sent the flotilla yet?'

Berthier drew closer. 'He must have done...'

Derrien looked to sea then back to Bonaparte and drew his horse closer. 'General, I do not under—'

'*Has Perrée sent the flotilla.*'

Derrien felt the words like a whiplash. He glanced at Berthier, who nodded. 'I believe so, General, according to the timetable...'

'Messenger,' Bonaparte said, removing his eye from the scope, his gaze burning at him. '*Messenger.*'

Derrien did not yet understand his sudden agitation, but turned and called, '*Despatch-rider!*'

There was a thudding of hooves as a horse clattered up behind them, a trooper of the 3rd Dragoon Cavalry saluting, his braided jacket slung over one shoulder, his eyes shadowed by the visor of his shako. '*Mon général!*'

'New orders... the flotilla is to stop in Jaffa – at once.'

Derrien began jotting a note for the rider. 'Go to Jaffa, to the *Ordinnateur Maritime*. He is to intercept the flotilla from Damietta. Captain Standelet must not proceed to Acre until further notice—'

The rider took the note and looked to the general for confirmation. Bonaparte turned to him and nodded. 'Go.' The rider spun his mount and charged into full gallop, *Make way, make way, despatch!*

Derrien moved his horse closer to the edge and raised his eyeglass, looking out to sea. Berthier and Lannes came forward. 'What is it...?'

Bonaparte swore under his breath, '*Ma foi – is everyone blind but I?*' He thrust his scope into Berthier's hands and pointed.

They all looked out. Derrien focussed the tube, and he stared, moving slowly across the grey sea until he too stopped dead. In his sights was a ship. At first he thought it the artillery flotilla and his heart leapt, then he saw the large red ensign flapping astern. It was not the flotilla. It was the British 74-gun HMS *Theseus*, coming round the north headland of Acre, and behind it a Turkish frigate and several small brigantine sloops.

'*Mon dieu,*' murmured Berthier. 'If we use the coast road they will blast us with their guns...'

'Where is the vanguard?' asked Lannes. 'They might yet have reached Haifa – we must send word at once and divert the main column.' He looked to Berthier and Bon. 'Through Tiberias, through Nazareth—'

Bon was hesitant. 'But that would add *miles* to the march, and they are exhausted.'

'It is but one battleship, surely,' said Bourrienne, looking out at the bay. 'And these others, are they mercantile…?'

'*And there*—' snapped Bonaparte, pointing further off, as if they were all to blame. Derrien swung the scope and looked.

On the horizon was another ship. It was HMS *Tigre*.

Sir William Sidney Smith had beaten them to it.

Capture

The three attack boats moved ahead, the marines using their short paddles, digging deep, hard and swift, the fog muffling most stray sounds. They had tied a line between each boat, the rope dipping and dropping into the water with every change of speed. They passed the first tartane, a dark shape to port, another visible to starboard, their bells clanging, and slipped astern the brig, lurching and pitching slightly in the wake.

In the rearmost boat, Hazzard looked up at the painted name: *Foudre*. He could hear the creak and strain of her rigging, the snap of her sails as they caught the breeze then lost it, conversation aboard muted, few hands yet up and about, dawn barely an hour gone. He put a hand to the Lorenzoni. It was damp, the grip slightly wet, the mist touching everything with moisture, and he feared for its powder. The scimitar hung heavy at his side, and he knew he might have to rely on that rather than the pistol.

He had no way of knowing how many ships were in the flotilla, nor what strength they were. *Foudre* was smaller than a corvette, suggesting to Hazzard she was more of a rearguard and that somewhere up ahead lay a larger command vessel. But the brig was doubtless carrying a greater amount of materiel than the tartanes either side; that much was certain. He began to feel the chill on his skin, his hand clenching the gunwale with too much tension. Perhaps it was too soon after Jaffa, too long after Egypt, too much at all.

Cook let go his line and his boat drifted to the left, going round the portside of the *Foudre*. Underhill's powered on through the water to get to the starboard bows. Hazzard followed him along the starboard side, Handley working the tiller. They could paddle silently, but the telltale knock of a gunwale against the hull would be enough to rouse any experienced hand – once alongside they had to be quick. Around him were Pettifer, De Lisle, Kite and Warnock – Warnock ever the Indian fighter from the Americas, his shoulders working under supreme control, his eyes fixed on the brig.

The wooden wall loomed above them and they churned in the wake, the roar louder as they edged ever nearer. Pettifer reached up and caught a knotted line trailing in the water, and pulled them in as they shipped their paddles quietly. The boarding steps drew closer. Pettifer looped the knot line to a cleat on the gunwale and hauled them over to the steps, Kite paddling on the starboard side to push them in. There came the inevitable hollow clunk and boom as the boat banged into the side of the brig. Pettifer looked back at Hazzard – they waited, but there was no cry of alarm, no response from above. Pettifer made the line fast to the boat. Up ahead they could see Underhill doing likewise, hands up to the ship, lines taut. One of Underhill's crew lobbed a grapple and it swung up to the shrouds, snagging the lines silently. Hazzard waited. On the far side of the brig, they all heard Cook's short whistle, three short notes.

Hazzard cupped his hands to form a stirrup for Pettifer. '*Go*,' he hissed.

Pettifer stepped up and onto the slippery steps – he climbed hand over hand just over a fathom, paused, and peered over the edge, then threw a leg over the rail. Hazzard followed, De Lisle and Warnock right after him, Handley keeping the tiller true. Pettifer dropped to the deck, and Hazzard reached the top to see first Cook and his crew climbing aboard directly opposite – and a French soldier, tin plate in hand, eating some bread and cheese. '*Qui est-ce?*'

Pettifer smiled. 'Mornin'—' and put his fist in the Frenchman's stomach, doubling him over, the mouthful of bread flying a good yard. There was a shout, and Hazzard threw himself over the rail, seeing half a dozen sailors sitting about on the decks, on the hatches, on upturned casks and crates, cloaks and blankets over their shoulders, eating from small bowls – Egyptians and Greeks. He aimed the Lorenzoni, and they put their hands up as the others stole stealthily over the rail behind him.

To his left the deck rose to a small poopdeck and helm, and steps down to the aft cabins and holds. Warnock and Handley charged up the afterdeck steps to the helm and Warnock battered two startled men to the deck, Handley taking the wheel as Cook's division scattered across the decks – Hesse, Lawler, Church and Rhys aiming up at the tops, Underhill, Napier and Cochrane storming the forward hatch and charging down the steps.

Hazzard and Pettifer dived for the aft stairs, Kite hard behind, De Lisle joining Warnock, his four-barrelled turnover pistol out, hissing up to the tops as the unarmed men above put their hands up, '*Slow and easy, en bas, en bas, venez. Get down 'ere, sharpish...*'

As they ran down the aft steps, Hazzard heard Underhill shout '*Ammo!*' followed by Cook, '*One round down each gullet 'Miah, come on ye dozy buggers!*' The *Foudre* had three 18-pounders each side, enough to destroy any of the ships in the flotilla – once they had command of these, they could threaten the other ships.

Half-dressed in tunic or bare-chested in tattered breeches, French gunners erupted from the midships hatch, one of them firing a pistol wild, and Rhys responded with a blast from his musket into the group. A man fell, another wounded by the buck and ball – but the alarm was sounded.

Rigging hands in rags began dropping from the foremast tops above, some putting their hands to their heads, others with knives out. But they were soon overwhelmed by the marines, backing away, *Leh, leh, leh! No, no,* startled to see the dark *Bedu* headdresses, *binish* robes and scarlet jackets; one of them lunging round the mainmast, Warnock catching his knife arm and dropping him with a short blow of his tomahawk; another falling to his knees, a Greek, pleading, '*Oxhi, oxhi! Parakalo! No, no, please!*'

Hazzard charged down the dark passage to the stern, light filtering behind him through the midships gratings, and found two men in army uniform. They charged, broad-bladed knives out, and Pettifer shoved Hazzard to one side and fired the musketoon. The blast was deafening, and the two men flew backwards, the wooden panels and cabin doors behind them flying into splinters. '*Thanks Pet,*' said Hazzard, and they ran onward. Up ahead were two doors – Hazzard kicked in one of them and found the captain trying to load a pistol. Hazzard aimed the Lorenzoni, point-blank, two feet from his chest.

'*Capitaine,*' declared Hazzard, '*Je suis officier anglais.* You are taken. Lay down your arms and surrender your vessel.'

The captain paused, his eyes wide, his hands poised in mid-air, the short brass ramrod halfway down his pistol barrel. He looked at the Lorenzoni, at Pettifer, already reloading the musketoon and cocking the action. His eyes flicked to Hazzard's face.

'*Anglais?*'

Hazzard nodded. '*Oui.*'

The Frenchman took this in with a slow exhalation. He was somewhat older than Hazzard, greying at the sides of his long hair. He nodded sadly and lowered his hands, tossing the useless pistol onto the cot. 'With whom am I speaking…?'

Hazzard noted his calm, and deduced he was a gentleman. He continued in French. 'I am Major William Hazzard of His Britannic Majesty's Marines.'

The captain nodded, looking him up and down. 'And I am *Lieutenant de vaisseau* Desjardins. Your French is very good, for an *anglais*.' He frowned. 'Or an Arab?'

There was a philosophical lack of concern about him, an officer performing his task but without enjoyment. Hazzard asked, 'Who is in command of this flotilla?'

Desjardins shrugged again. '*Capitaine de vaisseau* Standelet.'

'Where is he?'

'In the corvette, the flagship,' he raised his chin, nodding with his head. 'Up ahead somewhere, I do not know.' He had said it with a deprecatory wave of the hand – he did not think much of Standelet.

Hazzard nodded. 'Lieutenant Desjardins, please call your men to lay down their arms, or we destroy this ship and your cargo.'

Desjardins contrived a perplexed frown. 'My cargo…?'

'The siege guns and ammunition in your holds.'

'Ah…' He sighed, a weary task to perform. 'I am bound to tell you, Major, we have no such guns.' He shrugged. 'Or siege munitions…'

Hazzard looked at him. 'Really.'

When they emerged on deck they found the fog clearing, the wind picking up. The marines had some forty men of the captive crew sitting cross-legged on the main deck between the mainmast and foremast in morose clusters: a handful of regular soldiers in uniform, but mostly conscripted foreign seamen still holding their hands up, uncomprehending, fearful. Others emerged from below, Napier behind them, '*Garn, sit over there wiv them lot*,' his musket slung on his shoulder.

The grey dawn revealed the shoreline of Cape Carmel rising in the distance ahead, just off the starboard bow. Evidently they had made a loop out to sea, bypassing Jaffa, and cut inland to sail up along the coast – they had nearly reached Acre.

The other ships were now clearly visible: tartanes, *avisos*, and a larger sloop further on, their crews shouting, pointing across the water at them, alarm bells sounding – what few soldiers they had among them had run for weapons, some forming at the rails with muskets. Hazzard moved the captain forward in clear view of the ships off the port and starboard beam. 'Lt Desjardins,' he ordered, 'call those ships to lay down their arms.'

Desjardins shrugged and shook his head. '*Désolé*, I cannot do this.' He turned apologetically. 'Major, you have done well. And I do not know from whence you came. Ingenious. But we are fifty men, and you are but…' he counted quickly, '…fifteen?' He gestured to the lines of men with muskets at the ships' rails not twenty yards off each side. 'And more. *You* must lay down *your* arms.'

Hazzard had expected this, and he looked past him. 'Sar'nt Cook!'

Cook appeared from round the foremast, banged his boot down, coming to attention. '*Sir!*'

'Marines, prepare to disembark!' Hazzard then repeated the order in French.

'*Sir!*'

The other crews were thrown by the use of French, the captives looking more confused as the marines backed away towards the rails and the waiting boats, still keeping them at gunpoint, the armed men on the nearby ships looking uncertainly to their officers. Cook pulled a bag o'tricks from Napier's satchel, strode to the central hatch by the gratings and looked down. He held it up.

'Light the fuse, sir?'

Hazzard looked at the captain and spoke in French. 'It is an explosive device we use. Lime, magnesium, oil, Greek naphtha – you understand, incendiary. He asks me permission to light the fuse.'

Desjardins looked from Cook to Hazzard, his face white. 'What? I… I do not under—'

'Yes!' called Hazzard, 'light the fuse! All men prepare to evacuate!' then in French, '*Allumez! Tous hommes, sauve qui peut!*' *All hands, save yourselves!*

'*Yes sir!*' Cook yanked the snap-fuse on the bundle and the quick-match began to fizz brightly, the captive crew crying out, *Non, non, non!* Cook moved over the midships hatch, peering down, ready to throw it below. He pointed down into the hold. 'In here sir?'

The captain shouted, waving his arms, '*Non, non! Do not do this! Non!*'

Hazzard interrupted, 'Yes! Throw it in, Jory!'

347

Desjardins turned to Hazzard. '*Non!* We surrender, I surrender!' He called out to the tartane off the port beam, '*Lieutenant! Lieutenant! Lay down your arms! Lay down your arms! Munitions!*' He looked back to Hazzard. '*Je vous en prie!* There are *two thousand* cartridges and the Gomer mortar shells below! *You will destroy the entire convoy and kill us all!*'

The crew began to run to the rail, several diving overboard to swim for the nearest ship, while on the tartane to port the muskets were dropped hastily as the officers shouted across their decks, *Tous hommes à voilure! Tous hommes en haut! Vite, vite, vite! All hands make sail! Hurry!*

A cry arose from the rigging above their heads. Hazzard looked up as Rhys whistled loudly from the tops, '*Sir! Ship o'sail off the port bow! There she comes!*'

There was the rushing howl of a hurtling round overhead, and a geyser of water burst thirty yards off the flotilla's port beam, the spray bright against the grey sky. Another crashed into the waves just off the starboard side of the sloop ahead, as the crews cried out *Munitions! Sauve toi!*

Desjardins took his chance and made a dash for Cook. He seized the bag o'tricks bundle, tugging at the spitting fuse, but Cook stood quietly over him as the quickmatch spat and fizzled out, spent, the wool unravelling in Desjardins's hands – a length of old blanket, harmless. He looked at Cook, at Hazzard, at them all, then out to sea – at the looming silhouette of the 74-gun HMS *Tigre*, bearing down on them in full sail from the flotilla's port bow.

'*Mon dieu...*'

–

'Another two rounds, Mr Wright!' called Smith from the starboard shrouds on the quarterdeck. 'Bracket them properly this time if you please. I haven't the coin for extra powder this month...'

'Aye sir!' Wright turned from the starboard gangway rail and shouted below to the main gundeck. '*Bracketing shots, forward target, check your elevation if you please, Mr Tyte! Fire!*'

HMS *Tigre* roared again, two more 18-pound rounds howling off in a lazy arc, crashing into the sea either side of the flotilla. Two smaller gunboats from Smith's new Acre squadron fanned out to starboard, their foremast coursers and headsails braced to catch the southwesterly, sailing round the outer edge of the flotilla to catch any stragglers. Smith raised his eyeglass. 'Compliments to Mr Tyte, good shot. Bring us to starboard to bear down to wind'ard of them if you please... we'll shove them against the cape if need be.'

The Bo'sun shouted the orders, and *Tigre* heeled round to threaten the flotilla from the seaward side, trying to trap them against the leeward shoreline and push them in the direction of Acre. Wright raised his eyeglass and leaned out from the rail.

'Sloop haring off to starboard sir – looks like the flag. We shan't catch her... and possibly those two small *avisos*...' He tracked their first gunboat, a small sloop skidding round to the south side of the French, the barking of her small guns echoing flat and staccato against Cape Carmel. 'The first four in line have struck their colours now sir... and there's the *Torride*, sir, in the rearguard! Flotilla must have captured her—'

'Short-lived, thank God, but there it is,' admitted Smith, 'What's that astern of them?'

The dark heights of Mt Carmel danced in Wright's vision, then back down to the flotilla. 'I'll be damned. A poleacre – no, a Turkish chebek... and two tartanes, riding very heavy, merchantmen, packed with...' he leaned forward, twisting the focus, '...*civilians...?*' He raised the scope again. 'It's Captain Reiz – I see Captain Reiz on deck, sir. I see him clear as day, but...'

Smith pointed to the centre of the convoy. 'Port bow, I do believe, of the large brig in the rearguard. We are, as they rightly say, in the nick of time.'

Wright swung the scope slowly. The image blurred with the remaining mist, the sail of the first gunboat blocking the brig, the French colours dragged down to her deck, the spread of the flotilla contained. A figure in a black robe, the scarlet sleeves clearly visible, made his way along the portside and mounted the forward rail, holding onto the stays. He raised a hand. Wright smiled and lowered the scope.

'Why am I not surprised, sir.'

'I must confess Mr Hazzard continues to surprise me.' Smith moved off to the gangway and shouted down to the tweendecks. 'Bo'sun! Make room for passengers, and get us over there lickety-split if you please – we don't want them to scatter.' He glanced at Wright. 'And no word from our gallant Spaniard... I trust all is well.'

Wright nodded. 'I pity the Frenchman that encounters him sir.'

Smith looked out again at the chebek and the convoy. 'I am sure he will return when we least expect it. Kindly ask Mr Tyte to assemble his officers and prize-crews. Major Douglas may rouse his marines and lower the boats.'

'Yes sir.'

Smith looked out at the chebek, a tremendous relief evident. On the distant ships hats were waved aloft, men in the rigging of *Torride* and the marines on the chebek whistling, calling out. 'Seems we have found a lost tribe of Dan, Mr Wright. And Mr Hazzard was true to his word...' He looked out, his voice dropping. '—and saved as many as he could.'

–

Among the trees on the summit of Mt Carmel, with none to witness, a trembling hand lowered a telescope, the staring eye wide, the face bone-white in a shaking, tremulous, silent rage. Citizen Derrien watched HMS *Tigre* pounce on the artillery flotilla.

No.

Scarcely able to believe it, he raised the scope to his eye once again, his tongue licking at his dry lips, the wind harsh in his face as he faced the sea. He scanned the activity aboard the brigs, tartanes and *avisos*, laden with the only siege artillery and battering-train the army could boast – the only weapons capable of breaching the walls of Al-Djezzar.

On the ships below, men were in the rigging lowering the sails, striking the colours, slowing – but the leading corvette turned away, trying to outrun the heavy battleship as it bore down on them. It fired again, encircling seven or eight of the smaller ships, its crescent wake marking a vast track and a power the small tartanes could never dream to match. Still the corvette made a run, two of the smaller *avisos* following, slipping from the battleship's clutches, but they did not head to Haifa or Acre. The corvette headed back to Jaffa.

'*No...!*'

But none heard. The scope shook in his grip, his eye catching the crew, the captain, *Is that Standelet! He should be shot for this*, the decks alive with running men – men in scarlet, men in black Arab robes, attack boats being lowered by the British ship packed with yet more men in red.

Then he saw a figure on one of the brigs, standing clear of the rest – an Arab robe, a scarlet sleeve, pistol in hand, a sword in the other.

As Derrien watched, he turned to look up at the mountain, almost as if to gaze directly into Derrien's lens.

Derrien tried to breathe, his throat closing, threatening to choke him dead.

Hazzard.

With an inarticulate scream, Derrien bent double, retching, falling to one knee, his inner voice shrieking, *the army, the army*, and he saw it marching, marching through Nazareth, marching through Galilee, unstoppable, storming ladders aloft, bound at last for Acre – with what? *With what now?* No cannons, no hope.

Hazzard.

His right hand smashed the telescope to the rock of the mountain, again and again, its broken glass and metals flying in all directions as he exhorted the devil himself, *au diable, diable, diable, diable.* Though on the holy mount in the shadow of Elijah, no demon heard his call for fire and blood, until finally he sank to the ground, crippled by his own destructive will, stricken to his blackened soul.

Hazzard.

You shall pay.

–

The sun vanished, then flashed again – dark, then bright. A screech from high above, wings broad as clouds blotting out the sun, fingers spreading, feeling the winds. *Buzzards*, he thought, vultures, carrion crows, circling, crying, as they drifted lower and lower to feed.

Another screech and he blinked, his gummed eyes difficult to open, and he could smell that old, salty tang he knew so well – the smell of the dead, sweet with putrescence, bitter and rank with rot.

Sergent-chef-major Achille Caron felt a weight on his chest, *a body*, and he tried to fight it off, his eyes opening now, the bloated face contorted, the mouth agape, browning teeth crawling with ants, and he shoved in horror, but nothing moved. Hands scrabbling for purchase, he pulled himself out from underneath instead, pain lancing through his chest and shoulders, then he emerged, the heat of the day suddenly warming him – and collapsed.

He moved a trembling hand to his face and picked at the scabbed blood over his swollen eyelids, and slowly opened them again, narrowed against the light, his own ironic voice in his mind: *Putain.*

Welcome to the Holy Land. He blew sand out of his mouth, his lips swollen and cracked, his tongue a dry bulbous snake writhing between his teeth.

His tunic was gone, his shirt torn open, and he felt a wound, the torn leather of a shoulder-strap, *the bullet*, he thought, *the ball struck here*, and he pressed and gasped, crying out.

He twisted his neck to the left to look down at his body. His hand came away dry, *No blood… why not.* The small-bore bullet had struck the hard saddle leather of his shoulder-strap, slowed, then bored through his tunic, into the padded linen lining, and finally struck his chest, but had not penetrated deep. It had hurt enough to knock him out. He could see him, even now, *Le Croquemort* – his own personal Mephistopheles, quietly convincing him of his righteousness. Just before he shot him.

'*Putain…*'

Part of him, somewhere, began to laugh. Achille Caron had learned early on in his military career that the only pistol worth having in the field was a dragoon service or horse-pistol, a large-mouthed .58 or .65 calibre monster. Not a gentleman's pocket pistol or pepperbox. He reached slowly for his thigh, but knew his weapons would be gone. Even his boots were gone, his bare feet feeling the breeze.

He remembered falling back, his legs bouncing on a cushion of grass and dust, his back banging to the ground, the wind going out of him, his gasps belonging to someone else. Guardsmen from the back of the command tent had leaned over him, shouting, *Chef, Chef, what happened, what happened*, someone snapping quick orders, Derrien – '*Get him out of here.*' He had felt arms pulling him through the grass, dust in his mouth, his breathing painful, someone threatening, '*If the general discovers this you shall—*'

Rossy? No, not Rossy, someone else, that dog of Derrien's perhaps, *the one who shot me*, far, far away.

He had been paralysed, his body slung in a cart, the boards hard beneath him, '*hurry you fool,*' hooves thudding into the dirt, the world fading. He had woken when he was lifted again – by his hands, by his feet, a dead weight – and was thrown, into the ditch with the other dead, where he lay still, his eyes closing over that world of murder and lies.

He heard footsteps, the murmur of speech, those familiar sounds his brother had taught him long ago, from Egypt, the dry glottal stops.

'…*sadiqi um aadow.*'

'*Fransaya? Aadow.*'

Two figures were talking above him, *friend or enemy*, they asked each other.

I cannot help you, mon ami, he thought, *for I know not anymore.*

There were more of them now, gathered above, looking down, a figure crouching over him – a Bedouin, a bandolier across the chest, cartridges and pistols slung, a curved *khanjar* dagger in the front of the belt. The Bedouin pulled the *shemagh* away, and Caron looked into a pair of eyes narrowed against the harsh climes of a harsher world.

'You are deserter…?' the voice asked in French.

Caron gasped, croaking, pointing to his throat, but his arm hardly moved. Nothing would work correctly. A wet goatskin was put to his lips, water dribbling over his cheek as he swallowed. He took a breath. '*Hal… anta badawi…? Bedu?*' he asked, his Arabic poor, his voice a thousand miles away.

The Bedouin reacted, looking at the others, then replied in French, '*Oui*, we are *Bedu*, we are Mamluk. From Arish, from Sinai. From Negev. Awlad 'Ali, Khushmaan, Tarabin.'

Caron began to focus on the figures standing above him, their dark hooded faces looking down. 'I am to say…' he wheezed, the only thing he could think of: '*L'anglais.*'

The gathered *Bedu* exchanged glances, *Al-Injilizi?* Another responded, *wait wait*, and the Bedouin's expression changed. 'Hazar Pasha.'

Caron closed his eyes. '*L'anglais*, who saved me… at Cairo,' he said hoarsely. 'I am Caron.'

The Bedouin looked down quizzically. 'Caron. The French sergeant. You give food to the *Bedu*, and water, where others do not. Yet here you lie.'

He nodded. '*Tried to stop them…*' he whispered. 'At Jaffa…'

The Bedouin nodded. 'Hazar was to come. To help.'

I knew him in Malta. I knew him in the sand.

Caron shook his head wearily. 'He must not… come to this place…' The air sighed in and out of him, rough, sibilant. 'It brings *death*. And battle…' he sighed, *want to sleep*, '…shall claim him, without honour. At Jaf… at *Jaffa*… we have lost too much honour…'

There was a brief silence. The Bedouin translated his words for the others, and they discussed it, moved by Caron's sorrow. Willing hands reached down and pulled him upright, and he groaned, lightheaded, the gunshot a torrent of flame through his body, making him collapse forward. He blinked as they lifted him, dead men in heaps all about, the staring face with browning teeth, his new friend beside him, staring upwards now, forgotten like him, *the executed Turks*, and he felt the misery return.

He heard prayers being intoned, faces shadowed by the sun, pious men, women lamenting, and he felt part of mankind again, and recalled his brother who had lived and died among these generous, insular desert people.

He had no vestige of uniform but filthy, bloodied breeches and a torn shirt. He was just Achille Caron of Aix-en-Provence once again. He looked out over heaps of the dead and discarded, mounds of earth banked to one side, forming a low ridge.

They helped him up, taking an arm each around their shoulders, and he looked out to the distant mountains of Palestine. His eye was arrested by the sight of possibly two hundred horse and camels, all turned towards him. His helpers got him to the Bedouin's horse, pushing him up, his saviour reassuring him. 'You are safe for now, friend of the *Bedu*, friend of Hazar. We shall find him together.'

He drank again from the skin, the water stealing down his chin to his neck, and asked, 'Where do we go…?'

Perhaps it was only a vain hope – because he was a tired old soldier, betrayed now once too often, wounded, weak, sickened and dishonoured by his countrymen and their crimes – that Caron felt he had found at least temporary refuge as he looked into the determined eyes of Shajar al-Durr.

Shajar mounted behind him and took the reins around his waist, turning to the ragged battalion as one of her officers drew a sword and cried out, *Allahu akbar!* and the host replied, *Allahu akbar! Shajar Shajar Shajar!*

'We go to Acre,' she said, 'to find Hazar.'

The horse moved off, and all Caron could hear was the repeated shout by the Mamluk Turks behind, *Intikam! Intikam!*

Revenge.

Pasha

The unforgiving sea crashed against the walls of Acre, the swell bursting upon its thick stone bastions, the spray reaching up to its battlements, the souls within gathering their goods from the jetties and docks, possibly for the last time; foreign merchantmen from Cyprus, Crete and Puglia heavily laden with cotton and olive oil, staggered out to the waves, fighting to get away to a safer harbour at Larnaca or Rhodes.

The ancient port of Acre jutted into the Mediterranean at the north end of a long, curving bay, running for nearly six miles to Haifa and Cape Carmel in the south. Its great stone walls and docks surrounded on three sides by the sea, there was but one impregnable corner bastion facing east on its landward side. Within this corner stood the castle citadel, its square towers rising higher than the walls around, commanding the landscape for miles.

Out to sea in the rocking swell, the glare almost blinding, rode the heavy battleships HMS *Tigre* and *Theseus*, the newly arrived 22-gun *Alliance*, and the captured flotilla of seven French ships. All now had English crews, sited to rake the shoreline and marshes with fire from Haifa to Acre, the lean gunboats slicing through the waves, heeling in the wind as they prowled the waters.

Once they had brought the chebek round to sail under the protective wing of HMS *Tigre*, Hazzard and the marines had disembarked, Delphine along with them, the Turkish Captain Kourosh hoping to reach the Larnaca roads in Cyprus. The refugees would be tended by the Aga, so he swore upon his paper promise for gold, signed: *In the name of the Serdar-i Azam, Shafik Reiz, Yuzbashi, of the Nizam-i Djedid.* Hazzard had wanted Delphine to join them for safety on Cyprus, but she had busied herself in the cockpit of *Tigre* with the surgeon, pretending not to hear, she and Maria organising instruments, cleaning them, laying them out, the surgeon looking on, impressed.

'Had I the choice, Major,' he had said, 'I would rather like such efficient hands to assist.'

'And what *else* must I do,' asked Delphine bluntly in French, not looking up at Hazzard, moving from one surface to another, scalpels, bone saws, needles; wiping, cleaning, finally glancing up with a challenging look. '*Eh bien?*' then in heavily accented English, 'Well, William?'

'It is for your own sake, Delphine – when this ship becomes a target for every gun ashore, a stray cannon round, a—'

'*Oui, oui, d'accord*, yes of course, these many rounds that come raining down, yes, for I have never once been in battle, *non*.' She threw down her cloth, exasperated, and turned to him. Maria looked round. 'I work with Larrey and Desgenettes, you understand?' Delphine said. 'I helped create the *ambulance volante*, the stretchers on the camels, so fast to get the men off the field, hm?' She looked away and he could see she was shaking. He remembered the Lorenzoni in her hands as she shot down her own maddened countrymen to save the lives of innocents.

'But not like Jaffa.'

'That will not happen here.' She closed her eyes. 'I know it so. *Oh, William… je vous en prie!*' Then just as abruptly she embraced him, and would not let him go.

How very like her she is, the thought unbidden, from deep within. He pushed it away and looked at the beams, the spars and power of the *Tigre* all around her, and thought of Smith, his quick-thinking, his resourcefulness. There was possibly no safer place.

When Hazzard had heard that De la Vega had gone in search of him at Jaffa, he demanded to set sail in the launch to find them. But sense had prevailed – De la Vega would return, he had no doubt, and it would take more than a few French sloops off Jaffa to outwit the deft Spaniard in the *Volpone*. That he missed Wayland was evident, but something of Egypt lingered within Hazzard and he did not fret the separation. Fate would bring him home.

The inhabitants of Acre had been roused by the army from their homes, all aware of the dread siege descending upon them. Beyond the two thickest walls that had withstood half a millennium came the horde of *Ahriman*, the demons of *Shaytan*, now become Bonaparte, who had feasted on babes in the bloody ruins of Jaffa. And beyond the crusader walls and redoubts, demi-brigades of the French Republic ranged from the coastal road of the bay in the south, across to the northern marshes and wastes, cutting off the port from the rest of the world, to undermine the ancient stones and bring her castle towers tumbling down.

The thunder of the cannon had begun almost at once, Bonaparte not hesitating despite the loss of his siege artillery, despite the British navy, despite Sir William Sidney Smith. His 12-pounders barked, packs of dogs straining at the leash, their flat, percussive report timed to a rate of fire designed to weary the defenders as much as pound the walls – in places over twenty feet thick. Howitzers and mortars tossed explosive shells high into the air, the bursts sending the people screaming for shelter deep in the stone labyrinths of the ancient city – but the Turks atop the walls remained undaunted by musket-fire, clambering back up to their posts, firing their own cannon after each salvo, *Vur un, Vur un! Smite them, smite them!*

In the streets the soldiers of Djezzar Pasha marched in platoon columns from the armouries, their plumed turbans bright and hopeful among the dun stone of the city, shouts rising, onlookers ululating as they marched, *yataghan* or *kilij* blades held before them with the rigid discipline of the Mamluk, miquelet muskets ported across the breast of the new hope in their midst. The iron men of the *Nizam-i Djedid* had come – swift and terrible would be their response.

Days of barrages passed, the marines of *Tigre* and *Theseus* shared out between the ships and the port, and 9 Company was no exception, Hazzard helping Phélippeaux and the Turks site cannons on the walls. Acre had become a cramped, armed camp – it was not a large town, barely two hundred yards of its walls facing the French, a single castle tower rising above the walls several storeys high. The Turks fired from its battlements and loopholes at the French engineers as they dug their trenches and mines to bring the wall down from beneath. To them it was the *Tour Maudite*, the 'Damned Tower', for good reason – at its base were littered the remains of scores of French dead.

Turkish gunners fired flaming charges over the churned ground beyond the wall, lighting the scenes in flaring yellow and white light, revealing a landscape of shell-craters and bodies, grenadiers and *sapeurs* moving about, caught frozen in the moment, looking up, then dashing for cover. One night Hazzard looked out over it all through an eyeglass, thinking back to the dust-blown Theban Necropolis, wondering if Bonaparte were too proud to fail, using his troops as a blunted ploughshare to plunge into this rocky, unwilling soil, all for no obvious harvest.

The following morning Hazzard and Reiz marched through the decorative gardens of the mosque with Smith and Col. Phélippeaux, heading for the castle.

'An audience then, sir,' confirmed Hazzard.

'Of a sort, yes,' said Smith evasively.

Behind them came an immaculate platoon of HMS *Tigre*'s marines, led by Sgt Dickory and their lieutenant, their brightwork polished, their arms swinging sharp and precise, their boots tramping the stones as one. Behind these came the grim faces of 9 Company, in scarlet and their dark *binish* robes, their sawn-off muskets slung at the shoulder, at their head Sergeants Cook and Underhill.

'In the land o'the heathen again, eh, Jory boy,' sniggered Underhill, with his dry rasp.

Cook's eyes flicked about, at the people watching, the Turkish guards staring. 'They say God hisself couldn't keep this place, 'Miah...' he whispered back. 'By all that's holy in Bristol...'

'Aye...'

They passed through arched gates into the castle's broad, paved open court with its central patch of garden, tall palms rising above, the sun dazzling. Each side of the great courtyard was dotted with dark archways, troops marching through to flagstone gangways and corridors beyond. French guns boomed all around, the reverberating thud of their impacts making the air shudder.

The marines came to a halt, the lieutenant doing an about-turn and taking Cook's salute, *Sah*. Hazzard kept walking, but looked back at his sergeant as he stood the men at ease. Cook gave him his slow nod, his unspoken message clear – *be careful*.

Smith led the way. 'Djezzar is feared rather than beloved,' he explained, 'and doubtless hated by many. He is the Ottoman Governor of Syria, but in effect rules the Lebanon independently. Much as Murad and Ibrahim did in Cairo...'

They passed under a towering gatehouse and entered another smaller courtyard, more palms rising. 'He is an old man now,' continued Smith in a hushed voice. 'Consequently, he looks upon us, and Colonel Phélippeaux, as a gift of heaven, protecting his realm...'

Hazzard could well see why – Phélippeaux was tireless, and had already been hard at work mounting the captured cannon from the artillery flotilla. A tactical genius, he had been directing the Turkish engineers how and where to reinforce the aged walls, his determination indefatigable.

'He has some French, as do many of the senior military Ottomans,' said Smith. 'Some Greek, and Arabic, though little or no English. We shall use his court interpreters.' He hesitated, then added, 'He is a brute, Major. He has imprisoned, tortured or murdered victims from nearly every cultural group of people in his domain: Turks, Druze, Shia, Christian, Muslim – all.' They came to broad steps and an open doorway, the sun suddenly bright. 'He once immured a band of men in these walls, leaving only their heads visible, that all might watch them die.'

'Good God...'

'Indeed. But that's not all.' They ascended the steps and entered a hall, Mamluk guards everywhere. 'I might now explain the purpose of this meeting,' said Smith, 'as this is no mere diplomatic audience.'

'What, then?' asked Hazzard, alert. 'What's happened?'

'We need official sanction to anchor in the bay and defend Acre, a mere courtesy. But there are several French prisoners in his loving care we need to interrogate.'

'Prisoners? From where?'

They walked in step quickly, their heels echoing, the thud of the guns now distant booming. Reiz listened. 'I have heard of an ambush, an attack – is it this of which you speak, Sir Siddani?'

'Precisely, Reiz,' said Smith. 'A unit of French infantry were set upon by a mob of peasants, and damn near killed to a man, believe it or not. But an officer and a few others were spared and given up to the army here in Acre – and now Djezzar has them. I intend to get them to safety to the *Tigre* and ask them rather a lot of questions, before the Pasha gets his teeth into them.'

'What might he do to them?' asked Hazzard.

Smith looked at him. 'My dear fellow. Imagine your worst terrors, and that might suffice.'

They ascended the steps to a dark hall, vast vaults arcing above their heads, thick medieval pillars supporting the tons of stone in the upper storeys, the heat dropping away immediately. They passed through an arch, Turkish troopers in red fez spotting Reiz and cracking to attention, then falling in behind as escort.

They could hear the murmur of voices ahead, and two guardsmen opened a set of tall ornate doors. Inside was a stateroom. It was not unlike the diwan chamber which Hazzard had first seen in Cairo, where he had watched Murad Bey arguing with Abu Bakr and Ibrahim. It consisted of wide steps, columns and arches, the walls glowing white with limewash, hung with magnificent carpets, more lying thick on the floors, their clicking heels silenced as they approached, the muffled voices of brightly turbaned courtiers dying off as they entered. The *qadis* and officials of the surrounding districts stood in loose groups, looking into the central area. Seated on a low sofa virtually on the floor, and leaning against a curving, heavily upholstered sloping banquette, long curling pipe in hand, was Al-Djezzar.

Ahmed Pasha al-Djezzar, 'the Butcher', sat cross-legged on a broad rich carpet, a dark, voluminous fur-trimmed *kaftan* spread either side, draping over his knees and feet, revealing a *kushak* sash in gilt thread and the hint of opulent *shalvar* trousers and jewelled slippers beneath. From the *kaftan* emerged grey silk sleeves, studded with small pearls and rubies, his aged but powerful hands decorated with rings lying folded in his lap, holding the long pipe, a tendril of smoke rising and twisting in the draught from the bright windows.

After all Hazzard had heard, from Masoud, from the French, from Smith, and from the work of his own imagination, he had not expected as old a man as this. He seemed to be little less than seventy, his thick beard almost white, shaven from his face to the jaw, his wide white moustaches like spikes, a lined and worn face beneath a loosely folded *sarik* turban of silk, a central plume held in place by a jewelled brooch. He did not look Turkish to Hazzard, as he would have imagined, not with Reiz's smooth deep complexion, but more European. But beneath the bushing grey brows were hardened eyes, hooded, narrowed and calculating. The pasha looked at each of them in turn, weighing their potential value and their intent. Hazzard took care to follow Smith's lead.

Smith slowed, and they stopped. Reiz glanced at Hazzard. They bowed. Two interpreters stepped forward and bowed in return. One of them spoke in French, 'Djezzar Pasha welcomes *le Colonel* Phélippeaux and *le Commandant Seigneur* Smith, and officers to his court.'

Phélippeaux bowed. 'And we are grateful to see His Excellence.'

The interpreter bowed again and replied, 'Commodore Smith, your brother sends word from the Sublime Porte of English support, and we give thanks to His Majesty the King George of Greatest Britain.'

Smith smiled graciously. 'My ships stand to protect Acre at the pasha's pleasure,' replied Smith in French. 'To which end I humbly request permission to make enquiries of the captive French officers in the castle cells, and to anchor in the Bay of Acre and seek the best tactical disposition for our ships in defence of the city.'

The interpreter mumbled to the pasha. It was a clever ruse to make the request for the French amid the formality of the mooring request. But Djezzar was not concerned and waved a hand, the interpreter bowing once again to Smith. 'It is so granted.'

Smith continued. 'In addition to your two hundred and fifty cannon, we bring four thousand round-shot of iron, one thousand two hundred explosive bombshells, two heavy mortars and a battering-train of siege artillery captured by our ships, formerly the property of Bonaparte himself.' There was a gratified chattering among the gathered officials, some applauding, and Smith took the bow in return.

Djezzar spoke abruptly out of the corner of his mouth. Reiz darted a look at Hazzard and shook his head briefly as if to say, *I cannot understand*. The interpreter spoke again. 'Then there is no need to evacuate Acre, *S'ieur* Siddani.'

'I agree,' insisted Smith. 'We shall bombard them from the castle walls, bombard them from our ships, and Colonel Phélippeaux will strengthen your defences. Our marines – I beg your pardon – our infantry of the navy,' he corrected himself, using the French expression, *infanterie de la marine*, 'are hard at work. Acre will hold, your Excellency.'

Djezzar spoke again. The interpreter bowed and replied, 'If you are confident, we shall recall a portion of our great army assembling on Rhodes to meet the enemy. Among them are the *Nizam-i Djedid*.'

Hazzard glanced at Reiz. 'Rhodes?'

Reiz nodded. 'To attack Egypt...'

'The greater the number of the brave soldiers of the sultan, the better the odds,' said Smith. 'One among your officers did great deeds of daring at Jaffa, saving many of the people, and he comes before you today, *Yuzbashi* Reiz.'

Reiz cracked to attention, stepped forward, and bowed his head. '*Voivode. Pasha.*'

Djezzar nodded, pleased. *Voïvode* as an ancient title from the Balkans was rarely heard in the Levant – it pleased Djezzar to be called *warlord*. '*Odlicno*.' *Excellent*, he replied in Serbian. He raised a hand and indicated Reiz, turning to his court. '*Nizam-i Djedid. En Iyisi*.' *The best*.

The interpreter continued. 'So, despite your boats, says the Djezzar Pasha, you need the *Nizam-i Djedid* to protect us.'

It was something of a challenge and Djezzar watched him, eyes narrowed once again.

'We can help the brave troops of the pasha to defend the city, yes,' insisted Phélippeaux. 'And so, I have begun to reinforce the walls of your great city.'

Djezzar's eyes turned on him and he growled, the interpreter translating. 'You are French, why would you fight your countrymen? Explain.'

Phélippeaux blinked and smiled, somewhat taken aback, but not much – it was a question he had answered many a time. 'My country was taken by revolutionaries, Excellence, and General Bonaparte is one of them.'

Then Djezzar spoke, in French, bypassing the interpreter. Hazzard thought it a strange voice – deep, guttural, grating. 'I have had the heads of men for less.' He leaned forward, taking a piece of dried fruit from a nearby platter. 'I have had men impaled, *oui*? For only thinking of rebellion. Ha, how they cry.' He almost laughed, a sniggering chuckle, then spread his hands wide. 'And I am pasha still.'

Hazzard watched him. He had seen brutal warlords strap men screaming to the muzzles of cannon and blow them to pieces, and laugh, and without question he knew this man was worse. His stomach churned with disgust, his face blank. But clearly something was showing – Reiz cast a sidelong glance, watching him.

'They commit the massacre at Jaffa,' said Djezzar. 'Women, old men, children... the rape, the murder... and every soldier killed. My men, *les miens, oui*, of my garrison. Shot, stuck,' he said, chewing on a honey-soaked dried apricot, idly miming a bayonet lunge with a wave of his hand, 'with the bayonet. They leave Abdullah Aga living. So, for what, that I surrender, hm, that even if my soldiers all die, I shall live? They let fall their arms at Jaffa yes, with honour, but still are killed. Ha.'

Hazzard felt a jolt, his first thought: *Delphine.* How they had got her out of that place, got them all out, barely in time. He glanced at Reiz for confirmation but Reiz seemed equally surprised. As Djezzar continued in his tirade, Hazzard considered this new Bonaparte: here was Ramesses, Ozymandias reborn, sacker of cities – after the revolt he had been just as bloody in Cairo. But why French soldiers would condone such a massacre he could not imagine.

Smith shot a glance at Phélippeaux and Hazzard, the news clearly troubling him deeply. 'I am appalled, if it is true…'

'But of course it is true!' shouted Djezzar. 'All of my garrison! All! The Albanians, the Moroccans, the Turks!'

'Four and one half thousand men,' said the interpreter with a bow to the pasha.

Just as suddenly Djezzar was on his feet, waving a pointed finger at them all, even his Turkish and Mamluk courtiers, in his use a violent gesture. 'I did swear to throw Banaparteh Sultan *al-Kebir*…' Some of them laughed in agreement at the absurdity of the title, but still he raged. '…yes, into the fire! And I shall. Who would believe the word of the French now? Who?' He looked about furiously, then gathered his robes to sit once more. 'Not I, certainly.'

Someone spoke – one of the courtiers, another replying – a hand pointing, and Hazzard found Djezzar looking directly at him. Smith whispered, '*Major.*'

The old man had leaned to his left, to look round Phélippeaux, who had accordingly stepped aside. 'Is it he…' asked the old man, looking about for confirmation, '…whom they call *Hazar*?'

The interpreter leaned down to Djezzar's ear, and the old man laughed again. 'Ah yes… *al-Aafrit al-ahmar*, the Red Devil.' His eye went to the ivory-hilted scimitar at his hip. 'With the *shamshir*, who rides with Bedouins and lives in deserts.'

Reiz came to attention and bowed. In rapid Turkish he said, 'Pasha. Hazar rode the desert to warn Murad of the French, and saved the Mamluk at Shubra Khit, at Embabeh. He gave succour to the people of Cairo in revolt against Banaparteh Sultan and helped the people of Jaffa. He is feared by the French, Excellence, and loved by his men.'

The Mamluk courtiers nodded at this, some calling out at the back, *Evet, yes, it is so*, and Djezzar looked again, at the expression on Hazzard's face, the old Indian orders still pinned to the breast of his Bombay jacket, and narrowed his eyes once again with a knowing look. 'Ah yes… *kırmızı sheytan*…' he said, nodding. '*Red devil*… I see it. And now,' he said, with a note of warning, 'you are at *my* command.'

Hazzard met his eye. He could feel Smith stiffen next to him, *William*, and knew the truth was not required, merely obeisance. Hazzard bowed his head and replied in French. 'But of course, Excellence.'

Djezzar tilted back his head, smacking his hands together, delighted. 'Ha! I have the *diable rouge*, and the Siddani Smit! What does Banaparteh have! We shall impale them all. Ha!' The assembly laughed with him, and he clapped his hands. 'Bring tea, bring food.'

As they marched out, Hazzard stalked ahead of Reiz, Phélippeaux and Smith until they burst into the inner courtyard, Smith catching him up, taking Hazzard's elbow. 'William. for God's sake—'

'We are here,' said Hazzard, 'to defend *that*?' he rasped, pointing back at the doorway. 'Good *Christ*, I wish Bonaparte all the luck in the world with him.'

'We are here, dear boy,' instructed Smith in a low voice, Phélippeaux nervous, looking at the Turkish guards waiting for them, 'to defend Acre. Nothing else.'

Hazzard marched off to the steps out to the courtyard. '*Damn* him. Impale men? Good God. I—'

'You must understand, *M'sieur d'Azzard*,' said Phélippeaux, 'Acre is vital.'

'If we lose Acre,' whispered Smith, 'then the French take the port, bring in that fleet of Bruix, or another from Venice or Bari or the Ionian Isles, then threaten our friendly ports on Cyprus, Rhodes, or even Constantinople – and we will have *lost the Levant*.' He stared hard at him. 'If so, then we have given Mr Bonaparte Esquire leave to rule Egypt, Syria and the East without let or hindrance. To form a new army, to move on Persia, or march to *India*. By *heaven*, William – can't you *see*? This little place, this ageing crusader fortress, is all that stands in the path of a new Empire of France.'

They descended the steps to the quad and into the sunshine. Smith's words merely fed Hazzard's smouldering hatred for it all, and he heard his own dry husk of a voice, trapped in a cell in Malta and beaten – by gaolers, by Derrien. *Damn the king, damn all kings, bloody tyrants all*.

Two Turkish officers appeared under one of the archways ahead, flanked by Cook and Underhill, behind them three soldiers holding a ragged scarecrow of a figure, his bruised and bloody face looking down, his head hanging, his wrists manacled. Hazzard looked at them all, then at Smith. 'So, we are here for ourselves, for Rule Britannia, as always.'

Smith straightened up, softening. 'Of course we are, William. And in so doing we may continue to fight the good fight. Or at least try to. God forfend that this fight should stop, or that England should fall – as I know you would wish neither as well. But it is the nature of diplomacy, is it not, the nature of *kingship*, to treat with the untreatable, when matters dictate.'

Hazzard looked at the group, the French prisoner, Cook watching him with one of his looks. 'I am no king, thank God…' he muttered, then made a promise, grating through his clenched teeth. 'But my men shall not die in *that* man's service.'

Smith looked at Cook and Underhill, then squeezed Hazzard's arm warmly. 'Nor shall they. You have my word on that, for King George very much needs us out here. Now,' he said, looking at their escort, 'let us take this chap, quick. And save an unworthy despot.' He strode across the quad, glancing at the Frenchman. '*M'sieur De la Salle? Enchanté. Je suis anglais*, Sir Sidney Smith. Have no fear, you are now in my company. Come, we have much to do.'

–

The walls loomed high above the entrenchments, and the fourth sally of the day ended in yet another retreat: the 85th *demi de bataille* fell back in disarray, the Turks still atop their walls, the scaling ladders lying broken among the dead, exhausted men flying from the mud and tumult. As drums sounded the retreat, the disembodied howls of sergeants soared across the field, *Withering fire, you dogs! Turn and give withering fire!* Some did, slowing their flight, firing back, only to be shot down by musketry, the blasts of Turkish cannon shredding the companies with grape-shot.

Derrien looked on. He had kept far from Bonaparte for some days after the loss of the siege guns, giving himself a roving brief, moving from the rear echelons of the camp to the deep trenches and ramparts piling high with earth and the dead, not the least the dead labourers they had conscripted into digging.

Riding from the mines to the rear, he heard shouting among ranking men and their officers. He reined in his horse by a stand of trees, the thump of the guns making the earth shudder. The men before him were the Alphas – he recognised them at once by the sight of the giant Pigalle.

'*Sous-Lieutenant* Thierry says he has not seen him, *capitaine. Not once*,' insisted Rossy, spitting with anger. 'Permission to seek him out.'

Captain Moiret looked more than usually harassed, running a hand over his lank hair, tired, his eyes closed, staring at the ground, thinking. 'He is not at the hospital here, I have asked.' They were equals in each other's eyes in their concern for *Sergent-chef-major* Achille Caron. 'He must have been taken to the field hospital in Ramla,' suggested Moiret. 'I have sent word, but no runners from Jaffa have made it back alive, Rossy. He might have been hit somewhere.'

Rossy slung his Charleville over his shoulder and nodded to Pigalle and the others. 'Then we shall go and find him.'

Moiret stopped them dead. 'No you damn well shall not, and you all know why! He would say the same himself – it would be desertion, and one of those fine fellows who murdered three thousand Turks would happily put you against a wall and blast you! He would not want that.'

'I like this not,' said Pigalle. 'Must I take this *putain con* of a castle myself before I get the *Chef*? Then I shall.'

'Pig, *mon dieu*, do nothing so foolish,' said Moiret. '*Nothing*. You stay alive – that is how we win this, not by getting your damned silly head blown off by a stray Rif cannon-ball.' Moiret looked at them all gathered about him, in their motley uniforms, a few of them barefoot like peasants with tattered baggy Turkish trousers and turbans. 'He cannot be with you now. It is as simple as that – you boys have had the good run under Caron, hm? Old *Tartuf*? Well, now you must do as the bigwigs say.' He sighed, hands to his face. 'He is my friend, *mes braves*, my oldest friend. I have sent word to find him. I have.'

St Michel kicked a stone with the toe of his boot. 'The *Chef*, he believed in the general. Then we too must believe in the general…'

Rossy rounded on him and spat on the ground. '*Non*, Micheline. He shoots the unarmed soldiers like dogs, he lets the city be destroyed, he lets Raff be killed, *he lets them all die* – why should we follow such a one?'

Micheline gave as good as he got. 'Because the *Chef* would wish it so—'

Derrien watched as a *chef de bataillon* major on horseback trotted over to the group, a major Rémy. 'You there. The 75th *de bataille*? Heavy line?'

Moiret looked up. 'Yes, *Chef de bataillon*. I am *Capitaine* Moiret. But this is the light company, *chasseurs à pied*.'

Major Rémy chewed on a stub of bread, then spat out a mouthful of mould. '*Ma foi. Eh bien*,' he said with a sigh, a matter of official rote. 'Your company is required at the line for the next advance, to clear the walls of musket-fire for the storming battalion.'

'Which company?'

'Second battalion, first company.'

'That is not I,' said Moiret. 'You want Régeaires.'

Rémy shrugged. '*Tant pis*. Régeaires is dead, too bad.'

Moiret sighed and dropped his head low again. 'Very well, Major, but I cannot command the Alphas as well as the line.'

A figure emerged from the dirt road, an officer. It was Captain Andret, from El-'Arish and Jaffa. 'I can command them.'

Moiret looked at him. 'Andret? You must be mad.'

But Rossy recognised him, Pigalle turning to see. 'Oh yes, if it please you,' said Rossy. 'Do let him lead us into the breach, I should wish it so very much...' His grisly smile told Moiret all, and they all deduced that Andret would not last the first minute under fire before Rossy accidentally shot him dead. He had done it before – and saved lives in the process. Derrien trotted forward, then slowed his horse to a walk. They turned, Rossy's face hardening in an instant.

'*Putain de la merde*...' he whispered. '*You*.'

'No, *Capitaine* Andret,' said Derrien. 'They are all still mine.'

Moiret and Major Rémy looked at him. 'Yours?' he asked. 'Nonsense. They are the 75th, they are needed at the—'

Derrien did not even look upon him, but waved a dismissive hand. 'Begone, *Chef de bataillon*, and find other fodder.'

Moiret watched Rémy hesitate and shrug again. 'Huh. *Croquemort*...' He turned his mount, spitting the bread from his mouth once more – perhaps, this time, not just from mould.

Rossy stepped forward and looked up at him. 'Your contract, *M'sieur le diable*, was with the *Chef*, not with us. We have not pricked our finger and signed your paper in blood.'

'What is this?' asked Moiret. 'What do you mean?'

'They served in the revolt of Cairo,' said Derrien, 'under me. Sabotaging the barricades… bringing order.' Derrien looked down at Rossy, clouds of stinking gunsmoke swirling in the skies behind him, casting grey shadow on his face, his eyes sinking away into darkness. 'As to my contract, Fusilier Rossy,' he said, 'you will sign. Or be flung at the breach.'

Moiret sighed, exasperated, '*Eh bien.* I must command the line company. Do you then take command of the Alpha company of *chasseurs à pied*?'

'I do.'

Moiret looked at him gravely, bringing a taste of his own menace. 'Then I shall so report to my *chef de bataillon*, to my *chef de brigade* and *général de brigade* that responsibility for the elite *Alpha-Oméga* rests solely with one Citizen Derrien,' he said, with a glance at Andret who watched Derrien with simpering decotion. 'And if any of them are lost, the *général en chef* will look to you for an answer.'

Andret positively danced with excitement. 'So Moiret, you lose them at last eh? You see? I did warn you…' He laughed, flinching and twitching with every boom of the distant guns.

Moiret turned to Andret. 'Do not come within pistol-shot of my line, Andret, or there shall be a regrettable tragedy.'

He headed away, Andret calling after him, 'You do not have the stomach! Eh, Moiret! The stomach!'

Derrien watched as the captain trudged off, leaving him with the semi-circle of simmering Alphas. Andret looked on, a broad smile on his face which, even to Derrien, spoke volumes to his want of sanity.

Derrien led them off to the north, on the far side of the huge bastion of Acre's walls and the Damned Tower. The whole area had been hacked open by a network of zig-zagged trenches leading to the dried-out medieval moat, now a muddy ditch stinking with rotting corpses. They passed behind the forward 12-pounder breach batteries, still blasting at the ageing stonework but to little avail. They stopped to take it all in.

'I used to wonder if there was a Hell…' murmured St Michel.

Rossy looked around, up to the hills, at the army camp nearly a mile off to their right, spread out across the broad rising uplands, leading to distant Nazareth and Cana. They could see open pits and lines of bodies awaiting burial, figures moving slowly about, mule-carts arriving with another load. But for a few stands of shattered trees, every inch of ground lay strewn in devastation. 'Yes,' said Rossy, 'I think we have found it.'

They reached the ramparts of the engineers' northern mine, rolling tumuli of earth and stone heaped everywhere. Some distance off the track leading to the distant army camp, lay a ruined village – now nothing more than jagged, broken stone walls and rubble tumbled in heaps on old foundations. Rossy saw that just beyond this were several large tents and shacks of broken planks and thatch. An old, dark-faced Lebanese woman in rag skirts and shawls stood outside one of them, her hand shielding her eyes from the sun as she looked at them.

Some two hundred yards off to their left stood the northern angle of Acre's tower bastion, and to its immediate right, a broad, deserted stretch of open ground reaching not half a mile to the shining sea. The plain was littered with French dead, lying in shell-craters, earth heaved upwards in barrages, none daring to cross the ground to collect them. Pigalle murmured, 'It is a *champ des morts*.' *A field of the dead.*

The guns began once again, the muzzle-blasts followed by rushing howls of the shells and distant flat, crumping impacts. Derrien stopped at a long, descending trench. 'Here we are,' he said. Up the ramp came a line of army labourers and *sapeurs* laden with barrows – then local men, women, old and young, bent double with sacks of stone or dragging wheeled limbers of heaped earth.

'These people dig,' explained Derrien patiently to the Alphas, 'so that those people,' he pointed to the tents and stone ruins beyond the village, 'might live. They are paid, and fed. If they do not dig, then their families suffer the consequences.'

On the far side of the ruins they could see men digging more grave pits – and beside, heaps of the dead. Rossy looked at them and up at Derrien. 'You shot them.'

Derrien met his eye. 'No. The Turks do that. In error of course, one presumes.'

'*And...*' said Andret excitedly, running down the ramp to an old Arab, collapsed in the dirt, his burden abandoned as he fell, his short-handled army shovel fallen in the mud. Andret kicked him. '*Yallah!* Up! On your feet!' When he had no response he ran to a sapper sergeant nearby, watching; he held out his hand and the sergeant wearily complied, handing him a short whip. Andret ran back to the old man while looking up at them, his eyes wide with anticipation. 'And we do this...!'

St Michel already had a bead on him with his Austrian rifle, but Rossy put a hand on the barrel and lowered it. He indicated Derrien on his horse – he was aiming his own pistol at St Michel. 'This,' said Derrien, an arm extended, pointing at Andret and the old man in the trench, 'is discipline.'

'Yes!' cried Andret, as he began to beat the old Arab over the head and shoulders, his teeth clenched hard with a frenzied savagery. 'And *this*, and *this!*' he shouted, until the old man was no more than a motionless ball against the wall of the trench. Andret took a breath and stepped back with a vigorous nod. 'That is what we do!'

Rossy and the others said nothing, but watched Andret as if he were a freak show exhibit, and Andret's smile faded, his hands clenching and unclenching in quivering temper. 'Well? Well?!' He brandished his pistol at the old man. 'Do you want to see more!'

'Enough Captain,' said Derrien.

'But—'

'I said enough,' repeated Derrien.

Rossy squinted up at him. 'You will not be here all of the day, M'sieur le Croquemort. I will wait, and I will leave Andret's tiny head upon your pillow one night, and say it was the Nizami.'

Derrien leaned down. 'Then you shall all sleep in the fresh outdoors, *en plennair*, with them.' He indicated the dead in the field beyond, straightened in the saddle and gathered the rein. 'You will guard the families and administer punishment when so ordered, clear debris from the mine, and the sergeant here will report your good progress. Is that clear?'

Rossy watched him turn his mount. 'I am thinking you are not long for this world, m'sieur.'

Derrien chirruped to his horse and rode away, across to the east, the blast of the guns sharp and hollow across the landscape. Two *sapeurs* lifted the old man's body out of the trench and carried him off, to lie with the others, in the fresh air, outside. Andret ran after Derrien's horse, looking back at them, as if afraid they were in hot pursuit.

The sapper sergeant glanced at them, his face expressionless, as dead as the bodies before the walls. 'They have the small *canon*, hm? Up there?' He twisted round slightly, a pipe held tight in his right hand, and jabbed a thumb over his shoulder at Acre. 'I hear we lose some men… taken, understand? The Nizami Shedids come out, take them.' He drew on his pipe. 'Next day with their small *canon*, they fire a short charge, you know? No range, just the charge. *Boum*. And then they come down, all around us, *un, deux, trois*, hm? Bim, bom, boum. Their heads, bounce, bounce…' He spat. 'The love between enemies, hm? It is lost now, *oui*?'

The Alphas watched him, saying nothing. He drew on his pipe, nodding to himself, a truth spoken. 'We bring plague, we bring death where we go. After Jaffa,' he added, putting the pipe between his teeth, looking out, 'God has gone from this place.'

Raid

'I cannot thank you enough… *je vous remercie*,' said De la Salle, seated at the large table in the Great Cabin of HMS *Tigre*. Smith sat opposite, officers around him, the stars picked out in the night sky behind, glimmering dimly in the galleried window panes, their candlelit reflections mere flickering ghosts in the glass, soon to vanish. One of Smith's servants moved about the room, clearing away the dinner they had just enjoyed, the sparkle of crystal and gleam of silverware bright against the dark distant horizon.

The dining table was well attended: Lieutenant De la Salle, as an erstwhile prisoner of Al-Djezzar, had told them much. *Tigre* Marines commander Major Douglas, Captain Miller of the *Theseus* and his Marines commander Major Oldfield sat alongside Hazzard and other lieutenants and senior midshipmen. Beside De la Salle sat Delphine, in a Turkish gown of ornamented pale sage green, a gift from Smith. She watched De la Salle protectively, overwhelmed by the notable Englishmen around.

Delphine had confirmed for Wright and Hazzard after the surgeon's examination that the man had indeed been kicked and battered all over – and his fingernails extracted. Smith had immediately provided him with the luxury of a heated bath and a set of clean clothes; he now sat in a new shirt, collar, cravat, breeches and boots, and a Royal Navy bluejacket, his eyes, cheekbones and mouth cut and livid with bruising, Delphine having cleaned the worst. The room was quiet as they listened to his stark confessions.

'They beheaded my men, the Turks,' he said, staring numbly, a faraway sound to his voice, a shaking hand reaching and grasping his wine for support. 'They are promised coin for each head they take. It is true, about Jaffa – I… I do not understand why they did that…' He drank, only a sip, as if out of nerves, yet remaining dead cold sober after three courses. 'They threatened their officers. In the pillage. I know of two who were killed by their own men, trying to stop the madness, you see.' He seemed to speak to himself, a quizzical perplexity about his own statements. He looked at them with a queer half-smile, his eyes wide. 'After the Turks paraded the boys' heads at the gate, the men became drunk with vengeance...' He shook his head, bewildered, smiling round at them in disbelief. 'Yet now they pay the local people for their food, their drink, their homes. It is all madness.' He sipped again. 'All...'

They had not told him Hazzard and Delphine had been there and fought their way out of it. Delphine looked away, a kerchief to her nose and mouth, and Hazzard watched, remembering the doctor, whom she had called Pascal, and his ultimate sacrifice. Smith was calm, kind. 'And the executions? The Turkish prisoners?' he asked. 'I shudder to ask – but is that *really* true, sir...?'

Delphine looked at him fearfully, perhaps hoping he would say no. But De la Salle nodded, staring back at cruel memory, a terrible accountability wracking him. 'The generals... they said we could not feed them. Could not keep them. That they would... be a threat...' He set down his glass, and the base rattled briefly on the polished surface. 'The men were wild, angry,' he frowned, remembering, 'on the verge of revolt, when we gave the Turks their bread.' He thought a moment. 'It is *our* bread, they said, *ours*, for dead men. They could not find soldiers to... to do it... at first...' He nodded to Delphine primarily. 'I am that little proud to say. Then some from each company, each battalion, I... I do not recall... until all knew a bad duty was coming.'

He sat in silence a moment, then continued, his voice a whisper. 'On the second day they said the Turks used the bodies of their comrades as a wall to shield them.' He looked out the window, imploring. 'Their friends protecting them even in death...'

Delphine turned away. '*Oh, mon dieu...*'

Pained, Smith sought to intervene. '*Je vous en prie, madame*, please... you need not suffer this.'

'No, no...' she insisted.

De la Salle looked away, his breath coming in shaking gasps as his chest heaved, his voice a whisper. 'The soldiers b-*bayonetted* them in any case...' His jaw shook and he drank again. 'Forgive me...'

There was silence in the cabin, each one of the officers wondering how they might have fared on such a day, each wondering how they might have refused, their thoughts their own. They looked on, unmoving – their judgement harsh. But none would say so.

'It is a terrible tale,' declared Smith quietly. 'And General Bonaparte shall answer for it – before some greater authority than we, most assuredly.'

'He shall indeed, sir,' murmured Douglas.

'Hear hear,' said Oldfield.

De la Salle nodded. 'Perhaps so, *m'sieur*. But he is our *général*, and we obey him. What then, are we?'

Delphine was staring off out the window, her dark hair glowing in the candlelight, the ornamental comb in her coiffure twinkling from gems and pinpricks of gold; her throat, her bare arm, pale cream. Hazzard watched her.

She is beautiful.

'It could happen again,' said De la Salle. 'They might prepare the assault as at Jaffa, I have no idea. If they breach, they might...' He looked up, imploring them, 'You must stop it... you must.'

Smith looked at the others, all slightly discomfited. Hazzard wondered if this were dereliction of his duty or a man with greater conscience.

De la Salle hesitated. 'There is something else... an administrator, or... from the State. We know such men now, in France.' He swallowed nervously. 'He is forever with the *général en chef*. He gives commands. Men obey, out of fear. No, it is not just fear – it is *terror*.'

Hazzard looked at him. 'Derrien...'

Delphine caught the tone of his voice, the hatred, and was almost afraid.

De la Salle froze, remaining very still, the name having a clear effect on him. He nodded. 'That is so. They call him the, how you say...' He then looked as if he had a bad taste in his mouth. '...*le Morticien*, or some such...'

'*Le Croquemort*,' said Hazzard, feeling his blood rise. 'Do you know where he is?'

'He is at the *Quartier* – the, how is it, the head-quarter, with the general, or at the camp. They say it is he who has brought the plague upon us... and has hospital staff shot for disobedience, for fearing to treat the victims. While the great Desgenettes, he now tries to treat the plague, yet falls with the fever as well.'

The breath caught in Delphine's throat, and she sat rigid, her hands in her lap. She had told Hazzard what had transpired at the Cairo hospital, with Fahina, with Derrien. With Colonel Laval. Hazzard watched her and wondered at her thoughts. 'Dr Desgenettes is treating plague?' she asked. 'With success?'

He looked at her, surprised. 'I have not heard, *madame*, but he has fallen with it, as they say, as have many of the others... while this, this *Croquemort*, tramples on our honour.'

Delphine looked down.

'*Madame?*' asked De la Salle. '*Ça va?*'

'*Bien, merci*,' she said, her voice small, delicate.

De la Salle nodded. 'This Derrien is... a creature.' He drank again. 'Some say he pockets the funds intended for local labourers, and uses prisoners as slaves. There are stories, terrible stories, of beatings, of shootings. It brings further dishonour upon us...'

Derrien.

Smith met Hazzard's eye. He could sense the fires burning.

'Derrien has failed us with the heavy guns as well. When you captured the flotilla of artillery, Sir Sidney,' said De la Salle quite suddenly, 'those, er, how do you say, the sail-barges, the little Arabian ships...?'

'Ah, yes, *tartanes*, they say,' said Wright with a quick smile.

'*Oui d'accord*, those few *tartanes* which escaped you,' he said, shaking his head wearily, '...Now they have returned, we see they have little value to the army, truly. We know the battle is lost.'

'Returned?' Smith's face hardly moved a muscle, his ticking mind utterly concealed. 'Ah, the little tartanes, yes...' He glanced at Wright and Hazzard, knowing full well they were not little Arabian sail-barges in the slightest, but twin-masted Levantine gunships armed with cannon – but De la Salle was in the army, not the navy, and would not necessarily know the difference. 'Well,' said Smith philosophically, 'Such things happen.'

'Indeed sir,' said Wright. He glanced at Smith. 'Remind me sir, where did we see them at anchor? I can't recall...'

Hazzard guessed Wright was probing. De la Salle sipped at his wine. 'Caifa, they call it, or Haifa, I believe? The small port at the far end of the bay?'

Wright nodded earnestly, 'Ah of course, *Haifa*, I did forget.'

De la Salle looked about. 'But yes, you have seen the ships, no doubt, of no real value.'

The officers murmured, *Mm*, *oh yes*, and *of course*, yet avoided looking at each other. Wright laid his napkin on the table, and made an apologetic gesture to Smith. 'Would you mind awfully if I just popped through to the wardroom a moment, sir...?'

Smith looked at Wright brightly and smiled. 'Absolutely, Lieutenant, do so, please. *Madame* Lascelles, *mon cher lieutenant*,' Smith said to De la Salle, 'my dear sir, if you would excuse us just a moment, I shall leave you in the company of my junior officers here – Mr Gill, Mr Tyte, do enjoy this very fine Porto, and show our guest the quarter galleries as need requires. Major Douglas, Mr Oldfield and Mr Hazzard? Oh, and Captain Miller, would you mind if I borrowed you for just a few moments?' He smiled at Delphine and De la Salle, 'We shall be but a short while...'

They all pushed back their chairs and stood as Smith got to his feet and the senior officers filed out after Wright, De la Salle suspecting nothing, staring into his wineglass. They went quickly through to the adjoining wardroom, its candelabra lit, the glow of dark panelling warm, the murmur of voices and Delphine's soft tones, gentle laughter at the junior officers' schoolboy French filtering through to them.

'Those dashed gunships, by God,' said Smith. 'How ever did they sneak those in...'

Douglas closed the door behind him, his voice hushed, 'That area was to be patrolled, sir, by our own gunboats.'

Oldfield gave a slight shrug. 'It's at least five miles away to the south, Jack,' he said to Douglas. 'Our fellows can't be everywhere at once.'

Wright busied himself at a locked chest. 'They must have crept in during that new moon, black as pitch it was...' He opened it to find rolled charts in their leather tubes. 'And now they're a damned threat...'

'Quite so,' said Captain Miller. 'They could be used to land troops up here, on the docks of Acre itself.'

Wright found the correct tube. 'Here we are sir.' He unrolled the chart and laid it out on the table. 'They're so desperate for artillery they might well have stripped the ships to employ their guns against the walls of Acre – or put a battery on Mt Carmel sir. Even a set of Long Nines could command the southern approach to the bay...'

'If they did that, they could get another artillery convoy through,' said Oldfield.

Hazzard spoke bluntly. 'Bonaparte will already have sent for a new convoy to dock at Jaffa. And ordered the guns to be brought overland.'

'Overland?' asked Miller. 'Would he risk that?'

Hazzard looked up at him. 'I would, sir.'

And Derrien would.

There was silence.

Smith's eyes narrowed as he examined the chart, his wry smile creeping across his lean features. 'Thirty marines, shall we say? Small boats, cut out the French gunships and tow them up here...'

Wright nodded. 'By God yes, sir... right from under their very noses.'

Major Douglas glanced at Wright for support. 'Sir, since we're planning to hit the mine at the foot of the walls, we cannot spare men for a raid such as this.'

Smith pursed his lips. 'How many are slated for the mine operation?'

Wright answered, 'A hundred of the *Nizam-i Djedid*, and we thought fifty marines from the combined Acre company.' He glanced at Oldfield. 'Some of your chaps from *Theseus*, I believe.'

'Yes, and they're ready for it too,' confirmed Oldfield. 'But that's not for two days from now.'

Smith looked at Miller. 'Then let *Tigre* do the tartane gunships.'

Hazzard stared at the chart, his mind far away.

'Mr Hazzard,' said Smith, 'you've grown exceeding quiet.'

Hazzard analysed the chart: Acre on its promontory at the top, the shore of the bay sweeping down on the right in a gentle curve to Haifa some six miles to the south, the shore then reaching out to sea again to the left, to the cape and Mt Carmel. At the summit, near a monastery, was a rough cross, labelled in pencil:

Fr HQ?

He pointed at it and asked Smith. 'How accurate is this, sir?'

Smith looked at it carefully. 'Uncertain. The night before we picked you up with the convoy, we saw their advance guard moving through Haifa. Our Lt Bushby took an armed launch, gave them some smart salvoes of swivel-guns and grape-shot and sent them packing. Many retired back up the slope.'

'Up the slope? Of Mt Carmel?'

'Yes. According to the locals this was "where the French sultans go".'

'And if I may, sir,' said Wright, 'there is also word they have taken over the Stella Maris monastery on the mountaintop as a hospital. Makes sense, for the senior officers of an HQ.' He pointed at the roads crossing the inland marshes and rivers, and a block of structures marked, *Hospital*. 'They have a main field hospital here, well inshore, but we still favour the monastery for the senior echelon.'

Hazzard felt his heart pounding. The port, the distances, the monastery – a fire beginning to burn within his mind.

Smith and the others watched and waited. 'Mr Hazzard...?'

'Sir...' Hazzard said. 'One raid, three operations.' He pointed down at Haifa. 'One to the port, to cut out the gunships...' He traced his finger back up to Acre. 'A second under Major Douglas, taking advantage of the diversion, to attack the mine...' His eye fell repeatedly on the slope of Mt Carmel, and he pictured its gradient, its elevation. 'And a third, for 9 Company.'

Smith watched him. 'Have you something in mind, Major?'

Fr HQ.

'Yes sir.'

He was going to capture Derrien.

Or Bonaparte.

—

'No,' insisted Delphine, hurriedly gathering her few things into a small canvas bag, her movements fast, angry. 'How can I stay, William...' her voice dropping off to a series of oaths muttered under her breath, '*nom d'un nom, d'un nom, mon dieu...*'

Hazzard watched her throwing things onto her cot, rolling them rapidly in the military style, the field-nurse preparing. 'You want to go to their hospital, where they are treating *bubonic plague* – Delphine, that is utter *madness*.'

She looked up, tears in her eyes. 'I have treated the plague, *Guillaume*, I have watched it cured, *moi-même*, myself, and if Réné is taken by it then I must try—'

'Réné?'

She stopped, her eyes closed, under supreme control, on the verge of weeping, and he saw it all. *Oh you fool, of course.*

Réné Desgenettes.

'Dr Desgenettes…?'

She nodded slowly. 'When my Luc was killed… in Italy, so many years ago… Réné, he took care of me, put me where I could advance – a woman, alone. Who had heard such a thing?' She looked up, still in her Turkish gown, her wet eyes smudged. 'I am now a surgeon's assistant, not an orderly or nurse. I stitch wounds, close after operations, apply clamps and tourniquets during amputations, hold them tight to stop them *screaming*, and…'

He waited, but he knew it was coming.

'And… I love him.'

Hazzard felt a crushing weight applied to his heart. For a moment he thought he was having that same conversation with Sarah, about her tearing off for a Grand Tour to Naples and trying to stop her – but now he saw this was not the case. Delphine was not Sarah.

'Listen, *please*,' he said, 'Bonaparte will retreat eventually, and when he does the army will fall apart – from plague, from indiscipline, *anything*. God alone knows what might happen to you there.'

'If he is ill, I can help. Then Réné, his staff, will take care of me.'

'Yes, he *might*, but what if he cannot…?'

'And what better protection for you, William, than for a woman to be among your number? Hm? That you escort a senior member of the surgical staff? Did you think of this?'

'That is *ridiculous*. I couldn't *possibly*—'

Spars raining down on them, splinters flying, the savants running across the decks, the cannons blasting, a woman stopping. I am Madame Lascelles, surgeon's assistant – this way, come—

Delphine Lascelles at Shubra Khit.

'I cannot ask that of you,' he said.

'So let it be my wish,' she said, 'to keep you safe.'

He turned to the plank door, one hand on the latch. 'If anything goes wrong, I will bring us all back.'

She looked at him. 'You always do.'

He went out, closing the door, dearly wishing that were so.

–

They gathered on the decks, a waning crescent moon silvering a cloudy haze. Sgt Dickory readied the men from the *Tigre*, Major

Douglas standing by the portside rail as they climbed into the first jolly-boat. Nine Company waited in their ramshackle kit – they had daubed blacking on their buttons, buckles and the brightwork on their muskets, their *binish* robes over their vestigial scarlet. Tariq was virtually invisible, only the glow of a new English clay pipe giving him away. Warnock stood, tomahawk in hand, two red and black stripes bright on his cheeks, his Mohawk warpaint, his eyes staring, ready.

Smith came along the gangway to the next boat, Lt Wright following; the sailors in their dark blue donkey jackets, rigging hands armed with pistols and swords, all climbing in, the men who would sail the ships out of the harbour.

'Mr Gill,' Smith called.

The young midshipman turned. 'Yes sir.'

'You will do fine I am sure, Mr Gill, and do harken to Master's Mate Lambert and Petty Tillery here. They know a thing or two.' Smith nodded at the older Tillery hovering behind. '*I say I say, where be Jack Tillery, why guiding us safe on the tiller he be*, what?'

Petty Officer Tillery, older than Gill, chuckled and came to attention. 'Sir.'

Major Douglas joined Hazzard, clearly still disturbed by 9 Company's part in the operation. 'What if you find *nothing*, man? Just smoke and dazzle? What then?'

Hazzard took a breath. 'Then we follow the smoke to the fire.'

Wright joined them. 'If anyone has a nose for trouble it's Major Hazzard.' He looked at his black *binish* and *shemagh*, the ivory scimitar at his hip, the Lorenzoni slung in its holster under his left arm. Wright lowered his voice. 'You have the new munitions.'

Hazzard gave an imperceptible nod, his mind working. 'Yes, two each man.'

Wright shook his head. 'Are you sure of all this, William?'

'Exactly, man,' said Douglas. 'What if you're cut off and exposed. What then?'

Hazzard looked at him. 'Then we shall create hell on earth for them all.'

Douglas looked at him, shocked. 'Good God, you are as hard a head as I've heard.' He put out his hand. 'Good luck to you then Hazzard. I trust we shall see you on time.'

Hazzard heard a latch click and the creak of a cabin door. From the darkened quarterdeck passage behind came Delphine, in a plain dark skirt and midshipman's blue jacket, her dark hair pulled back and wound tight, her meagre bag over her shoulder. Smith escorted her over to the starboard rail, not the least bit happy. '*Madame,*' he said, 'I do beg you to reconsider...'

She hesitated, then turned and quickly kissed him on the cheek. 'You have been very kind,' she said in French. 'I must help in the hospital if I can... I have seen it cured. I can help them.'

Smith bowed his head, took her hand and kissed it. 'Madam, such steadfast bravery. I shall commend you forever to my memory.'

Hazzard met her eye, then glanced at his watch. Timing was tight: they had to execute their plan and get out by dawn. 'Nine Company...' They looked up, and he nodded to Cook. 'Jory, in the boat.'

Pulling at his *binish* robe, Cook slung his musket over one shoulder and lowered his patterned blue *keffiyah* headdress onto his brow. '*Hasanan.*'

The large cutter and launch rowed out into the dark towards the *Alliance* and other gunboats waiting in the bay, four jolly-boats laden with sailors and marines already being lowered to meet them. The craft streamed out across the dark waters of the Bay of Acre, oars dipping swift and strong, their silver wakes glowing among the waves.

They soon covered the three miles to the approaches of Haifa and Cape Carmel, fighting the swirling current from the headland. The moon broke through the cloud, the sea gleaming, a light breeze skimming the surface into a gentle swell. At their agreed dispersal point they separated, Gill and Tillery in the launch, the cutter ahead, and four boats to port – and in the fifth, swinging further into the dark and out to sea – Delphine Lascelles and the black-clad men of 9 Company.

Hazzard watched Gill and Tillery's group head for the harbour-mouth of Haifa, then disappear, blotted out by the roaring waters round Cape Carmel. The swell rose as they paddled out of the bay. Handley gripped the tiller hard over as they rounded the rocks and shoals, the swell lifting and dropping them, the boat plunging. Delphine clung to the gunwale and Hazzard put an arm about her waist, and she held onto him.

Handley soon pointed into the dark. '*Sir, got a nice 'ole over there...*' he whispered.

Hazzard heard the rhythmic clash of pebble and shell in the surf before he saw it – a small cove of shingle beach. They kept their voices low, uncertain if there could be enemy sentries on the shoreline, but the area seemed deserted.

'*Take us in, Handley. Ready on the bows.*'

'*Clear aye.*'

They pulled for the shoreline, the boat swinging to port around an outcrop, the narrow strip of beach revealing itself in the white glow of the foaming surf. The prow struck the shingle, and they leapt out, splashing into the water, each taking hold of the gunwale and hauling the boat in, landing it on the beach.

Sand and shingle spread inland over rough grasses and scrub, the ridge of the mountain rising before them. Hazzard could see the lights of the monastery high above, glinting through the pines, a beacon shining out to sea. There were hard-worn paths everywhere, a coastal track up ahead heading south, to their right, and a clear trail up the side of the slope, leading to the church on the summit, guessed Hazzard – and the French HQ.

Delphine drew close and whispered, '*The hospital is at the church? Up there?*'

He nodded. 'So they believe.' He looked at her, her clothes, her bag. She had already slung it across her shoulders like a satchel. 'Ready?'

She shivered with the cold night air, or with nerves. She looked at him, her eyes gleaming in the dark. She swallowed nervously. 'Yes.' He looked round for Cook and gave him the nod.

'Jory.'

Cook jabbed finger and thumb over his shoulder. '*Right. By twos, Hesse and Kite pathfinders – Pet, bring up the rear.*'

The Cornishman whispered back, '*Clear aye.*'

Kite and Hesse moved past Hazzard up the track, Hesse going first with small, quick steps, Kite crouching, waiting. Hesse reached a bend by a dark clump of trees and sank down, waving him on. Kite dashed up the path past him to the next bend and squatted, then waved in turn – and Hesse carried on, the only sound the scuffle of boots in the sand and stone as they ascended the winding track, the rest following.

Hazzard took Delphine by the hand. '*Do as I do.*' She had the same look in her eye as she had in Jaffa – quick, assessing, aware. They set off after Napier and Cochrane, Pettifer coming at a trot, turning, looking back, the heavy musketoon ready.

When they were halfway up the sloping track, they encountered their first glimmer of light in the depth of shadow. The yellow wash of a lantern threw crazed patterns all around, lighting a ledge where the track widened. They all stopped. Tariq came back down to Hazzard and tapped the side of his nose, then Hazzard smelled it – tobacco. Hazzard put a hand to his lips to Delphine, and crept forward.

He saw them through the leaves of the trees: two sentries, white facings to their tunics, one wearing a sheepskin jerkin for the cold. They were smoking pipes, both wandering about, trying to keep warm, one kicking at the stones as they argued quietly, their voices rendered into murmurs, occasionally rising, then a soft laugh.

Up ahead, Kite pointed forward, two fingers walking, then drew a finger across his throat. Cook gave a thumbs-up and settled back. Through the trees Hazzard watched as one of them began to undo his buttons, fumbling with his sheepskin. Finally, he let them drop forward and began to urinate off the ledge. He hummed a tune, but stopped abruptly – there was the slight sound of sand underfoot and Hazzard watched the man crumple silently. He looked up the track – Kite had gone on, Hesse reappearing, giving a wave to continue. When they passed the ledge, no trace of the sentries remained.

It was a long, rising route to the summit, steep in places but with little climbing over rocks or through trees and thick undergrowth. They moved in near total silence – not even Porter's remedy bottles clinked, each wrapped in cloth in his shoulder-bag. Hazzard looked out at the glow of the dark sea and the height of the trees above, and calculated they were nearly there. He ran ahead to meet Kite and Hesse and saw the twinkle of lights through the leaves. Then he heard shouts, and the world erupted with gunfire.

From far below the mountain came the rattle and pop of musketry, and the percussive thud of cannons booming, disembodied shouts drifting upwards. The boats must have reached the port – and been discovered.

With the diversion of action at the base of the mountain, all eyes would be focussed on the port below – not on their most exposed weakness, the seaward slope they had just climbed. '*On me,*' said Hazzard, hurrying on, the others behind, and found Kite at the top of the track. They came to the edge of the trees and dropped down low into the brush.

The terrain was flat and open, dotted with clumps of brush and grass beneath only a few tall pines and wind-dried thorn. Some twenty yards to his left was a large marquee tent, positioned to overlook the bay to the north – but only one, not enough for an HQ or small garrison. There were men in uniform, many half-dressed, roused from sleep, running to the post-and-rail fence they had built at the edge, looking down at the source of the gunshots, the flash of a howitzer and the booming report, an officer looking down through an eyeglass, giving orders to note the time, the direction, *'Regardez! Faites la note alors!'*

Kite dropped onto one knee in the bushes behind Hazzard, and they both looked up in wonder: before them rose the magnificent Stella Maris Church and monastery.

'Blimey eh, sir...' he murmured reverently.

Hazzard gazed at the holiest of holies, built over the cave-grotto of Elijah, prophet of Jehovah, who slew the Philistine priests and crushed their god Baal. Tall palms, small ornamental trees in front, garden paths, a fountain, and above, its dome reflecting the indigo gleam of the sky, its windows dimly lit with glowing lamplight.

Hazzard saw a shadow flitting through the undergrowth on the far right, moving towards them steadily. A moment later Hesse appeared, breathing hard, speaking in German. 'Some commotion. Despatch-post, several horses, fifteen or twenty men, a line of tents behind the church – all empty, *Herr Major*, as they look down the mountain. That is all. No support troop, guards unit, nothing. *Kein Hauptquartier.'*

No HQ.

No Bonaparte.

He looked at the church and monastery. It could still be the senior officers' hospital as Wright suggested. The marines moved into the brush and trees, carefully, quietly. Hazzard glanced at Cook. *'We'll tread softly now. Clear?'*

The big man peered through the leaves and nodded in agreement. *'Clear aye.'*

Delphine joined him, slightly breathless, kneeling in the bushes beside him. He looked at Kite.

'Ready?'

'Yessir.'

'Hesse?'

'Jawohl.'

That they were wrong about the HQ forced Hazzard into their second option for the Mount, one he did not relish. He looked left and

384

right – everyone was in position. Delphine looked up at the church, then at Hazzard. She nodded. '*Prête.*'

Ready.

A new salvo of explosions and the tearing sound of rapid musket-fire lit up the edge of the slope from beyond the French at the rail like distant fireworks, and Hazzard knew it was time.

The four of them got to their feet, broke cover, and strode for the church.

It was an unnerving sensation for Hazzard, suddenly to be walking in full view, the French soldiers from the marquee leaning over their rail fence far off to the left, some turning, seeing them, then remarking to others, one pointing. Hazzard knew the best course was not to look, that everything should seem as routine as possible. He felt the Lorenzoni bump against him, smelling its oil and powder.

The first call came faster than he had expected.

'*Eh, tiens – qui est-ce...?*'

They kept walking. The church and monastery drew closer.

'*Sir...*' hissed Kite, '*here they bloody come...*'

'Do not look round,' grated Hazzard to the three of them. 'Nearly there...'

'*Vous là – il faut que... ehh! Arrêtez alors!*'

It was an officer, calling them to halt.

Delphine coughed, said something to Hazzard, touched his arm, very natural, and he blessed her for it, *excellent*. '*Oui, c'est vrai,*' he replied. They marched through the stones of the garden, a palm rising high above, blotting out the stars. More explosions erupted below, the flat percussion of them echoing across the bay. The same voice shouted now, '*J'ai dit – arrêtez!*' *I said, halt.*

But still Hazzard ignored him, feigning fatigue, removing his dark Arab headdress, a side door of the church so very close now, barely ten yards, a light in a window beckoning them. The door opened, a curious friar in the doorway, a long medical apron over his habit, looking out, first at Hazzard and Delphine, then to the shouting men. Hazzard thought if he could just reach him then they would be safe – but he heard one of the French running now, coming at a jog, hearing the rattle of the buckles and sling of his musket, another joining him, and the man who had been shouting trying to catch them up, still calling. Hazzard knew it would be unnatural for him not to look round now. Just an arm's length from the friar and their safe haven, he stopped and turned.

'*Quoi? Qu'est-ce qui est?*' Hazzard demanded, outraged. 'Well! What is it? You address me like that? *Me!*'

The running men stopped short, two privates with muskets, the officer in shirtsleeves suddenly slowing, all taken aback by Hazzard's indignant French. Hazzard looked at them each in turn. '*Alors?* We haven't time for this – who in hell are you?'

The officer stood more upright, sensing trouble. 'I… pardon, but… there is a raid in progress below and you failed to present yourself—'

'I am *Chef de bataillon* St Juste, 2nd of the 14th *Tirailleurs* from Jaffa,' he indicated Delphine, 'escorting *Assistante de Chirurgien, Madame* Lascelles, for the hospital to Dr Desgenettes, which you would have known if your men had challenged me when I first set foot up here. Where is your *damned discipline*, man!' He looked him up and down, taking an aggressive pace forward, and barked that question no soldier likes to hear: 'Name?'

The officer stiffened. '*Capitaine* Furat, 3rd battalion the engineers – I command the observation post. Our night watch spotted English boats in the bay,' he said, pointing out to the sea, 'an attack below, in Haifa, and we notified the—'

Hazzard interrupted him. 'Is the Chief Surgeon Desgenettes in the hospital or not? I was told he was at the hospital near the *Quartier général.*'

Furat looked perplexed, the friar emerging from the doorway, concerned, not understanding their rapid French. 'This was the *Quartier* for a brief time, Major, but it has moved now inland, with the camp and, *je m'excuse*… I do not know where Dr Desgenettes might be. Have you a passport or order, or—'

The friar approached, 'Ah, Major St Juste,' and took his hand, bowing, and in halting French saying, 'We hope you to come with *madame. Beneditto, beneditto…*'

Hazzard looked at the friar's inscrutable expression, his olive skin and generous eyes, and guessed he was a native Levantine. Hazzard bowed his head. '*As-salamu aleikum. Hel'helalthin al-musteshfa?*' *Is this the hospital?*

The friar's face lit with delight at the sound of Arabic, and he bowed. '*Nahm, effendi.*' *Yes.* '*Vennez, vennez,*' he said again in his thick accent, perhaps so the captain would understand. *Come, come.*

Hazzard waved a hand at Furat and made for the door. '*Eh bien*, we shall see for ourselves. You have been no help at all.'

The two sentry guards looked at Furat, hesitant. Furat called out, 'No, no, wait! They... they say they have the plague fever in there and—'

Hazzard looked at him, angry. 'Then what by God are you doing standing about here for? Back to your posts and keep watch for any ships coming into the *damned* harbour, and do your *damned* duty.' He turned sharply and ushered Delphine through the door after the friar, Kite and Hesse following.

Furat snapped at one of his men, 'Oh *putain*, go with them for God's sake.'

'But *cap'taine*, the fever...'

'Then wait for him, *ma foi...*' He turned and trudged back to the rail, shouting for his sergeant.

Inside, the church was at once breathtaking and horrifying. The friar led them through a passage to the foyer, where they saw polished stone floors, soaring pillars topped with golden capitals beneath a dome hovering over an elaborate altar, and a carven statue of the Virgin Mary, Our Lady of the Star of the Sea. She looked down upon them all, and Hazzard wondered if she should not be covered, to protect her gaze from the shames of Man.

But before the altar, in the nave and in the adjoining rooms, were cots, examination tables and bedrolls filled with the sick. Delphine gasped and Hazzard held her hand. He looked down at the friar. 'Thank you,' he said, in Arabic, *shokran*, 'for your help.'

The friar made a face and shrugged, a gesture from a land where a few important things matter, but not little things like this. '*Médecin*,' he said, and gestured for them to follow to the doctor. He led them to a corridor to the monastery quarters, and stopped at a small lamplit anteroom.

Inside they saw a doctor, cramped by various orderlies crowding round a patient on a table. He wore a close white cap like a Muslim, a white kerchief over his mouth and nose, and was swathed in a spattered white gown and apron tight up to his throat. The friar called to him, and he looked up, seeing Hazzard's garb, his eye falling on Delphine. He pulled the mask from his mouth, and blinked. '*Madame... Lascelles...?*'

It took Hazzard a moment, but his face was vaguely familiar – and then he remembered a fleeting glimpse, on the gunboat on the Nile at Shubra Khit. He had been one of the *savants* running with her to the stern of the ship.

'*Gilles…?*' said Delphine in disbelief.

He set down his instrument on a metal tray and wiped his hands on a cloth. 'Delphine…? B-but how…?' The orderlies stepped back, and he hurried to her, then stopped himself, remembering the contagion, his urge to embrace her cut short. 'It is plague, but we are not to call it so – it is the High Fever.'

Hesse and Kite immediately covered their mouths and noses with their Arab *shemagh*, Kite muttering under his breath, '*Christ Jaysus an' all…*'

'Is Réné here?' asked Delphine. 'I have come to find him…'

He looked down, shaking his head. 'Delphine… he…'

She put a hand to her mouth, and Hazzard could feel her tense. '*Oh no… no, please…*'

'He has given himself the disease. Deliberately.'

'*What?*'

'An experiment, he said, putting his hand into the tainted blood and infectious buboes of a patient who then died… putting it into incisions in his arms… he was determined. Larrey says he is in a wretched state.'

She looked about 'Where? Can I go to him?'

He looked surprised. 'No, no, he is at the main hospital, by the army camp. These,' he said, spreading his hands, 'are favoured officers they thought to keep separate at first. But it has spread from Jaffa.'

'From the army or the town?' asked Hazzard. '*Chef de bataillon* St Juste, the 14th.'

'Oh, yes, er, that is to say, no – the fever was with the army, and now is in Jaffa.' He cleared his throat. 'So far it has stricken nearly everyone in the garrison there. You must leave here.'

'Good God,' murmured Hazzard. 'Where can we find the hospital and *Quartier*?'

The doctor seemed puzzled. 'Why… the main road, a few kilometres to the rear…'

Hazzard muttered under his breath, '*Delphine, come. Now.*'

He made to turn from the room, Delphine in hand, but she hung back. 'Gilles, we must find Réné – I… I shall see you, soon? At the *Quartier*…'

He looked pained. 'Delphine, it is not safe here, why are you along? *Why?*'

She looked back at him, shaking her head. 'I... because I *must.*' She turned for the door, then looked back. 'Gilles... Gilles, we cut open the bubo in Cairo, and Alexandria... treated the abscess... and some lived. Wash them all in seawater—'

The doctor nodded. 'I shall try. Be careful, *je vous en prie...*'

They went out, the friar showing them the way. Hazzard looked at him, his head bobbing, wreathed in smiles. He looked Hazzard in the eye. '*Dominus vobiscum.*'

God be with you.

But instead of Latin, or Rome, or High Church, Hazzard thought instead of Egypt, and that this was why he had come, that he could pass on to others some measure of hope, to whom he had no idea. '*Walyakun Rabbena ma'ak.*'

And God be with you.

The friar bowed his thanks and watched them go, then closed the door.

When they hurried from the garden entrance, across the gravel, around the fountain and passed the tall palms, Kite and Hesse slowed and came to a stop. Half a dozen French soldiers were waiting, now with powder and cartridge pouches over their shoulders, muskets levelled, Captain Furat in the centre, a man in a grey-blue tunic beside him. Behind, across their path to the trees by the white marquee, stood the others, no longer looking over the mountain into the bay below. Hazzard stopped, his left hand at the hilt of the scimitar, his thumb easing the blade from the neck of the scabbard.

'*Chef de bataillon... Madame,*' said Furat grandly with a slight bow of the head, 'This is *Caporal* Franche, just up from the port and the English raid. He says he knows of another boat, not accounted for, which they think landed somewhere on the shore, down here, by us.'

Hazzard flicked a glance at the stone-faced corporal standing to one side.

'They seemed to be in black, so he says, much like you, but, *eh bien*, the boat was seen.' Furat held up his arms, *oh the fortunes of war.* 'So, I must insist that you put up your arms, and—'

He had little time to finish, as there came a low rushing noise and a dull thud, and Corporal Franche gasped and fell forward, a red-feathered Huron tomahawk buried in his spine. Furat stared. Next came a short whistle.

Hazzard swept Delphine behind him and down, covering her in a crouch with his robe as Cook and Underhill blanketed the area in a rapid cross-fire of volleys, the first shots taking five of Furat's men down at once, two more falling in a cloud of powder as Kite fired his buck and ball from the hip, more shots erupting in the dark, peppering the white canvas of the marquee as men tried to run, only to be met by the thunderous roar of Pettifer's musketoon.

Furat spun back to face Hazzard as he rose and drew the scimitar, the tip of the blade flying to Furat's throat, quivering just under his chin.

'Turn,' said Hazzard in French. 'Tent.'

Delphine looked on, a hand to her mouth, Kite helping her up from the ground. '*Be awright, Miss, just you see.*'

The door to the church opened, the light spilling out, faces at windows, a pair of friars coming hesitantly to the doorway to see what had happened. Hazzard shouted at them, '*C'est trop dangereux! Stay inside!*' Immediately they shut the door with a clatter of locks and bolts.

Hazzard marched Furat to the marquee, Underhill waiting with four prisoners, hands behind their heads. The dead lay all around, some hit while in flight for the distant hill road. Hazzard could not see Porter or De Lisle, until he heard horses and a shrill whistle from behind, De Lisle running out from a walled quad on the stony track, waving an arm with a thumbs-up.

The marines gathered the abandoned Charleville muskets and slung them spinning over the edge of the slope into the night, hearing them crash through the trees below. Underhill, Napier and Cochrane then drove Furat and the remaining French down the forested track they had just ascended, all bound at the wrists. Furat looked back at Hazzard, calling, '*Qui êtes vous!*' Who are you! The rest of them evidently feared the worst, calling in shaking voices, *Non, non, je vous en prie, m'sieur! M'sieur l'anglais!* Underhill said nothing, and the group disappeared down the hillside.

Hazzard examined the observation post marquee – there were three large tripod-mounted telescopic eyeglasses in the entrance. Hazzard looked through one and saw a greatly enlarged port of Acre, the ships at the docks, the telescope reaching some five miles with ease. There were also a number of charts laid out on tables, lists of dates and times, ships' names standing out: *La Tigre, La Théseus, L'Alliance, La Torride.*

They had seen the raid coming before it had even begun, and passed the word to the port below. 'Smash them up. Every eyeglass you can find, then over the edge with them,' Hazzard said, walking out.

Cook appeared next to him, Delphine staring at the dead as Pettifer and the others laid them out. Hazzard looked at Delphine. 'This is what I meant.'

Her eyes closed, and she gave a brief nod. 'We must get to the hospital…'

'Yes.'

Underhill, Napier and Cochrane reappeared from the mountain track, coming at the run.

'Done?' asked Cook.

Underhill gave his dry rasping laugh. 'Aye, Jory. We guv 'em a kiss and tucked 'em in for the night.'

Cochrane said, 'Chucked their boots n'breeches away so they'll get a bit chilly, lashed to the pines.'

'Prickly an' all,' added Napier. 'But no scorpiums.'

Hazzard nodded. 'Good. Come on.'

He headed off, Cook whistling to the others. 'Porter an' 'Andy got a few horses, sir,' he said, 'and a cart.'

'We'll need it,' said Hazzard. 'Their HQ is inland.'

'Like Cap'n Smith feared.'

They reached the carriageway to the monastery quad and saw Porter and Handley with the horses, Porter struggling with a girth strap, Handley with a saddle, '*Come on you lot, give us a ruddy 'and.*' One was already saddled and bridled, a tough dark bay Turkoman, snorting impatiently, Corporal Franche's presumably, thought Hazzard – he mounted it quickly, its hooves clattering out onto the pounded earth of the road. 'Jory, get them mounted up.' He glanced at Delphine. 'Nearly there. You go with Sergeant Cook, I'm going ahead.'

She nodded, her eyes wide, nervous, her initial excitement now dwindled to quiet fear. 'Yes, William,' she said in English. 'Be careful…'

Pettifer buckled two of the horses into the wagon harness and the marines clambered into the back, fitting themselves in, Cochrane and Warnock coming behind them, carrying one of the dead soldiers. 'You sure 'bout this sir?' asked Cochrane. They hefted him up into the back, the others taking him, Porter covering him with a torn horse-blanket.

'Yes, he might help.' Hazzard headed past them down the sloping road, tall dark pines rising either side, Cook's misgivings evident as he called after him. 'And you reckon he'll be there…?'

'*He better be*,' Hazzard shouted back over his shoulder, '*Because I'm not leaving this bloody place without him*—' He kicked his heels in and charged on ahead down the hill.

Trap

Fifty yards out from their targets on the bay, the launch, cutter and jolly-boats from HMS *Tigre* had met a curtain of fire, the surface of the black water fizzing with musketry from the anchored tartanes and from atop the walls of Haifa. No longer mere Levantine sail-barges, the tartanes had been converted into ketch-rigged gunships with small-bore cannon, the largest of them a sloop of war at the head of the line. By the time the English jolly-boats drew within range, the French crews were already manning their 6- and 8-pounders, shredding the sea with grape-shot.

Tillery tried to bring the launch around, but they were caught in a cross-fire, the ships moored in an L against the port quays on one side and the shoreline on the other. Their only chance seemed to be to duck under the targets themselves.

'*Mr Gill! We must make for the shoreline ships sir!*' shouted Tillery. '*Pull inshore under their bows where they can't use their guns!*'

'*Right you are, Tilly!*' cried Gill. '*Hard a'starboard! Make for the gaps between the ships! Pull! Pull!*'

The launch pitched on the swell as she swung round on her oars and charged for the sharp, rising prow of the heavy sloop. The large cutter followed – but the exposed jolly-boats turned away, the oarsmen trying to escape the fire, and headed back into the bay. When the French saw the launch streaking for the bows of the sloop by the shore, they redoubled their efforts, men on the town walls firing a constant hail of musketry, muzzle-flashes flickering all along the parapets, the reports punctuated by thundering blasts from the ships' guns.

'*Make ready,*' called Gill, as the high bows of the French ship rolled overhead. A moment later they felt the shudder of the beach beneath the keel, all thrown forward as she grounded. '*Back! Back! Pull her off!*'

Lambert, the Master's Mate, called from the cutter beyond, '*Ahoy the launch! Ahoy! Take a line! Take a line in tow!*'

Tillery nearly fell as the launch heeled, and saw Lambert in the cutter behind, thrown back from the bows with a cry, clutching his arm. The cutter turned about, and the fire increased once more, volleys rapping, the tartanes trying to swing out on their anchors to use their guns. Hands in the stern of the cutter shouted out over the roar of the gunfire and threw two lines, the loops of rope suspended for a moment high in the air, then dropping, several of the launch hands reaching to catch them, lashing them round the pins.

Gill called back to the cutter, '*Tow is secure!*' and the cutter heaved round on the swell, trying to pull the launch off the beach.

Renewed fire poured down from the walls, and Tillery saw near sixty men charging along the shoreline, the cutter rocking with impacts, the gunwales bursting with splinters. A howitzer opened up on shore with a *whump* of powder and an orange cloud of flame; there was a hurtling rush of air and an explosive shell burst on the water beside them, men crying out as the heavy boat heeled over.

Marine Sergeant Dickory stood amidships and called out, '*Volley fire ashore! Call off ready!*' Shouts came back, *ready aye*, and Dickory roared, '*Fire!*' A loose volley boomed out and men ashore fell, others diving for cover, '*Reload! Volley fire the gunboats, call ready! Fire!*'

Dickory's volley fire now struck the tartanes, and several French gunners fell, one dropping a linstock, a flare of powder bursting, one man toppling overboard. Taking endless bursts of musket-fire, the cutter heaved the launch from under the French sloop – until something cut the line to her bow.

'*She's let go the bloody painter! They cut us off!*' cried one of the hands. Tillery looked out at the cutter, being raked with musket-fire – Dickory was struck, once, twice, then fell to one knee, '*Give me another volley you lazy bastards...! Fire!*' and the marines fired again, the scene obscured by gunsmoke, a sailor pulling Dickory to cover as they tried to row away.

Still attached at the stern, the launch was dragged out by the cutter and swung round parallel to shore, her broadside now exposed. The French immediately resumed steady fire, musket-balls whipping off every surface, men falling, crying out, one struck in the eye, his head snapping back, his face a mass of blood and powder-burns.

'*Mr Gill's hit, Tilly!*' cried one of the sailors, and Tillery grabbed the tiller, swinging the arm about to shift her to the swell, anything to get them out of range. The launch pitched against the waves and dropped again, the beach grinding beneath them, the surf lifting her and finally crashing her ashore with a shudder – before it stopped moving at last. The French ceased fire, the troops on the beach running, then slowing, moving towards them at walking pace.

Tillery looked at the crew – there was scarcely a man among them not wounded. Gill lay at the bows, across the laps of several of the sailors. Tillery gave the order. 'Arms down lads, arms down. Ye've done enough... more than enough.'

The remaining jolly-boats were pulling back, the cutter limping away, picking up a few swimmers, dragging them in, returning a withering fire at the walls. Tillery looked out at the port, the gunships, the lights, lanterns swinging in the hands of running men, the French now crowding round the bows of the grounded launch, others standing off, muskets aimed and ready.

Soldiers waded the few yards out to them in the surf, helping the walking wounded onto their feet. Two of the launch's sailors carried Gill to the beach and laid him down. A bare-headed sergeant jogged towards the boy, knelt over him and put an ear to his heart. He then straightened and pounded a fist on Gill's chest, listened, then pounded again, and finally listened once more. He opened Gill's eyes, peering into them, then looked back at the sailors apologetically, shaking his head. They all stood round, looking down at the young, torn body. Another was laid reverently next to him – Kircher, thought Tillery, a volunteer. Haifa, at last, was quiet.

'*Merde alors*,' swore one of the French, as they led Tillery out at gunpoint. Some of the soldiers shouted at them, angry, shoving them along to the others. A senior officer waited – a seaman perhaps, thought Tillery, his bluejacket braided, with gold epaulettes, several orders on his breast, a dark, weathered face. Beside him was another younger man, also an officer. The senior officer held up a hand and the prisoners came to a halt. '*Qui est l'officier?*'

The younger man translated. 'Who is your officer?' he asked.

Tillery looked about. With Gill dead and the other lieutenant gone back in the boats and cutter, he stepped forward. 'I am, sir. Petty Officer John Tillery, His Majesty's Ship *Tigre*.'

The officer murmured this to his superior. The older man nodded and spoke again, the other interpreting in a heavy accent. 'The commandant says, if you have any of the questions, you may be asking me, *Capitaine* Chac. I was prisoner in England some time. Who was your captain tonight? On *La Tigre*? It was Sir Sidney?'

They looked at each other and then to Tillery.

Tillery nodded. 'Yes sir.'

The officer seemed pleased. 'I know of him well. *Eh bien, le commandant*, he says that you are very lucky, in consequence of being in your boats and to escape, *sans être tués*, without being killed.' He looked at Tillery directly and bowed his head briefly in salute. 'There were no less than two thousand men who fired upon you constantly from the walls of Haifa.'

Tillery nodded. He did not feel very lucky. 'Mm. Thank you sir.'

The commandant spoke again and put out a hand to them, waving them to come along, the interpreter translating once more. 'Come, a doctor is called, and we will go to the hospital, for the wounded – but first come now with us to the port.' He detected their hesitation, and reassured them, 'For a hot supper – I am sure you are in need.'

Tillery looked out at the bay, the remaining boats rowing out into the darkness towards the safety of the *Tigre*. He thought of the cutter – was it just shot and shrapnel that cut the painter line, he wondered, or simple self-preservation? When he caught up to the rest of the men one of the bloodied sailors tramped alongside, and said, '*S'like they was waitin' fer us, eh... Not bloody fair that were. Not bloody fair.*'

'Just bad luck, Ned,' said Tillery, but he began to wonder how it all could have gone so very wrong.

–

The Alpha-Omegas usually kept themselves to themselves on the outskirts of any camp – but they did so especially now, when the High Fever was raging, so they said. They set out their bell tents in a protective ring at a safe distance, but it did not keep out all comers. There came the loud snap of a twig – their alert signal.

Immediately Rossy sat up on his bedroll in his tent, Pigalle lying a yard away already looking, both with the muzzles of their loaded muskets at their sides, pointing at the entrance flap. It flew open, and the blaze of a lantern dazzled them. It was Antonnais.

'R-Rossy...?' he whispered. 'It is... *it is that man...*'

Rossy groaned and threw himself back onto his woollen bed. 'Anton, it is the middle of the night is what it is. I have beetles in my socks, I smell like a dead badger, and my hairdresser has said I must rest my eyes... or I get those terrible bags under them.' He rolled over, nestling his grimy, unshaven face into his folded cloak as if it were a silken pillow, pulling up his striped Bedouin blanket. Pigalle watched as a new face appeared.

'Rossy...' rumbled Pigalle.

It was Jules-Yves Derrien.

Rossy looked up. '*Putain...*'

'There was a raid at the south port,' said Derrien. 'Englishmen, in boats,' he added, his eyes shining. 'Some have been captured.'

Rossy sat forward. '*Anglais?*' he asked. 'Real ones? In red?'

Derrien nodded. 'So they say.'

Rossy glanced at Pigalle. 'Our *anglais?*'

Derrien nodded. 'So we shall discover.'

—

Hazzard reached the forest at the base of the sloping road and threw himself out of the saddle, running to the edge of the trees. He peered down at Haifa through his eyeglass: the port was lit up, troops everywhere, gathering in groups, many looking on at a column of ragged men in half-undress and uniform. He thought he recognised Tillery, but could not be certain. It was clear the raid had been a failure, spotted by Captain Furat and the observation post on Mt Carmel, and now there were wounded captives.

With an escort of camels carrying the worst cases, the column of walking wounded headed along a road just behind the beach area. It was mostly floodplain, studded with scrub and low trees, marsh in all directions. The group crossed a junction of roads and headed inland. There was only one place they could be going: the main field hospital, as marked on Wright's map, and as described by the French surgeon at the monastery.

Hazzard swung the scope to the right and saw distant tent lines, partially collapsed structures, but all across the far hillsides he could see campfires – enough, he guessed, for some eight to ten thousand men.

Caesar.

He heard hoofbeats behind, and the rattle and clank of the wagon drawing to a halt by his own horse on the road. '*Jory,*' he hissed. Cook joined him and surveyed the scene.

'*By all that's ruddy holy in Bristol…*' mumbled the old sergeant. He looked down at the train of wounded prisoners. 'They scooped the lot.'

Hazzard glanced at Cook. 'We won't have to go into their camp. Now we know where he'll be.'

Cook looked thoughtfully at him. 'Clear aye… they're goin' to that field hospital. And wherever they go, that bastard'll want to be there. To interrogate the poor buggers…'

Derrien.

Moth to a flame.

'Let's hope,' said Hazzard. 'Otherwise they went through hell for nothing.'

They hurried back through the brush to the road where Delphine sat waiting on a horse, the others gathered on the wagon, Pettifer up front on a rough bench seat, holding the reins. Cook and Hazzard climbed into their saddles.

Hazzard pulled a watch from his pocket – it was Wayland's. As he popped its lid open he gave a thought to his missing second in command. He would be pleased to know they were being so precise. 'Time. Half-past four. Sunrise in ninety minutes, dead-time to send signal: one hour. Then rdv and out.'

Cook and Underhill brought out their own watches and synchronised. 'Half four, clear aye.'

He looked at them all in turn, none of their faces blurring as they had on the *Esperanza* that first day, each one known to him, each one important. His eye fell on Warnock, his savage warpaint grim and fitting under his dark robes, the Marine scarlet jerkin barely more than an open black military collar at his neck, the *binish* covering all. He remembered their first meeting aboard the *Esperanza* – the man's reluctance, his suspicion and anger. Napier, the boxer, with his big boots and special English, Cochrane the presbyter hangman, Kite the cut-purse and Handley the pirate; De Lisle, quick as a cat, and Pettifer, the Cornish rock tying them all secure. And Porter, worth all the king's horses and all the king's men, his round spectacles flashing. Hesse and Tariq sat dressed in grey-blue French army tunics, Hesse wearing Corporal Franche's, with cross-belt and pistols liberated from the observation post on the Mount. They could have been twins.

What have they all sacrificed?

They were there, he knew, not just for him, but had their own reasons, perhaps for each other – as he was for them. He glanced at Underhill, tough as oak, the steadiest hand indeed. 'You know what to do, Underhill,' he said, then added, 'Not a man left overboard. Not one.'

They murmured their assent, *aye*, some adding, *not jack nor jolly*. He took the reins and turned his horse, ready, glancing at Delphine and Cook – and nodded at them all. '*Bien. Allons-y.*'

Good. Let's go.

–

The prisoners of the failed raid had marched along the shore then inland, away from the bay, behind the stretcher-bearing camels – '*L'ambulance volante,*' explained Captain Chac, the interpreter. They half-carried the remainder of the walking wounded, their arms in slings, the lame given sticks as crutches or the supporting arms of their fellows, an escort of guards either side.

They crossed a bridge over a low-lying river, its black waters sliding past, cold and threatening, the marshland dark around them, the pitted surface of the moon. Tillery looked out at distant Acre, lit by sporadic gunfire, the Turks now quite content to engage the French at night if they so demanded.

When they reached the hospital, his hopes were raised by finding a square-topped Levantine building in a broad courtyard, with flanking outbuildings and stables, its colonnades and arches glowing. They moved past a set of sentries, one of them spitting at them as they passed, cursing – a sergeant then cuffing the offender across the head.

They crossed an open lamplit forecourt to a pair of double doors. Orderlies and soldiers guided the walking-wounded away, a sergeant taking the man from Tillery's shoulder. Tillery watched him go, the sergeant giving him a brisk nod, some kind of approbation from an old hand – as much as anyone could hope for.

Chac took him aside as the rest were led through to *triage*. He followed the interpreter and a guard with a lantern, down a white-washed corridor to an office or guard room. He looked behind him to find he was going alone. Inside was a table and several chairs, a cabinet and desk with an inkstand, a cracked, peeling door to his right, and another on the far wall to the left, leading outside, and a window with no glass, shuttered against the cold night. It was a doctor's office.

'You will all be given a rice and mutton ration for several days,' said Chac, moving to the internal door behind Tillery, opening it, seeing the dark storeroom inside, closing it and waving the guard away. He put the lantern on the table, the pair of them lit by the reeded refraction of its glass case, the corners of the room still dark. Chac pulled three chairs to the rickety wooden table and sat down, Tillery doing likewise. 'These rations are for your stay, until you are exchanged. Perhaps only in some few days, hm.'

'Exchanged?' Tillery was surprised. 'Lads all think they're goin' to be shot.'

Chac looked back at him, appalled. 'But why should they think this?'

Tillery sat. 'It seems your custom.'

Chac took a deep breath. 'Jaffa.' He nodded. '*Mon dieu. Quel horreur.* That was... a different thing. A terrible thing. Here, you are our honoured enemy. Just as we are for you, as I once was.'

The door behind Chac opened to the night air, a sudden cold draught blowing in, and he got to his feet as Colonel Junot entered, flapping off his cloak and beating his hat against his arm. A soldier outside closed the door behind him. 'The *dirt*, the *mire*... it is everywhere here.' He slapped a sheaf of pages on the table, pulled a bottle of ink and a quill from his pocket and banged them down as well. 'You will clerk for me today, hm, *Capitaine* Chac.'

'*D'accord, Colonel.*'

Junot looked at Tillery. 'So. I am *Chef de brigade* – er, how you say – *Colonel* Junot, of *le Quartier général*, the ehh, Head-Quarter. My Henglish is... ah, *limité, alors*, we talk here with...' he waved a hand at Chac, '...*cet officier-ci, le capitaine*, hm?' He busied himself with the sheaf of papers, giving some to Chac, keeping some for himself, not looking at Tillery as he spoke. '*Vous êtes Jean Till'ry, un second-maître de vaisseau de 74, la Tigre.*'

Chac relayed the statement. 'You are Petty Officer John Tillery of HMS *Tigre* of 74 guns?'

'Yes sir.'

Junot fired out his next question – Chac interpreted. 'What then is the fleet disposition at Constantinople?'

Taken aback, Tillery hesitated a moment and considered. 'Eleven sail of the line, sir, frigates and bombs. Fitting out for fifty-thousand troops.'

Junot showed no reaction, his sunken eyes deep hollows in his cadaverous skull-like face. He sighed, wiping a hand over his eyes. 'We have perceived that Sir Sidney has changed the *Tigre* into three decks of guns?'

Tillery nodded. 'Yes sir. She's an eighty now, at least.'

'How many French prisoners are there aboard?'

Tillery tried to remember. 'I'd say some 300, sir. Including those saved from Al-Djezzar Pasha as well.'

Chac recorded every word, the pen scratching. Without a change of expression Junot asked, 'What ships have you cruising off Alexandria? In the blockade.'

Tillery saw no harm in answering, as anyone could see for themselves through an eyeglass. '*Swiftsure*, 74, the *Lion*, 64, *Culloden*, 74, and others, sir.'

'Where then is Captain Hood of the *Zealous*?'

Tillery glanced at Junot, his eyes mostly on Chac. 'Sir Samuel was relieved and has gone to England I believe, sir.'

There was silence for a moment, Junot staring at him. Then without a flicker he asked, 'Is there talk of peace in England?'

The question took both Tillery and Chac by surprise. But before Tillery could give an answer, there was a commotion outside the back door, the latch working, a muffled voice protesting, '*You may not enter here, Citizen, by order of*—' but the door was opened, the rusted hinges shrieking. In stepped Jules-Yves Derrien, his face ruddy from the cold, his eyes bright and blank as he stared in, noting Junot, Chac, the pen, ink and notes. He turned his gaze on Tillery. In the doorway behind appeared Rossy and Antonnais, looking over his shoulder, satisfied the room was safe.

'You have no business here,' said Junot.

Derrien looked at him. 'I fear I do. You are requested at the *Quartier*, to report on the prisoners. The *général en chef* has an interest in them. You may take your tin soldiers and go.'

'Tin soldiers, indeed,' scoffed Junot, slowly getting to his feet. 'What then are those mongrels with you? Trained apes, I presume?'

Rossy stepped in behind Derrien, his Charleville at the port. 'We prefer dogs, *mon colonel.*'

Junot looked at him, at Antonnais and his matted blond curls. 'I will see about this,' he said with a sigh, gathering Chac's notes, his pen and ink, and marched for the door.

Satisfied, Derrien removed his black cloak, folding it neatly over one arm and laying it on a chair. Rossy stepped outside and closed the door.

'Well now,' Derrien said to Tillery in his best English. 'What shall we discuss…?'

—

Hazzard, Cook and Delphine rode hard down the slope from the Mount, Hazzard fretting at the twisting descent, *too long, taking too long*, worried about the hour they had left before they had to signal Major Douglas and Sir Sidney on the *Tigre*. He found the road leading out of the port, the dust laid by the dew of the night, the stars cold above – it then split into a forked beaten track: to the left lay the distant lights of Acre and its fortress some five miles off; to the right was the track taken by the captives, leading eventually to the hillside camps of the French army.

They did not wait for Underhill and the marines in the cart behind, but heeled round the corner to the right to follow the route taken by the prisoners, the pot-holed track wide, graded by marching troops, horses and gun-limbers. They passed squads of soldiers trudging back from watches or the raid itself, calling and cursing as the mud flew up from their hooves.

Hazzard saw the distant campfires and lanterns of Caesar's army growing in intensity far ahead. There were thousands of them, in neat rows across the backdrop of rising hills, blocks of flickering fires for blocks of men, division after division.

Good God.

Maybe it was here, he reflected, somewhere, in this place near Cana of Galilee, Nazareth and Bethlehem, where messiahs were born and sacrificed, that one would find that place of terror named in the New Testament. A plain like this perhaps – he was unsure, but thought it might be here somewhere. When he looked out at the shocked and stricken land around Acre – the distant flash and thud of Turkish cannon blazing from the walls, the constant flares of light and fire, dwarfing the small dark figures of men, reduced to shadows against the world, soon to be forgotten with the rising of the sun – he thought, *Yes, it's here. This could be Armageddon.*

'There it is,' cried Delphine, pointing ahead.

At the side of the road on the left was a cluster of buildings glowing white in the darkness, the windows bright with lamps, men moving on the road before it, some hopping off mule-carts, helping fellows to the ground or carrying stretchers. There was a rough cordon and a squad of sentries, just then letting in a cart, calling for attendants and staff.

They slowed and turned off, Hazzard riding forward, his Arab headdress off, his *binish* laced tight, his Bombay collar black, gold and red standing up from beneath. A sergeant held up a hand to slow the horses, but Hazzard spoke first. '*Chef de bataillon* St Juste, 14th *Tirailleurs* of Jaffa, I escort *Madame* Lascelles here to Dr Desgenettes. Is he here? It is most urgent.'

The man looked at them each, at Delphine, and bowed his head courteously. '*Enchanté, madame.* Is this so?'

'Yes, yes please, Dr Desgenettes seeks to treat the High Fever, and I bring the cure from Cairo for him.'

Hazzard glanced at her, impressed – they had not rehearsed that at all.

'Cure? *Mon dieu*, can it be so…? Open the gate.' The sergeant stepped smartly aside to attention and saluted. '*À vos ordres, Chef de bataillon.*'

They cantered across the front court, past the cart offloading the wounded at the main doors, and followed Delphine round the side. 'There will be a staff entrance,' she said, 'it must be back here, with access to the stores…'

They found a quad, carts, horses, and a side door, two soldiers coming out, lighting pipes with a taper they were protecting from the wind. Cook and Hazzard strode up the steps behind Delphine and the two men did not look at them twice, billows of sweet smoke rising up around them.

It was much as the monastery hospital on the Mount, thought Hazzard – exhausted, sallow-faced orderlies moving quickly, carrying sheets, blankets, buckets, canvas bags, the stench abominable, distant cries and shouts, men and women in pain, some in final agonies. Delphine knew her place and led them through to a staff area, shelves stacked with folded linens and bandages, metal bowls and jars. She took a young Turkish woman aside. 'Where are the senior patients? Dr Desgenettes?'

The woman looked at her wide-eyed, then swallowed nervously and nodded, her French very rough. 'Y-yes... the man Monge... and the General Caffarelli... but you must not enter—'

Delphine closed her eyes in thanks. 'Oh, *mon dieu*, thank you. Where? *Please.*'

The girl hesitated then gave in, and led them down an airless rear corridor, barely wide enough for two abreast, the noise subsiding behind them as they went. The nurse stopped at a doorway – Delphine nodded and the nurse ran back to the main ward. Hazzard could hear a man inside coughing, gasping. Delphine went in, and they moved to the doorway behind her.

There were four metal-framed cots, supported by stretchers of canvas beneath, sheets draped over the sides, blankets heaped on each patient. Mosquito netting hung from the ceiling around each, diaphanous curtains floating on the breeze from a small square window aperture high on the wall. In the corner was Desgenettes.

Delphine put her hands to her mouth. 'Oh *mon dieu*... Réné...' She hurried to the bed in the far-left corner, where lay the *Médecin en chef* of Bonaparte's expedition, stricken with bubonic plague. He saw her and struggled onto one elbow.

'Delphine...' he gasped, 'Wh-what do you do here...? My heavens...'

She threw the mosquito netting aside and embraced him. 'Oh, *mon cher... mon cher...*'

Hazzard's eye was arrested not by the sight of the famous doctor, but by the old man in the opposite corner, at the far right. Leaving Cook at the door, he moved slowly between the beds, the smells of alcohol sharp, the sour tang of bodies worse. The scimitar bumping as he walked, he felt his heart beat as he looked down at Professor Gaspard Monge.

The old man now looked ancient, his eyes wide, unseeing, his pale skin paper-thin, his body wracked with shivers, a bowl of broth of some kind on a nightstand beside him. The blanket lay low by his knees, and Hazzard remembered his own fevers – the raging heat, throwing off the covers, only to shudder with cold the next moment. He raised the net and leaned in, pulling the blanket carefully up to his chest, the old man's shaking hands taking it. His tongue licked at dry lips, his head turning to see him, nodding, his voice a tremulous dry husk. '*Th-thank you...*' he clasped Hazzard's hand. '*My son, mon général… you w-were always a g-good boy. I… I knew you would c-come…'* Hazzard looked down at him. Monge was delirious, yet Hazzard well knew that truth was often told in such ill humours. He remembered their meeting on the *Orient*, and Monge's thunderous frown: *My 'field', m'sieur, is the physical. The optical. The sun. The Earth. Light. Heat. The furnace, the steam. Smelting, casting, the iron – fire. Life, m'sieur. These things are my 'field'.* The old man squeezed his hand, and Hazzard felt such sorrow, that this great man's closest companion in this awful place was Bonaparte himself, an adopted son, and chief architect of the surrounding horrors.

'It is the least I can do,' said Hazzard. He looked over at Delphine with Desgenettes, Cook standing at the door keeping watch, then glanced at Monge's bowl of broth.

Hazzard took the bowl and held a spoonful to the old man's lips. He tilted Monge's white head forward so he could drink, spluttering weakly as he did. Monge lay back, exhausted. The old man shook his head. 'Never have I… doubted such a thing…' he said, his mind rambling.

Hazzard set down the bowl, feeling Cook's eyes on him. He set Monge's quaking hands under the blanket and stood up. 'Jory.'

Delphine looked round and said to Desgenettes, 'Réné, I am here to tend you, we must get you to your own tent…'

'I am already improved. The temperature, it is high, but not what it was. I… I do not understand – it does not infect as I thought, not as a poison…' He looked up at Hazzard. 'Thank you, *m'sieur*, for bringing her to me, but you must go from this place, get her away to safety—'

'No, Réné, I am staying—'

'You will not, *mon dieu*, Delphine…' He began to cough.

Hazzard touched her shoulder. 'Delphine, listen to him.'

She straightened reluctantly. 'But—'

'We *must* go.'

Hazzard headed out, Cook following, looking over his shoulder, the corridor clear as they moved to the main ward. Delphine followed, hurrying along, angry, frustrated, '*Guillaume… wait, je vous en prie!*'

Hazzard strode onwards, then slowed as he came to a grand doorway, and looked in. It was a vast hall in polished stone: beneath a decorative high ceiling a colonnade of torchlit arches divided the space into two large chambers, broad stone steps leading from one to the other, beds packed in tight on either side, many places merely straw heaped on the floor, men in bedrolls and threadbare blankets, the scene cast hellish in the dull orange flicker of the torches. Attendants moved with lanterns among the patients, bare, sweating limbs hanging from beds; some wandered about, dazed, naked, or retching, before collapsing on the steps, their heads leaning against the stone plinths of columns, while others were dragged back to their place. Hazzard held his *shemagh* over his nose and mouth and led the way down the central aisle quickly. 'I cannot leave you in this wretched place.'

'You must, William, it is where I belong. I shall find the commissar.'

'This is madness. It is not Cairo.'

'*That is why I am needed.*'

Hazzard looked at her. 'Desgenettes is right. We must get you out of here. When these men get back to Cairo they will be in a terrible state, you will be more needed there surely. What then if you throw your life away here?'

She had no answer. 'I cannot leave him…'

Hazzard looked up and down the crowded ward. 'Good God I need some air. We've got to see if the prisoners are here…'

She shook her head. 'But why? We cannot free them. Why any of this if you will not leave me, where I must—'

Hazzard kept his voice low and grated. 'Because this place is a *trap.*'

She looked at him in fear. '*Trap?*'

'Not for us,' he said, 'for *him.*'

Hazzard pushed his way through the ward to the opposite doorway to the foyer, and a pair of men in uniform. He called, '*Eh, tiens*, where are the English prisoners, from the raid? The colonel wishes to speak with them.'

The soldier straightened somewhat. 'No idea, *mon Chef*. Some in the ward, some talk now. Down there, office of the doctor, maybe.'

Hazzard and Cook marched down the hallway, Hazzard pulling Delphine by the hand. He saw the open double doors of the main entrance ahead, flanked by two sentries leaning on their muskets, one stuffing the bowl of a pipe. From the lamplit interior the dark outside seemed deeper, foreboding, the cold of the pre-dawn blowing in. To the left just inside the door was a passage.

He slowed as he came to it and stood a moment, peering down it. He looked at one of the men at the door. '*Les anglais?*'

The sentry nodded. 'One of them,' he said, tamping down his new tobacco. 'Down there.'

Hazzard looked again. He did not move.

Cook came closer behind him, concerned. 'What is it?'

Hazzard stared down the whitewashed passage. He could hear voices. There were two recessed doorways on the right-hand side – the first open, a storeroom, an internal connecting door just visible. The second at the end was lit by a glowing lantern, and standing before it was a man in turban and heavy robes, a Berber or Mamluk, his arms folded across his chest. An orderly emerged from the first door and pulled it closed behind him.

Despite the general murmur and irregular racket of the hospital, the shouts, the sudden bang of equipment being shifted or a door slamming – despite all this, he sensed something.

Sweat sprang to his brow and his hand began slowly reaching for his sword.

Cook waited behind him, knowing the signs. 'Sir. What *is* it?'

'He's here,' said Hazzard. He would know that voice anywhere.

It was Derrien.

And Napoleon Bonaparte.

Pettifer drove the carthorses fast, their hooves drumming on the hard-packed road, De Lisle next to him on the bench, shouting, '*Forty-five minutes, Pet!*'

'*Goin' fast as I can, Lil...*'

They had all pored over the map in Hazzard's briefing and knew their ground, but not where they might encounter enemy troops in any precise concentration. But no strangers to army camp life, they knew the drill, as Underhill summed it up: '*eads down, eyes front, and get on with yer business.*

They had clattered past the hospital and ridden inland as fast as they could, time of the essence, passing squads on the road – with Hesse and Tariq standing in the back in their French army tunics, no one challenged them.

There seemed to be only three usable roads to Acre: one they had passed, from Haifa along the shore; another further inland from the back of the French camp, heading out to Nazareth; and a middle track forced by the army across the scrub and marsh, a great wedge of routes leading to the hellish frontline. When they came to a junction Pettifer hauled the horses round to the left and stopped. They looked down the forced track.

'This must be it,' said Pettifer.

'It's an artillery run,' said Underhill, leaning over the backboard of the bench seat, looking down the road and back up the hill. 'Right,' he said, 'come on Petty, quick as mustard.'

'Awright, awright,' muttered the big Cornishman and gee'd the horses with a smack of the reins, and the cart rattled onto the wagon trail, marsh water spraying up from the spinning wheels. Kite notice the dead Frenchman staring up at them.

'Gorblimey, Doc, cover him up,' complained Kite. 'Puts me right off, he does...'

'God's in his heaven, tha' lad…' murmured Porter gently, and covered the body of the dead French soldier more carefully with the blanket.

They passed a platoon of troops and Pettifer slowed; the French officer looked up as they passed, Hesse standing behind the driver's backboard like a conquering general, raising a hand sharply to his forehead in salute. The officer nodded back and Pettifer lashed the horses again, the cart shooting onwards, the marines slouched in the back, yet another cartload of Levantine mercenaries headed for the front.

After a mile they saw the distant French artillery batteries, and followed their bright muzzle-flashes. Men moved across the landscape, lanterns swinging, mules plodding along muddy duckboards and marsh-tracks. Squads of French troops gathered in quiet groups at the sides of the road, a lantern for each, the darkness thick behind them, none looking up, none noticing their passage.

Before them lay the stricken zig-zag of mining access trenches, scarring the ground up to the walls of Acre. The dark castle of Al-Djezzar glowered at them from two hundred yards off to their left, lamplight in the medieval windows and loopholes lending it a demonic air. Fifty yards to their right the artillery batteries blasted, each dazzling flash capturing the scene, stark and frozen in time, a tableau of the unmoving and immovable, streaks of fire soaring, marking the passage of the twisting shells crashing into the stonework of an earlier unholy crusade.

'Over there,' said De Lisle. 'The village.'

Underhill leaned over the bench and looked. 'Must be.'

On the other side of the batteries stood the ruined village they knew so well from their briefing. One or two buildings were barely standing among heaps of masonry and rubble. 'That's it,' said Underhill, 'the rdv. But what's all this here then…?'

At the end of the track, just before the ruins was a small marshalling yard, surrounded by a defensive rampart of earth facing the castle, and behind, the remains of a shattered stone building. A dozen troops and labourers moved about, lanterns in hand, points of light in the darkness. Opposite the entrance on the far side was a track leading to the guns and the trenches – and the ruined village.

'This ain't on the ruddy map…' muttered Pettifer, and they slowed. 'Must be new…'

Lined up in the yard were a number of neatly parked, low four-wheeled wagons – on each, a long, chained strongbox. They watched one being led out, two mules pulling, the front wheels turning to a sharp angle, the rear then following on its articulated chassis.

'Caissons,' said Underhill with a grin.

'What?' asked De Lisle.

Underhill winked at them. 'Things that go bang, Lil.' He smiled nastily, looking out. 'It's their little artillery supply train.'

'*Christ Jaysus…*' mumbled De Lisle, '*shite an' all…*'

Hesse looked at the track to the guns beyond. 'It is a stage-post. They bring shot from the artillery park back there, and take it from here to the guns over there.' He looked at Tariq. 'It is perfect.'

Underhill patted Pettifer on the shoulder. 'Let's give 'em the shite of their lives. Lock yer cocks, lads. Tariq, you ready?'

The little Bedouin saluted. '*Oui, m'sieur.*'

Pettifer chucked to the horses and they moved on, turning into the yard. A soldier stepped out, a lantern swinging high, but they clattered in regardless and he leapt back, calling out as they came to a stop in front of the partially demolished house, the artillery caissons a bare fifteen yards away. An overweight and angry quartermaster sergeant stormed towards them.

'*Requisitions d'abord! Papiers! Demandes de quartier-maître de bataillon, brigade ou division!*'

Kite began climbing down. 'Why don't none of 'em ever speak bloody English…'

They jumped out and got busy, bustling with the stiff bundle in the back, pulling him out, the blanket dropping as Porter very deliberately yanked it off, crossing himself, '*Oh mon dieu…*' The corpse sagged in their hands and they dropped it to the ground, with much hand-waving and swearing in French and Arabic, *Ah putain alors, salaud de merde hein, hassanan, hassanan*, Warnock and Handley turning away, making a meal of it, their black *shemagh* pulled over their mouths. The sentry with the lantern and the large sergeant stopped and looked on, appalled, kerchiefs to their noses, his shouts now muffled. 'What do you do here, eh, eh? What is this!'

Sergent Hesse snapped back at the man without hesitation. 'We are the 14th *Tirailleurs* from Jaffa – where do you put the dead around here, because the hospital did not want him!'

The sentry looked at them, aghast. '*Jaffa…?*'

'Yes, Jaffa!' shouted Hesse. They took a pace back, eyes bulging in terror as they stared down at the body.

'B-but you all have plague in Jaffa...'

'*Plague?* I have a dead man in my cart! Do I leave him with you?' He snapped his fingers at the marines. '*Oui, zut alors*, we leave him – I have had enough...'

'No, no!' called the quartermaster sergeant. Hesse's Swiss-accented French aside, their eyes flitted over their Arab robes, their muskets, swords and Arabian daggers, his eye catching Warnock and his fierce face-paint – he pointed round to the back of the ruined walls and shouted, 'There! There, back there!'

They fussed over who was to pick up the body, the heavyset sergeant so fearful he showed them the way – leaving De Lisle and Pettifer on the front driver's bench of the cart. No one noticed Tariq, who had slipped away into the dark.

His army satchel over his shoulder, the little Bedouin marched with great aplomb in his grey corporal's tunic around the edge of the yard, and slipped behind the guard tent. He scuttled round behind the caisson wagons parked below the heaped ramparts of earth and wattle. Behind the caissons were stacked separate small groups of kegs and large crates, some marked '*Cartouche – Canon de 12*'.

He squatted by a stack of crates. A team of mules appeared from the battery trail to his right, the supply troops hurrying over to the driver, calling to each other, one uncoupling the wagon, another two taking the nearest loaded caisson wagon and hauling it round to the mules' harness.

Tariq reached into his satchel and pulled out a bag o'tricks and a large pouch. Normally equipped with quickmatch, which could burn at a rate of one foot per second, this particular bundle had the opposite – a slowmatch fuse of treated cotton, adulterated to burn at one foot per quarter-hour. He cut the fuse accordingly, pushed the glass-paper and phosphor igniter onto the thick frayed end and yanked the cap. It flared and snapped briefly, then died to a sizzling glow. He jammed the bundle in a hollow behind the bottom crate and emptied the pouch of black powder on the ground and across the stores of gun cartridges – then backed away into the yard in full view, his hands fiddling at his crotch. One of the supply troop saw him and shouted.

'*Eh tiens! Personne par là, eh!*'

Tariq ignored him and began to urinate on one of the parked caissons. The soldier swore and waved a dismissing hand, '*Merde alors...*'

'*J'arrive, j'arrive alors,*' *coming already,* called Tariq, turning, hurrying past the soldier to the cart, doing up a fly button on his falls, straightening his tunic. Tariq strode straight across the small yard to the cart, nodded at De Lisle and Pettifer and followed the lamplight behind the ruined walls to find the others.

They had carried the dead soldier round the back, following the large quartermaster. Tariq found them among the dim glow of more lanterns – stumps of broken walls, piles of stone, hit by past barrages. He saw a line of dead French laid out before a large shallow pit. Inside the pit were a dozen older men and women, digging at the earth.

'Mary an' Joseph,' murmured Cochrane to Napier. 'Dead Frogs...'

On the far side of the long, shallow pit were more dead – Turks, possibly locals, the gravediggers mournful, downcast, their sorrows writ in their silence.

'Poor buggers,' murmured Pettifer.

The overfed quartermaster sergeant shouted at the diggers, shooing them away from the main mass grave they had dug for the dead French. 'They do the digging, the peasants here, hm, from that village over there, a dirty people.' He jerked a thumb in the vague distance. Prayers were being intoned, lanterns glowing, their faces cast in a sickly yellow pallor and saddening shadow. Hesse, Kite, Handley and the others watched them.

'We got to get 'em out of here...' whispered Handley. They could see a few miserable tents and shacks clustered together in the flash of the batteries' endless barrage.

They had laid their corpse with the other dead and the sergeant looked at them imperiously. 'Well? Is that all you had?' He saw them looking at the labourers. 'They work on the mine. Too many dead, then they work here. Huh. Captain Andret says they are shiftless lazy dogs, I can tell you...'

The gravediggers looked at the marines, their robes, their *keffiyah* headdresses, their weapons – some stopped working and stared. Tariq raised his voice in Arabic to them and many turned, then looked at the sergeant, then at the marines.

'Wh-what did he say...?' demanded the quartermaster sergeant, then with a dawning realisation, backing away, 'Wh-who *are* you?'

Warnock glanced at Underhill. 'Sarge?'

Underhill nodded. 'By all bloody means, my lad.'

Warnock took a step forward, simmering with rage. '*Psst*.'

The sergeant turned, his face slick with sweat. He raised his lantern. 'Y-yes?'

'*Knock knock, twat.*'

The thud of the tomahawk coincided with a new salvo, and they were spared the sounds of bone cracking as Warnock smashed his stone axe upward into the man's fat chin, sending his head back with a loud snap. He dropped like a poleaxed boar. Warnock kicked his corpse, his knife out, ready to peel off the man's scalp, but Underhill stopped him.

'Put 'im in the bloody hole with the other heroes,' said Underhill. He shook his head. 'Look at 'em... bloody misery made flesh, they are. What says the boat?'

They nodded back their *ayes*, and Underhill gestured for the older man of the group. He came closer – he was perhaps sixty, short white hair at his temples, bald sun-browned pate, a farmer in better days. 'Parlay Fransay?' asked Underhill, 'Speako Englees?'

The man's face lit with surprise. '*Ingliz?*'

Underhill smiled. 'That's right, King Georgie's best. Tariq, tell 'im.'

Tariq bowed to the man '*Injilizi. Min Misr.*'

It was the strangest message of hope to bring, yet it seemed to help. *Englishmen*, he had said, *from Egypt*.

'Right,' said Underhill, 'signal prepared. Now, let's go save the ruddy day.'

–

A sense of otherworldliness stealing into him, not quite feeling the ground beneath his feet, Hazzard went outside through the main doors of the hospital, Delphine and Cook hanging back, aware something was amiss. He had recognised the voices, his skin crawling, the hairs on the nape of his neck standing on end, but still he wanted to be certain. His left hand clutching the scabbard of the scimitar, Hazzard moved cautiously past the guards and round the front of the building.

In the glow of a coach lamp hung on the hospital wall he saw elite dragoon troopers on fine horses, one without a rider, all waiting in the forecourt, the beasts stamping and snorting, their breath steaming. There were a few common soldiers milling about, several junior officers in their best uniforms. One of the soldiers broke from the group, wandering slowly, a dishevelled man with his back to Hazzard, his head low, bent over a pipe perhaps, or a mouthful of food.

Even with his back turned, Hazzard knew him, knew his moustache and unshaven chin, how he held himself, always ready; he recognised the mismatched pack, tunic and breeches – French, Turkish, Egyptian. Hazzard knew him at once, from Malta, from Embabeh, and a barricade in Cairo – it was Rossy, of the Alpha-Omega.

Delving into his pocket for his tobacco pouch, Rossy stopped dead. He looked slowly over his shoulder, then turned – and stared straight at Hazzard.

For all their combined instinct, the pair stood in silence, both startled by each other, yet not, the weight of mutual debt and counter-debt in each other's minds, flashing memories of their past encounters – at Valletta, in Lacroix's camp, of the sun and heat, and the water that had saved him, the barricade, the mob, their rescue. They stood motionless, held fast by uncertainty, calculation and conscience.

Hazzard drew the Lorenzoni and stumbled backwards to the doors, as Rossy dropped his pipe and he too moved backwards, reaching for his musket and began to shout – nothing intelligible at first, just an animal cry that there was great danger, until he found his voice, '*To arms! To arms! Anglais! There are anglais here!*'

Hazzard staggered into the sentries at the double doors, Cook pulling him inside, Delphine gasping with shock. Hazzard dived down the passageway, Cook seizing Delphine and shoving her after. The Berber or Mamluk at the end turned too late as Hazzard threw himself against the first door into the storeroom. He saw shelves, jars, linens, files and folders – and the communicating door to the voices he could now hear clearly, mingling with more inarticulate shouts.

Hazzard crashed through the door and the scene seemed to slow, every movement sharp in his mind, Tillery turning to look back at him, his eyes wide, Derrien rising slowly to his feet on the far side of the table, one hand reaching forward, his mouth open, shouting something that Hazzard could not hear. Deputy Blais was behind him, a hand to Derrien's shoulder – and Bonaparte in the chair to the right, a grey cloak over a dark brocaded army tunic, looking round, cool eyes wide, a dragoon reaching for him – though Bonaparte did not move, a call coming from outside, *Protect the general!*

He spoke.

'Mister Hazzard.'

Hazzard had no words, stopped again in his mind by thoughts of Caesar's *Gallic Wars* and an inscription, '*For practice*', but brought the Lorenzoni to the aim, Bonaparte not breaking his gaze at Hazzard, as if aware of the inevitable protection of Fate, his long hair suddenly wild as he was pulled from his chair, Derrien reaching for him, his wounded gloved hand producing his screw-barrelled pocket pistol. He saw Delphine, and his eyes widened madly as he raised the gun.

'*Traitor!*'

Delphine gasped, '*You!*'

There was a shot, the room bright with the flash, the smoke dense and choking, and Hazzard hit the wall out of instinct, the bullet whining off the doorframe. Delphine shouted, falling back into the storeroom behind as the Lorenzoni boomed, its large-calibre shell howling between Derrien and Bonaparte, hitting Blais, his eyes wide as he fell back, his throat bursting. Figures crowded Hazzard's vision, Rossy dropping low, pulling Bonaparte after him, the dragoons shouting, *Away! Get him away*, the wooden shutter at the window exploding into fragments with gunshots. Tillery dropped flat for cover, Cook shouting, '*Sir*,' dragging Hazzard down and back, Derrien's voice filled with rage, '*Arrest her! Traitor! Traitor! After them!*'

They burst out into the passage, the Mamluk down, blood dark on the wall behind – Hazzard thought, *Jory, well done*, and they ran, Delphine's hand in his charging back through the hospital into the main ward, the troops rushing past them to the main entrance, and Hazzard called, 'Quickly! *Aux armes!* Men at the front!'

Hazzard pulled Delphine along, Cook running behind as they found the side passage and corridor where they had seen Desgenettes and Monge, and the door to the side quad. It had gone wrong, but Cook knew what to do, Hazzard thinking only – *horses, rdv* – and they threw open the door into the cold darkness, running to the rail where they had tied them, Hazzard lifting Delphine up but she was very heavy – he saw her sagging and pulled her close, the red patch on her left shoulder. *Derrien's bullet? Ricochet?*

'She's hit! Put her on—'

Her voice was a gasp. 'I am… all right,' she said in a scarcely audible whisper.

Cook heaved her into his saddle in front and climbed up behind as Hazzard turned and lunged for his own mount, tugging the reins round, Cook calling, 'Them dragoons'll be all over the place—'

'No, they won't...' Hazzard pulled the horse about and they rode for the forecourt, charging through the knot of spectators, the last of the dragoons already gone, galloping off up the road to escort Bonaparte. Hazzard saw Rossy and another Alpha leap aside as he and Cook made the gate, a sentry brandishing a musket, the Lorenzoni booming again, knocking him down.

He looked behind at Delphine in Cook's arms – the men behind were too close, running out into the road, muskets in hand. Hazzard groped at the satchel slung on the saddle and pulled out a bag o'tricks. He spun the horse about as Cook rode past, pulled the snap-igniter and hurled it at the gate. The bundle hit the posts and rails and bounced, fizzing, the more seasoned men diving into the mud as it went off with a whump and flashing spray of naphtha, white and green in the dark, some unlucky, crying out. Hazzard hesitated on the road, turning his mount, the horse frantic to ride, the troops running across the quad to the gate – then he saw him, Derrien, running for a horse, screaming, '*After them! After them!*'

Hazzard kicked his heels in, '*Come on,*' and galloped up the road to the camp, several lengths behind Cook and Delphine, Cook's broad back shielding her, and Hazzard likewise shielding them both.

They reached the junction and he watched Cook take the left turn, the horse leaning into the curve, Hazzard seeing Delphine's head sagging at times, images of burning ships and the *Orient*, and lying in the boat, dark stains across Sarah's body—

No...

He heeled round the corner after them, towards Acre, away from Bonaparte, away from the quarry, *but never mind, we had a try didn't we; yes, we can say that,* he thought, the horse's hooves a constant battering, thundering on the hard-packed mud, water spraying as they splashed through the edge of the marsh and the pot-holes.

A musket-ball thwacked into the ground beside them, and he looked over his shoulder – three cavalry, skidding round the corner after him, Rossy and another of the Alphas, and charging up the middle, Derrien, his voice bright with rage, '*After them!*'

It might work, thought Hazzard, *it just might work*, presenting the hunter with a quarry and luring him on, letting him follow, *but the risk*, and he saw Izzam and Alahum at Alexandria smiling and nodding as Masoud translated his name for them, *Ahh! Khatar.*

Risk: hazard.

Bloody fool, letting her talk you into healing the bloody sick, let them die of the bloody plague they brought, a curse upon you all and may the plagues of Egypt fall upon thee.

Another bullet, whining off into the dark, a hammer at his left hip, the saddle thudding him hard in the back. The horse screamed, but all stopped short, the horses skittering left and right, as the road ahead vanished in a thunderclap of light and flame. The deadline had passed – Tariq's bomb had gone up.

–

'There is the signal,' called Smith from the quarterdeck of HMS *Tigre*. 'Mr Tyte, signal all gunboats to open fire and give cover.'

'*Aye sir*,' called Tyte from behind on the poopdeck. '*Theseus* signalling sir, moving into second position.'

'Very good, Mr Tyte,' replied Smith, as the guns rumbled on their trucks and were run out, 24-pounders, 32s and Long 18s. 'Bring her round, upper and middle per broadside, and let her bounce on her springs, Bo'sun!'

The call came back, '*Aye-aye! Helm hard a-starboard! Run yer guns a-portside and give 'em hellfire my lads!*'

The gunboats that had been unable to support Tillery's raid now drew in close to Haifa, blazing away, the road, shoreline and fortified walls exploding in a series of bursts, the port flying to pieces under the barrage, each ship firing in chain to maintain a constant bombardment, the gunships they had sought to cut-out and capture now flying to splinters and matchwood.

Troops ran along the shoreline to get away, but *Tigre* opened up, the first shots rising high and crashing down along the shore, the running figures of men transfixed in silhouette, then obliterated. *Tigre* swung on her springs as she fired, spreading the blazing shot all along the coast, the barrage creeping inland, pounding the trench network – not fifty yards from the corner of the walls of Acre.

Smith looked through his eyeglass at the bursting smoke and flame of the incendiary shot, the landscape a blaze of fire. He lowered the eyeglass, thinking of Hazzard, thinking of Wright. 'Come on, man… You can do it.'

Major Douglas of the marines and Lt Wright jerked back in alarm as Tariq's bomb in the marshalling yard exploded, lighting up the sky – the few French manning the line scattered, the batteries falling momentarily silent. They turned to their mixed company of marines and *Nizam-i Djedid*, swords in hand. Wright nodded at *Yuzbashi* Reiz. 'Ready?'

Reiz straightened his red fez, his gold brocaded red coat, and drew his gleaming and deadly *kilij* sword. 'Yes, Wright Pasha.'

'Good luck.'

Reiz blinked, his mind elsewhere, but smiled warmly. 'And you, Wright Pasha. I go for Hazar.'

Wright understood. 'Of course.'

Reiz looked at the *Nizami* and raised the long, bent-angled *kilij* and cried '*Hucuuum!*'

The company of one hundred *Nizami* roared, and stormed up the incline from the shore leading to the Acre seagate, up through the mud and earth to the French trenches beyond, *Hucum! Allah, Allah, Allah!* The incessant bombardment of HMS *Tigre* sent up soaring mountains of earth and rubble just beyond, the French pickets falling back and running to the rear lines. Reiz was determined to reach Hazzard and get him back to the shores of Acre, to the seagate. He charged across the stricken surface, looking, ever looking to the distant roads, hoping to catch a glimpse of him, his legs pumping, plunging into sudden craters, stumbling on stones, on bodies, the mud heavy on his boots, his *kilij* high as the *Nizam-i Djedid* poured through the frontline trenches of their enemy to a cacophony of screams, swords swinging, the French flying in stark terror.

Reiz reached his first ditch. He slid down the earth parapet on his backside, his boots foremost, and dropped to the bottom, a white-faced tunic leaping up before him, a burst of powder-smoke blooming in his vision as the man fell, Wright passing him, grabbing him up and pulling him along, shoving his empty pistol into his belt. Another Frenchman came at him from ahead, bayonet levelled, but Reiz spun in a tight circle, as he had seen Hazzard do, the *kilij* driving the bayonet into the mud wall, his sword rising and swinging at the neck. The man fell, the *Nizami* behind raging, gathering up the heads, *Intikam! Intikam!*

Revenge.

The red-coated *Nizami* troopers flooded along the trenchline, some hit by flying shrapnel from the bombardment, others ducking beneath the low parapet, following Reiz and a *Mulazim* lieutenant, the land around them erupting, the impacts of the barrage creeping ahead of the troops to clear their path, courtesy of Sir William Sidney Smith.

Guns firing from the battlements of the castle above, the French sappers and miners dashed across the torn open ground, the traversing fire from the castle's cannons sweeping them away in a hurricane of shot. The French night watch fell back in disordered clusters, clambering out of the trenches with their siege ladders and running, then reforming, moving backwards in disciplined ranks, some managing to fire musket volleys, unwilling to yield, men falling, the cannonfire blasting the ground around them.

Wright appeared up ahead from round a corner in the trench. 'Reiz! The entrance to the mine! To the left! Some go ahead, the rest go left, *sola, sola! Kalanlar sola!*'

Reiz ran to him and looked. At the end of a sloping lane cut into the earth, shored up with wattle and rock either side, was a low, dark tunnel entrance framed by stone and timber. It seemed to lead to the castle walls and the southern corner of the Damned Tower, which rose fifty yards away into the gloom of the cloudy sky. 'We have it, Wright Pasha! This is the mine!'

He stood on the corner and funnelled a squad of the *Nizami* down the ramp, leading them to the mine entrance. Keeping close to the trench wall, Reiz crouched to the dark tunnel mouth and shouted in fluent French, '*Sapeurs! Engineers! We are the Nizam-i Djedid! You have one minute to come out and lay down your arms!*'

The trench flashing with the detonations of gunfire overhead, he looked into the mine entrance, waiting, the sweat pouring off his forehead beneath his long-tailed red fez. His sergeant crouched beside him on one knee, peering inside, his miquelet musket aimed ready. '*Yuzbashi...*' he said with a warning note.

In reply came a burst of light and the report of a musket cracking in echo, the sergeant dropping back in alarm but unhurt. Reiz had seen enough. '*Evet!*' Yes!

Three *Nizami* ran up and threw fizzing bombs inside. They all dashed back to the main trench, throwing themselves against the trench wall around the corner. There was a muffled series of blasts and a rushing cloud of smoke rolled into the trench. Wright and Douglas came running at a crouch – the tunnel mouth still stood open.

'All we need do is collapse the entrance,' said Douglas. 'Physics will do the rest...'

'Bring up the locker!' called Wright to the marines behind.

Passed up from the rearward men came a long, flat box, two marines carrying it by leather strap handles. They set it down in the main trench, and Wright opened it.

Inside was a tight row of four fat paper cartridges for a 24-pounder naval gun, the smell of cordite and quickmatch strong, the locker lined with langrage scrap iron. He pulled the quickmatch fuse out and closed the locker, the fuse dangling. 'Right, get this into the tunnel.'

'For God's sake, that's enough to bring the castle down, Wright,' protested Douglas. 'Too close to the wall and you've done the job for them—'

Wright carried on, not looking up. 'All prepared by a Welsh miner from the Rhondda, sir. Come on lads, let's make a bang.'

–

The barrage sent up by the *Tigre* was to last no more than ten minutes. Hazzard could not imagine how much time had elapsed since it began, but he saw the smouldering wreckage of the village up ahead as the *Tigre's* guns fell silent.

Cook and Delphine darted right then left off the track, a dogleg to join the Nazareth road, Delphine hanging onto the saddle bow, Cook enormous behind her, his arms enfolding her, the blazing French batteries not far off, the ruined village visible in the lightening pre-dawn gloom. Troops had begun to gather in platoons, coming down from the camp. Hazzard could not go much faster and began to slow, looking behind – Rossy and a younger Alpha were there, Derrien at the front, confident with his weight of numbers. But more dragoons and cavalry had followed, pistols cracking, and he heard the whine and howl of their bullets as he danced the horse from side to side, ducking low, feeling the inevitable grasp of Fate.

Is this where? he thought, *Here? Shot in the back on a road to a siege?*

He had always wondered where it would be, but he had his prefer-ence now, after being in Egypt. He had always imagined he would be wounded, and crawl away into the desert, and fall into a waiting pit, the sand to cover him forevermore, as it had Cambyses and his army and countless others: as if he had never been – a small relic of a brief time on earth, a desiccated memento for a land that remembered the world, but kept silent.

Going to the seagate at the dockside of Acre's port would be impossible now that he was so far inland, the marching troops too numerous. He looked beyond the French artillery, out to the far side of the castle. He saw the empty north shore – no troops, no lines to be seen, an empty desert plain controlled by English naval guns out to sea. It had been his alternative escape route – simple, but utterly exposed, and now their only option.

Hazzard followed the dogleg, dodging right then left, up a rise and onto the road, and saw the cart and two horses waiting on the verge, *perfect*, and put himself lower in the saddle in preparation, just in case, leaning to one side as Pettifer hurled a bag o'tricks. Hazzard's horse whinnied at the sound of the first explosion, and he hauled on the rein, turning in the road. Another bundle landed just in front of Derrien, and the road burst with a whump, the boy with Rossy crying out. Rossy shouted, *Anton!* and tried to control his own mount, but slid from the saddle, crashing to the ground. Hazzard saw Derrien fall, eyes wide, his horse staggering and rearing in a cloud of smoke, toppling on its side, crushing him to the track. Derrien roared with pain – just as the pursuing cavalry rode into Underhill's ambush: 9 Company opened fire from the scrub, utterly invisible in their black robes.

The buck and ball loads sprayed across the road, shredding the horses' fetlocks and sending them skidding and collapsing in a screaming tangle. Pettifer's musketoon boomed, a dragoon trooper flying from his saddle, another firing back, his pistol empty, drawing his sword, a second volley bringing the last of them down. Cook turned about, Delphine holding on to the pommel of the saddle, calling *William!* and Hazzard rode back to the scene.

Eight horses lay near the corner of the track where it met the road, one struggling to rise, the others barely breathing, the dragoons and cavalrymen sprawled across the track, or lying dead in the scrub. Rossy lay on his side by the verge, an arm moving slowly, and Hazzard was grateful, *he lives.*

Derrien was still very much alive, scrabbling out from underneath his fallen mount, his legs kicking and scraping at the earth as he pushed and thrust himself backwards, straining, the horse trapping his leg, his voice a constant whisper of panic to himself '*Hazz... Hazzard...*'

With a final jerk he tugged himself free, pushing himself awkwardly to his feet, trying to stand, his hand on his damaged leg. He hobbled back to the dead troopers – to run to safety, Hazzard could not tell, watching him dispassionately, not even with the hatred he had come to know so well.

The marines stood and watched as Derrien stumbled along the track, his leg dragging as he went, no walking-stick any longer, limping, looking back, his lank hair swinging either side of his bruised and bloodied face, his coat torn at the shoulder, his chest heaving, his breath coming in gasps. Then Hazzard saw what he was doing – reaching for one of the dead trooper's swords.

His right leg stiff behind him, he stooped and pulled a blade from a dead man's scabbard, the steel scraping, the effort making him gasp. He swung round and turned to face Hazzard. He raised the heavy blade *en garde*, and waited, the breath sawing in and out of his open mouth.

Hazzard dismounted, sliding down from the saddle. He drew the scimitar and walked towards him, and stopped five paces away. Derrien licked his lips, his eyes wide, his gaze flicking from Hazzard to the marines and back, the upright sabre shaking in his hand. He lunged but Hazzard knocked it away without a thought. Derrien then swung the blade in a lateral swipe, grunting with the force and intent of the blow. Again, an easy parry, Hazzard looking at him, impassive, moving only his sword.

'Come, Englishman with no king,' Derrien raged in English, 'Damn the king! Your own... your own words, the *thinking* man, the *thinking...*'

The marines gathered round as Derrien swung again, his whole body lunging with the blow to cut at Hazzard's elbow, falling forward, losing his footing – but again Hazzard simply raised the scimitar and the blades clanged.

'*Come, damn you!*' he screeched, chopping down at Hazzard from above.

Hazzard parried the blade at an angle and tipped it to one side, the sabre digging into the dirt of the road. Derrien fought for breath. 'I am... *I am...*' he gasped, reverting to French, 'I am the *Republic...*'

Hazzard looped the tip of the scimitar round Derrien's blade and twisted the sabre from his hand. It fell to the road. Derrien stared, his lungs wheezing in shuddering gasps. He looked round at the marines, at Cook on the horse behind, and saw Delphine. His face twisted with loathing.

'*You...*' he hissed, 'You should be *shot*... with all your damned *nurses*... and *orderlies*, and—' He dug a hand into his coat for his second pocket pistol, and fired wild.

Underhill smashed the butt of his musket into Derrien's neck, and he fell with a grunt. Kite aimed his musket down at him. 'You're bloody nicked, mate.'

The cart rattled onto the road and Napier took the unconscious Derrien in two hands, lifted him bodily, and slung him in the back like a sack of coal, De Lisle and Hesse gagging him with a *shemagh*, pulling his hands behind his back and binding his wrists tightly. Porter took Delphine up with him, already examining her wound as Hazzard climbed stiffly into his saddle – part of him unable to believe that they had, in the end, captured Derrien, a creature who had become as abstract to him as Lucifer. He felt numb, distracted, almost lost.

The sky brightened in the misty half-light of dawn. The artillery batteries were visible a hundred yards off, and beyond, the village ruins and open northern plain beckoned – their escape route.

The cart clattered onto the Nazareth road and down towards the French batteries. Troops in column came across the scrub and marsh, along the road, down from the camps in the hills, none paying the slightest attention to a rushing cart full of mercenaries and robed riders on horseback.

They passed the former munitions marshalling yard, now a blackened crater, filled with sappers and engineers searching through the rubble of the explosion. They rode up the pot-holed track behind the guns to the sprawling remains of the ruined village, and took cover by the shattered walls. Cook jumped down from his horse and saw Hazzard climb down slowly, staggering slightly, looking at his right hand.

'What is it?' demanded Cook.

Hazzard shook his head. 'Nothing... come on...'

Cook took his hand and looked – it was red with blood. '*Christ.*' Derrien's pistol-ball had caught him in the side.

'Wait – just listen, Jory...' Hazzard leaned against the stone wall behind and sank down to the grass. He looked out at the grey north shore, the lights of the castle shining on the left, its parapets winking with muzzle-flashes. The surf crashed against the port walls, the grey mist rising along a deserted stretch of beach reaching northwards for miles – across only a few hundred yards of empty ground. 'We make the dash, using the raid on the mine as cover. Wright said they would blow the mine as a signal, just as we did for them...'

'*Christ Jaysus*...' He turned and shouted, 'Porter! Get o'er here now!'

Porter scrabbled his way out of the cart and dropped beside them. Hazzard lost his patience, tired.

'Will you *listen*, Jory – *Theseus*... she's not there yet. Might be too shallow for her... to pick us up.'

Porter found the blood patch, then swore. 'Damn these things.' He pulled off the black *binish* from Hazzard's shoulders and opened the Bombay Marine jacket. 'It's skinned your ribs sir.' He put a pad of linen against it and Hazzard grimaced. 'Hold that,' Porter said, putting Hazzard's hand on it.

'Can't feel a thing...'

Porter checked round his side to his back, and looked at Cook. 'It's broke a rib, Sarge, and bounced in, don't know how. Needs to be dug out.'

'No bloody time for that...' muttered Hazzard, trying to push himself up.

'Sit *still*, damn ye,' cursed Cook.

Porter looked as worried as he had with Wayland. 'I'll... I'll bandage it...'

Delphine joined them, her bare shoulder likewise wrapped. 'William...'

He looked up at her. 'You cannot stay... not here...'

She held his face, her hands cool, and he felt relief wash over him. *No burning ship, not this time.*

She handed Porter a roll of linen crepe, lifting Hazzard's arm out of the way, and Porter began to wrap him round the waist, binding him tight. 'Oh lord, man... It's over a kidney... God above...' Porter whispered. 'I'd give you a ruddy corset if I had one, sir...'

A shot rang out and stone chips flew from one of the broken walls nearby. Kite shouted out, '*Mine*,' and fired his musket in reply. There followed another shot and more chips flew. They all ducked below the stone walls, the unconscious Derrien still in the cart.

Hazzard looked to Warnock and Kite. 'Split up, go around, keep each other in sight.'

'Hold on,' said Cook, 'look at this now...'

Hazzard pushed himself forward and looked over the smashed wall by his head. He saw a white flag waving.

'Stay down.' Hazzard looked about, accounting for everyone. He took a breath and called out in French, '*What do you want?*'

The voice came back, deep, sonorous. '*You are the anglais?*'

Hazzard looked at Cook. 'Yes!'

'*Come to speak,*' said the voice. '*I stand now.*'

They looked out and saw the giant shape of Pigalle rise in his grey and sandy desert garb, his hands out. 'That's him,' said Cook. 'Bloke I took down at Embabeh... from the barricade and all.'

'It's one of Caron's Alphas,' said Hazzard, 'who saved me...' He looked at the marines. 'Hold your fire.'

With a wince, Hazzard stood up, pulling his short jacket across the bandage. He moved round the corner of the stone wall, his hands out. Cook rose behind him, but Underhill snatched at his sleeve. 'Hold hard there, Jory boy...'

Cook glanced at him. 'Strange times, 'Miah...'

Underhill got to his feet, looked across the shell-shattered stone ruins and saw Pigalle waiting. 'By God they be strange, aye...'

Warnock murmured, '*Sarge... Christ Jaysus...*'

Pigalle moved forward into the ruins, his dusty grey *shemagh* blowing from the end of his long Charleville musket. He looked about, then nodded at Cook in recognition. 'John Bull.'

Cook nodded back, boxers acknowledging each other in the ring. 'Aye.'

Pigalle looked down at the ground, kicked something with his boot. 'I lose Rossy. And Antonnais.'

Hazzard watched as the other Alphas appeared, one by one, predatory animals coming out of the dark into the dull dawn light. One joined Pigalle, a rifle with mounted sight in his hands – St Michel, who had doubtless been sniping at them. There must have been a dozen in all, half-dressed as Arabs, just as 9 Company were. The two units looked across at each other, the ruined village become a looking-glass.

'Rossy is injured,' said Hazzard in French, 'on the Nazareth road, but alive. He saved the general. Antonnais was with him.'

Pigalle nodded, satisfied. '*Merci.*' He looked round. 'You go now? To the ships?' His hand waved out at the distant shore.

Hazzard said nothing.

Pigalle shrugged, looking down, then out to sea. He glanced at St Michel who nodded his assent, a decision agreed among them. 'We give you the cover fire.'

Hazzard stared at the huge man, Underhill suddenly dead still behind as Cook murmured, '*By all that's holy in bloody Bristol…*'

'But one demand,' said Pigalle, 'Andret, he uses the people here, from Achzib, from Cana, beats them, to dig until they die. You must take them away, to safety.'

Hazzard did not understand. 'Take who? Which people?'

The skies began to lighten and the hills dipped deeper in shadow by contrast – they had not much time left, Hazzard knew. And still *Theseus* had not appeared. Pigalle pointed, indicating through the ruins the tents and hovels on the rising ground to the rear. Two dozen Lebanese peasants had gathered, old men, women, and several older children – Andret and Derrien's unofficial labour for the mining operation.

'My God…' gasped Hazzard.

Pigalle looked at St Michel, who urged him on. 'And, if you take the people,' said Pigalle, 'Andret,' he added with a decided nod of appreciation, 'he will suffer.' Beside him, St Michel smiled.

Underhill confirmed it all for Hazzard. 'Frogs been usin' them to dig graves and all, sir. Saw 'em before Tariq blew the ammo dump. If we can get 'em across that ground, they got a chance.'

Hazzard stared at them, their misery, their wretched state. 'They could be shot to pieces…' But he wondered if much could be worse than what they had already suffered.

'You go now,' said Pigalle, 'Andret gets the light company to come. *Mercenaires.* North Africans… Maghrib, Berbers, thieves. We do not like them. We will help you. Rossy, and our *Chef*,' he said, his head dropping slightly as he looked down with sadness, 'they teach me much about honour.' He looked around at the trenches, at the guns and the castle. 'There is no honour here – only between us.' He nodded his head firmly again, a bargain struck. 'We are the *Alpha-Oméga*,' he said, sealing their promissory bond, 'and you are the *anglais*.'

'*William*,' called Delphine, 'over there!' She pointed to the north.

They looked round – behind Pigalle and the Alphas, across the open plain to the dark scrub hills beyond, lanterns had appeared, swaying in the shadows of a low rise, several hundred yards from their road to safety and the beach: the French mercenaries.

'It is Andret,' said Pigalle. 'He comes.'

Hazzard glanced at Cook. 'If they reach the shoreline first they'll cut us off…'

As he spoke they saw a dim flash deep in the shadows behind the lanterns, then heard a distant thump, and a round-shot hurtled towards them. Cook shouted, '*Down!*'

Twenty yards away a 12-pound ball thudded into the ground, skipped, and crashed into the perimeter of the stone ruins, taking down a wall and corner, the masonry exploding into a cloud of stone, blocks tumbling and rolling. Hazzard shouted to Pigalle. '*Allons-y!* Pettifer! Bring that bloody cart! Marines to me!'

Pigalle called to the others as the next round came howling down, well short, crumping into the earth on the far side of the village. They ran through the ruins, 9 Company and the Alphas, past the shattered walls and heaps of rubble to reach the civilians running from the bombardment, Pettifer now far ahead, the cart rattling up a dirt track alongside, Cochrane, Napier, Hesse and Tariq in the back, Derrien lying flat, gagged, his hands bound, writhing, screaming out.

Pigalle began herding the group to the cart, Pettifer and the others jumping down, handing up a pair of boys to the bench seat, others clambering up over the backboard to the rear. 'Tell them,' said Hazzard, 'I cannot get them all through—'

'They know,' said St Michel.

Another round came down, bursting further off. The old farmer-turned-gravedigger helped a woman up to the cart, and another, the space filling quickly, Napier hauling Derrien to a sitting position, his head thrashing as he screamed behind his gag in frustrated rage. The rest would have to run behind and hope.

'You go straight, by the castle walls,' said Pigalle, 'We go right, to the Berber *Tirailleurs*, hm?'

Hazzard nodded. '*Bonne chance.*'

Pigalle looked at him, his big face frowning. 'And you, *M'sieur l'anglais.*'

'*Tiens,*' said St Michel. '*On y va!* We go!'

The Alphas leading them out beyond the ruins to the trenchline, they reached the open ground, the light increasing by the moment, when Warnock and Kite came at the run from behind. 'Sir, a company o'the heavy mob closing in on the left now, from the trenches.'

St Michel looked. 'Grenadiers. Madmen.'

Hazzard looked round at them all. '*On me in twos, covering fire, the wagon! Go!*'

Pettifer lashed the horses. They all began to run.

Armageddon

Sergent-chef-major Achille Caron clambered onto his camel, its legs folded beneath itself, resting low on the ground, the blankets of his saddle warm. He hooked his leg round the pommel, taking the rein, and the beast rose up from behind then pushed itself to full height with a plaintive roar. He gave the command, *hat-hat*, and the camel moved forward slowly, its long neck swinging left and right looking at the others, at the horses, as the company of *Bedu* mounted in their saddles all around. He stopped by the horse of Shajar al-Durr.

She stood quiet, her arms out to the sides, as two Tarabin draped her with a sleeveless jerkin of mail, a dark blue *binish* overtop, pulling her long black hair free. Her servant Zeinab waited, in her hands a small mail and silver tiara, decorated with pearls. Zeinab raised it onto her head, fitting the tongs into Shajar's thick hair, the pearls and mail descending over her forehead to a point between her eyes.

'You are indeed the Tree of Pearl, then,' said Caron.

She looked up at him with a slight smile, and inclined her head, then climbed into her saddle. She took the reins and wrapped them in her fists. 'They must see me, to know I am here and have faith,' she replied, hands reaching up, checking her straps and stirrups, a curved scimitar slipped into a sheath on the saddle. 'To see another, truly, is the greatest gift any soul can bestow upon another.'

'Did the *anglais* see you?' he asked.

She inclined her head again. 'He did.'

He trotted the camel closer. 'You know where he is?'

'We shall find him. You shall not fight with us, Caron, friend of the *Bedu*, for we face your countrymen.'

Caron looked off at the lightening hills, off into Palestine, Nazareth in the distance, Bethlehem beyond. Somewhere, he thought, there was still grace. 'There is only one I seek, and I shall find him once you have gone. But thank you, for an old man's life.'

Shajar looked round as Zeinab mounted and rode up beside her. 'Then follow,' she said to Caron, 'watch, and wait. And be as wise as you have been.'

She leapt into a light gallop, a troop of horse behind, a sense of greatness emanating from her, as if she were a ghost from another time. The Mamluks wheeled round in formation, their white robes a flashing river, the Tarabin, Khushmaan and Awlad 'Ali following, carbines raised, the horses charging to the south, their voices rising all around him, *Shajar, Shajar, Shajar! Allahu akbar!*

Caron gave the camel a gentle swat with a switch and lurched forward into the trailing dust storm, thinking of a chase, and a quarry – feeling somehow that something good would come of this day.

–

Reiz pushed through his men in the trench and looked out at the land beyond the Damned Tower. The ground opened for nearly half a mile, old entrenchments now abandoned thanks to the fire given by the English ships that had once stood offshore, their guns sweeping the area of French troops. But as he stared across the plain, his eye caught movement where there should have been none.

A French company was moving in from the north, from the dark hills. He looked across the misty trenches to the French batteries to his right, and saw another company of infantry, some in dark tunics and some in pale coats with the tall caps of grenadiers – moving across the trench line, not coming in to attack the walls or castle. Together the companies were forming a pincer, to meet on the plain – but he could not see why.

'*Yuzbashi!*' cried his sergeant and pointed. Far off to the right near the remains of the ruined village, from beyond the French batteries, came a galloping horse cart. It was packed with civilians – and charging across the open plain. Behind it came a platoon of infantry, some in black *binish* and Arab *shemagh*, running. They were making a straight run to the shoreline. At the front was a man in red with a curved sword.

Reiz could see stage after stage playing out before him – by the time the cart drew within fifty yards of the shore, the two French companies would have closed the pincer and surrounded them.

'Wright Pasha!' he called, 'Doogalas Pasha! It is Hazar!'

Wright and the marines shoved the explosive locker into the mine entrance, a marine unwinding the line of quickmatch to the corner of the main trench. Douglas hurried up behind Reiz and looked through his eyeglass.

'Good God... Wright!' he called over his shoulder, 'Come quickly!'

Wright came at a run, taking the eyeglass form Douglas. 'It's Hazzard,' he said. 'He's got civilians with him... they're on the wrong side of the blasted castle—'

'But they'll never see him to pick him up,' said Douglas, '*Theseus* is standing off the port to the west but *Tigre*'s in the bay in the south.'

'I shall go,' said Reiz. 'This company here will protect his flank.'

Wright did not like it. 'Reiz, please – when the mine blows it will be a sufficient diversion, and the French will come running straight into the castle guns.'

'For Hazar it will be too late.' Reiz turned to the *Nizami* behind, all watching the French moving across the landscape. '*Nizam-i Djedid!*' he cried, '*Hazar Pasha saves our people! Will you help him! Yes or no!*'

As one, the Turks roared, and Reiz scrambled out of the trench, '*Saldir...!*'

The *Nizam-i Djedid* poured out of the trench behind him, a stream of red coats cutting across the cratered terrain, the cannon on the Damned Tower blazing, the French grenadiers turning, the shells crashing among them, some diving for cover. Reiz kept his eye on the marines and the distant cart, not feeling the ground beneath his pounding feet, a French officer appearing from a trench, a sword rising. He swung his *kilij* – another roar from the men behind, *Reiz, Reiz, Reiz!*

Wright and Douglas raced back to the trench wall and entrance ramp to the mine, a line of French running towards them, vaulting over the ditches, the marines answering with volley-fire. Wright knelt by the end of the quickmatch fuse and drew his pistol. He glanced at Douglas, who nodded. Wright pulled the trigger, the flintlock flashing, the flare from the priming-pan lighting the fuse. It fizzed and spat, rushing along its length. Wright called to the marines, '*All out and down!*'

Far behind Reiz and the *Nizami*, the ground shuddered, a vast tower of earth rising with a thunderclap. Clods of mud and debris raining down behind them, the *Nizami* roared again, speeding their charge across the No Man's Land of ditches and shellholes, squads of French infantry clambering out of their trenches, only to be cut down by the swords of the red-coated Turks. Reiz saw the swathe of French in blue and white less than a hundred yards away, heading for the open ground. He turned the *Nizami* to intercept them, leading the charge from the Damned Tower, knowing they might never get back, his only thought – *Hazzard*.

–

Pettifer lashed at the horses and they galloped along one of the tracks criss-crossing the cratered marshland, water spraying from their hooves, the overloaded cart bouncing and shaking behind, the people crying out. De Lisle fired another salvo of buck and ball to their left at the approaching French, the ground bursting around them as two 12-pound rounds struck and heaved up fountains of earth. The horses whinnied, one twisting in his harness, its forelegs folding, dragging the other horse with it, and they ploughed into the mud and marsh, a great wave of water washing up as the cart twisted, bucked and tipped with a scream of metal and splintering wood, the passengers sent tumbling.

Underhill and Warnock were on them in moments, '*Get 'em out, Knocky lad!*' Pettifer clambered to his feet and fired a salvo from the musketoon, Kite and Handley running in, pulling them up, the younger lifting their elders, staggering forward in twos and threes, limping, falling, crying out in fear, '*Quick! Isri ya!*'

The ground shook again as another round burst beside them, and they screamed, Hazzard shouting, '*Pettifer! Get out of there!*' Still another round whistled overhead, striking the side of the cart, the wood leaping, exploding, Kite throwing himself flat, Handley picking him up, *C'mon Mick!* Porter and Delphine running, the shore barely two hundred yards distant.

'*Delphine!*' Hazzard ran for her, taking her hand, she holding Porter's, pulling him along – Hazzard could hear him gasping, his spectacles gone, his head bare, his face flushed. Far to his right Hazzard saw them coming, a ragged line of running men, possibly two hundred, a great curving arc of them, the Berber and Maghrib mercenaries, some heading to the sea, trying to cut them off. He ran, looking about, ticking them off in his mind, *Cook, Underhill, Hesse, Cochrane, Tariq, Napier, good*, his right hand clutching the wound at his side, the wind going out of him too fast, *come on*. He let go of Delphine's hand.

'*William!*'

'*Go! Get to the shore! Whatever happens!*'

He ran to the Lebanese, struggling through the marsh, pulling them along, calling to them, '*Yallah! Isri ya!*' remembering Reiz in the streets of Jaffa, '*Chabuk! Chabuk!*'

Twenty yards to their right the Alphas dropped, Pigalle firing into the approaching arc of Berber troops, some distant shapes in robes falling, flying off their feet, St Michel shouting, '*Allez, allez! Go, go!*' Underhill coming behind Hazzard, pulling him along, '*Come, sir,*' his mud-caked boots heavy beneath him, *hundred and fifty yards to the sea,* he thought, and found he was shouting, '*Only a hundred and fifty yards!*'

The massed cry of the Berbers was now audible, an inarticulate shout, and they could see an officer at the front, waving a sword. St Michel pointed: '*Andret!*'

The Alphas began firing at the figure, the earth leaping around his feet – the lone man fell into the marsh, dropping his sword, picked himself up and ran back to his lines screaming, St Michel loading up another shot, firing, missing, cursing, waving the others on.

Hazzard looked to his left and saw the second company of French charging towards them from their left. Warnock and Cochrane went onto one knee, firing, Hesse and Tariq making a two-rank firing party – their volleys boomed, the buck spreading, hitting, spattering in the mud, men toppling backwards into the trenches, a musket falling, a bonnet flying.

One of the Lebanese, the ageing farmer, ran with heavy leaping strides, trying to pull two of the women along behind him, but one stumbled, falling. The old man stooped to lift her, an arm under her shoulder, a bullet striking him, and he staggered, dropping to one knee, then stood again, shouting, lifting her bodily. Pettifer ran to him – Hazzard saw the musket-balls bursting around Pettifer's feet, one hitting his leg, another his shoulder, and the big Cornishman shouted with pain as he dropped into the marsh.

'*Petty!*' De Lisle ran for him, Underhill and Cook close behind, Warnock and Kite lying prone, firing in volleys to cover them, Warnock screaming at the French in a rage, wanting them to close, so he could tear into them. But it all seemed useless, Hazzard knew – the sea, the shoreline, shuddering before him, in the distance, *what for*, he thought, *no boats, no bloody boats, no ship, nothing*, and they too

433

would dive into the sea, try to swim, and be picked off one by one by the patient French or Berbers or whoever they might be.

But it had given them hope, just for some moments, and that was all he had ever wanted, just to pass that much on at the very least, to any of them, to the marines, to the forgotten people whose homes had become a battlefield, whose lives had been trampled by yet another tyrant. May he inherit the wind, he thought, may he inherit the void, *Ozymandias, may you stare at the ruins of your temple and the empty skies for the rest of eternity.*

The French muskets were closer now, bullets snapping and whizzing at the ground, and he saw some of the villagers fall, arms out, some stopping, pulling them up, dragging them, shouting in fear; and all began to gather in the centre, the approach of the French on the right, the French on the left, the fear driving all into the centre, into a knot, Cook shouting, '*Keep your distance.*'

Underhill cried out, then dropped, '*Jory!*'

It was more a scream than anything, his hand out, reaching for him over twenty feet off, but he was falling and wanted him to come, and Cook stopped, turned and ran back, '*'Miah!*' He pulled him through the mud by his arm, not letting go.

Hazzard looked across the plain, the French on the right firing at will, one of the Alphas falling, Pigalle lifting him onto his back, carrying him, running to a shellhole – filled with dead. Pigalle skidded into it, other Alphas following, the marines pulling the Lebanese down to cover among the bodies below. As Hazzard slid down the blast wall of the crater, he had a memory of De la Salle in the Great Cabin, his confessions, and the tale of the massacre of the Moroccans at Jaffa.

'*The bodies!*' he cried, '*Use the bodies for cover!*' A Lebanese mother and child fell into the hole beside him, and he snatched at the nearest corpse, lifting it by its jacket front, shouting at himself, at everything, hauling the trunk upright, the stench making him want to retch, as a bullet thwacked into it. He called to the sobbing woman cradling her daughter in her arms, and she nodded, sheltering under the dead man, others doing likewise.

From the trenchlines came a wave of pale coats, *grenadiers*, he thought, seeing their tall mitre caps, bayonets held out. He heard himself shouting, '*These are the men who burned Jaffa! These are the men who murdered the families!*' Without hesitation, an Alpha flung himself down in the mud beside him, aimed his Charleville and fired into them, hitting the first man, tangling three others in the charge. The Alpha took a pistol from his belt and fired, then spat, drawing a knife, putting it in his teeth and began to reload. He looked at Hazzard, furious. '*Pour l'honneur*,' he declared, and fired another round into the hated grenadiers.

Hazzard got to his feet, his vision clouded with the powder-smoke all around. He drew the scimitar. '*Derrien! Where is Derrien!*' He charged over the marshland, a knot of French infantry close, five men, ten, he cared little, the scimitar sweeping aside the first bayonet, and he spun round, the sword flashing across the soldier's throat, '*Damn you!*' Hazzard spun again, chopping down, cleaving a Charleville in half. '*Derrien!*'

A hand smacked him on the back and dragged him down, '*Wotchit sir!*' Handley holding him tight, the call coming late – *bag o'tricks!* He saw the bundles flying, and covered his head – there was a dull whump, and men screamed before them, iron fragments smacking into the mud, fizzing across the marsh, black smoke rising. '*Up!*'

Warnock was soon beside him, thrashing into the squad of French with his tomahawk, a short sword in his left hand, '*Come on ye bloody shites, ye bloody piss-shites!*' Closing with them, his axe whipping left and right, taking faces, eyes, throats, until a bayonet went through his thigh and he roared, his hand lashing out, goring the soldier with the spike of the axe-head. He tugged out the bayonet, and Handley and Hazzard lifted him, running back to the crater.

They slid down the mud wall, and one by one the others stood with the explosive bundles, pulling the snap-igniters, the quickmatch hissing, lashing, and flung them – Cook's arm the strongest, Pigalle roaring, throwing two into the grenadiers, ducking down behind their parapet of dead men. The explosions thudded, one after the other, erupting through the charging soldiers, each bag blasting the men around, one running in flames, screaming, falling into the mud just yards from the crater's edge.

Hazzard stood, wheezing, his right side burning, his mind in a fog, musket-fire rapping out overhead. He looked round at them, Cook holding Underhill, the old pirate pale, shaking, firing pistols off to the right, Napier lying prone on the parapet, firing off left, Handley reloading, Hesse face down, curled up, unmoving, Warnock, Cochrane, Porter with Delphine, holding her down, the bullets kicking up the earth in spouts – and he thought, *I would not die in*

435

any other company, and realised he was shouting it from the edge of the shellhole, Delphine crying out, '*William!*'

The French grenadiers and infantry had fallen back on the right to regroup and were now fifty yards off, the Berbers a hundred yards off to the left, and he looked for a desperate man – in black, limping, struggling – but saw nothing. *Nothing.* And he began to give up that little hope he had clung to, the sea just fifty yards away. He turned to look across the devastation that would claim them – and he saw it.

A pillar of fire.

Just as he had seen at Shubra Khit, a storm following the cavalry of Murad Bey. He spun, hit, the first bullet creasing his left shoulder-blade, reverberating through his neck and chest, and he dropped to one knee, his mouth open in a rage of pain, the clouds swimming before his eyes – another bullet kicked up the earth before him, its olive and tawny scrub spraying back at him, a broad lash of fire across his thigh, but still he looked, and pointed, so they could see. The pillar rose behind the Berbers and spread, engulfing them, tearing through them, a stream of white gossamer and chainmail, Mamluk swords high, cutting through the fleeing Berbers, through the Maghrib, and he thought of Memnon, and dead tyrants, and laughed at how Murad would have liked to have seen it. Behind came a troop of Bedouin horse, their faces wrapped in blue and checked *shemagh*, their robes flapping. *Saif Ali...! Allah, allah, allah!*

At the front, just ahead of the others, he saw a rider in dark blue, no headdress, a glint of pearl and silver from a diadem over those gleaming, almond-shaped eyes, a stream of dark hair flying behind.

Shajar al-Durr.

He was shouting, standing, trying to hold himself upright, '*Up! Get up! Marines to me!*' And Cook was on him, his arm round his waist, pulling him, Underhill beside him, pushing himself up, '*Nine Comp'nay!*' Warnock was up, the clouds of dust rising as the first riders reached them and tore around them in a broad protective arc behind them, the grenadiers falling, the Mamluks dipping low, their swords taking heads and arms, muskets flying to pieces, men screaming as they fell.

The marines dragged themselves out of the crater, the clouds of dust and sand behind them a shield as they forced their way forward, the water so close, the surf breaking, Hazzard now shouting, '*To the shore!*'

Shadows in the rising dust, the sand blowing in the wind, some French getting through, looming out of the cloud, then turning – there came a rising shout from behind, *Reiz, Reiz, Reiz*, and the *Nizam-i Djedid* fell upon them, their swords cleaving a swathe through the pale coats of the grenadiers as they turned their bayonets too late, either to be trampled by the Mamluk or cut down by the *Nizami*.

Horsemen tumbled in the melee, musket-balls flying through the cloud. Cochrane fell, '*Arthur!*' and Napier charged through them, '*Cocky!*' the cries of the Tarabin and Mamluk rolling, the old Turkish warcry, *Vur un Vur un! Smite them!*

Out to sea, Hazzard saw the distant shadow of the heavy *Theseus*, standing far off, too far, four boats drawing towards them, oars digging deep, men at the prow shouting, *Pull! Pull!* Her guns fired and there was a roar overhead, hurtling rounds crashing far behind them. He saw Kite fall and turned to gather him up, *Where's Hesse, where is he!* He watched Shajar behind them, at the tip of an arrowhead, curving again in a great arc, the Mamluk crescent moon come down to them, the French falling back, the red coats of the *Nizami* a blood-red spear thrust into the backs of the grenadiers, turning to face them at the bayonet, the bayonet not enough, their volleys broken, *Retirez! Retirez!* The 32-pounders of the *Theseus* crashed deep into the plain, a line of bursts, driving them back to the trenchline.

Hazzard slipped an arm under Kite's shoulder and tried to pull him, *no strength*, his leg engulfed in pain, his left arm useless, hanging, blood sticky on his hand. They lurched forward at a limping run for the shore, the dunes rising then sloping down. '*Come on sir, nearly bloody there,*' said Kite.

All around them Hazzard saw *Nizami* red coats in a defensive ring, *Turks*, and he sensed Reiz beside him, a protective spirit, a *kilij* swinging, a line of them behind firing into the fleeing French grenadiers, *Hazirla! Atesh!* The blasts deafening, and the French falling into the wall of flying dust, a whirlwind to shield them as they reached the water.

Hazzard fell to the sand and pushed Kite towards the surf and the approaching boats, his voice a whisper. '*Go, man, go on…*'

The first boat struck the shingle, men running, '*Theseus to me!*'

Hands reached for him, but he fought them off, *Delphine, where is she*, and saw Cook hauling Porter and Hesse into the water, Tariq close behind, De Lisle dragging Pettifer, almost a dead weight, Warnock taking his other arm, shouting, '*There's too bloody many!*'

Cook made it to the boat, throwing Underhill inside, the old sergeant collapsing into the arms of the oarsmen. A sailor fired a pistol into the storm of dust, a French grenadier falling, and Hazzard saw some had reformed, coming in again. Pigalle waded into the grenadiers and Berbers, two muskets swinging, '*I am Pigalle! And where I plant my boot, there shall I not be moved!*' The Moorish *Tirailleurs* fled, swept away by the giant's hand. Hazzard reached for the Lorenzoni, his hand shaking, *weak*, and saw Cook stop suddenly in the water, throwing his arms outward.

Jory.

His back arching, the big man fell into the water, oarsmen jumping out of the boat, a young midshipman trying to lift him, getting him in, Hazzard dropping now to all fours, unable to move, *Jory*, and began to shout, '*Jory!*'

Hazzard could not breathe, the air insufficient, his blood in the sand before him. *Here is my pit, at last*, a square patch of shoreline north of Acre, where he would be covered as were the princes of Tyre and bloody crusader barons before him, where Saladin jousted with Richard. He took a last sight of Shajar, riding, her sword high, the jewelled diadem on her forehead glinting, her head twisting left and right, her kohl-lined Egyptian eyes seeking him out, and he let go, *I will take her then as my last view of this world*.

He let his face fall into the sand, its harsh crystals grinding into his skin. He then heard a hurtling overhead, a thunder from out at sea – but not from *Theseus*. This was low, fast, different. Instinctively the marines threw themselves flat, the Turks doing likewise.

The front of the reformed French *Tirailleurs* erupted in a line of flaming explosions, the grenadiers turning, thrown in all directions, more bodies for the field of dead. Hazzard tried to turn his face to look – and found his hope reflected back upon him: racing inshore without fear of the shoals, the prow swinging sharply to starboard, came a frigate, the guns on her top deck rippling with fire all along her broadside, the wasteland roaring with more shell-bursts and the cries of men. She heeled over, her copper hull plates bright in the sunrise bathing the shore.

The *Volpone*.

She dropped three boats outboard onto the water with a crash, the spray bursting as they struck the surface. The oars swung, pulling fast towards the shore, a figure standing in the prow of the first, in a long pale cutaway coat, a Toledo rapier in hand – behind him another, in Marine scarlet.

Hazzard wanted to call out, to try to reach him, his voice a dry husk, '*Mr Wayland…*'

In danger of being hit by the naval shells, the Tarabin rode out, through the centre of the fleeing Berber *Tirailleurs*, the company scattering, the Mamluks hacking at them as they charged through them. Abandoned on the field, running on his own, was a single officer shouting to the *Tirailleurs*, calling them to come back. It was Andret. He stopped, alone in the marsh, and turned to look back. St Michel raised his rifle, aimed, and fired. In the distance, the figure spun, then fell forward into the mud.

Hazzard pushed himself up in the sand, his arms shaking, and forced himself to one knee, looking out through the swirling dust left by Shajar's Mamluks, and saw a man, trying to run, staggering through the marsh, tearing the loose cord from his wrists.

Derrien.

One hand to his leg, Jules-Yves Derrien limped along the marsh as if to follow the Berbers to safety – then stumbled down a dune to the shore, and lay still in the surf. Hazzard wanted to charge after him, but could not. He collapsed, the surf splashing around him, soaking him, red with his blood, *mine this time, not Harry's.* He gazed along the beach and saw Derrien in the distance, a black shape among the blue and white of the shore, dragging himself painfully through the sand – and felt a strange euphoria wash over him as he let Derrien go from him forever. *He is nothing, nothing.*

Hands pulled at his foot, turning him, and then his wrist, dragging him round, and the pain roared. It was Delphine, looking down on him, sobbing, calling to him, but he had not heard, *William, William!* Sarah was behind her, helping her to pull him, her kindest smile, her softest voice calling him as well, *William…*

The light blossomed above, *sunrise*, he realised, *sunrise at last*, and Sarah faded from view, vanishing into the blue of the sky behind Delphine. '*William! Can you hear me!*' He heard her, and Alfonso, De la Vega's son, pulling him in, his dark hair long and curling, shouting at someone behind to help.

Hazzard sagged in their arms, his vision clouding, *Sarah, not yet, but soon*, feeling her miniature digging into his side, still in its place, *not yet*, as the Spaniards lifted him into a boat.

Derrien lay still, the ebb and flow of the surf washing around him, slapping his cheeks, filling his mouth, his nose – and he coughed and spluttered. He pushed himself up and staggered, his bad leg worse. His hand groped for his walking-stick of bleached sycamore, but, not finding it, he fell again, among the bodies of the dead Berber and Maghrib company all around, kicking at them in frustration. He crawled through the sand to the top of a low dune, his head down, and lay still for a moment, face-down, a man at prayer.

He heard the grunting of a horse, its teeth cropping at grasses, and he looked up.

Camel.

There was a faint footfall on the sand near his head. When he opened his eyes, he saw the toes of a pair of boots before him. He looked up.

It was an Arab, in shadow from the rising sun behind. Derrien held up a hand to shield his eyes. The Arab removed the dusty *shemagh* from his face and spoke slowly and clearly, so that Derrien might understand, 'I am *Sergent-chef-major* Achille Mérové Caron, of the 75th Invincibles…' Derrien tried to push himself upright to look properly, but still could not see, '…veteran of the Americas, the Indies, Lodi, the Adige, saviour of Bonaparte at the Bridge at Arcole.'

'No…' gasped Derrien. 'You… you *fell.* You…'

Along the shore came a group of *Tirailleurs*, in their robes and bandoliers, back for easier pickings, sorting through the dead, looking for purses, coin, gold, anything, their chatter low on the wind. Caron bent lower. 'And what are you, Citizen *Croquemort?*'

Derrien struggled to his knees and looked up. 'What… *am I?*' he asked with a gasp, 'What *am I?* I am the *Republic…*' he said, his voice shaking, looking up at Caron. '*I am the Republic.*'

Caron stepped back, and three *Tirailleurs* filled Derrien's vision. They looked him over briefly. Simultaneously they leaned forward, the breath suddenly going out of him, a sledgehammer to his body. His head shaking, he looked down, and saw their three spike bayonets thrust into him, two to his chest and one in the abdomen. He tried to gasp, his eyes bulging, but could not, and they yanked out the shafts and moved on, indifferent.

Derrien tried to stand, but fell again to his knees, looking down at the spreading patches on his coat and shirt, the mud and sand on it all.

'I... I am the *Republic*,' he hissed to Caron. 'I *am*. I...' He sank slowly into the surf, collapsing backwards, looking up at the sky. Pigalle joined Caron, and they looked down at him, then to St Michel and the other Alphas. Derrien's last view was of Caron giving his world-weary nod.

'*Alors*. The world,' said Caron, 'is at last a better place.'

–

Hazzard blinked, the light dazzling, Reiz's face coming into focus. He smiled and nodded. 'Yes,' he said to someone, 'he is here.'

Hazzard could feel the rocking of the boat, hear the oars in the rowlocks – and smell the sweet scent of a cheroot. De la Vega's voice was quiet, reflective, beside him, 'Ehh, *amigo*, you do the mad things when you are not with me, hm.' De la Vega exhaled, a blue cloud swirling on the sea breeze. 'I think I am the – how you say – steadying influence for you. You say this? Steadying?'

Hazzard felt De la Vega's hand clasp his and he clutched it tight in return.

De la Vega looked down at him, no different, same as ever. '*Mio hermanito del mar*. My little brother of the sea. My new gun officer, he say, do this, do that, and I say, but I not know these things of which you speak, but he does he says, and ba-boum, *Volpone* has her vengeance at last.'

His neck stiff, Hazzard tried to look to the other side, uncertain but hopeful. 'Mr Wayland...?'

'Yes, sir,' said the familiar voice, another hand on his shoulder. 'Here sir.'

Hazzard felt the relief flood into him. 'How...?'

'One of Sir Sidney's rippling broadsides, sir,' he said, 'with a certain Spanish dash.'

Hazzard closed his eyes, a question he did not want to ask but had to. 'Jory? The men?'

There was hesitation, then De la Vega said, 'All. All with the wounds, some bad, some not, but all here.'

Delphine took his other hand, small and cool in his. 'William... *le sergent* is hit, in the back, but will live. Oh... look at you.' She began to weep again, the bright blue of the sky behind her dazzling, her blood-smeared face, her bandaged shoulder. No Sarah intervened this time, though he waited, and he felt at ease that she was gone. 'I am sorry... to have put you through this...'

'And eighteen of the people,' said Reiz proudly. 'You bring eighteen of them. Only six were lost. A great feat, Hazar.'

Hazzard's heart sank, and he tried to breathe.

The bystanders, the unwilling, the hapless and forgotten.

Six.

'Derrien.'

There was silence.

Delphine put a hand to his forehead, and he saw her faint smile.

'No,' he said with a whisper, 'don't tell me... I don't care.'

'The siege is not over, sir,' said Wayland, 'but Reiz managed to blow one of their mines, with Lt Wright and Major Douglas. Sir Sidney will be staying to help Al-Djezzar.'

'The *Nizami*,' whispered Hazzard, 'Reiz... *Teshekir ederim.*' *Thank you.*

Reiz's black eyes, lined and tired as they were, wrinkled into a smile, his moustache rising. 'As you came for us at Jaffa, Hazar Pasha, so we have come for you at Akka. May God protect you.'

Hazzard thought of Masoud in Egypt, and his similar words. He wondered whether he would get back, to find that shallow pit in the desert, wherever it might be, so he might be blown across the dunes with the endless sands – yet another grain within the great hourglass of Anubis, keeping time for the world, each soul marking an endless moment.

Overhead, a flock of sacred ibis called, white wings flashing in the sun, heading south to summer in the wetlands of the Delta. He took the message as a blessing of hope from Thoth, and closed his eyes.

Epilogue

Rubicon

Commander Charles Blake knocked and entered the small, cramped and cluttered office. Before a tall sash window opposite, there stood a carved partners' desk heaped with stacks of paper in oak trays, file cabinets and bookshelves to left and right, the whole giving the effect of a busy solicitor's rooms. The echoing sounds of Whitehall drifted up from below, carriages clattering past, crossing-sweepers calling and, above it all, the chimes of the Horse Guards clock sounding eleven. Out of uniform for the first time in some years, Blake felt somewhat uncomfortable, but was glad of his lightweight summer coat, London already glowing in the warmth of the July sunshine. He presumed he would grow accustomed to his civilian garb – as he knew he must.

At the desk sat a vigorous, periwigged figure in frock coat and cravat, pen in hand. He looked up and got quickly to his feet. 'Charles, my dear fellow, do come in,' he began with a laugh. 'So, have we poached you at last?'

William Wickham was a quick, dynamic man of nearly forty, with an easy smile and elegant manner. Diplomat and civil servant, he had applied these qualities to become the Under-Secretary of the Home Department, and only the previous year had been appointed Supervisor of Britain's new centralised intelligence agency, the Alien Office.

'Almost, William, almost,' said Blake, sitting in a leather-backed chair opposite. 'Sir Rafe does wonder where I get to…'

'Well, anything to annoy Sir Rafe,' Wickham said generously.

Blake smiled to himself. 'If you're still certain, I can begin the secondment next week. The First Sea Lord is retiring, in favour of Lord St Vincent, and seems happy to spare me for a six-month.'

'Excellent. The sooner you start the better.'

Blake hesitated, knowing he had already tested his new appointment and possibly his friendship with Wickham: 'If I might ask, how have you managed with that other matter, so far?'

Wickham held up his hands and sat back in his chair. 'It's very tricky, Charles. Breaking up 9 Company seems impossible, as there's no record of it anywhere.'

Blake nodded. 'Yes, I have removed them from the single Admiralty file Sir Rafe had created, and eradicated all trace.'

Wickham seemed helpless. 'And that was it, you see? As individual marines they're vulnerable. Their pay, promotions, service records and so forth are all with the Admiralty and their divisions, Plymouth or Portsmouth, aren't they? And Hazzard himself is Chatham – it's an administrative nightmare.'

Blake thought of Hazzard, and Sarah Chapel, even young Wayland. He glanced at the file cabinets, stocked, he knew, with names, descriptions, lives – Hazzard's perhaps, and quite possibly his own. 'I want him to be free of Sir Rafe. After what he has suffered, he deserves that much at the very least.'

Wickham sympathised, and grew almost angry at the thought of it. 'I understand, Charles, really I do. The Nile, Acre, all of it, his *fiancée* by God – that action of his at Acre should be gazetted, and come with a knighthood and a pension... but for the damnable Sir Rafe Lewis, if you'll pardon me.'

'Indeed. I believe Hazzard has suffered at his hand for long enough. The affair on the *Tigre* was too much.'

Wickham looked down at his desk, at the page he had been reading just before Blake had arrived. He handed it over. 'For next week. This is the latest comment from the French Committee – about Egypt and our mutual friend. If he behaves as Sidney thinks he will, then either we shall have peace, or a prelude to something far worse.'

Blake read the report. Mostly it concerned Bonaparte. The French Committee had been very accurate in the past few years, their exiled pre-Revolution ministers and civil servants extrapolating from known facts, providing possible political outcomes – a Brain Machine, Wickham had once called them. And what they thought now seemed very dangerous indeed.

'If this is accurate,' began Blake, 'they might very well be right.'

'We've had the notion for months, and Sidney has been working towards it, but—' Wickham paused. 'Wait a moment. Is Hazzard still out there?'

'I believe they are all on Cyprus, recuperating. At least, Sir Sidney has put in there regularly since the Turkish attack on Aboukir Bay.'

'Jolly good...' said Wickham, reaching for his pen. 'Let's give them a new start, shall we? And put them beyond the reach of Sir Rafe Lewis for good...'

—

Seabirds wheeled high above, their calls almost inaudible amid the crashing of the waves on the rocks and cliffs of ancient Crete, the spray bursting bright against the Aegean blue of the sea and the sky. Hazzard sat on a boulder in the sun, staring out across the water towards Egypt, the wind tugging at his hair, his shirtsleeves flapping and billowing like so much sail.

It had been over three months now since their break-out from Acre in May. They had gone in the *Tigre* straight to an Ottoman hospital on Cyprus – all of them hit, all of them torn and bloody – and spent the first three weeks in surgery and fever, Wayland and Smith obtaining the finest quinine and *Mkwalabo* treatments from the imperial apothecaries.

Hesse had been struck in the abdomen, and nearly died on the voyage, but Tariq had tended him well; Napier had taken three .65 calibre Charleville rounds and lived to tell the tale, Cochrane two, Underhill had a bad hit to the left side of his upper chest, a bullet smashing his clavicle, leaving his arm splinted out to the side. Pettifer, too, had been in a winding-corset for the bullets to his back, saved by a stiff leather jerkin no one had known he wore regularly under his Marine scarlet: 'Got the idea from Admiral Nelson,' he said, 'keeps him warm, they say.' Even so, he had limped about on crutches for weeks. The bayonet thrust into Warnock's thigh had missed the bone and his femoral artery by mere inches. Kite, Handley and De Lisle had been peppered with shell fragments and powder burns, and Porter had taken a bayonet blade across his left hand and forearm and a blow to the back, leaving him in a sling and propped on a single crutch for over a month. During their convalescence, Wayland had travelled back and forth between Constantinople and the blockade fleet on the *Tigre* with Smith and on the *Volpone* with De la Vega, and managed a few visits en route.

Cook's bullet to the back had broken a rib, one of the fractured ends scraping a lung, but not sufficiently to puncture it. As the weeks had gone by, he had been able to walk for ever-increasing periods of time. On Crete he had walked with Hazzard from the base to explore the interior – they had found the tunnel entrances mentioned by Pococke, supposedly the Labyrinth inhabited by the mythical Minotaur, but without Wayland, Hazzard had lacked the heart to delve deeper.

Hazzard's own wounds had been cuts, burns and glancing shots, one over his left shoulder-blade, the other into a torn thigh. After some weeks he could hobble, then walk and eventually run once again. The left arm stiffened at times, but the left side of his back was no longer wracked with spasm. The worst had been the injury to his side, from Derrien's pistol, but an Ottoman surgeon found no bullet, instead fragments of glass-enamel – from Sarah's miniature. It was his opinion that the small picture had taken the greatest shock, and saved his life.

Smith had then moved them from Cyprus to Crete, another Ottoman possession, to keep them away from prying Admiralty eyes – in the hope, perhaps, that Lewis and Melville would forget about them, or at least leave them in peace while they recovered. Delphine had returned to Egypt with Tariq. She had recuperated from her own shoulder wound, and chafed to get back.

Smith had agreed to take her after his reconnaissance operations off the Levantine coast. HMS *Tigre* had patrolled the French retreat from Acre to Jaffa, going so far as to take wounded men aboard to save them from the vengeful Turks; many had been abandoned by their comrades for fear of plague. Bonaparte's final farewell to the siege had been a request to have his plague-stricken soldiers put down like dying horses. The rag-tag army had dragged itself back to the Nile, declaring victory, celebrating a Caesarean triumph in Cairo. Delphine, believed Smith, was needed there more than ever before.

The only other report of interest they received was that Derrien was dead. The news had left Hazzard numb, empty, his last link to Sarah gone. His vengeance had somehow kept her alive, but now he waved her goodbye, mourning not only her loss – but also a loss of purpose.

Now, weeks later, Hazzard sat, feeling spent, hopes unfulfilled, seeing little on the path ahead to cheer him. He so wished to see the ibis again, to travel up the Nile, and see it all, but truly *see* it, as Shajar had wanted him to see her.

But he knew that first Bonaparte would have to be dislodged – and this seemed less and less likely. Fifteen thousand Turks had landed at

Aboukir Bay in a brave but fruitless invasion, and within several hours Bonaparte's exhausted army had thrown them back into the sea. The news had been a blow, to all of them, as if this single hope too had now been dashed.

Hazzard heard footfall on the sand and turned to see Cook approaching with an even stride, no signs of puffing up the incline, the rugged wind-blasted rocks rising behind him. They both had taken to wearing the undress uniform of wounded men, long white duck trousers, belt and shirt, Hazzard their only officer, no sick-parade to attend. When they gathered they looked like a gang of sailing hands. Cook looked older, but still as powerful as ever before. He stopped some way off, his head down, something wrong.

'What is it?' asked Hazzard.

'Sir Sid wants us,' he said. 'Bad bloody news.'

–

'Break us up?' demanded Hazzard. 'They can't – we're with Room 63, not the regular Active List—'

They had gathered in the Great Cabin, the bright blue sea dazzling in the windows. The *Tigre* was docked at the quayside for repairs, booms swinging outboard, a hoist raising a new mainmast topyard as the sound of hammers mingled with calls from the Cretan shipwrights on the quay. Lt Wright stood to one side, Smith behind the long table now strewn with despatches and papers, very much the man under siege.

'It's not bloody *fair*,' complained Warnock.

'*Mind yer tone, Private Knock-bloody-knock*,' growled Underhill. He cleared his throat and said to them all, 'We been on a fine holiday, ain't we, lads? Time to pay the devil's dues once more, aye.'

Smith seemed confused, and cast a puzzled glance at Wright, equally lost. 'A moment, gentlemen. Have you, then, received orders?' asked Smith. 'Specific orders? How?'

'Signals Officer gave it to me, sir,' said Cook, taking the folded letter from his back pocket. 'This morning, when the *Seahorse* put in.'

Wright took it and glanced over it briefly. 'It was in the despatch bag, sir,' said Wright. 'Looked like Admiralty bumf addressed to Sar'nt-Major Cook... But it's all here, an official record addressed to the senior sergeant.'

Hazzard was livid. 'According to this, some idiot wants to post Cook and Underhill to Portsmouth to drill recruits on the parade ground or some such nonsense.'

Kite spoke up, 'An' me an' Lil have to join the *Turps* – sorry sir, the *Terpsichore* – Knocky and Hesse the *Lion*, Arfur Napier's goin' home unfit on half-pay and Cocky's bein' posted to some guard duty in Belfast—'

Smith shook his head. 'No, no, gentlemen, you don't quite under-stand...' he said, trying to placate them. 'This is indeed nonsense, all of it...' He leafed through the various pages before him, 'John, where the devil is the...'

Wright looked through another pile. 'Here it is, sir—'

'Ah,' Smith took it from him. 'Yes, here we are...' He glanced over it briefly then stopped. 'Yes... *previous status rescinded, 9 Company His Majesty's Marine Forces hereby removed active service*, so forth, *ceding from previous authority, to be redeployed Special Executive Branch, henceforward Special Landing Squadron, reporting operations authority the Alien Office, and Under-Secretary of the Home Department, pending procedures heretofore, et cetera, et cetera, et cetera...*' He looked round at them, holding the paper up for them to see, 'Signed, William Wickham, Permanent Under-Secretary of State... and here, the seal of the Prime Minister's office, No. 10 Downing St, London.' He looked at their baffled faces and smiled. 'You have all been *released* from the Royal Navy and the Marines—'

'But wh—' Hazzard took the letter to read himself. 'I do not—'

'—and been absorbed into the Alien Office.' Smith looked at them but they still did not understand. 'Gentlemen, you have been promoted to the Special Executive Branch of the intelligence service.' He straightened, hands behind his back, pleased. 'No longer respons-ible to the Admiralty, or Sir Rafe Lewis, or Room 63, but only to the Home Secretary and the Prime Minister.'

'So,' said Cook slowly, 'those orders...'

'To be ignored, Sar'-Major,' said Smith.

Kite looked round. 'No *Turps*, or *Lion*, then sir? Or half-pay for Napier...?'

'No,' he said. 'No *Turps*. No half-pay. Promise.'

They stood staring at him a moment, then at Cook, and then at Hazzard. Hazzard sighed. 'Sir Sidney...'

'Mr Hazzard, you and 9 Company now have a singular mission, with me as your Local Control – the expulsion of the French from Egypt. And we shall do it,' he said, leaning forward onto the table, casting his eye over each of them, 'by *hook* or, by God, by *crook*.' He cocked an eyebrow. 'You game?'

They waited for Hazzard. He stared at the table-top, at the papers, pages and sheets that controlled their lives, then looked round at them all.

There was a knock at the door. Second Lieutenant Tyte entered. 'Sir, the *Volpone*'s just put in. Captain De la Vega is headed this way,' he said with alarm. 'In a hurry.'

Without answering Smith's question, Hazzard got to his feet and they all followed him through the passage out to the quarter-deck beyond. Dickory and several marines banged to attention. The marines of 9 Company hung back, watching, and Dickory murmured to Underhill, 'Trouble coming, 'Miah…'

'Always does, Docky…'

The small, rock-lined harbour had only one rickety quayside and a few rotting jetties for the local fishing fleet. Hazzard saw the *Volpone* standing just offshore, a jolly-boat being moored, and De la Vega and Alfonso striding along the bouncing deckboards of the quay towards the *Tigre*.

De la Vega was piped aboard and leapt up the last few steps to the portside rail. His hand out to Hazzard, he met Smith and Wright, shaking his head. 'It has come, *señor*,' he began, giving him a despatch, 'We must be quick, *muy rápido*.'

Smith read the note. 'Good God. John,' he said to Wright, 'it worked…'

Hazzard asked De la Vega, 'What is it?'

'From Hassan and Masoud,' said De la Vega. He handed him the note. *Two frigates Alexandria, Muiron and Carrère, now loaded. Activity al-Elfi Bey palace, carriages, Monge, Berthollet, Denon, general staff.*

'One day to Hassan,' said De la Vega, 'then two days for me to get here. Time, she has gone.'

Smith looked over the rigging and turned quickly to Wright. 'How much longer before we can make sail?'

Wright shook his head. 'An hour for the topyard at least, sir, and another hour for the decks and pumps, but we can delay other repairs—'

De la Vega cut in, 'I go, *señor. Volpone* is faster and ready to turn about.' He looked at Hazzard. 'I came for these *hombres*.'

Hazzard turned to Smith, 'What in hell's been going on?'

Smith spoke quickly and quietly, taking him to one side, Cook joining them. 'Hassan, Masoud's man in Rosetta, discovered these very frigates moored at Alex in early July. No one noticed them, but now they've been armed to the teeth – both ready to go at a moment's notice.'

Hazzard felt a frisson of ice shoot up his spine. 'And?'

Smith nodded. 'We think he's going to use them.'

'Good God...' He recalled his thoughts before the Battle of the Nile, thoughts of Nelson, of tethered goats – of the great general needing a means of escape:

Where is the coachman, oh, he is where, waiting here, waiting there, waiting waiting for his fare...

Hazzard turned to the rest of them. 'Jory – desert kit, locks, blades, bags, *now*.'

Cook looked at them both, 'Will one o'ye tell me what the *blazes*—'

Hazzard flicked a glance at Smith. 'We're going after Bonaparte.'

Cook stared back at them both a moment, his face blank. '*Jaysus...*' He turned and bawled at them as the marines scattered across the decks, '*Nine Comp'nay!* Get yer kit and make for the *Volpone* like Davy wants ye!'

Smith looked up at the rigging again, frustrated. 'We'll be but hours behind you, William,' he said, Wright dashing off to consult with the bo'sun, shouts going up to the tops, *Hurry it up aloft!* 'Flush him out,' said Smith, 'and beat him towards our guns. Then we shall have him.'

Hazzard strode to the steps down to the main deck, his hands shaking at the prospect. Smith must have read something in his expression, for he leaned on the quarterdeck rail and called down after him, adamant, 'Alive, William, *alive*. To negotiate, to get them *out*.'

For the first time, Hazzard saw that Smith did not fully understand – he was no student of Caesar. But Hazzard knew: to take power, Caesar had to return to Rome – and this Caesar would be no different.

I fight all battles as I did my first. Much as Caesar.

Gleaming silverware, chilled Pouilly and a rich Margaux, a dinner on the flagship *Orient*, the candlelit glow of expectant faces – and William John Hazzard, Marine, honoured guest of Caesar.

In Bonaparte's mind, he had just conquered the Gauls, sent his punitive raid to Britannia and returned victorious. There remained only one last step:

To cross the Rubicon and take the Republic.

Smith called again, 'I do mean it, William. *Alive.*'

Hazzard stopped and looked back at him – then hurried down to the main decks.

–

The *Volpone* heeled across the Libyan Sea to the Levant on a strong westerly, then caught the prevailing northerly and dived southward upon the coast of Egypt. Hazzard manned the fo'c'sle, transfixed, holding onto the shrouds as the spray burst at the bows and the Catalans around him leapt to their tasks. It was the chase from England for Sarah all over again, the chase to Malta, to Alexandria, every stitch of canvas billowing overhead, dolphins leaping at the prow to guide them.

Hazzard had been thrown into chaos by the realisation of what he was about to do – and he would do it alone, not with Cook, not with the marines, of that he was determined: this was his affair, his alone. To confront the architect of the endless mayhem and destruction that had so ravaged his world was beyond his comprehension. Standing opposite Derrien in the gloom of the Nazareth road had been strange enough, but this was beyond his darkest imaginings. He did not move from the forward stays for the first day of their voyage, at one point the Catalans backing away from him as if he were possessed by demons, his hands on the lines, shaking them as he raged against this Caesar, this new Ozymandias.

Hazzard understood Smith's demands: capture the commander, demand the peace. Without their invincible god-general, the army would awaken to the reality of their plight: cut off, abandoned, hated in a foreign land, merely waiting to be destroyed. Smith had made perfect sense.

But, for Hazzard, his solution did not incorporate *justice*. It brought no justice for the thousands murdered, on the battlefields, in Cairo, in El-'Arish, in Jaffa, in Acre. Caron and his men would have demanded justice from the great general, the would-be sultan of the Orient, justice for the name of France, so besmirched by this lust for power.

I come to bury Caesar, not to praise him.

Oh, by God, I do.

It was nearly five in the morning when they reached the waters of Alexandria, the lights winking from the port, from the quaysides and ships. *Volpone* was running dark, and had doused sail, drifting in silently, standing off a quarter of a mile. Cook and De la Vega joined Hazzard at the bows and they surveyed the port and the horizon. There was no sign of the blockade fleet.

Cook lowered his eyeglass and swore. 'Where in hell is everyone? Supposed to be half a dozen heavies out there...'

De la Vega watched the shoreline. 'Masoud leaves us the two torches, *dos antorchas sí*? If they burn, he is still here. If not, he is gone.'

'He is here,' said Hazzard, 'I *know* it...'

De la Vega glanced at Cook but neither said a word. Hazzard had been in his own world since they had set sail, focussed, obsessed. Hazzard turned the scope back to the coastline and slowly swung left, to the east and Aboukir Bay.

There was no moon, and not a breath of wind, but under the starlit dome of night he could see the Aboukir headland reaching out to sea, with its small lamplit fortress tower, where Wayland and Handley had ridden against French artillery positions and saved the *Culloden*. Large Egyptian *djerms*, *feluccas* and small boats plied everywhere along the shore, rowing in the still air, sloops, tartanes, and traders further out, all with lanterns burning bright, sparkling on the water. To find the *Muiron* or *Carrère* among them would be nigh impossible.

'*There*,' said De la Vega. 'East of the port. Is it...? It is only one torch. Masoud's signal, *amigo*?'

Hazzard looked more closely. It was not a torch, but a lantern, black undergrowth and thickets behind. There was no other light on that stretch of beach, and it was far from anything at the port, perfect for a clandestine rendezvous – or escape.

He peered to the left and right, finding the darkest spot, halfway between Alexandria's eastern harbour and the fort on the Aboukir headland. 'Over there,' said Hazzard, pointing. 'Lower the boat.' He clapped the eyeglass shut and stalked off to the tweendecks.

Within a few minutes the boat splashed into the water, the Catalan crew of four manning the oars; Hazzard took the tiller, De la Vega and Cook beside him, Warnock and Pettifer at the bow, checking their weapons. Alfonso followed in a second boat with the rest of the marines – and they began to row towards the shore, Hazzard staring ahead at the coast, watchful, intent.

The air hung dead in the August heat. The palms rose black against the indigo night, the undergrowth thick, the shore ringing with the surf on the sand and shingle. Hazzard hauled the tiller over and the boat nudged further eastwards, heading deeper into the darkness and the darkest patch of shoreline, the glow of the lantern still far to their left. Cook looked to their target and flicked a glance back at him, '*There's nothing there, sir…*'

The keel grounded gently on the shingle and before the crew had shipped their oars, Hazzard was out and into the water, moving silently through the surf to the beach, his Bombay scarlet rendered a dull grey in the darkness. De la Vega hissed at him, '*Wait, amigo! Madre de Dios—*'

Cook swore, '*Damnation… get after him!*'

In their dark *kaftan* and *binish*, Warnock and Pettifer jumped out and waded waist-deep through the water after the flitting shadow of Hazzard, De la Vega and Cook close behind, beaching the boat with the oarsmen.

Hazzard reached the brush along the shore, some of it reaching out to touch the water. He pushed his way through the undergrowth and palm thickets, his boots seeking submerged rocks, slipping, then finding a purchase, the scimitar at his hip trailing in the rise of the swell.

He ducked below hanging palm leaves and fallen brush into deeper water, and saw a deserted stretch of sand ahead, a short, curving beach and another dark thicket beyond. He clambered out of the water and onto the sand and stones, the surf thrashing loud. He jogged along the shingle, the beach rising to his right to tussocks of grass and more undergrowth – until he heard something else.

Horses.

He reached the distant thicket and quietly moved into its shadows, pressing forward through the shoots and branches, the leaves brushing his face. His left hand gripped the neck of the scimitar's scabbard, his right ready to draw the Lorenzoni. Through the frame of palm leaves he saw a sloping shingle beach ahead, shell and pebble clashing musically in the drag of the surf. The lantern was clearly visible fifty yards off, now very dim, nearly spent. In the water a short distance to the other side he saw what he was looking for:

Boat.

A painted gig, fifteen feet long, broad in the beam. Oarsmen sat inside, waiting. He wondered if he should seize the boat and force them to take it out to find one of the frigates – when a man stepped in front of him, not three feet away. Hazzard froze.

The figure was looking up the beach, his back to the thicket. He smelled of horses, the earthy tang of manure mingling with leather and gun-oil, a slung holster pistol hanging at his thigh. It was a dragoon. Hazzard sank lower in the bushes.

He then saw a group of dragoons ahead move into the glow of the lantern, shuffling about, murmuring, one chuckling. He counted six of them – just waiting, their horses on the coastal path, presumably. He shifted slightly to his left, moving a spear-bladed palm from his vision.

Further along the beach two lone figures approached, moving towards the dragoons and the boat: one slight, angular, in a cocked hat, wearing low, turned-down boots and white breeches – the other was the same height, only more portly. He recognised the outline of General Jacques-François Menou, from the affair at Kafr-Shahabas.

The other was Napoleon Bonaparte.

For a moment he stared, then found himself pushing through the trees to his left into the surf, drawing the scimitar and lashing out to his right, burying it deep into the neck of the dragoon who had blocked his view. He jerked the blade out and the man fell. There was a shout, *le general, le general*, the six dragoons turning, one trooper coming at a run – and Hazzard ran at him.

He was tall, powerful, his blade shining, coming down at his head. Hazzard caught it with the scimitar, side-stepping left into the surf, throwing the dragoon forward and down, turning the scimitar blade and whipping it upwards on the return, across the man's neck.

A pistol boomed, the bullet smashing into the pebbles, another shot, and Hazzard stumbled into the water, sheathing the sword and drawing the Lorenzoni, his arm numb, his limbs weightless, his breathing rasping through his mouth and clenched jaw.

The horses clattered and he saw the shape of Menou running up the dune with three men pushing him along, *run run, au secours, au secours!* Another bullet kicked up the stones at Hazzard's right foot, but he dropped to his left knee into the water, firing, a man going down – he cranked the loading-arm of the pistol and fired again. Two other dragoons fired and Hazzard replied, the pistol bucking in his hand, a man dropping. He heard the sound of horses galloping off, a voice crying, '*Protect the Governor!*'

Two figures pulled Bonaparte to the boat and Hazzard found himself running deeper into the water, his arm stiff, *hit*, the hand sticky, breathing difficult but no pain, *no pain*, the Lorenzoni growing heavier. Three troopers charged, one lagging, wounded, their pistols out, one raising a sword and Hazzard felt an impact, spinning away, a sledgehammer to his left shoulder.

Three shots rang out from the undergrowth and two of the dragoons stumbled, one falling face-down as De la Vega appeared, Cook behind, Warnock and Pettifer close by – the musketoon roared and the last two dragoons flew backwards into the surf and lay still.

His chest heaving, Hazzard stumbled, twenty yards from the white-painted boat, the oarsmen poised, staring, two troopers standing in the boat, one aiming a carbine, the other a heavy pistol. Between them stood Bonaparte, his pale face glowing amid the darkness of his coat, hat and cravat. He seemed calm, one hand outstretched, as if telling his men to hold their fire. All was still.

For a moment they looked at each other. Hazzard looked down the barrel of the Lorenzoni in his extended right hand, trembling in his tight grip.

'Mr Hazzard.'

Hazzard could scarcely force words from his throat. His breathing sawed between his lips, his chest heaving. '*What now then, great Caesar?*' he spat. '*Leave* them? *Leave them all to die?*'

Bonaparte stared back at him, his wide eyes unblinking. 'I go to save my country. Would you not do the same for yours?'

The French was short and clipped, just as he remembered.

'*Liar.* Thief in the night, stealing away, *sans tambour, sans trompette.*'

The expression seemed to cut Bonaparte deep and his breath hissed. 'We had the drums and trumpets. Did you not hear them? At my triumph, after our victory.'

'*Victory?* The murder of *thousands*. Proud, proud *liberator*. You have brought nothing but destruction and *death*.'

Bonaparte lashed back at him, '*Look about you!* This land is testament to destruction and death! What could I have destroyed that was not already lying in ruin!'

Hazzard squeezed the grip of the Lorenzoni more tightly, the heavy barrel wavering. His left shoulder throbbed, his booming pulse loud in his ears. 'Is this, then, to be your legacy? Your *empire*?'

Bonaparte looked thoughtful, then disappointed in him. 'You of all men should know, Mr Hazzard. History proves it. Empire is what the people want, what they need. Or they fall into dissolution and chaos. I shall save them, give them that peace.'

'And take *everything* from them—'

Bonaparte raised his chin, angry, 'And when I am gone, Mr Hazzard, what then? Who shall they remember? Who? Djezzar? Mustafa? Murad? Barras? No. They will remember *me*,' he shouted, jabbing a finger at his chest, his voice cracking with rage. '*Me!*'

Hazzard's gun-arm began to shudder. 'Six thousand at Jaffa, butchered,' he rasped. '*Two* thousand at El-'Arish *in their sleep. Your own men with plague to be poisoned*?' Hazzard took a deep breath. 'In England, we would cry *villain!*'

Bonaparte said nothing, his hands clamping angrily behind his back, as if trying to control himself. He looked to his bodyguards. 'I could give the order.'

'And you would be the first to fall.'

He thought of Smith: *Alive, William, alive. To negotiate, to get them out.*

Hazzard's finger felt the spring of the trigger.

Bonaparte scoffed. '*Non*,' he said, with another sorry shake of the head, '*Pas du tout*. I am so confident in Fate, Mr Hazzard, that I know you will not shoot. Even your own admirals wish it so.' He put his arms out, his hands raised up in mock puzzlement. 'Where,' he asked, 'is the English fleet? Gone. Do you see?' He lowered his hands. 'I am to reach home. I shall reconquer our lost lands, and rescue my army from this desert.' His voice grew quiet, reflective. 'There are some things greater than ourselves, would you not say? Caesar knew this. All great men do.'

Hazzard blinked, the perspiration running into his eyes. The first glimmers of dawn broke in the sky behind Bonaparte, revealing Aboukir Bay.

Hazzard's heart hammered in his chest, the heavy Lorenzoni drooping slightly, his breathing the only sound he could register. It was a conversation from Homer, he thought, Odysseus in the shade-world speaking with the dead, or with Hades himself, discussing right and wrong. 'You will pay, *damn* you.'

Bonaparte considered this, looking down, nodding. 'Perhaps. One day. But for now, let us save what we can of our worlds. You to yours, and I to mine.' He spoke quietly, as if commiserating with Hazzard. 'We have done too much,' he said, 'to stop now.'

Bonaparte snapped his fingers at the cox'n, and the crew lowered their oars slowly into the water, and began to row.

'*Do not...*' gasped Hazzard, barely a whisper, the Lorenzoni shaking, its weight unbearable. 'Do not...'

Warnock moved beside Cook, watching from the beach. '*What do we do, Sarge...?*'

Cook put out a hand, afraid to disturb the spell manifested before them. '*Still, boy... still now...*'

'*Amigo,*' called De la Vega softly to Hazzard. 'It is over.'

Hazzard did not hear him, could hear nothing. He looked at Bonaparte, recalling the man he had met, their strange and rare kinship. The boat pulled slowly from the pebbles and into the water, the soft splash of the oars the only sound. The dragoon guards maintained their aim, their weapons levelled, and Bonaparte remained standing in the boat, watching Hazzard – then abruptly he turned and sat down in his seat, and the dragoons lowered their arms. Within minutes, the boat had pulled out to sea, a heavy sloop moving on the horizon, weighing anchor.

Cook and De la Vega ran into the surf to catch Hazzard as he fell, and dragged him to the shore, De la Vega pulling open his Bombay jacket, examining the shoulder, a dark patch spreading. '*Amigo, madre de Dios... why did you not shoot?*'

Hazzard raised the Lorenzoni slowly, and squeezed the trigger. The flintlock fell with a dead click in the pan. '*Empty.*'

De la Vega stared at it, 'No...' He took it, looking into it, shaking it, as Cook sank back, cursing, '*By all that's bloody holy in Bristol, lad...*'

Hazzard struggled upright in the surf beside them, the rest of the marines coming at the run along the shoreline, Porter pushing through them to see to the shoulder wound, one hand delving into his bag. Hazzard heard them chattering about the approaching French, and Cook cutting them short: '*Nine Company – on yer feet.*' They pulled Hazzard up, the pain coming in waves, and they hurried through the shallows.

Hazzard looked back, into the distant darkness of the desert, the gleam of dawn brightening the scene with every passing moment, and he felt some faint measure of hope for the future. Free of Lewis and the Admiralty, free of Derrien, the weight of Karnak left him – Ozymandias had gone. Above, a flight of ibis flapped and cried in the streaks of gold, home at last.

Historical Note

The first casualty of the corps of *savant* academics was young Louis Auguste Joly, a landscape artist and painter whom Denon referred to as a 'draughtsman'. His end is described accurately here: although they were fêted like royalty at the previous stop, the tourists led by Generals Menou and Marmont were set upon outside the gates of Kafr-Shahabas in September 1798. All diaries give the same dreadful report – that Joly panicked and jumped from his saddle, crying out for help yet refusing to climb up to safety with his colleagues; they were soon overrun. General Menou did all that he could, and the party was forced to flee. The escorting cavalry later found Joly's headless body.

Shajar al-Durr and Baibars were real figures, but from the 13th century. Baibars rode from Egypt to defeat the Mongols, and Shajar (or Shajarat) was the only queen ever to lead the Mamluks, voted to rule Egypt by the *diwan*. She remains a heroic figure in Egyptian history, and it seemed fitting she should be the face of Egyptian resistance – especially with the Tarabin *Bedu*. The Al-Tirabin or Tarabin are a fiercely effective Bedouin warrior tribe in the Sinai; for centuries they have been known as the gatekeepers to Egypt, and stand guard even today.

The Cairo revolt was organised chiefly by the Al-Azhar Mosque, the *muezzin* and *imams* spreading the word openly via the minarets and in the streets on the Sunday morning of 21st October 1798. Muskets were handed round and gatherings increased until the mob swelled to breaking point. Riot swept through the city, the crowd destroying virtually everything it touched, looting, burning and battering to death anyone in their path – including their own people. They killed the doctors and nurses at the military hospital, and ran from bed to bed stabbing their helpless victims to death. Some Egyptian leaders tried to restore order where they could, and Sheikh al-Mansur represents those brave few.

The scenes at the Institute are similarly true to life: led by Monge, the *savants* largely defended themselves, his stirring speech encouraging even the pompous poet Parseval-Grandmaison to step up alongside the few troops supporting them. The mob gathered at the entrance to their cul-de-sac, some running forward and throwing stones, others firing their guns while pot-shots rained down on them from academics in overlooking windows. In the end, the *savants* were saved by a company of infantry.

Bonaparte's response was to bombard the area around the Al-Azhar and clear the barricades to allow the cavalry to charge along the main roads. The next day, the gigantic and doubtless terrifying West Indian General Dumas (father of Alexandre, soon-to-be author of *The Three Musketeers*) crashed through the Al-Azhar gates with his cavalry and crushed the defenders. In the aftermath, thousands of captives were beheaded and their bodies thrown into the Nile. Napoleon Bonaparte had become a tyrant.

Whether Admiralty Intelligence took so bold a step as to finance the revolt is unknown, but what is certain is that the revolt was the bloody and catastrophic failure Lord Keith might have wanted, and galvanised the sleeping leviathan that was the Ottoman Empire. Subsequently, Al-Djezzar Pasha gathered an army and prepared to strike.

Bonaparte had already expressed his wishes for a grand Oriental empire, from Egypt to India – yet the Syria campaign was more a pre-emptive strike than an invasion ('Syria' was a loose term for a largely undefined area east of Sinai and south of Turkey, incorporating Palestine, Lebanon and other regions). However, if successful, the opportunity was there for Bonaparte to march clear to Constantinople if he could, just as the Directory had so kindly suggested. In his more grandiose dreams, Bonaparte imagined foreign troops flocking to his banner as they marched, he the great Caesar leading them. But almost nothing went according to plan.

He took barely half his forces, as Hazzard and Wayland calculated, leaving his heavy artillery behind and sending it onwards by sea in a flotilla commanded by a Captain Standelet. Reynier led the attack on the sleeping Mamluk camp at El-'Arish as described, and Bonaparte called it a 'most beautiful victory'; though I have given Reynier a troubled conscience it is uncertain how he felt about it. From there things grew darker still.

Starving and infected with bubonic plague, the army trudged through muddy, rainswept scrub on the Levant coast, often in freezing temperatures. The plague had come on the march from Egypt, just as Delphine Lascelles had warned; Private Millet really did cut open the bubo in his groin, and lived to tell the tale, thanks to the treatment from nurses and assistants like Delphine and Fahima. However, many hospital orderlies were untrained and fearful – and some ran from the plague victims. They were put against walls and shot, from Alexandria to Damietta and down to Cairo. Execution seems to be the motif of this period.

Meanwhile, the straggling column reached Gaza. The Turks fell back to gather their forces and abandoned the town to the native Christians – though its doors were opened happily to the French, Gaza was looted for several days straight. Ramla (mistakenly called 'Er Ramieh' by French cartographers at the time) gave them some respite, and Dr Desgenettes took over the monastery of St Nicodemus and Joseph of Arimathea as a hospital for their fevered and dying soldiers. The Mamluk attack on the Jaffa road was a real event, and one can only wonder what became of the prisoners.

The attack on Jaffa (also Joppa, Yafa, and Yafo – known best today around the world as Tel Aviv) happened much as described here, including the near-miss of a lone Ottoman rifleman, who managed to shoot off Bonaparte's hat. The tipping-point seems to have been the parley: after several hours of bombardment, a young French subaltern and trumpet-boy went in to demand Abdullah Aga's surrender. Their severed heads were put on pikes and brandished over the gates in triumph, the bodies thrown over the wall like so much bloody meat. The army was outraged.

The ancient walls were eventually breached, grenadiers pouring into the town in fury. Once inside, French troops killed every Turkish soldier they encountered, even as they surrendered. They looted shops and homes, murdered civilians, women, children, old men, raped young girls and bludgeoned their screaming mothers. Officers were unable to control the pillage, some threatened by their own men and several killed. The only Turks to escape were those who retreated to the central block, often called the 'citadel'. When Eugène de Beauharnais and Croisier returned proudly with their captives, Bonaparte's words were recorded by Bourrienne. He was furious.

Apologists have cited the paltry supplies of the French army, their logistical inability to take the entire garrison as prisoners. Even at the time, Citizen Peyrusse knew this was untrue: as he declares to Derrien, having looted Gaza and Jaffa for food, the invading army had in its possession 400,000 rations of biscuit, and several hundred tonnes of rice. Yet historians have claimed there was not enough to feed the prisoners, therefore they had to be shot. The military objections make some sense: Bonaparte could hardly release an enemy force of four thousand men into the wilderness – what then could he do, many have asked with a shrug.

Bourrienne, Bonaparte's diarist, knew this was a difficult matter to explain away. He claims a 'war council' was held, collective arguments raging – but no other officer mentions this in his diaries. There is no doubt the senior generals would have had something to say, such as General Miot, but nothing would have affected the decision of the *général en chef*.

The victims were dealt with more or less as Caron witnessed: over a period of several days they were shot, drowned, trampled and bayonetted to death. Major Detroye of the engineers, killed later at Acre, kept an accurate record. In his diaries is a little chart:

On March 7	during the attack there died more than	2,000 Turks
On March 8	there were shot	800 Turks
On March 9	there were shot	600 Turks
On March 10	there were shot	1,041 Turks
		4,441

Even this does not account for all of the dead of Jaffa. The term 'Turk' is often applied in this period to all Ottomans, yet the garrison was mostly Albanian ('Arnauts'), Syrians, Turks and some Moroccan/Maghrib troops – that is to say, peoples from the west of North Africa (many Maghrib and Berber troops formed mercenary units in Bonaparte's army – as Hazzard later discovered).

There must be no doubt whatsoever that Napoleon Bonaparte ordered these executions. Historian J. Christopher Herold's suggestion that it was an example to Djezzar Pasha at Acre of what to expect is possibly the only explanation – as Derrien said, 'a bold stroke'.

Yet, Lt De la Salle (who really was captured by the Turks and rescued by Smith) also told us the truth aboard the *Tigre*: common French soldiers did not queue up eagerly to execute the prisoners – many refused, but many were unaware of what was happening until they were told to form a line and open fire. Others were on the verge of riot, still in bloodthirsty mood from the pillage of the town – perhaps they were the men who rowed out in boats to bayonet the swimming captives. I leave it to *Sergent-chef-major* Achille Caron to stand as the conscience of France, which was clearly torn.

When Bonaparte reached Acre, he took Mt Carmel on the exposed headland of the cape and set up a temporary HQ, just as Hazzard had been led to believe before his night raid. Instead of seeing his siege-artillery flotilla sailing safely into the harbour below, Bonaparte looked through his telescope to find HMS *Tigre* and HMS *Theseus*. He sent his panicked despatch to call off the convoy, even to send it back – anything. But it was too late.

In HMS *Tigre*, Sir William Sidney Smith swooped down upon the flotilla, gave chase and bagged all but three of the ships. In so doing, he deprived Bonaparte of the only means of breaching the walls of Acre. In that first action, Sir Sidney had saved the day. He almost always did. Few officers so epitomised the bold Englishman in the Age of Sail, with such cool courage and sheer dash, as Sir William Sidney Smith. Of all the British naval forces thrown against Napoleon over the next sixteen years, the exiled emperor named Smith as the greatest thorn in his side: without Smith, Napoleon confessed on St Helena, he would have taken Acre.

In the first major attack on Acre the seventy-year-old Djezzar Pasha sat upon his walls firing a pistol, offering a bounty for French heads. His name, al-Djezzar, 'the Butcher', was no exaggeration. He impaled men, beheaded them, built them into walls so their heads could be seen and all could hear their screams, and during the siege had several hundred Christian prisoners publicly strangled in the castle courtyard. Smith was unable to prevent him but Bonaparte condemned Smith for allowing it to happen.

The night raid on Haifa comes to us straight from the little-known diary of John Tillery: over two thousand French muskets and cannon opened up on the handful of British boats coming in to attack. Only two men in the launch were killed, Midshipman Gill and Seaman Kircher; the rest had no choice but to surrender. After hearing tales of Jaffa, Tillery was convinced they were going to be shot, but were well-treated. Tillery was indeed interrogated by 'several officers' – and then by Bonaparte himself.

The area around Acre would have resembled the Somme in 1916. HMS *Tigre*, *Theseus* and other gunboats cleared the shores with regular barrages, blasting the marshes from Haifa to the seagate of Acre. The shore north of the walls of Acre was a No Man's Land of shell-craters and French dead, where Hazzard and 9 Company made their escape. The trenches before the walls were hellish by any standards, historians counting as many as forty different attacks mounted by the French, each one beaten back by the Turkish defenders.

Of these defenders, the most visible would have been several hundred of the highly disciplined *Nizam-i Djedid* (a phonetic form often used for *Çedid*), represented by the young, brave *Yuzbashi* Reiz. Trained by Europeans, they were the 'New Order' Army of Sultan Selim III, and memoirs stand testament to their ferocity and unflinching courage.

Major John Douglas and Lt John Wright did attack the French mine near the Damned Tower, with some success, though not on the same night as Tillery's raid. The raid of Major Oldfield from HMS *Theseus* was even more gallant, but led to the deaths of fifteen British marines, and Oldfield himself, who fought off the French with his sword before being overcome. So heroic was his conduct that General Berthier mentioned him in his memoirs, relating that they recovered Oldfield's body and buried him with honours.

We shall see more of Lt Wright, who was without question an officer working with Admiralty Intelligence or the Alien Office. He was captured with Sidney Smith in Paris and thrown into the Temple Prison, but was sprung by Phélippeaux in an operation worthy of the Scarlet Pimpernel: Phélippeaux convinced the guardroom at the Temple that Smith and Wright were to be moved to another prison, had them marched to a waiting carriage, and whisked into the night back to England.

Phélippeaux was given the rank of colonel in the British army, and fought with Smith and the Turks against Bonaparte at Acre, managing the reinforcement of the walls. Bonaparte believed he would take Acre in two weeks – he was there for two and a half months. When finally they broke through the wall, they encountered Phélippeaux's master-stroke: a second wall. Caught in crossfires and exhausted, the French retreated and Bonaparte fell back. Phélippeaux died of exhaustion some short time later.

The Syria campaign is largely obscured by the grand imperial frills of later years. True, Bonaparte did encourage his men by attending the plague victims, holding their hands – yet at the same time suggested to

Dr Desgenettes that the worst cases be given an overdose of laudanum and put to death: they would infect the remainder of his army and hamper the return to Cairo. There is no question that he did this. Though some have tried, it is not a matter of debate.

Desgenettes refused, and the walking wounded staggered back to Egypt. Though they had not taken Acre, they had defeated the Turks in several running battles, among them one at Mt Tabor: consequently Bonaparte declared the campaign a victory, and held a triumph for himself in Cairo. However, within a month, the Turks landed at Aboukir Bay, where Brueys had watched Nelson descend upon his battle-fleet the previous year. Here Bonaparte won his greatest victory, and threw the Turks back into the sea – Kléber was so overwhelmed he even hugged Bonaparte.

In the weeks that followed, Sir Sidney sowed the seeds of dissatisfaction. Two French officers came aboard the *Tigre* to parley over an exchange of prisoners, and Smith kindly provided them with European newspapers: the reports spoke mostly of French reversals in the field, the loss of Italy, of Rome, of nearly all that Bonaparte had won. Smith knew his enemy well. In the first week of August, Bonaparte hurried back to Cairo to gather his travel companions and pack his trunk.

The night of 23rd August 1799 was somewhat inauspicious. There was no moon, and no wind. Bonaparte waited on the beach at sunset for Menou to arrive, and presented him with a parcel of paperwork: orders for Kléber, and a proclamation to the army and the Cairo *diwan*. They strolled a while, chatting. By 9 p.m. it was so dark the boarding party lit lanterns so the boats from *La Muiron* and *La Carrère* could find them. History says Bonaparte was aboard at 5 a.m., but it is possible he had one last task to accomplish ashore with Menou – and was caught by Hazzard just before dawn. By 8 o'clock he had set sail for France, crossing his own personal Rubicon – Caesar was coming home.

The army received no warning that their beloved general was to steal away into the night. Neither did the rest of his generals – as we shall see. The only man to question the future emperor, to demand an explanation for his excess, for his crimes, was William John Hazzard. It seems Bonaparte was right to trust the gods: that the Lorenzoni was empty we can blame only on Fate.

–

And here the poem, grown from that broken masonry at the mortuary temple of Thebes, where Hazzard's stone gods are seated even today, staring into the east to bring forth every new day, in the hope of golden Eos:

OZYMANDIAS

I met a Traveller from an antique land
Who said: 'Two vast and trunkless legs of stone
Stand in the desert. Near them, on the sand,
Half sunk, a shattered visage lies, whose frown,
And wrinkled lip, and sneer of cold command,
Tell that its sculptor well those passions read
Which yet survive, stamped on these lifeless things,
The hand that mocked them and the heart that fed:
And on the pedestal these words appear:
"My name is OZYMANDIAS, king of kings,
Look on my works, ye Mighty, and despair!"
Nothing beside remains. Round the decay
Of that Colossal Wreck, boundless and bare
The lone and level sands stretch far away.'

Percy Bysshe Shelley, 1818

Acknowledgements

I would like to thank Daniel Gosling at the National Archives, and the staff at the Caird Library & Archives at the National Maritime Museum in Greenwich; Alistair France and Anthony Gray; interpreters and transliterators Muhammad Wafa, Essam Edgard Samné, and former Naval Intelligence officer Hassan Eltaher; agents Jon Wood, Mike Bryan and Heather Adams, and my editor at Canelo, Craig Lye.

Jonathan Spencer, 2021